STARSTRUCK

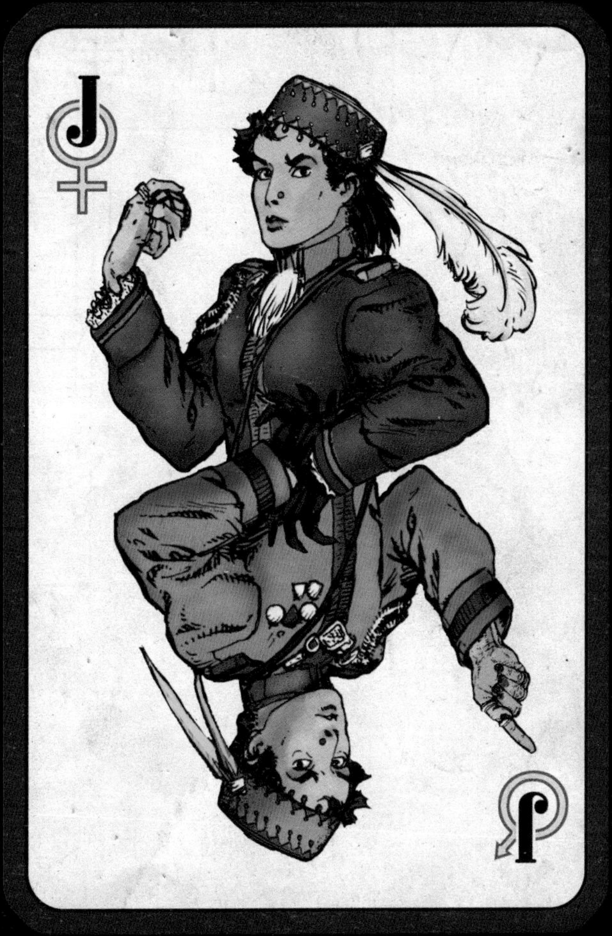
J
J

ELAINE LEE M^W^ KALUTA LEE MOYER

IDW

ISBN: 978-1-61377-439-7

24 23 22 21   3 4 5 6

IDW®

www.IDWPUBLISHING.com

Nachie Marsham, Publisher • Blake Kobashigawa, VP of Sales • Tara McCrillis, VP Publishing Operations • John Barber, Editor-in-Chief • Mark Doyle, Editorial Director, Originals • Lauren LePera, Managing Editor • Joe Hughes, Director, Talent Relations • Anna Morrow, Sr. Marketing Director • Keith Davidsen, Director, Marketing & PR • Topher Alford, Sr. Digital Marketing Manager • Shauna Monteforte, Sr. Director of Manufacturing Operations • Jamie Miller, Sr. Operations Manager • Nathan Widick, Sr. Art Director, Head of Design • Neil Uyetake, Sr. Art Director, Design & Production • Shawn Lee, Art Director, Design & Production • Jack Rivera, Art Director, Marketing

Ted Adams and Robbie Robbins, IDW Founders

Facebook: facebook.com/idwpublishing • Twitter: @idwpublishing
YouTube: youtube.com/idwpublishing • Instagram: @idwpublishing

STARSTRUCK

Elaine Lee – *Writer*
Michael Wm. Kaluta – *Artist*
Lee Moyer – *Painter*
Todd Klein – *Letterer*
Charles Vess – *Galactic Girl Guides Inker*
John Workman – *G.G.G. Letterer*
Scott Dunbier – *Editor*

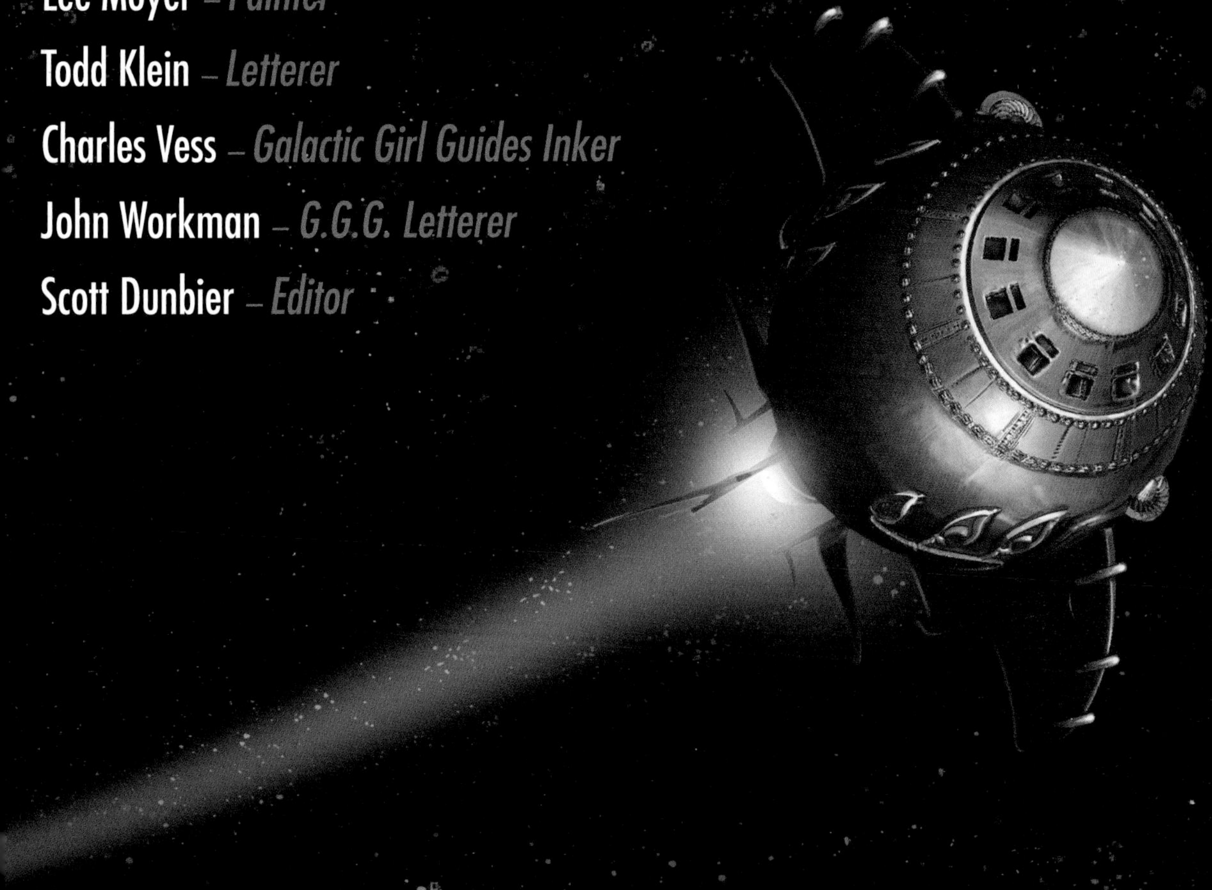

COLLECTED EDITION

Michael Wm. Kaluta – *Cover Artist*
Mike Carey and Lin Carey (A.J. Lake) – *Introduction*
Tym Stevens – *A Starstruck History*
Elaine Lee and Lee Moyer – *Book Designers*

ADDITIONAL MATERIALS

Linda Medley – *Vector*
Walt Carter – *3D Ship Renderings*
Jim Mueller – *Jumpin' Jills*

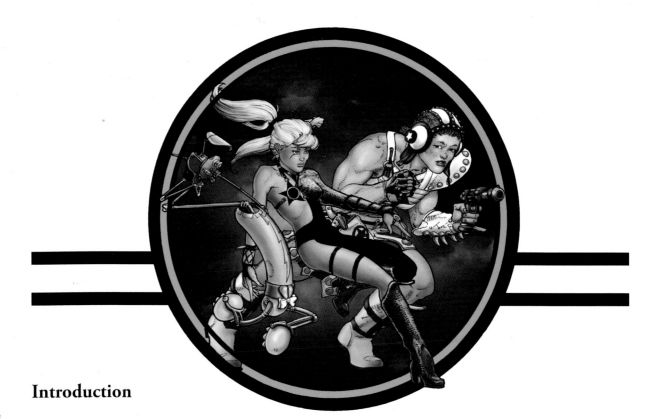

Introduction

There are some books that detonate inside your head like a ton of intra-cranial plastique the first time you read them: others oh-so-gradually get under your skin till they become, almost without you realizing it, a part of your life. *Starstruck* is both.

To explain: We first came across Lee and Kaluta's wondrous creation in the autumn of 1984. In those days, we were a couple of ex-English students trawling the comics shops around London's Leicester Square in search of a fix for our shared SF/fantasy addiction: usually super-team stuff in those days, to be honest. And then one day... we were browsing the shelves in an idle way when the cover of a graphic novel caught our attention. Two female warriors leaping out of the frame, one armed and muscled, one scarred and lacking a breast. And a blue mechanical dildo on legs. Title: "The Luckless, The Abandoned And Forsaked." Inside, it got weirder. A random perusal revealed a blank-eyed scion of the aristocracy in love with a headless pleasure-doll, a space attack with a payload of scrambled egg, and a troupe of larcenous Girl Guides. We wondered what the hell it was we'd got our paws on, but we knew that – whatever it was – we wanted it.

So we got the instant high; oh yes. But we got the slowburn, too. Over the next year or so, as we snapped up and devoured all six issues of the tragically short-lived ongoing, we found ourselves increasingly expressing ourselves in the book's unique and wondrous argot. "Nothing important in head," one of us would say, if we whacked our skull on the underside of a cupboard door. Or, when caught out in a lie, "truth as far as it goes." Or – one that was called into service a whole lot in those dark, Thatcherite days: "The mother is paradox – ever present, and never there when you need her." We even composed our own stark verse (qv).

We'd actually hit the story rather late. *Starstruck* had been around as a stage play since 1980 and a comic strip since 1982 (in *Heavy Metal* magazine). So how cool is it that at the end of the first decade of the the 21st century, it still reads as being ahead of its time?

The truth is, there just never was another book out there that did what *Starstruck* did. We could ramble on about the epic scale, but there had been space operas with epic scale before. Asimov had epic scale. Heinlein had epic scale. Hell, even E.E. Smith had epic scale. But *Starstruck... Starstruck* wasn't just epic, it was polyphonic. Accompanying the main narrative you had whole skeins of quotes, sometimes from outside sources, sometimes from the book's own densely populated universe of imagined voices and cultures. You had the encyclopaedia entries which were part footnote, part set-up, part mini-essays on mind-bending concepts put in there just for the sheer joy of it. (Want to know how to win the coveted "Sign of

1

the Nova" Guide badge? Or what to do with your Vercadian Protector Android, assuming you're rich enough to own one? Or why so many planets are called Alias? It's all there.) You had letters, vid-casts, recordings, official documents, telepathic playback from android consciousnesses; you had poetry, drama and song; you had switches of viewpoint, a cast of billions; in short, you had a whole – expanding – universe.

And at this point, let's ditch the nostalgia and switch to the present tense: because we're not just reliving the heady days of our youth, we're talking about the book – the living, breathing, quivering, fawn-like thing – that you're holding in your hands right now. *Starstruck*, the beacon that lit up our past with visions of an implausibly rich and phantasmagorical future, is actually very much a thing of the present. IDW have finally provided a stage big enough for Lee and Kaluta's vision, and the result is this collection.

If this is your first exposure – if the present volume is your gateway drug – we can tell you a little about what to expect. Reading *Starstruck* is like reading sci-fi written and drawn by J.S. Bach in the middle of an acid trip: fugues and choruses and multi-part harmonies of narrative, playing off each other in unexpected ways to produce delayed reveals, sting-in-the-tail pay-offs, devastating, poignant and ironic juxtapositions.

And none of this does justice to the sheer breakneck, lunatic energy of the storytelling. This is a universe of unceasing political intrigue; it's like a giant chess game, if you can imagine a chess game played at near-light speed by a couple of dozen players, some of them power-crazed, some simply crazed, and one or two just in it for the laughs. And out of this plethora of amazingly realised, amazingly varied characters, a bigger, all-inclusive story emerges: a story that pits two great dynasties against each other, across worlds and generations, and defines the stakes – with total conviction – as the soul, identity and destiny of an entire civilisation.

Meanwhile, around the feet of the great movers and shakers swarm the Galactic Girl Guides, a comic creation worthy of a Twain or a Waugh. Young girls need to be thoroughly trained and equipped to survive in the Starstruck universe, and the G.G.G. (slogan: "It's a TOUGH GALAXY, but SOMEBODY'S gotta live in it, and it might as well be YOU!") is an institution designed to fill that need – adding a wondrous comic operetta counterpoint to the grand space opera of the main narrative, and ultimately connecting with it through the character of Brucilla the Muscle, one half of the greatest comics partnership since Batman and Robin.

Which brings us to another kick-in-the-pants feature of Lee and Kaluta's universe: most of it's run by women. All the great characters in the book's first run were female. This in the 1980s, mind you, when female characters in the comics cosmos tended to be token, big-breasted and desperately overshadowed by the men. Well, not here. Ronnie Lee Ellis, family saboteur and best-selling author, the revolutionary Mary Medea, the evil Verloona Ti, Galatia-9 and the sublime Brucilla – these women define the dimensions of the story space and make its many, many strands cohere into something truly unique. They're people you have to keep watching.

We've kept watching ever since, like the adherents of some crazed sect, and the hour so long foretold is now at hand.

Lee. Kaluta. Vess. Moyer. Klein. Homage them. Praise the words they speak. Honor to the mind that replicates their pattern.

Mike Carey   Lin Carey (A.J. Lake)

London, Dec 2010

In memory of...

Elaine's dad,
Frank Hackney Lee,
for buying her all those comic books

and

Michael's mom,
Clotilde G. Kaluta,
for throwing his comic books away.

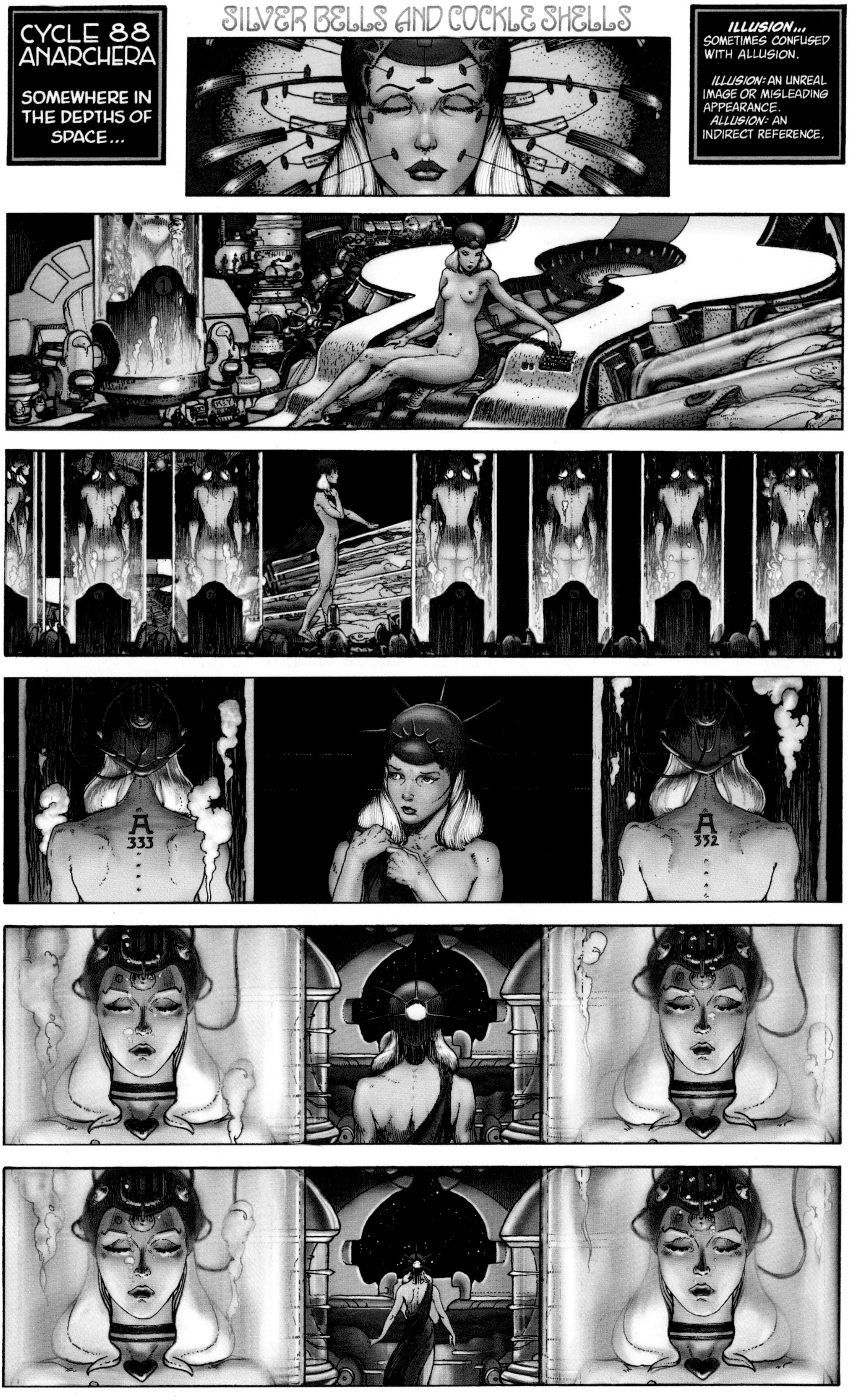

CYCLE 88
ANARCHERA
SOMEWHERE IN THE DEPTHS OF SPACE...
SILVER BELLS AND COCKLE SHELLS
ILLUSION... SOMETIMES CONFUSED WITH ALLUSION.
ILLUSION: AN UNREAL IMAGE OR MISLEADING APPEARANCE.
ALLUSION: AN INDIRECT REFERENCE.
KEY
A 333
A 332

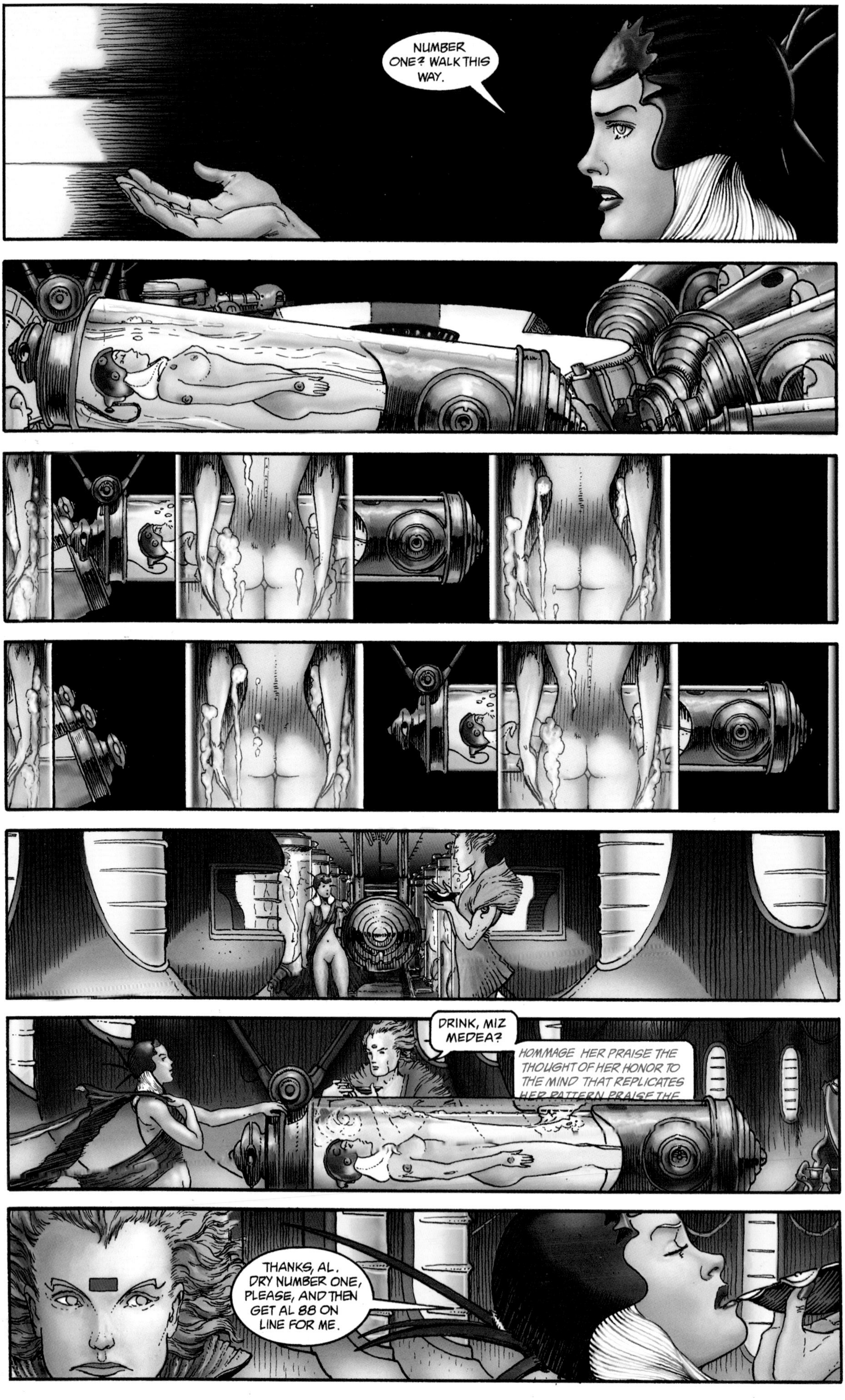
NUMBER ONE? WALK THIS WAY.
DRINK, MIZ MEDEA?
HOMMAGE HER PRAISE THE THOUGHT OF HER HONOR TO THE MIND THAT REPLICATES
THANKS, AL. DRY NUMBER ONE, PLEASE, AND THEN GET AL 88 ON LINE FOR ME.

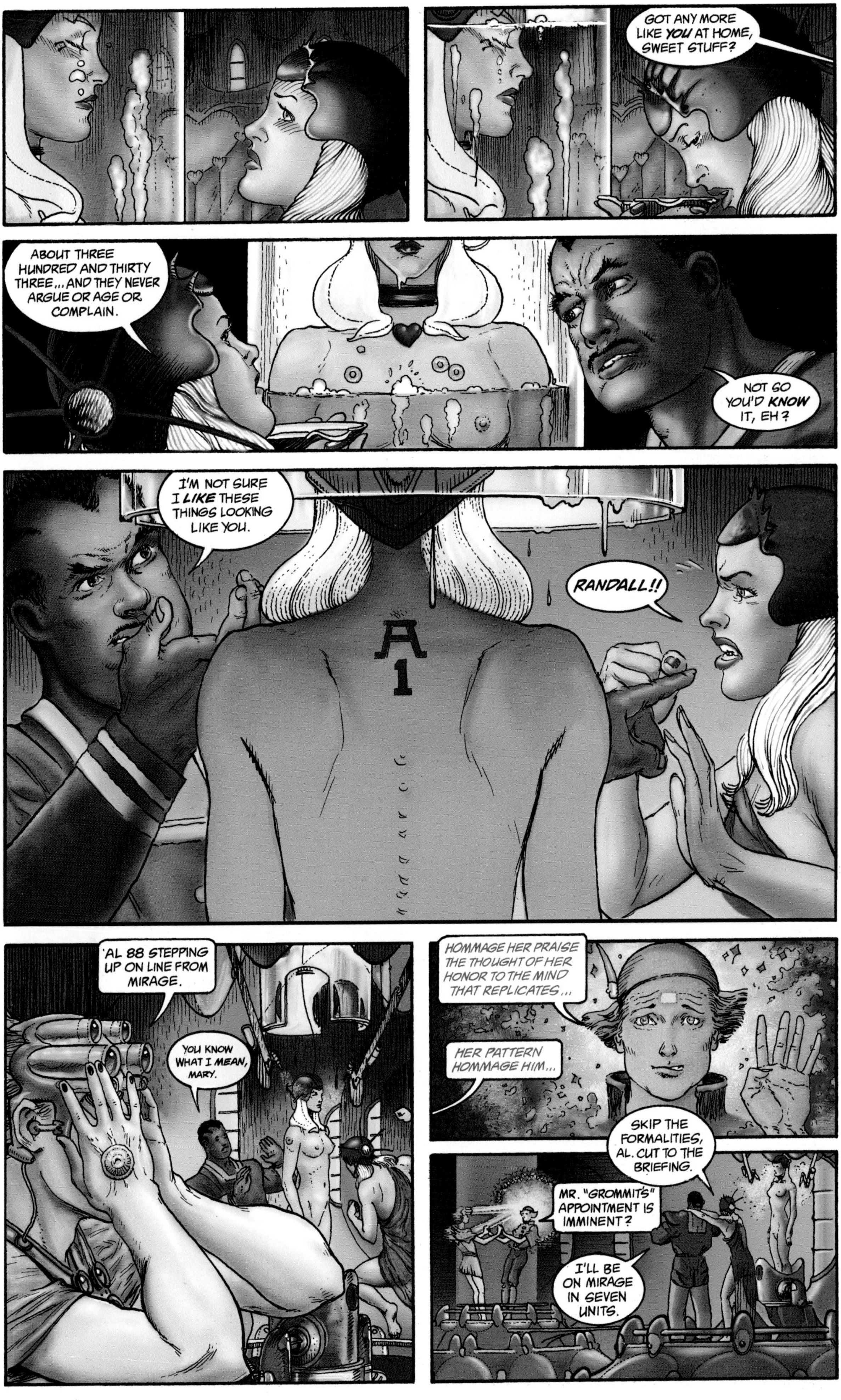

GOT ANY MORE LIKE YOU AT HOME, SWEET STUFF?
ABOUT THREE HUNDRED AND THIRTY THREE,.. AND THEY NEVER ARGUE OR AGE OR COMPLAIN.
NOT SO YOU'D KNOW IT, EH?
I'M NOT SURE I LIKE THESE THINGS LOOKING LIKE YOU.
RANDALL!!
A 1
'AL 88 STEPPING UP ON LINE FROM MIRAGE.
YOU KNOW WHAT I MEAN, MARY.
HOMMAGE HER PRAISE THE THOUGHT OF HER HONOR TO THE MIND THAT REPLICATES...
HER PATTERN HOMMAGE HIM...
SKIP THE FORMALITIES, AL. CUT TO THE BRIEFING.
MR. "GROMMIT'S" APPOINTMENT IS IMMINENT?
I'LL BE ON MIRAGE IN SEVEN UNITS.

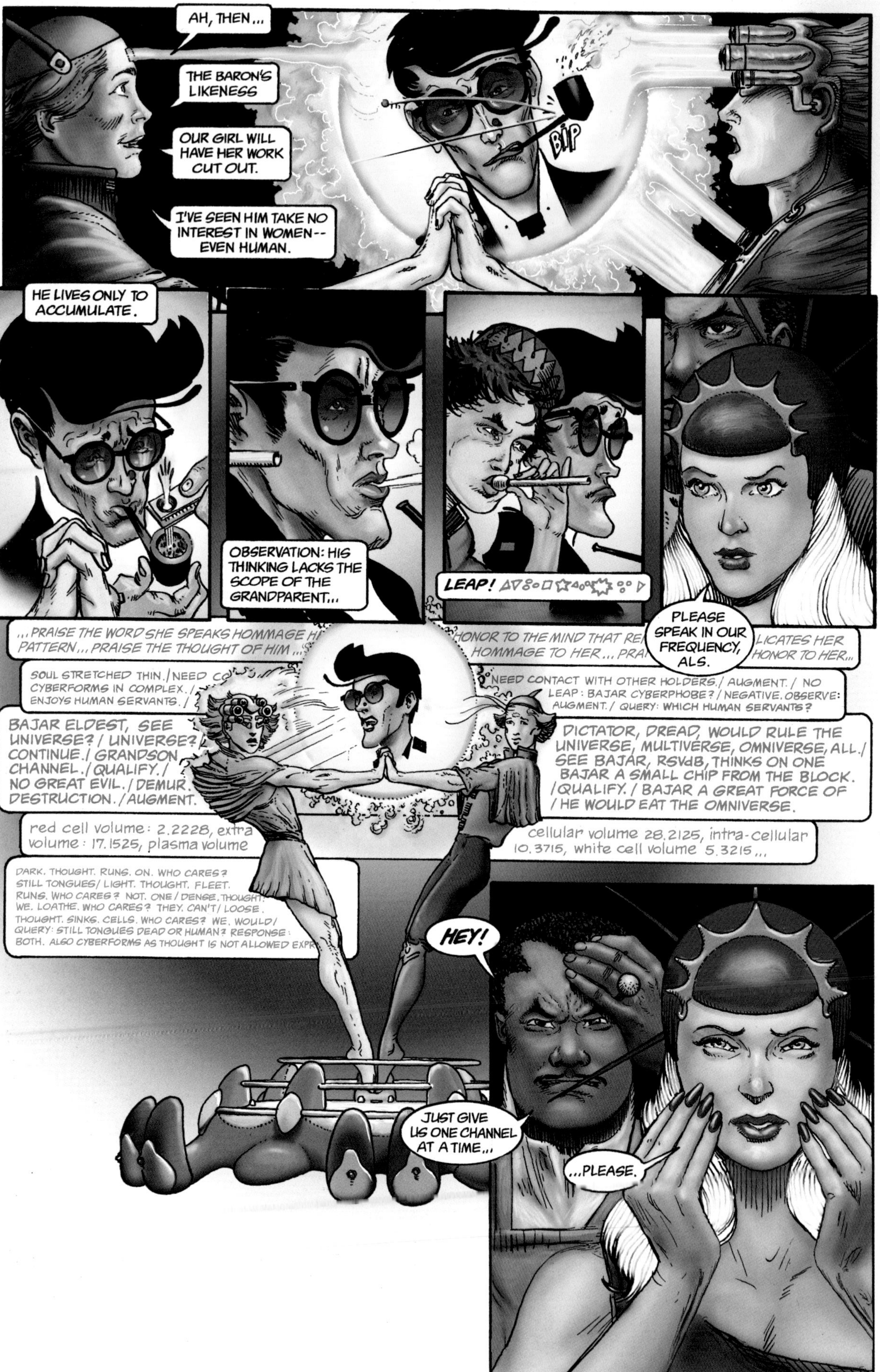
AH, THEN...
THE BARON'S LIKENESS
OUR GIRL WILL HAVE HER WORK CUT OUT.
I'VE SEEN HIM TAKE NO INTEREST IN WOMEN-- EVEN HUMAN.
BIP
HE LIVES ONLY TO ACCUMULATE.
OBSERVATION: HIS THINKING LACKS THE SCOPE OF THE GRANDPARENT...
LEAP!
...PRAISE THE WORD SHE SPEAKS HOMMAGE H
PATTERN... PRAISE THE THOUGHT OF HIM...
HONOR TO THE MIND THAT RE
HOMMAGE TO HER... PRA
LICATES HER
HONOR TO HER...
PLEASE SPEAK IN OUR FREQUENCY, ALS.
SOUL STRETCHED THIN./NEED C
CYBERFORMS IN COMPLEX./
ENJOYS HUMAN SERVANTS./
NEED CONTACT WITH OTHER HOLDERS./ AUGMENT./ NO
LEAP: BAJAR CYBERPHOBE?/ NEGATIVE. OBSERVE:
AUGMENT./ QUERY: WHICH HUMAN SERVANTS?
BAJAR ELDEST, SEE UNIVERSE?/ UNIVERSE? CONTINUE./ GRANDSON CHANNEL./QUALIFY./ NO GREAT EVIL./DEMUR. DESTRUCTION./AUGMENT.
DICTATOR, DREAD, WOULD RULE THE UNIVERSE, MULTIVERSE, OMNIVERSE, ALL./ SEE BAJAR, RSVdB, THINKS ON ONE BAJAR A SMALL CHIP FROM THE BLOCK. /QUALIFY./ BAJAR A GREAT FORCE OF / HE WOULD EAT THE OMNIVERSE.
red cell volume: 2.2228, extra volume: 17.1525, plasma volume
cellular volume 28.2125, intra-cellular 10.3715, white cell volume 5.3215...
DARK. THOUGHT. RUNS. ON. WHO CARES? STILL TONGUES/ LIGHT. THOUGHT. FLEET. RUNS. WHO CARES? NOT. ONE/ DENSE. THOUGHT. WE. LOATHE. WHO CARES? THEY. CAN'T/ LOOSE. THOUGHT. SINKS. CELLS. WHO CARES? WE. WOULD/ QUERY: STILL TONGUES DEAD OR HUMAN? RESPONSE: BOTH. ALSO CYBERFORMS AS THOUGHT IS NOT ALLOWED EXPR
HEY!
JUST GIVE US ONE CHANNEL AT A TIME...
...PLEASE.

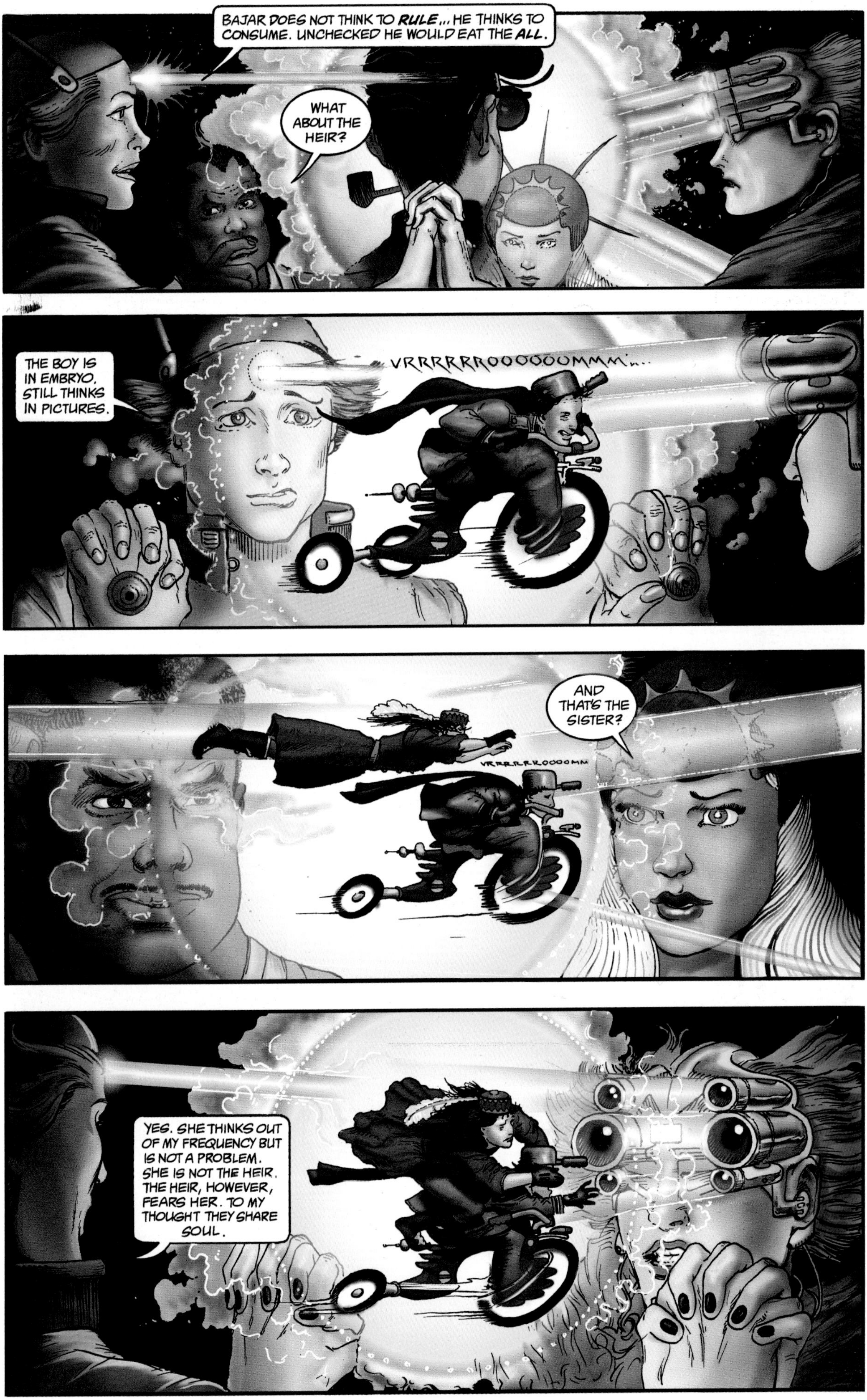
BAJAR DOES NOT THINK TO RULE... HE THINKS TO CONSUME. UNCHECKED HE WOULD EAT THE ALL.
WHAT ABOUT THE HEIR?
THE BOY IS IN EMBRYO, STILL THINKS IN PICTURES.
VRRRRRROOOOOOMMM...
VRRRRRROOOOMM
AND THAT'S THE SISTER?
YES. SHE THINKS OUT OF MY FREQUENCY BUT IS NOT A PROBLEM. SHE IS NOT THE HEIR. THE HEIR, HOWEVER, FEARS HER. TO MY THOUGHT THEY SHARE SOUL.

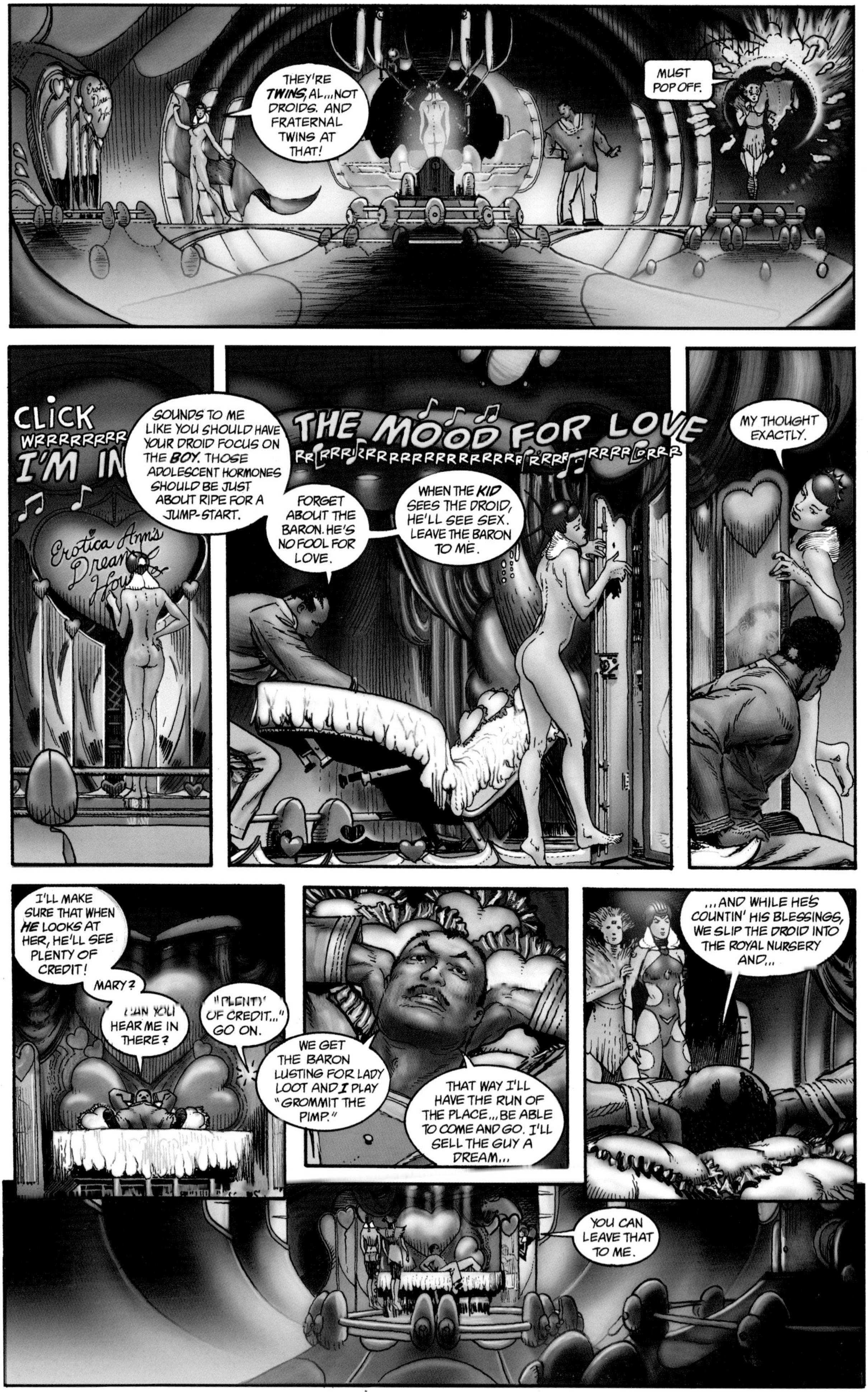

THEY'RE TWINS, AL... NOT DROIDS. AND FRATERNAL TWINS AT THAT!
MUST POP OFF.
CLICK
WRRRRRRRR
I'M IN
THE MOOD FOR LOVE
RRRRRRRRRRRRRRRRRRRRRRRRRRRRRRRRRRR
SOUNDS TO ME LIKE YOU SHOULD HAVE YOUR DROID FOCUS ON THE BOY. THOSE ADOLESCENT HORMONES SHOULD BE JUST ABOUT RIPE FOR A JUMP-START.
FORGET ABOUT THE BARON. HE'S NO FOOL FOR LOVE.
WHEN THE KID SEES THE DROID, HE'LL SEE SEX. LEAVE THE BARON TO ME.
Erotica Ann's Dream House
MY THOUGHT EXACTLY.
I'LL MAKE SURE THAT WHEN HE LOOKS AT HER, HE'LL SEE PLENTY OF CREDIT!
MARY?
CAN YOU HEAR ME IN THERE?
"PLENTY OF CREDIT..." GO ON.
WE GET THE BARON LUSTING FOR LADY LOOT AND I PLAY "GROMMIT THE PIMP."
THAT WAY I'LL HAVE THE RUN OF THE PLACE... BE ABLE TO COME AND GO. I'LL SELL THE GUY A DREAM...
...AND WHILE HE'S COUNTIN' HIS BLESSINGS, WE SLIP THE DROID INTO THE ROYAL NURSERY AND...
YOU CAN LEAVE THAT TO ME.

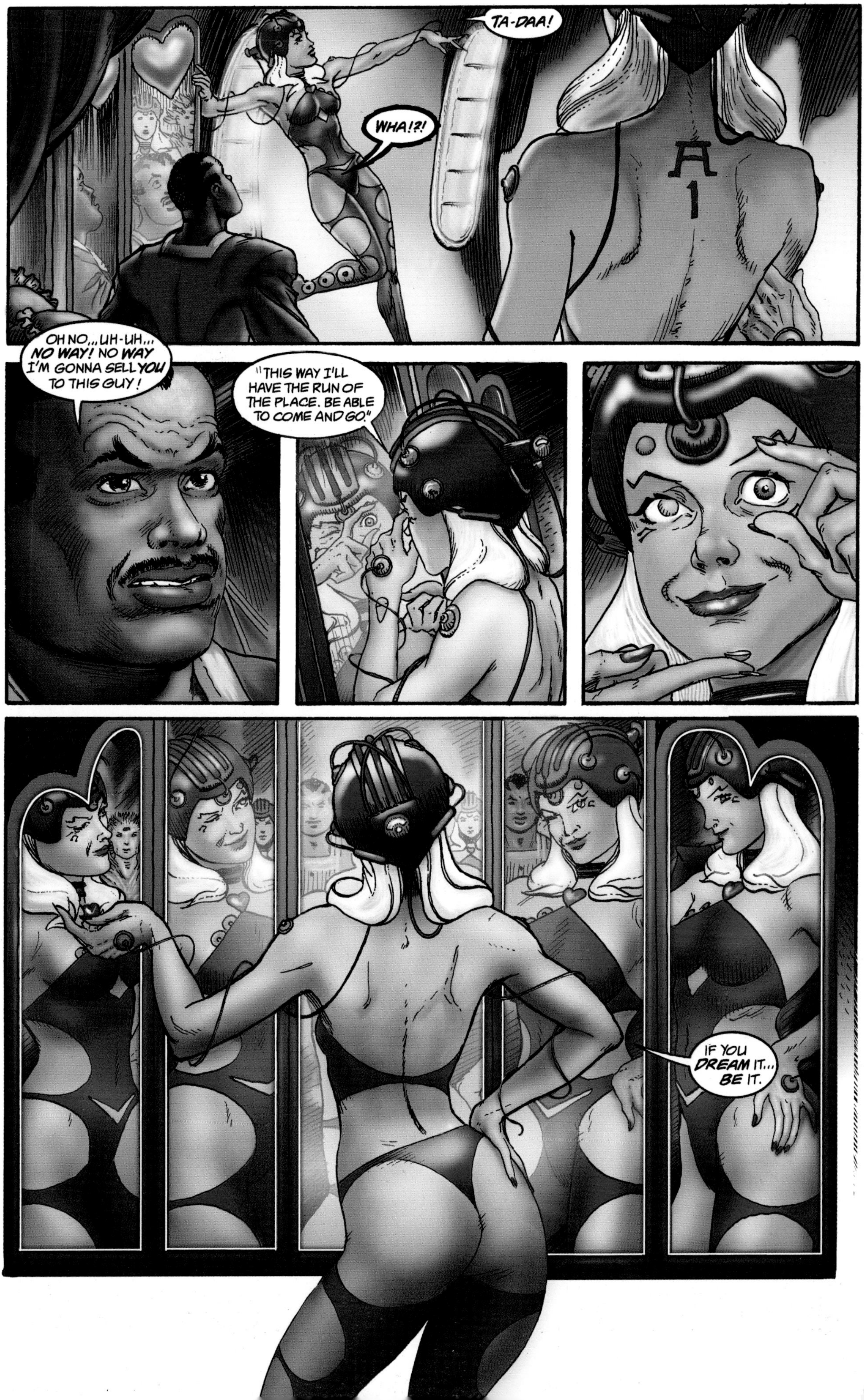
TA-DAA!
WHA!?!
OH NO,,, UH-UH,,, NO WAY! NO WAY I'M GONNA SELL YOU TO THIS GUY!
"THIS WAY I'LL HAVE THE RUN OF THE PLACE. BE ABLE TO COME AND GO."
IF YOU DREAM IT... BE IT.

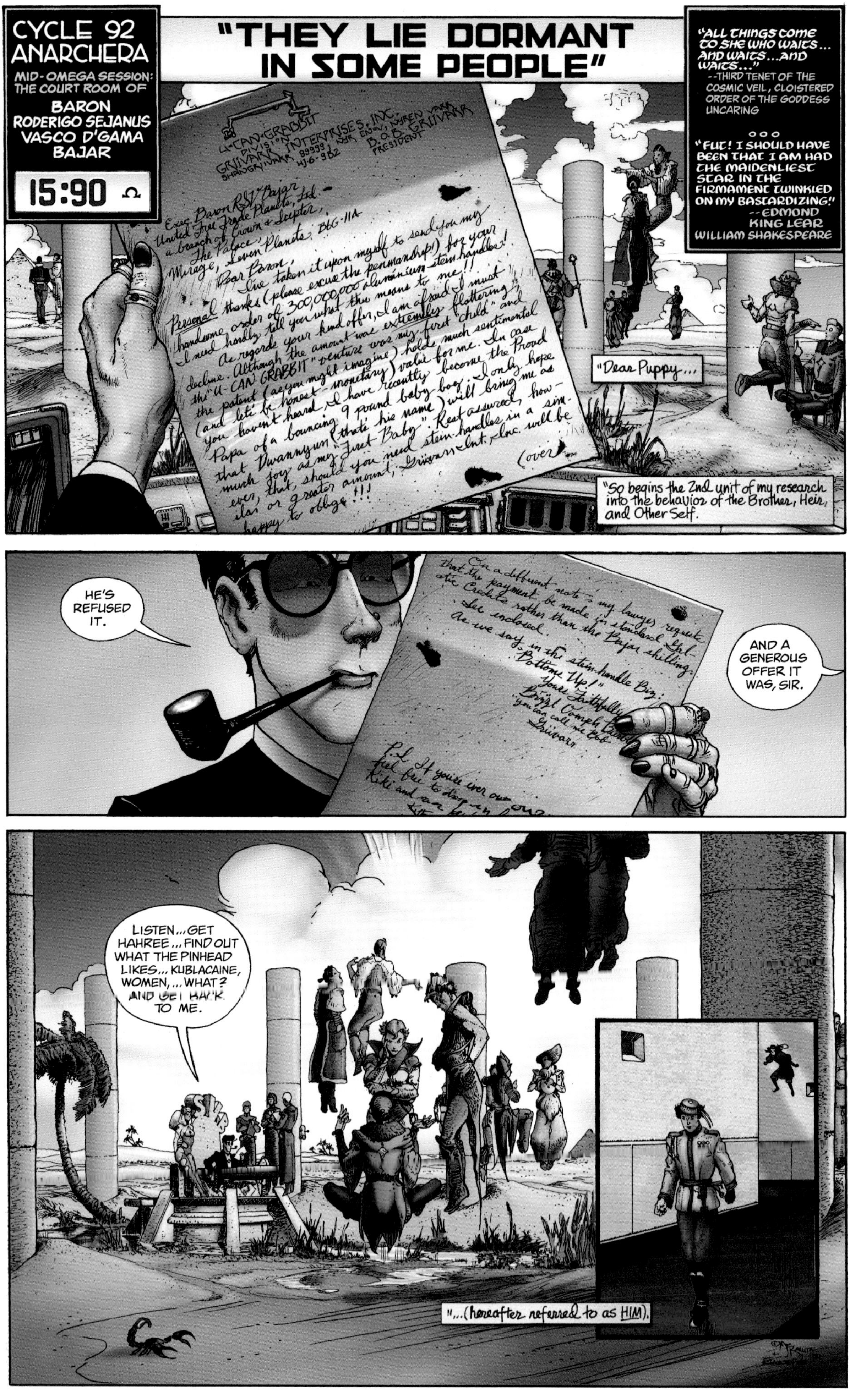
CYCLE 92
ANARCHERA
MID-OMEGA SESSION: THE COURT ROOM OF
BARON RODERIGO SEJANUS VASCO D'GAMA BAJAR
15:90 Ω
"THEY LIE DORMANT IN SOME PEOPLE"
"ALL THINGS COME TO SHE WHO WAITS... AND WAITS... AND WAITS..."
--THIRD TENET OF THE COSMIC VEIL, CLOISTERED ORDER OF THE GODDESS UNCARING
"FUT! I SHOULD HAVE BEEN THAT I AM HAD THE MAIDENLIEST STAR IN THE FIRMAMENT TWINKLED ON MY BASTARDIZING!"
--EDMOND KING LEAR WILLIAM SHAKESPEARE
U-CAN-GRABBIT DIVISION
GRIIVARR INTERPRISES, INC.
99999, NYR ENV, NYREN VARR
HJ-6-9B2
B.O.B. GRIIVARR PRESIDENT
Exec. Baron RSVD Bajar
United Free Trade Planets, Ltd.
a branch of Crown & Scepter,
The Palace, BBG-11A
Mirage, Seven Planets
Dear Baron,
I've taken it upon myself to send you my
Personal thanks (please excuse the penmanship!) for your
handsome order of 300,000,000 aluminium stein-handles!
I need hardly tell you what this means to me!!
As regards your kind offer, I am afraid I must
decline. Although the amount was extremely flattering,
the "U-CAN-GRABBIT" venture was my first "child" and
the patent (as you might imagine) holds much sentimental
(and let's be honest - monetary) value for me. In case
you haven't heard, I have recently become the Proud
Papa of a bouncing 9 pound baby boy. I only hope
that Dwannyun (that's his name) will bring me as
much joy as my First Baby". Rest assured, however, that, should you need stein-handles in a similar or greater amount, Griivarr Int., Inc. will be
happy to oblige!!!
(over)
"Dear Puppy...
"So begins the 2nd unit of my research into the behavior of the Brother, Heir, and Other Self.
HE'S REFUSED IT.
On a different note, my lawyer request
that the payment be made in standard Gal-
otic Credits rather than the Bajar shilling.
See enclosed.
As we say in the stein-handle Biz:
Bottoms Up!"
Yours Faithfully,
Brigit Oomph
you can call me Bob
Griivarr
P.S. If you're ever out our way
feel free to drop in
Kiki and
AND A GENEROUS OFFER IT WAS, SIR.
LISTEN... GET HAHREE... FIND OUT WHAT THE PINHEAD LIKES... KUBLACAINE, WOMEN,... WHAT? AND GET BACK TO ME.
"...(hereafter referred to as HIM).

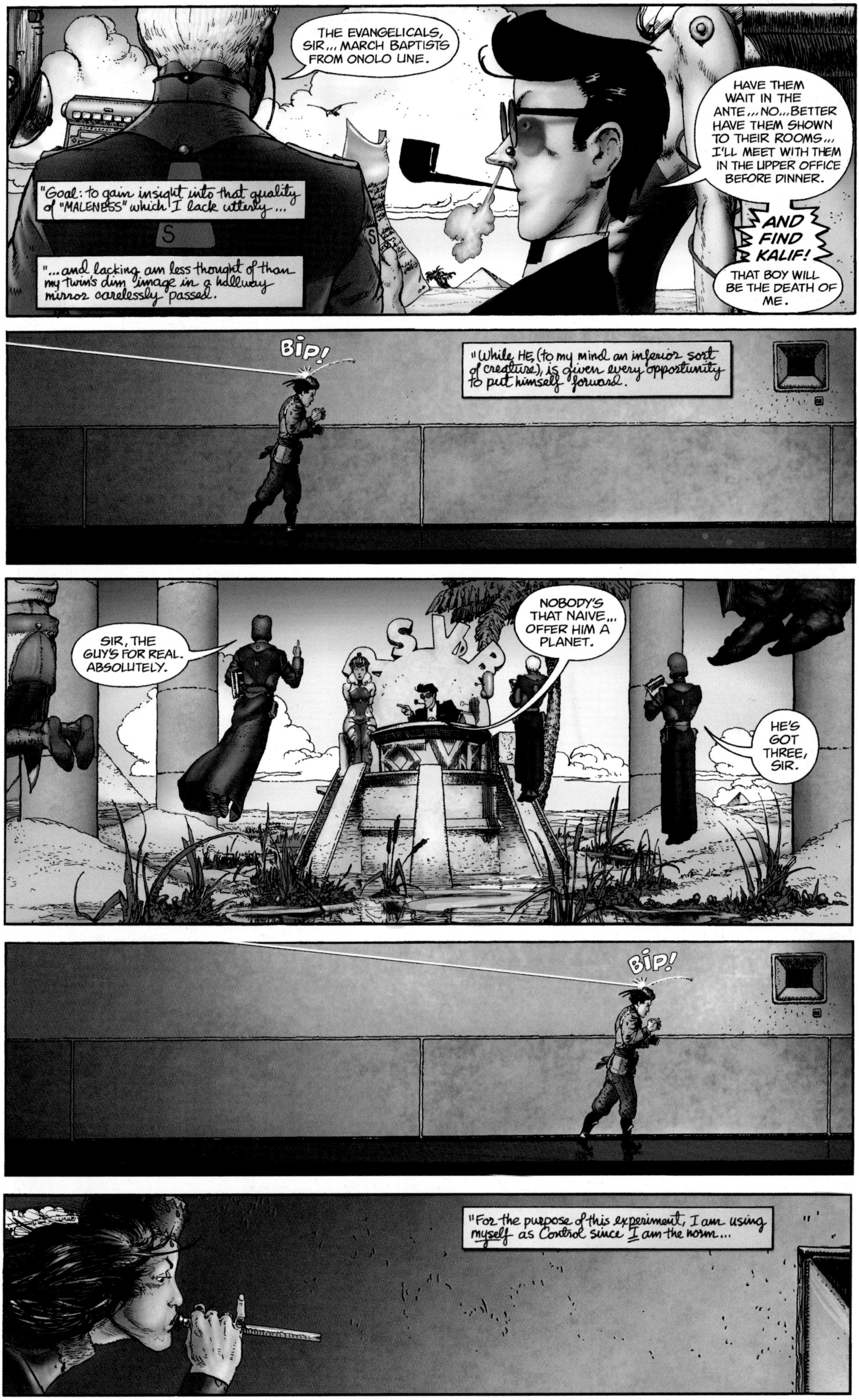
THE EVANGELICALS, SIR... MARCH BAPTISTS FROM ONOLO LINE.
"Goal: to gain insight into that quality of "MALENESS" which I lack utterly...
"...and lacking am less thought of than my twin's dim image in a hallway mirror carelessly passed.
HAVE THEM WAIT IN THE ANTE... NO... BETTER HAVE THEM SHOWN TO THEIR ROOMS... I'LL MEET WITH THEM IN THE UPPER OFFICE BEFORE DINNER.
AND FIND KALIF!
THAT BOY WILL BE THE DEATH OF ME.
BIP!
"While HE, (to my mind an inferior sort of creature), is given every opportunity to put himself forward.
SIR, THE GUY'S FOR REAL. ABSOLUTELY.
NOBODY'S THAT NAIVE... OFFER HIM A PLANET.
HE'S GOT THREE, SIR.
BIP!
"For the purpose of this experiment, I am using myself as Control since I am the norm...

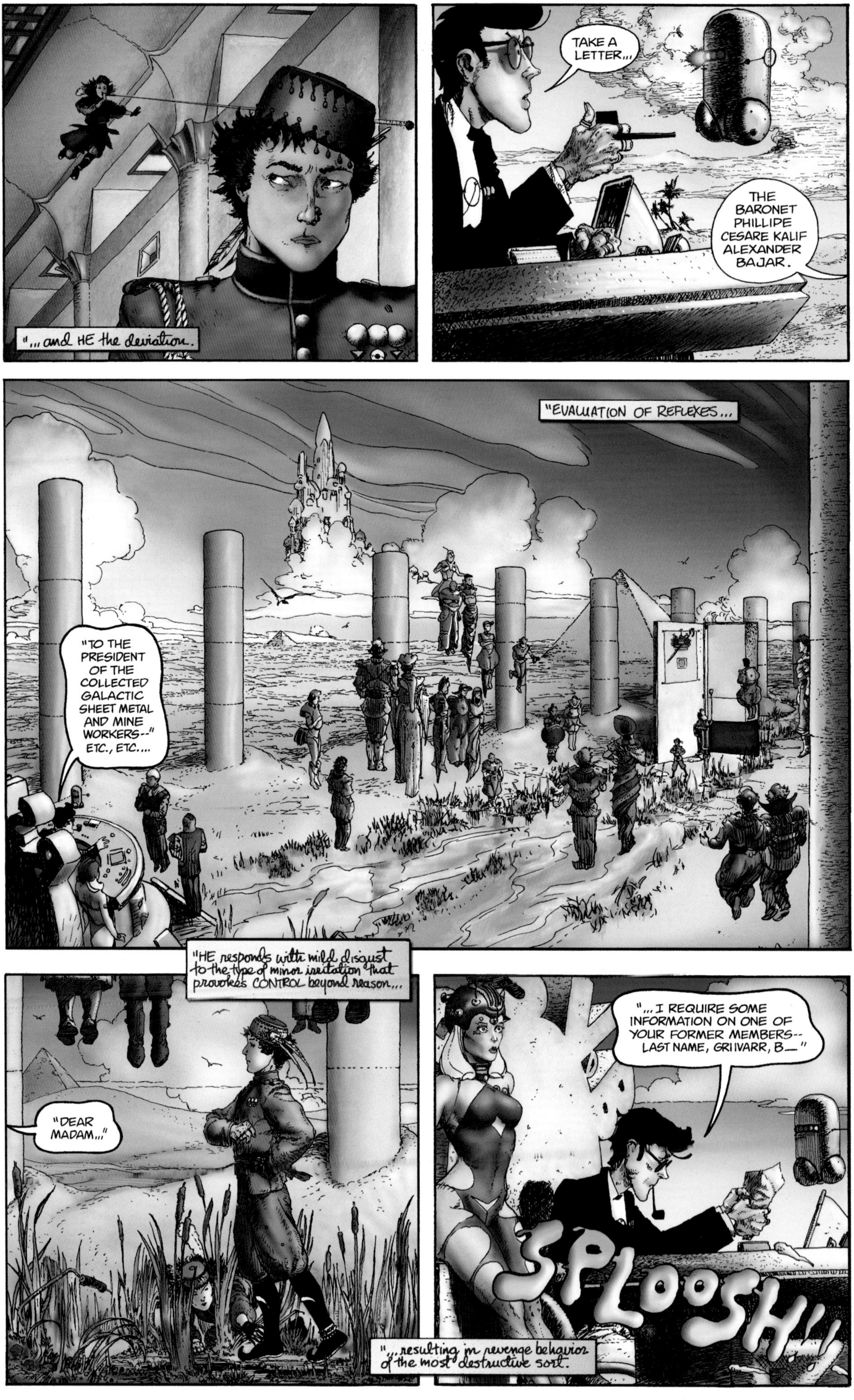
"... and HE the deviation.
TAKE A LETTER...
THE BARONET PHILLIPE CESARE KALIF ALEXANDER BAJAR.
"EVALUATION OF REFLEXES...
"TO THE PRESIDENT OF THE COLLECTED GALACTIC SHEET METAL AND MINE WORKERS--" ETC., ETC....
"HE responds with mild disgust to the type of minor irritation that provokes CONTROL beyond reason...
"DEAR MADAM..."
"... I REQUIRE SOME INFORMATION ON ONE OF YOUR FORMER MEMBERS-- LAST NAME, GRIIVARR, B__"
SPLOOSH!!
"... resulting in revenge behavior of the most destructive sort.

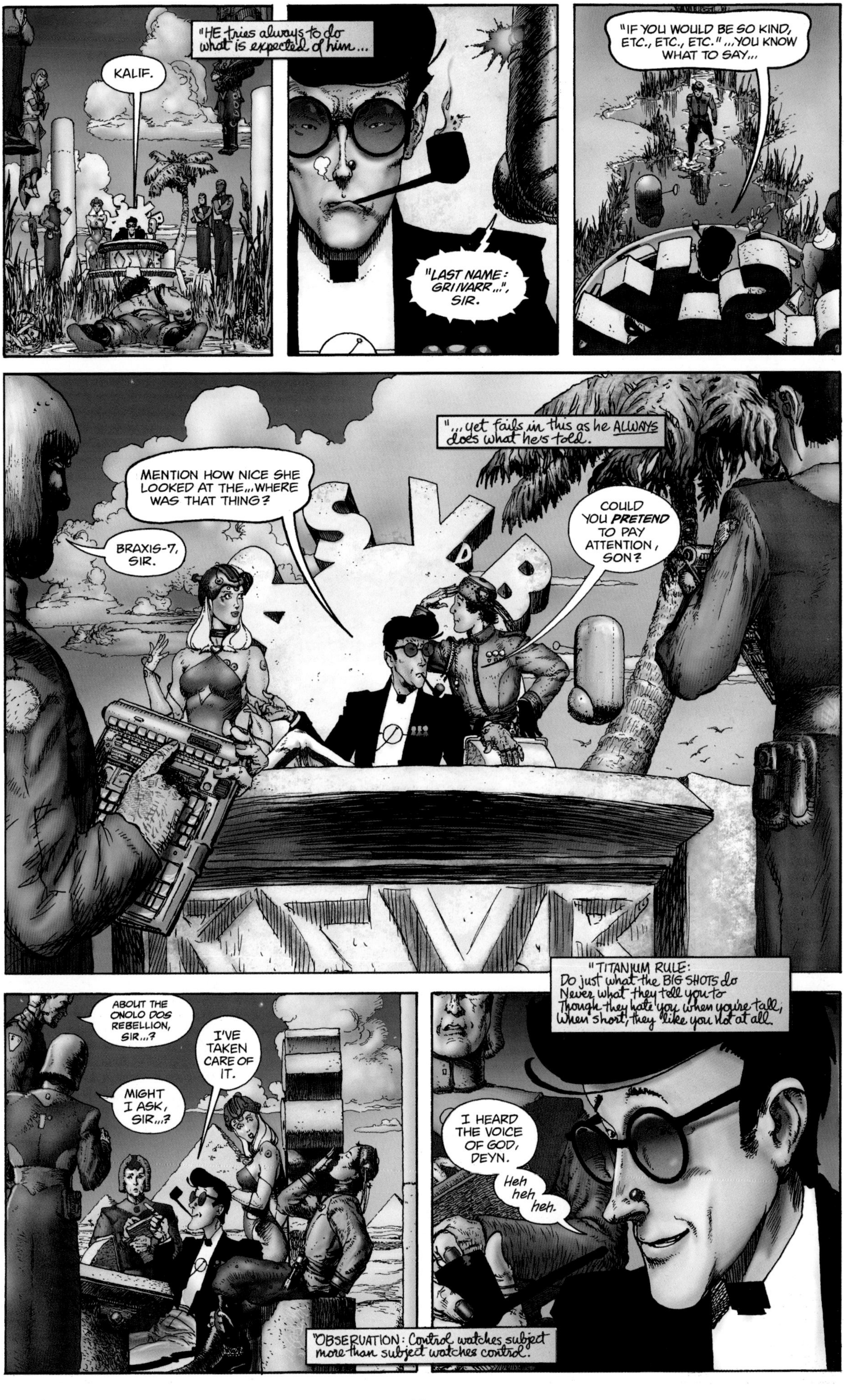
"HE tries always to do what is expected of him...
KALIF.
"LAST NAME: GRIVARR...", SIR.
"IF YOU WOULD BE SO KIND, ETC., ETC., ETC." ...YOU KNOW WHAT TO SAY...
"...yet fails in this as he ALWAYS does what he's told.
MENTION HOW NICE SHE LOOKED AT THE... WHERE WAS THAT THING?
BRAXIS-7, SIR.
COULD YOU PRETEND TO PAY ATTENTION, SON?
ABOUT THE ONOLO DOS REBELLION, SIR...?
I'VE TAKEN CARE OF IT.
MIGHT I ASK, SIR...?
"TITANIUM RULE:
Do just what the BIG SHOTS do
Never what they tell you to
Though they hate you when you're tall,
When short, they like you not at all.
I HEARD THE VOICE OF GOD, DEYN.
Heh heh heh.
"OBSERVATION: Control watches subject more than subject watches control.

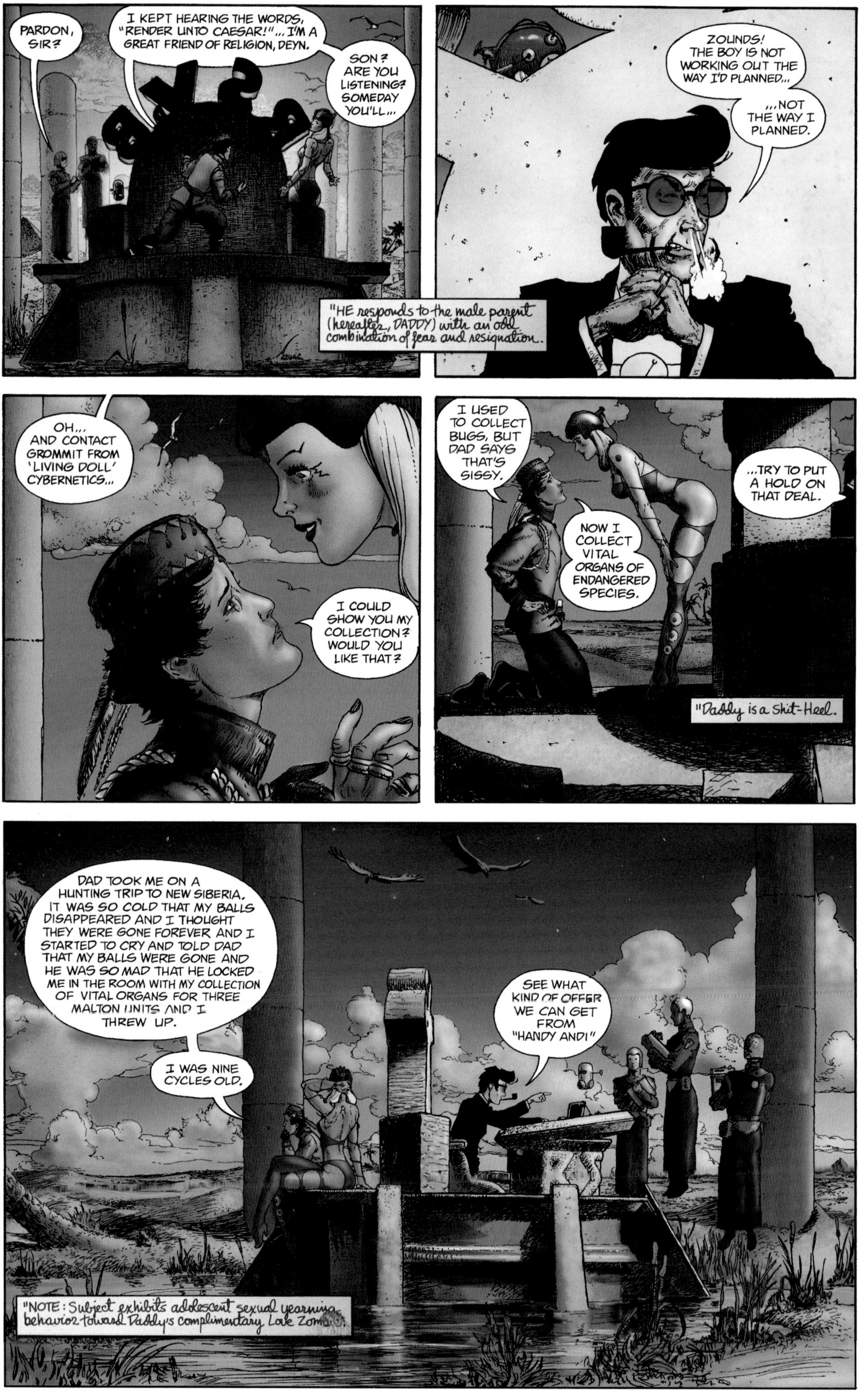
PARDON, SIR?
I KEPT HEARING THE WORDS, "RENDER UNTO CAESAR!"... I'M A GREAT FRIEND OF RELIGION, DEYN.
SON? ARE YOU LISTENING? SOMEDAY YOU'LL...
"HE responds to the male parent (hereafter, DADDY) with an odd combination of fear and resignation.
ZOUNDS! THE BOY IS NOT WORKING OUT THE WAY I'D PLANNED...
...NOT THE WAY I PLANNED.
OH... AND CONTACT GROMMIT FROM 'LIVING DOLL' CYBERNETICS...
I COULD SHOW YOU MY COLLECTION? WOULD YOU LIKE THAT?
I USED TO COLLECT BUGS, BUT DAD SAYS THAT'S SISSY.
NOW I COLLECT VITAL ORGANS OF ENDANGERED SPECIES.
...TRY TO PUT A HOLD ON THAT DEAL.
"Daddy is a Shit-Heel.
DAD TOOK ME ON A HUNTING TRIP TO NEW SIBERIA. IT WAS SO COLD THAT MY BALLS DISAPPEARED AND I THOUGHT THEY WERE GONE FOREVER AND I STARTED TO CRY AND TOLD DAD THAT MY BALLS WERE GONE AND HE WAS SO MAD THAT HE LOCKED ME IN THE ROOM WITH MY COLLECTION OF VITAL ORGANS FOR THREE MALTON UNITS AND I THREW UP.
I WAS NINE CYCLES OLD.
SEE WHAT KIND OF OFFER WE CAN GET FROM "HANDY ANDI"
"NOTE: Subject exhibits adolescent sexual yearning behavior toward Daddy's complimentary Love Zom

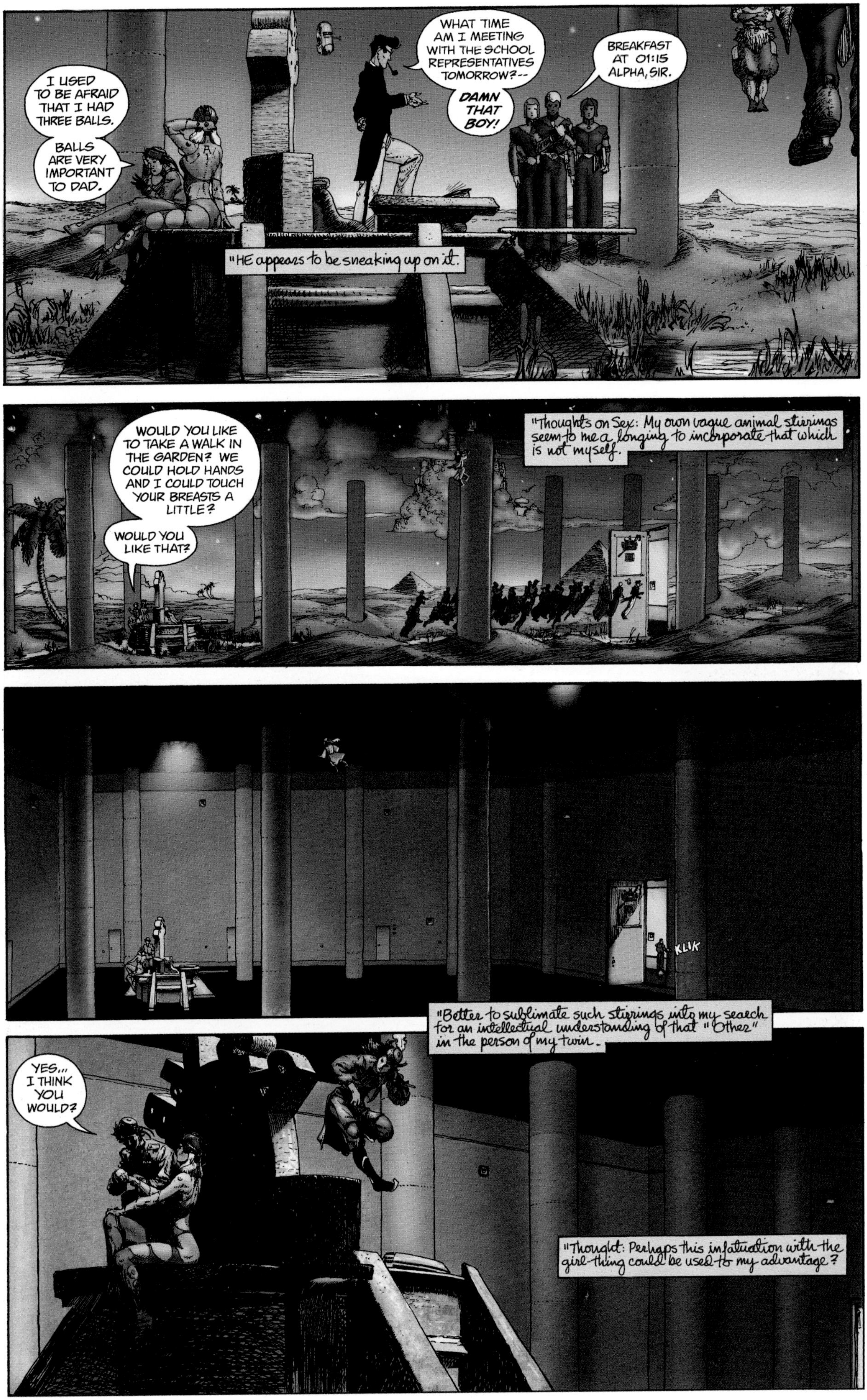
I USED TO BE AFRAID THAT I HAD THREE BALLS.
BALLS ARE VERY IMPORTANT TO DAD.
WHAT TIME AM I MEETING WITH THE SCHOOL REPRESENTATIVES TOMORROW?--
DAMN THAT BOY!
BREAKFAST AT 01:15 ALPHA, SIR.
"HE appears to be sneaking up on it.
"Thoughts on Sex: My own vague animal stirrings seem to me a longing to incorporate that which is not myself.
WOULD YOU LIKE TO TAKE A WALK IN THE GARDEN? WE COULD HOLD HANDS AND I COULD TOUCH YOUR BREASTS A LITTLE?
WOULD YOU LIKE THAT?
KLIK
"Better to sublimate such stirrings into my search for an intellectual understanding of that "Other" in the person of my twin.
YES... I THINK YOU WOULD?
"Thought: Perhaps this infatuation with the girl-thing could be used to my advantage?

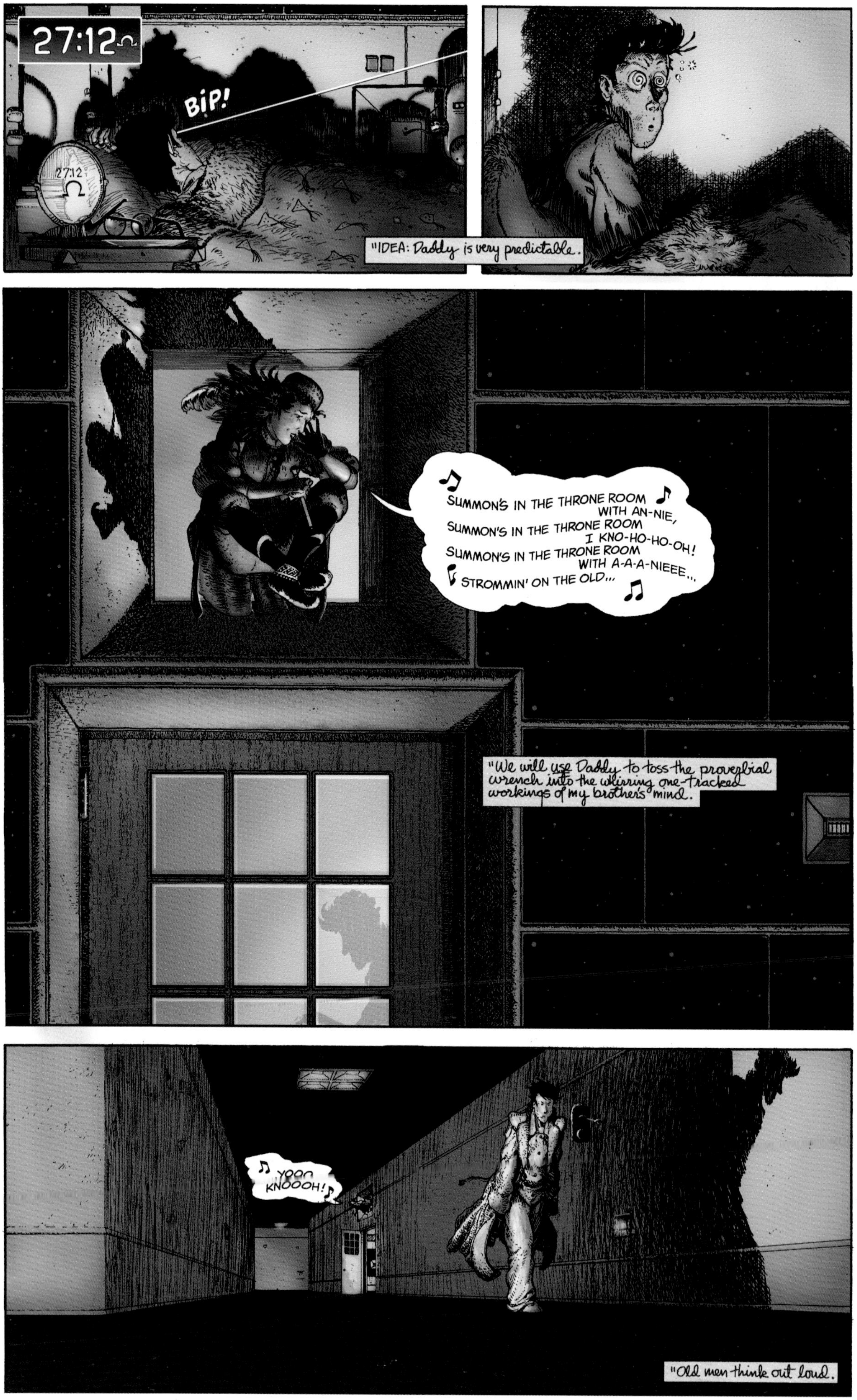
27:12
BIP!
"IDEA: Daddy is very predictable.
SUMMON'S IN THE THRONE ROOM WITH AN-NIE, SUMMON'S IN THE THRONE ROOM I KNO-HO-HO-OH! SUMMON'S IN THE THRONE ROOM WITH A-A-A-NIEEE... STROMMIN' ON THE OLD...
"We will use Daddy to toss the proverbial wrench into the whirring one-tracked workings of my brother's mind.
YOON KNOOOH!
"Old men think out loud.

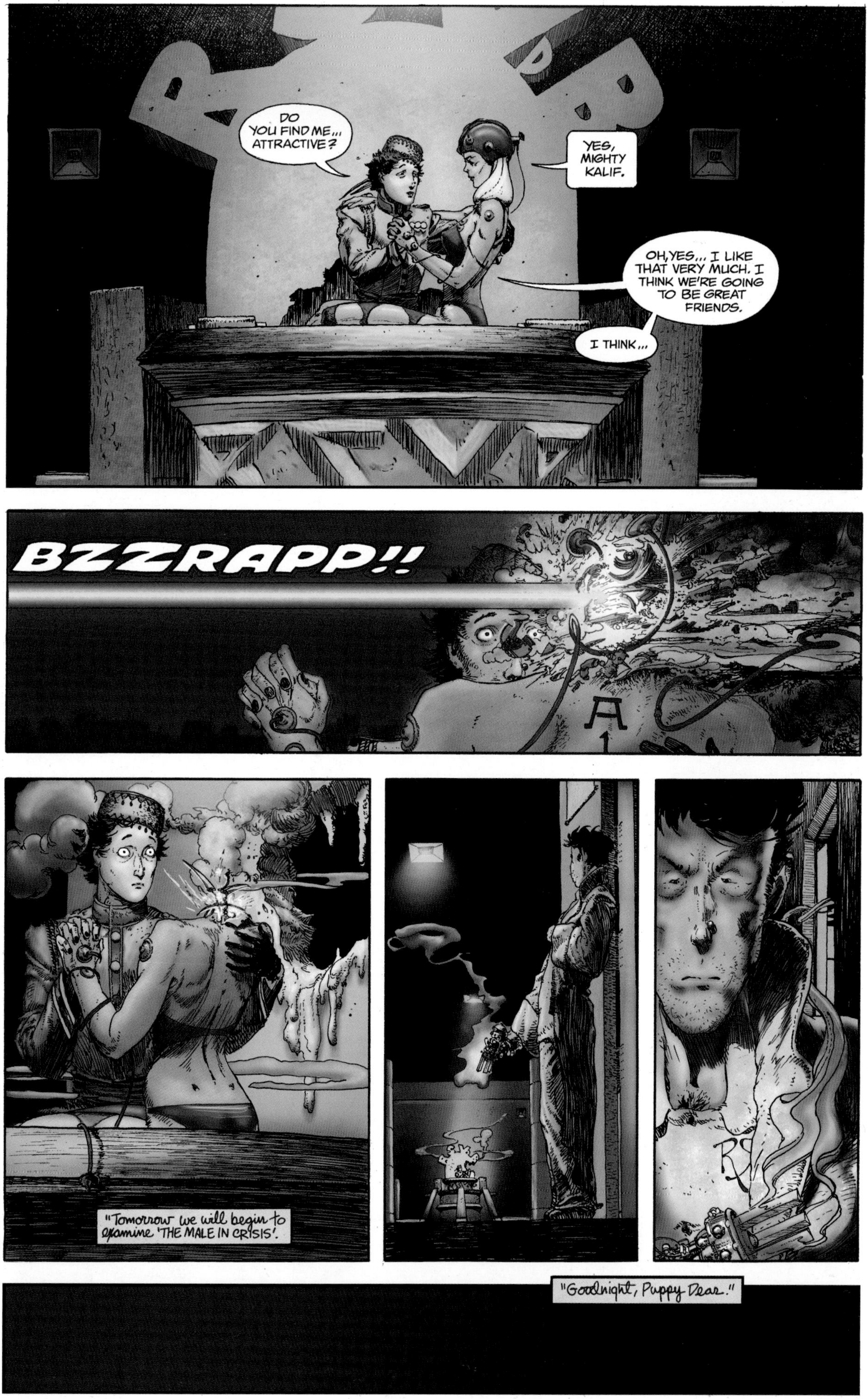
DO YOU FIND ME... ATTRACTIVE?
YES, MIGHTY KALIF.
OH, YES... I LIKE THAT VERY MUCH. I THINK WE'RE GOING TO BE GREAT FRIENDS.
I THINK...
BZZRAPP!!
"Tomorrow we will begin to examine 'THE MALE IN CRISIS'.
"Goodnight, Puppy Dear."

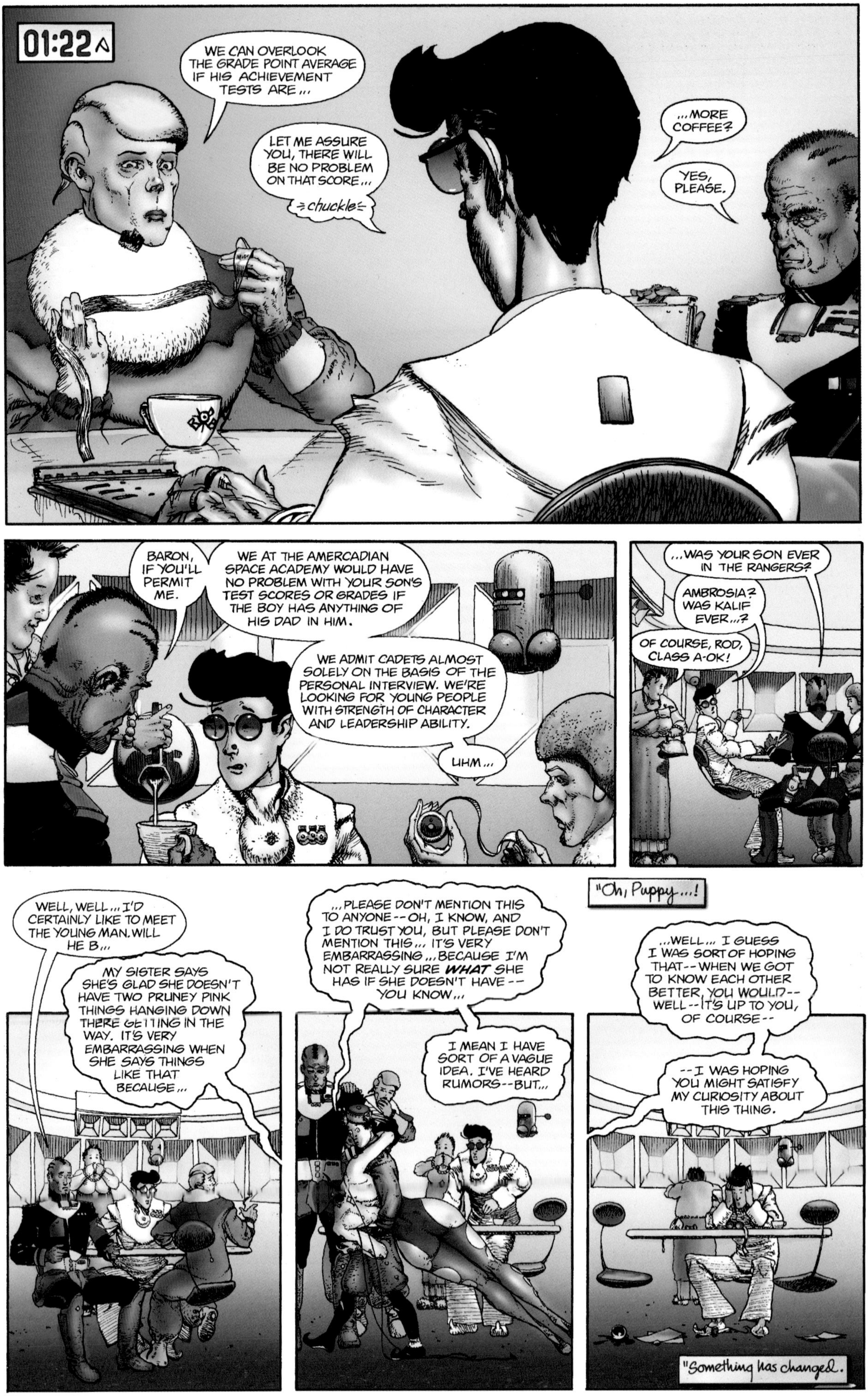
01:22
WE CAN OVERLOOK THE GRADE POINT AVERAGE IF HIS ACHIEVEMENT TESTS ARE...
LET ME ASSURE YOU, THERE WILL BE NO PROBLEM ON THAT SCORE...
chuckle
...MORE COFFEE?
YES, PLEASE.
BARON, IF YOU'LL PERMIT ME.
WE AT THE AMERCADIAN SPACE ACADEMY WOULD HAVE NO PROBLEM WITH YOUR SON'S TEST SCORES OR GRADES IF THE BOY HAS ANYTHING OF HIS DAD IN HIM.
WE ADMIT CADETS ALMOST SOLELY ON THE BASIS OF THE PERSONAL INTERVIEW. WE'RE LOOKING FOR YOUNG PEOPLE WITH STRENGTH OF CHARACTER AND LEADERSHIP ABILITY.
UHM...
...WAS YOUR SON EVER IN THE RANGERS?
AMBROSIA? WAS KALIF EVER...?
OF COURSE, ROD, CLASS A-OK!
WELL, WELL... I'D CERTAINLY LIKE TO MEET THE YOUNG MAN. WILL HE B...
MY SISTER SAYS SHE'S GLAD SHE DOESN'T HAVE TWO PRUNEY PINK THINGS HANGING DOWN THERE GETTING IN THE WAY. IT'S VERY EMBARRASSING WHEN SHE SAYS THINGS LIKE THAT BECAUSE...
...PLEASE DON'T MENTION THIS TO ANYONE--OH, I KNOW, AND I DO TRUST YOU, BUT PLEASE DON'T MENTION THIS... IT'S VERY EMBARRASSING... BECAUSE I'M NOT REALLY SURE WHAT SHE HAS IF SHE DOESN'T HAVE--YOU KNOW...
I MEAN I HAVE SORT OF A VAGUE IDEA. I'VE HEARD RUMORS--BUT...
"Oh, Puppy...!
...WELL... I GUESS I WAS SORT OF HOPING THAT--WHEN WE GOT TO KNOW EACH OTHER BETTER, YOU WOULD--WELL--IT'S UP TO YOU, OF COURSE--
--I WAS HOPING YOU MIGHT SATISFY MY CURIOSITY ABOUT THIS THING.
"Something has changed.

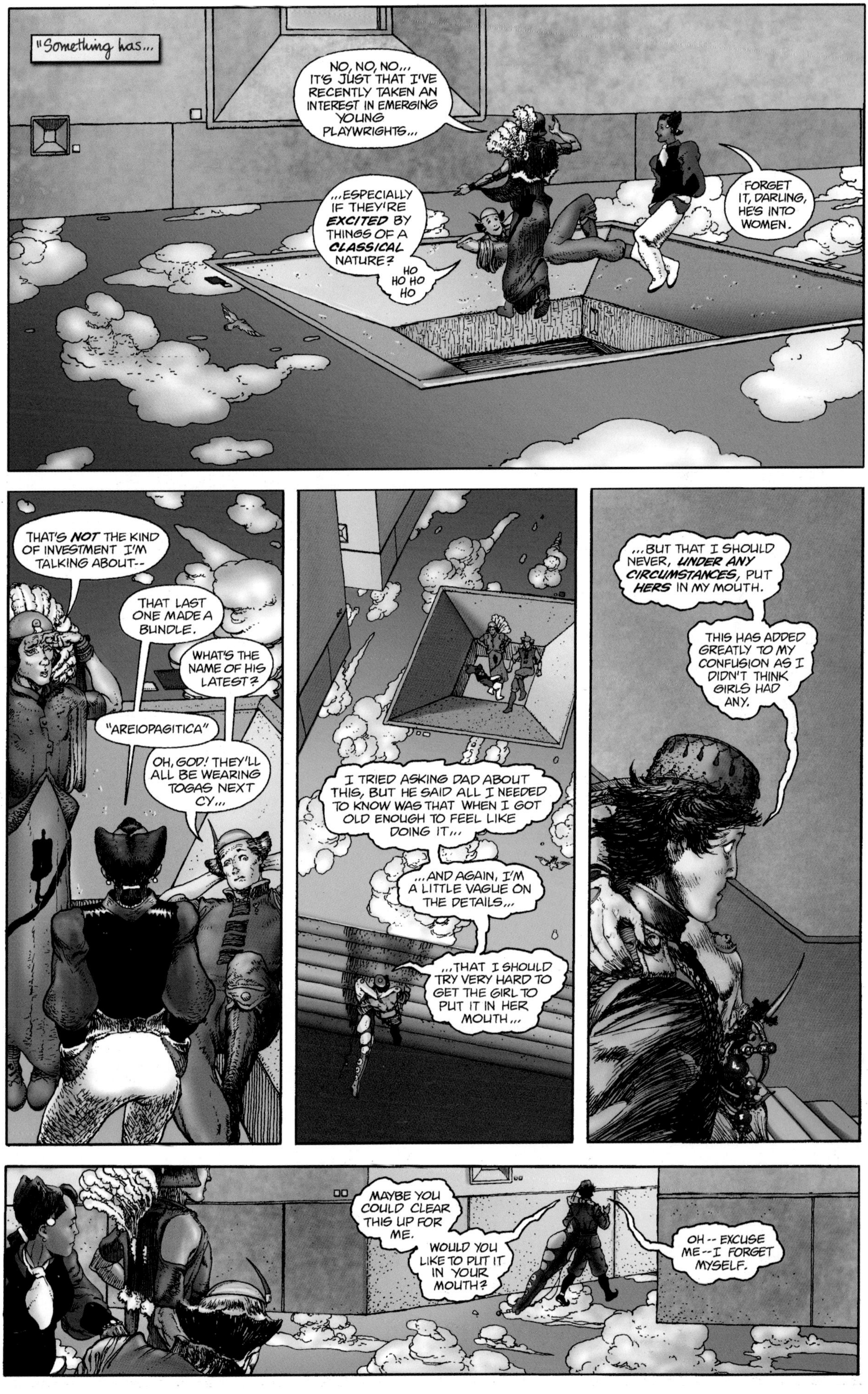
"Something has...
NO, NO, NO,.. IT'S JUST THAT I'VE RECENTLY TAKEN AN INTEREST IN EMERGING YOUNG PLAYWRIGHTS...
...ESPECIALLY IF THEY'RE EXCITED BY THINGS OF A CLASSICAL NATURE?
HO HO HO HO
FORGET IT, DARLING, HE'S INTO WOMEN.
THAT'S NOT THE KIND OF INVESTMENT I'M TALKING ABOUT--
THAT LAST ONE MADE A BUNDLE.
WHAT'S THE NAME OF HIS LATEST?
"AREIOPAGITICA"
OH, GOD! THEY'LL ALL BE WEARING TOGAS NEXT CY...
I TRIED ASKING DAD ABOUT THIS, BUT HE SAID ALL I NEEDED TO KNOW WAS THAT WHEN I GOT OLD ENOUGH TO FEEL LIKE DOING IT...
...AND AGAIN, I'M A LITTLE VAGUE ON THE DETAILS...
...THAT I SHOULD TRY VERY HARD TO GET THE GIRL TO PUT IT IN HER MOUTH...
...BUT THAT I SHOULD NEVER, UNDER ANY CIRCUMSTANCES, PUT HERS IN MY MOUTH.
THIS HAS ADDED GREATLY TO MY CONFUSION AS I DIDN'T THINK GIRLS HAD ANY.
MAYBE YOU COULD CLEAR THIS UP FOR ME.
WOULD YOU LIKE TO PUT IT IN YOUR MOUTH?
OH -- EXCUSE ME -- I FORGET MYSELF.

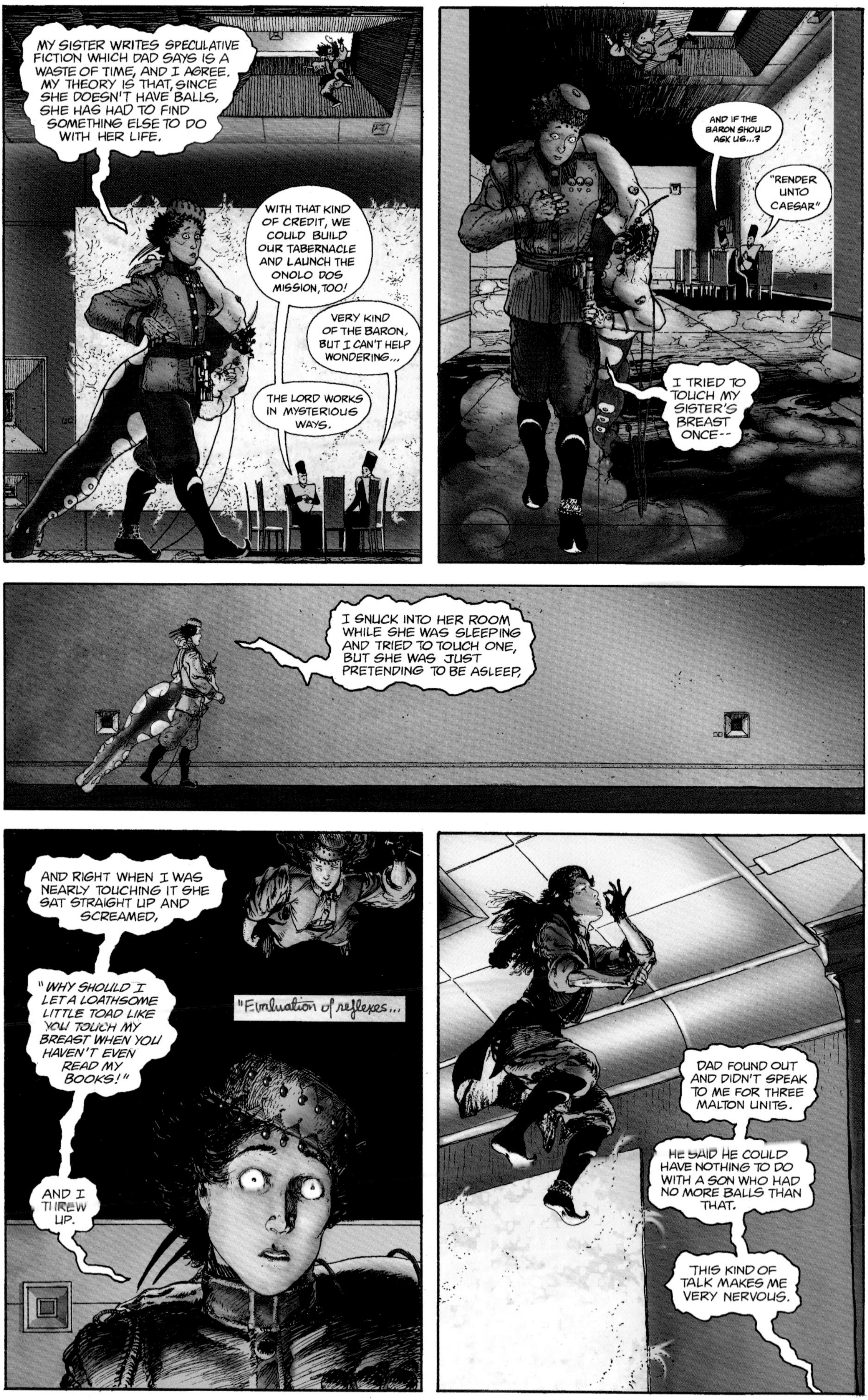
MY SISTER WRITES SPECULATIVE FICTION WHICH DAD SAYS IS A WASTE OF TIME, AND I AGREE. MY THEORY IS THAT, SINCE SHE DOESN'T HAVE BALLS, SHE HAS HAD TO FIND SOMETHING ELSE TO DO WITH HER LIFE.
WITH THAT KIND OF CREDIT, WE COULD BUILD OUR TABERNACLE AND LAUNCH THE ONOLO DOS MISSION, TOO!
VERY KIND OF THE BARON, BUT I CAN'T HELP WONDERING...
THE LORD WORKS IN MYSTERIOUS WAYS.
AND IF THE BARON SHOULD ASK US...?
"RENDER UNTO CAESAR"
I TRIED TO TOUCH MY SISTER'S BREAST ONCE--
I SNUCK INTO HER ROOM WHILE SHE WAS SLEEPING AND TRIED TO TOUCH ONE, BUT SHE WAS JUST PRETENDING TO BE ASLEEP,
AND RIGHT WHEN I WAS NEARLY TOUCHING IT SHE SAT STRAIGHT UP AND SCREAMED,
"WHY SHOULD I LET A LOATHSOME LITTLE TOAD LIKE YOU TOUCH MY BREAST WHEN YOU HAVEN'T EVEN READ MY BOOKS!"
"Evaluation of reflexes...
AND I THREW UP.
DAD FOUND OUT AND DIDN'T SPEAK TO ME FOR THREE MALTON UNITS.
HE SAID HE COULD HAVE NOTHING TO DO WITH A SON WHO HAD NO MORE BALLS THAN THAT.
THIS KIND OF TALK MAKES ME VERY NERVOUS.

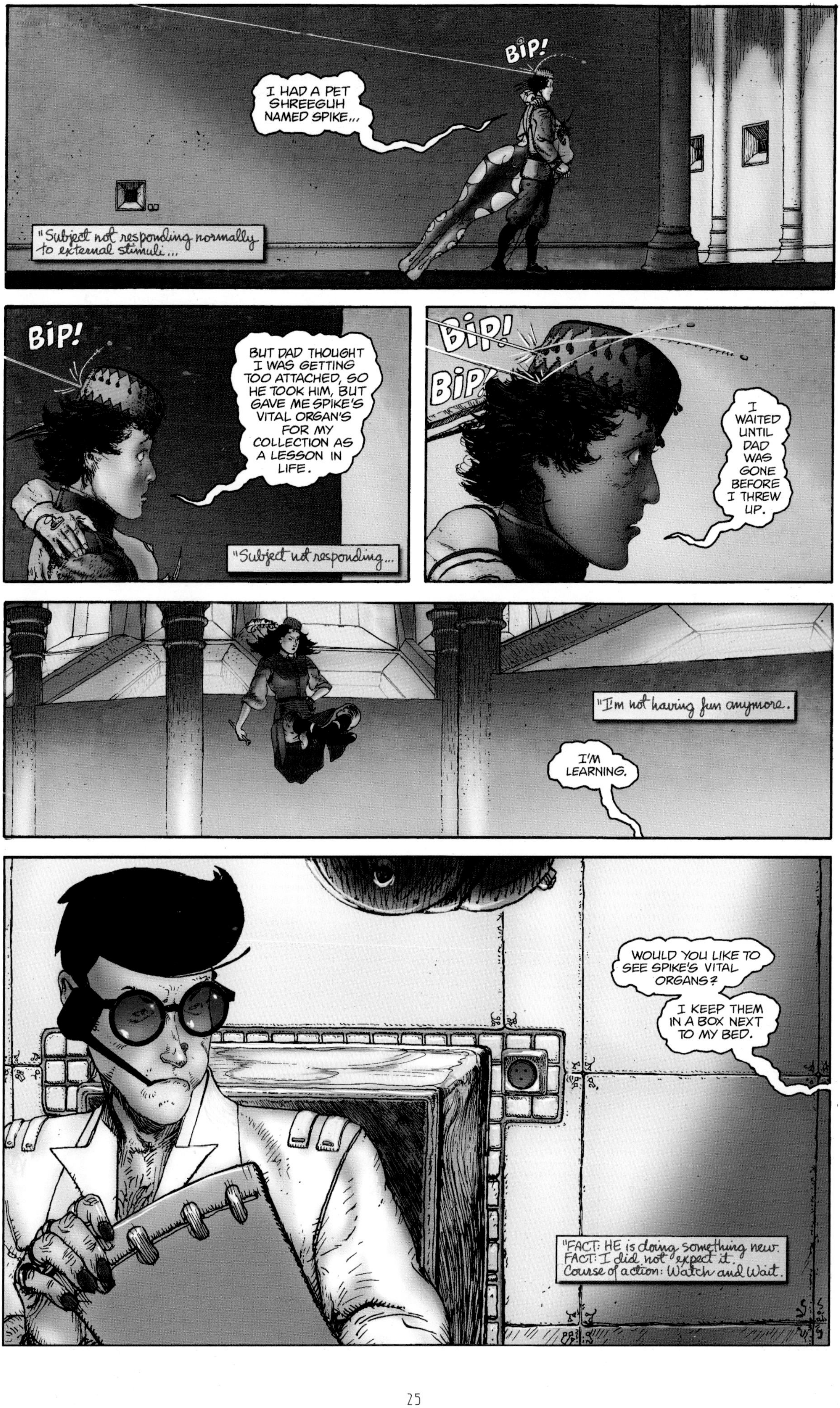
BIP!
I HAD A PET SHREEGUH NAMED SPIKE...
"Subject not responding normally to external stimuli...
BIP!
BUT DAD THOUGHT I WAS GETTING TOO ATTACHED, SO HE TOOK HIM, BUT GAVE ME SPIKE'S VITAL ORGAN'S FOR MY COLLECTION AS A LESSON IN LIFE.
"Subject not responding...
BIP!
BIP!
I WAITED UNTIL DAD WAS GONE BEFORE I THREW UP.
"I'm not having fun anymore.
I'M LEARNING.
WOULD YOU LIKE TO SEE SPIKE'S VITAL ORGANS?
I KEEP THEM IN A BOX NEXT TO MY BED.
"FACT: HE is doing something new.
FACT: I did not expect it.
Course of action: Watch and Wait.

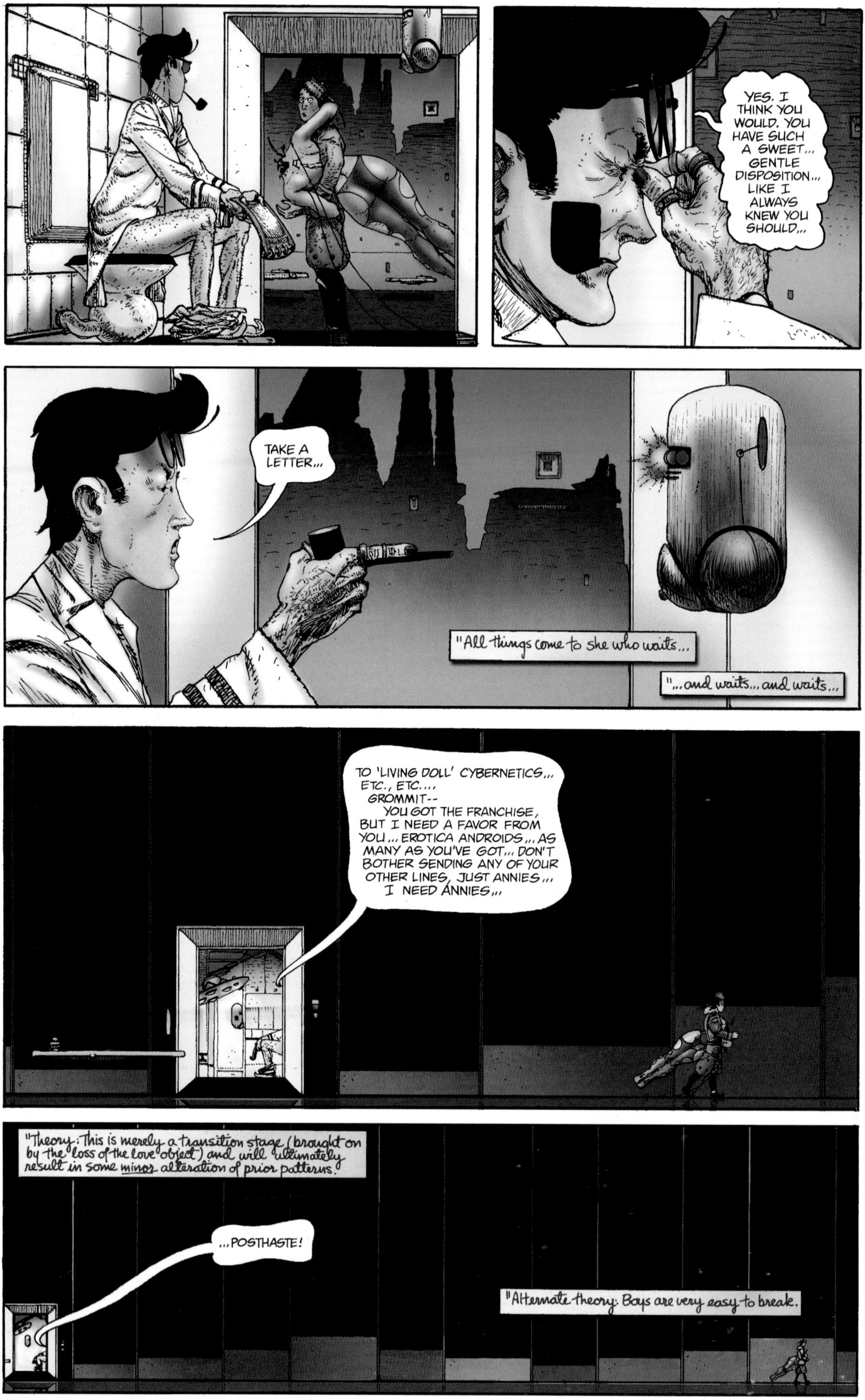
YES. I THINK YOU WOULD. YOU HAVE SUCH A SWEET... GENTLE DISPOSITION... LIKE I ALWAYS KNEW YOU SHOULD...
TAKE A LETTER...
"All things come to she who waits...
"...and waits... and waits...
TO 'LIVING DOLL' CYBERNETICS... ETC., ETC.... GROMMIT-- YOU GOT THE FRANCHISE, BUT I NEED A FAVOR FROM YOU... EROTICA ANDROIDS... AS MANY AS YOU'VE GOT... DON'T BOTHER SENDING ANY OF YOUR OTHER LINES, JUST ANNIES... I NEED ANNIES...
"Theory: This is merely a transition stage (brought on by the loss of the love object) and will ultimately result in some minor alteration of prior patterns.
...POSTHASTE!
"Alternate theory: Boys are very easy to break.

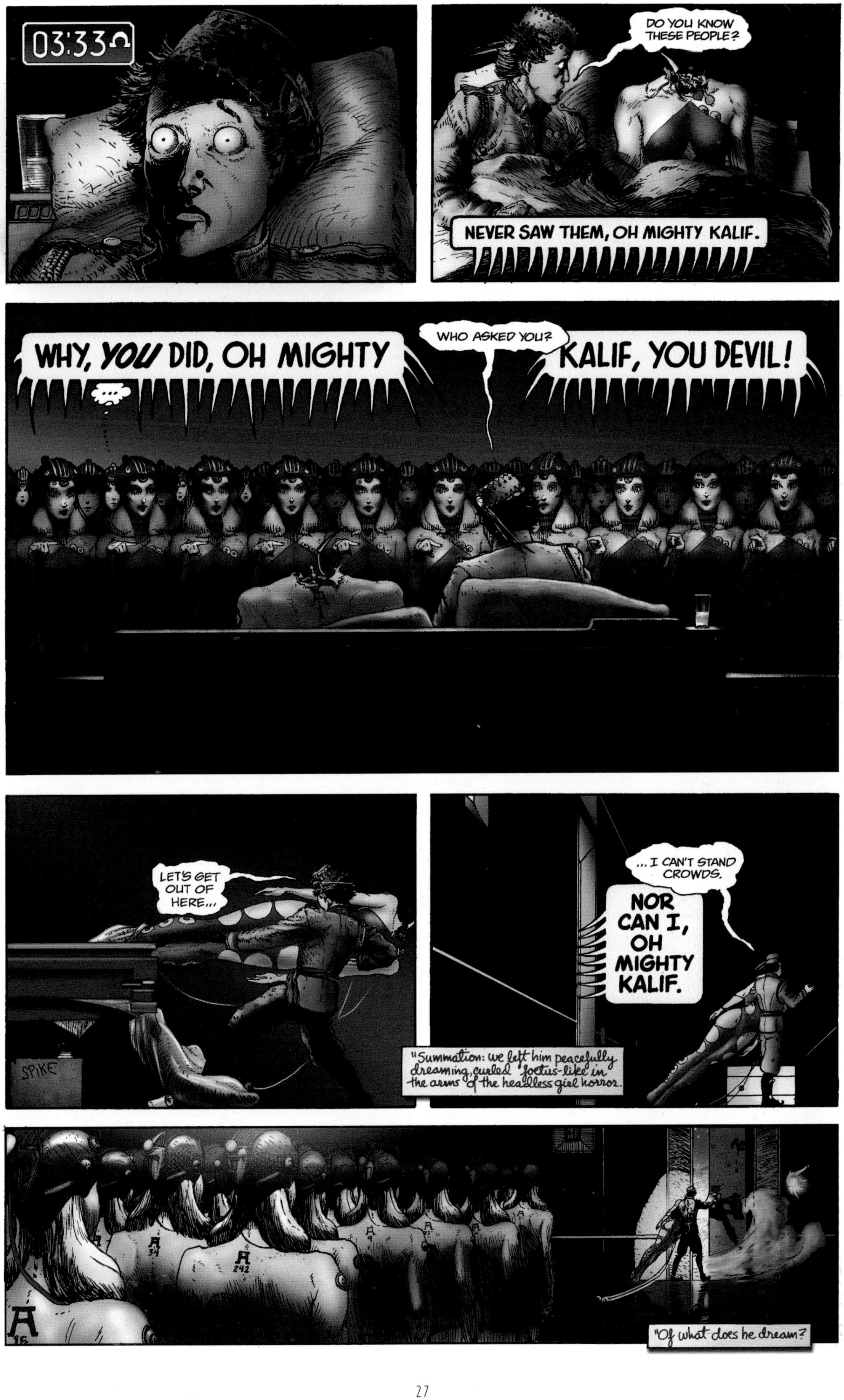
03:33
DO YOU KNOW THESE PEOPLE?
NEVER SAW THEM, OH MIGHTY KALIF.
WHY, YOU DID, OH MIGHTY
WHO ASKED YOU?
KALIF, YOU DEVIL!
...
LET'S GET OUT OF HERE...
SPIKE
...I CAN'T STAND CROWDS.
NOR CAN I, OH MIGHTY KALIF.
"Summation: we left him peacefully dreaming, curled foetus-like in the arms of the headless girl horror.
"Of what does he dream?

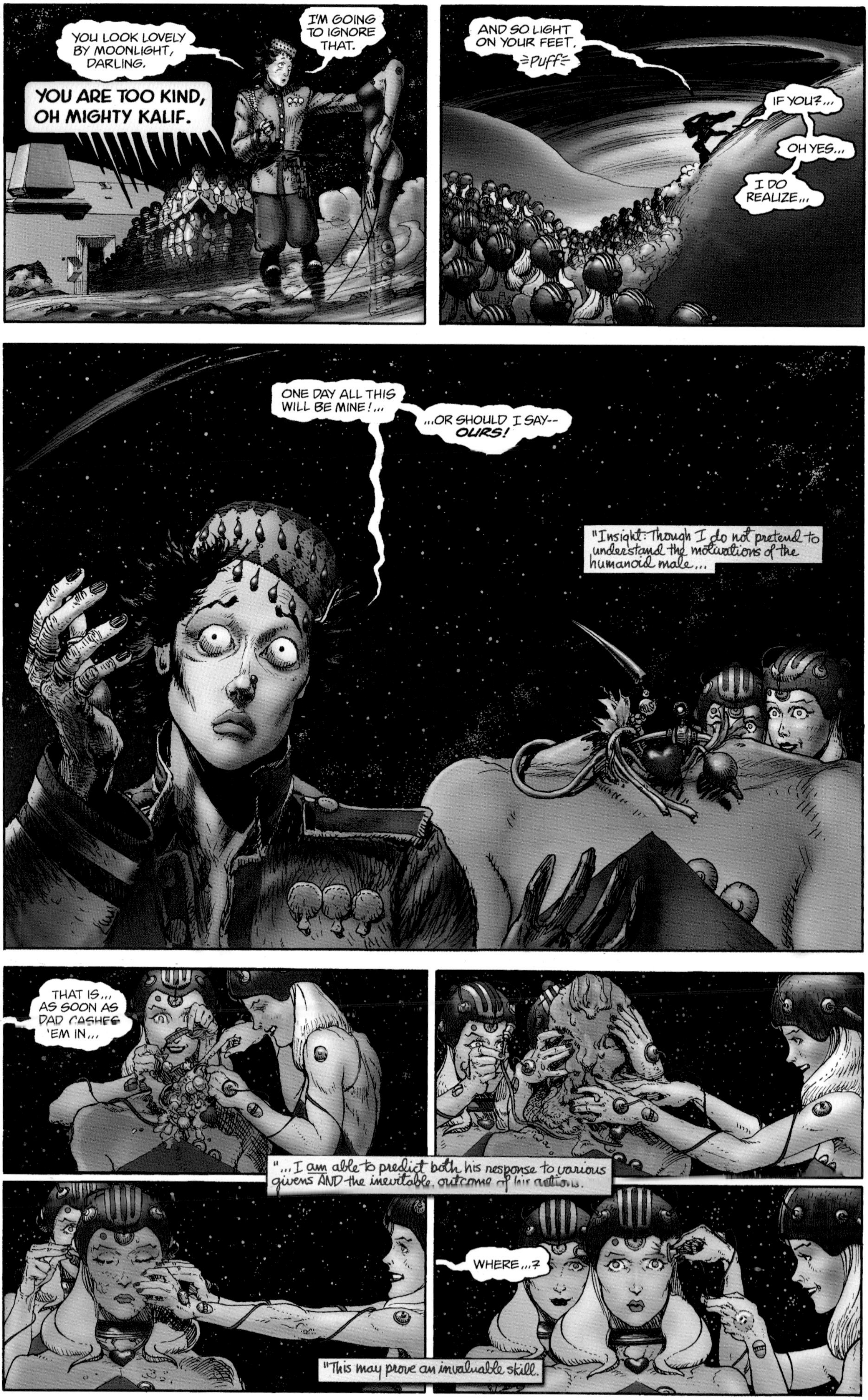
YOU LOOK LOVELY BY MOONLIGHT, DARLING.
I'M GOING TO IGNORE THAT.
YOU ARE TOO KIND, OH MIGHTY KALIF.
AND SO LIGHT ON YOUR FEET.
PUFF
IF YOU?...
OH YES...
I DO REALIZE...
ONE DAY ALL THIS WILL BE MINE!...
...OR SHOULD I SAY-- OURS!
"Insight: Though I do not pretend to understand the motivations of the humanoid male...
THAT IS... AS SOON AS DAD CASHES 'EM IN...
"...I am able to predict both his response to various givens AND the inevitable outcome of his actions.
WHERE...?
"This may prove an invaluable skill.

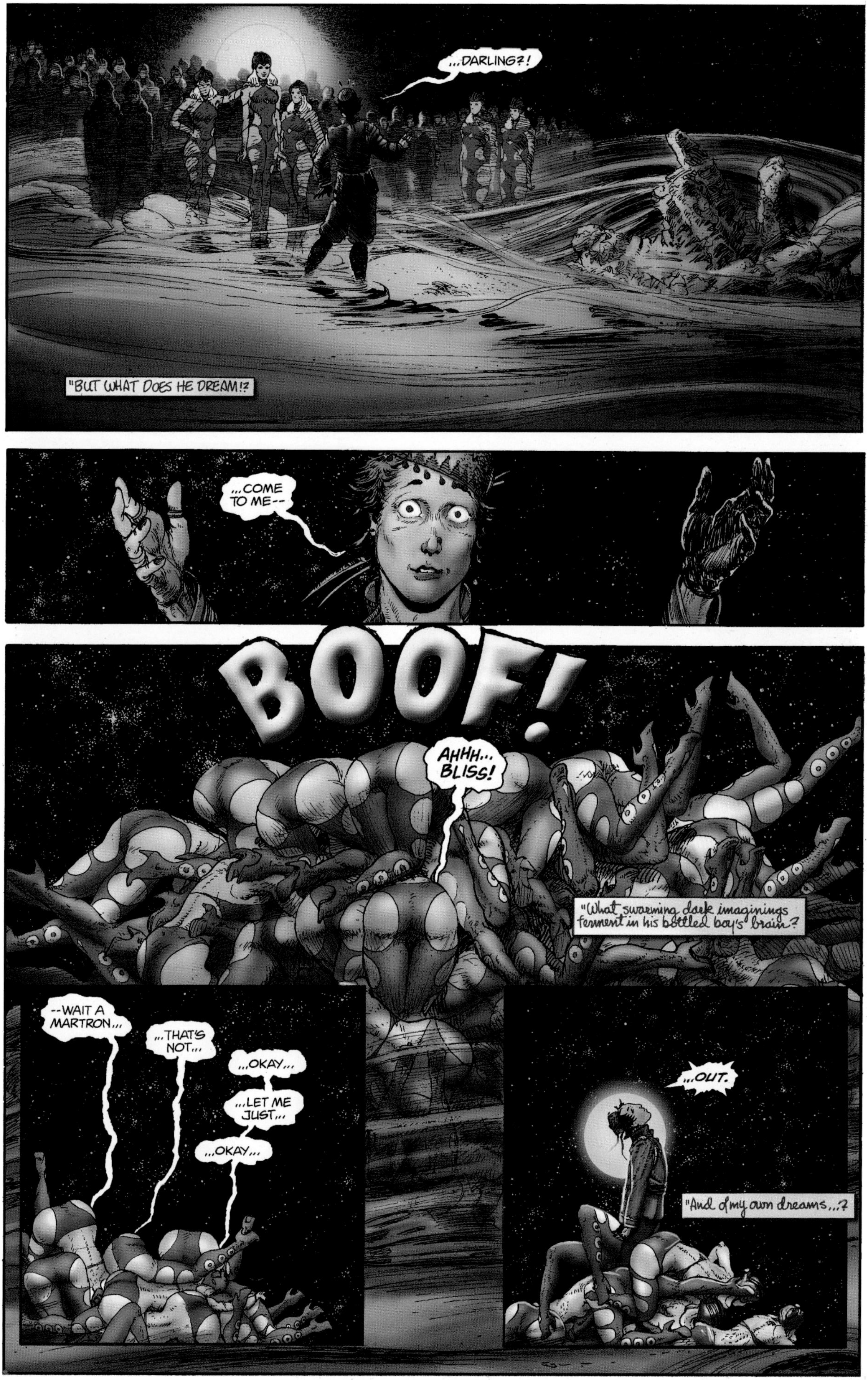

...DARLING?!
"BUT WHAT DOES HE DREAM!?
...COME TO ME--
BOOF!
AHHH... BLISS!
"What swarming dark imaginings ferment in his bottled boy's brain?
--WAIT A MARTRON...
...THAT'S NOT...
...OKAY...
...LET ME JUST...
...OKAY...
...OUT.
"And of my own dreams...?

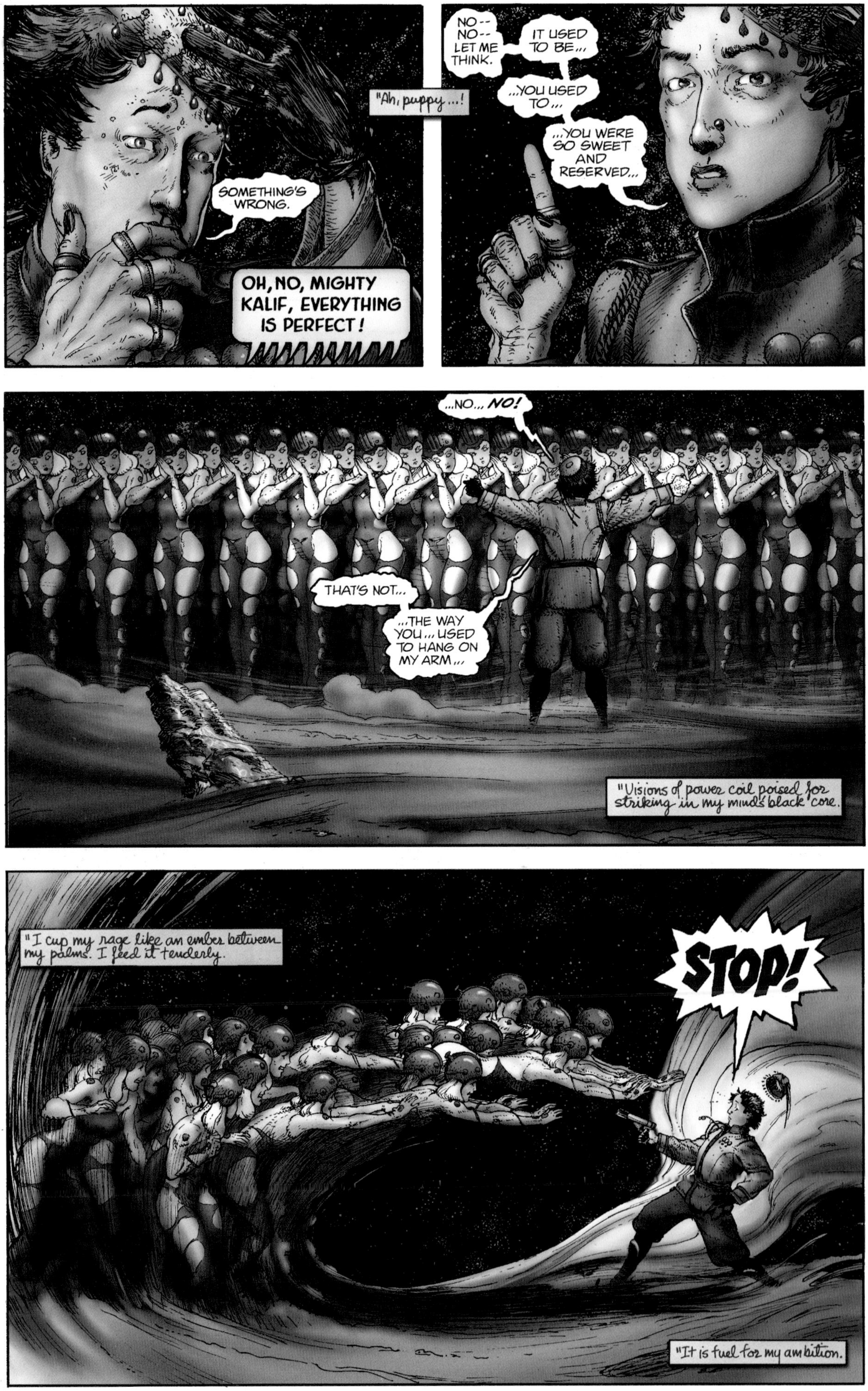
SOMETHING'S WRONG.
OH, NO, MIGHTY KALIF, EVERYTHING IS PERFECT!
"Ah, puppy...!
NO-- NO-- LET ME THINK.
IT USED TO BE...
...YOU USED TO...
...YOU WERE SO SWEET AND RESERVED...
...NO... NO!
THAT'S NOT...
...THE WAY YOU... USED TO HANG ON MY ARM...
"Visions of power coil poised for striking in my mind's black core.
"I cup my rage like an embers between my palms. I feed it tenderly.
STOP!
"It is fuel for my ambition.

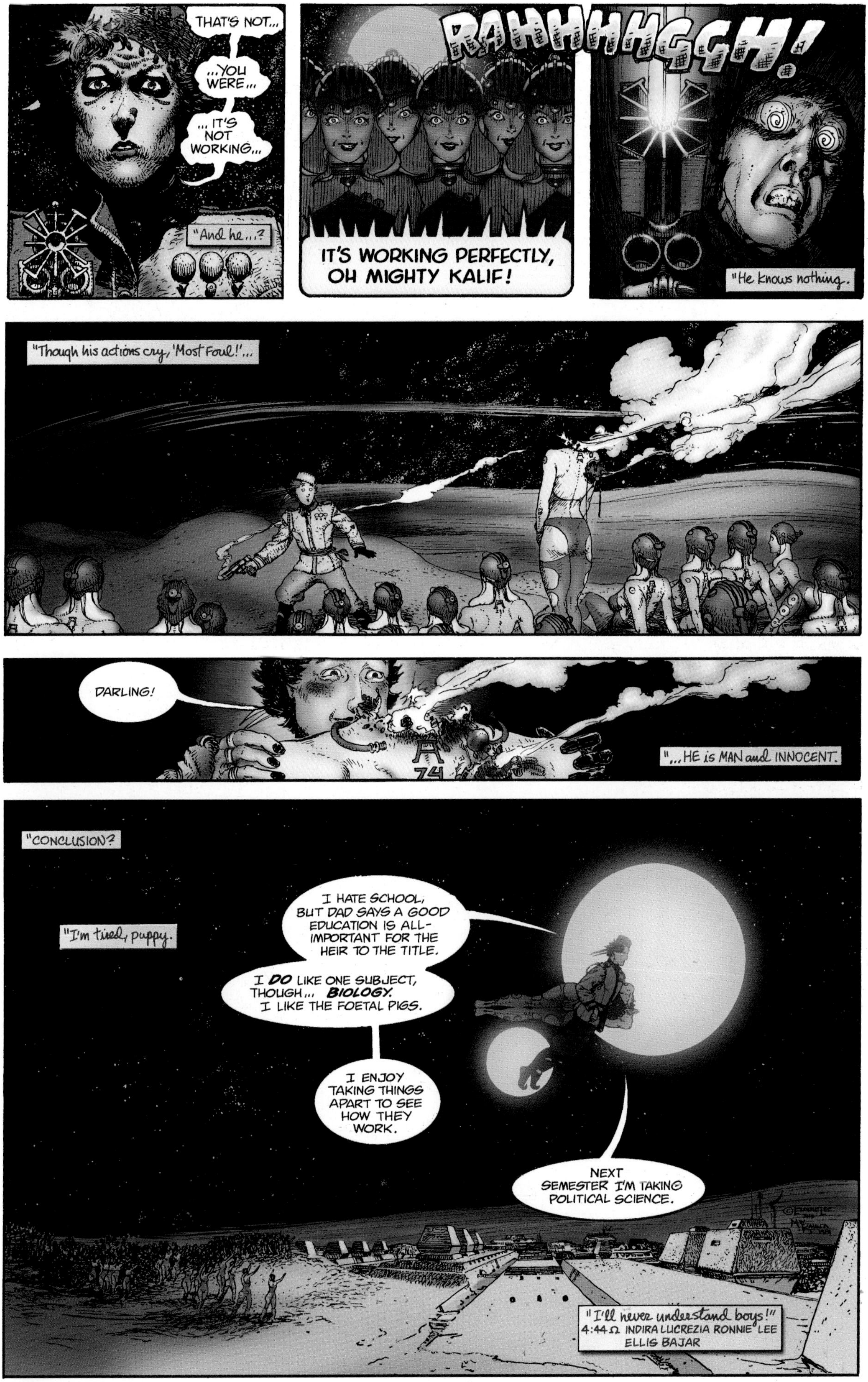
THAT'S NOT...
...YOU WERE...
...IT'S NOT WORKING...
"And he...?
RAHHHHGGH!
IT'S WORKING PERFECTLY, OH MIGHTY KALIF!
"He knows nothing.
"Though his actions cry, 'Most Foul!'...
DARLING!
"...HE is MAN and INNOCENT.
"CONCLUSION?
"I'm tired, puppy.
I HATE SCHOOL, BUT DAD SAYS A GOOD EDUCATION IS ALL-IMPORTANT FOR THE HEIR TO THE TITLE.
I DO LIKE ONE SUBJECT, THOUGH... BIOLOGY. I LIKE THE FOETAL PIGS.
I ENJOY TAKING THINGS APART TO SEE HOW THEY WORK.
NEXT SEMESTER I'M TAKING POLITICAL SCIENCE.
"I'll never understand boys!"
4:44 Ω INDIRA LUCREZIA RONNIE LEE ELLIS BAJAR

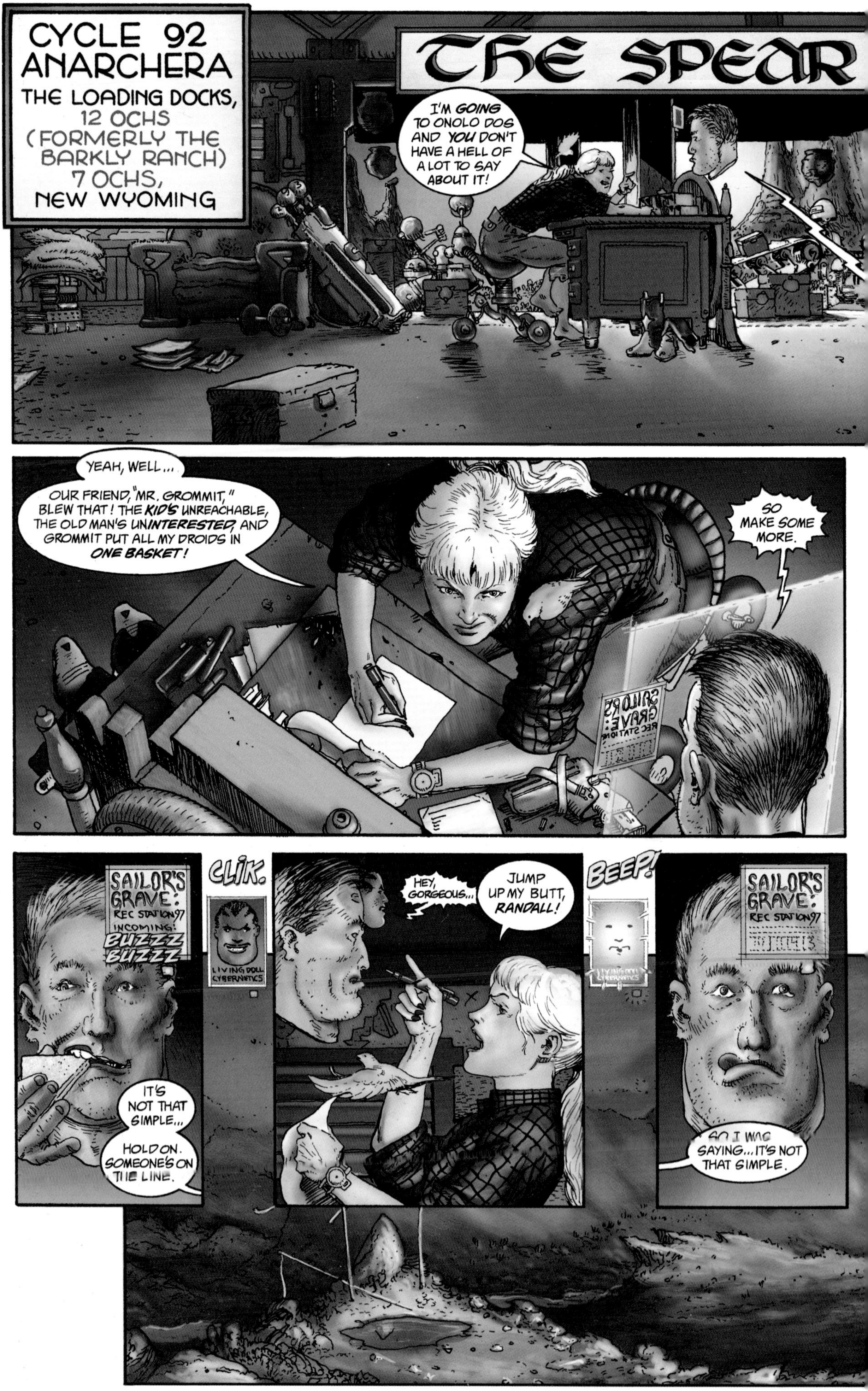

CYCLE 92
ANARCHERA
THE LOADING DOCKS,
12 OCHS
(FORMERLY THE
BARKLY RANCH)
7 OCHS,
NEW WYOMING
THE SPEAR
I'M GOING TO ONOLO DOS AND YOU DON'T HAVE A HELL OF A LOT TO SAY ABOUT IT!
YEAH, WELL...
OUR FRIEND, "MR. GROMMIT," BLEW THAT! THE KID'S UNREACHABLE, THE OLD MAN'S UNINTERESTED, AND GROMMIT PUT ALL MY DROIDS IN ONE BASKET!
SO MAKE SOME MORE.
SAILOR'S GRAVE: REC STATION 97 INCOMING!
BUZZZ BUZZZ
IT'S NOT THAT SIMPLE...
HOLD ON. SOMEONE'S ON THE LINE.
CLIK.
LIVING DOLL CYBERNETICS
HEY, GORGEOUS...
JUMP UP MY BUTT, RANDALL!
BEEP!
LIVING DOLL CYBERNETICS
SAILOR'S GRAVE: REC STATION 97
SO I WAS SAYING... IT'S NOT THAT SIMPLE.

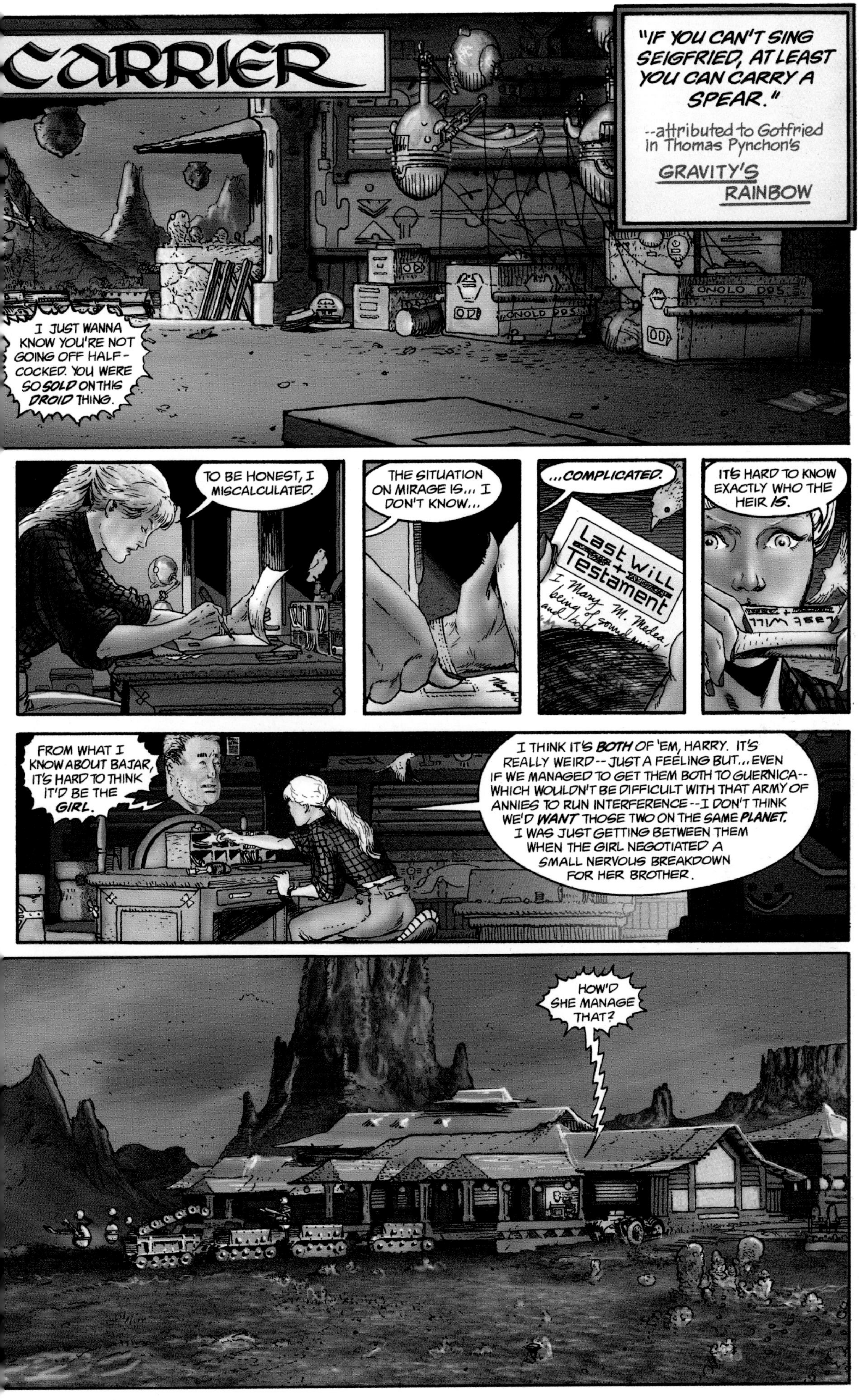
CARRIER
"IF YOU CAN'T SING SEIGFRIED, AT LEAST YOU CAN CARRY A SPEAR."
--attributed to Gotfried in Thomas Pynchon's GRAVITY'S RAINBOW
ONOLO DDS
I JUST WANNA KNOW YOU'RE NOT GOING OFF HALF-COCKED. YOU WERE SO SOLD ON THIS DROID THING.
TO BE HONEST, I MISCALCULATED.
THE SITUATION ON MIRAGE IS... I DON'T KNOW...
...COMPLICATED.
Last will + Testament
I Mary M. Medea being of sound mind and body
IT'S HARD TO KNOW EXACTLY WHO THE HEIR IS.
FROM WHAT I KNOW ABOUT BAJAR, IT'S HARD TO THINK IT'D BE THE GIRL.
I THINK IT'S BOTH OF 'EM, HARRY. IT'S REALLY WEIRD--JUST A FEELING BUT... EVEN IF WE MANAGED TO GET THEM BOTH TO GUERNICA--WHICH WOULDN'T BE DIFFICULT WITH THAT ARMY OF ANNIES TO RUN INTERFERENCE--I DON'T THINK WE'D WANT THOSE TWO ON THE SAME PLANET. I WAS JUST GETTING BETWEEN THEM WHEN THE GIRL NEGOTIATED A SMALL NERVOUS BREAKDOWN FOR HER BROTHER.
HOW'D SHE MANAGE THAT?

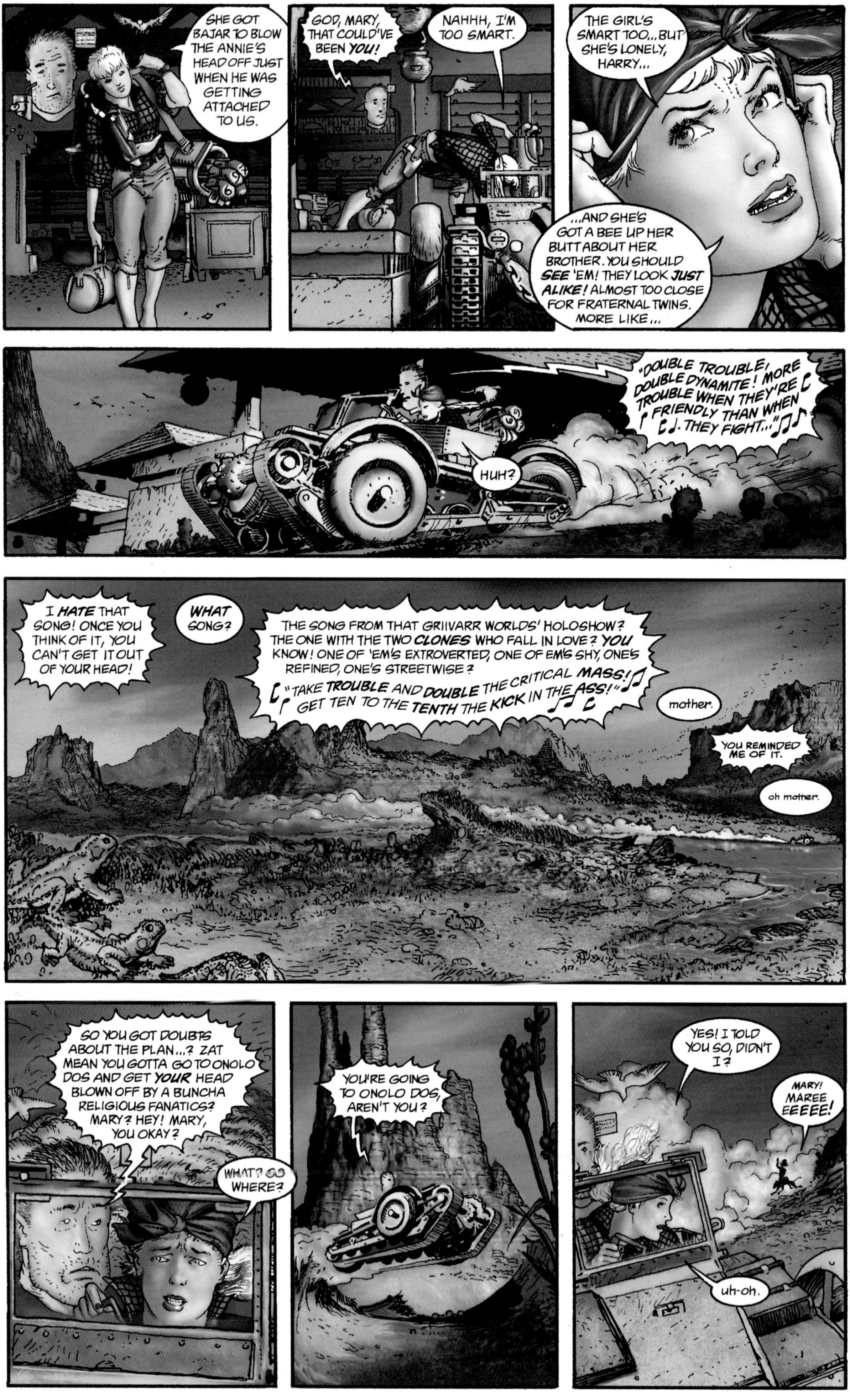
SHE GOT BAJAR TO BLOW THE ANNIE'S HEAD OFF JUST WHEN HE WAS GETTING ATTACHED TO US.
GOD, MARY, THAT COULD'VE BEEN YOU!
NAHHH, I'M TOO SMART.
THE GIRL'S SMART TOO... BUT SHE'S LONELY, HARRY...
...AND SHE'S GOT A BEE UP HER BUTT ABOUT HER BROTHER. YOU SHOULD SEE 'EM! THEY LOOK JUST ALIKE! ALMOST TOO CLOSE FOR FRATERNAL TWINS. MORE LIKE...
"DOUBLE TROUBLE, DOUBLE DYNAMITE! MORE TROUBLE WHEN THEY'RE FRIENDLY THAN WHEN THEY FIGHT..."
HUH?
I HATE THAT SONG! ONCE YOU THINK OF IT, YOU CAN'T GET IT OUT OF YOUR HEAD!
WHAT SONG?
THE SONG FROM THAT GRIIVARR WORLDS' HOLOSHOW? THE ONE WITH THE TWO CLONES WHO FALL IN LOVE? YOU KNOW! ONE OF 'EM'S EXTROVERTED, ONE OF EM'S SHY, ONE'S REFINED, ONE'S STREETWISE?
"TAKE TROUBLE AND DOUBLE THE CRITICAL MASS! GET TEN TO THE TENTH THE KICK IN THE ASS!"
mother.
YOU REMINDED ME OF IT.
oh mother.
SO YOU GOT DOUBTS ABOUT THE PLAN...? ZAT MEAN YOU GOTTA GO TO ONOLO DOS AND GET YOUR HEAD BLOWN OFF BY A BUNCHA RELIGIOUS FANATICS? MARY? HEY! MARY, YOU OKAY?
WHAT? GO WHERE?
YOU'RE GOING TO ONOLO DOS, AREN'T YOU?
YES! I TOLD YOU SO, DIDN'T I?
MARY! MAREE EEEEE!
uh-oh.

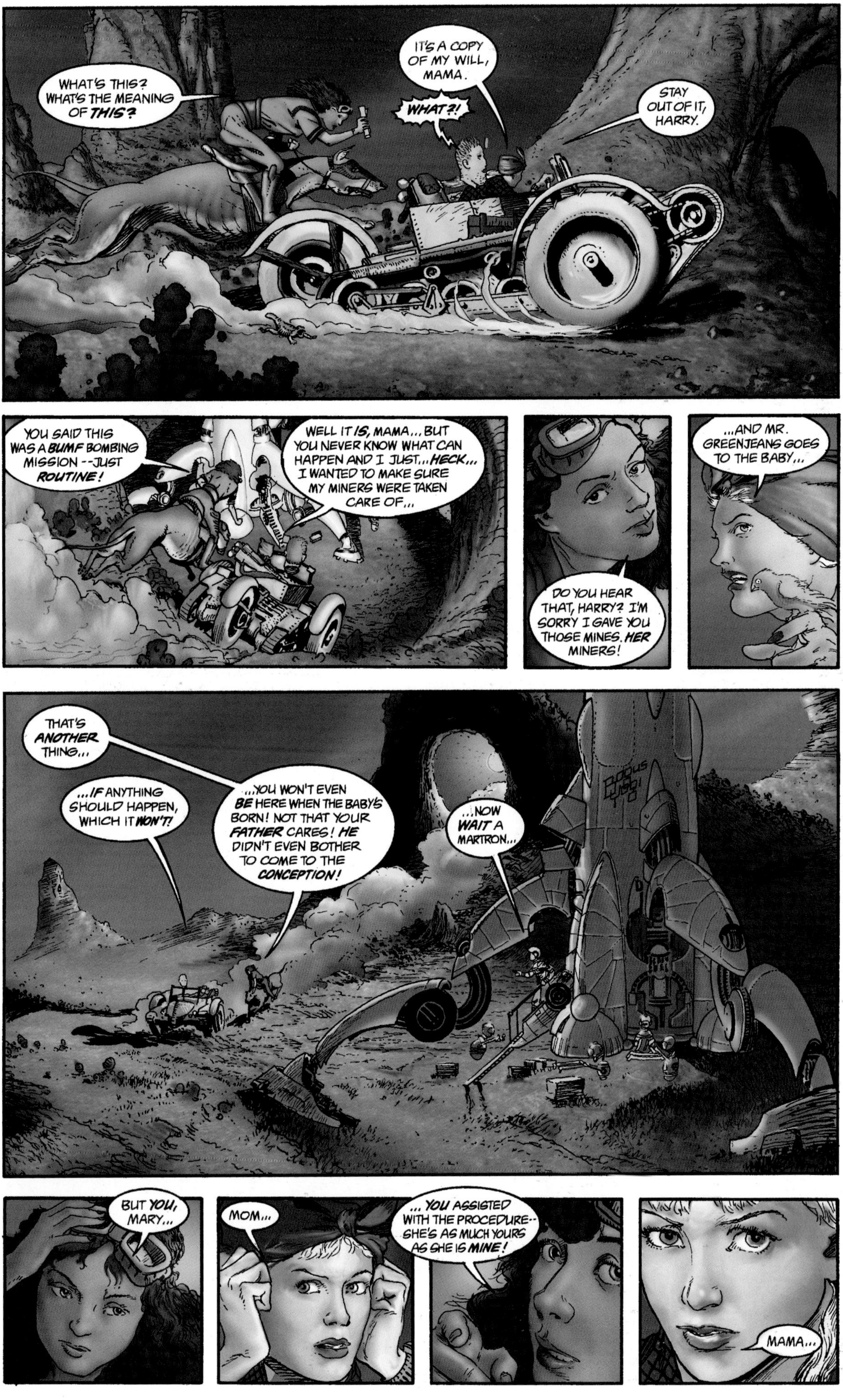
WHAT'S THIS? WHAT'S THE MEANING OF THIS?
IT'S A COPY OF MY WILL, MAMA.
WHAT?!
STAY OUT OF IT, HARRY.
YOU SAID THIS WAS A BUMF BOMBING MISSION --JUST ROUTINE!
WELL IT IS, MAMA... BUT YOU NEVER KNOW WHAT CAN HAPPEN AND I JUST... HECK... I WANTED TO MAKE SURE MY MINERS WERE TAKEN CARE OF...
DO YOU HEAR THAT, HARRY? I'M SORRY I GAVE YOU THOSE MINES. HER MINERS!
...AND MR. GREENJEANS GOES TO THE BABY...
THAT'S ANOTHER THING...
...IF ANYTHING SHOULD HAPPEN, WHICH IT WON'T!
...YOU WON'T EVEN BE HERE WHEN THE BABY'S BORN! NOT THAT YOUR FATHER CARES! HE DIDN'T EVEN BOTHER TO COME TO THE CONCEPTION!
...NOW WAIT A MARTRON...
BUT YOU, MARY...
MOM...
...YOU ASSISTED WITH THE PROCEDURE-- SHE'S AS MUCH YOURS AS SHE IS MINE!
MAMA...

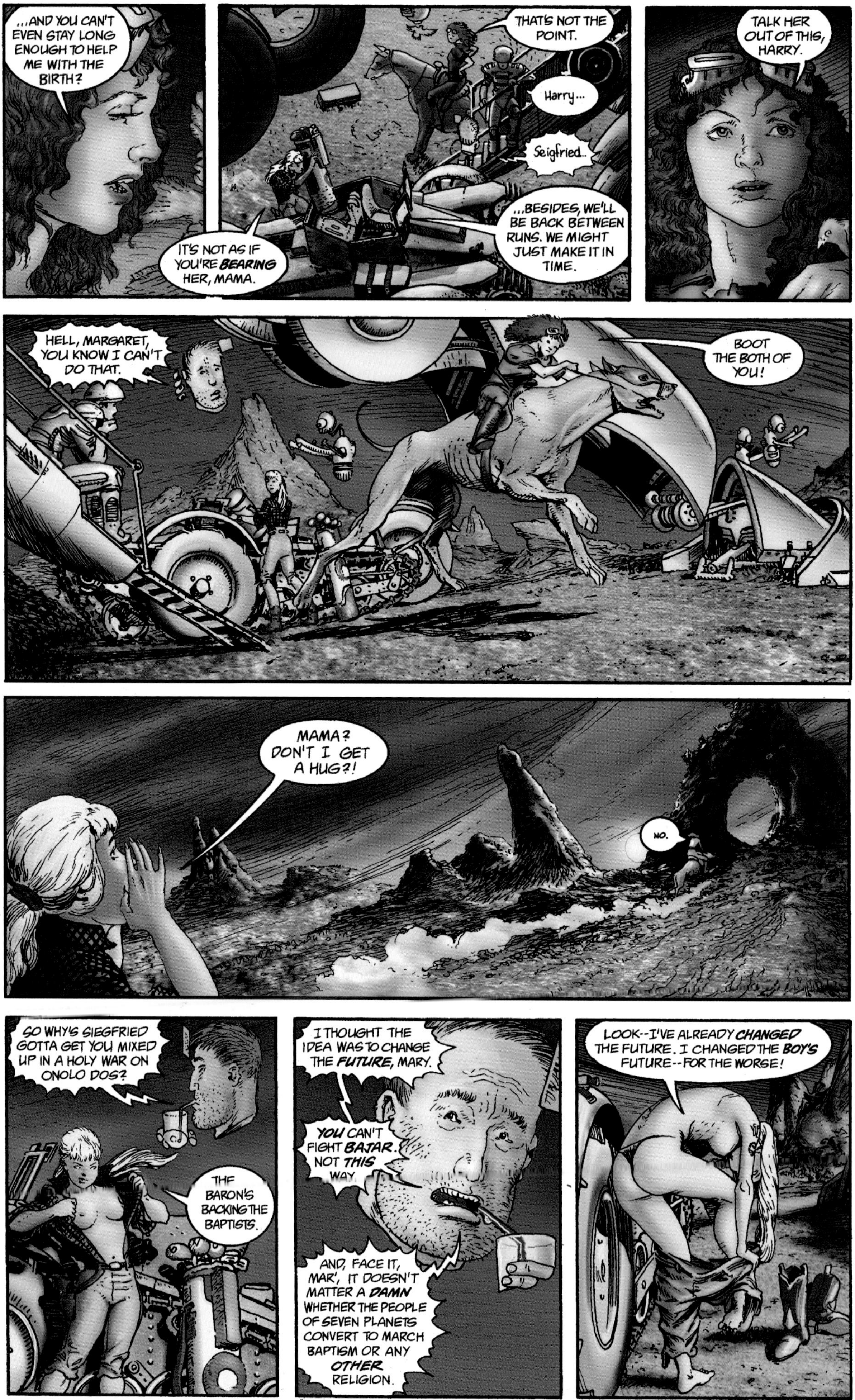
...AND YOU CAN'T EVEN STAY LONG ENOUGH TO HELP ME WITH THE BIRTH?
THAT'S NOT THE POINT.
Harry...
Seigfried...
IT'S NOT AS IF YOU'RE BEARING HER, MAMA.
...BESIDES, WE'LL BE BACK BETWEEN RUNS. WE MIGHT JUST MAKE IT IN TIME.
TALK HER OUT OF THIS, HARRY.
HELL, MARGARET, YOU KNOW I CAN'T DO THAT.
BOOT THE BOTH OF YOU!
MAMA? DON'T I GET A HUG?!
NO.
SO WHY'S SIEGFRIED GOTTA GET YOU MIXED UP IN A HOLY WAR ON ONOLO DOS?
THE BARON'S BACKING THE BAPTISTS.
I THOUGHT THE IDEA WAS TO CHANGE THE FUTURE, MARY.
YOU CAN'T FIGHT BAJAR. NOT THIS WAY.
AND, FACE IT, MAR', IT DOESN'T MATTER A DAMN WHETHER THE PEOPLE OF SEVEN PLANETS CONVERT TO MARCH BAPTISM OR ANY OTHER RELIGION.
LOOK--I'VE ALREADY CHANGED THE FUTURE. I CHANGED THE BOY'S FUTURE--FOR THE WORSE!

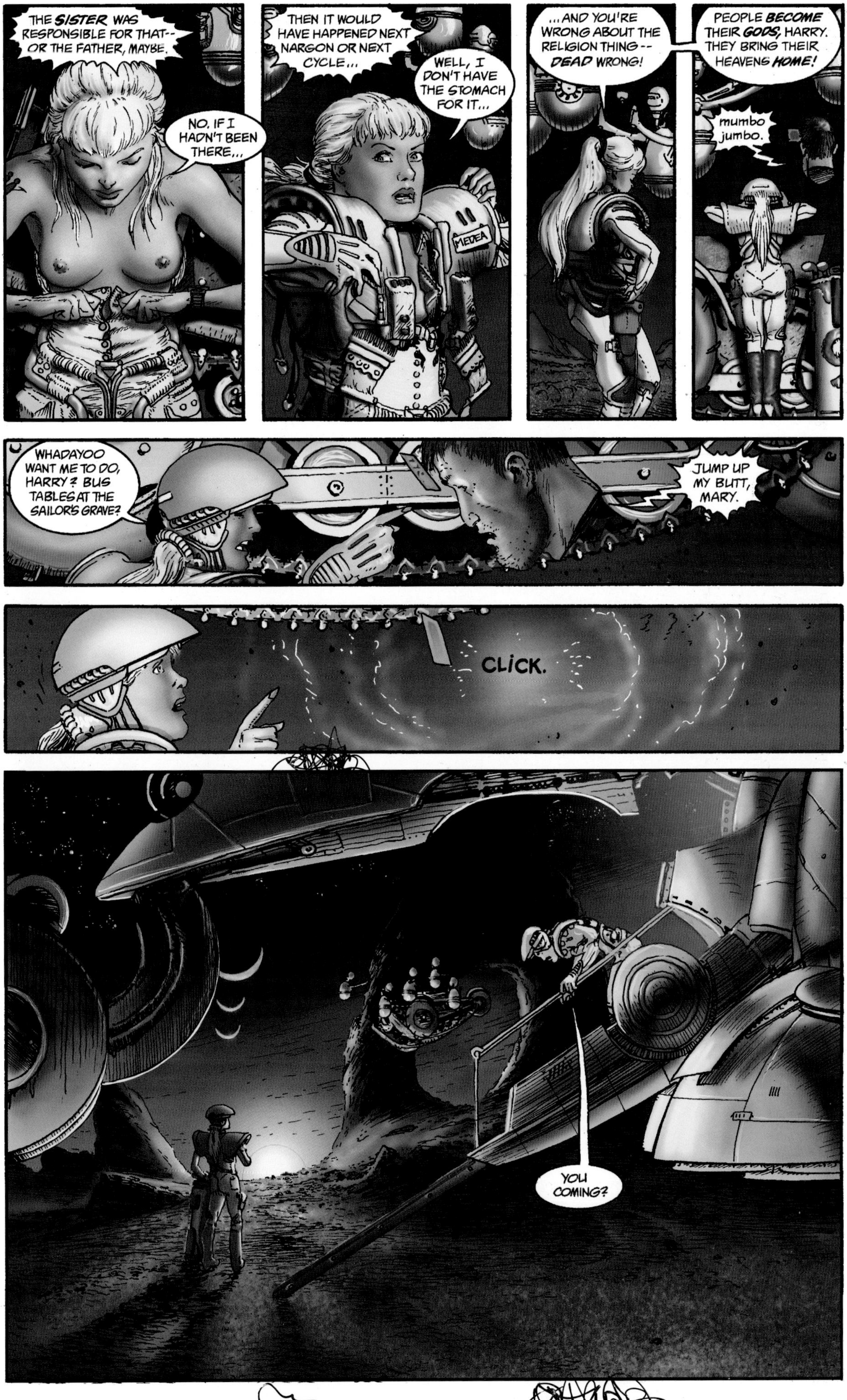
THE SISTER WAS RESPONSIBLE FOR THAT-- OR THE FATHER, MAYBE.
NO. IF I HADN'T BEEN THERE...
THEN IT WOULD HAVE HAPPENED NEXT NARGON OR NEXT CYCLE...
WELL, I DON'T HAVE THE STOMACH FOR IT...
MEDEA
...AND YOU'RE WRONG ABOUT THE RELIGION THING -- DEAD WRONG!
PEOPLE BECOME THEIR GODS, HARRY. THEY BRING THEIR HEAVENS HOME!
mumbo jumbo.
WHADAYOO WANT ME TO DO, HARRY? BUS TABLES AT THE SAILOR'S GRAVE?
JUMP UP MY BUTT, MARY.
CLICK.
YOU COMING?

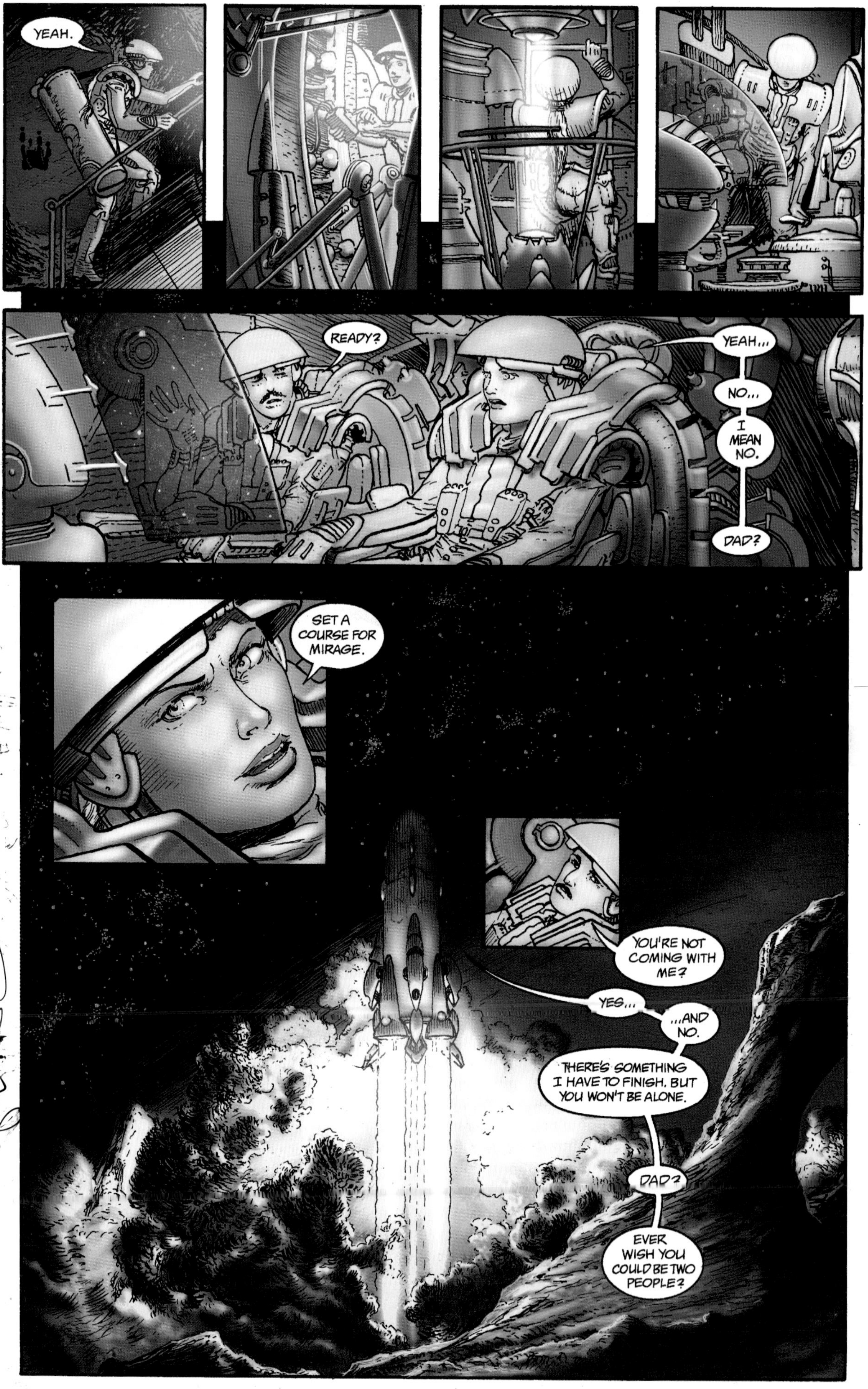
YEAH.
READY?
YEAH...
NO...
I MEAN NO.
DAD?
SET A COURSE FOR MIRAGE.
YOU'RE NOT COMING WITH ME?
YES...
...AND NO.
THERE'S SOMETHING I HAVE TO FINISH. BUT YOU WON'T BE ALONE.
DAD?
EVER WISH YOU COULD BE TWO PEOPLE?

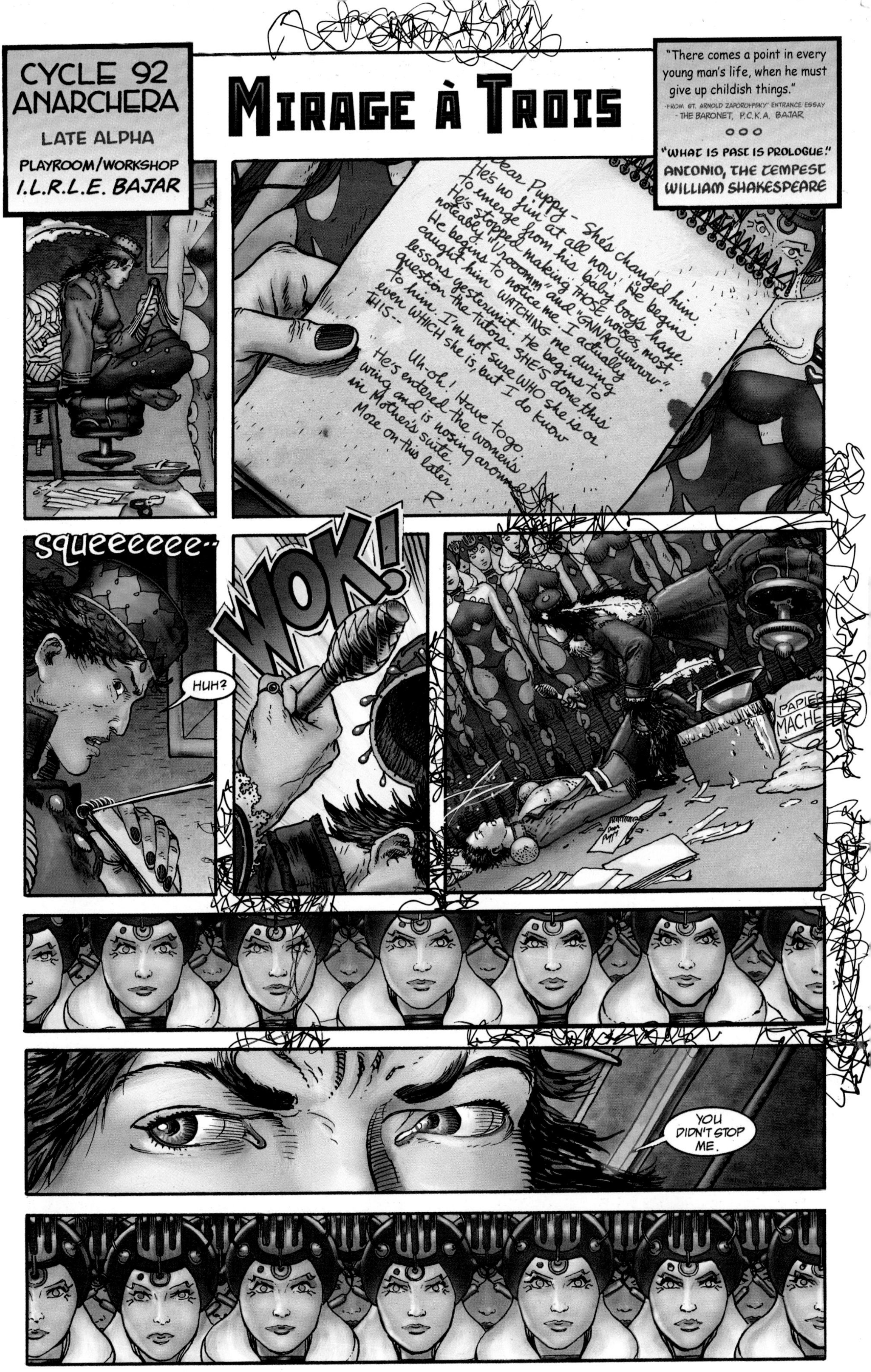
CYCLE 92
ANARCHERA
LATE ALPHA
PLAYROOM/WORKSHOP
I.L.R.L.E. BAJAR
MIRAGE À TROIS
"There comes a point in every young man's life, when he must give up childish things."
-FROM ST. ARNOLD ZAPOROHFSKY' ENTRANCE ESSAY
- THE BARONET, P.C.K.A. BAJAR
"WHAT IS PAST IS PROLOGUE!"
ANTONIO, THE TEMPEST
WILLIAM SHAKESPEARE
Dear Puppy - She's changed him. He's no fun at all now; He begins to emerge from his baby boy's haze. He's stopped making THOSE noises, most noteably "Vrooomm" and "GNNAOuuuww". He begins to notice me. I actually caught him WATCHING me during lessons yesterunit. He begins to question the tutors. SHE'S done this to him. I'm not sure WHO she is or even WHICH she is, but I do know THIS--
Uh-oh! Have to go. He's entered the women's wing and is nosing around in Mother's suite. More on this later.
-R
squeeeeee--
HUH?
WOK!
PAPIER MACHE
YOU DIDN'T STOP ME.

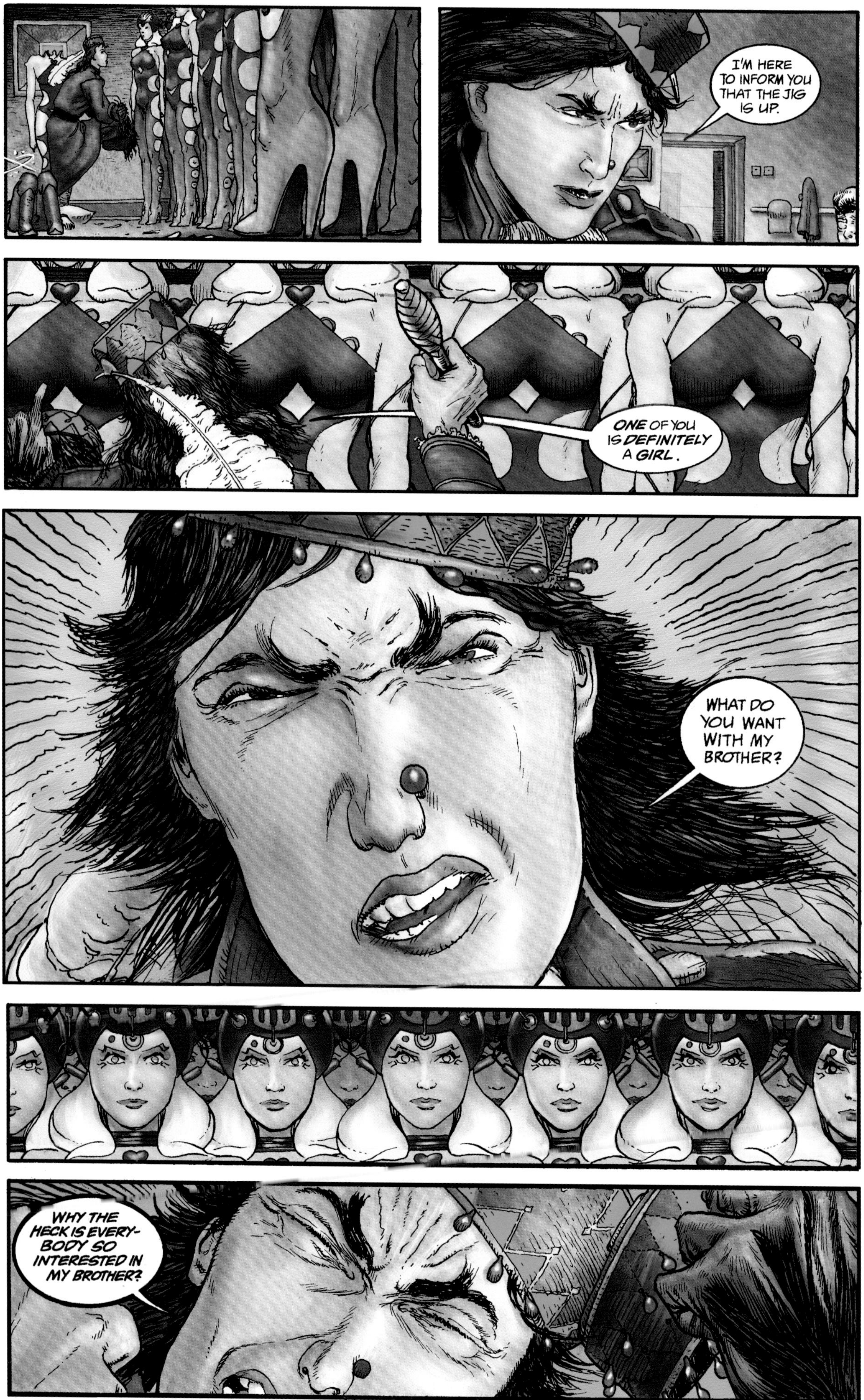
I'M HERE TO INFORM YOU THAT THE JIG IS UP.
ONE OF YOU IS DEFINITELY A GIRL.
WHAT DO YOU WANT WITH MY BROTHER?
WHY THE HECK IS EVERY-BODY SO INTERESTED IN MY BROTHER?

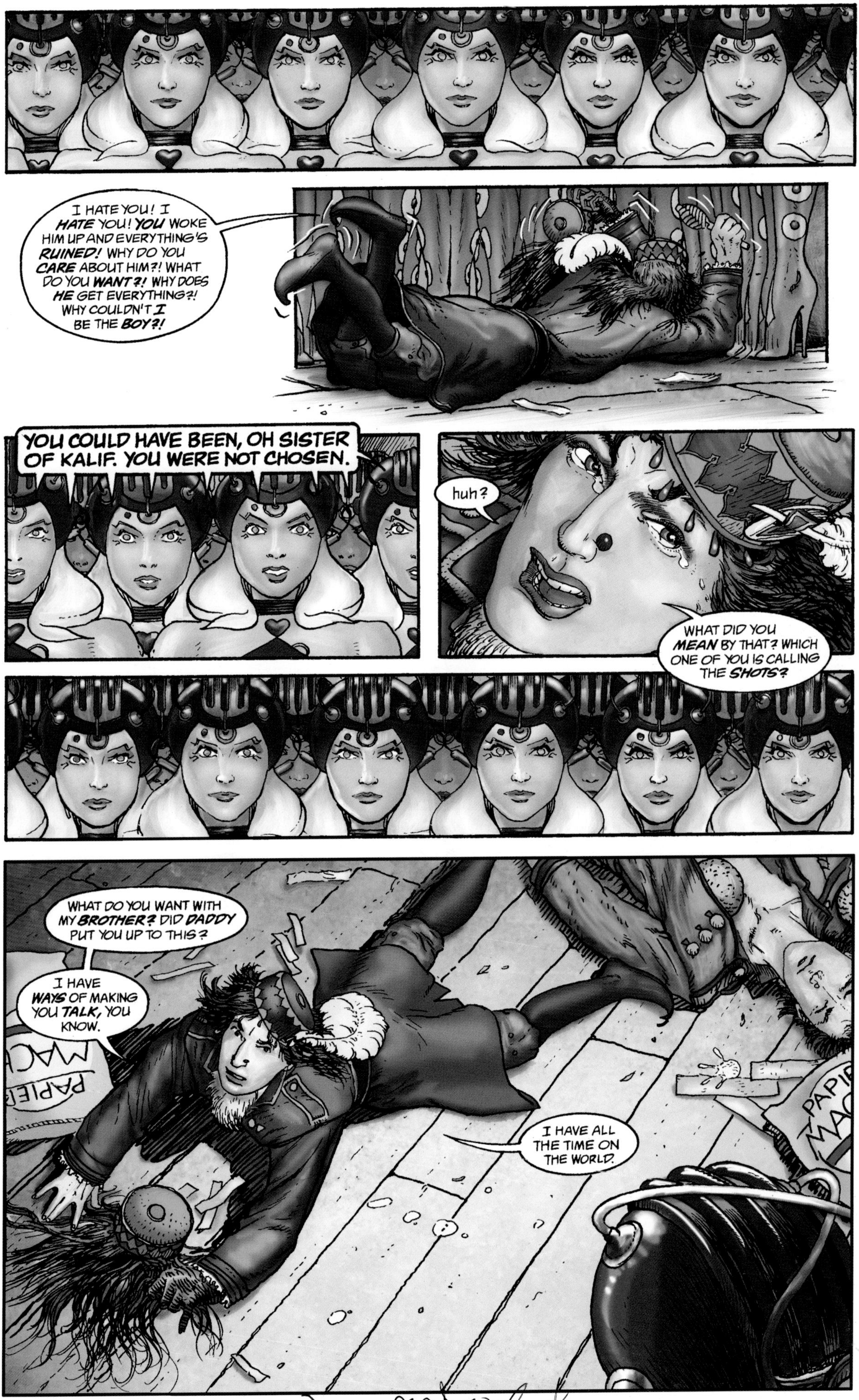
I HATE YOU! I HATE YOU! YOU WOKE HIM UP AND EVERYTHING'S RUINED! WHY DO YOU CARE ABOUT HIM?! WHAT DO YOU WANT?! WHY DOES HE GET EVERYTHING?! WHY COULDN'T I BE THE BOY?!
YOU COULD HAVE BEEN, OH SISTER OF KALIF. YOU WERE NOT CHOSEN.
huh?
WHAT DID YOU MEAN BY THAT? WHICH ONE OF YOU IS CALLING THE SHOTS?
WHAT DO YOU WANT WITH MY BROTHER? DID DADDY PUT YOU UP TO THIS?
I HAVE WAYS OF MAKING YOU TALK, YOU KNOW.
I HAVE ALL THE TIME ON THE WORLD.
PAPIER MACH
PAPIER MAC

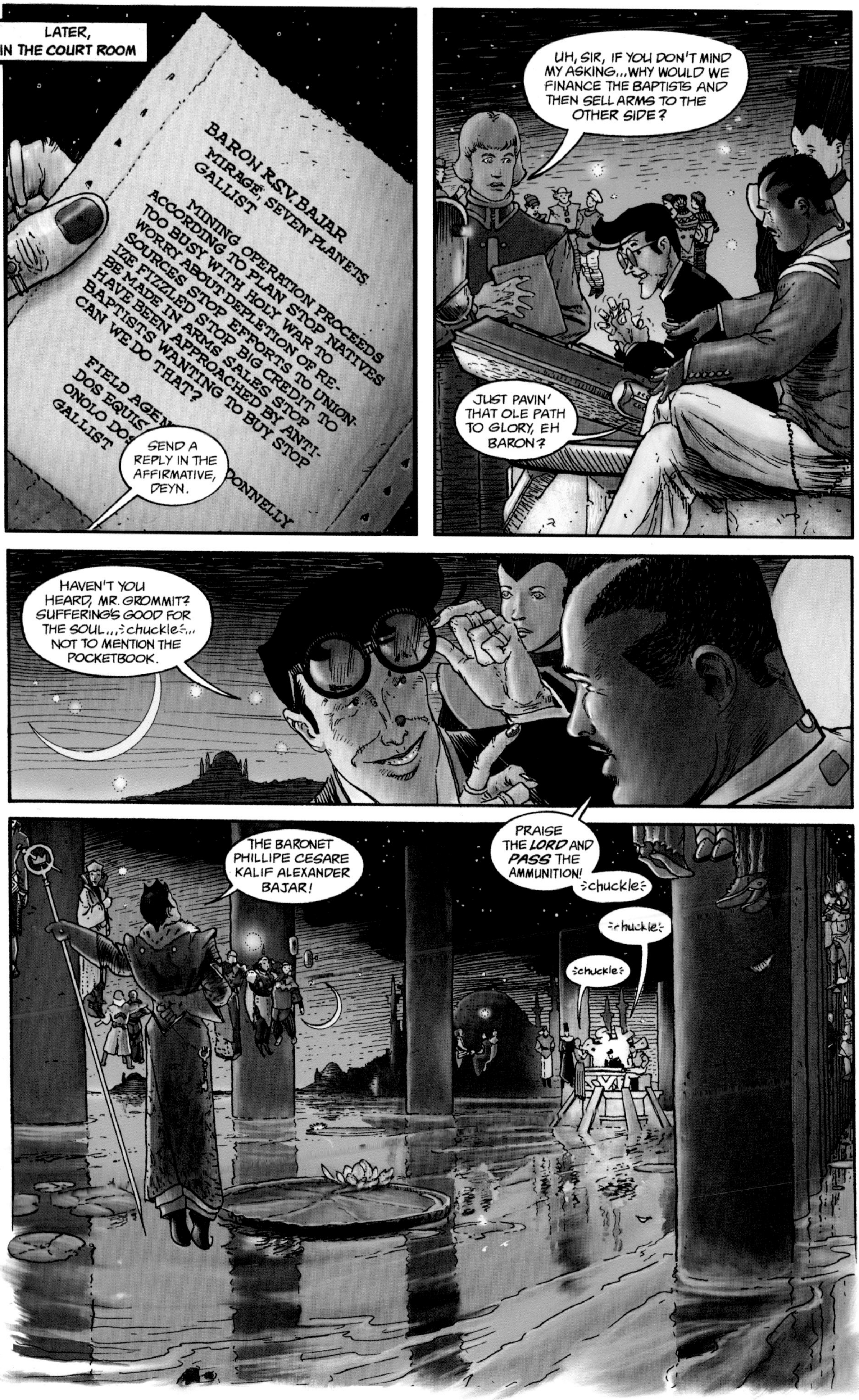

LATER, IN THE COURT ROOM
BARON R.S.V. BAJAR
MIRAGE, SEVEN PLANETS
GALLIST
MINING OPERATION PROCEEDS
ACCORDING TO PLAN STOP NATIVES
TOO BUSY WITH HOLY WAR TO
WORRY ABOUT DEPLETION OF RE-
SOURCES STOP EFFORTS TO UNION-
IZE FIZZLED STOP BIG CREDIT TO
BE MADE IN ARMS SALES STOP
HAVE BEEN APPROACHED BY ANTI-
BAPTISTS WANTING TO BUY STOP
CAN WE DO THAT?
FIELD AGEN
DOS EQUIS
ONOLO DOS
GALLIST
DONNELLY
SEND A REPLY IN THE AFFIRMATIVE, DEYN.
UH, SIR, IF YOU DON'T MIND MY ASKING... WHY WOULD WE FINANCE THE BAPTISTS AND THEN SELL ARMS TO THE OTHER SIDE?
JUST PAVIN' THAT OLE PATH TO GLORY, EH BARON?
HAVEN'T YOU HEARD, MR. GROMMIT? SUFFERING'S GOOD FOR THE SOUL... :chuckle:... NOT TO MENTION THE POCKETBOOK.
THE BARONET PHILLIPE CESARE KALIF ALEXANDER BAJAR!
PRAISE THE LORD AND PASS THE AMMUNITION! :chuckle:
:chuckle:
:chuckle:

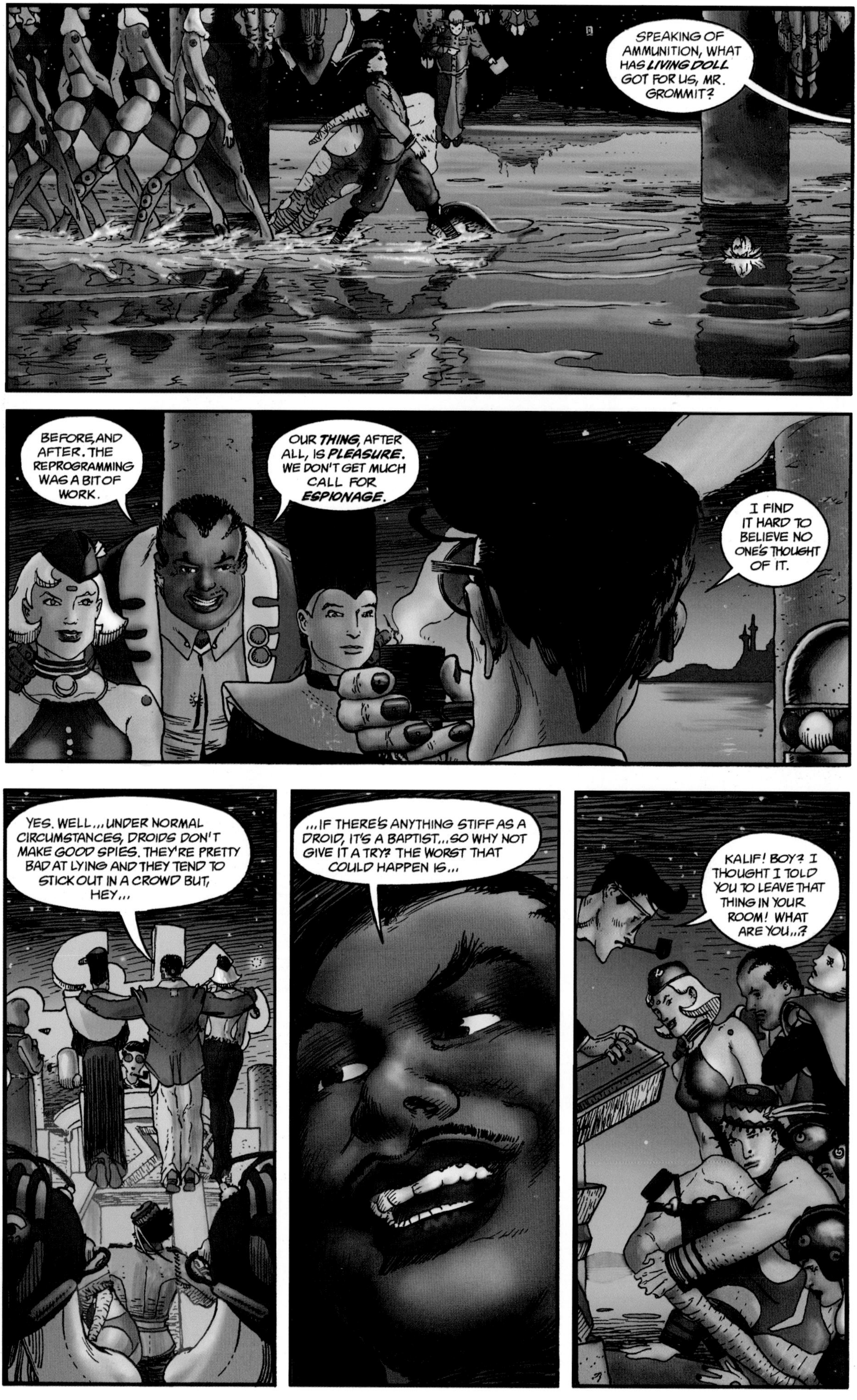
SPEAKING OF AMMUNITION, WHAT HAS LIVING DOLL GOT FOR US, MR. GROMMIT?
BEFORE, AND AFTER. THE REPROGRAMMING WAS A BIT OF WORK.
OUR THING, AFTER ALL, IS PLEASURE. WE DON'T GET MUCH CALL FOR ESPIONAGE.
I FIND IT HARD TO BELIEVE NO ONE'S THOUGHT OF IT.
YES. WELL... UNDER NORMAL CIRCUMSTANCES, DROIDS DON'T MAKE GOOD SPIES. THEY'RE PRETTY BAD AT LYING AND THEY TEND TO STICK OUT IN A CROWD BUT, HEY...
...IF THERE'S ANYTHING STIFF AS A DROID, IT'S A BAPTIST... SO WHY NOT GIVE IT A TRY? THE WORST THAT COULD HAPPEN IS...
KALIF! BOY? I THOUGHT I TOLD YOU TO LEAVE THAT THING IN YOUR ROOM! WHAT ARE YOU...?

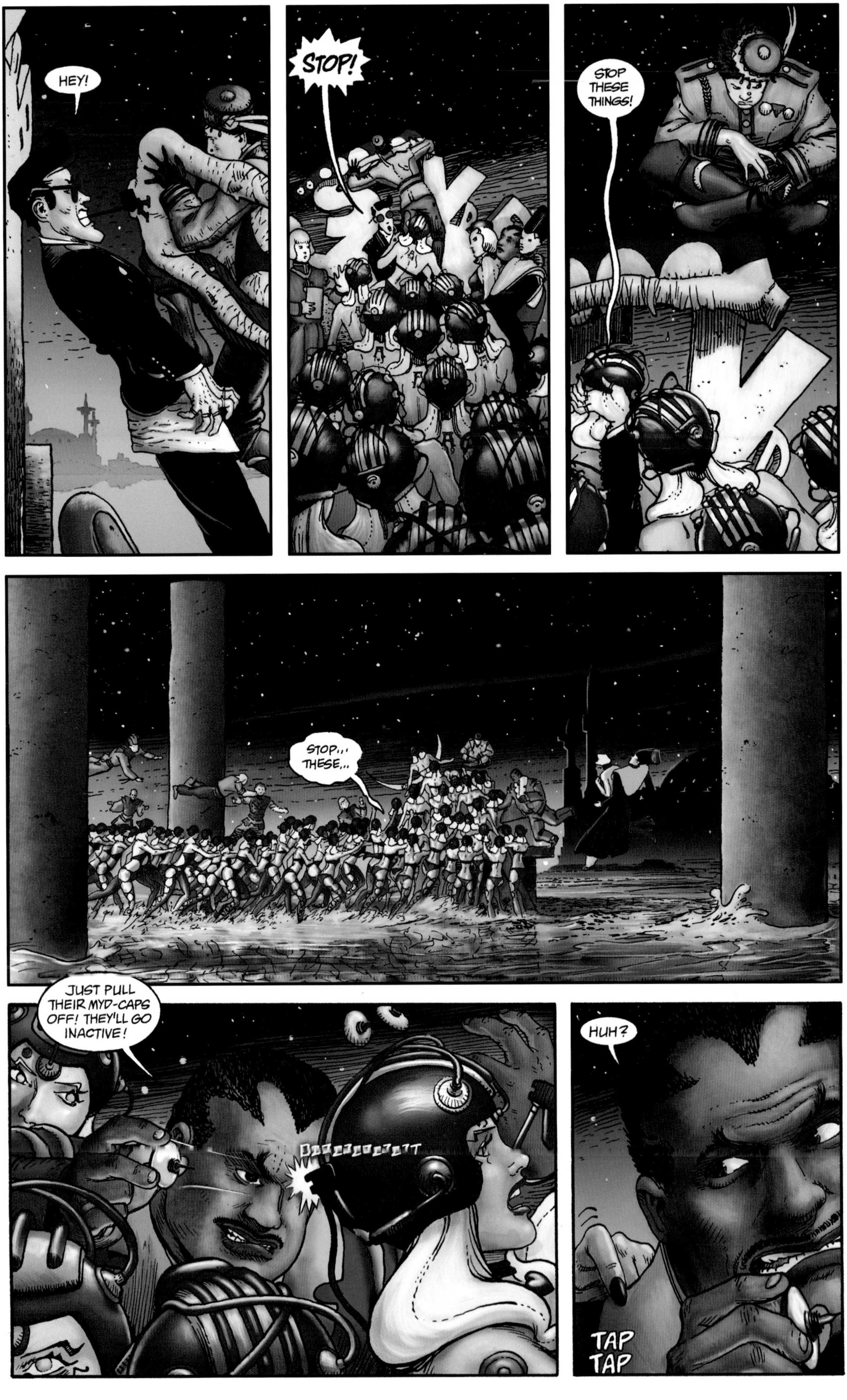

HEY!
STOP!
STOP THESE THINGS!
STOP... THESE...
JUST PULL THEIR MYD-CAPS OFF! THEY'LL GO INACTIVE!
HUH?
TAP TAP

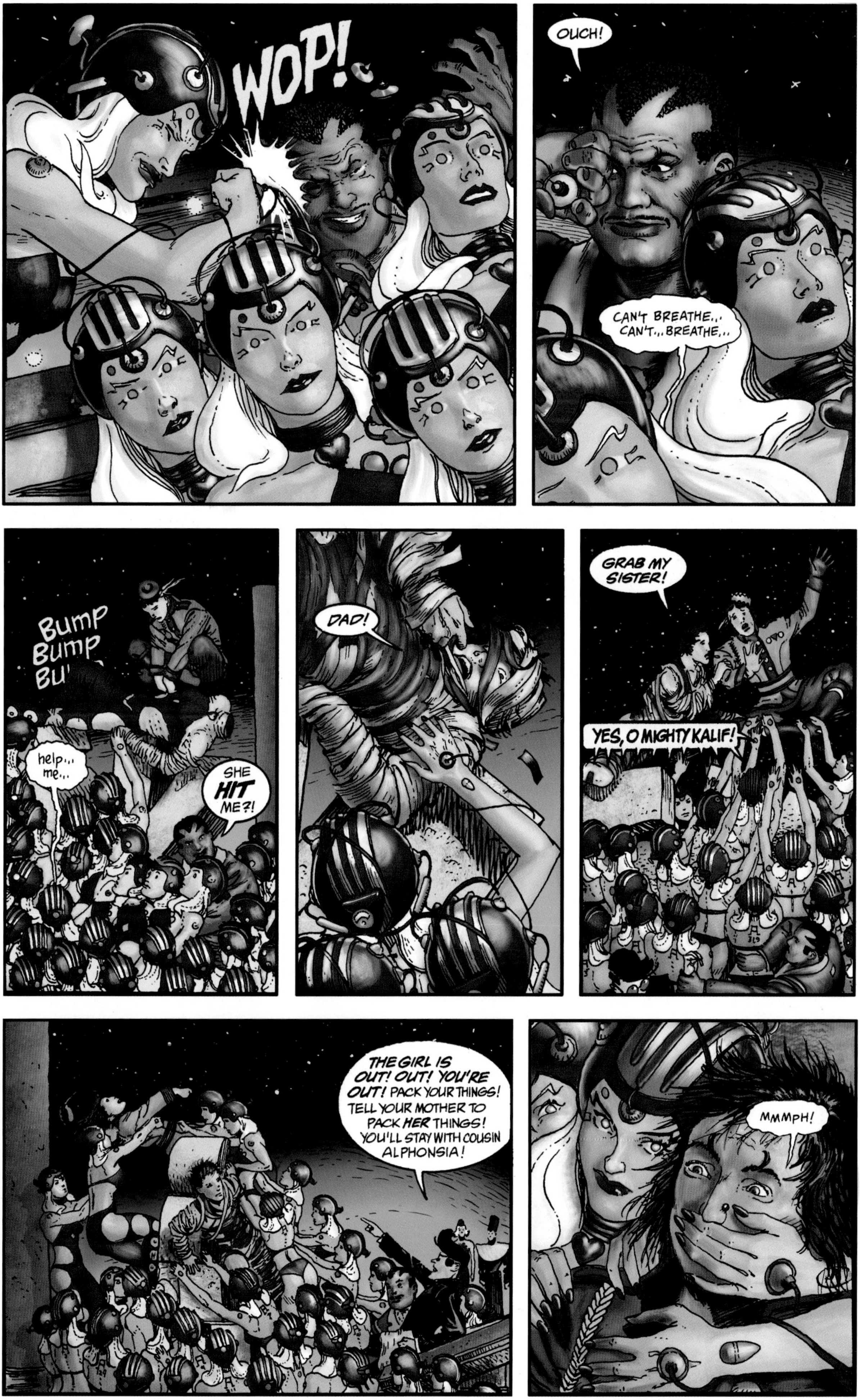
WOP!
OUCH!
CAN'T BREATHE... CAN'T... BREATHE...
Bump
Bump
help... me...
SHE HIT ME?!
DAD!
GRAB MY SISTER!
YES, O MIGHTY KALIF!
THE GIRL IS OUT! OUT! YOU'RE OUT! PACK YOUR THINGS! TELL YOUR MOTHER TO PACK HER THINGS! YOU'LL STAY WITH COUSIN ALPHONSIA!
MMMPH!

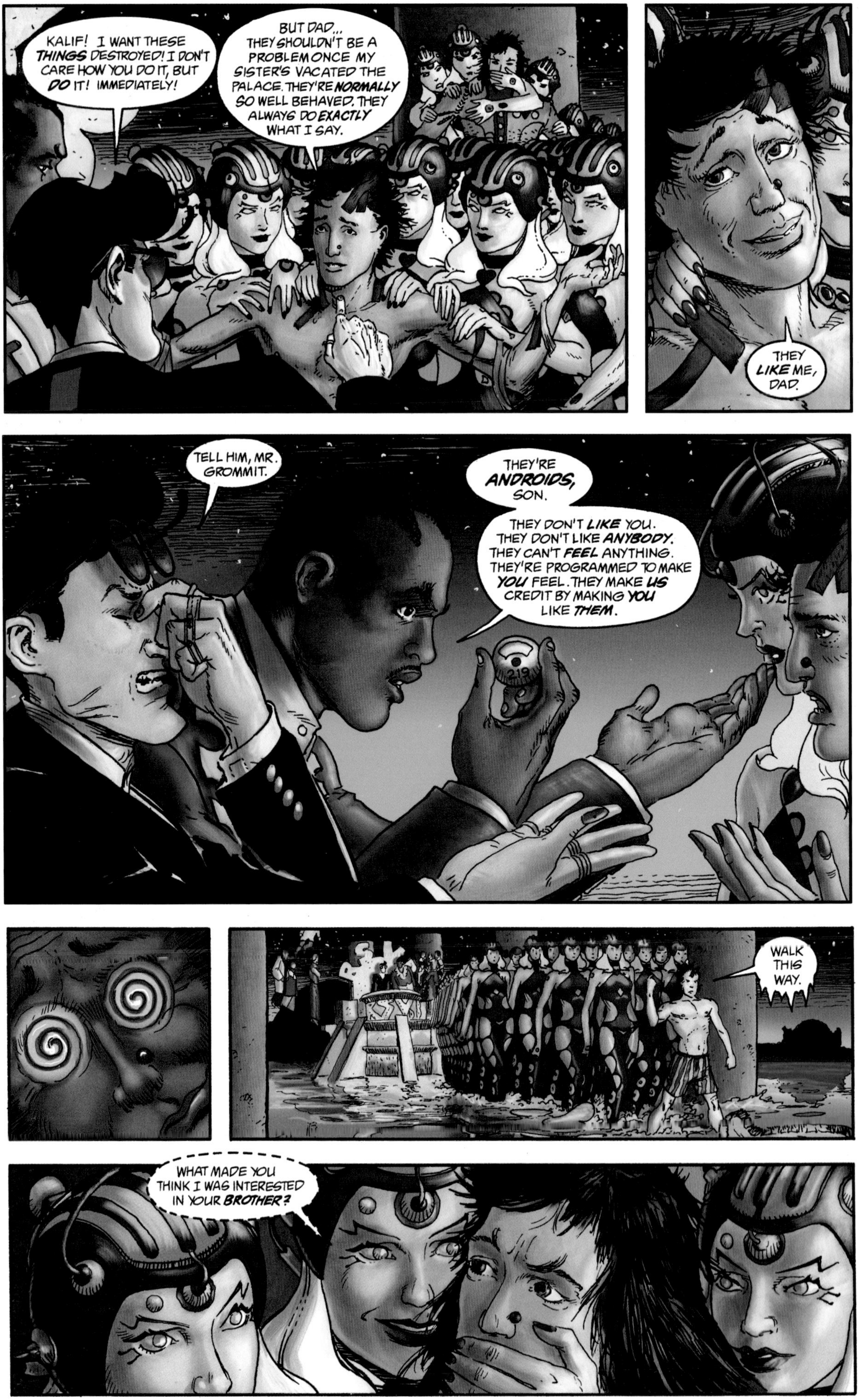
KALIF! I WANT THESE THINGS DESTROYED! I DON'T CARE HOW YOU DO IT, BUT DO IT! IMMEDIATELY!
BUT DAD... THEY SHOULDN'T BE A PROBLEM ONCE MY SISTER'S VACATED THE PALACE. THEY'RE NORMALLY SO WELL BEHAVED. THEY ALWAYS DO EXACTLY WHAT I SAY.
THEY LIKE ME, DAD.
TELL HIM, MR. GROMMIT.
THEY'RE ANDROIDS, SON.
THEY DON'T LIKE YOU. THEY DON'T LIKE ANYBODY. THEY CAN'T FEEL ANYTHING. THEY'RE PROGRAMMED TO MAKE YOU FEEL. THEY MAKE US CREDIT BY MAKING YOU LIKE THEM.
219
WALK THIS WAY.
WHAT MADE YOU THINK I WAS INTERESTED IN YOUR BROTHER?

CYCLE 92
ANARCHERA

PLAYROOM/WORKSHOP
OF THE BARONET
PHILLIPE CESARE
KALIF ALEXANDER
BAJAR

Pretty Maids All in a Row

"GLORIANNA (READ GLORIOUS ANNIE) WAS ONE OF THE *'IN TUNE'*... MOVING WITH THE RHYTHM OF THE UNIVERSE, RIDING HER CURRENTS, APPEARING SIGH-SOFT WHERE OPPORTUNITY KNOCKED."

-- FROM *Dear Puppy* THE DIARY OF I.L.R.L.E. BAJAR

"I'M GOING TO BUY A PAPER DOLL THAT I CAN CALL MY OWN, A *DOLL* THAT OTHER FELLOWS CANNOT STEAL. AND THEN THE FLIRTY,

FLIRTY GUYS WITH FLIRTY, FLIRTY EYES WILL HAVE TO FLIRT WITH DOLLIES THAT ARE REAL. WHEN I COME HOME AT NIGHT SHE

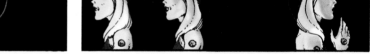

WILL BE WAITING, SHE'LL BE THE TRUEST DOLL IN ALL THIS WORLD. I'D RATHER HAVE A PAPER DOLL TO CALL MY OWN THAN

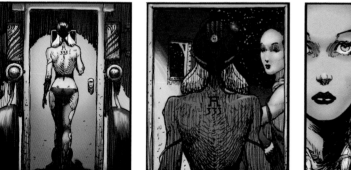

HAVE A FICKLE-MINDED REAL LIVE GIRL."

LYRICS AND MELODY BY JOHNNY S. BLACK © 1942

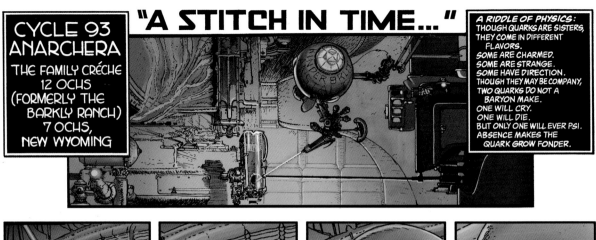

"A STITCH IN TIME..."
CYCLE 93 ANARCHERA
THE FAMILY CRÉCHE 12 OCHS (FORMERLY THE BARKLY RANCH) 7 OCHS, NEW WYOMING
A RIDDLE OF PHYSICS: THOUGH QUARKS ARE SISTERS, THEY COME IN DIFFERENT FLAVORS. SOME ARE CHARMED. SOME ARE STRANGE. SOME HAVE DIRECTION. THOUGH THEY MAY BE COMPANY, TWO QUARKS DO NOT A BARYON MAKE. ONE WILL CRY. ONE WILL DIE. BUT ONLY ONE WILL EVER PSI. ABSENCE MAKES THE QUARK GROW FONDER.
...TWELVE MILLION REFUGEES PACKED INTO THE REC STATION SPACE FRONT WAITING DEPORTATION...
A LETTER FROM MARY, AL--SHE SENDS GREETINGS.
...AND SPEAKING OF RELIGIOUS REPRESSION... OUR LAST STORY TONIGHT TAKES US TO ONOLO DOS, SECOND WORLD OF THE ONOLOS, SEVEN PLANETS WHERE...
2
couldn't get any--not even toilet pa
So this was my first chance to write!
Sorry we didn't make it back for little
Molly's B-Day. It's hard to get off world
since the March Baptists deployed the
tabernacle.
Enclosed find one silk scarf worn by
the much acclaimed hero of the battle
of Dos Equis--yours truly--a gift for
my baby sister. Don't be alarmed by the
bullet holes and powder burns. As they
say, a miss is as good as a spaelon, and
I haven't felt this alive since the droid
wars ended.
Greetings to the al's and a kiss for
Molly.-I'll want that hug I get
home.
Love
Mary Mary

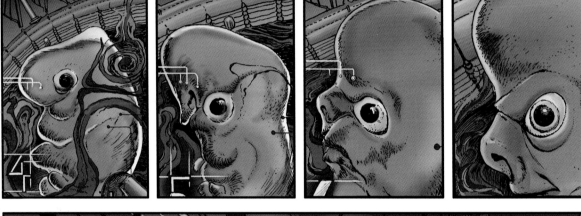

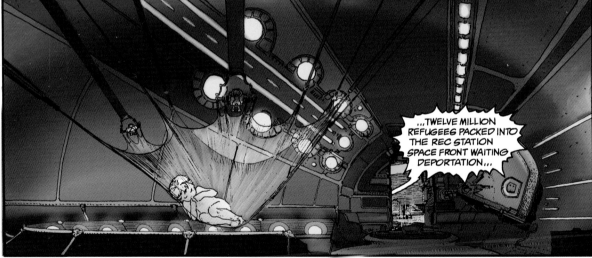

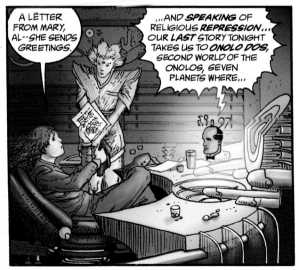

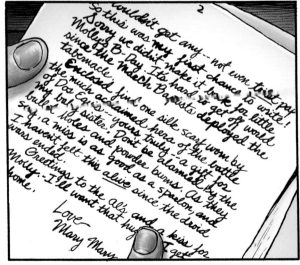

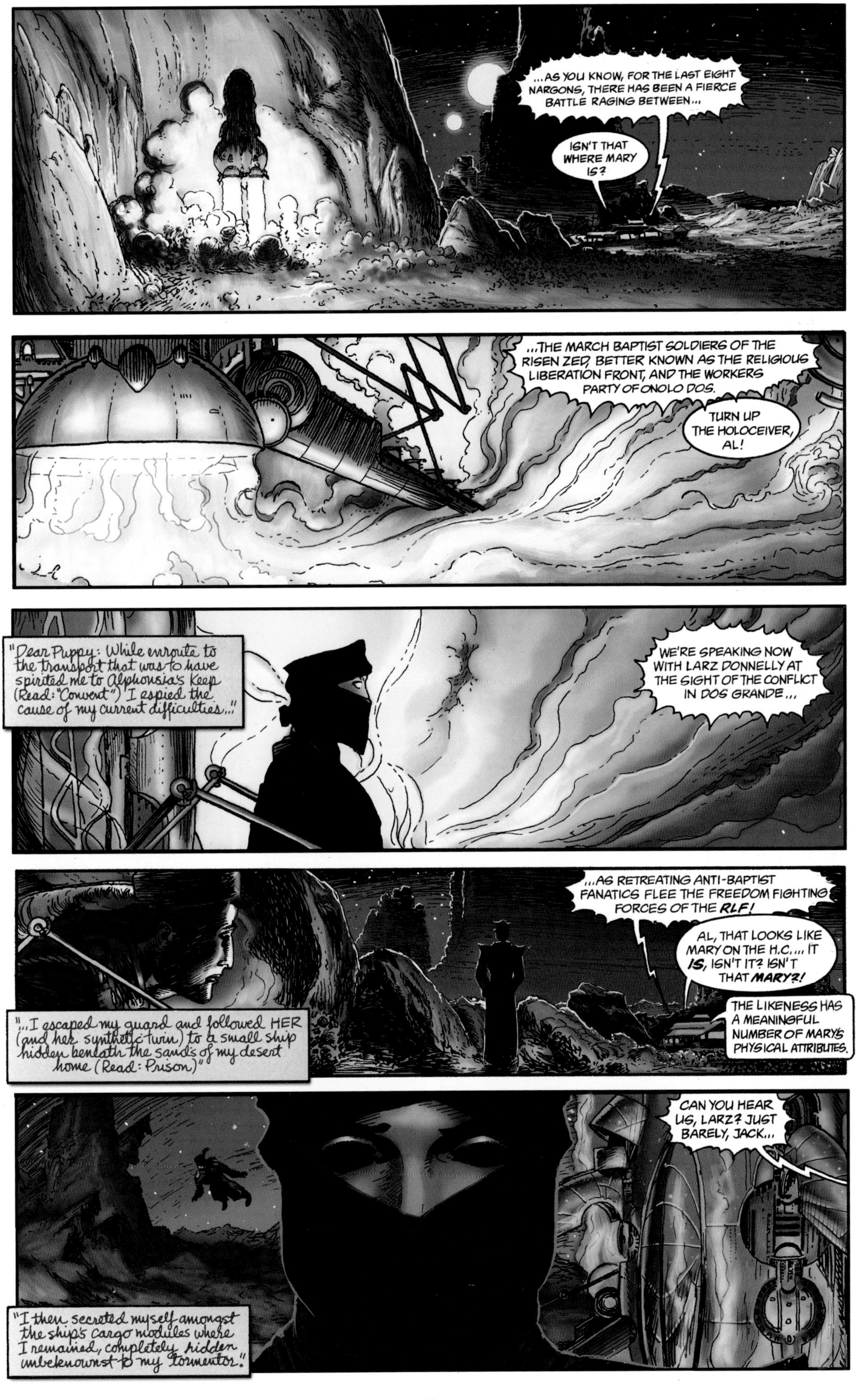
...AS YOU KNOW, FOR THE LAST EIGHT NARGONS, THERE HAS BEEN A FIERCE BATTLE RAGING BETWEEN...
ISN'T THAT WHERE MARY IS?
...THE MARCH BAPTIST SOLDIERS OF THE RISEN ZED, BETTER KNOWN AS THE RELIGIOUS LIBERATION FRONT, AND THE WORKERS PARTY OF ONOLO DOS.
TURN UP THE HOLOCEIVER, AL!
"Dear Puppy: While enroute to the transport that was to have spirited me to Alphonsia's Keep (Read: "Convent") I espied the cause of my current difficulties..."
WE'RE SPEAKING NOW WITH LARZ DONNELLY AT THE SIGHT OF THE CONFLICT IN DOS GRANDE...
...AS RETREATING ANTI-BAPTIST FANATICS FLEE THE FREEDOM FIGHTING FORCES OF THE RLF!
AL, THAT LOOKS LIKE MARY ON THE H.C.... IT IS, ISN'T IT? ISN'T THAT MARY?!
THE LIKENESS HAS A MEANINGFUL NUMBER OF MARY'S PHYSICAL ATTRIBUTES.
"...I escaped my guard and followed HER (and her synthetic twin) to a small ship hidden beneath the sands of my desert home (Read: Prison)"
CAN YOU HEAR US, LARZ? JUST BARELY, JACK...
"I then secreted myself amongst the ship's cargo modules where I remained, completely hidden unbeknownst to my tormentor."

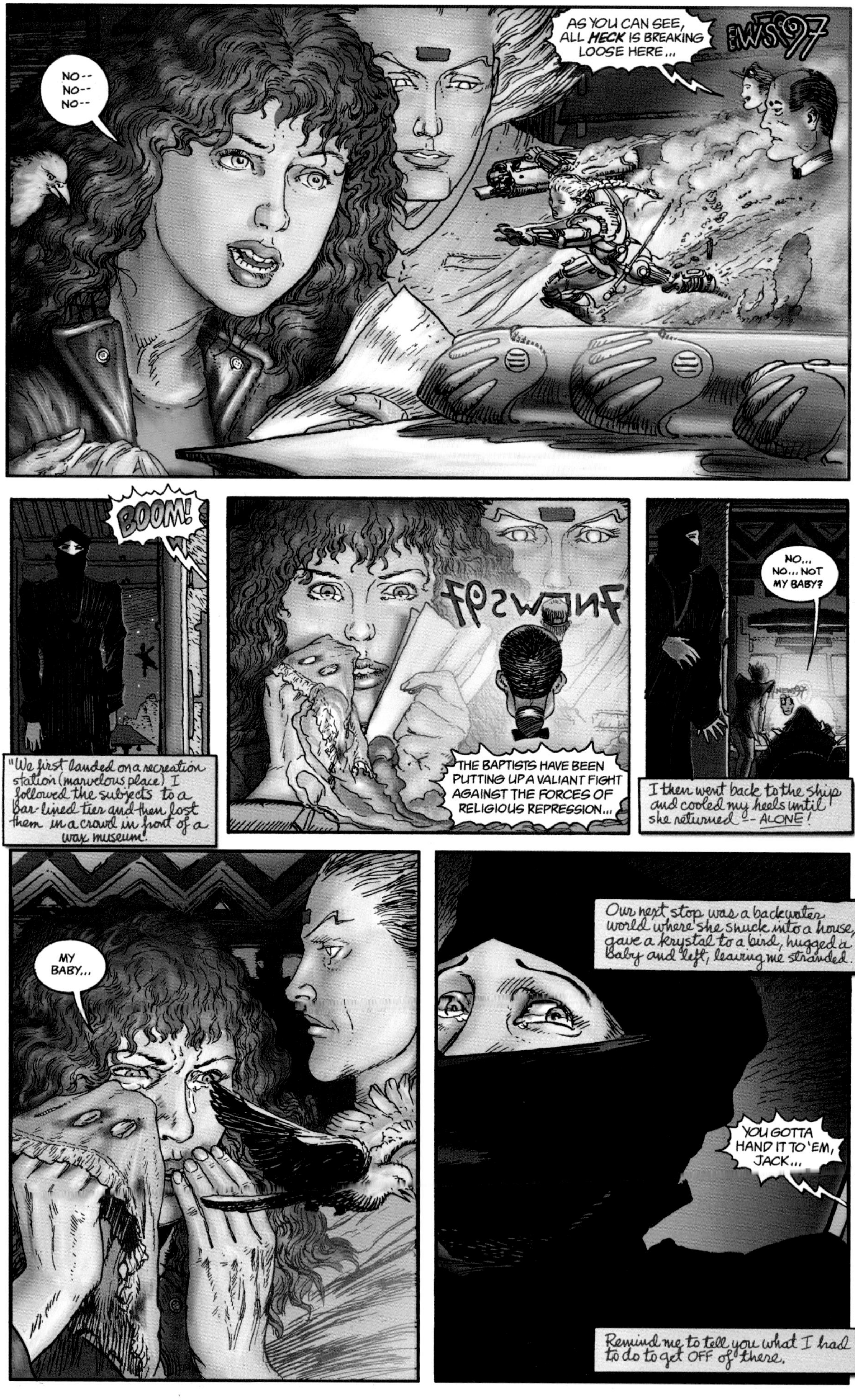

NO-- NO-- NO--
AS YOU CAN SEE, ALL HECK IS BREAKING LOOSE HERE...
BOOM!
"We first landed on a recreation station (marvelous place) I followed the subjects to a bar-lined tier and then lost them in a crowd in front of a wax museum."
THE BAPTISTS HAVE BEEN PUTTING UP A VALIANT FIGHT AGAINST THE FORCES OF RELIGIOUS REPRESSION...
NO... NO... NOT MY BABY?
I then went back to the ship and cooled my heels until she returned -- ALONE!
MY BABY...
Our next stop was a backwater world where she snuck into a house, gave a krystal to a bird, hugged a baby and left, leaving me stranded.
YOU GOTTA HAND IT TO 'EM, JACK...
Remind me to tell you what I had to do to get OFF of there.

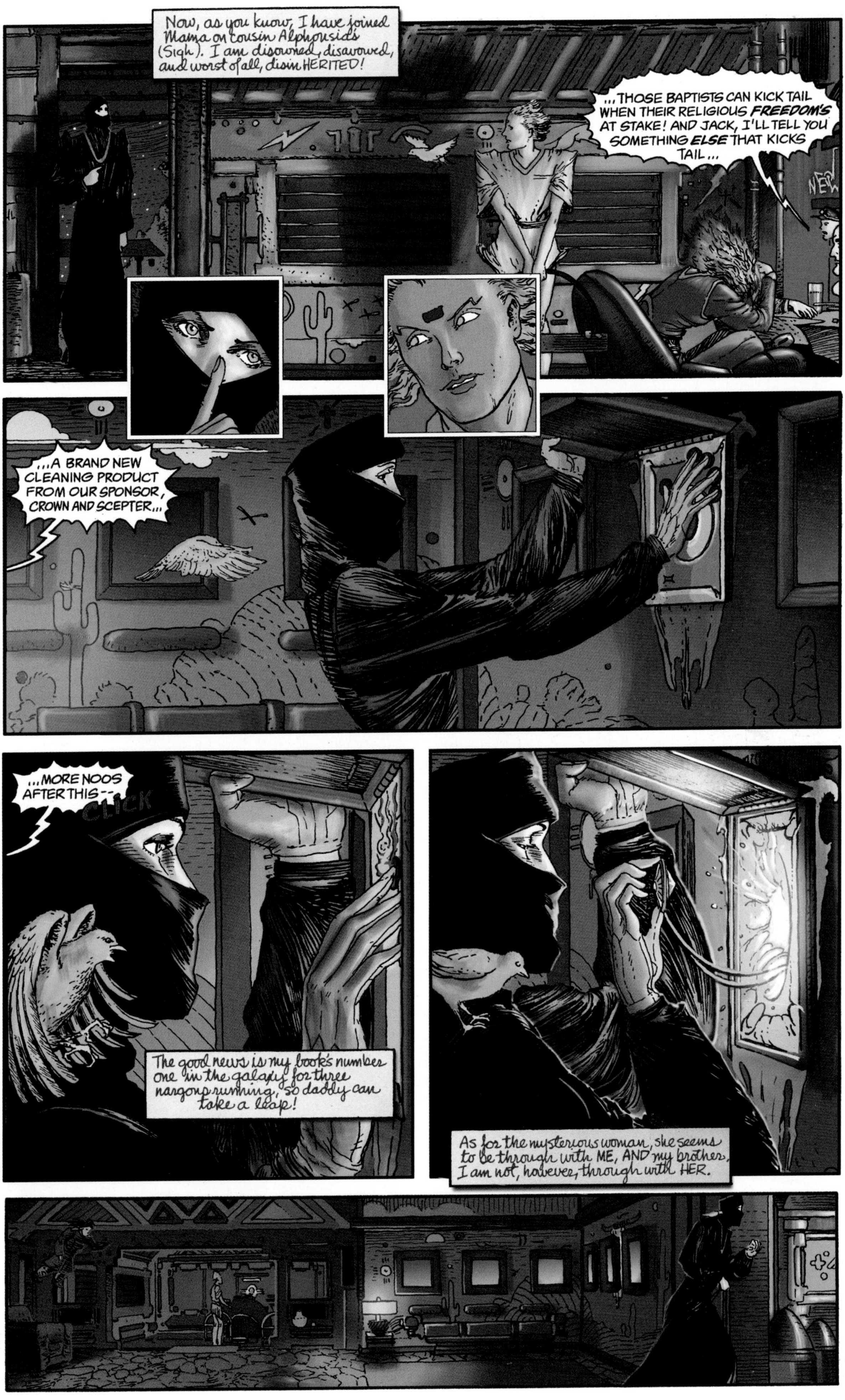

Now, as you know, I have joined Mama on cousin Alphousid's (Sigh). I am disowned, disavowed, and worst of all, disinHERITED!
...THOSE BAPTISTS CAN KICK TAIL WHEN THEIR RELIGIOUS FREEDOM'S AT STAKE! AND JACK, I'LL TELL YOU SOMETHING ELSE THAT KICKS TAIL...
...A BRAND NEW CLEANING PRODUCT FROM OUR SPONSOR, CROWN AND SCEPTER...
...MORE NOOS AFTER THIS--
CLICK
The good news is my book's number one in the galaxy for three nargons running, so daddy can take a leap!
As for the mysterious woman, she seems to be through with ME, AND my brothers. I am not, however, through with HER.

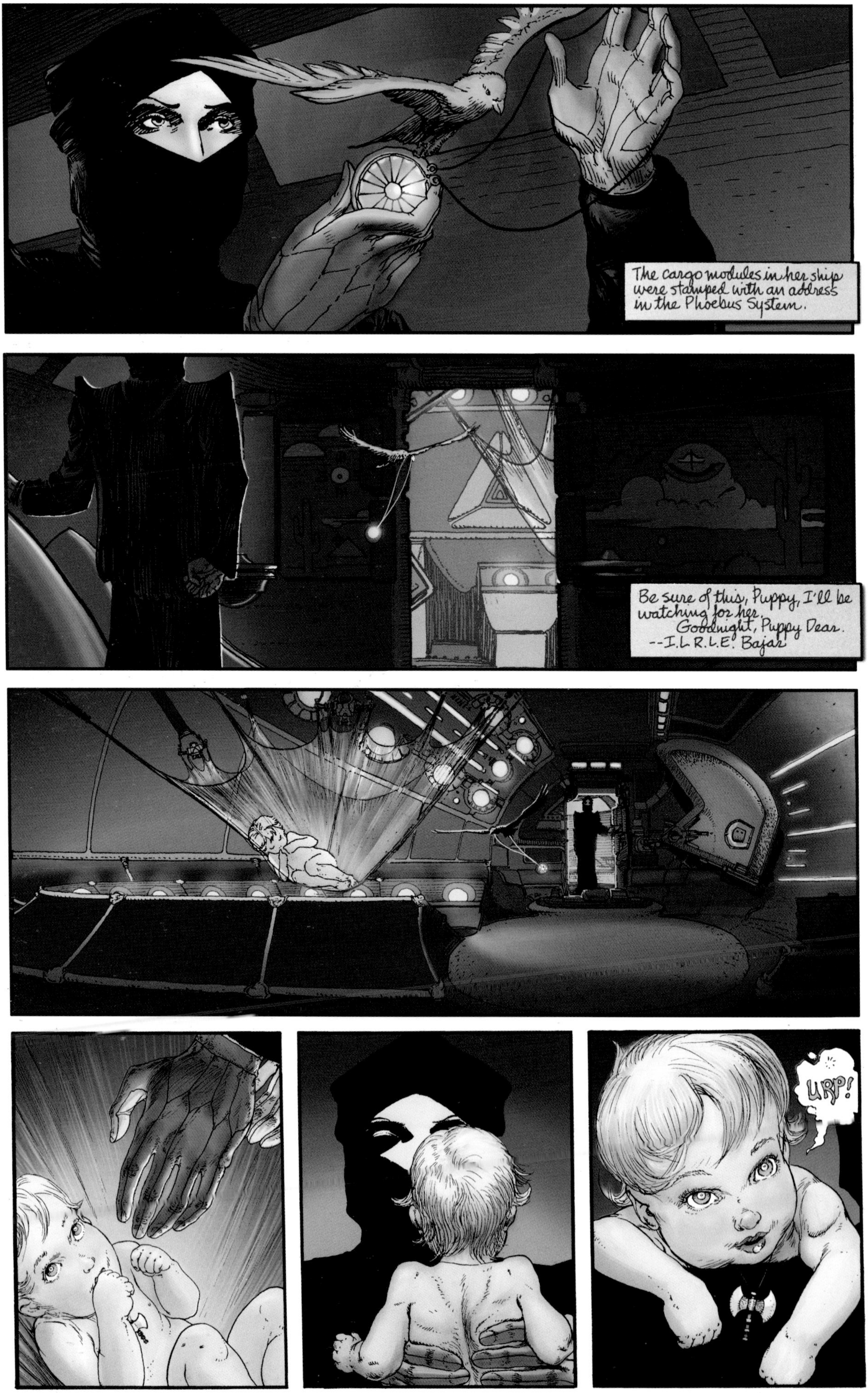
The cargo modules in her ship were stamped with an address in the Phoebus System.
Be sure of this, Puppy, I'll be watching for her.
Goodnight, Puppy Dear.
--I.L.R.L.E. Bajaz
URP!

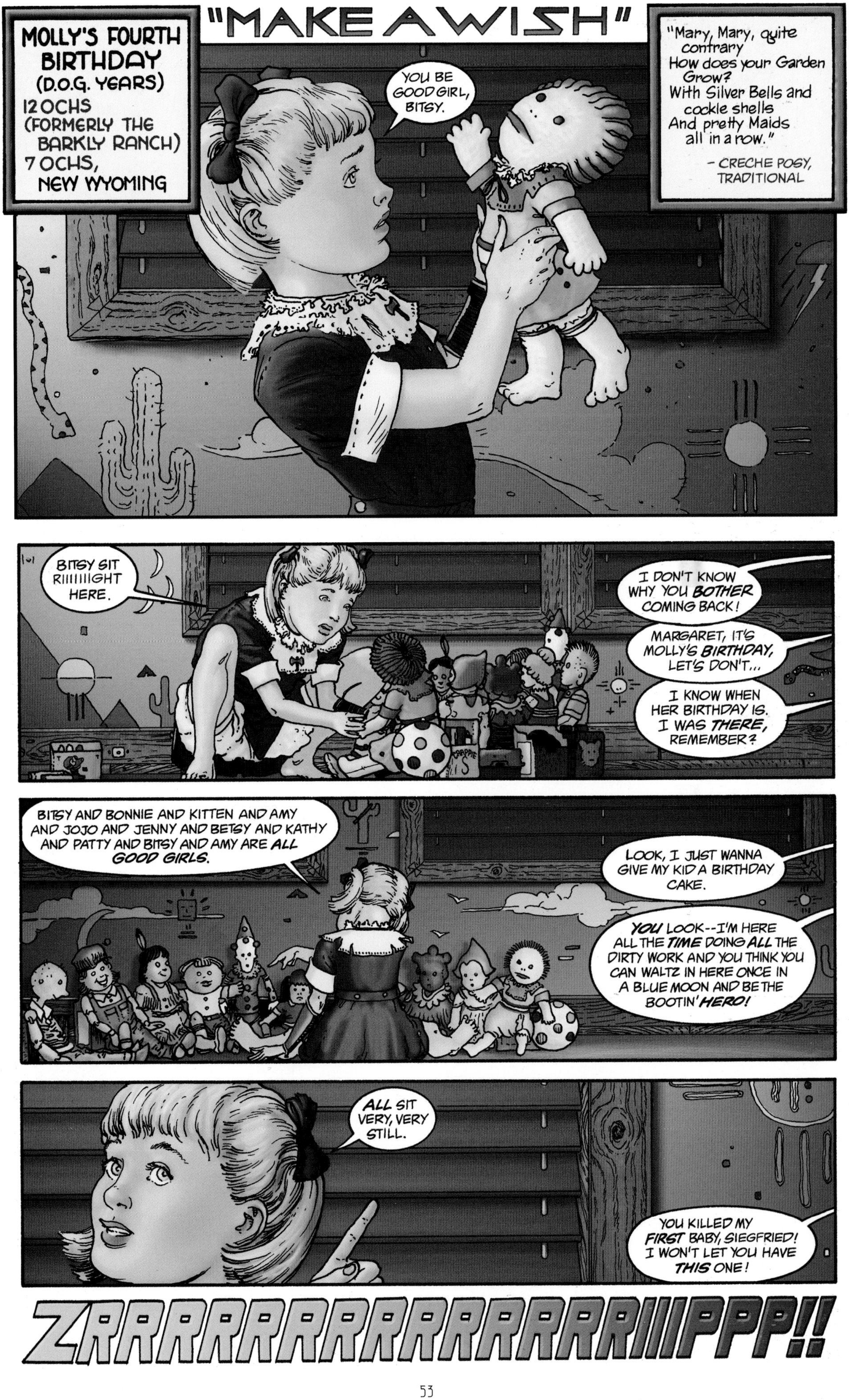
"MAKE A WISH"
MOLLY'S FOURTH BIRTHDAY (D.O.G. YEARS) 12 OCHS (FORMERLY THE BARKLY RANCH) 7 OCHS, NEW WYOMING
YOU BE GOOD GIRL, BITSY.
"Mary, Mary, quite contrary How does your Garden Grow? With Silver Bells and cockle shells And pretty Maids all in a row." – CRECHE POSY, TRADITIONAL
BITSY SIT RIIIIIIGHT HERE.
I DON'T KNOW WHY YOU **BOTHER** COMING BACK!
MARGARET, IT'S MOLLY'S **BIRTHDAY,** LET'S DON'T...
I KNOW WHEN HER BIRTHDAY IS. I WAS **THERE,** REMEMBER?
BITSY AND BONNIE AND KITTEN AND AMY AND JOJO AND JENNY AND BETSY AND KATHY AND PATTY AND BITSY AND AMY ARE **ALL GOOD GIRLS.**
LOOK, I JUST WANNA GIVE MY KID A BIRTHDAY CAKE.
YOU LOOK--I'M HERE ALL THE **TIME** DOING **ALL** THE DIRTY WORK AND YOU THINK YOU CAN WALTZ IN HERE ONCE IN A BLUE MOON AND BE THE BOOTIN' **HERO!**
ALL SIT VERY, VERY STILL.
YOU KILLED MY **FIRST** BABY, SIEGFRIED! I WON'T LET YOU HAVE **THIS** ONE!
ZRRRRRRRRRRRRRRIIIPPP!!

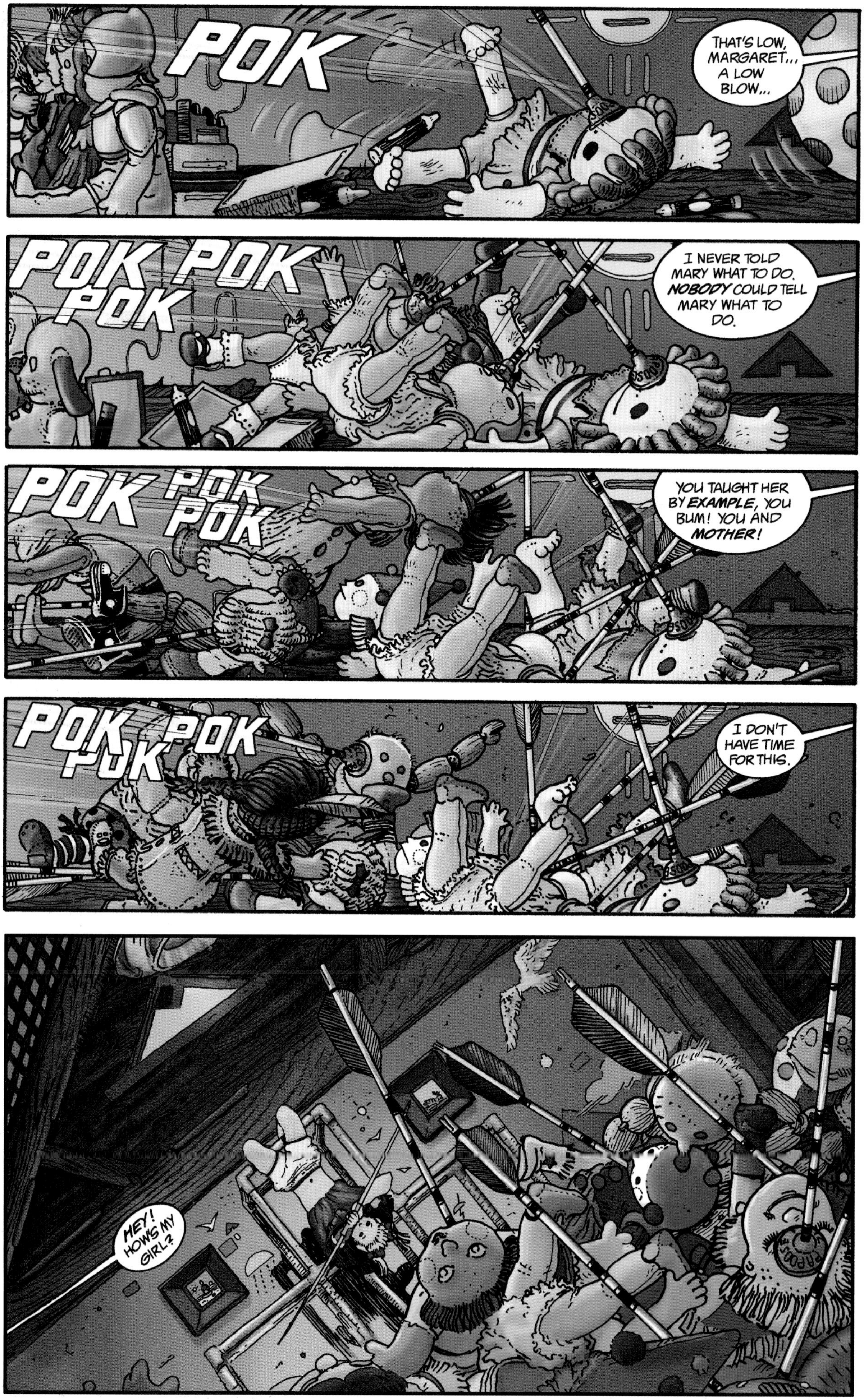
POK
THAT'S LOW, MARGARET... A LOW BLOW...
POK POK POK
I NEVER TOLD MARY WHAT TO DO. NOBODY COULD TELL MARY WHAT TO DO.
POK POK POK
YOU TAUGHT HER BY EXAMPLE, YOU BUM! YOU AND MOTHER!
POK POK POK
I DON'T HAVE TIME FOR THIS.
HEY! HOW'S MY GIRL?
PAPOOSE

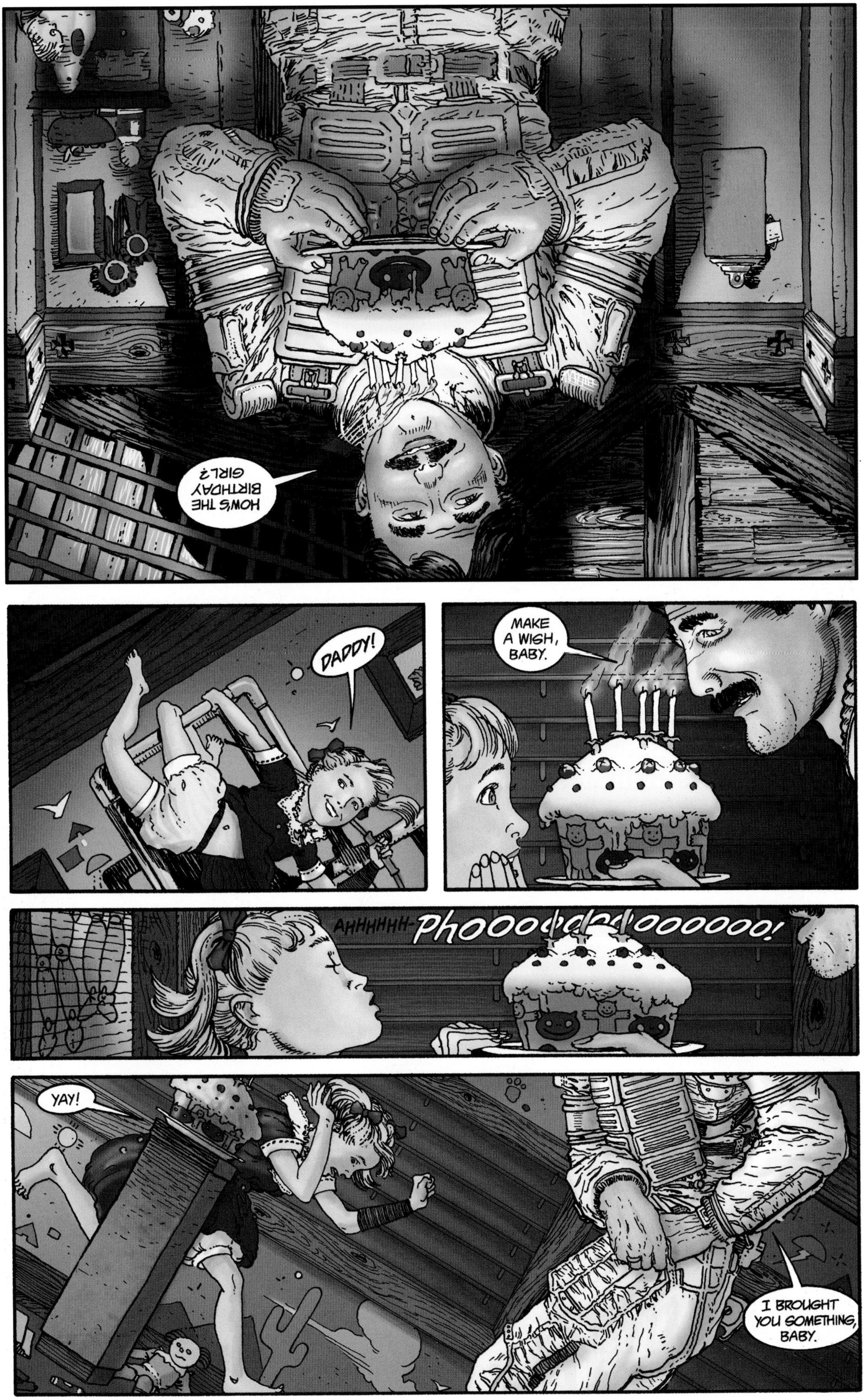
HOW'S THE BIRTHDAY GIRL?
DADDY!
MAKE A WISH, BABY.
AHHHHHH-PHOOOOOOOOOOOOO!
YAY!
I BROUGHT YOU SOMETHING, BABY.

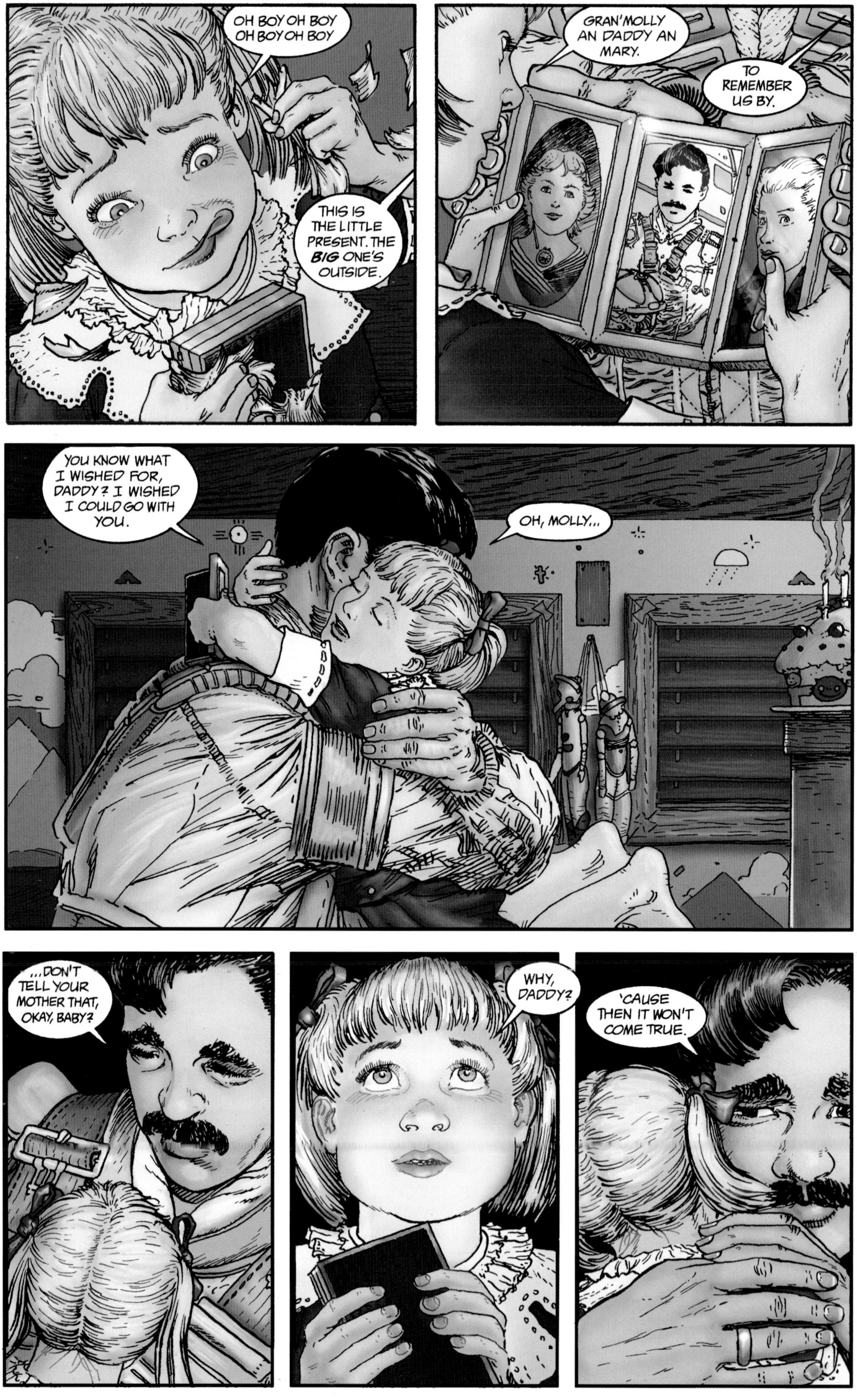
OH BOY OH BOY OH BOY OH BOY
THIS IS THE LITTLE PRESENT. THE BIG ONE'S OUTSIDE.
GRAN'MOLLY AN DADDY AN MARY.
TO REMEMBER US BY.
YOU KNOW WHAT I WISHED FOR, DADDY? I WISHED I COULD GO WITH YOU.
OH, MOLLY...
...DON'T TELL YOUR MOTHER THAT, OKAY, BABY?
WHY, DADDY?
'CAUSE THEN IT WON'T COME TRUE.

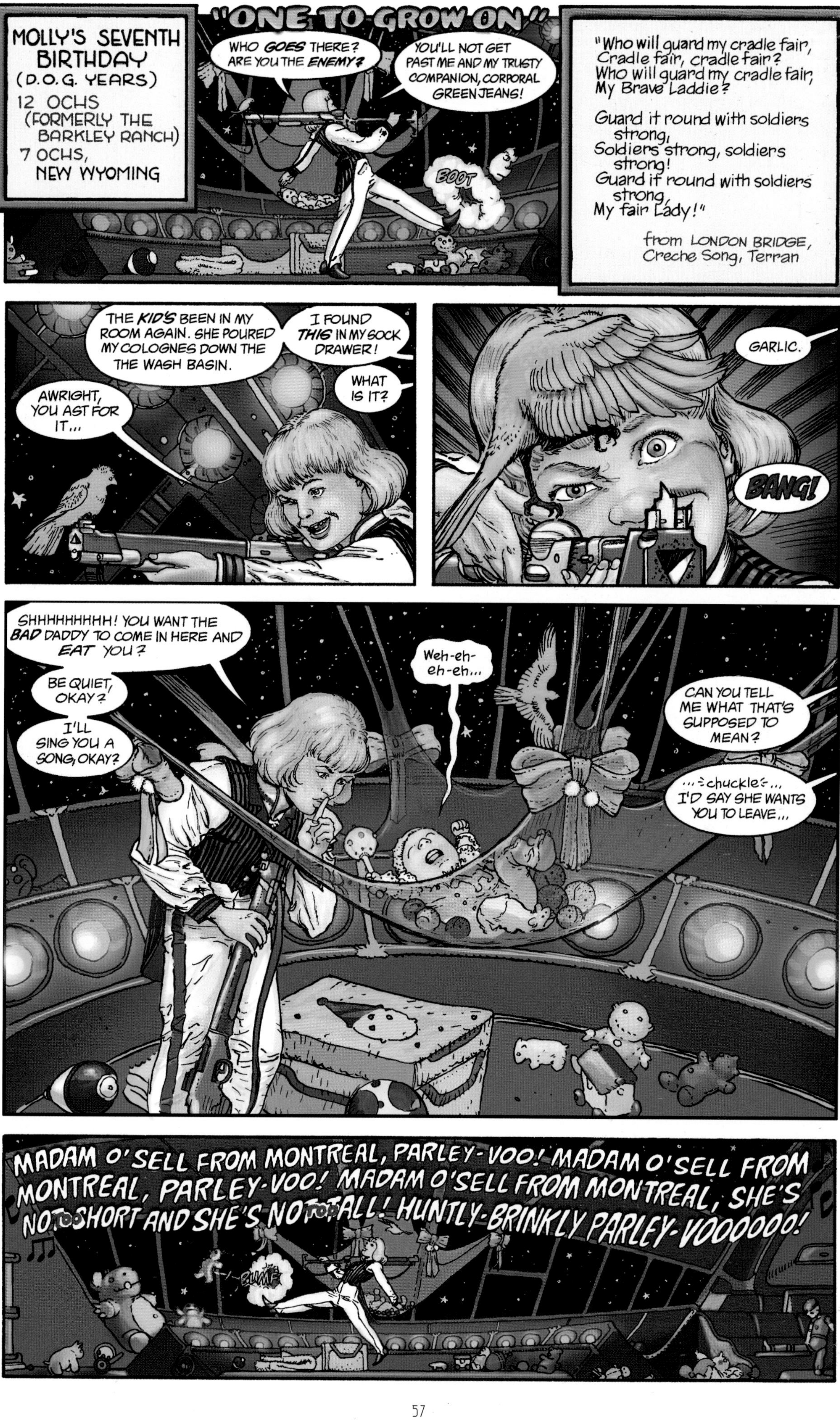
"ONE TO GROW ON"
MOLLY'S SEVENTH BIRTHDAY (D.O.G. YEARS) 12 OCHS (FORMERLY THE BARKLEY RANCH) 7 OCHS, NEW WYOMING
WHO GOES THERE? ARE YOU THE ENEMY?
YOU'LL NOT GET PAST ME AND MY TRUSTY COMPANION, CORPORAL GREEN JEANS!
BOOT
"Who will guard my cradle fair, Cradle fair, cradle fair? Who will guard my cradle fair, My Brave Laddie?
Guard it round with soldiers strong, Soldiers strong, soldiers strong! Guard it round with soldiers strong, My fair Lady!"
from LONDON BRIDGE, Creche Song, Terran
THE KID'S BEEN IN MY ROOM AGAIN. SHE POURED MY COLOGNES DOWN THE THE WASH BASIN.
I FOUND THIS IN MY SOCK DRAWER!
WHAT IS IT?
AWRIGHT, YOU AST FOR IT...
GARLIC.
BANG!
SHHHHHHHHH! YOU WANT THE BAD DADDY TO COME IN HERE AND EAT YOU?
BE QUIET, OKAY?
I'LL SING YOU A SONG, OKAY?
Weh-eh-eh-eh...
CAN YOU TELL ME WHAT THAT'S SUPPOSED TO MEAN?
...chuckle... I'D SAY SHE WANTS YOU TO LEAVE...
MADAM O'SELL FROM MONTREAL, PARLEY-VOO! MADAM O'SELL FROM MONTREAL, PARLEY-VOO! MADAM O'SELL FROM MONTREAL, SHE'S NOT SHORT AND SHE'S NOT TALL! HUNTLY-BRINKLY PARLEY-VOOOOOO!

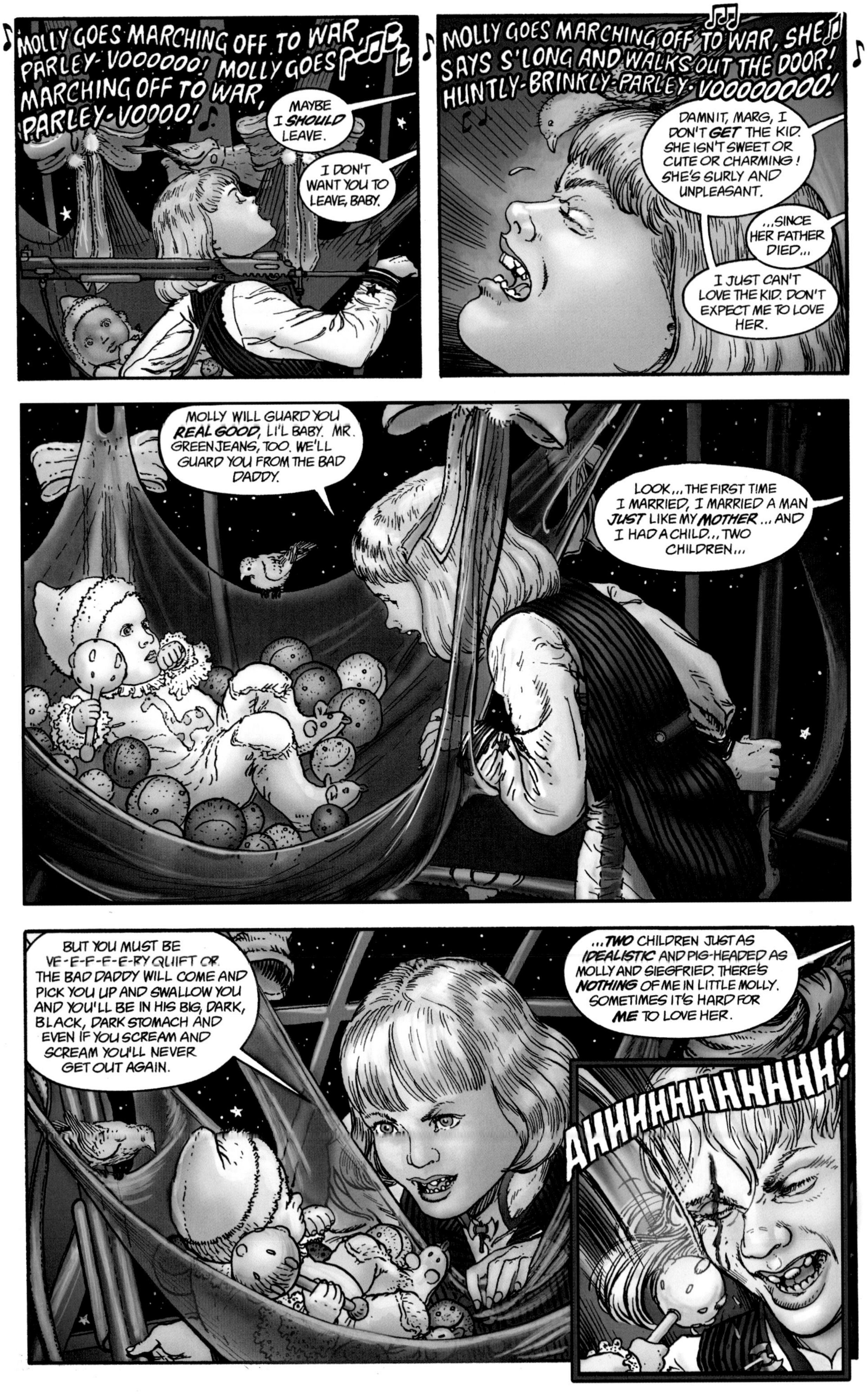
MOLLY GOES MARCHING OFF TO WAR, PARLEY-VOOOOOO! MOLLY GOES MARCHING OFF TO WAR, PARLEY-VOOOO!
MAYBE I SHOULD LEAVE.
I DON'T WANT YOU TO LEAVE, BABY.
MOLLY GOES MARCHING OFF TO WAR, SHE SAYS S'LONG AND WALKS OUT THE DOOR! HUNTLY-BRINKLY-PARLEY-VOOOOOOOO!
DAMNIT, MARG, I DON'T GET THE KID. SHE ISN'T SWEET OR CUTE OR CHARMING! SHE'S SURLY AND UNPLEASANT.
...SINCE HER FATHER DIED...
I JUST CAN'T LOVE THE KID. DON'T EXPECT ME TO LOVE HER.
MOLLY WILL GUARD YOU REAL GOOD, LI'L BABY. MR. GREEN JEANS, TOO. WE'LL GUARD YOU FROM THE BAD DADDY.
LOOK... THE FIRST TIME I MARRIED, I MARRIED A MAN JUST LIKE MY MOTHER ... AND I HAD A CHILD... TWO CHILDREN...
BUT YOU MUST BE VE-E-E-E-E-RY QUIET OR THE BAD DADDY WILL COME AND PICK YOU UP AND SWALLOW YOU AND YOU'LL BE IN HIS BIG, DARK, BLACK, DARK STOMACH AND EVEN IF YOU SCREAM AND SCREAM YOU'LL NEVER GET OUT AGAIN.
...TWO CHILDREN JUST AS IDEALISTIC AND PIG-HEADED AS MOLLY AND SIEGFRIED. THERE'S NOTHING OF ME IN LITTLE MOLLY. SOMETIMES IT'S HARD FOR ME TO LOVE HER.
AHHHHHHHHHHHH!

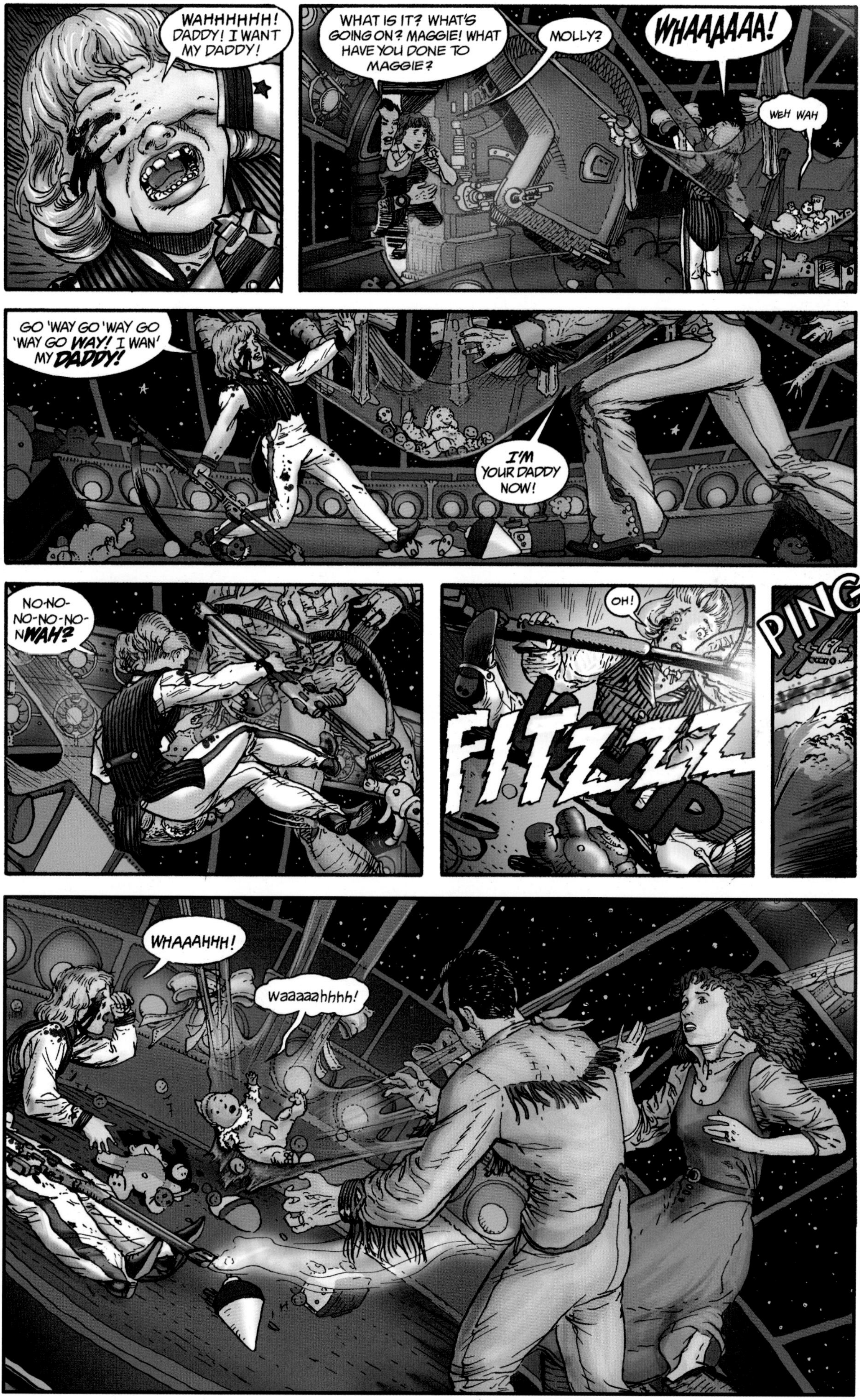

WAHHHHHH! DADDY! I WANT MY DADDY!
WHAT IS IT? WHAT'S GOING ON? MAGGIE! WHAT HAVE YOU DONE TO MAGGIE?
MOLLY?
WHAAAAAA!
WEH WAH
GO 'WAY GO 'WAY GO 'WAY GO WAY! I WAN' MY DADDY!
I'M YOUR DADDY NOW!
NO-NO-NO-NO-NO-NWAH?
OH!
FITZZZ
UP
PING!
WHAAAHHH!
Waaaaahhhh!

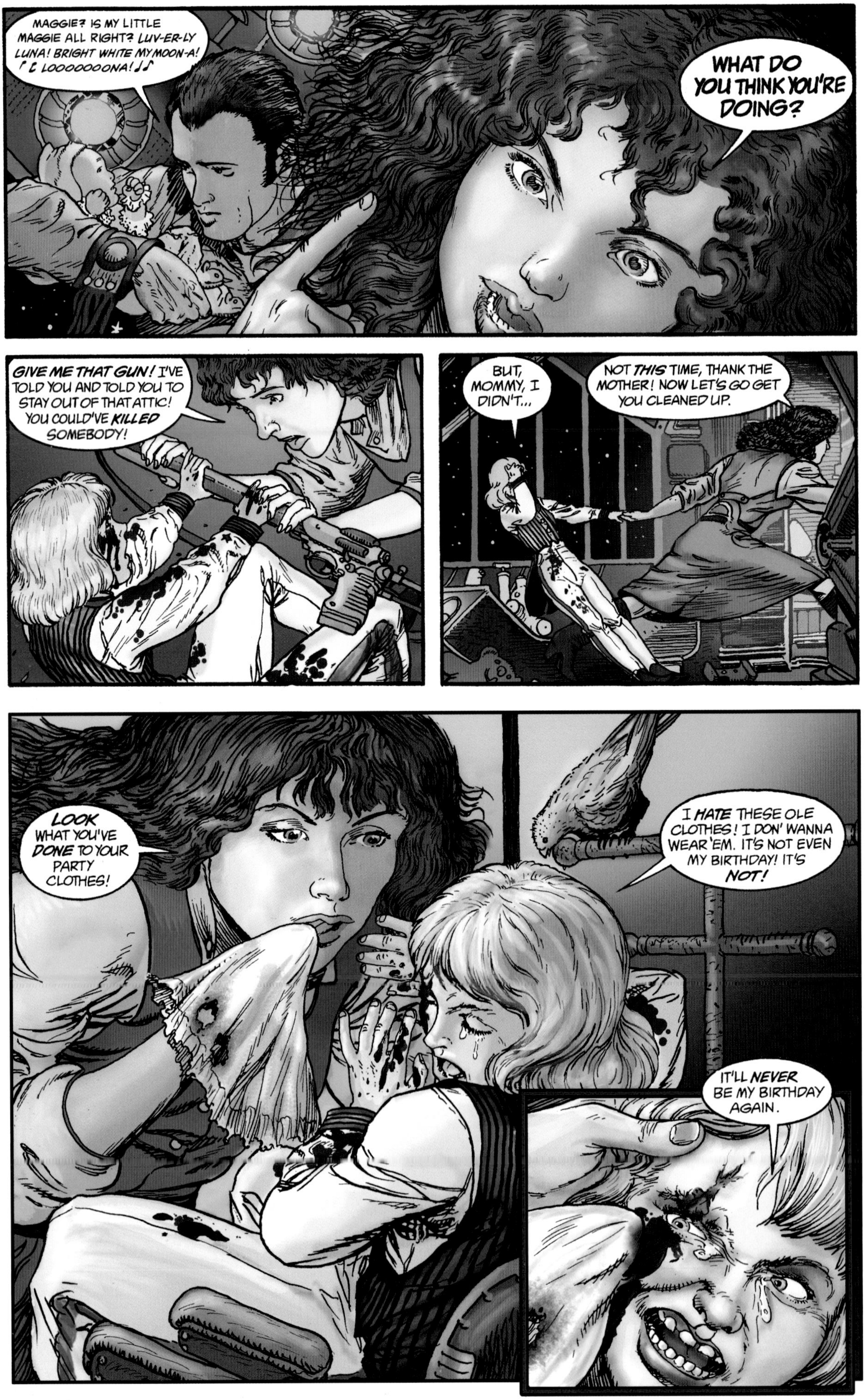
MAGGIE? IS MY LITTLE MAGGIE ALL RIGHT? LUV-ER-LY LUNA! BRIGHT WHITE MY MOON-A! LOOOOOOONA!
WHAT DO YOU THINK YOU'RE DOING?
GIVE ME THAT GUN! I'VE TOLD YOU AND TOLD YOU TO STAY OUT OF THAT ATTIC! YOU COULD'VE KILLED SOMEBODY!
BUT, MOMMY, I DIDN'T...
NOT THIS TIME, THANK THE MOTHER! NOW LET'S GO GET YOU CLEANED UP.
LOOK WHAT YOU'VE DONE TO YOUR PARTY CLOTHES!
I HATE THESE OLE CLOTHES! I DON' WANNA WEAR 'EM. IT'S NOT EVEN MY BIRTHDAY! IT'S NOT!
IT'LL NEVER BE MY BIRTHDAY AGAIN.

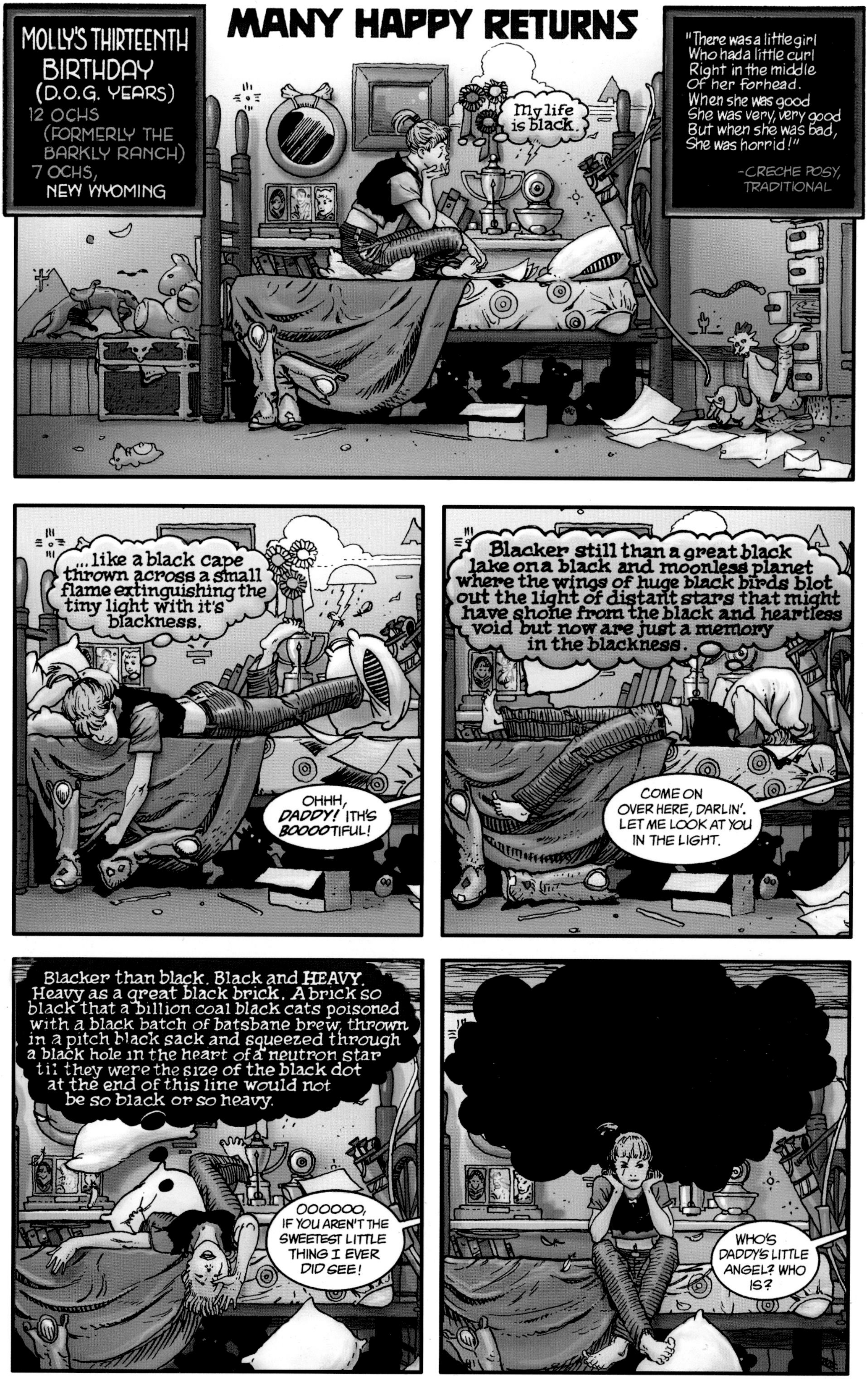
MANY HAPPY RETURNS
MOLLY'S THIRTEENTH BIRTHDAY (D.O.G. YEARS) 12 OCHS (FORMERLY THE BARKLY RANCH) 7 OCHS, NEW WYOMING
"There was a little girl Who had a little curl Right in the middle Of her forhead. When she was good She was very, very good But when she was bad, She was horrid!" -CRECHE POSY, TRADITIONAL
My life is black.
...like a black cape thrown across a small flame extinguishing the tiny light with it's blackness.
OHHH, DADDY! ITH'S BOOOOTIFUL!
Blacker still than a great black lake on a black and moonless planet where the wings of huge black birds blot out the light of distant stars that might have shone from the black and heartless void but now are just a memory in the blackness.
COME ON OVER HERE, DARLIN'. LET ME LOOK AT YOU IN THE LIGHT.
Blacker than black. Black and HEAVY. Heavy as a great black brick. A brick so black that a billion coal black cats poisoned with a black batch of batsbane brew, thrown in a pitch black sack and squeezed through a black hole in the heart of a neutron star til they were the size of the black dot at the end of this line would not be so black or so heavy.
OOOOOO, IF YOU AREN'T THE SWEETEST LITTLE THING I EVER DID SEE!
WHO'S DADDY'S LITTLE ANGEL? WHO IS?

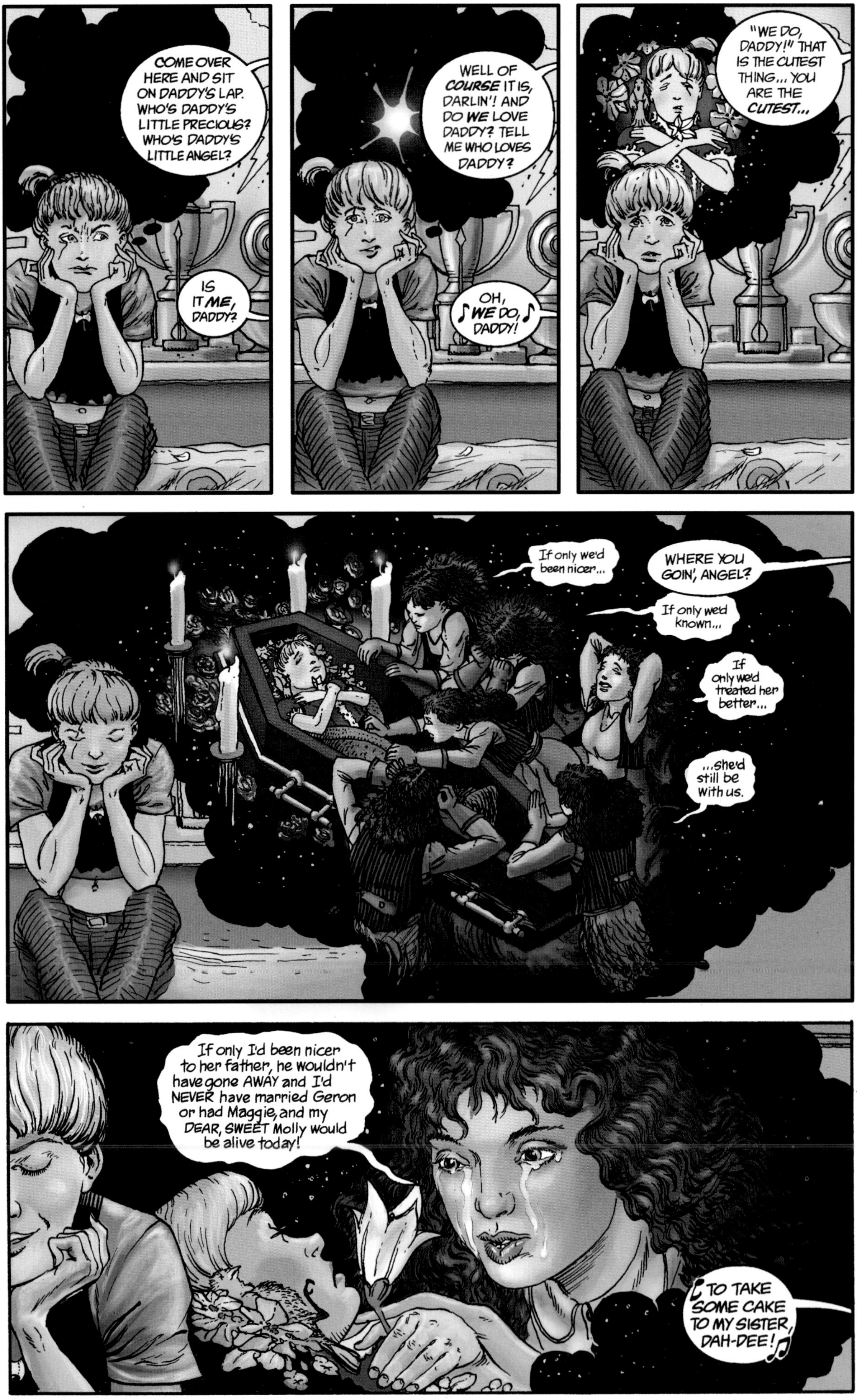
COME OVER HERE AND SIT ON DADDY'S LAP. WHO'S DADDY'S LITTLE PRECIOUS? WHO'S DADDY'S LITTLE ANGEL?
IS IT ME, DADDY?
WELL OF COURSE IT IS, DARLIN'! AND DO WE LOVE DADDY? TELL ME WHO LOVES DADDY?
OH, ♪WE DO,♪ DADDY!
"WE DO, DADDY!" THAT IS THE CUTEST THING... YOU ARE THE CUTEST...
If only we'd been nicer...
WHERE YOU GOIN', ANGEL?
If only we'd known...
If only we'd treated her better...
...she'd still be with us.
If only I'd been nicer to her father, he wouldn't have gone AWAY and I'd NEVER have married Geron or had Maggie, and my DEAR, SWEET Molly would be alive today!
♪TO TAKE SOME CAKE TO MY SISTER, DAH-DEE!♪

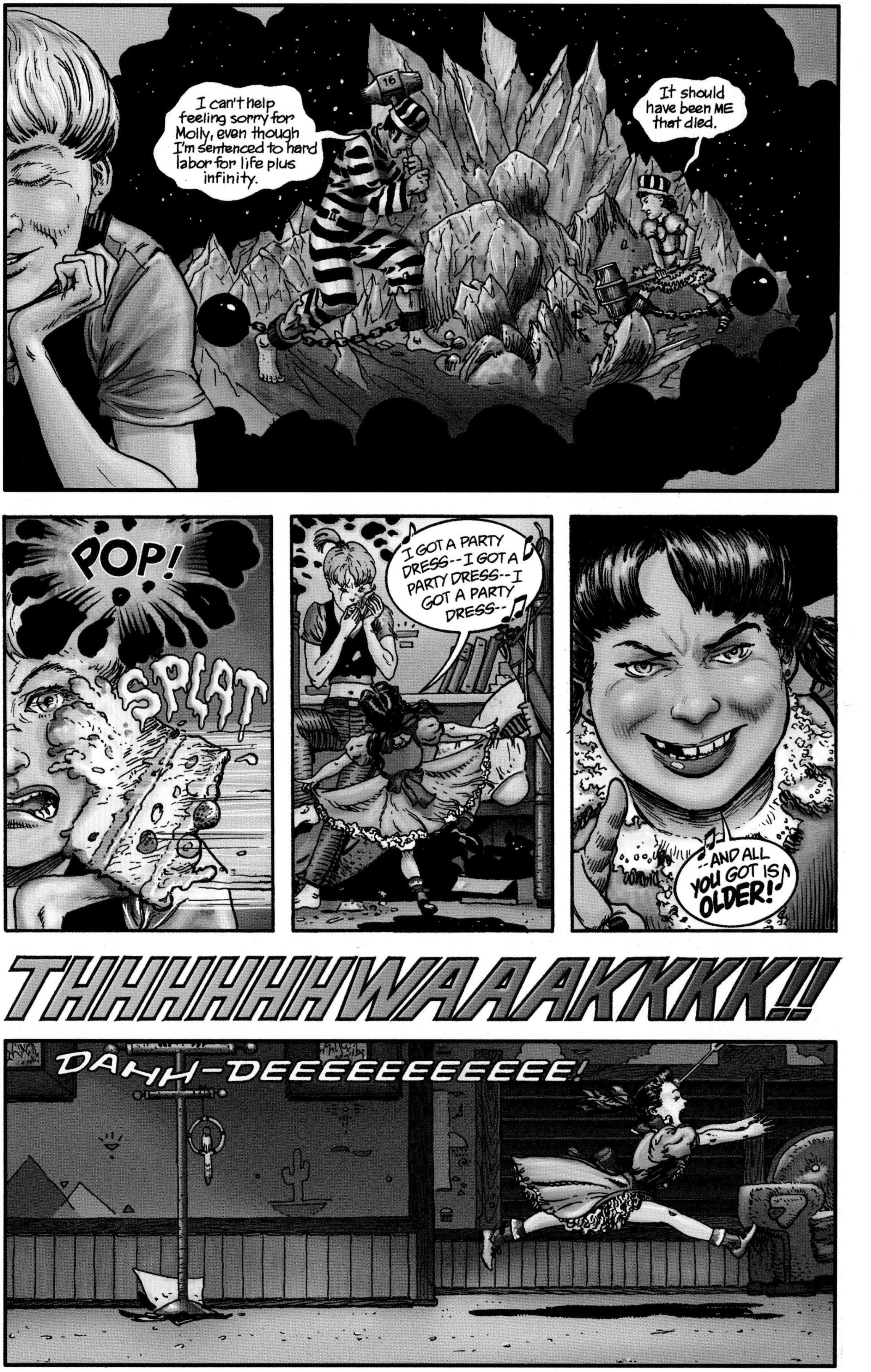
I can't help feeling sorry for Molly, even though I'm sentenced to hard labor for life plus infinity.
It should have been ME that died.
16
POP!
SPLAT
I GOT A PARTY DRESS--I GOT A PARTY DRESS--I GOT A PARTY DRESS--
--AND ALL YOU GOT IS OLDER!
THHHHHHWAAAAKKKK!!
DAHH-DEEEEEEEEEEE!

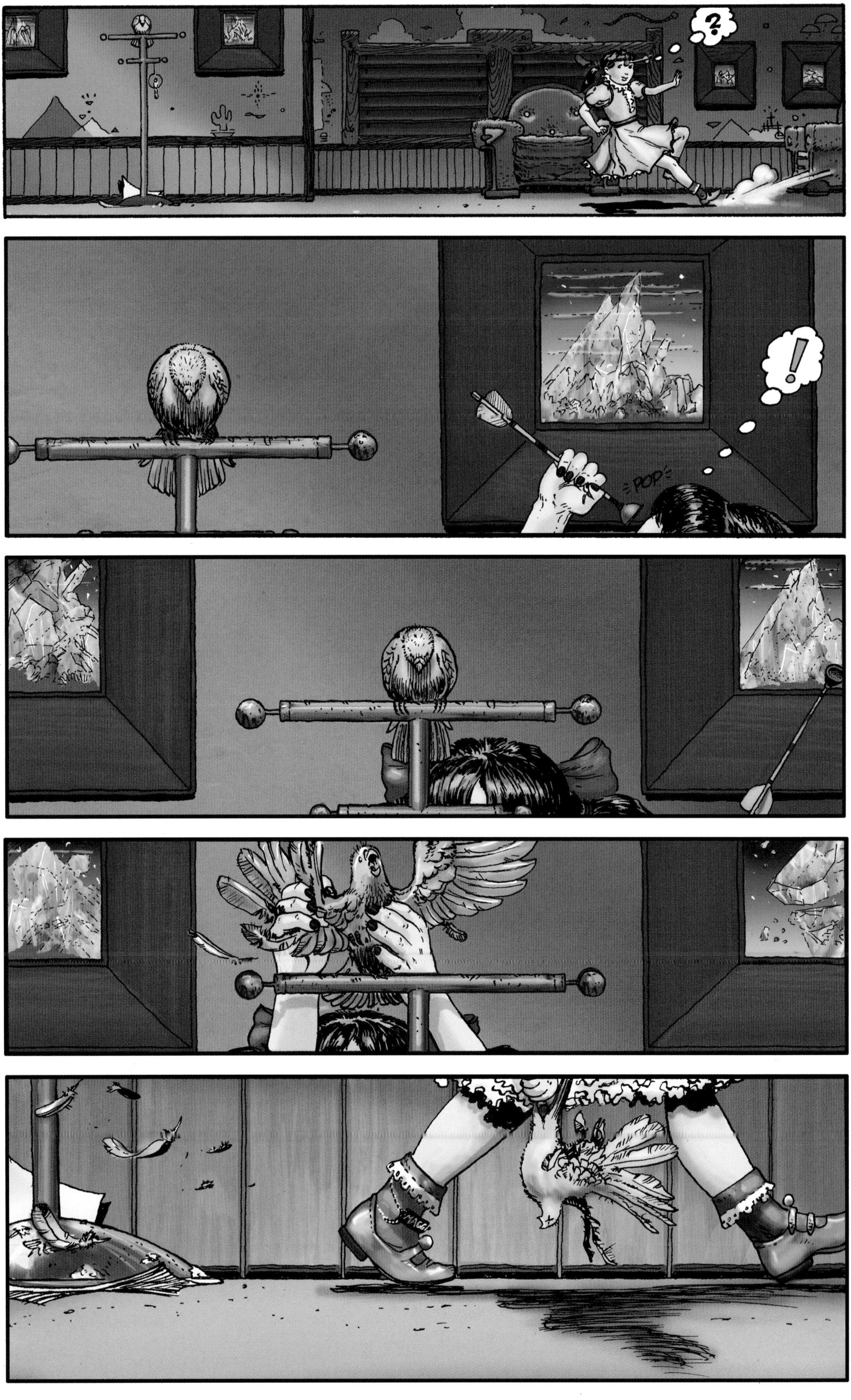
?
!
POP
MAGGI

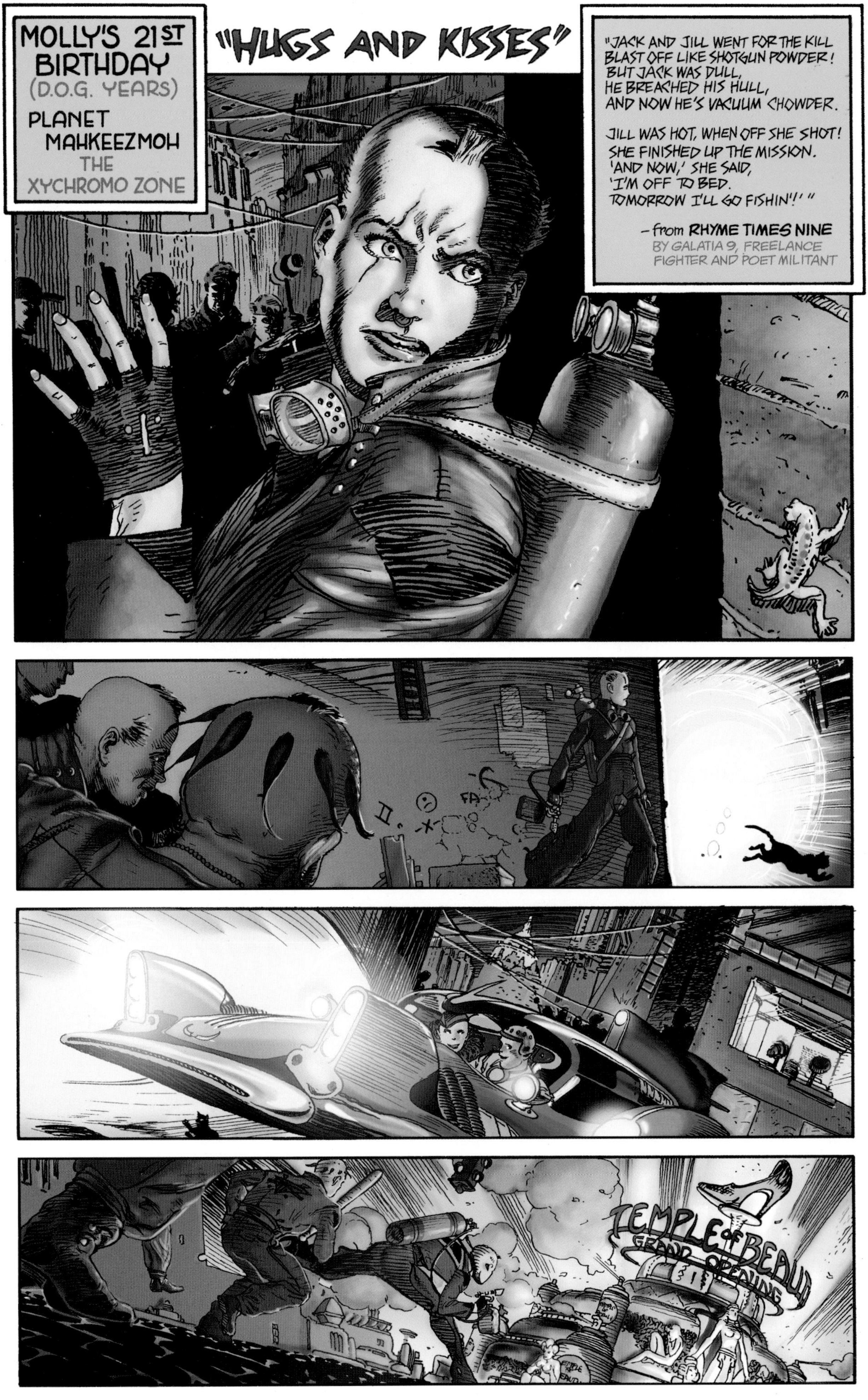
MOLLY'S 21ST BIRTHDAY
(D.O.G. YEARS)
PLANET MAHKEEZMOH
THE XYCHROMO ZONE
"HUGS AND KISSES"
"JACK AND JILL WENT FOR THE KILL
BLAST OFF LIKE SHOTGUN POWDER!
BUT JACK WAS DULL,
HE BREACHED HIS HULL,
AND NOW HE'S VACUUM CHOWDER.
JILL WAS HOT, WHEN OFF SHE SHOT!
SHE FINISHED UP THE MISSION.
'AND NOW,' SHE SAID,
'I'M OFF TO BED.
TOMORROW I'LL GO FISHIN'!' "
– from RHYME TIMES NINE
BY GALATIA 9, FREELANCE FIGHTER AND POET MILITANT
TEMPLE of BEAU
GRAND OPENING

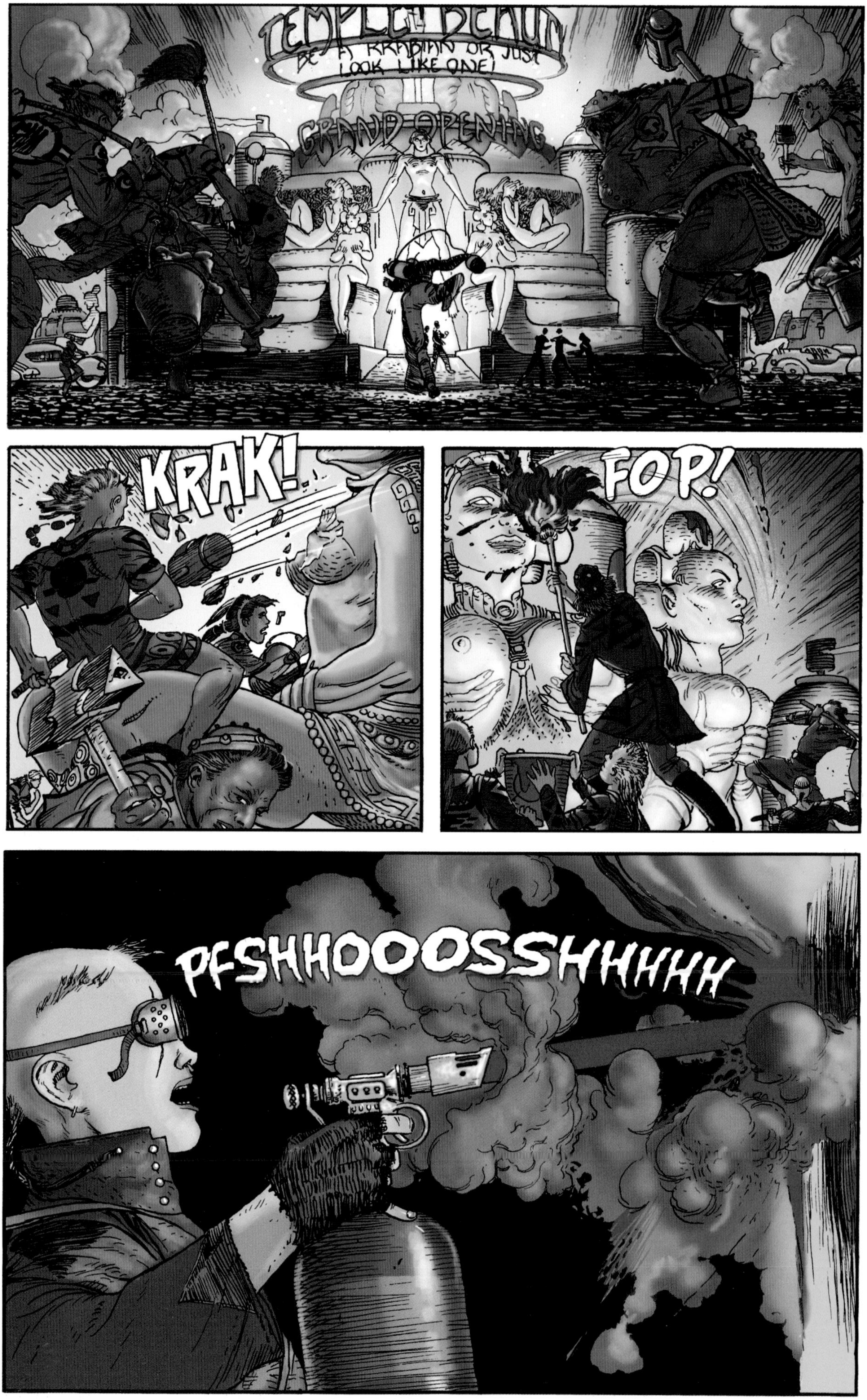
TEMPLE
BE A KRABIAN OR JUST LOOK LIKE ONE!
GRAND OPENING
KRAK!
FOP!
PFSHHOOOSSHHHHH

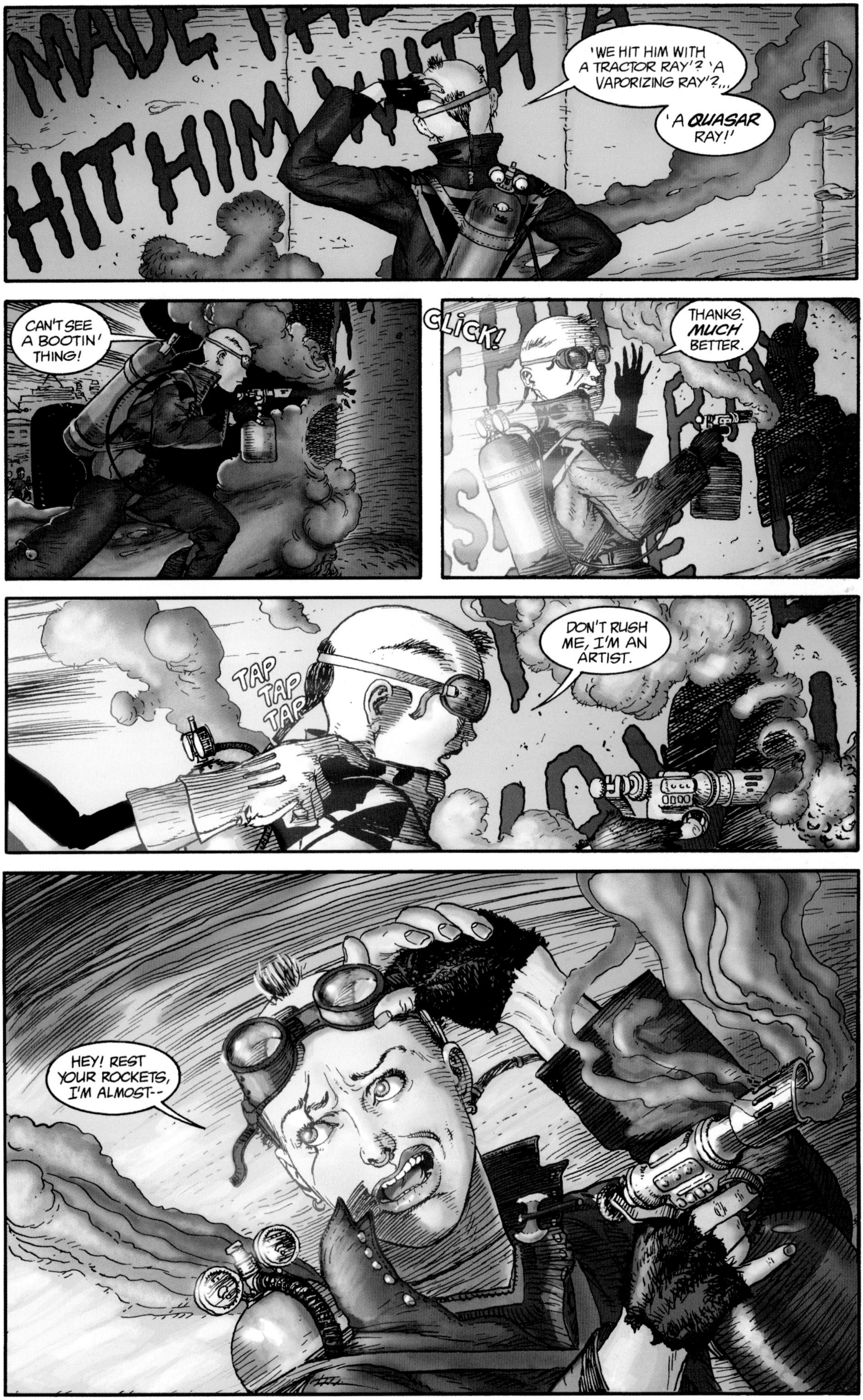
'WE HIT HIM WITH A TRACTOR RAY'? 'A VAPORIZING RAY'?...
'A QUASAR RAY!'
CAN'T SEE A BOOTIN' THING!
CLICK!
THANKS. MUCH BETTER.
TAP TAP TAP
DON'T RUSH ME, I'M AN ARTIST.
HEY! REST YOUR ROCKETS, I'M ALMOST--

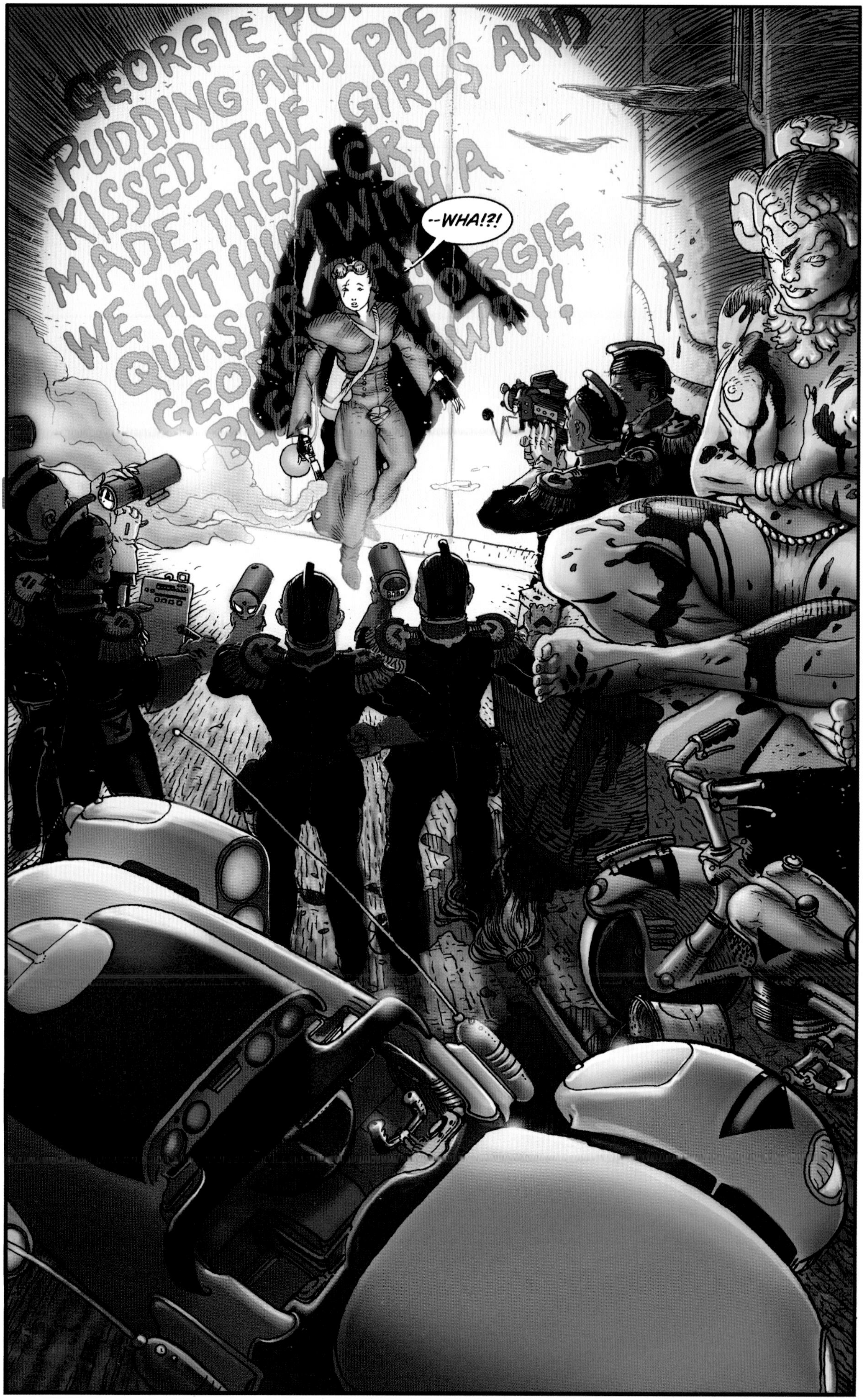
PUDDING AND PIE
KISSED THE GIRLS AND
MADE THEM CRY
--WHA!?!

...APPREHENDED ONLY MARBECS AGO. AUTHORITIES BELIEVE MIZ ROE TO BE THE INFAMOUS POET MILITANT...

QUASAR RAY GEORGIE PORGIE BLEW AWAY!

...RESPONSIBLE FOR THE DESECRATION OF 38 TEMPLE OF BEAUTY FRANCHISES THROUGHOUT THE *XYCHROMO ZONE*.

I *KNEW* IT HAD TO BE HER.

KETTLE BLACK, SELF-PROCLAIMED LEADER OF THE GUERNICAN ART SQUAD, HAS CANONIZED MIZ ROE, MAKING HER AN OFFICIAL SQUAD *MARTYR*.

TURN IT OFF, DADDY.

...AND I WAS *RIGHT*.

...SHE *COULDN'T* RESIST THAT GRAND OPENING.

DADDY'S PRETTY LITTLE GENIUS.

LUV-ER-LY *LUNA!* LIGHT WHITE MY *MOON-A!*

GEORGIE PORGIE, MY *ASS!*

HEART KNOX WOMEN'S PRISON, PLNT 007, XYCHROMO ZONE

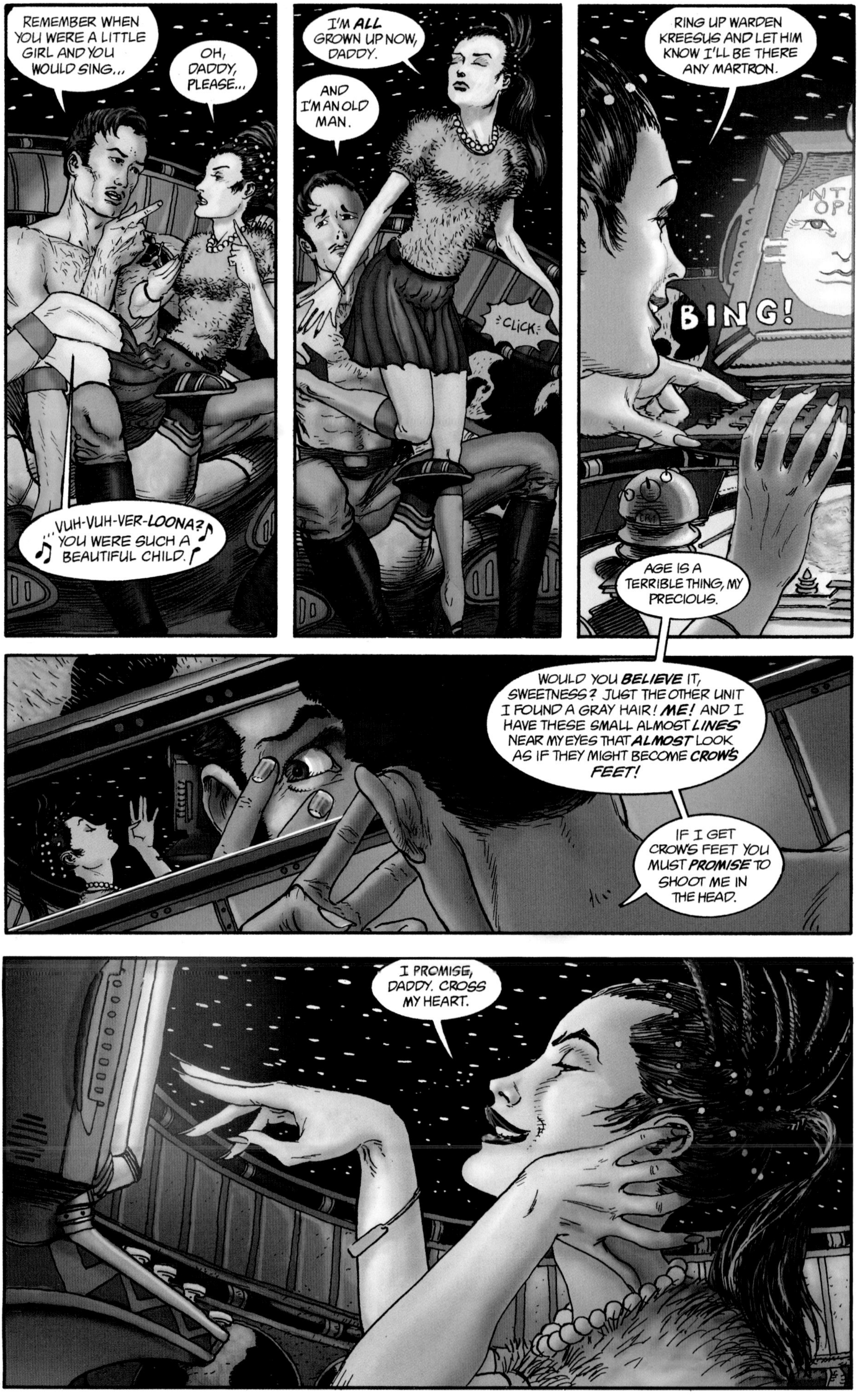

REMEMBER WHEN YOU WERE A LITTLE GIRL AND YOU WOULD SING...
OH, DADDY, PLEASE...
...VUH-VUH-VER-LOONA? YOU WERE SUCH A BEAUTIFUL CHILD.
I'M ALL GROWN UP NOW, DADDY.
AND I'M AN OLD MAN.
CLICK
RING UP WARDEN KREESUS AND LET HIM KNOW I'LL BE THERE ANY MARTRON.
BING!
AGE IS A TERRIBLE THING, MY PRECIOUS.
WOULD YOU BELIEVE IT, SWEETNESS? JUST THE OTHER UNIT I FOUND A GRAY HAIR! ME! AND I HAVE THESE SMALL ALMOST LINES NEAR MY EYES THAT ALMOST LOOK AS IF THEY MIGHT BECOME CROW'S FEET!
IF I GET CROW'S FEET YOU MUST PROMISE TO SHOOT ME IN THE HEAD.
I PROMISE, DADDY. CROSS MY HEART.

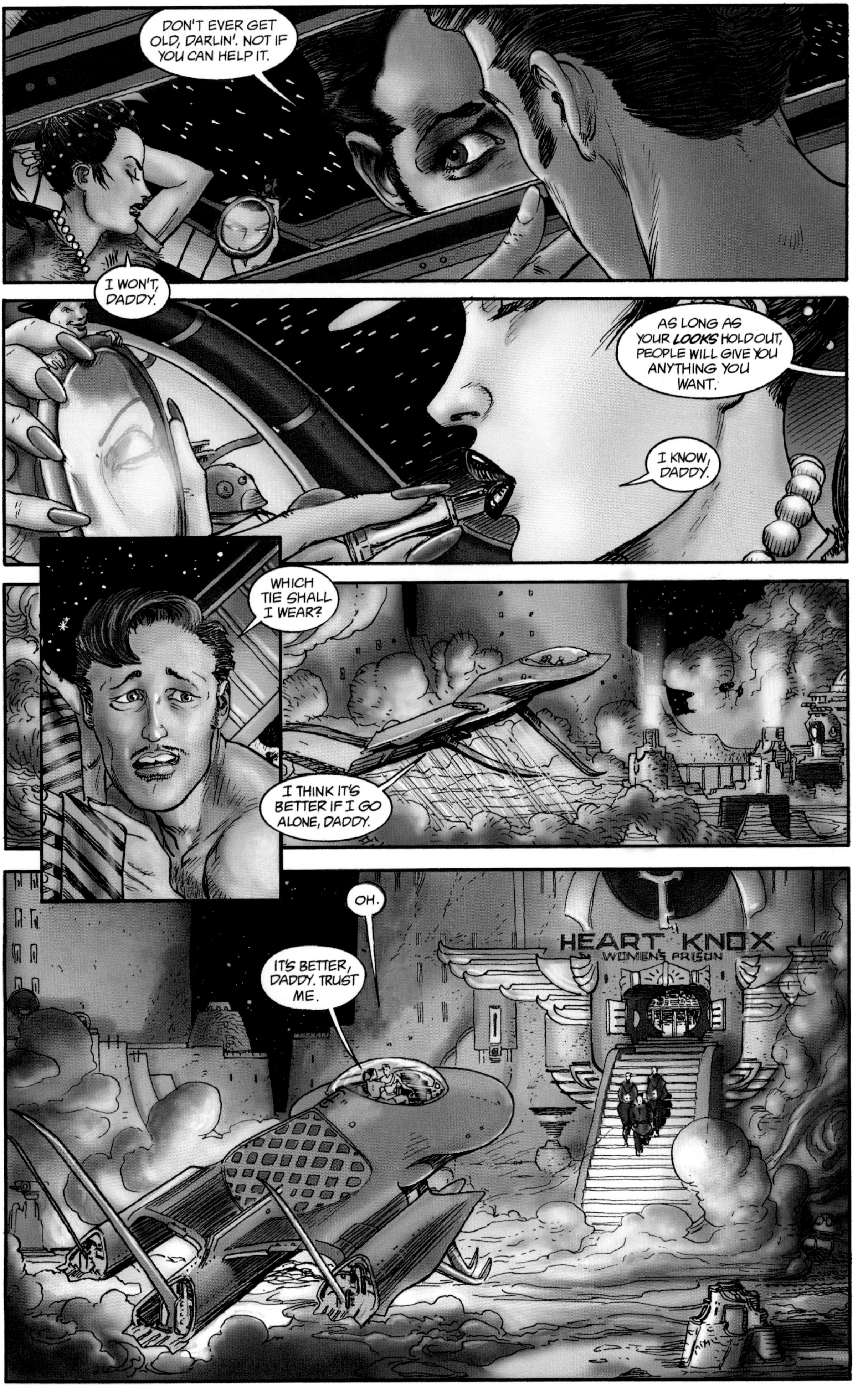
DON'T EVER GET OLD, DARLIN'. NOT IF YOU CAN HELP IT.
I WON'T, DADDY.
AS LONG AS YOUR LOOKS HOLD OUT, PEOPLE WILL GIVE YOU ANYTHING YOU WANT.
I KNOW, DADDY.
WHICH TIE SHALL I WEAR?
I THINK IT'S BETTER IF I GO ALONE, DADDY.
OH.
IT'S BETTER, DADDY. TRUST ME.
HEART KNOX
WOMEN'S PRISON

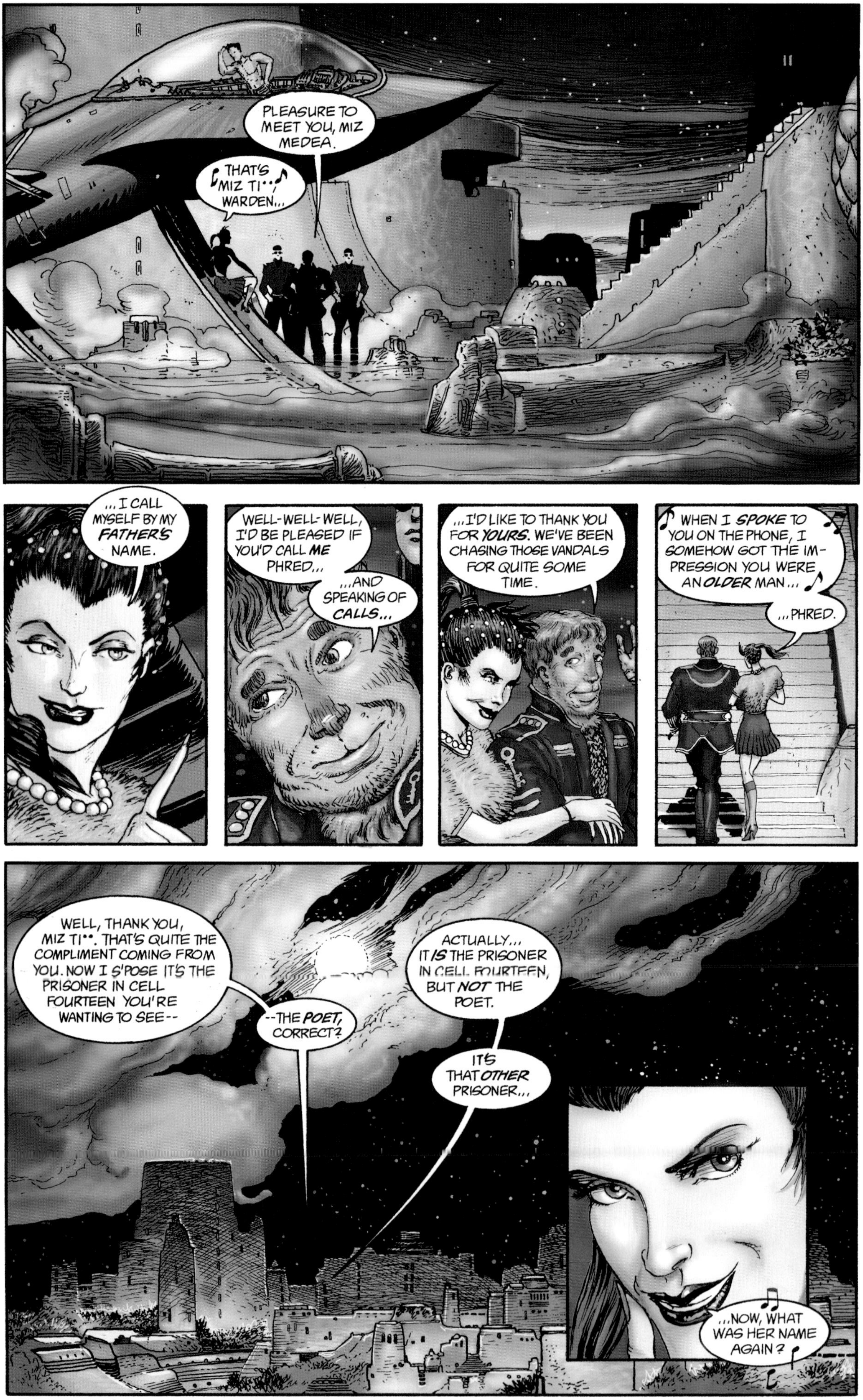
PLEASURE TO MEET YOU, MIZ MEDEA.
THAT'S MIZ TI••, WARDEN...
...I CALL MYSELF BY MY FATHER'S NAME.
WELL-WELL-WELL, I'D BE PLEASED IF YOU'D CALL ME PHRED...
...AND SPEAKING OF CALLS...
...I'D LIKE TO THANK YOU FOR YOURS. WE'VE BEEN CHASING THOSE VANDALS FOR QUITE SOME TIME.
WHEN I SPOKE TO YOU ON THE PHONE, I SOMEHOW GOT THE IM-PRESSION YOU WERE AN OLDER MAN...
...PHRED.
WELL, THANK YOU, MIZ TI••. THAT'S QUITE THE COMPLIMENT COMING FROM YOU. NOW I S'POSE IT'S THE PRISONER IN CELL FOURTEEN YOU'RE WANTING TO SEE--
--THE POET, CORRECT?
ACTUALLY... IT IS THE PRISONER IN CELL FOURTEEN, BUT NOT THE POET.
IT'S THAT OTHER PRISONER...
...NOW, WHAT WAS HER NAME AGAIN?

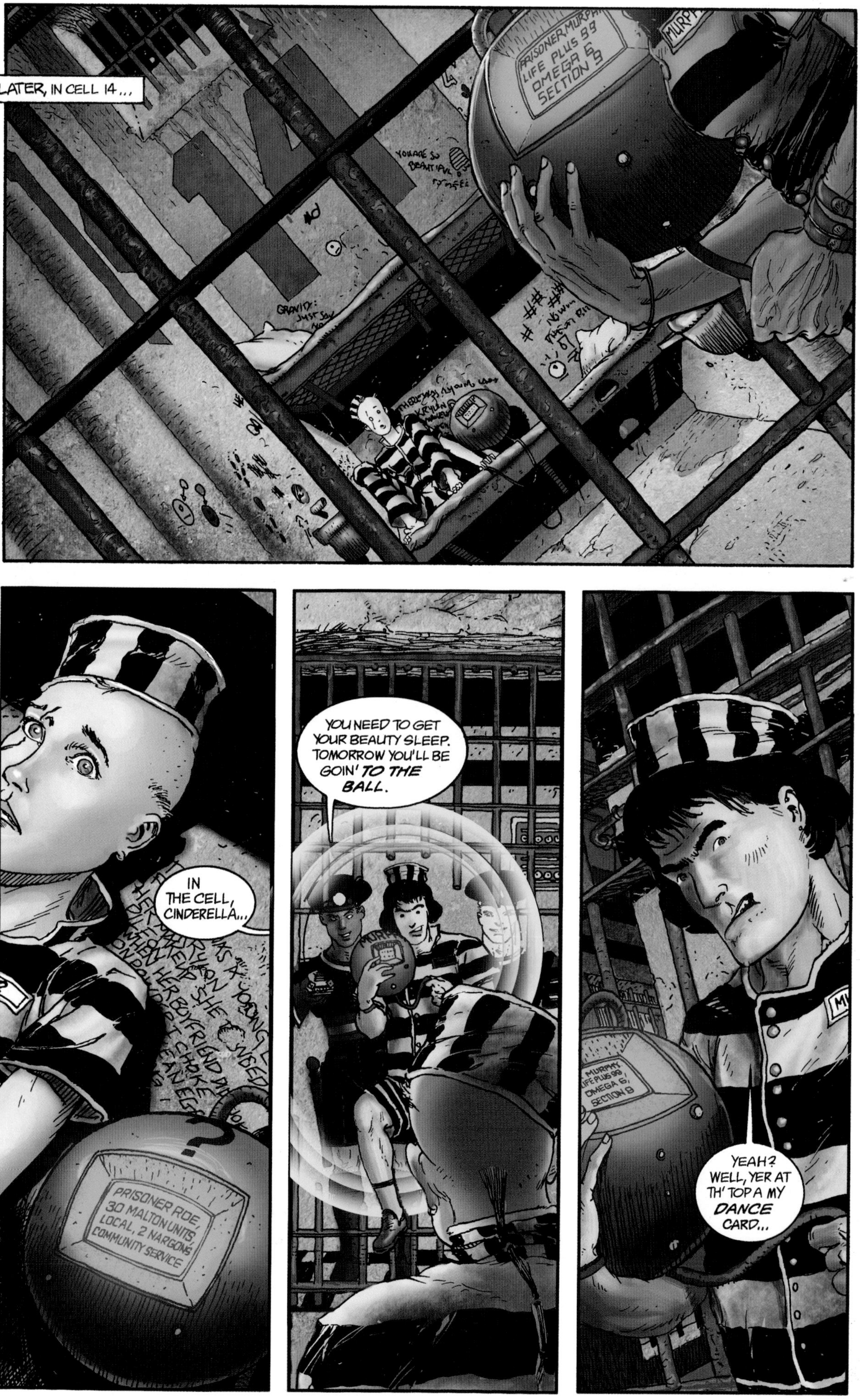
LATER, IN CELL 14...
IN THE CELL, CINDERELLA...
PRISONER ROE, 30 MALTON UNITS, LOCAL, 2 NARGONS COMMUNITY SERVICE
YOU NEED TO GET YOUR BEAUTY SLEEP. TOMORROW YOU'LL BE GOIN' TO THE BALL.
YEAH? WELL, YER AT TH' TOP A MY DANCE CARD...

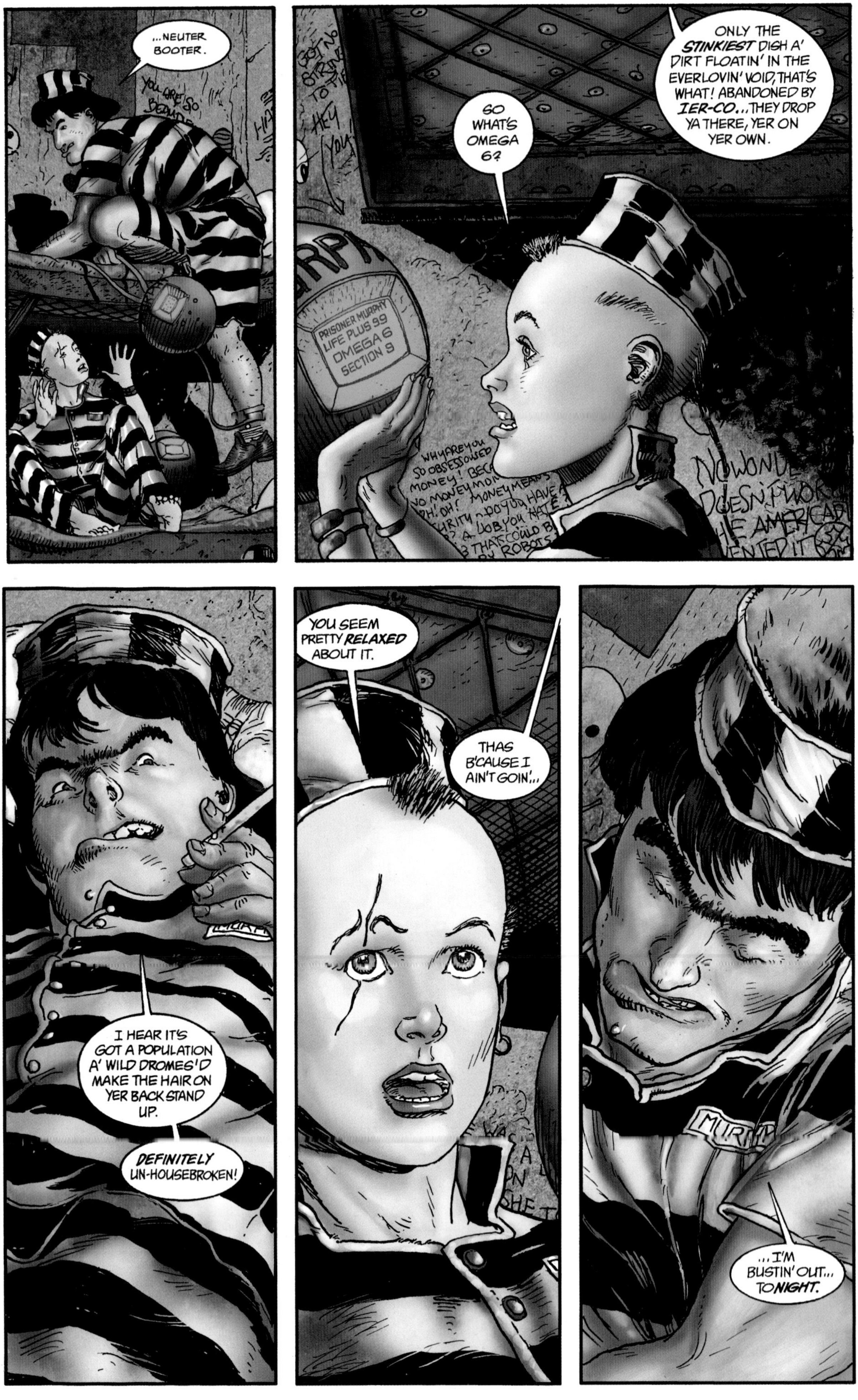
...NEUTER BOOTER.
SO WHAT'S OMEGA 6?
ONLY THE STINKIEST DISH A' DIRT FLOATIN' IN THE EVERLOVIN' VOID, THAT'S WHAT! ABANDONED BY IER-CO... THEY DROP YA THERE, YER ON YER OWN.
PRISONER MURPHY
LIFE PLUS 99
OMEGA 6
SECTION 9
I HEAR IT'S GOT A POPULATION A' WILD DROMES'D MAKE THE HAIR ON YER BACK STAND UP.
DEFINITELY UN-HOUSEBROKEN!
YOU SEEM PRETTY RELAXED ABOUT IT.
THAS B'CAUSE I AIN'T GOIN'...
...I'M BUSTIN' OUT... TONIGHT.

PLAY YER CARDS RIGHT, I'LL TAKE YA WIT ME.
WHAT YA GOT IN MIND?
CATCH!
WHADIZIT?
A ONEWAY TICKET TO OUTSVILLE. YOU HOP ON MY BACK, I'LL SCRATCH YOURS. C'MON, BALDIE, WE AIN'T GOT ALL UNIT!
HEY!
WATCH THE EARS, SIS!
WORKS!
THIS A GOOD IDEA?

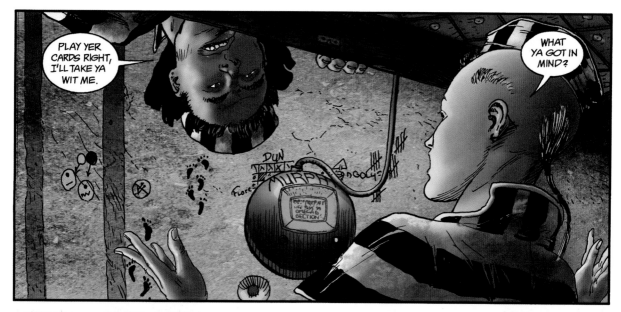

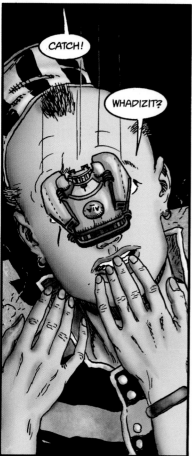

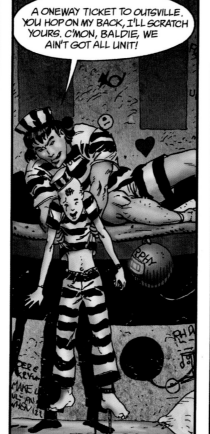

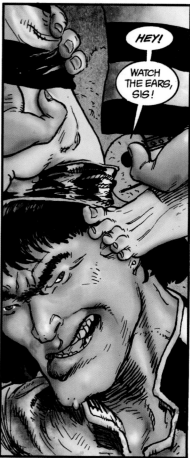

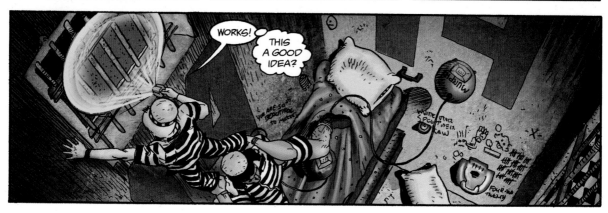

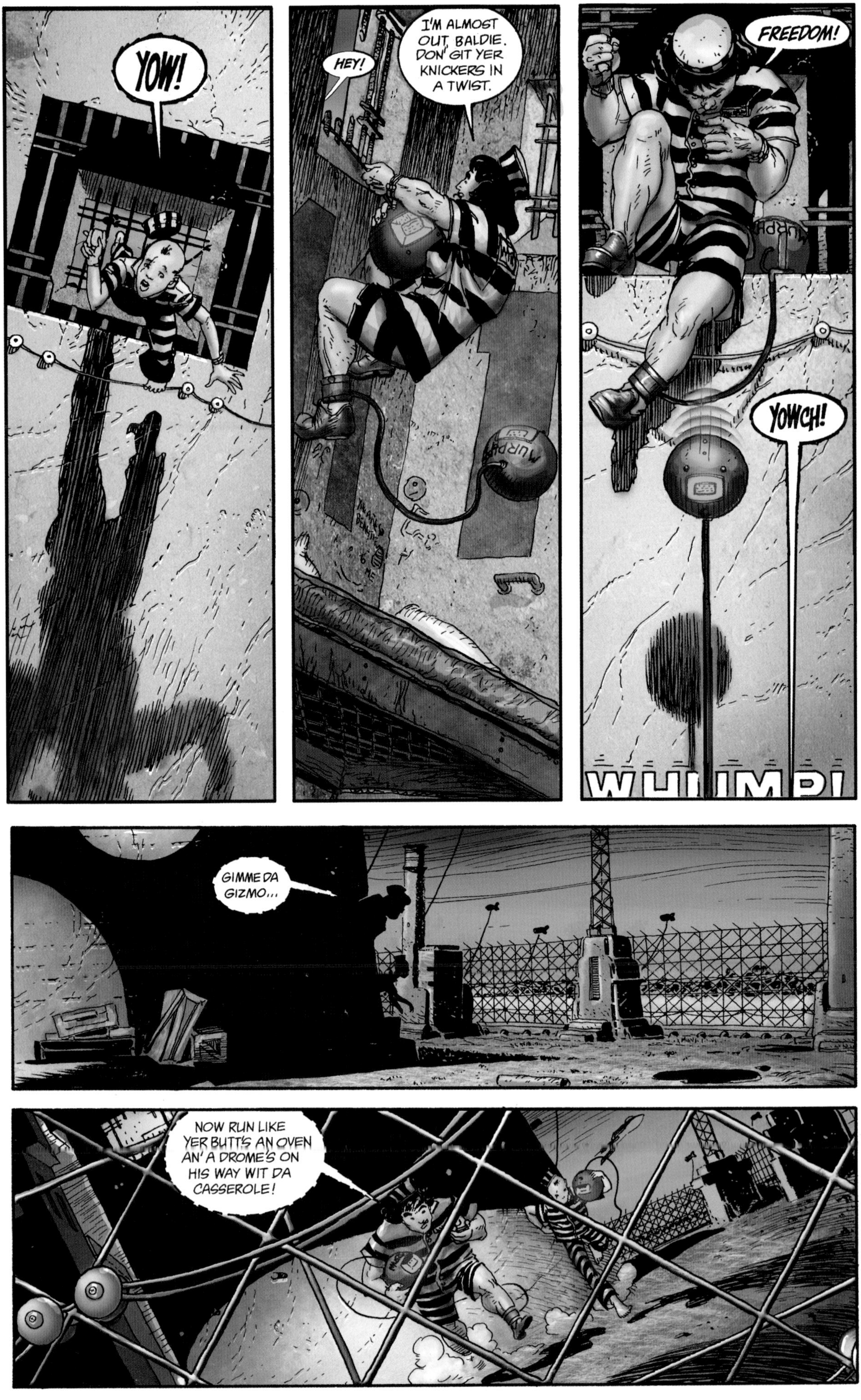
YOW!
HEY!
I'M ALMOST OUT, BALDIE. DON' GIT YER KNICKERS IN A TWIST.
FREEDOM!
YOWCH!
WHUMP!
GIMME DA GIZMO...
NOW RUN LIKE YER BUTT'S AN OVEN AN' A DROME'S ON HIS WAY WIT DA CASSEROLE!

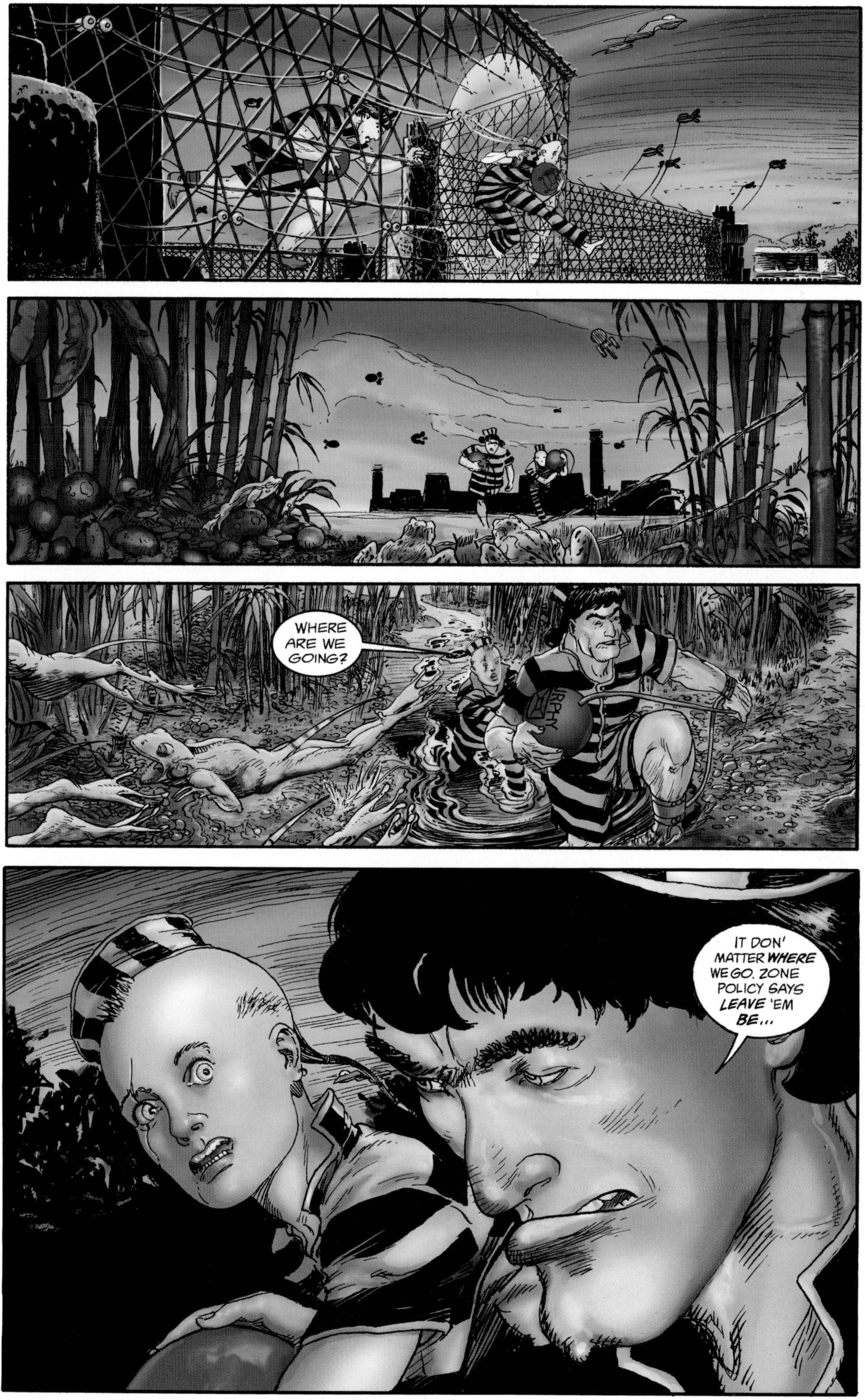
WHERE ARE WE GOING?
IT DON' MATTER **WHERE** WE GO. ZONE POLICY SAYS **LEAVE** 'EM **BE**...

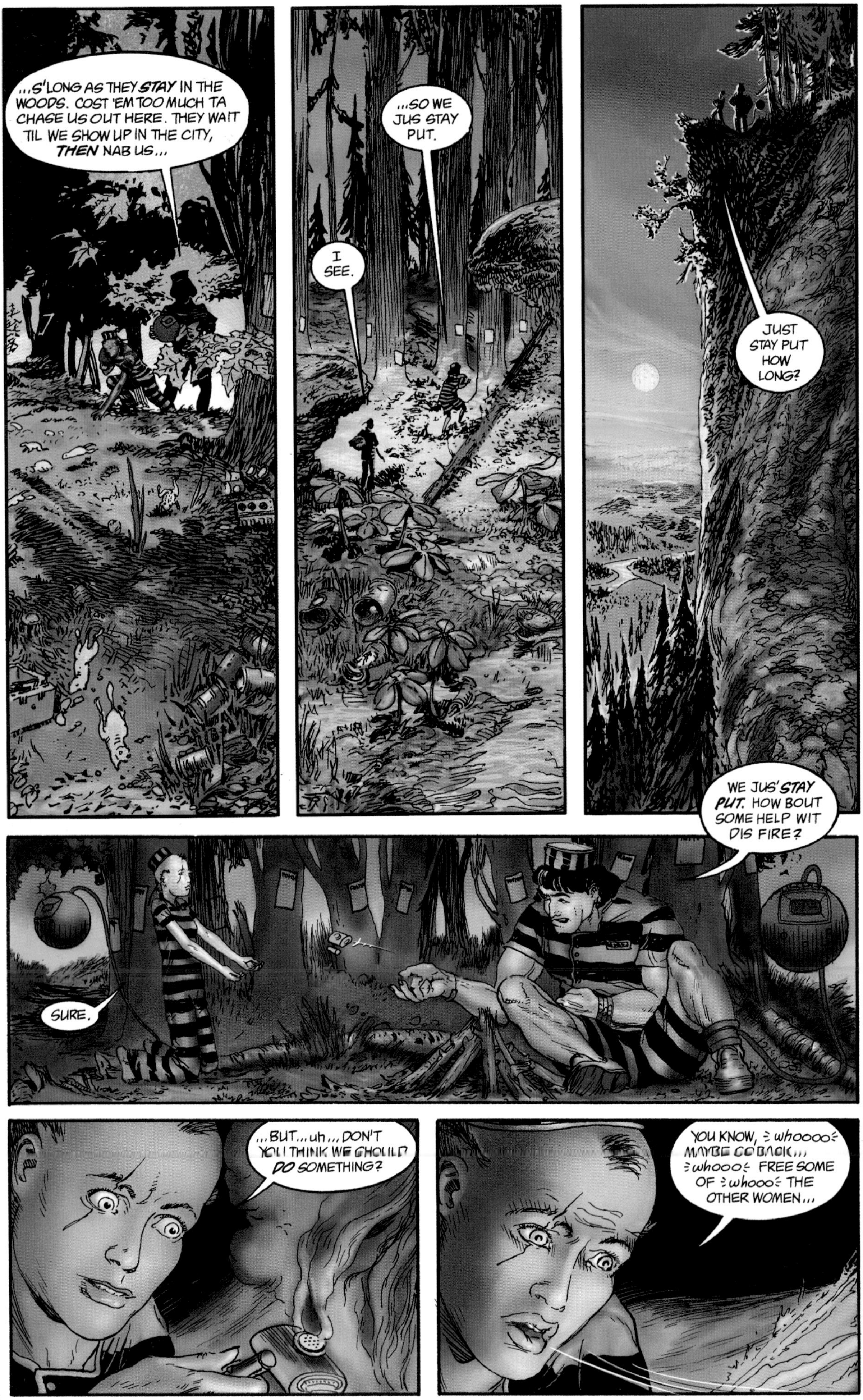
...S'LONG AS THEY STAY IN THE WOODS. COST 'EM TOO MUCH TA CHASE US OUT HERE. THEY WAIT TIL WE SHOW UP IN THE CITY, THEN NAB US...
...SO WE JUS STAY PUT.
I SEE.
JUST STAY PUT HOW LONG?
WE JUS' STAY PUT. HOW BOUT SOME HELP WIT DIS FIRE?
SURE.
...BUT...uh...DON'T YOU THINK WE SHOULD DO SOMETHING?
YOU KNOW, whoooo MAYBE GO BACK... whooo FREE SOME OF whooo THE OTHER WOMEN...

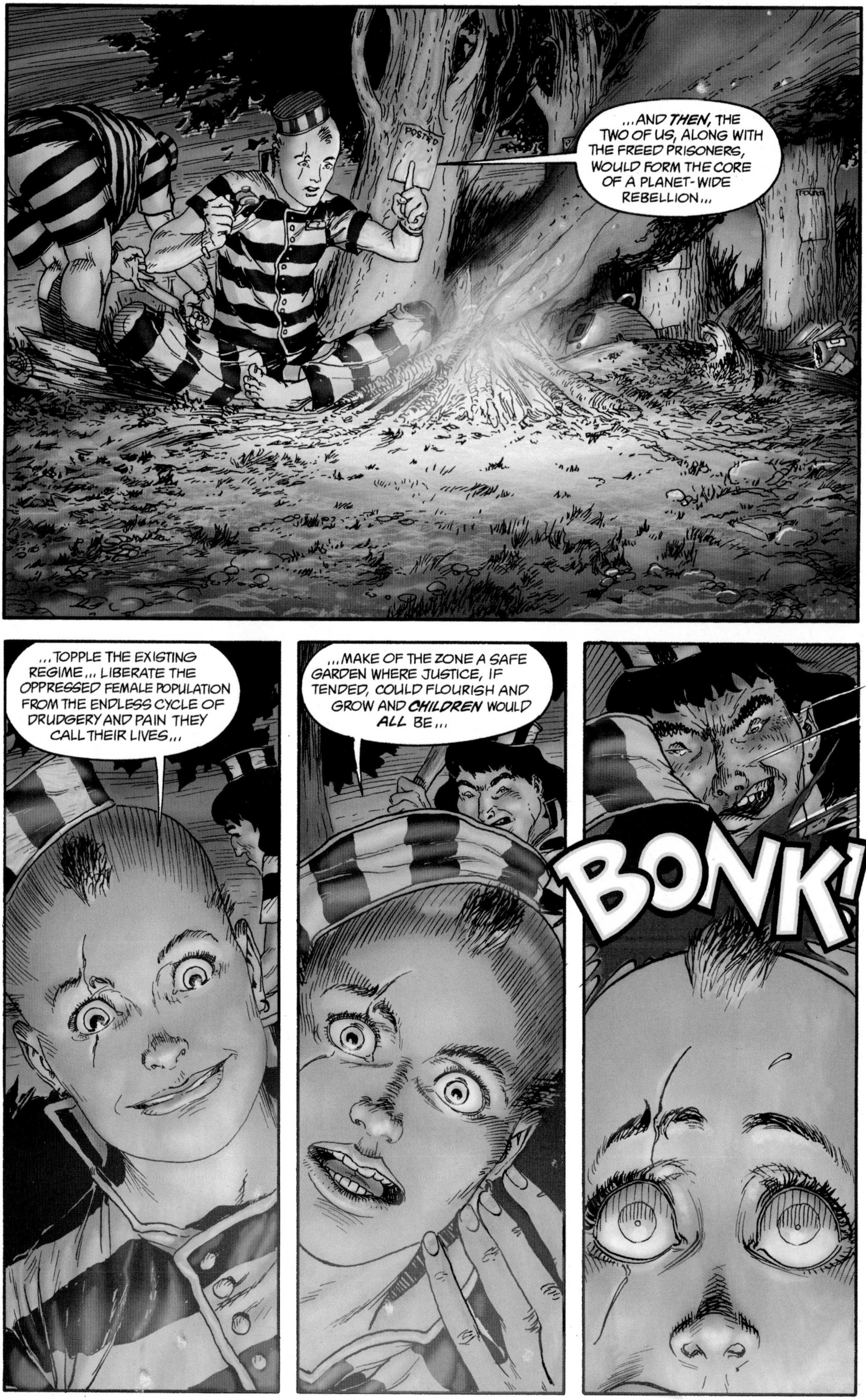
...AND THEN, THE TWO OF US, ALONG WITH THE FREED PRISONERS, WOULD FORM THE CORE OF A PLANET-WIDE REBELLION...
POSTED
...TOPPLE THE EXISTING REGIME... LIBERATE THE OPPRESSED FEMALE POPULATION FROM THE ENDLESS CYCLE OF DRUDGERY AND PAIN THEY CALL THEIR LIVES...
...MAKE OF THE ZONE A SAFE GARDEN WHERE JUSTICE, IF TENDED, COULD FLOURISH AND GROW AND CHILDREN WOULD ALL BE...
BONK!

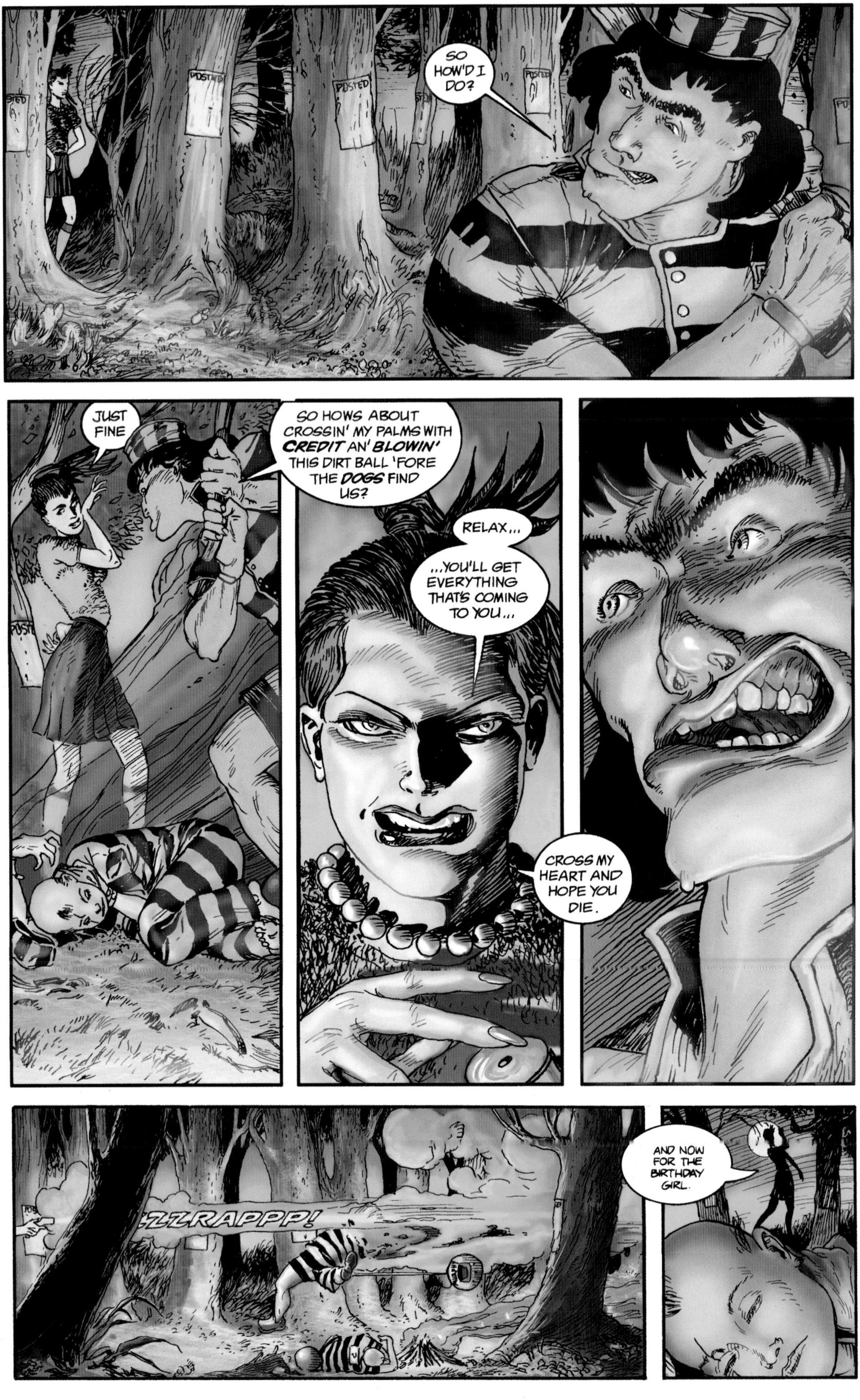
POSTED
SO HOW'D I DO?
JUST FINE
SO HOWS ABOUT CROSSIN' MY PALMS WITH **CREDIT** AN' **BLOWIN'** THIS DIRT BALL 'FORE THE **DOGS** FIND US?
RELAX...
...YOU'LL GET EVERYTHING THAT'S COMING TO YOU...
CROSS MY HEART AND HOPE YOU DIE.
ZZRAPPP!
AND NOW FOR THE BIRTHDAY GIRL.

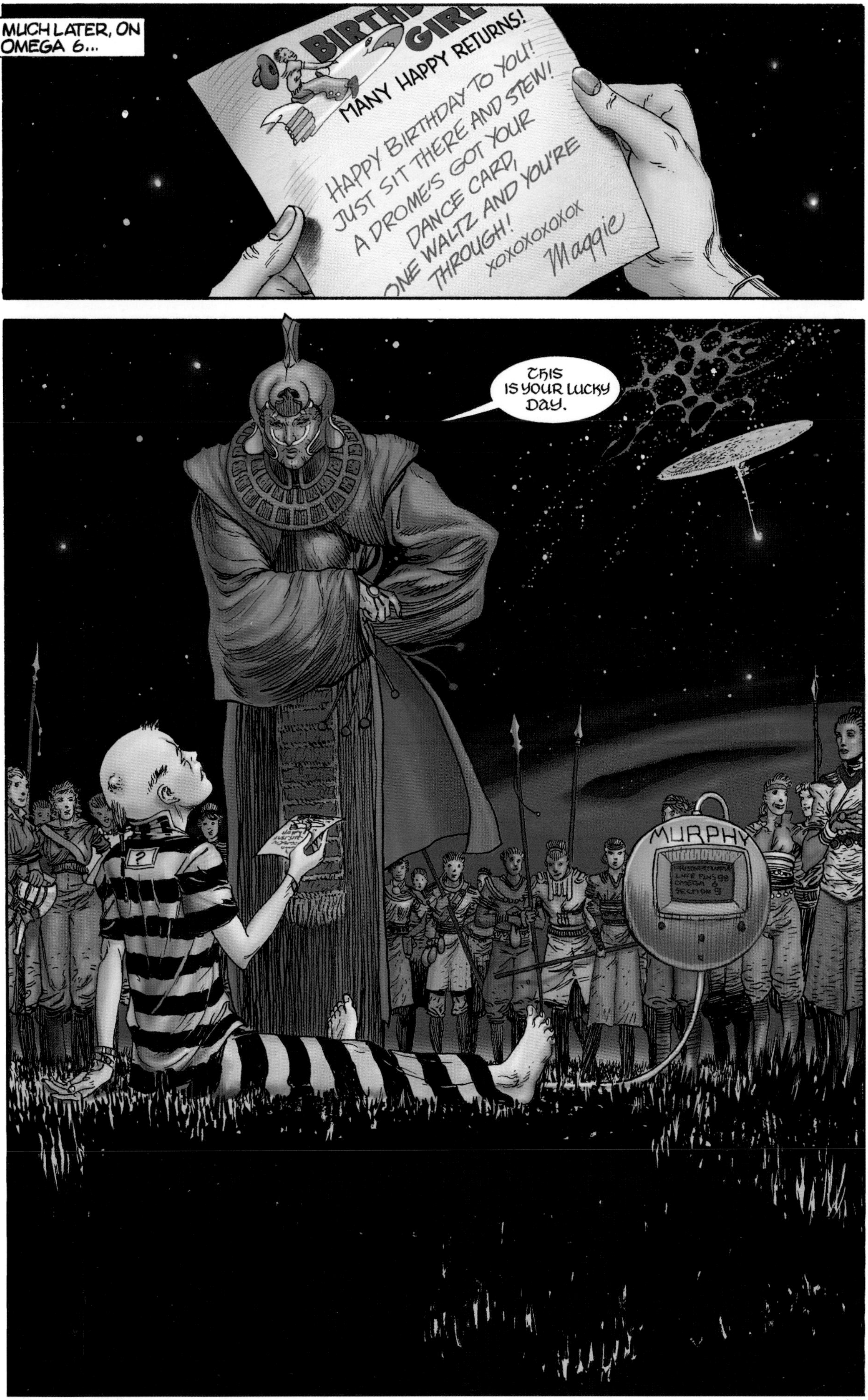
MUCH LATER, ON OMEGA 6...
MANY HAPPY RETURNS!
HAPPY BIRTHDAY TO YOU!
JUST SIT THERE AND STEW!
A DROME'S GOT YOUR
DANCE CARD,
ONE WALTZ AND YOU'RE
THROUGH!
XOXOXOXOXOX
Maggie
THIS IS YOUR LUCKY DAY.
MURPHY

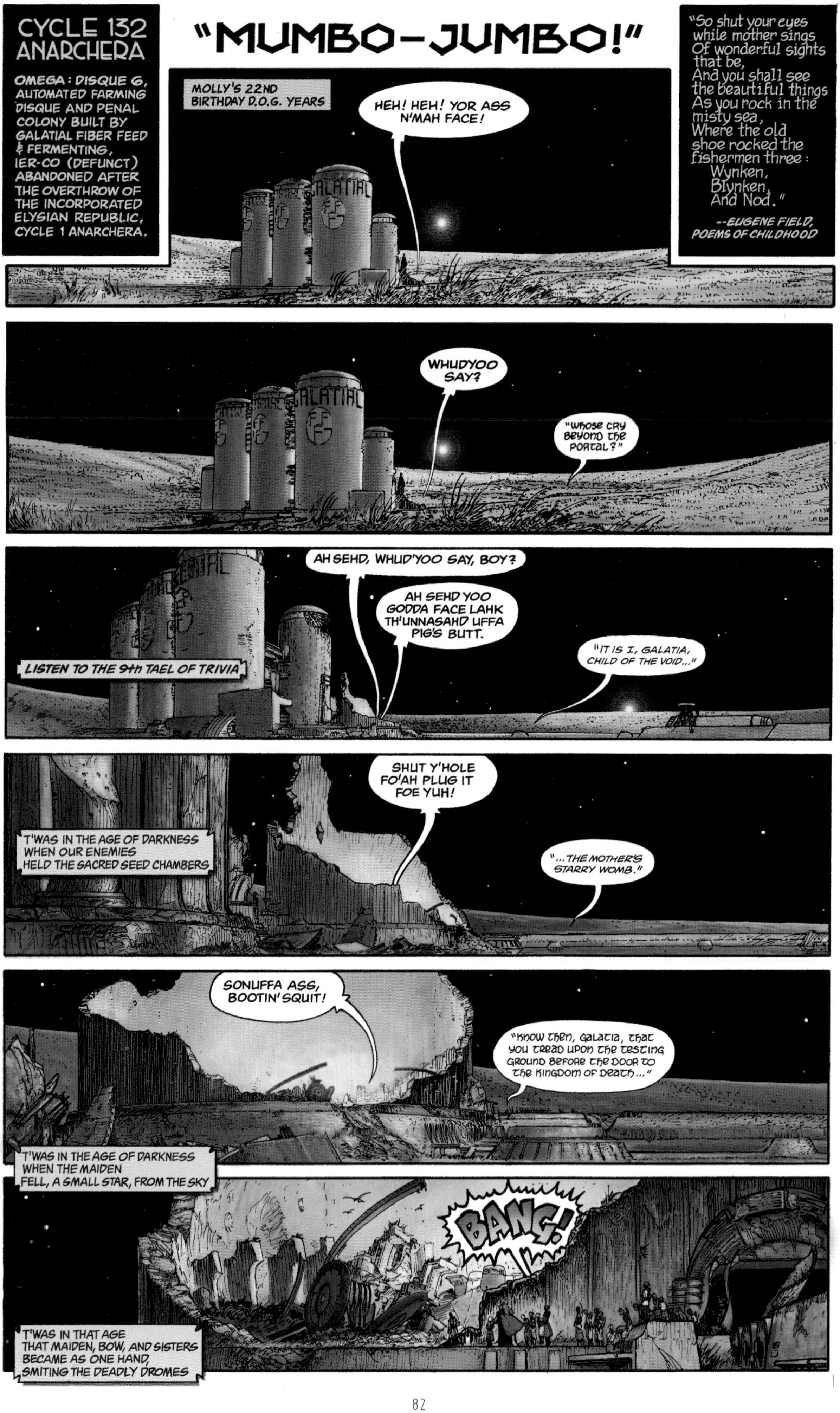
CYCLE 132 ANARCHERA
OMEGA : DISQUE 6, AUTOMATED FARMING DISQUE AND PENAL COLONY BUILT BY GALATIAL FIBER FEED & FERMENTING, IER-CO (DEFUNCT) ABANDONED AFTER THE OVERTHROW OF THE INCORPORATED ELYSIAN REPUBLIC, CYCLE 1 ANARCHERA.
"MUMBO-JUMBO!"
"So shut your eyes while mother sings Of wonderful sights that be, And you shall see the beautiful things As you rock in the misty sea, Where the old shoe rocked the fishermen three : Wynken, Blynken, And Nod."
--EUGENE FIELD, POEMS OF CHILDHOOD
MOLLY'S 22ND BIRTHDAY D.O.G. YEARS
HEH! HEH! YOR ASS N'MAH FACE!
GALATIAL
WHUDYOO SAY?
"WHOSE CRY BEYOND THE PORTAL?"
AH SEHD, WHUD'YOO SAY, BOY?
AH SEHD YOO GODDA FACE LAHK TH'UNNASAHD UFFA PIG'S BUTT.
LISTEN TO THE 9th TAEL OF TRIVIA
"IT IS I, GALATIA, CHILD OF THE VOID..."
SHUT Y'HOLE FO'AH PLUG IT FOE YUH!
T'WAS IN THE AGE OF DARKNESS WHEN OUR ENEMIES HELD THE SACRED SEED CHAMBERS
"...THE MOTHER'S STARRY WOMB."
SONUFFA ASS, BOOTIN' SQUIT!
"KNOW THEN, GALATIA, THAT YOU TREAD UPON THE TESTING GROUND BEFORE THE DOOR TO THE KINGDOM OF DEATH..."
T'WAS IN THE AGE OF DARKNESS WHEN THE MAIDEN FELL, A SMALL STAR, FROM THE SKY
BANG!
T'WAS IN THAT AGE THAT MAIDEN, BOW, AND SISTERS BECAME AS ONE HAND, SMITING THE DEADLY DROMES

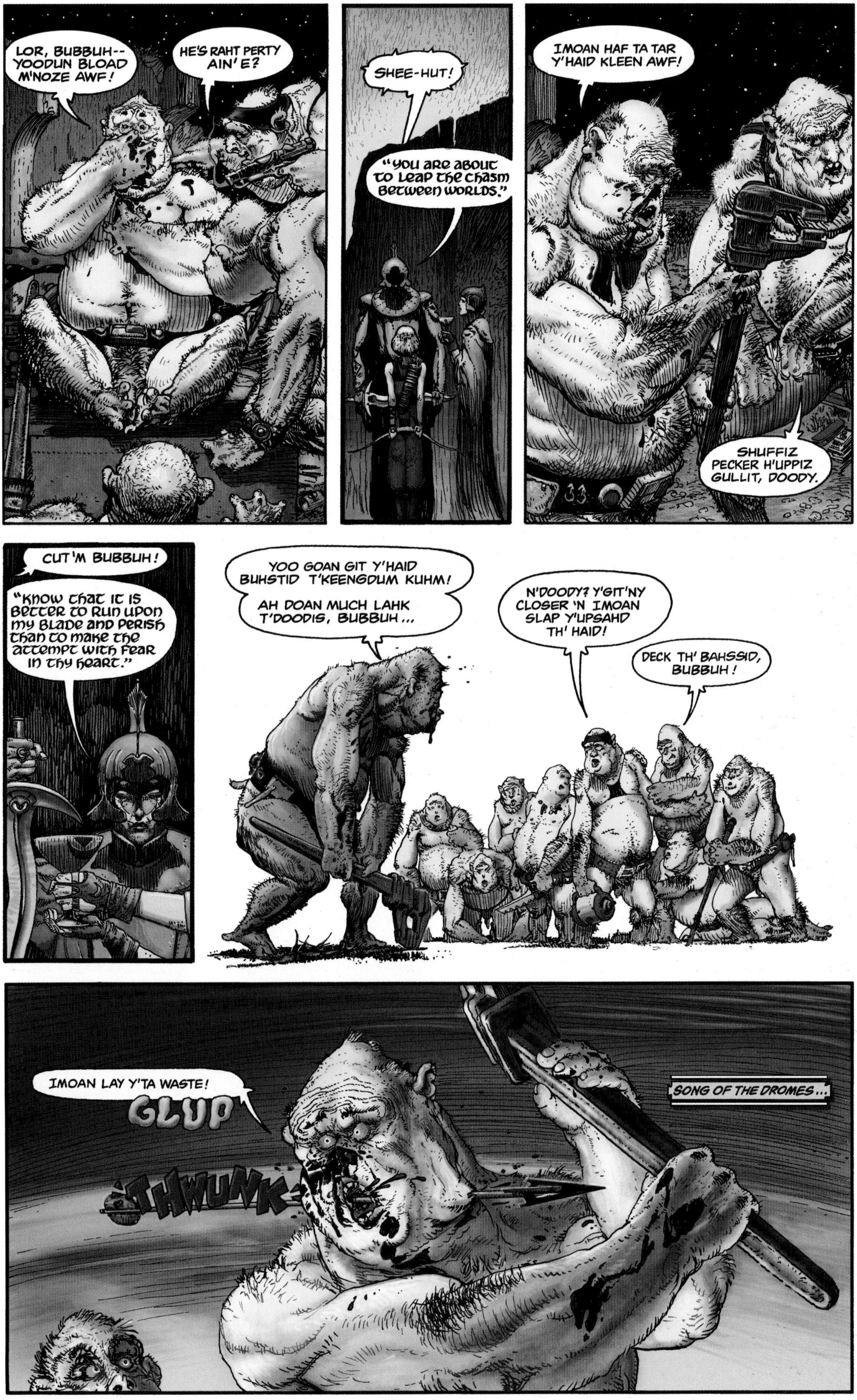
LOR, BUBBUH-- YOODUN BLOAD M'NOZE AWF!
HE'S RAHT PERTY AIN' E?
SHEE-HUT!
"YOU ARE ABOUT TO LEAP THE CHASM BETWEEN WORLDS."
IMOAN HAF TA TAR Y'HAID KLEEN AWF!
SHUFFIZ PECKER H'UPPIZ GULLIT, DOODY.
CUT'M BUBBUH!
"KNOW THAT IT IS BETTER TO RUN UPON MY BLADE AND PERISH THAN TO MAKE THE ATTEMPT WITH FEAR IN THY HEART."
YOO GOAN GIT Y'HAID BUHSTID T'KEENGDUM KUHM!
AH DOAN MUCH LAHK T'DOODIS, BUBBUH...
N'DOODY? Y'GIT'NY CLOSER 'N IMOAN SLAP Y'UPSAHD TH' HAID!
DECK TH' BAHSSID, BUBBUH!
IMOAN LAY Y'TA WASTE!
GLUP
SONG OF THE DROMES...
THWUNK

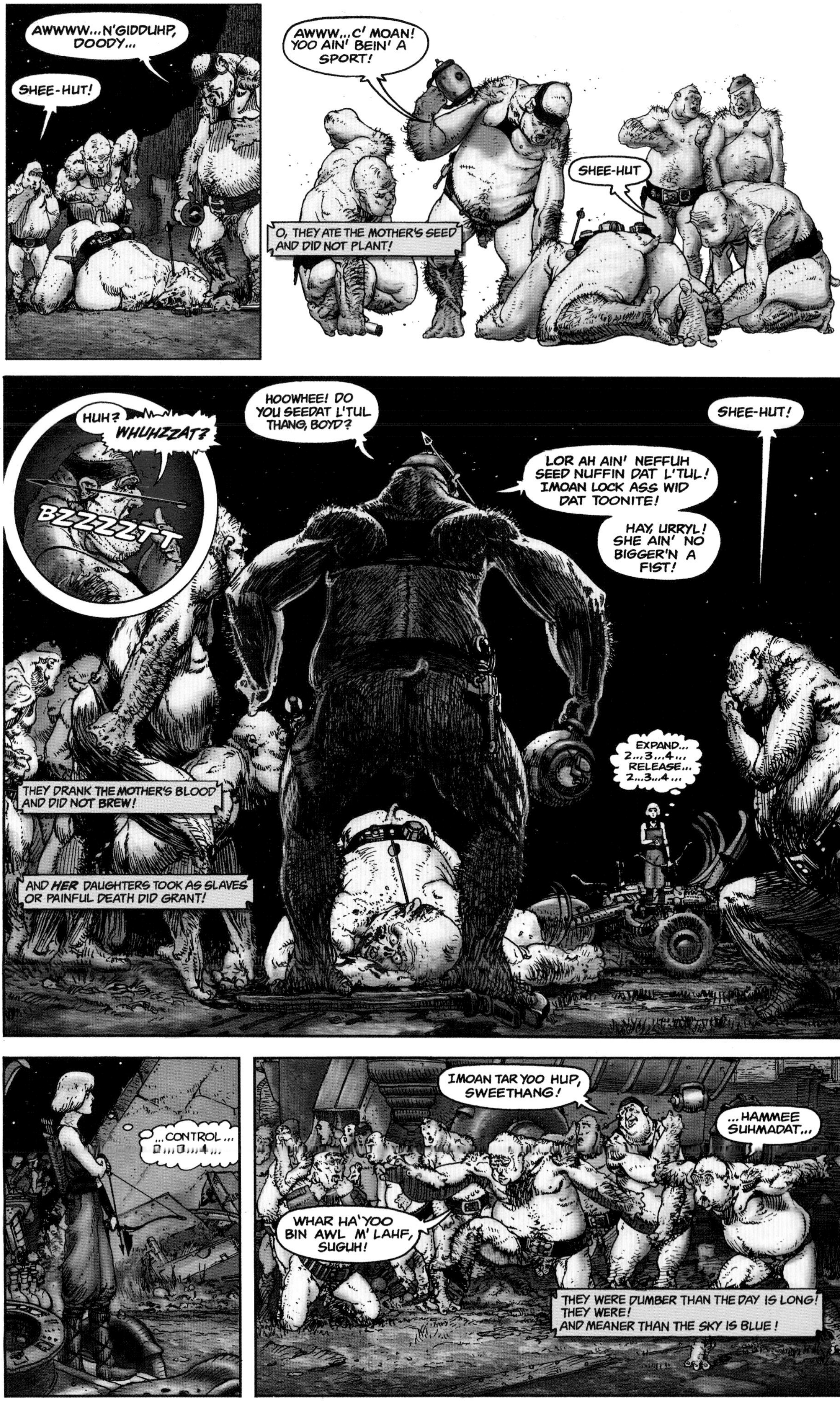
AWWWW... N'GIDDUHP, DOODY...
SHEE-HUT!
AWWW... C' MOAN! YOO AIN' BEIN' A SPORT!
O, THEY ATE THE MOTHER'S SEED AND DID NOT PLANT!
SHEE-HUT
HUH? WHUHZZAT?
BZZZZZTT
HOOWHEE! DO YOU SEEDAT L'TUL THANG, BOYD?
LOR AH AIN' NEFFUH SEED NUFFIN DAT L'TUL! IMOAN LOCK ASS WID DAT TOONITE!
HAY, URRYL! SHE AIN' NO BIGGER'N A FIST!
SHEE-HUT!
EXPAND... 2...3...4... RELEASE... 2...3...4...
THEY DRANK THE MOTHER'S BLOOD AND DID NOT BREW!
AND HER DAUGHTERS TOOK AS SLAVES OR PAINFUL DEATH DID GRANT!
...CONTROL...
IMOAN TAR YOO HUP, SWEETHANG!
...HAMMEE SUHMADAT...
WHAR HA'YOO BIN AWL M' LAHF, SUGUH!
THEY WERE DUMBER THAN THE DAY IS LONG! THEY WERE! AND MEANER THAN THE SKY IS BLUE!

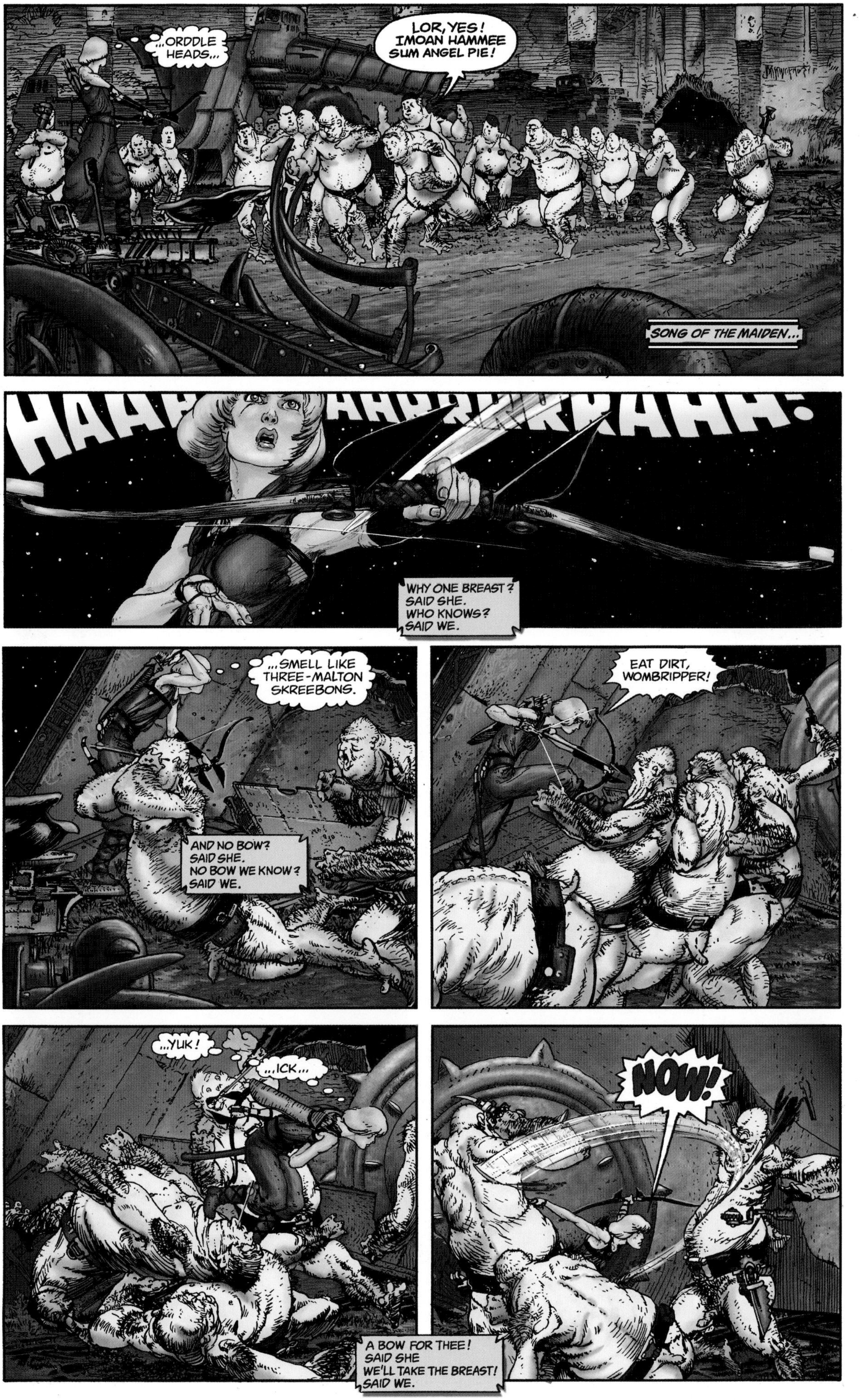
...ORDDLE HEADS...
LOR, YES! IMOAN HAMMEE SUM ANGEL PIE!
SONG OF THE MAIDEN...
WHY ONE BREAST? SAID SHE. WHO KNOWS? SAID WE.
...SMELL LIKE THREE-MALTON SKREEBONS.
AND NO BOW? SAID SHE. NO BOW WE KNOW? SAID WE.
EAT DIRT, WOMBRIPPER!
...YUK!
...ICK...
NOW!
A BOW FOR THEE! SAID SHE WE'LL TAKE THE BREAST! SAID WE.

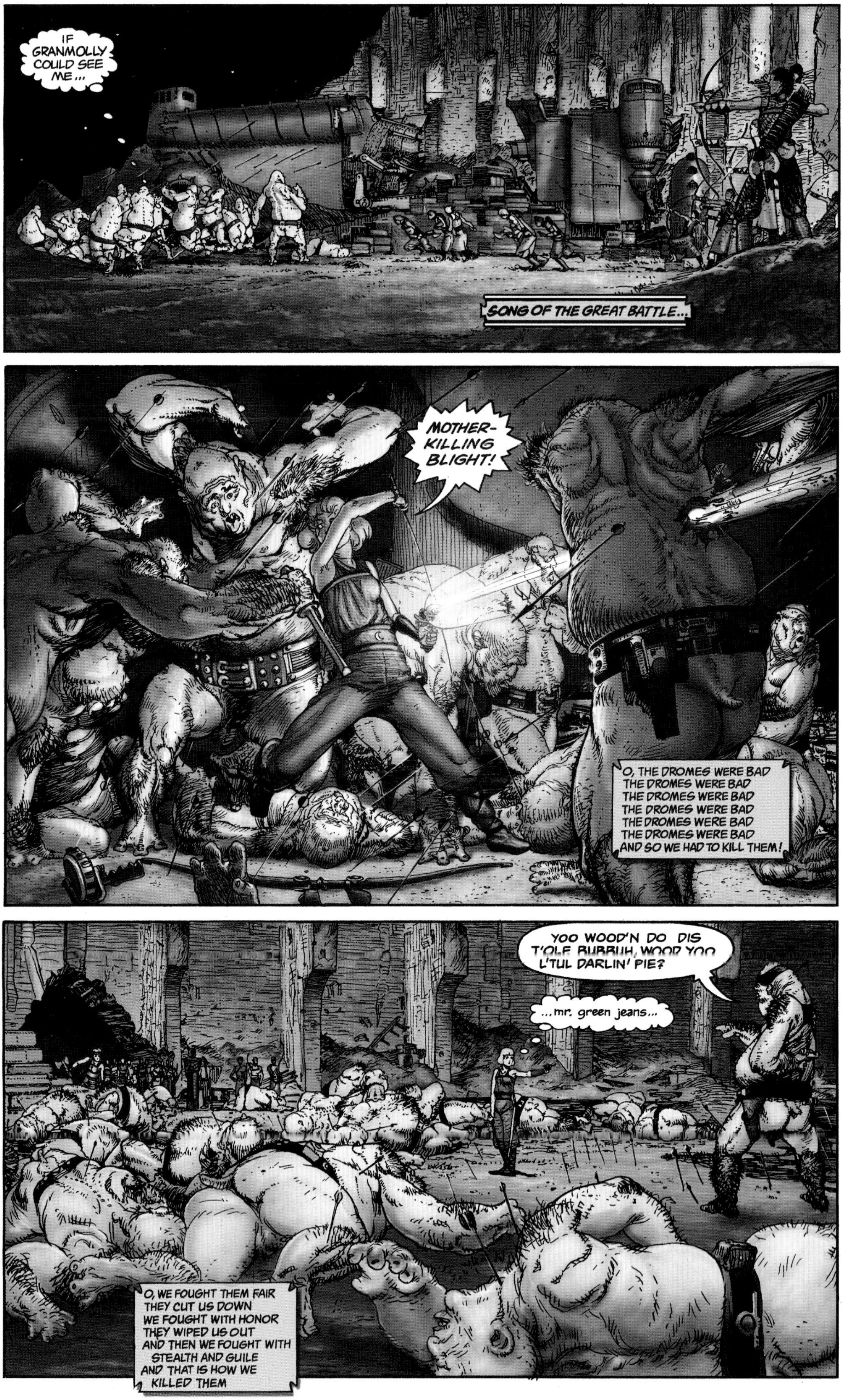
IF GRANMOLLY COULD SEE ME...
SONG OF THE GREAT BATTLE...
MOTHER-KILLING BLIGHT!
O, THE DROMES WERE BAD
THE DROMES WERE BAD
THE DROMES WERE BAD
THE DROMES WERE BAD
THE DROMES WERE BAD
THE DROMES WERE BAD
AND SO WE HAD TO KILL THEM!
YOO WOOD'N DO DIS T'OLE BUBBUH, WOOD YOO L'TUL DARLIN' PIE?
...mr. green jeans...
O, WE FOUGHT THEM FAIR
THEY CUT US DOWN
WE FOUGHT WITH HONOR
THEY WIPED US OUT
AND THEN WE FOUGHT WITH
STEALTH AND GUILE
AND THAT IS HOW WE
KILLED THEM

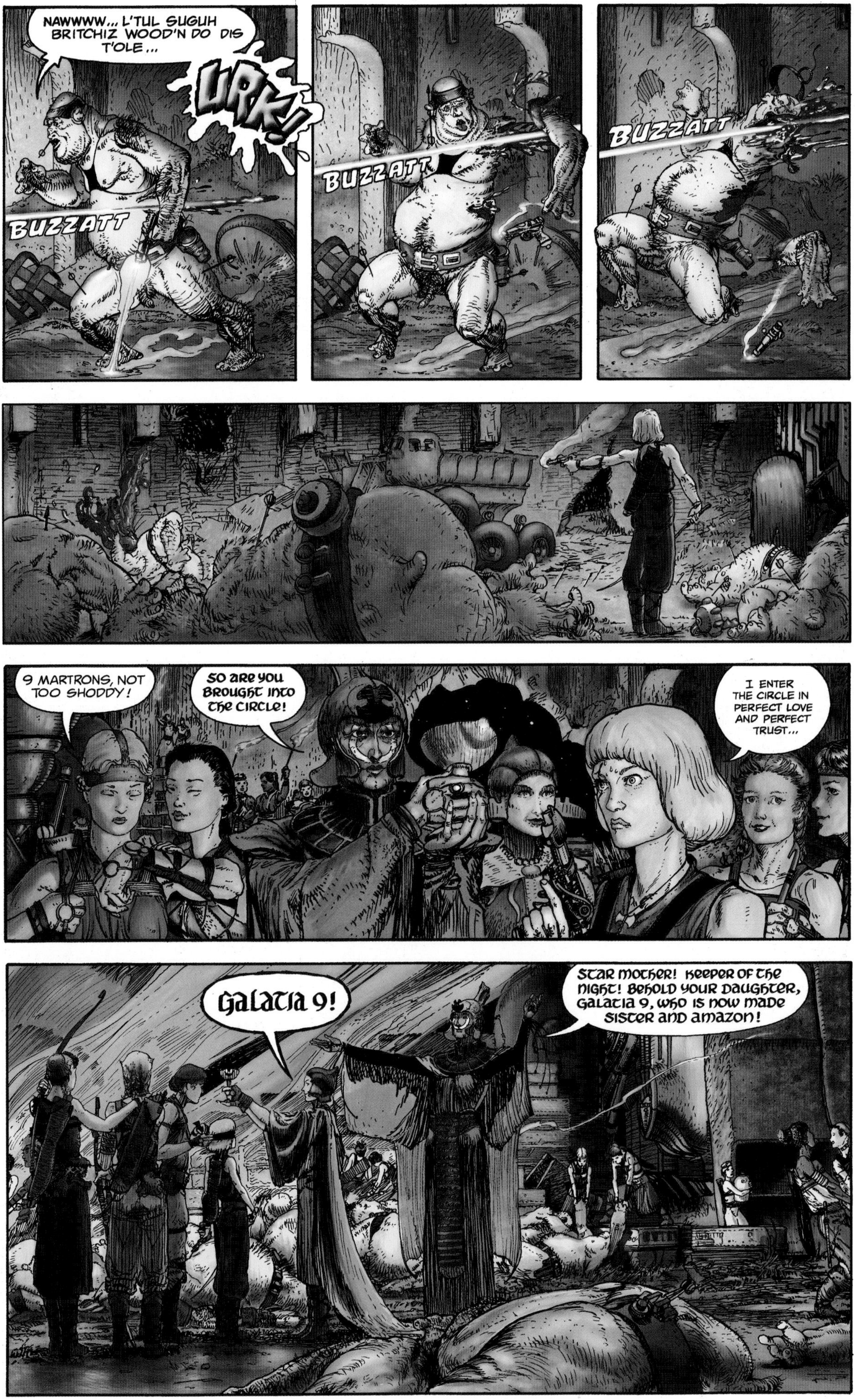

NAWWWW... L'TUL SUGUH BRITCHIZ WOOD'N DO DIS T'OLE...
URK!
BUZZATT
BUZZATT
BUZZATT
9 MARTRONS, NOT TOO SHODDY!
SO ARE YOU BROUGHT INTO THE CIRCLE!
I ENTER THE CIRCLE IN PERFECT LOVE AND PERFECT TRUST...
GALATIA 9!
STAR MOTHER! KEEPER OF THE NIGHT! BEHOLD YOUR DAUGHTER, GALATIA 9, WHO IS NOW MADE SISTER AND AMAZON!

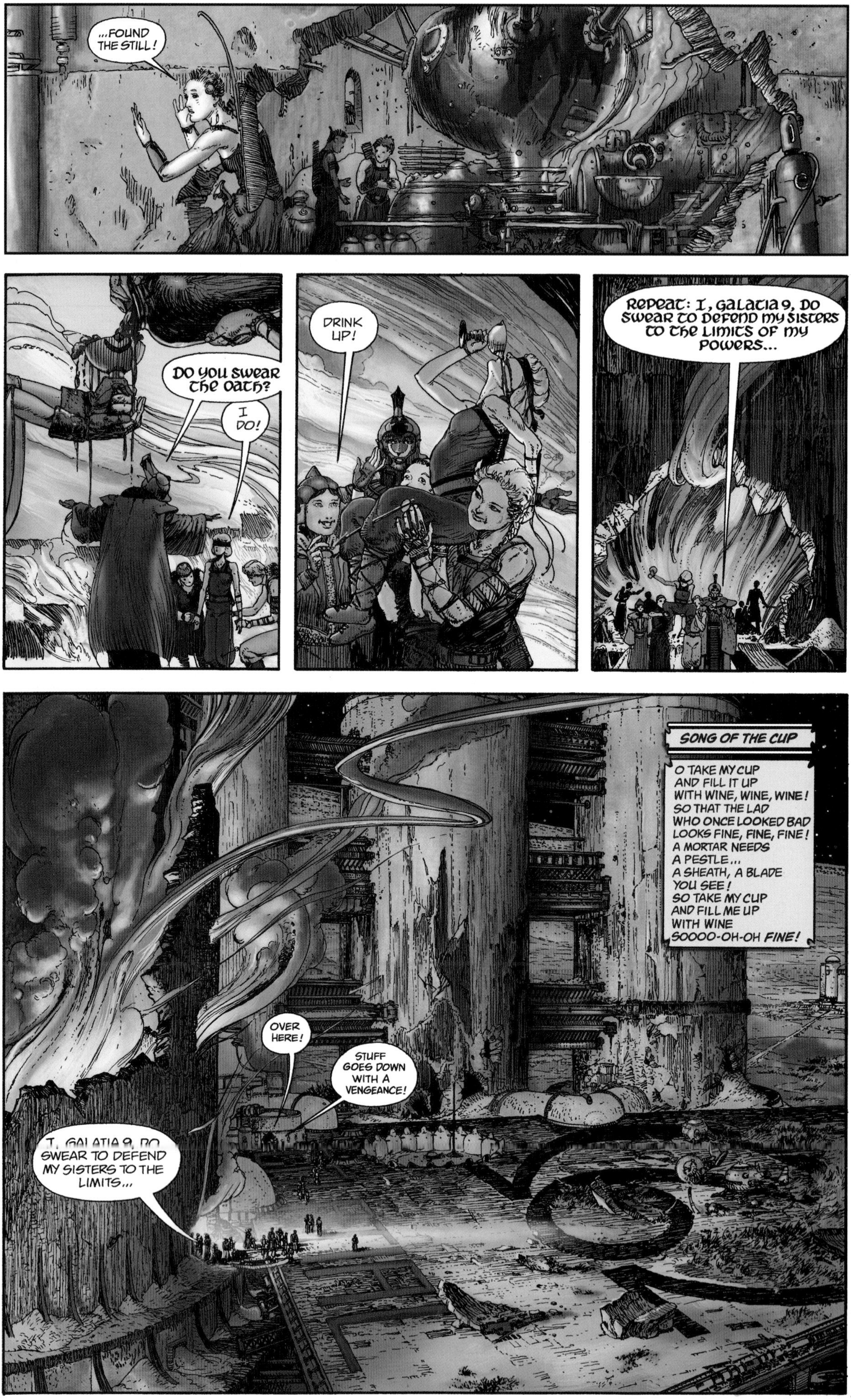
...FOUND THE STILL!
DO YOU SWEAR THE OATH?
I DO!
DRINK UP!
REPEAT: I, GALATIA 9, DO SWEAR TO DEFEND MY SISTERS TO THE LIMITS OF MY POWERS...
SONG OF THE CUP
O TAKE MY CUP
AND FILL IT UP
WITH WINE, WINE, WINE!
SO THAT THE LAD
WHO ONCE LOOKED BAD
LOOKS FINE, FINE, FINE!
A MORTAR NEEDS
A PESTLE...
A SHEATH, A BLADE
YOU SEE!
SO TAKE MY CUP
AND FILL ME UP
WITH WINE
SOOOO-OH-OH FINE!
OVER HERE!
STUFF GOES DOWN WITH A VENGEANCE!
I, GALATIA 9, DO SWEAR TO DEFEND MY SISTERS TO THE LIMITS...

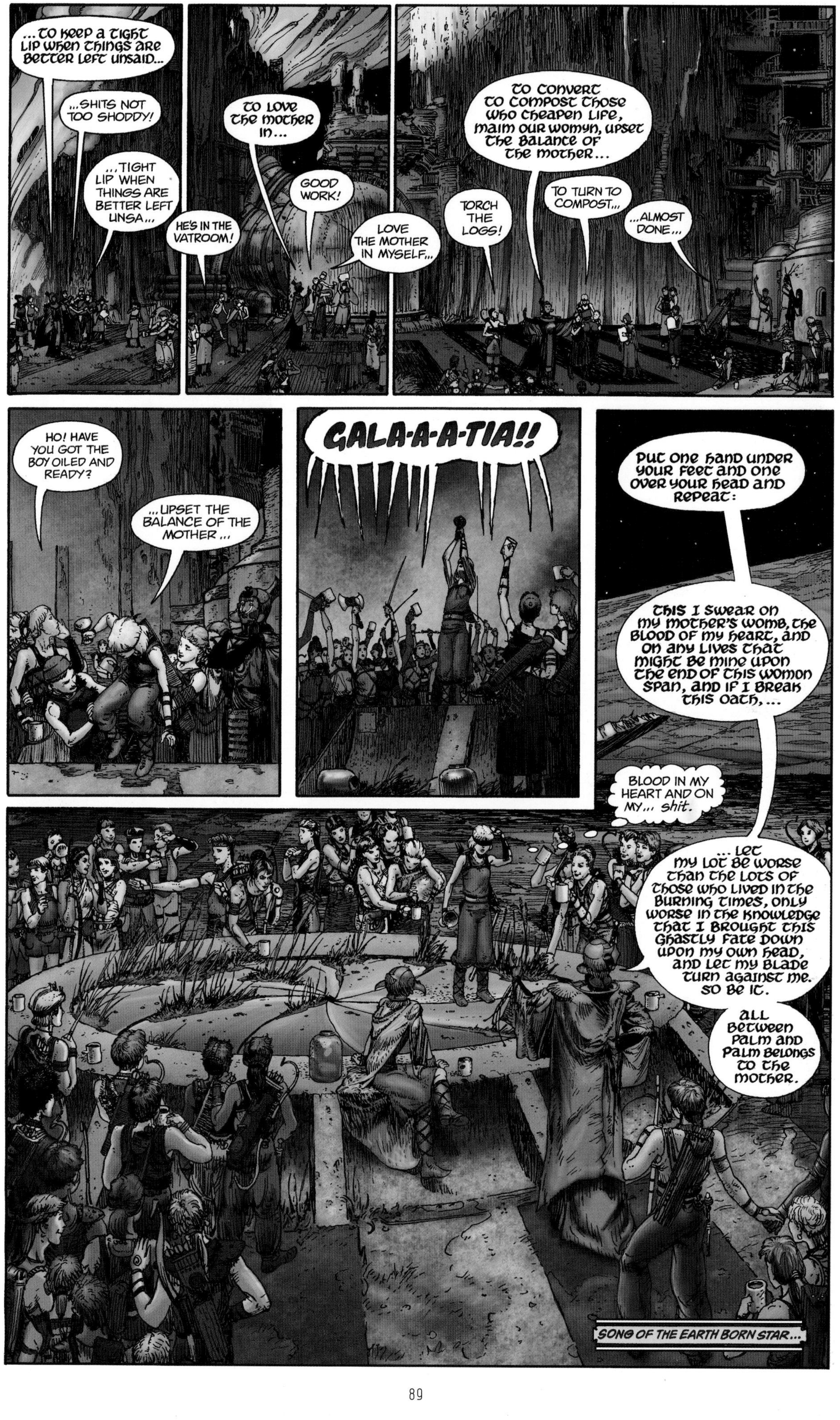
...TO KEEP A TIGHT LIP WHEN THINGS ARE BETTER LEFT UNSAID...
...SHITS NOT TOO SHODDY!
...TIGHT LIP WHEN THINGS ARE BETTER LEFT UNSA...
HE'S IN THE VATROOM!
TO LOVE THE MOTHER IN...
GOOD WORK!
LOVE THE MOTHER IN MYSELF...
TO CONVERT TO COMPOST THOSE WHO CHEAPEN LIFE, MAIM OUR WOMYN, UPSET THE BALANCE OF THE MOTHER...
TORCH THE LOGS!
TO TURN TO COMPOST...
...ALMOST DONE...
HO! HAVE YOU GOT THE BOY OILED AND READY?
...UPSET THE BALANCE OF THE MOTHER...
GALA-A-A-TIA!!
PUT ONE HAND UNDER YOUR FEET AND ONE OVER YOUR HEAD AND REPEAT:
THIS I SWEAR ON MY MOTHER'S WOMB, THE BLOOD OF MY HEART, AND ON ANY LIVES THAT MIGHT BE MINE UPON THE END OF THIS WOMON SPAN, AND IF I BREAK THIS OATH, ...
BLOOD IN MY HEART AND ON MY... *shit.*
...LET MY LOT BE WORSE THAN THE LOTS OF THOSE WHO LIVED IN THE BURNING TIMES, ONLY WORSE IN THE KNOWLEDGE THAT I BROUGHT THIS GHASTLY FATE DOWN UPON MY OWN HEAD, AND LET MY BLADE TURN AGAINST ME. SO BE IT.
ALL BETWEEN PALM AND PALM BELONGS TO THE MOTHER.
SONG OF THE EARTH BORN STAR...

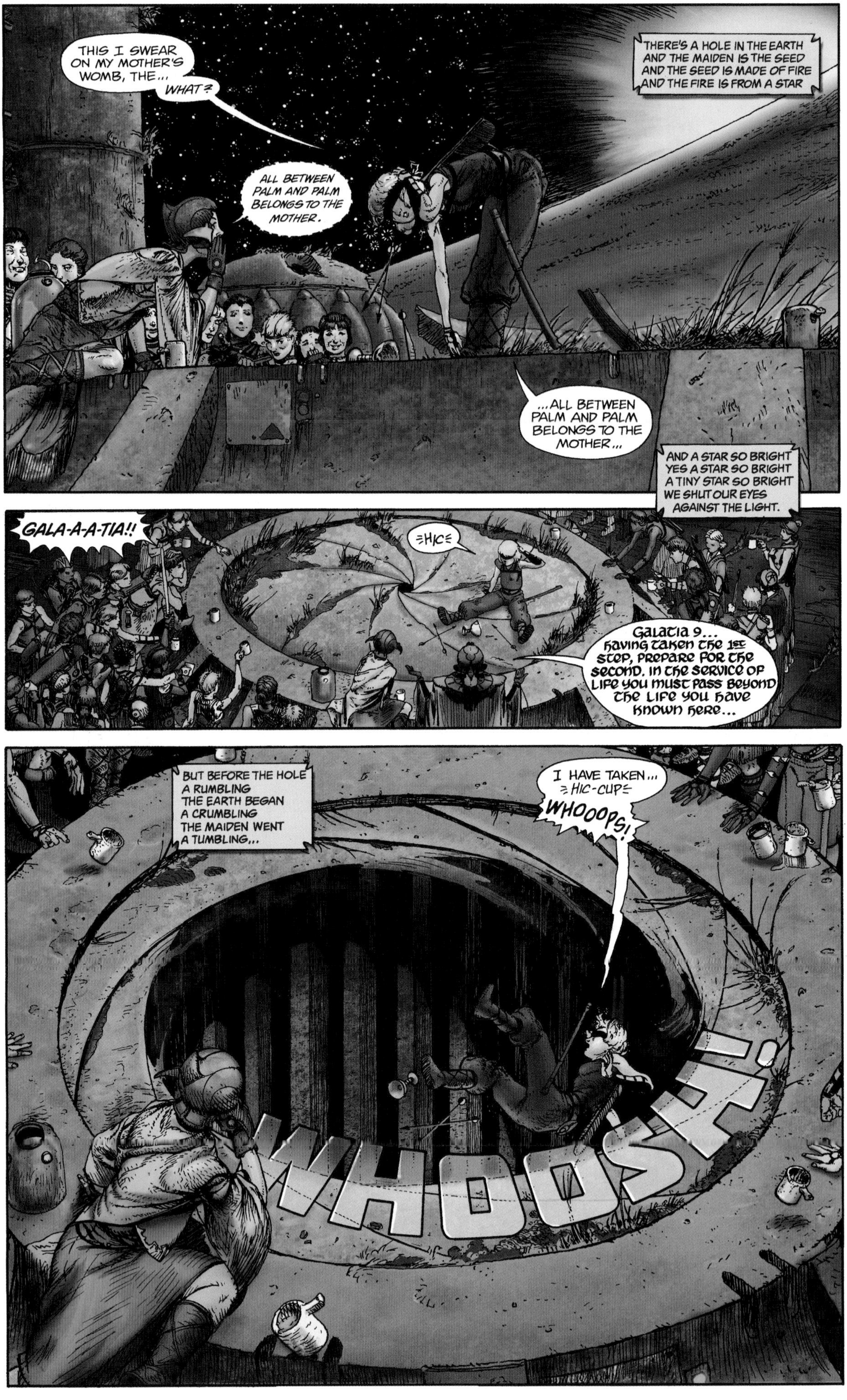
THIS I SWEAR ON MY MOTHER'S WOMB, THE... WHAT?
THERE'S A HOLE IN THE EARTH AND THE MAIDEN IS THE SEED AND THE SEED IS MADE OF FIRE AND THE FIRE IS FROM A STAR
ALL BETWEEN PALM AND PALM BELONGS TO THE MOTHER.
...ALL BETWEEN PALM AND PALM BELONGS TO THE MOTHER...
AND A STAR SO BRIGHT YES A STAR SO BRIGHT A TINY STAR SO BRIGHT WE SHUT OUR EYES AGAINST THE LIGHT.
GALA-A-A-TIA!!
HIC
Galatia 9... having taken the 1st step, prepare for the second. In the service of life you must pass beyond the life you have known here...
BUT BEFORE THE HOLE A RUMBLING THE EARTH BEGAN A CRUMBLING THE MAIDEN WENT A TUMBLING...
I HAVE TAKEN... HIC-CUP
WHOOOPS!
WHOOSH!

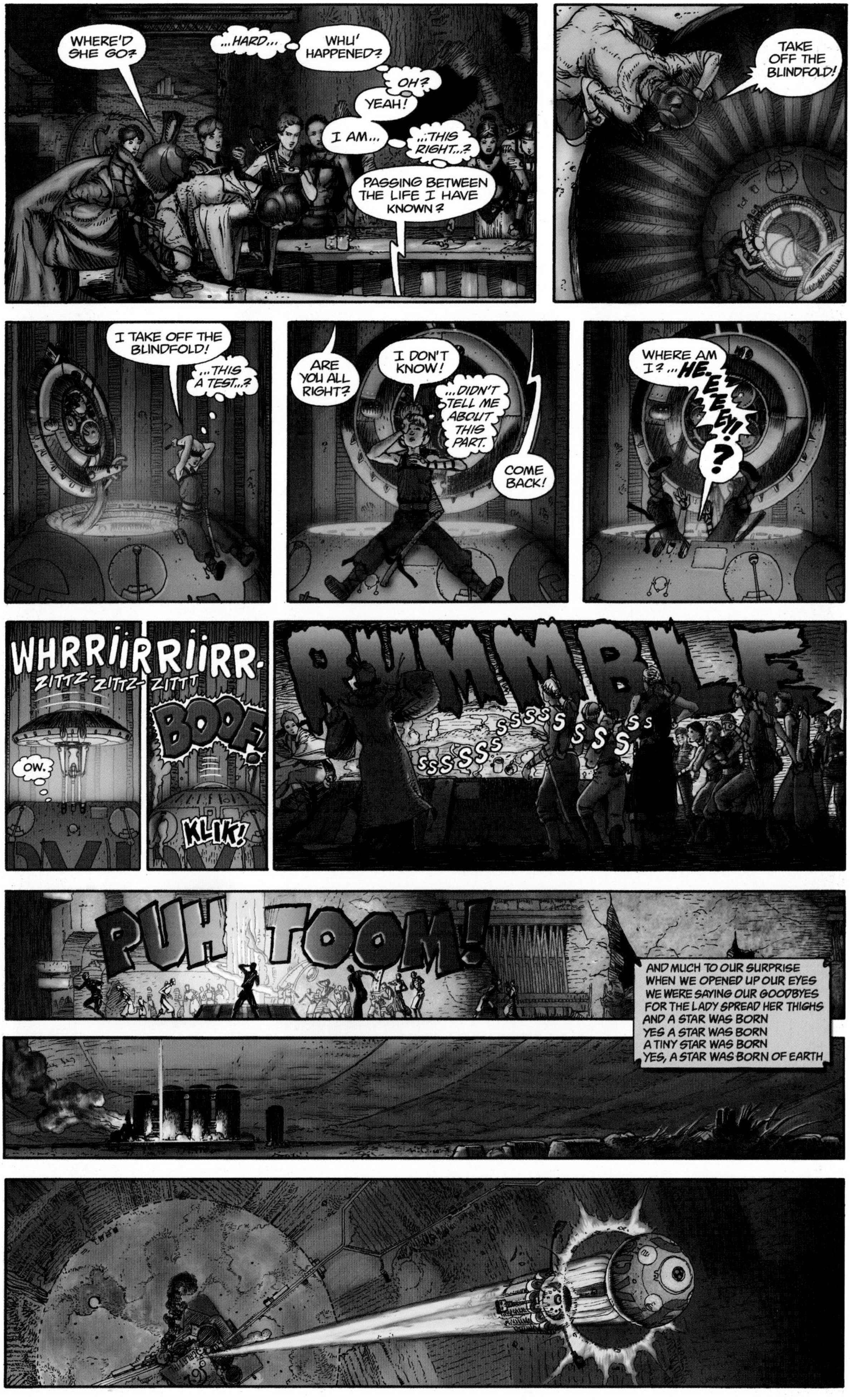
WHERE'D SHE GO?
...HARD...
WHU' HAPPENED?
OH?
YEAH!
I AM...
...THIS RIGHT...?
PASSING BETWEEN THE LIFE I HAVE KNOWN?
TAKE OFF THE BLINDFOLD!
I TAKE OFF THE BLINDFOLD!
...THIS A TEST...?
ARE YOU ALL RIGHT?
I DON'T KNOW!
...DIDN'T TELL ME ABOUT THIS PART.
COME BACK!
WHERE AM I? ...HE.EEEEY!!
?
WHRRIIRRIIRR-
ZITTZ-ZITTZ-ZITTT
OW.
BOOF!
KLIK!
RUMMBLE
SSSSSSSSSSSS
PUH TOOM!
AND MUCH TO OUR SURPRISE
WHEN WE OPENED UP OUR EYES
WE WERE SAYING OUR GOODBYES
FOR THE LADY SPREAD HER THIGHS
AND A STAR WAS BORN
YES A STAR WAS BORN
A TINY STAR WAS BORN
YES, A STAR WAS BORN OF EARTH

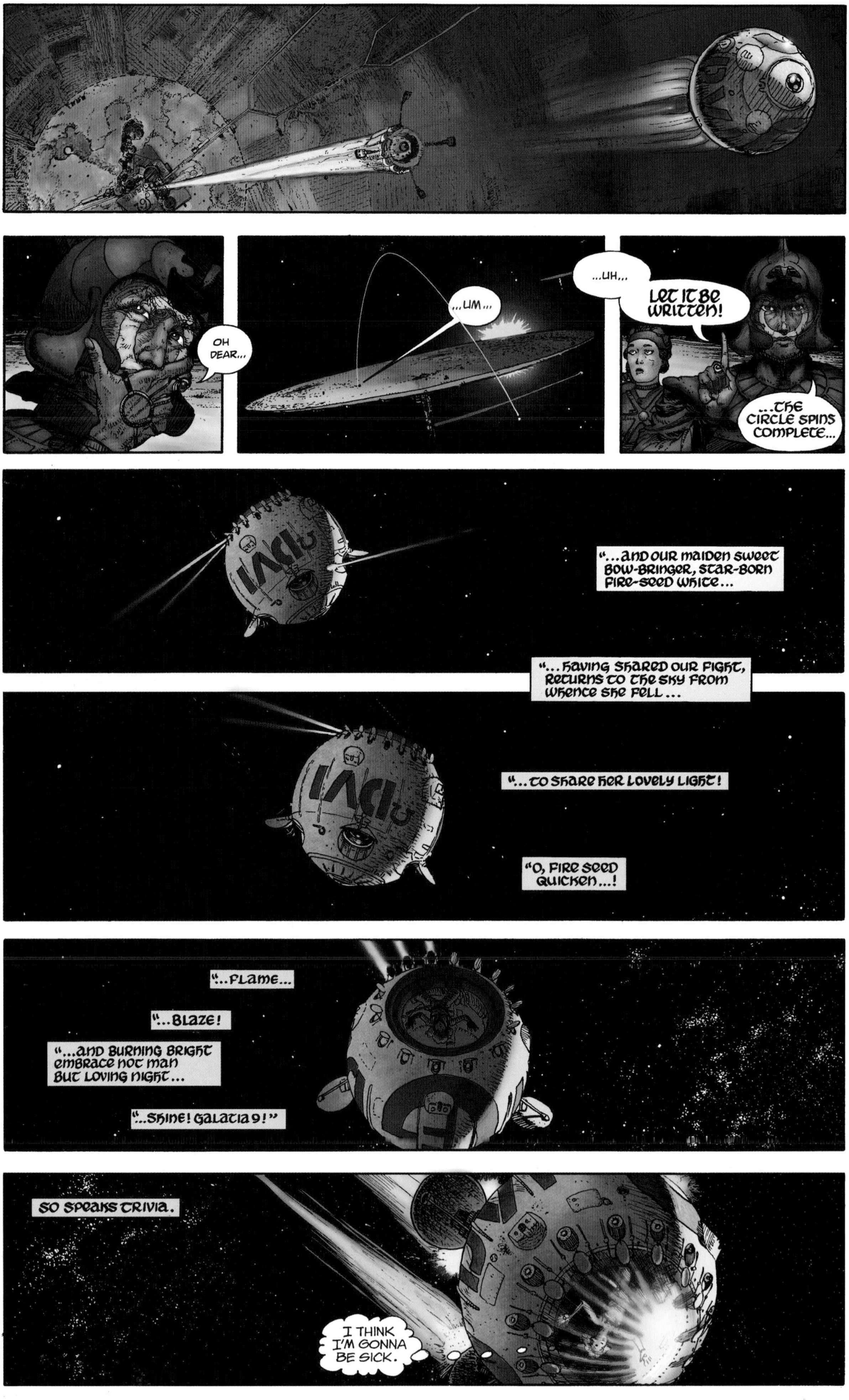
OH DEAR...
...UM...
...UH...
LET IT BE WRITTEN!
...THE CIRCLE SPINS COMPLETE...
"...AND OUR MAIDEN SWEET BOW-BRINGER, STAR-BORN FIRE-SEED WHITE...
"...HAVING SHARED OUR FIGHT, RETURNS TO THE SKY FROM WHENCE SHE FELL...
"...TO SHARE HER LOVELY LIGHT!
"O, FIRE SEED QUICKEN...!
"...FLAME...
"...BLAZE!
"...AND BURNING BRIGHT EMBRACE NOT MAN BUT LOVING NIGHT...
"...SHINE! GALATIA 9!"
SO SPEAKS TRIVIA.
I THINK I'M GONNA BE SICK.

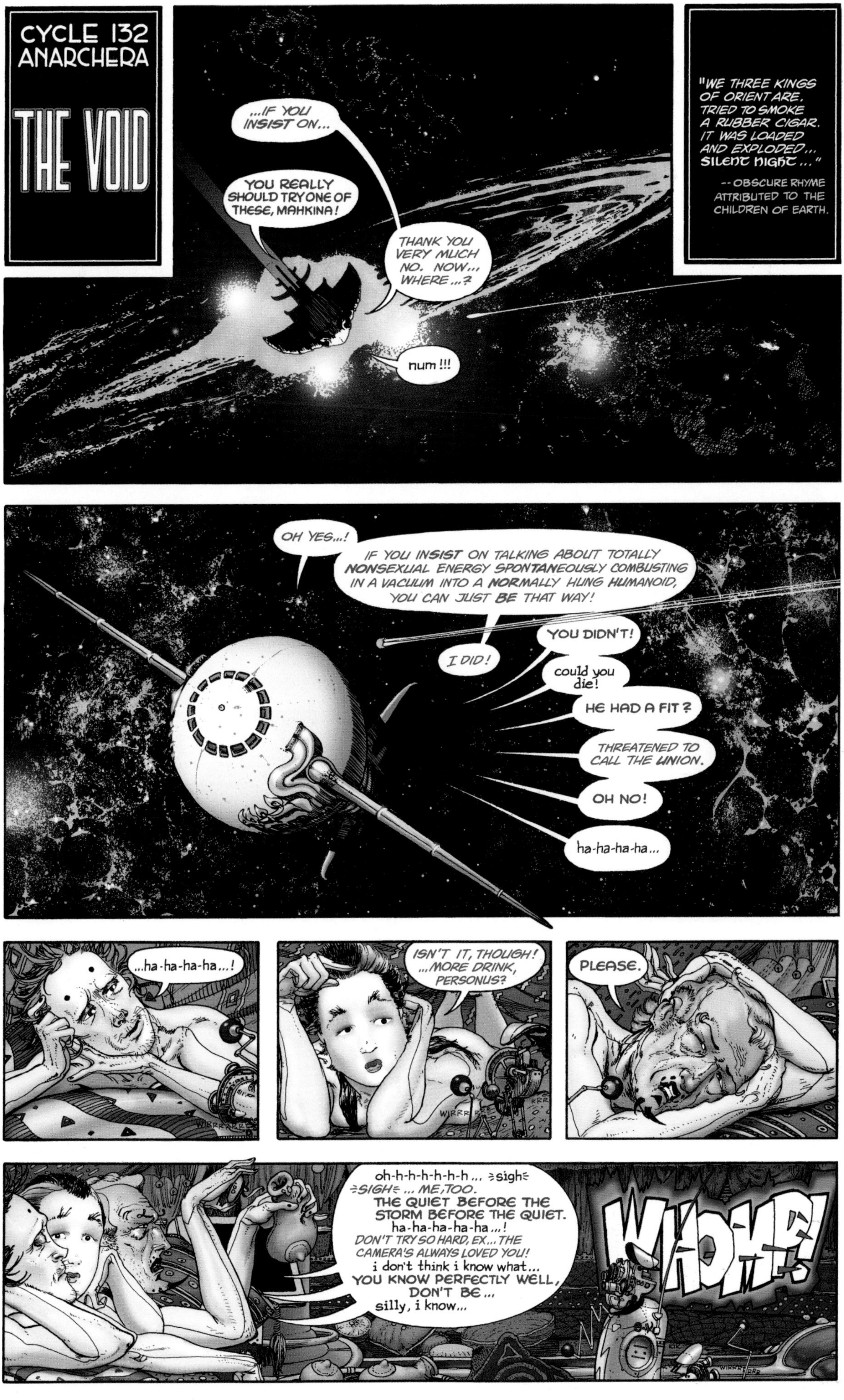

CYCLE 132
ANARCHERA
THE VOID
"WE THREE KINGS OF ORIENT ARE. TRIED TO SMOKE A RUBBER CIGAR. IT WAS LOADED AND EXPLODED... SILENT NIGHT..."
-- OBSCURE RHYME ATTRIBUTED TO THE CHILDREN OF EARTH.
...IF YOU INSIST ON...
YOU REALLY SHOULD TRY ONE OF THESE, MAHKINA!
THANK YOU VERY MUCH NO. NOW... WHERE...?
num!!!
OH YES...!
IF YOU INSIST ON TALKING ABOUT TOTALLY NONSEXUAL ENERGY SPONTANEOUSLY COMBUSTING IN A VACUUM INTO A NORMALLY HUNG HUMANOID, YOU CAN JUST BE THAT WAY!
I DID!
YOU DIDN'T!
could you die!
HE HAD A FIT?
THREATENED TO CALL THE UNION.
OH NO!
ha-ha-ha-ha...
...ha-ha-ha-ha...!
ISN'T IT, THOUGH! ...MORE DRINK, PERSONUS?
PLEASE.
oh-h-h-h-h-h-h... ≥sigh≤
≥SIGH≤ ... ME, TOO.
THE QUIET BEFORE THE STORM BEFORE THE QUIET.
ha-ha-ha-ha-ha...!
DON'T TRY SO HARD, EX... THE CAMERA'S ALWAYS LOVED YOU!
i don't think i know what...
YOU KNOW PERFECTLY WELL, DON'T BE...
silly, i know...
WHOMP!

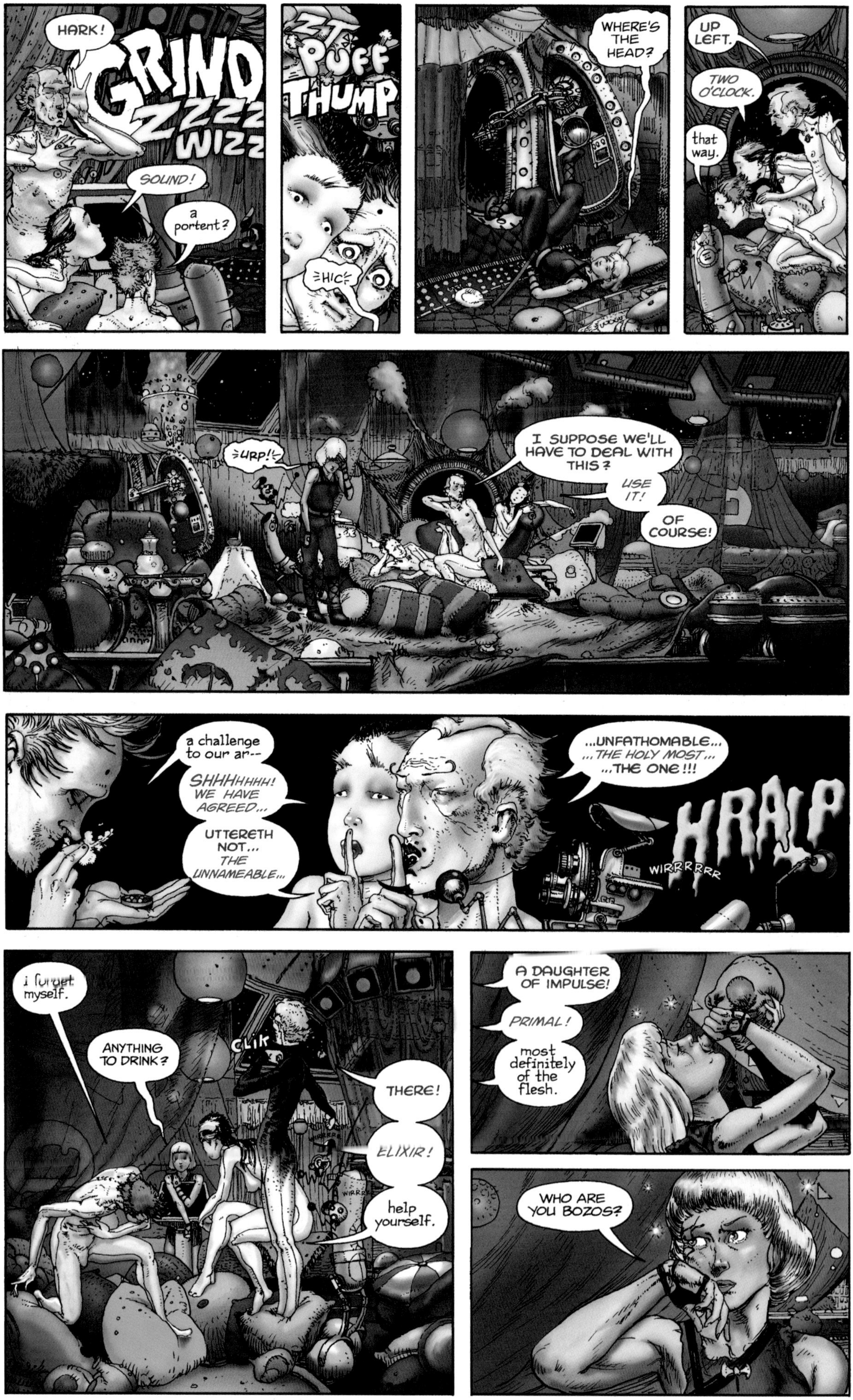
HARK!
GRIND
ZZZZ
WIZZ
SOUND!
a portent?
ZT
PUFF
THUMP
HIC
WHERE'S THE HEAD?
UP LEFT.
TWO O'CLOCK.
that way.
URP!
I SUPPOSE WE'LL HAVE TO DEAL WITH THIS?
USE IT!
OF COURSE!
a challenge to our ar--
SHHHHHHH! WE HAVE AGREED...
UTTERETH NOT... THE UNNAMEABLE...
...UNFATHOMABLE... ...THE HOLY MOST... ...THE ONE!!!
HRALP
WIRRRRRR
i forget myself.
ANYTHING TO DRINK?
CLIK
THERE!
ELIXIR!
help yourself.
A DAUGHTER OF IMPULSE!
PRIMAL!
most definitely of the flesh.
WHO ARE YOU BOZOS?

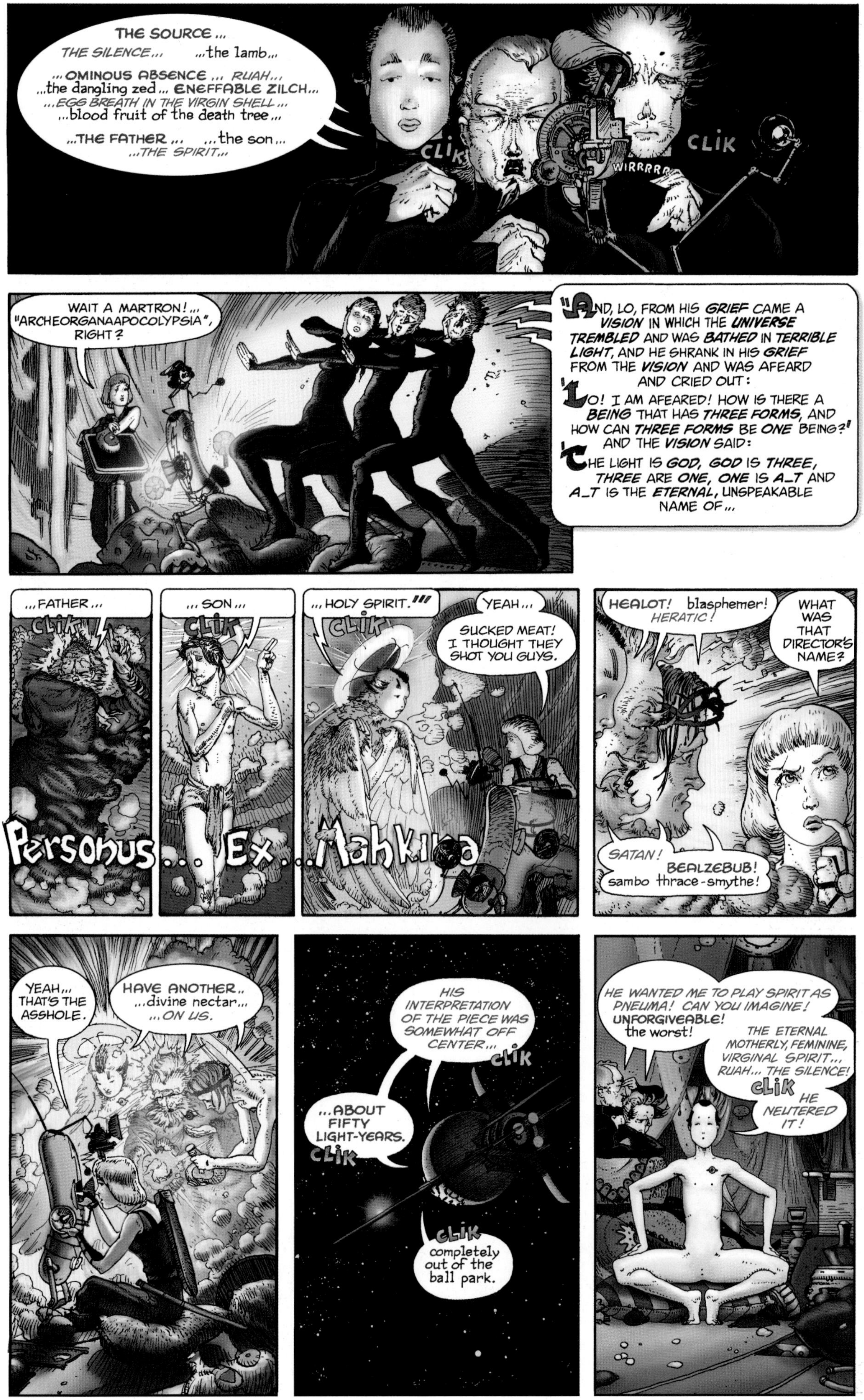
THE SOURCE... THE SILENCE... ...the lamb... ...OMINOUS ABSENCE... RUAH... ...the dangling zed... ENEFFABLE ZILCH... ...EGG BREATH IN THE VIRGIN SHELL... ...blood fruit of the death tree... ...THE FATHER... ...the son... ...THE SPIRIT...
CLIK
WIRRRRR
CLIK
WAIT A MARTRON!... "ARCHEORGANAAPOCOLYPSIA", RIGHT?
"AND, LO, FROM HIS GRIEF CAME A VISION IN WHICH THE UNIVERSE TREMBLED AND WAS BATHED IN TERRIBLE LIGHT, AND HE SHRANK IN HIS GRIEF FROM THE VISION AND WAS AFEARD AND CRIED OUT:
'LO! I AM AFEARED! HOW IS THERE A BEING THAT HAS THREE FORMS, AND HOW CAN THREE FORMS BE ONE BEING?' AND THE VISION SAID:
'THE LIGHT IS GOD, GOD IS THREE, THREE ARE ONE, ONE IS A_T AND A_T IS THE ETERNAL, UNSPEAKABLE NAME OF...
...FATHER...
CLIK
...SON...
CLIK
...HOLY SPIRIT."'
CLIK
YEAH...
SUCKED MEAT! I THOUGHT THEY SHOT YOU GUYS.
Personus... Ex... Mahkina
HEALOT! blasphemer! HERATIC!
WHAT WAS THAT DIRECTOR'S NAME?
SATAN! BEALZEBUB! sambo thrace-smythe!
YEAH... THAT'S THE ASSHOLE.
HAVE ANOTHER.. ...divine nectar... ...ON US.
HIS INTERPRETATION OF THE PIECE WAS SOMEWHAT OFF CENTER...
CLIK
...ABOUT FIFTY LIGHT-YEARS.
CLIK
CLIK
completely out of the ball park.
HE WANTED ME TO PLAY SPIRIT AS PNEUMA! CAN YOU IMAGINE! UNFORGIVEABLE! the worst!
THE ETERNAL MOTHERLY, FEMININE, VIRGINAL SPIRIT... RUAH... THE SILENCE!
CLIK
HE NEUTERED IT!

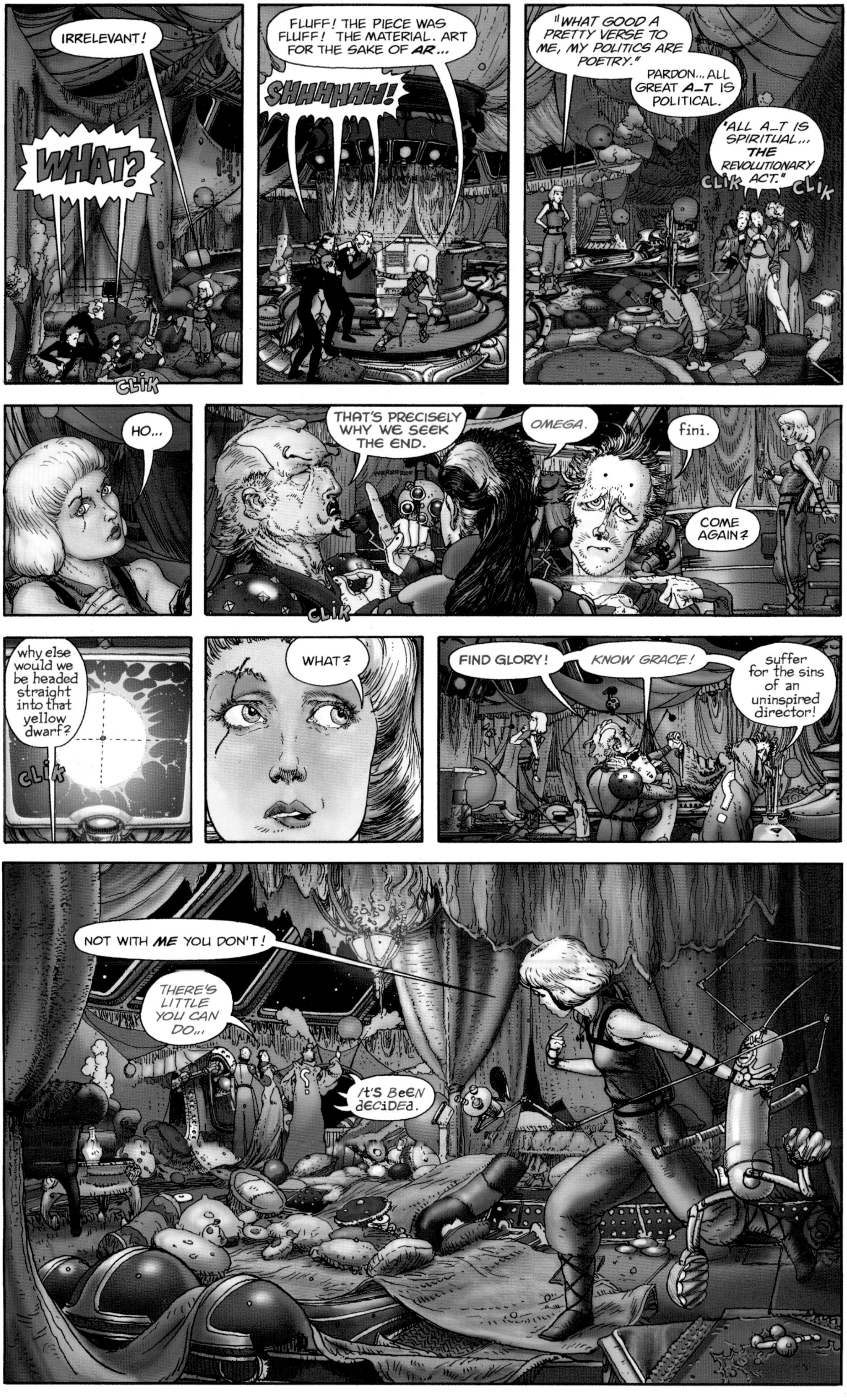
IRRELEVANT!
WHAT?
CLIK
FLUFF! THE PIECE WAS FLUFF! THE MATERIAL. ART FOR THE SAKE OF AR...
SHHHHHH!
"WHAT GOOD A PRETTY VERSE TO ME, MY POLITICS ARE POETRY."
PARDON... ALL GREAT A_T IS POLITICAL.
"ALL A_T IS SPIRITUAL... THE REVOLUTIONARY ACT."
CLIK
CLIK
HO...
THAT'S PRECISELY WHY WE SEEK THE END.
OMEGA.
fini.
COME AGAIN?
CLIK
why else would we be headed straight into that yellow dwarf?
CLIK
WHAT?
FIND GLORY!
KNOW GRACE!
suffer for the sins of an uninspired director!
NOT WITH ME YOU DON'T!
THERE'S LITTLE YOU CAN DO...
IT'S BEEN DECIDED.

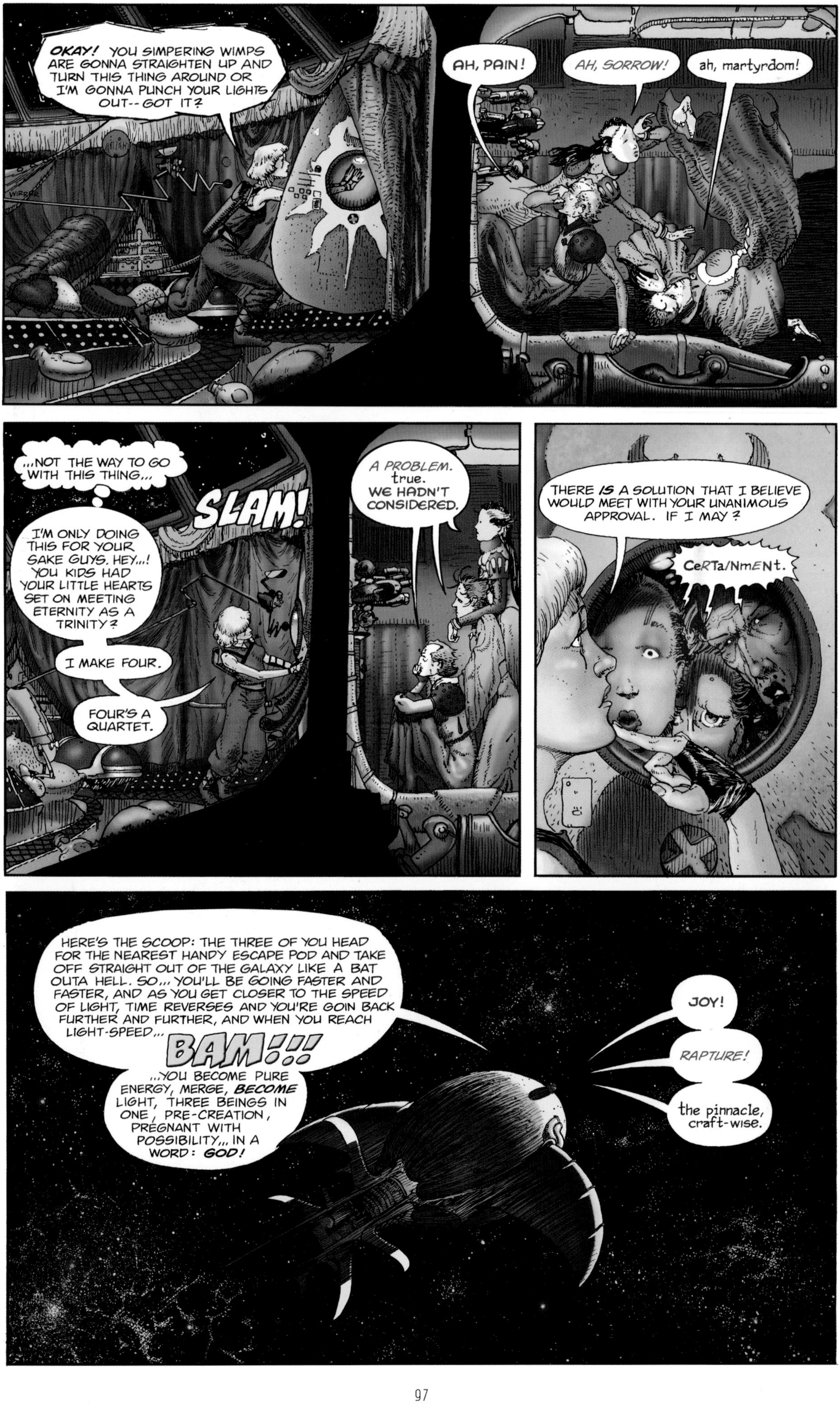

OKAY! YOU SIMPERING WIMPS ARE GONNA STRAIGHTEN UP AND TURN THIS THING AROUND OR I'M GONNA PUNCH YOUR LIGHTS OUT--GOT IT?
AH, PAIN!
AH, SORROW!
ah, martyrdom!
...NOT THE WAY TO GO WITH THIS THING...
SLAM!
I'M ONLY DOING THIS FOR YOUR SAKE GUYS. HEY...! YOU KIDS HAD YOUR LITTLE HEARTS SET ON MEETING ETERNITY AS A TRINITY?
I MAKE FOUR.
FOUR'S A QUARTET.
A PROBLEM.
true.
WE HADN'T CONSIDERED.
THERE IS A SOLUTION THAT I BELIEVE WOULD MEET WITH YOUR UNANIMOUS APPROVAL. IF I MAY?
CeRTa/NmENt.
HERE'S THE SCOOP: THE THREE OF YOU HEAD FOR THE NEAREST HANDY ESCAPE POD AND TAKE OFF STRAIGHT OUT OF THE GALAXY LIKE A BAT OUTA HELL. SO... YOU'LL BE GOING FASTER AND FASTER, AND AS YOU GET CLOSER TO THE SPEED OF LIGHT, TIME REVERSES AND YOU'RE GOIN BACK FURTHER AND FURTHER, AND WHEN YOU REACH LIGHT-SPEED...
BAM!!!
...YOU BECOME PURE ENERGY, MERGE, BECOME LIGHT, THREE BEINGS IN ONE, PRE-CREATION, PREGNANT WITH POSSIBILITY... IN A WORD: GOD!
JOY!
RAPTURE!
the pinnacle, craft-wise.

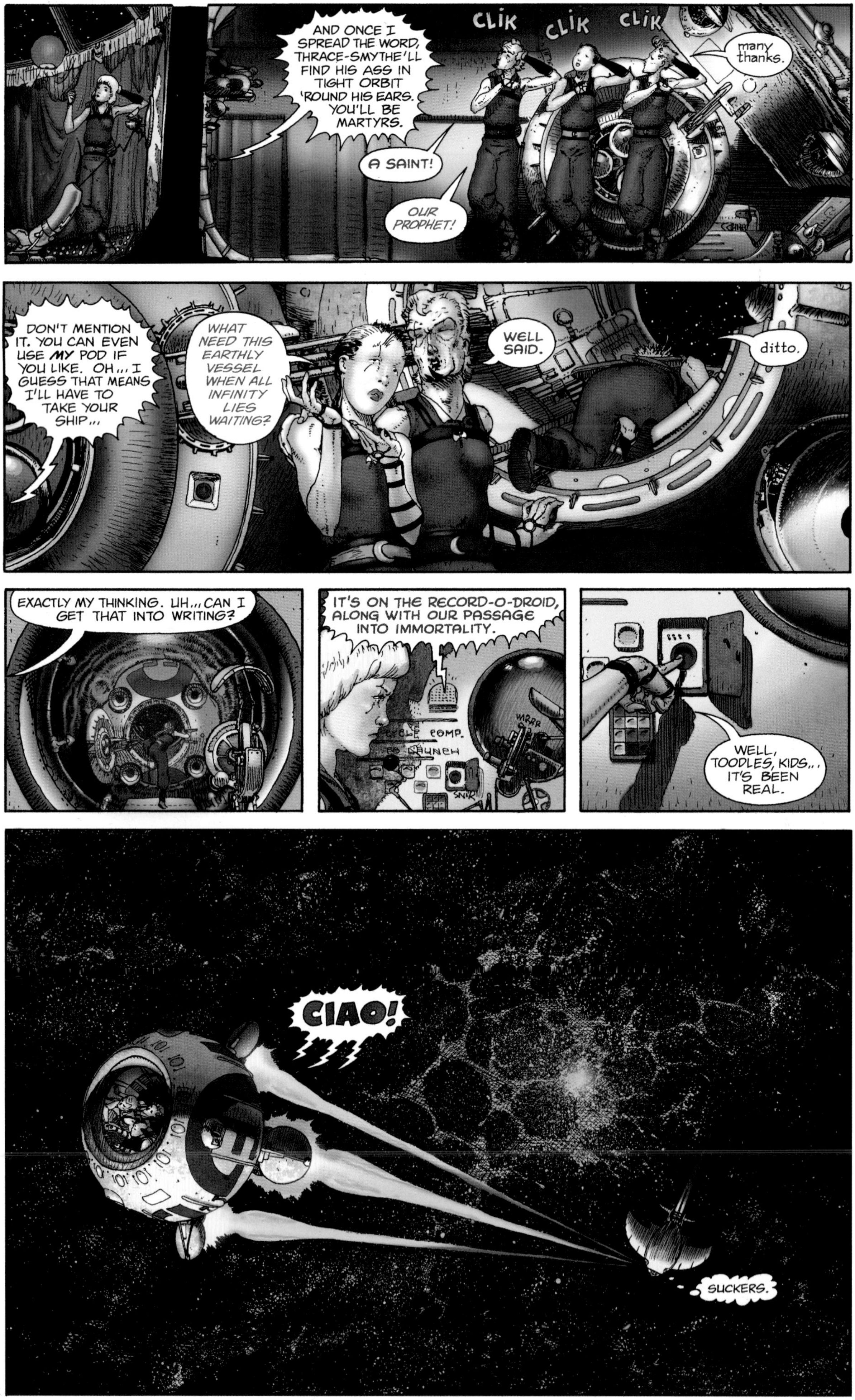
AND ONCE I SPREAD THE WORD, THRACE-SMYTHE'LL FIND HIS ASS IN TIGHT ORBIT 'ROUND HIS EARS. YOU'LL BE MARTYRS.
CLIK
CLIK
CLIK
many thanks.
A SAINT!
OUR PROPHET!
DON'T MENTION IT. YOU CAN EVEN USE MY POD IF YOU LIKE. OH... I GUESS THAT MEANS I'LL HAVE TO TAKE YOUR SHIP...
WHAT NEED THIS EARTHLY VESSEL WHEN ALL INFINITY LIES WAITING?
WELL SAID.
ditto.
EXACTLY MY THINKING. UH... CAN I GET THAT INTO WRITING?
IT'S ON THE RECORD-O-DROID, ALONG WITH OUR PASSAGE INTO IMMORTALITY.
WELL, TOODLES, KIDS... IT'S BEEN REAL.
CIAO!
SUCKERS.

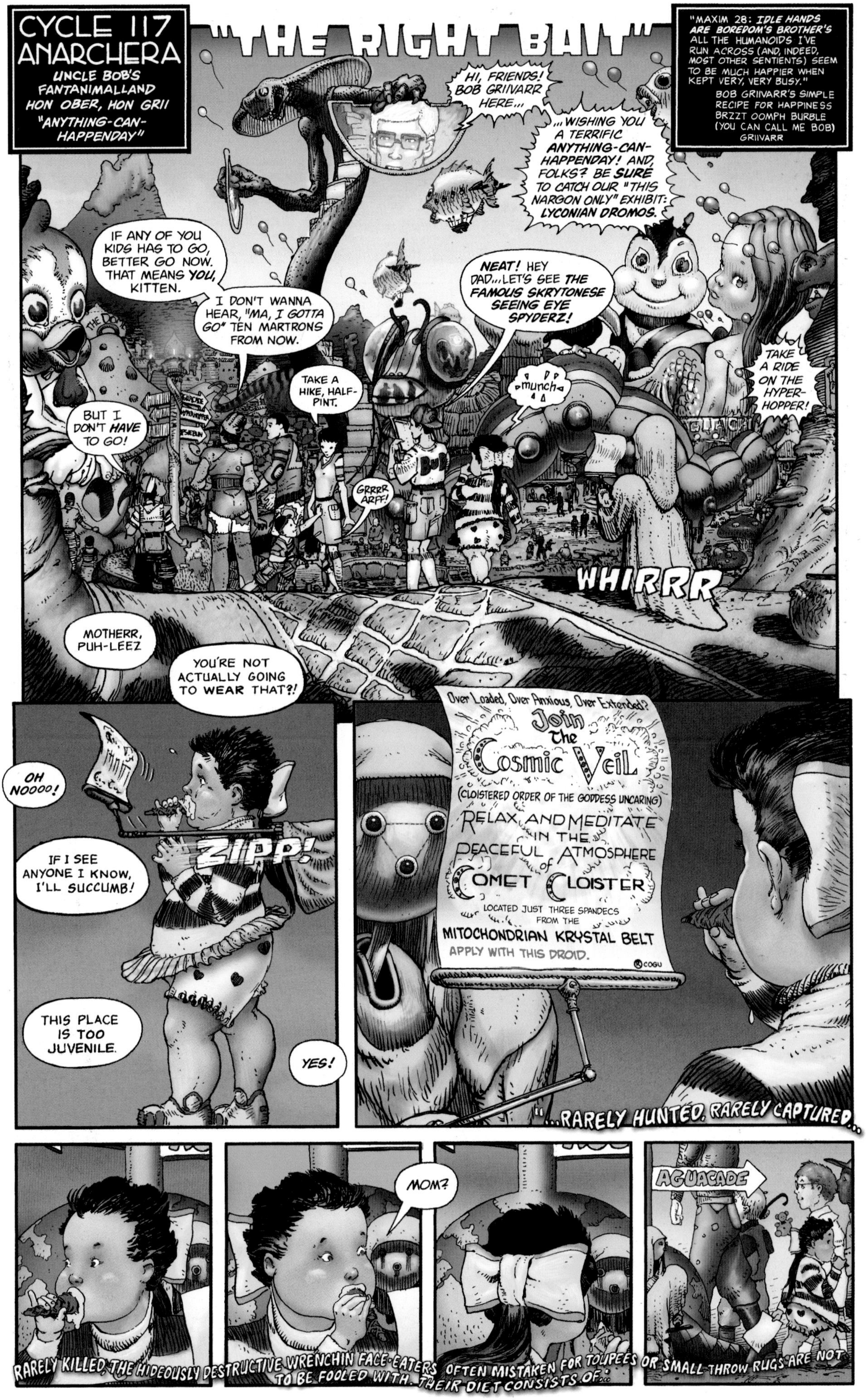
CYCLE 117
ANARCHERA
UNCLE BOB'S FANTANIMALLAND
HON OBER, HON GRII
"ANYTHING-CAN-HAPPENDAY"
"THE RIGHT BAIT"
"MAXIM 28: IDLE HANDS ARE BOREDOM'S BROTHER'S ALL THE HUMANOIDS I'VE RUN ACROSS (AND, INDEED, MOST OTHER SENTIENTS) SEEM TO BE MUCH HAPPIER WHEN KEPT VERY, VERY BUSY."
BOB GRIIVARR'S SIMPLE RECIPE FOR HAPPINESS
BRZZT OOMPH BURBLE (YOU CAN CALL ME BOB) GRIIVARR
HI, FRIENDS! BOB GRIIVARR HERE...
...WISHING YOU A TERRIFIC ANYTHING-CAN-HAPPENDAY! AND, FOLKS? BE SURE TO CATCH OUR "THIS NARGON ONLY" EXHIBIT: LYCONIAN DROMOS.
IF ANY OF YOU KIDS HAS TO GO, BETTER GO NOW. THAT MEANS YOU, KITTEN.
I DON'T WANNA HEAR, "MA, I GOTTA GO" TEN MARTRONS FROM NOW.
NEAT! HEY DAD...LET'S SEE THE FAMOUS SKRYTONESE SEEING EYE SPYDERZ!
TAKE A HIKE, HALF-PINT.
munch
TAKE A RIDE ON THE HYPER-HOPPER!
BUT I DON'T HAVE TO GO!
GRRRR ARFF!
WHIRRR
MOTHERR, PUH-LEEZ
YOU'RE NOT ACTUALLY GOING TO WEAR THAT?!
OH NOOOO!
ZIPP!
IF I SEE ANYONE I KNOW, I'LL SUCCUMB!
THIS PLACE IS TOO JUVENILE.
YES!
Over Loaded, Over Anxious, Over Extended?
Join the Cosmic Veil
(CLOISTERED ORDER OF THE GODDESS UNCARING)
RELAX AND MEDITATE IN THE PEACEFUL ATMOSPHERE of COMET CLOISTER
LOCATED JUST THREE SPANDECS FROM THE
MITOCHONDRIAN KRYSTAL BELT
APPLY WITH THIS DROID.
COGU
"...RARELY HUNTED, RARELY CAPTURED...
MOM?
AGUACADE
RARELY KILLED, THE HIDEOUSLY DESTRUCTIVE WRENCHIN FACE-EATERS OFTEN MISTAKEN FOR TOUPEES OR SMALL THROW RUGS ARE NOT TO BE FOOLED WITH. THEIR DIET CONSISTS OF...

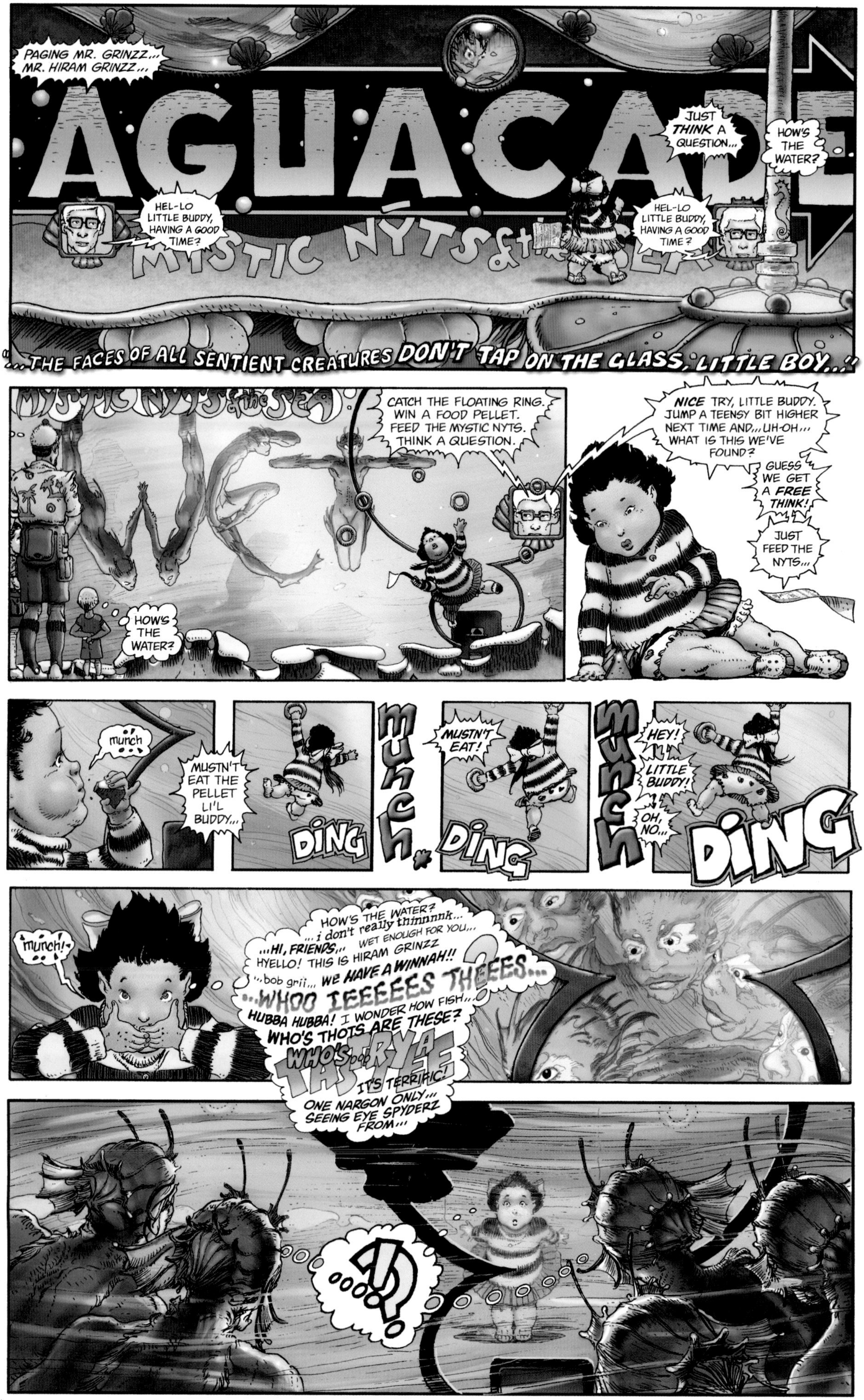

PAGING MR. GRINZZ... MR. HIRAM GRINZZ...
AGUACADE
HEL-LO LITTLE BUDDY, HAVING A GOOD TIME?
MYSTIC NYTS
JUST THINK A QUESTION...
HOW'S THE WATER?
HEL-LO LITTLE BUDDY, HAVING A GOOD TIME?
"...THE FACES OF ALL SENTIENT CREATURES DON'T TAP ON THE GLASS, LITTLE BOY..."
MYSTIC NYTS of the SEA
CATCH THE FLOATING RING. WIN A FOOD PELLET. FEED THE MYSTIC NYTS. THINK A QUESTION.
HOW'S THE WATER?
NICE TRY, LITTLE BUDDY. JUMP A TEENSY BIT HIGHER NEXT TIME AND... UH-OH... WHAT IS THIS WE'VE FOUND?
GUESS WE GET A FREE THINK!
JUST FEED THE NYTS...
munch
MUSTN'T EAT THE PELLET LI'L BUDDY...
DING
munch
MUSTN'T EAT!
DING
munch
HEY! LI'L LITTLE BUDDY!
OH, NO...
DING
munch!
HOW'S THE WATER?
...i don't really thinnnnk...
...HI, FRIENDS... WET ENOUGH FOR YOU...
HYELLO! THIS IS HIRAM GRINZZ
...bob grii... WE HAVE A WINNAH!!
...WHOO IEEEEES THEEES...
HUBBA HUBBA! I WONDER HOW FISH...
WHO'S THOTS ARE THESE?
WHO'S... TRY A TASTEE
IT'S TERRIFIC!
ONE NARGON ONLY... SEEING EYE SPYDERZ FROM...
OOO

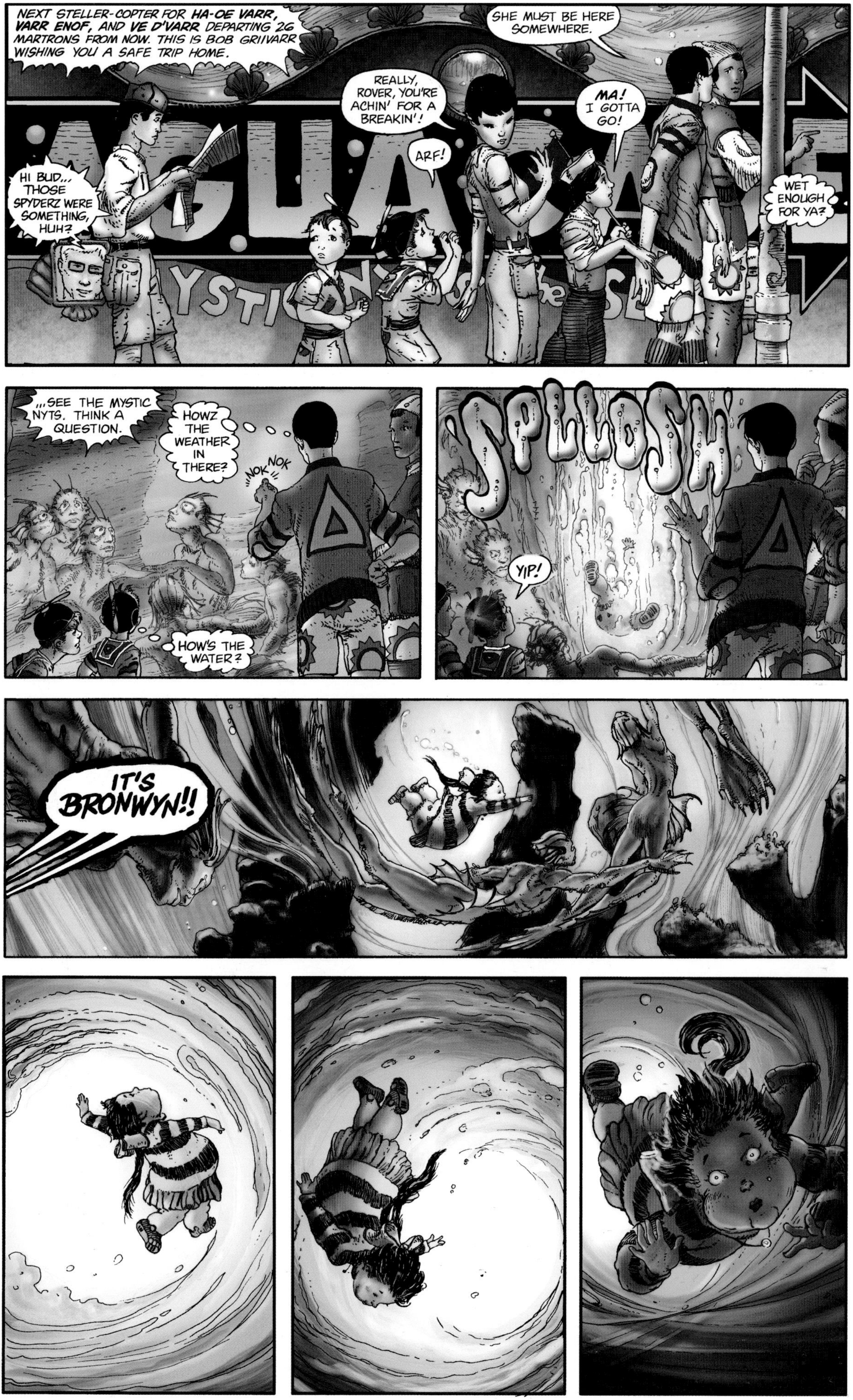
NEXT STELLER-COPTER FOR HA-OE VARR, VARR ENOF, AND VE D'VARR DEPARTING 26 MARTRONS FROM NOW. THIS IS BOB GRIIVARR WISHING YOU A SAFE TRIP HOME.
SHE MUST BE HERE SOMEWHERE.
REALLY, ROVER, YOU'RE ACHIN' FOR A BREAKIN'!
ARF!
MA! I GOTTA GO!
HI BUD... THOSE SPYDERZ WERE SOMETHING, HUH?
WET ENOUGH FOR YA?
...SEE THE MYSTIC NYTS. THINK A QUESTION.
HOWZ THE WEATHER IN THERE?
NOK NOK
HOW'S THE WATER?
SPLLOSH
YIP!
IT'S BRONWYN!!

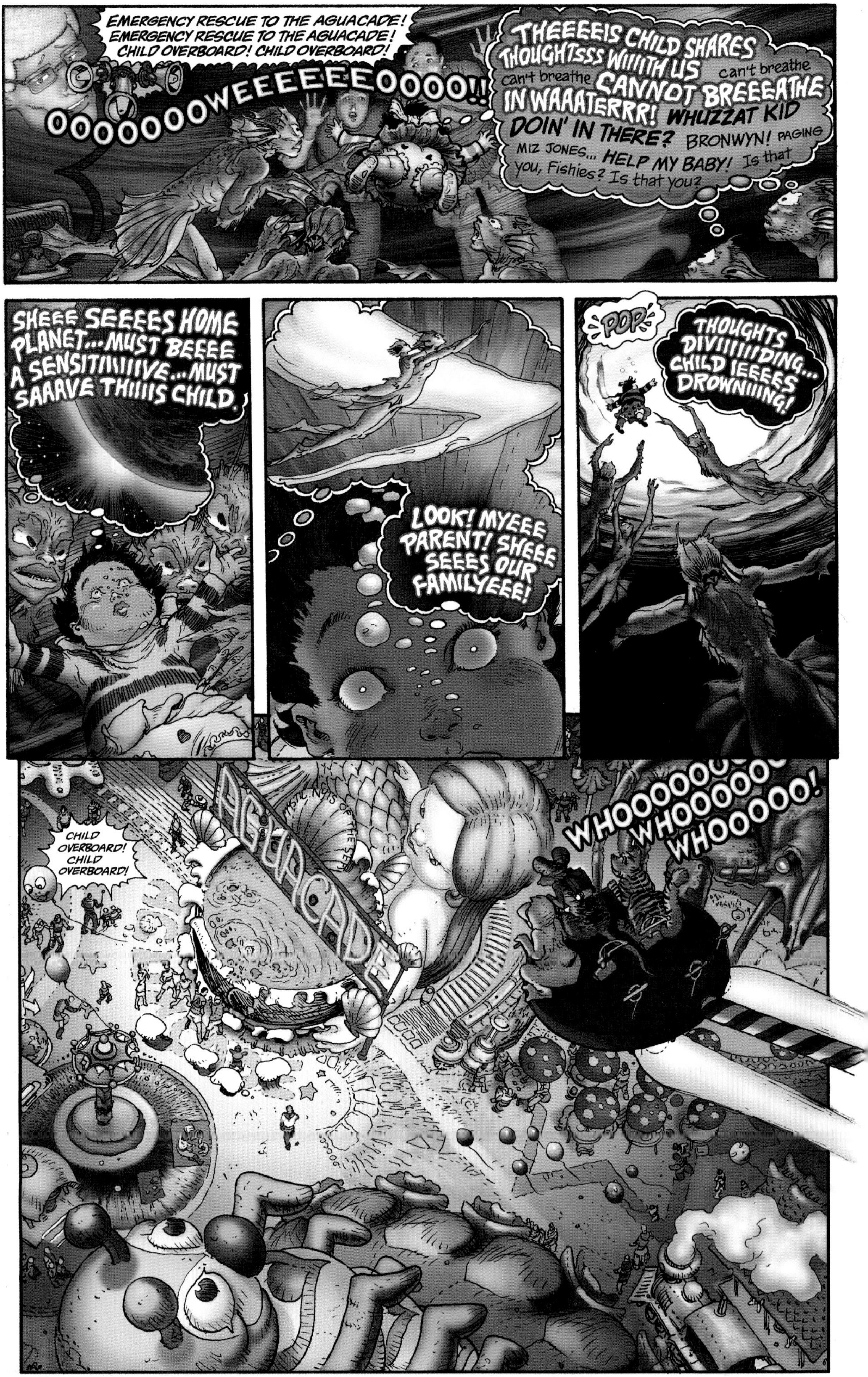
EMERGENCY RESCUE TO THE AGUACADE! EMERGENCY RESCUE TO THE AGUACADE! CHILD OVERBOARD! CHILD OVERBOARD!
OOOOOOOOWEEEEEEEOOOO!!
THEEEEIS CHILD SHARES THOUGHTSSS WIIIITH US can't breathe can't breathe CANNOT BREEEATHE IN WAAATERRR! WHUZZAT KID DOIN' IN THERE? BRONWYN! PAGING MIZ JONES... HELP MY BABY! Is that you, Fishies? Is that you?
SHEEE SEEEES HOME PLANET... MUST BEEEE A SENSITIIIIIIVE... MUST SAAAVE THIIIIS CHILD.
LOOK! MYEEE PARENT! SHEEE SEEES OUR FAMILYEEE!
POP
THOUGHTS DIVIIIIIIDING... CHILD IEEEES DROWNIIIING!
AGUACADE
CHILD OVERBOARD! CHILD OVERBOARD!
WHOOOOOOO WHOOOOOO WHOOOOOO!

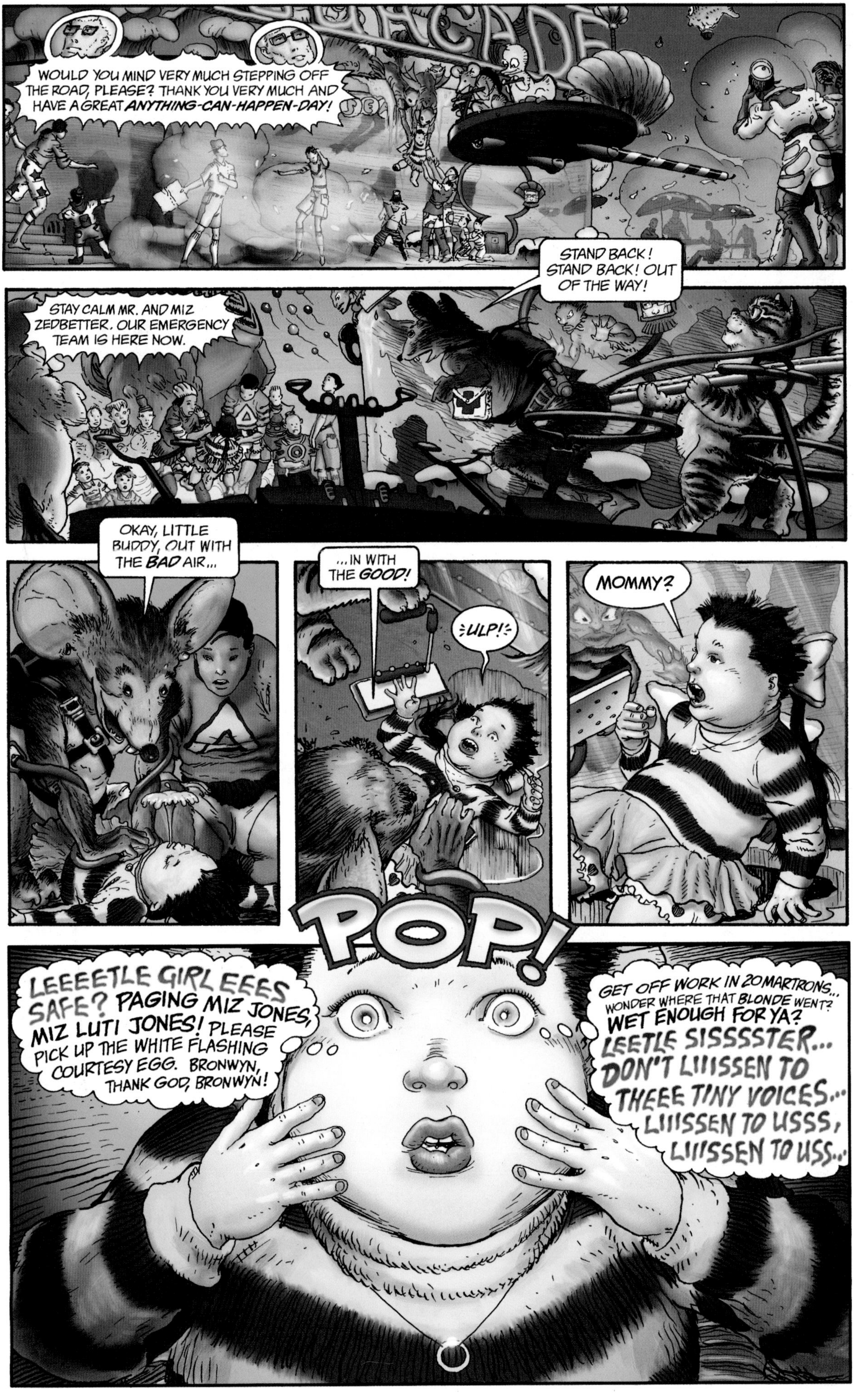
WOULD YOU MIND VERY MUCH STEPPING OFF THE ROAD, PLEASE? THANK YOU VERY MUCH AND HAVE A GREAT ANYTHING-CAN-HAPPEN-DAY!
STAND BACK! STAND BACK! OUT OF THE WAY!
STAY CALM MR. AND MIZ ZEDBETTER. OUR EMERGENCY TEAM IS HERE NOW.
OKAY, LITTLE BUDDY, OUT WITH THE BAD AIR...
...IN WITH THE GOOD!
ULP!
MOMMY?
POP!
LEEEETLE GIRL EEES SAFE? PAGING MIZ JONES, MIZ LUTI JONES! PLEASE PICK UP THE WHITE FLASHING COURTESY EGG. BRONWYN, THANK GOD, BRONWYN!
GET OFF WORK IN 20 MARTRONS... WONDER WHERE THAT BLONDE WENT? WET ENOUGH FOR YA? LEETLE SISSSSTER... DON'T LIIISSEN TO THEEE TINY VOICES... LIIISSEN TO USSS, LIIISSEN TO USS...

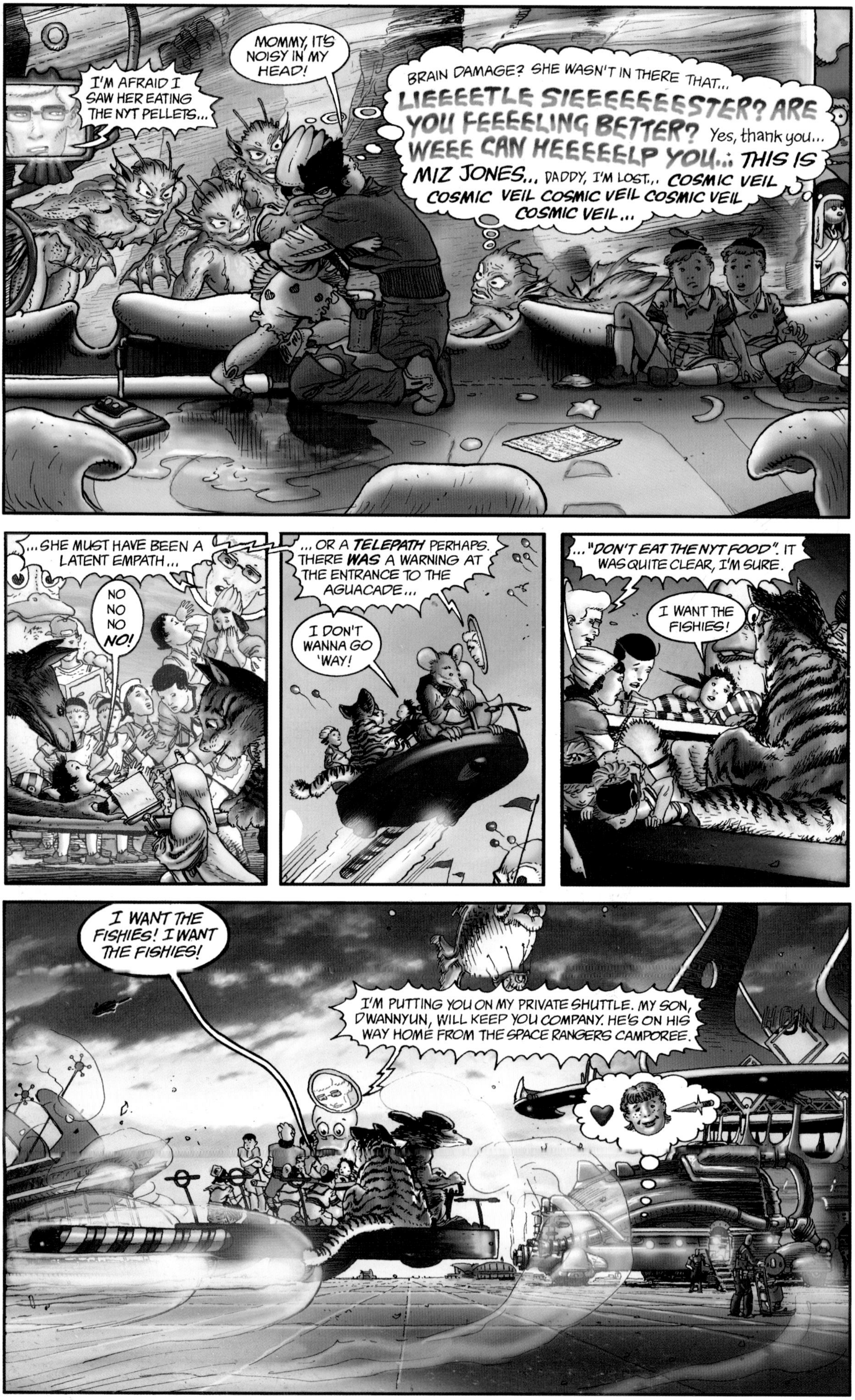

MOMMY, IT'S NOISY IN MY HEAD!
I'M AFRAID I SAW HER EATING THE NYT PELLETS...
BRAIN DAMAGE? SHE WASN'T IN THERE THAT...
LIEEEETLE SIEEEEEEESTER? ARE YOU FEEEELING BETTER? Yes, thank you... WEEE CAN HEEEEELP YOU... THIS IS MIZ JONES... DADDY, I'M LOST... COSMIC VEIL COSMIC VEIL COSMIC VEIL COSMIC VEIL COSMIC VEIL...
...SHE MUST HAVE BEEN A LATENT EMPATH...
NO NO NO NO!
...OR A TELEPATH PERHAPS. THERE WAS A WARNING AT THE ENTRANCE TO THE AGUACADE...
I DON'T WANNA GO 'WAY!
..."DON'T EAT THE NYT FOOD". IT WAS QUITE CLEAR, I'M SURE.
I WANT THE FISHIES!
I WANT THE FISHIES! I WANT THE FISHIES!
I'M PUTTING YOU ON MY PRIVATE SHUTTLE. MY SON, DWANNYUN, WILL KEEP YOU COMPANY. HE'S ON HIS WAY HOME FROM THE SPACE RANGERS CAMPOREE.

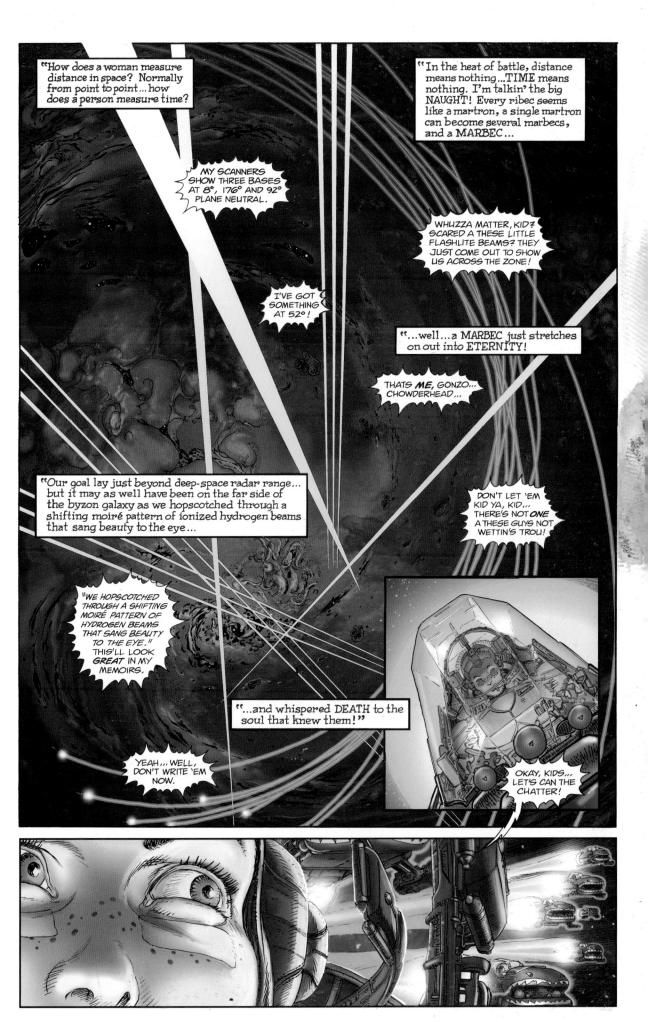

"How does a woman measure distance in space? Normally from point to point... how does a person measure time?

"In the heat of battle, distance means nothing... TIME means nothing. I'm talkin' the big NAUGHT! Every ribec seems like a martron, a single martron can become several marbecs, and a MARBEC...

MY SCANNERS SHOW THREE BASES AT 8°, 176° AND 92° PLANE NEUTRAL.

WHUZZA MATTER, KID? SCARED A THESE LITTLE FLASHLITE BEAMS? THEY JUST COME OUT TO SHOW US ACROSS THE ZONE!

I'VE GOT SOMETHING AT 52°!

"...well...a MARBEC just stretches on out into ETERNITY!

THATS *ME*, GONZO... CHOWDERHEAD...

"Our goal lay just beyond deep-space radar range... but it may as well have been on the far side of the byzon galaxy as we hopscotched through a shifting moiré pattern of ionized hydrogen beams that sang beauty to the eye...

DON'T LET 'EM KID YA, KID... THERE'S NOT *ONE* A THESE GUYS NOT WETTIN'S TROU!

"WE HOPSCOTCHED THROUGH A SHIFTING MOIRÉ PATTERN OF HYDROGEN BEAMS THAT SANG BEAUTY TO THE EYE." THIS'LL LOOK *GREAT* IN MY MEMOIRS.

"...and whispered DEATH to the soul that knew them!"

YEAH,... WELL, DON'T WRITE 'EM NOW.

OKAY, KIDS... LET'S CAN THE CHATTER!

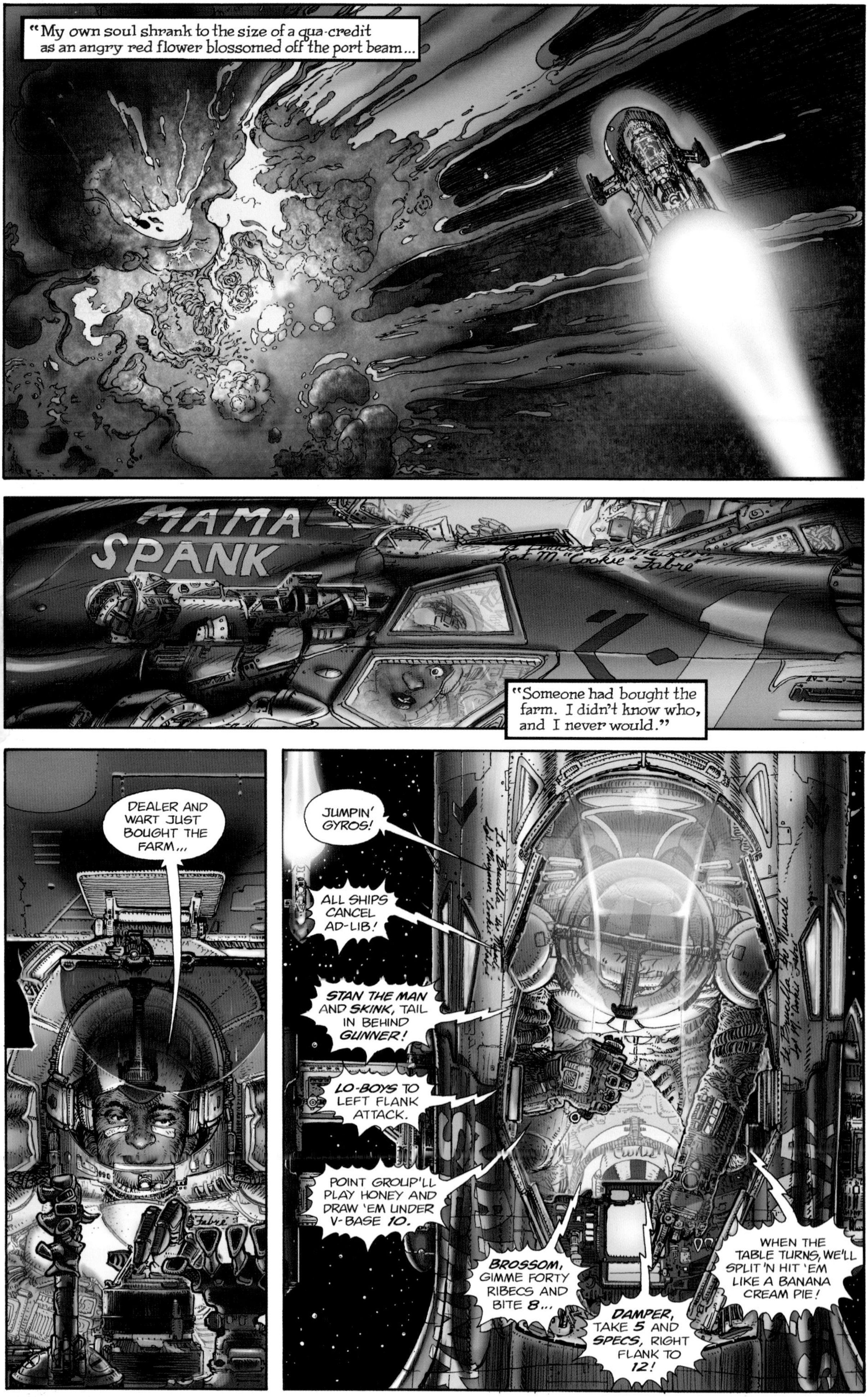
"My own soul shrank to the size of a qua-credit as an angry red flower blossomed off the port beam...
MAMA SPANK
"Someone had bought the farm. I didn't know who, and I never would."
DEALER AND WART JUST BOUGHT THE FARM...
JUMPIN' GYROS!
ALL SHIPS CANCEL AD-LIB!
STAN THE MAN AND SKINK, TAIL IN BEHIND GUNNER!
LO-BOYS TO LEFT FLANK ATTACK.
POINT GROUP'LL PLAY HONEY AND DRAW 'EM UNDER V-BASE 10.
BROSSOM, GIMME FORTY RIBECS AND BITE 8...
DAMPER, TAKE 5 AND SPECS, RIGHT FLANK TO 12!
WHEN THE TABLE TURNS, WE'LL SPLIT 'N HIT 'EM LIKE A BANANA CREAM PIE!

"My lips moved in a silent prayer to the Mother as point group crawled under Vercadian Base 10, drawing their H-beams like so many Pryfromian Phlys. And suddenly...

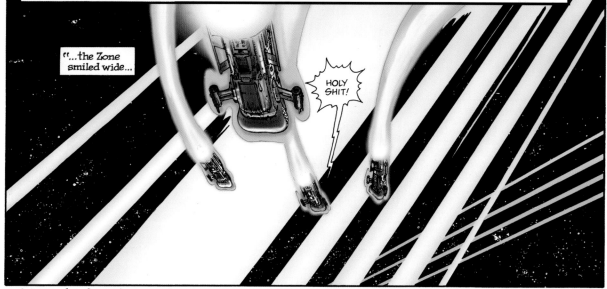

"...the Zone smiled wide...

HOLY SHIT!

"...belching bile from its great churning gut, and each brave Brigader of Point Group saw his or her face reflected in its omnivorous teeth as he or she stared grim-faced down the trembling throat of death!

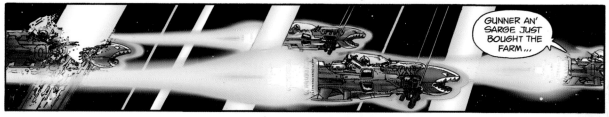

GUNNER AN' SARGE JUST BOUGHT THE FARM...

"Unbeknownst to me, "Damper" and the Hi-Boys had cut out the malignant Base 5 like the cancer it was. My full attention was, at the time, primarily focused on keepin' Point Group clear of the fast-fryin' fangs of the death-dealin' droids.

My full attention proved to be worth less than a BAJAR SHILLING.

SKINK AND WEEBLE JUST BOUGHT THE FARM!

"There was a hell of a lotta real estate auctioned off in that Neutral Zone an' my kids thought they were pickin' it whole-sale! To my mind, they were paying top dollar...

OH MOTHER OH MOTHER OH MOTHER! STAN...!

"...they were paying with BRIGADER BLOOD!

"...I saw it comin' at 'em, but before I could say 'Stan! Claw off to Port!', Stan and "Butcher" had been reduced to a fond memory...

"...and just as suddenly--

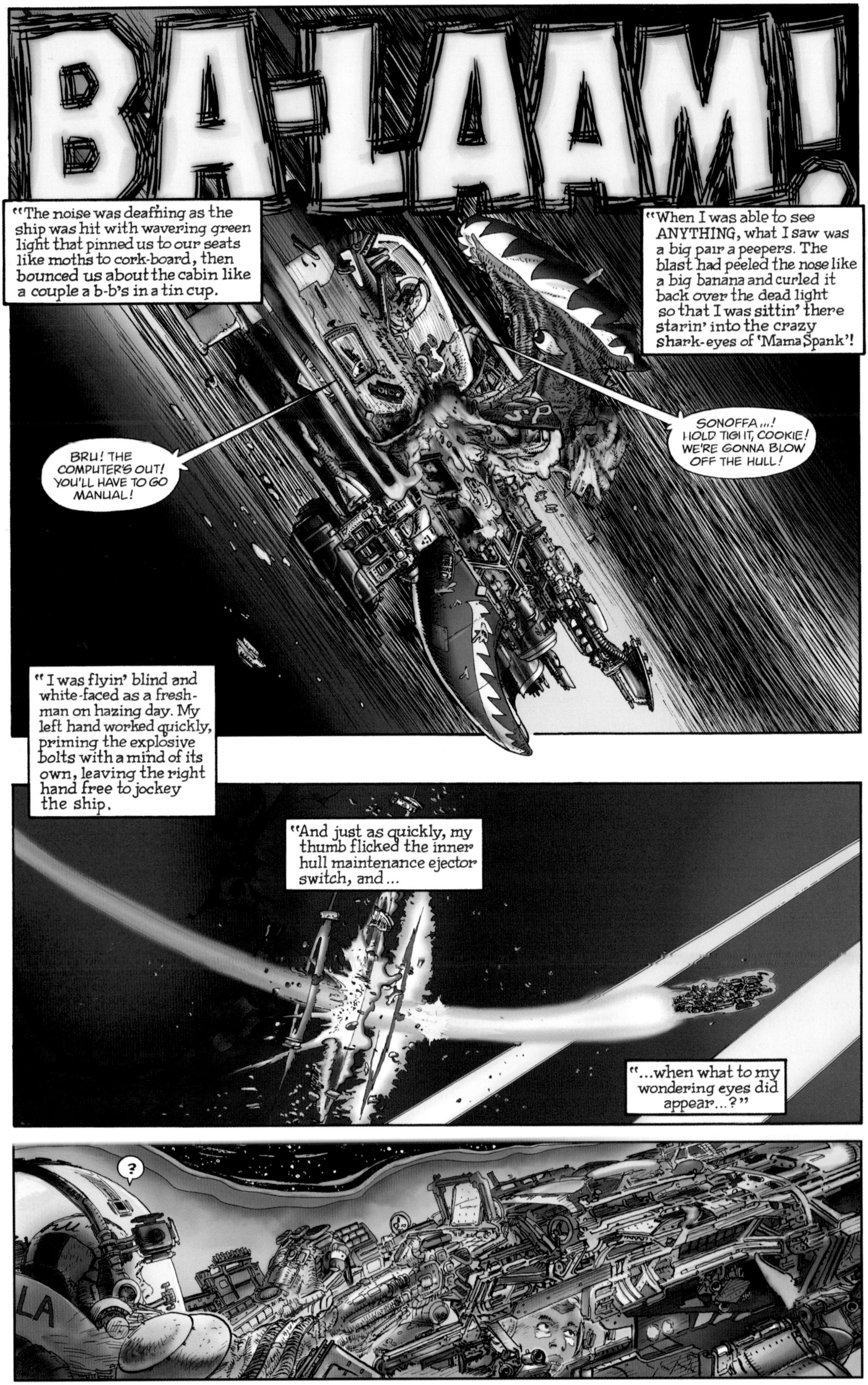
BA-LAAM!
"The noise was deafning as the ship was hit with wavering green light that pinned us to our seats like moths to cork-board, then bounced us about the cabin like a couple a b-b's in a tin cup.
"When I was able to see ANYTHING, what I saw was a big pair a peepers. The blast had peeled the nose like a big banana and curled it back over the dead light so that I was sittin' there starin' into the crazy shark-eyes of 'Mama Spank'!
BRU! THE COMPUTER'S OUT! YOU'LL HAVE TO GO MANUAL!
SONOFFA...! HOLD TIGHT, COOKIE! WE'RE GONNA BLOW OFF THE HULL!
" I was flyin' blind and white-faced as a fresh-man on hazing day. My left hand worked quickly, priming the explosive bolts with a mind of its own, leaving the right hand free to jockey the ship.
"And just as quickly, my thumb flicked the inner hull maintenance ejector switch, and...
"...when what to my wondering eyes did appear...?"
?

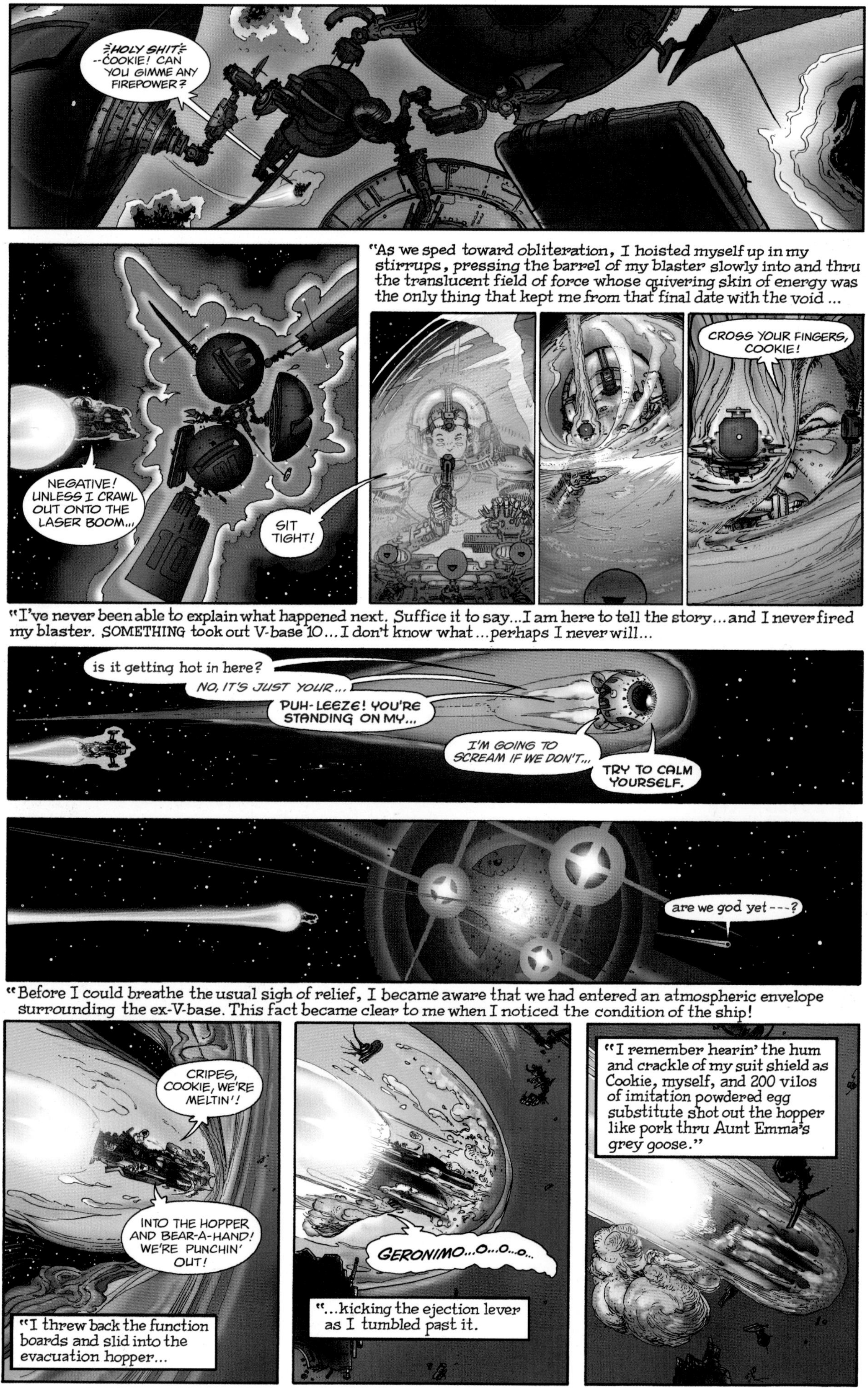
HOLY SHIT --COOKIE! CAN YOU GIMME ANY FIREPOWER?
"As we sped toward obliteration, I hoisted myself up in my stirrups, pressing the barrel of my blaster slowly into and thru the translucent field of force whose quivering skin of energy was the only thing that kept me from that final date with the void ...
NEGATIVE! UNLESS I CRAWL OUT ONTO THE LASER BOOM...
SIT TIGHT!
CROSS YOUR FINGERS, COOKIE!
"I've never been able to explain what happened next. Suffice it to say...I am here to tell the story...and I never fired my blaster. SOMETHING took out V-base 10... I don't know what...perhaps I never will...
is it getting hot in here?
NO, IT'S JUST YOUR...
PUH-LEEZE! YOU'RE STANDING ON MY...
I'M GOING TO SCREAM IF WE DON'T...
TRY TO CALM YOURSELF.
are we god yet---?
"Before I could breathe the usual sigh of relief, I became aware that we had entered an atmospheric envelope surrounding the ex-V-base. This fact became clear to me when I noticed the condition of the ship!
CRIPES, COOKIE, WE'RE MELTIN'!
INTO THE HOPPER AND BEAR-A-HAND! WE'RE PUNCHIN' OUT!
"I threw back the function boards and slid into the evacuation hopper...
GERONIMO...O...O...O...
"...kicking the ejection lever as I tumbled past it.
"I remember hearin' the hum and crackle of my suit shield as Cookie, myself, and 200 vilos of imitation powdered egg substitute shot out the hopper like pork thru Aunt Emma's grey goose."

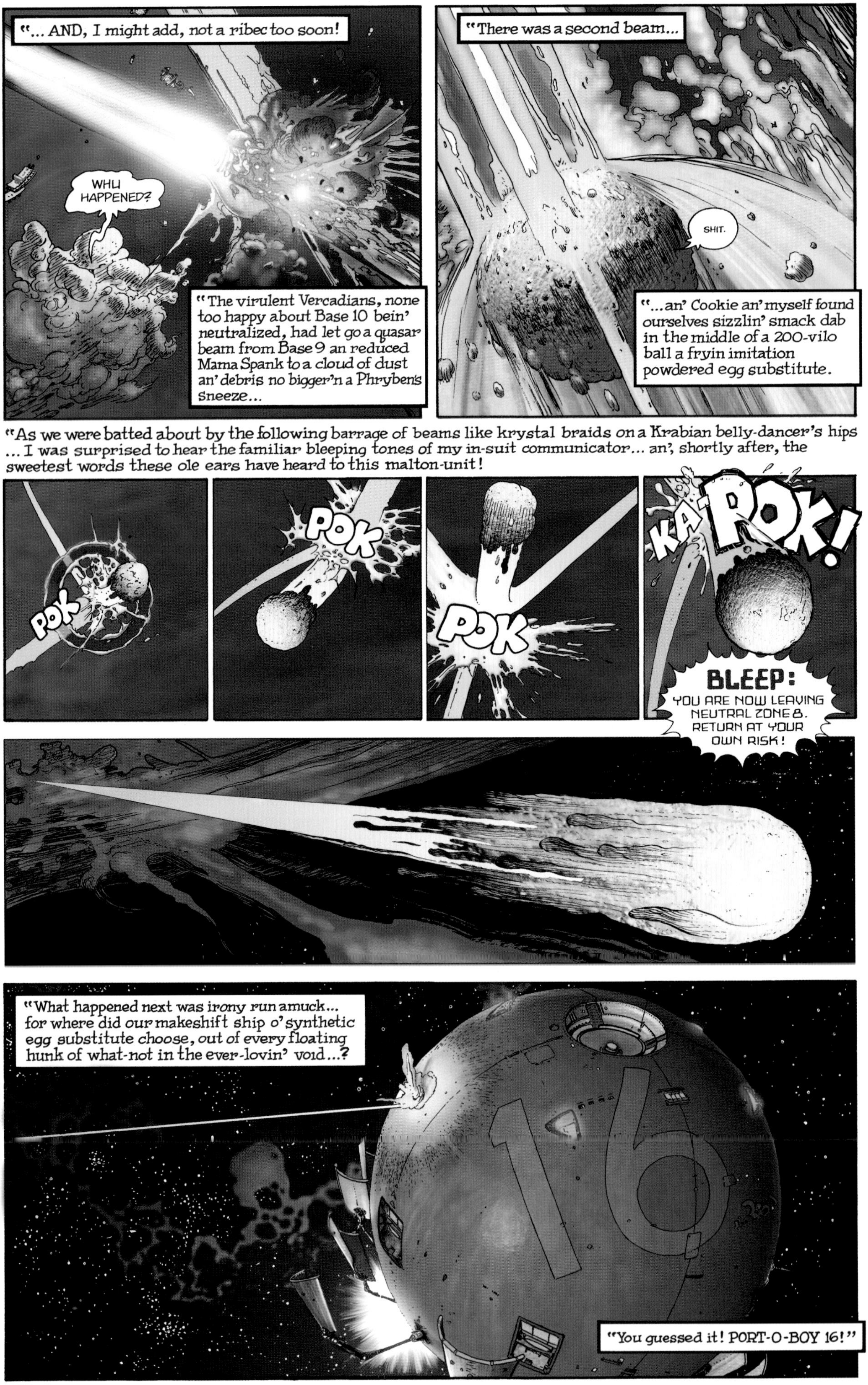
"... AND, I might add, not a ribec too soon!
WHY HAPPENED?
"The virulent Vercadians, none too happy about Base 10 bein' neutralized, had let go a quasar beam from Base 9 an reduced Mama Spank to a cloud of dust an' debris no bigger'n a Phryben's sneeze...
"There was a second beam...
SHIT.
"...an' Cookie an' myself found ourselves sizzlin' smack dab in the middle of a 200-vilo ball a fryin imitation powdered egg substitute.
"As we were batted about by the following barrage of beams like krystal braids on a Krabian belly-dancer's hips ... I was surprised to hear the familiar bleeping tones of my in-suit communicator... an', shortly after, the sweetest words these ole ears have heard to this malton-unit!
POK
POK
POK
KA-POK!
BLEEP: YOU ARE NOW LEAVING NEUTRAL ZONE 8. RETURN AT YOUR OWN RISK!
"What happened next was irony run amuck... for where did our makeshift ship o' synthetic egg substitute choose, out of every floating hunk of what-not in the ever-lovin' void...?
16
"You guessed it! PORT-O-BOY 16!"

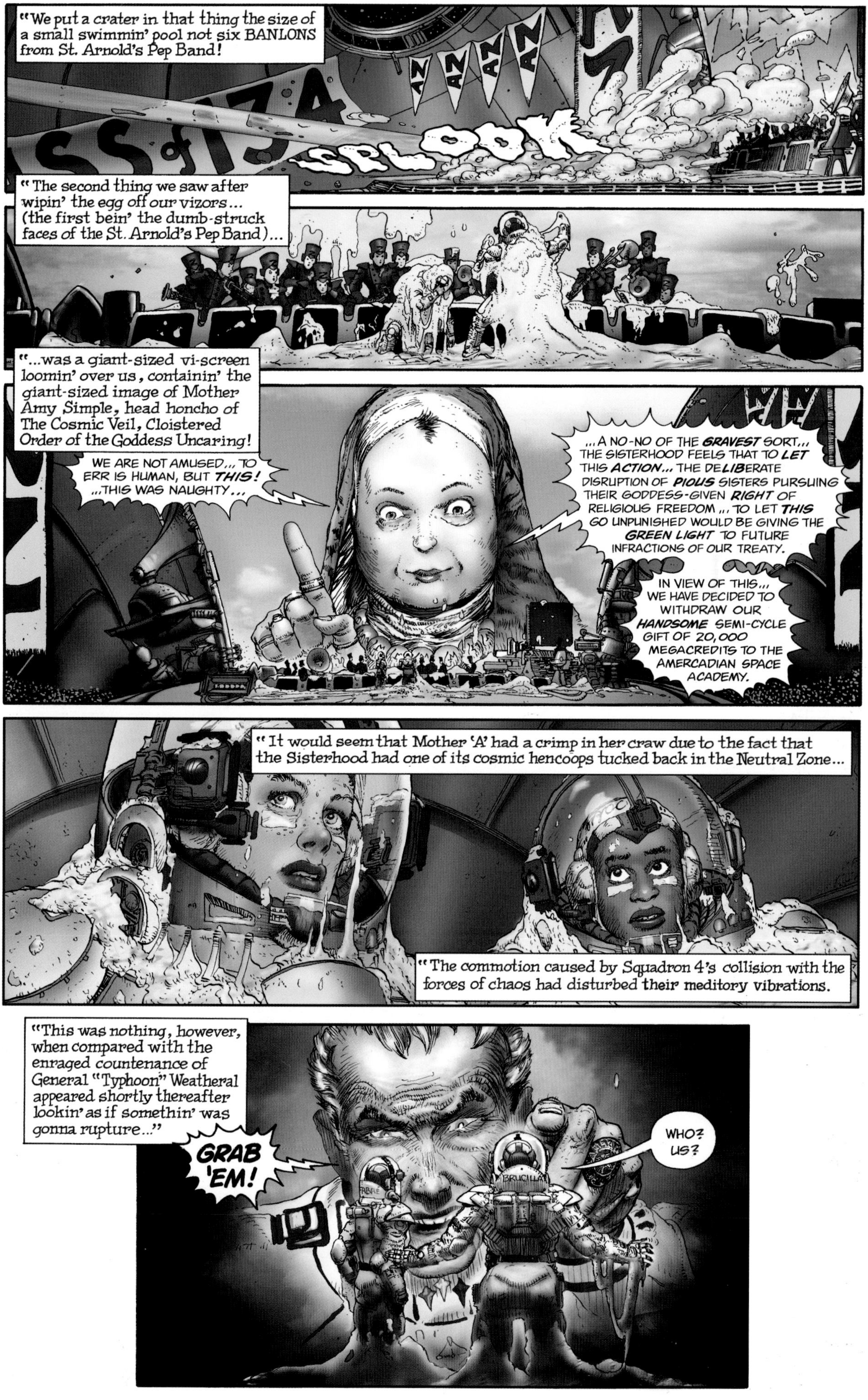

"We put a crater in that thing the size of a small swimmin' pool not six BANLONS from St. Arnold's Pep Band!
SPLOOK
"The second thing we saw after wipin' the egg off our vizors... (the first bein' the dumb-struck faces of the St. Arnold's Pep Band)...
"...was a giant-sized vi-screen loomin' over us, containin' the giant-sized image of Mother Amy Simple, head honcho of The Cosmic Veil, Cloistered Order of the Goddess Uncaring!
WE ARE NOT AMUSED... TO ERR IS HUMAN, BUT THIS! ...THIS WAS NAUGHTY...
...A NO-NO OF THE GRAVEST SORT... THE SISTERHOOD FEELS THAT TO LET THIS ACTION... THE DELIBERATE DISRUPTION OF PIOUS SISTERS PURSUING THEIR GODDESS-GIVEN RIGHT OF RELIGIOUS FREEDOM... TO LET THIS GO UNPUNISHED WOULD BE GIVING THE GREEN LIGHT TO FUTURE INFRACTIONS OF OUR TREATY.
IN VIEW OF THIS... WE HAVE DECIDED TO WITHDRAW OUR HANDSOME SEMI-CYCLE GIFT OF 20,000 MEGACREDITS TO THE AMERCADIAN SPACE ACADEMY.
"It would seem that Mother 'A' had a crimp in her craw due to the fact that the Sisterhood had one of its cosmic hencoops tucked back in the Neutral Zone...
"The commotion caused by Squadron 4's collision with the forces of chaos had disturbed their meditory vibrations.
"This was nothing, however, when compared with the enraged countenance of General "Typhoon" Weatheral appeared shortly thereafter lookin' as if somethin' was gonna rupture..."
GRAB 'EM!
WHO? US?

"The next few marbecs were a nightmare. Little did I suspect that I was to play the pawn in a drama of deception that made a travesty of justice and a mockery of the words 'fair play'.

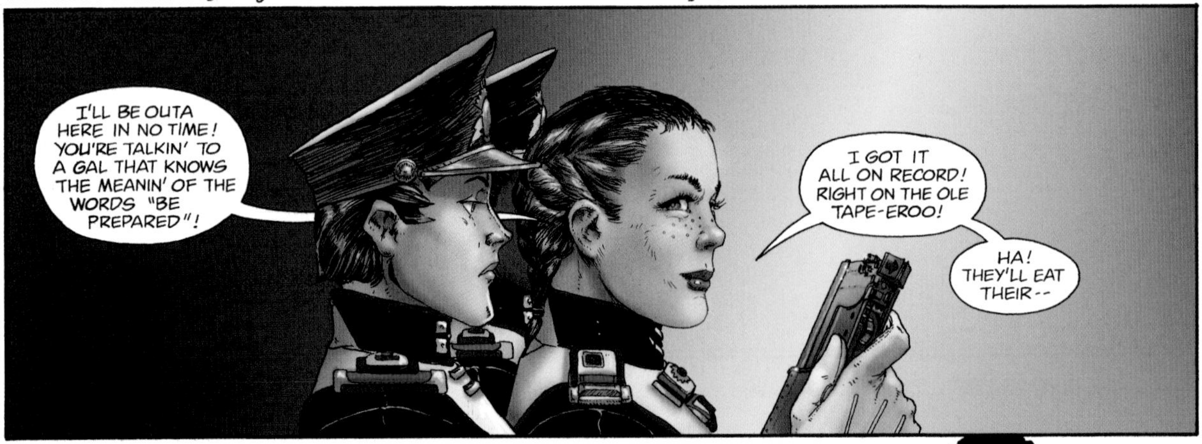
I'LL BE OUTA HERE IN NO TIME! YOU'RE TALKIN' TO A GAL THAT KNOWS THE MEANIN' OF THE WORDS "BE PREPARED"!
I GOT IT ALL ON RECORD! RIGHT ON THE OLE TAPE-EROO!
HA! THEY'LL EAT THEIR--

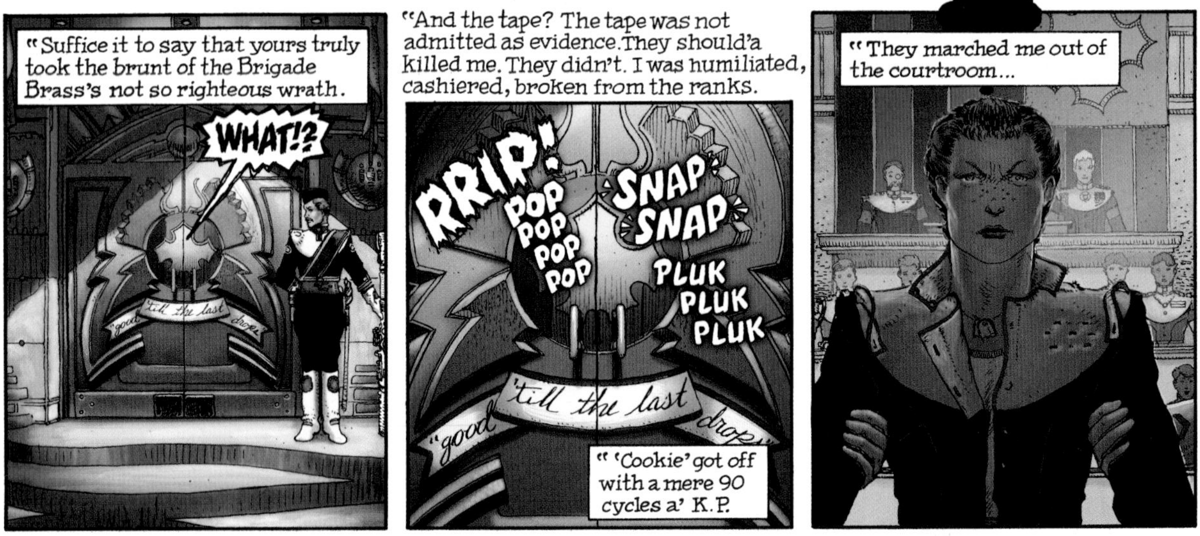
"Suffice it to say that yours truly took the brunt of the Brigade Brass's not so righteous wrath.
WHAT!?
"good 'till the last drop"
"And the tape? The tape was not admitted as evidence. They should'a killed me. They didn't. I was humiliated, cashiered, broken from the ranks.
RRIP!
POP POP POP POP
SNAP SNAP
PLUK PLUK PLUK
"good 'till the last drop"
"'Cookie' got off with a mere 90 cycles a' K.P.
"They marched me out of the courtroom...

"... down deep into and through the dank gray back corridors of Brigade Headquarters. I hung my head, so filled was I with shame and burning rage and then, by yet another foul turn of fate, found myself face to face with the last guy in Amercadia I wanted to run into at this moment."

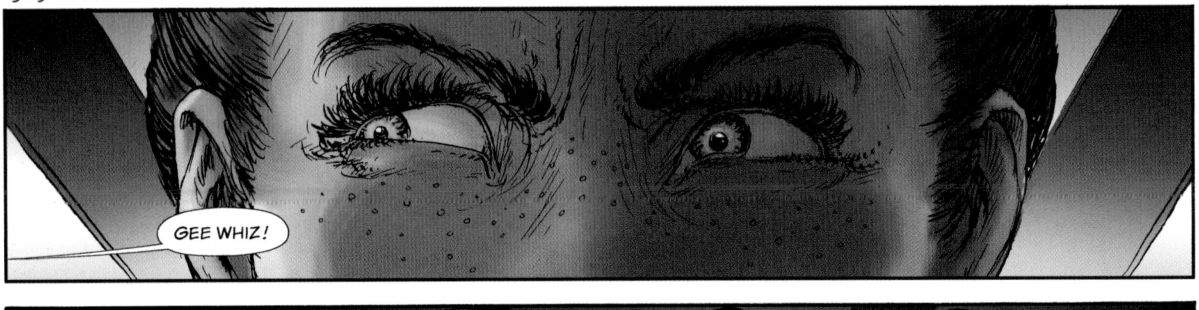
GEE WHIZ!

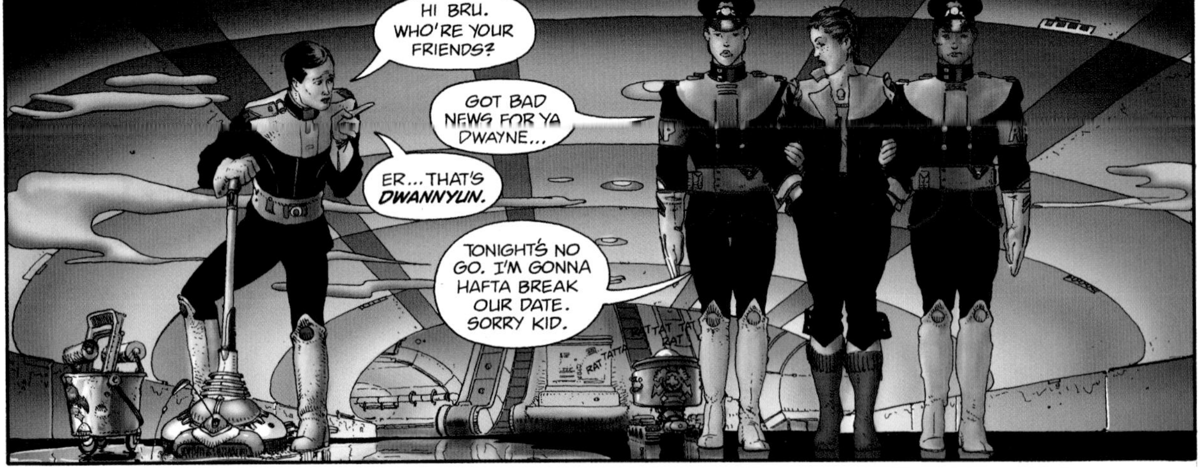
HI BRU. WHO'RE YOUR FRIENDS?
GOT BAD NEWS FOR YA DWAYNE...
ER...THAT'S DWANNYUN.
TONIGHT'S NO GO. I'M GONNA HAFTA BREAK OUR DATE. SORRY KID.

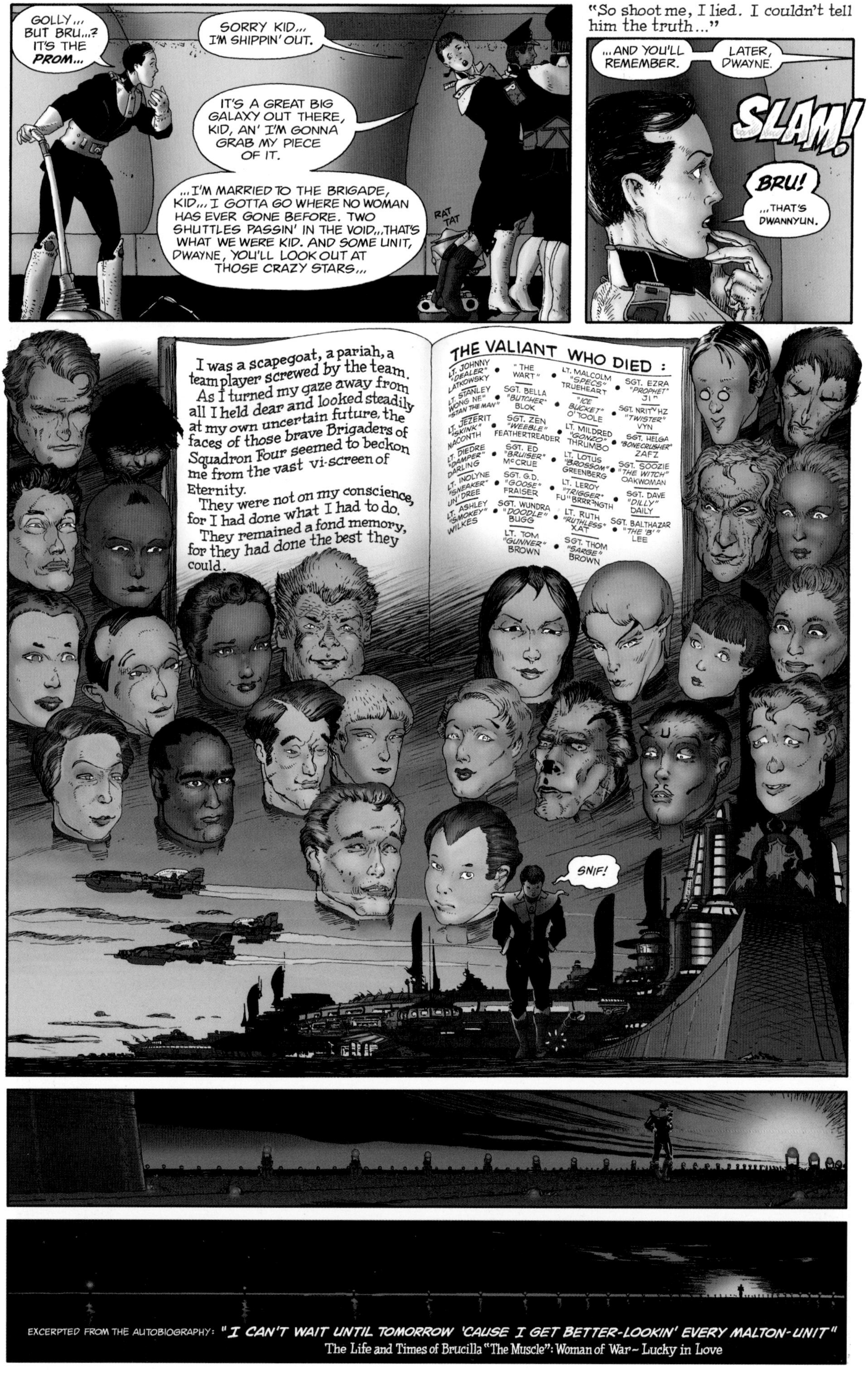
GOLLY,,, BUT BRU,,,? IT'S THE PROM...
SORRY KID,,, I'M SHIPPIN' OUT.
IT'S A GREAT BIG GALAXY OUT THERE, KID, AN' I'M GONNA GRAB MY PIECE OF IT.
...I'M MARRIED TO THE BRIGADE, KID,,, I GOTTA GO WHERE NO WOMAN HAS EVER GONE BEFORE. TWO SHUTTLES PASSIN' IN THE VOID,,,THAT'S WHAT WE WERE KID. AND SOME UNIT, DWAYNE, YOU'LL LOOK OUT AT THOSE CRAZY STARS,,,
RAT TAT
"So shoot me, I lied. I couldn't tell him the truth..."
...AND YOU'LL REMEMBER.
LATER, DWAYNE.
SLAM!
BRU!
...THAT'S DWANNYUN.
I was a scapegoat, a pariah, a team player screwed by the team. As I turned my gaze away from all I held dear and looked steadily at my own uncertain future, the faces of those brave Brigaders of Squadron Four seemed to beckon me from the vast vi-screen of Eternity.
They were not on my conscience, for I had done what I had to do.
They remained a fond memory, for they had done the best they could.
THE VALIANT WHO DIED:
LT. JOHNNY "DEALER" LATKOWSKY
LT. STANLEY WONG NE" "STAN THE MAN"
LT. JEZERIT "SKINK" NACONTH
LT. DIEDRE "DAMPER" DARLING
LT. INOLYNE "SNEAKER" UN'DREE
LT. ASHLEY "SMOKEY" WILKES
"THE WART"
SGT. BELLA "BUTCHER" BLOK
SGT. ZEN "WEEBLE" FEATHERTREADER
SGT. ED "BRUISER" McCRUE
SGT. G.D. "GOOSE" FRAISER
SGT. WUNDRA "DOODLE" BUGG
LT. TOM "GUNNER" BROWN
LT. MALCOLM "SPECS" TRUEHEART
"ICE BUCKET" O'TOOLE
LT. MILDRED "GONZO" THRUMBO
LT. LOTUS "BROSSOM" GREENBERG
LT. LEROY "TRIGGER" FU"BRRRNGTH
LT. RUTH "RUTHLESS" XAT
SGT. THOM "SARGE" BROWN
SGT. EZRA "PROPHET" JI
SGT. NRITVHZ "TWISTER" VYN
SGT. HELGA "BONECRUSHER" ZAFZ
SGT. SOOZIE "THE WITCH" OAKWOMAN
SGT. DAVE "DILLY" DAILY
SGT. BALTHAZAR "THE 'B'" LEE
SNIF!
EXCERPTED FROM THE AUTOBIOGRAPHY: "I CAN'T WAIT UNTIL TOMORROW 'CAUSE I GET BETTER-LOOKIN' EVERY MALTON-UNIT"
The Life and Times of Brucilla "The Muscle": Woman of War ~ Lucky in Love

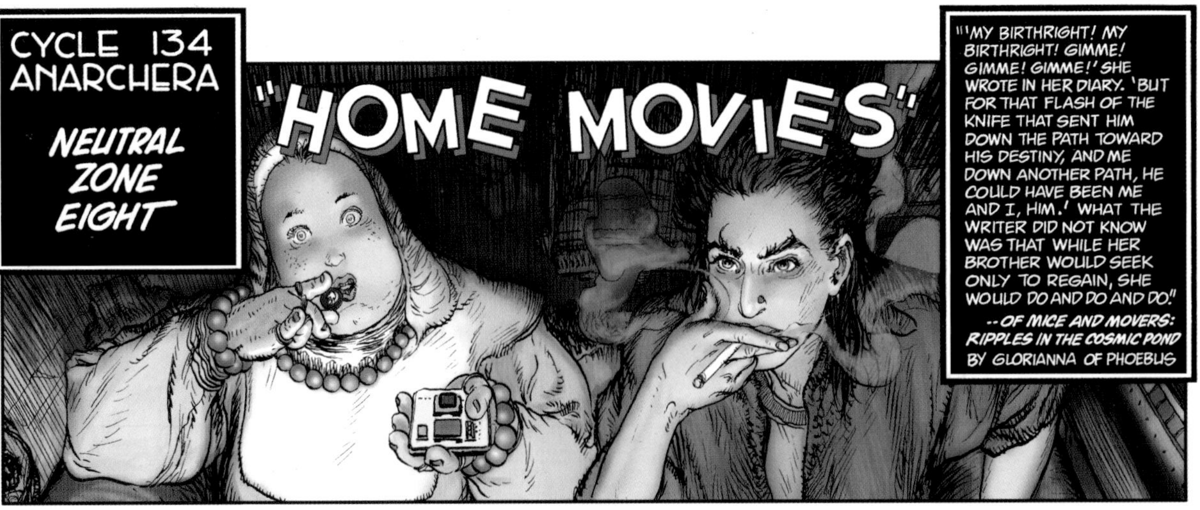
CYCLE 134
ANARCHERA
NEUTRAL ZONE EIGHT
"HOME MOVIES"
"'MY BIRTHRIGHT! MY BIRTHRIGHT! GIMME! GIMME! GIMME!' SHE WROTE IN HER DIARY. 'BUT FOR THAT FLASH OF THE KNIFE THAT SENT HIM DOWN THE PATH TOWARD HIS DESTINY, AND ME DOWN ANOTHER PATH, HE COULD HAVE BEEN ME AND I, HIM.' WHAT THE WRITER DID NOT KNOW WAS THAT WHILE HER BROTHER WOULD SEEK ONLY TO REGAIN, SHE WOULD DO AND DO AND DO."
--OF MICE AND MOVERS: RIPPLES IN THE COSMIC POND BY GLORIANNA OF PHOEBUS

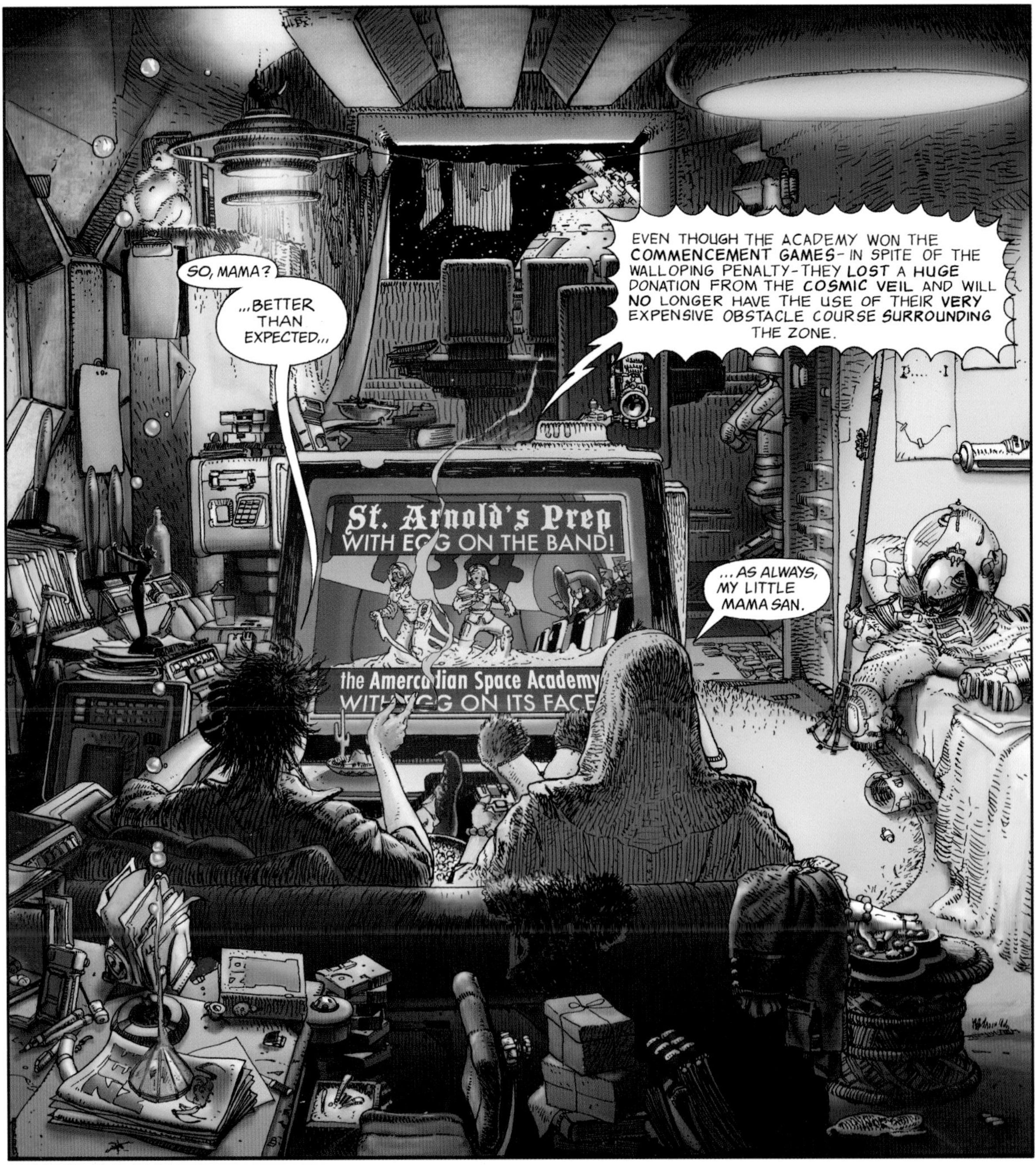
SO, MAMA?
...BETTER THAN EXPECTED...
EVEN THOUGH THE ACADEMY WON THE COMMENCEMENT GAMES- IN SPITE OF THE WALLOPING PENALTY- THEY LOST A HUGE DONATION FROM THE COSMIC VEIL AND WILL NO LONGER HAVE THE USE OF THEIR VERY EXPENSIVE OBSTACLE COURSE SURROUNDING THE ZONE.
St. Arnold's Prep
WITH EGG ON THE BAND!
Space Academy
ON ITS FACE
...AS ALWAYS, MY LITTLE MAMA SAN.

"WHENEVER YOU BLOCK, PARRY OR TRANSFORM, BE SURE TO THINK THE MOVES THROUGH TO A BURN, A CUT, OR TO WHITE DEATH. PONDER THIS."

--MASTERING DREAM ENHANCEMENT GAMES
BY VIRGIL H., INTERSOLAR PROTOARCHETYPAL ID-IMEX LEVEL TOUCHÉMENTO CHAMPION

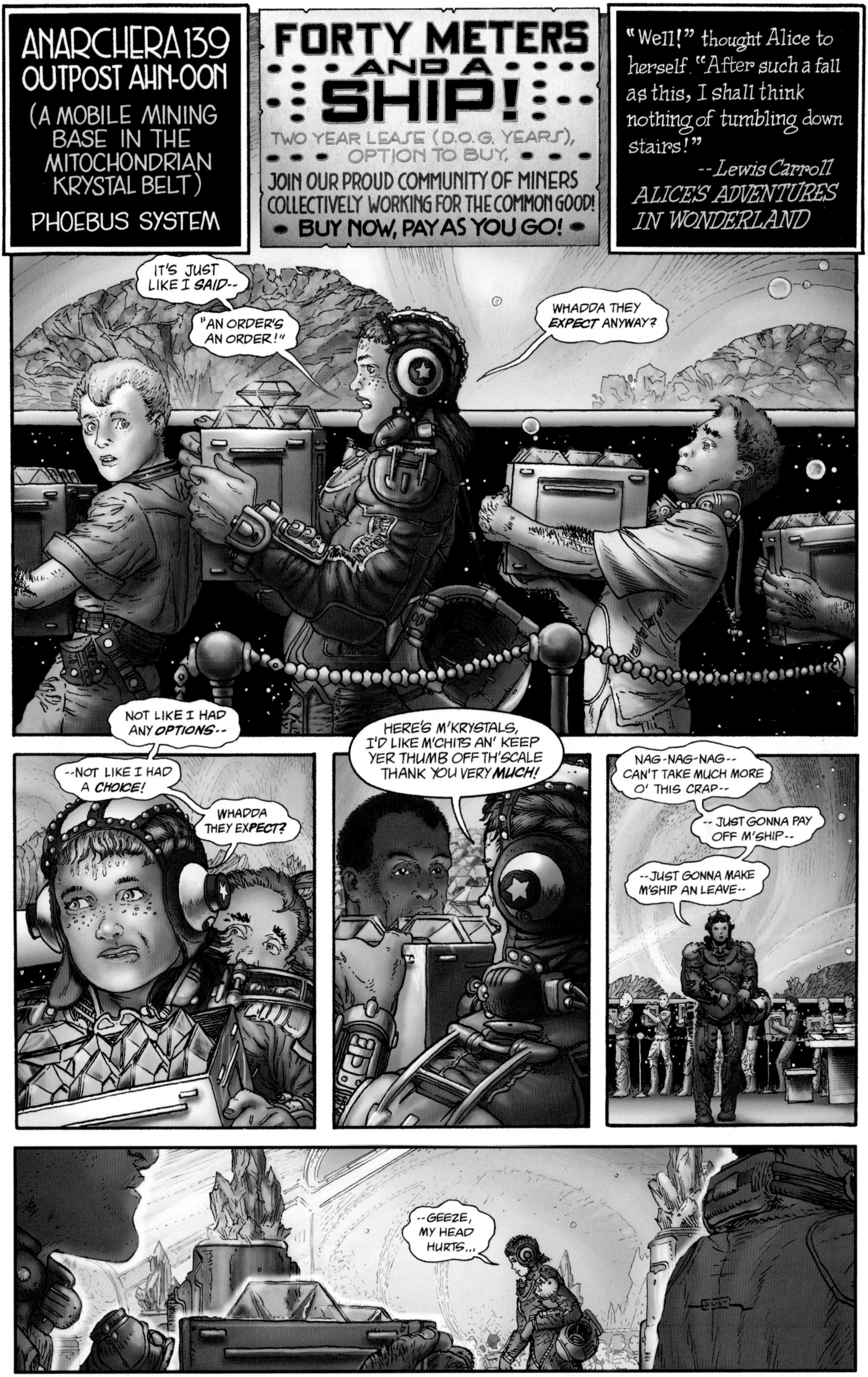
ANARCHERA 139
OUTPOST AHN-OON
(A MOBILE MINING BASE IN THE MITOCHONDRIAN KRYSTAL BELT)
PHOEBUS SYSTEM
FORTY METERS AND A SHIP!
TWO YEAR LEASE (D.O.G. YEARS), OPTION TO BUY,
JOIN OUR PROUD COMMUNITY OF MINERS COLLECTIVELY WORKING FOR THE COMMON GOOD!
BUY NOW, PAY AS YOU GO!
"Well!" thought Alice to herself. "After such a fall as this, I shall think nothing of tumbling down stairs!"
--Lewis Carroll
ALICE'S ADVENTURES IN WONDERLAND
IT'S JUST LIKE I SAID--
"AN ORDER'S AN ORDER!"
WHADDA THEY EXPECT ANYWAY?
NOT LIKE I HAD ANY OPTIONS--
--NOT LIKE I HAD A CHOICE!
WHADDA THEY EXPECT?
HERE'S M'KRYSTALS, I'D LIKE M'CHITS AN' KEEP YER THUMB OFF TH'SCALE THANK YOU VERY MUCH!
NAG-NAG-NAG-- CAN'T TAKE MUCH MORE O' THIS CRAP--
--JUST GONNA PAY OFF M'SHIP--
--JUST GONNA MAKE M'SHIP AN LEAVE--
--GEEZE, MY HEAD HURTS...

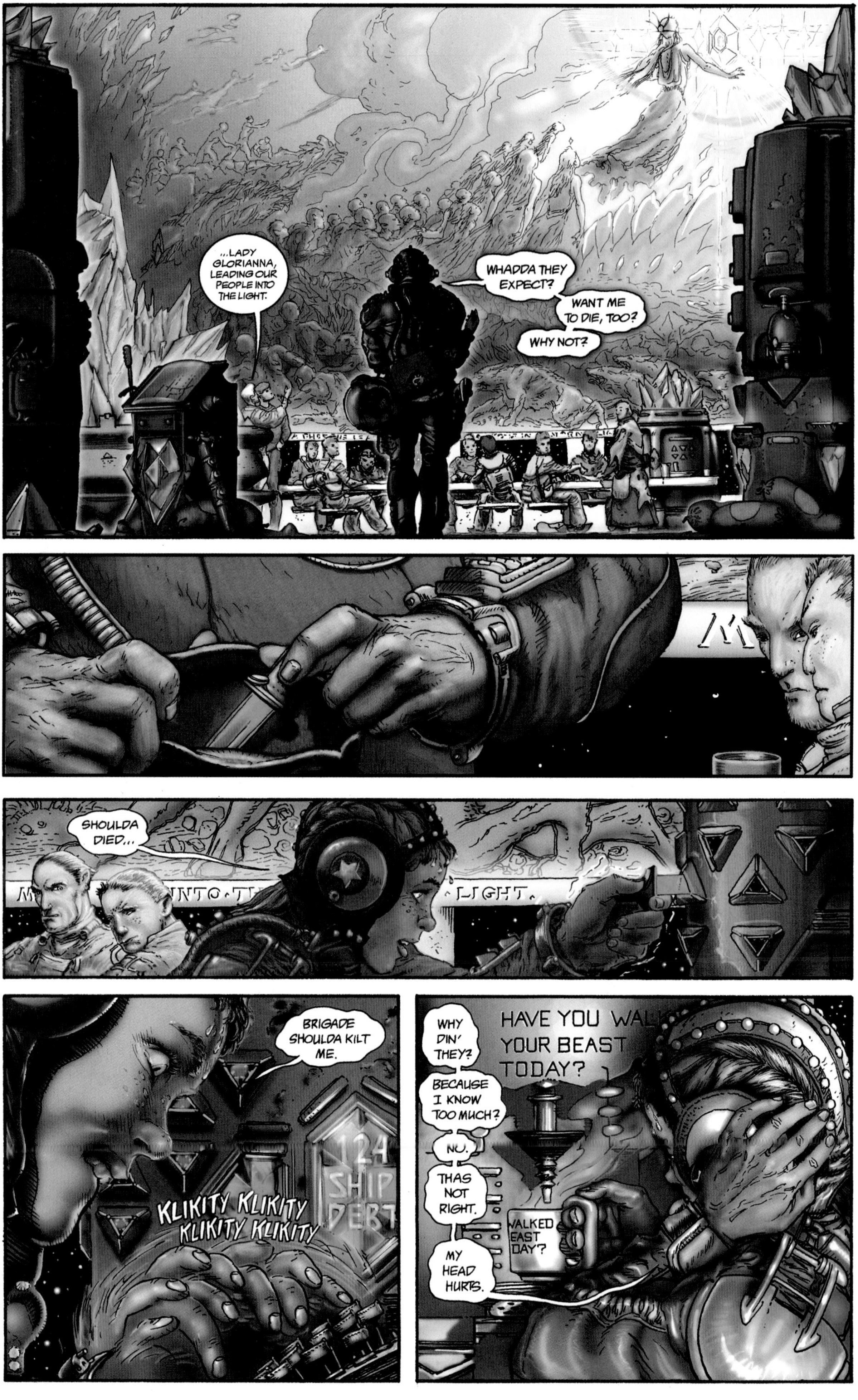
...LADY GLORIANNA, LEADING OUR PEOPLE INTO THE LIGHT.
WHADDA THEY EXPECT?
WANT ME TO DIE, TOO?
WHY NOT?
SHOULDA DIED...
BRIGADE SHOULDA KILT ME.
KLIKITY KLIKITY
KLIKITY KLIKITY
WHY DIN' THEY?
BECAUSE I KNOW TOO MUCH?
NO.
THAS NOT RIGHT.
MY HEAD HURTS.

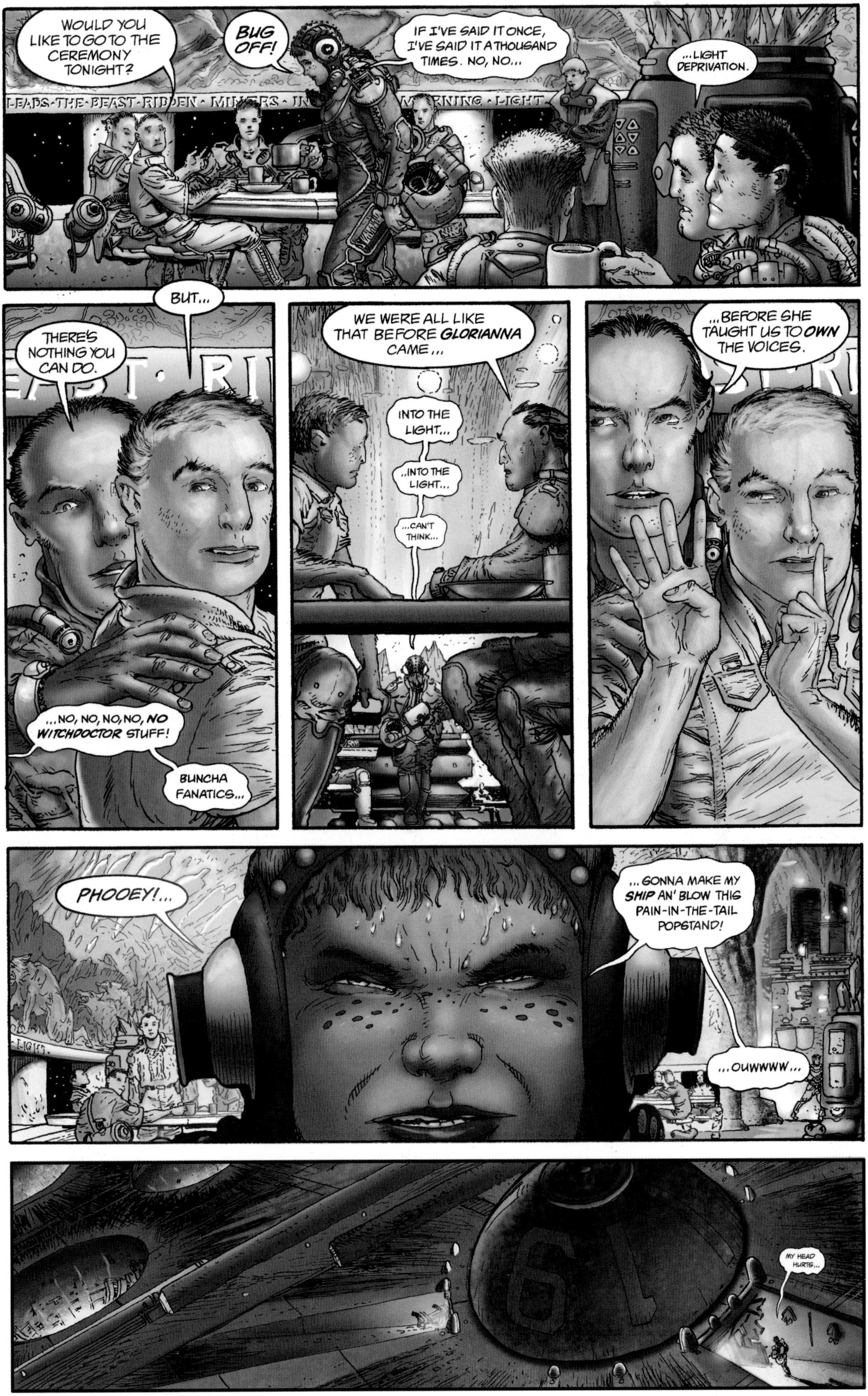
WOULD YOU LIKE TO GO TO THE CEREMONY TONIGHT?
BUG OFF!
IF I'VE SAID IT ONCE, I'VE SAID IT A THOUSAND TIMES. NO, NO...
...LIGHT DEPRIVATION.
THERE'S NOTHING YOU CAN DO.
BUT...
...NO, NO, NO, NO, NO WITCHDOCTOR STUFF!
BUNCHA FANATICS...
WE WERE ALL LIKE THAT BEFORE GLORIANNA CAME...
INTO THE LIGHT...
...INTO THE LIGHT...
...CAN'T THINK...
...BEFORE SHE TAUGHT US TO OWN THE VOICES.
PHOOEY!...
...GONNA MAKE MY SHIP AN' BLOW THIS PAIN-IN-THE-TAIL POPSTAND!
...OUWWWW...
MY HEAD HURTS...

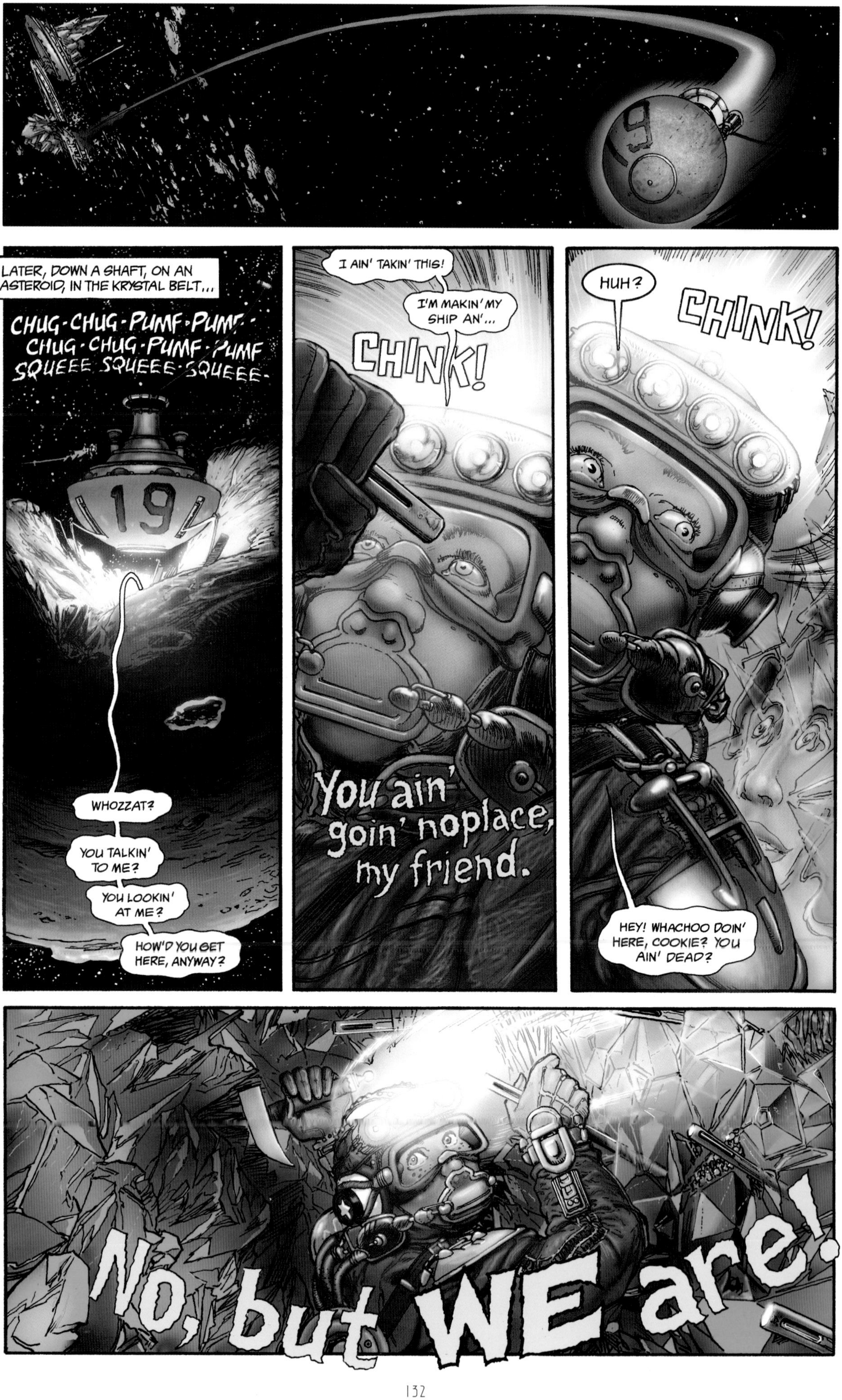

LATER, DOWN A SHAFT, ON AN ASTEROID, IN THE KRYSTAL BELT...
CHUG-CHUG-PUMF-PUMF-
CHUG-CHUG-PUMF-PUMF
SQUEEE-SQUEEE-SQUEEE-
WHOZZAT?
YOU TALKIN' TO ME?
YOU LOOKIN' AT ME?
HOW'D YOU GET HERE, ANYWAY?
I AIN' TAKIN' THIS!
I'M MAKIN' MY SHIP AN'...
CHINK!
You ain' goin' noplace, my friend.
HUH?
CHINK!
HEY! WHACHOO DOIN' HERE, COOKIE? YOU AIN' DEAD?
No, but WE are!

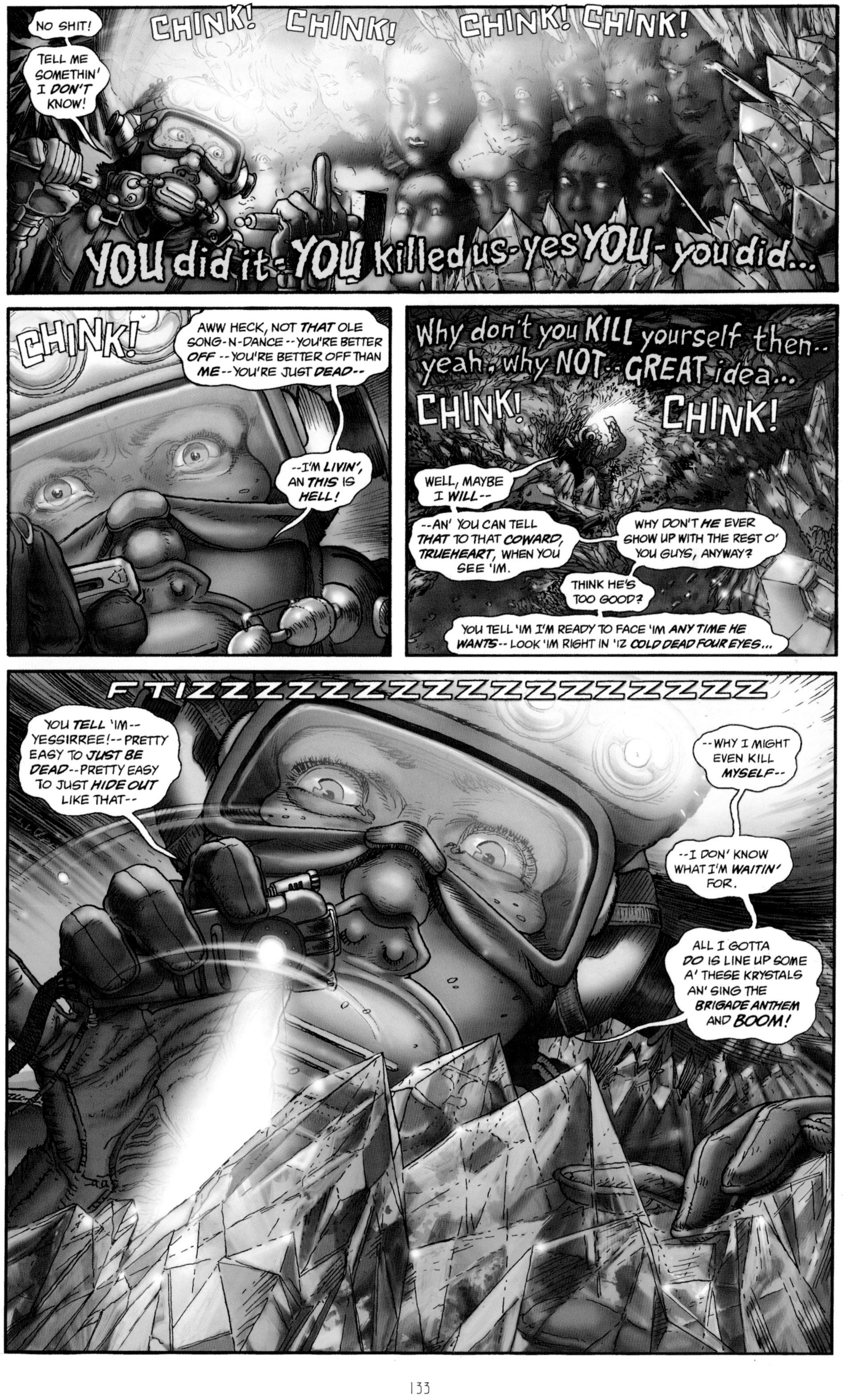
NO SHIT!
TELL ME SOMETHIN' I DON'T KNOW!
CHINK! CHINK! CHINK! CHINK!
YOU did it - YOU killed us - yes YOU - you did...
CHINK!
AWW HECK, NOT THAT OLE SONG-N-DANCE -- YOU'RE BETTER OFF -- YOU'RE BETTER OFF THAN ME -- YOU'RE JUST DEAD--
--I'M LIVIN', AN THIS IS HELL!
Why don't you KILL yourself then.. yeah, why NOT.. GREAT idea...
CHINK! CHINK!
WELL, MAYBE I WILL--
--AN' YOU CAN TELL THAT TO THAT COWARD, TRUEHEART, WHEN YOU SEE 'IM.
WHY DON'T HE EVER SHOW UP WITH THE REST O' YOU GUYS, ANYWAY?
THINK HE'S TOO GOOD?
YOU TELL 'IM I'M READY TO FACE 'IM ANY TIME HE WANTS-- LOOK 'IM RIGHT IN 'IZ COLD DEAD FOUR EYES...
FTIZZZZZZZZZZZZZZZZZZZZZZ
YOU TELL 'IM-- YESSIRREE!-- PRETTY EASY TO JUST BE DEAD-- PRETTY EASY TO JUST HIDE OUT LIKE THAT--
--WHY I MIGHT EVEN KILL MYSELF--
--I DON' KNOW WHAT I'M WAITIN' FOR.
ALL I GOTTA DO IS LINE UP SOME A' THESE KRYSTALS AN' SING THE BRIGADE ANTHEM AND BOOM!

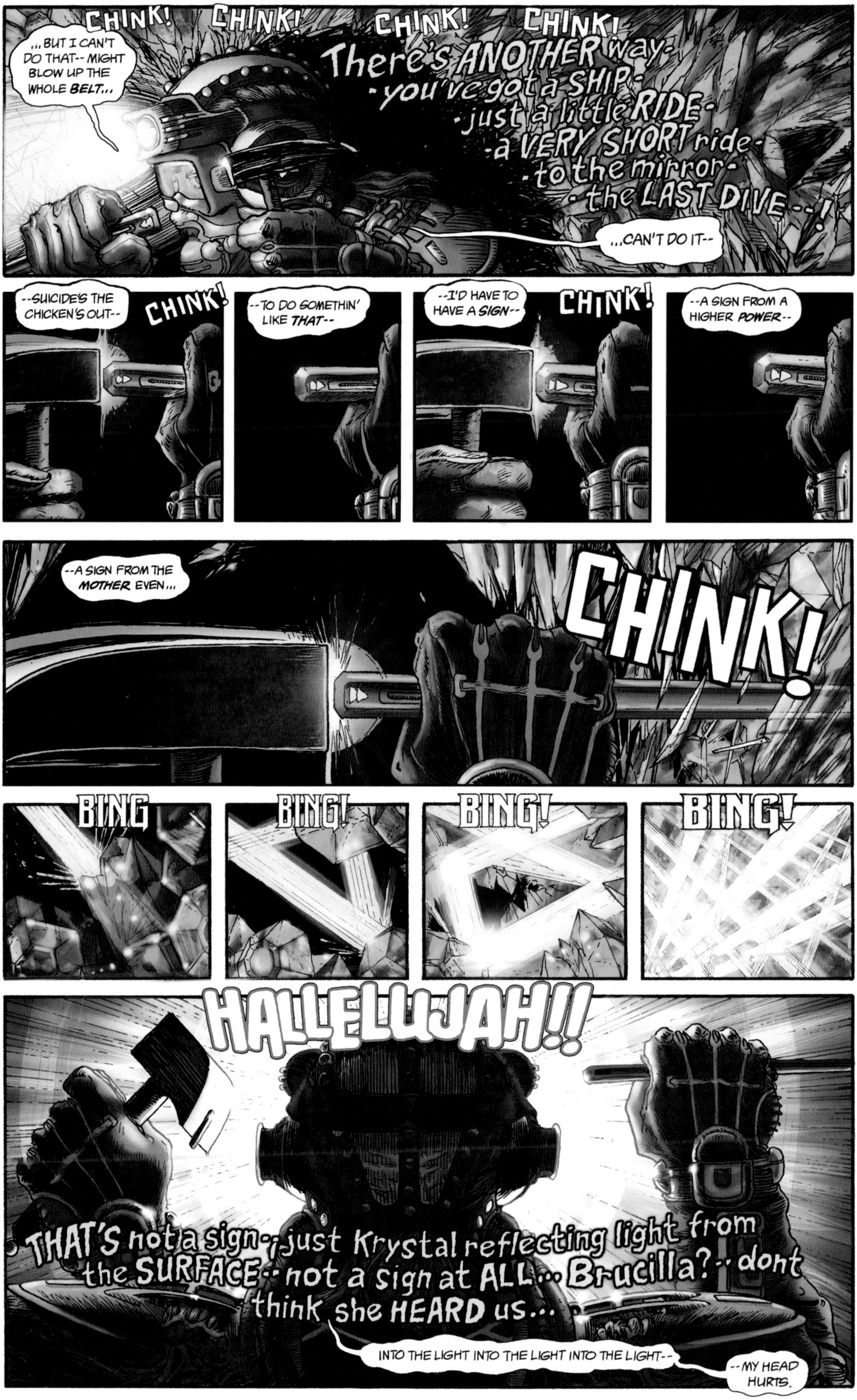
CHINK! CHINK! CHINK! CHINK!
...BUT I CAN'T DO THAT-- MIGHT BLOW UP THE WHOLE BELT...
There's ANOTHER way- -you've got a SHIP- -just a little RIDE- -a VERY SHORT ride- -to the mirror- -the LAST DIVE--!
...CAN'T DO IT--
--SUICIDE'S THE CHICKEN'S OUT--
CHINK!
--TO DO SOMETHIN' LIKE THAT--
--I'D HAVE TO HAVE A SIGN--
CHINK!
--A SIGN FROM A HIGHER POWER--
--A SIGN FROM THE MOTHER EVEN...
CHINK!
BING
BING!
BING!
BING!
HALLELUJAH!!
THAT'S not a sign-- just Krystal reflecting light from the SURFACE-- not a sign at ALL... Brucilla?-- dont think she HEARD us...
INTO THE LIGHT INTO THE LIGHT INTO THE LIGHT--
--MY HEAD HURTS.

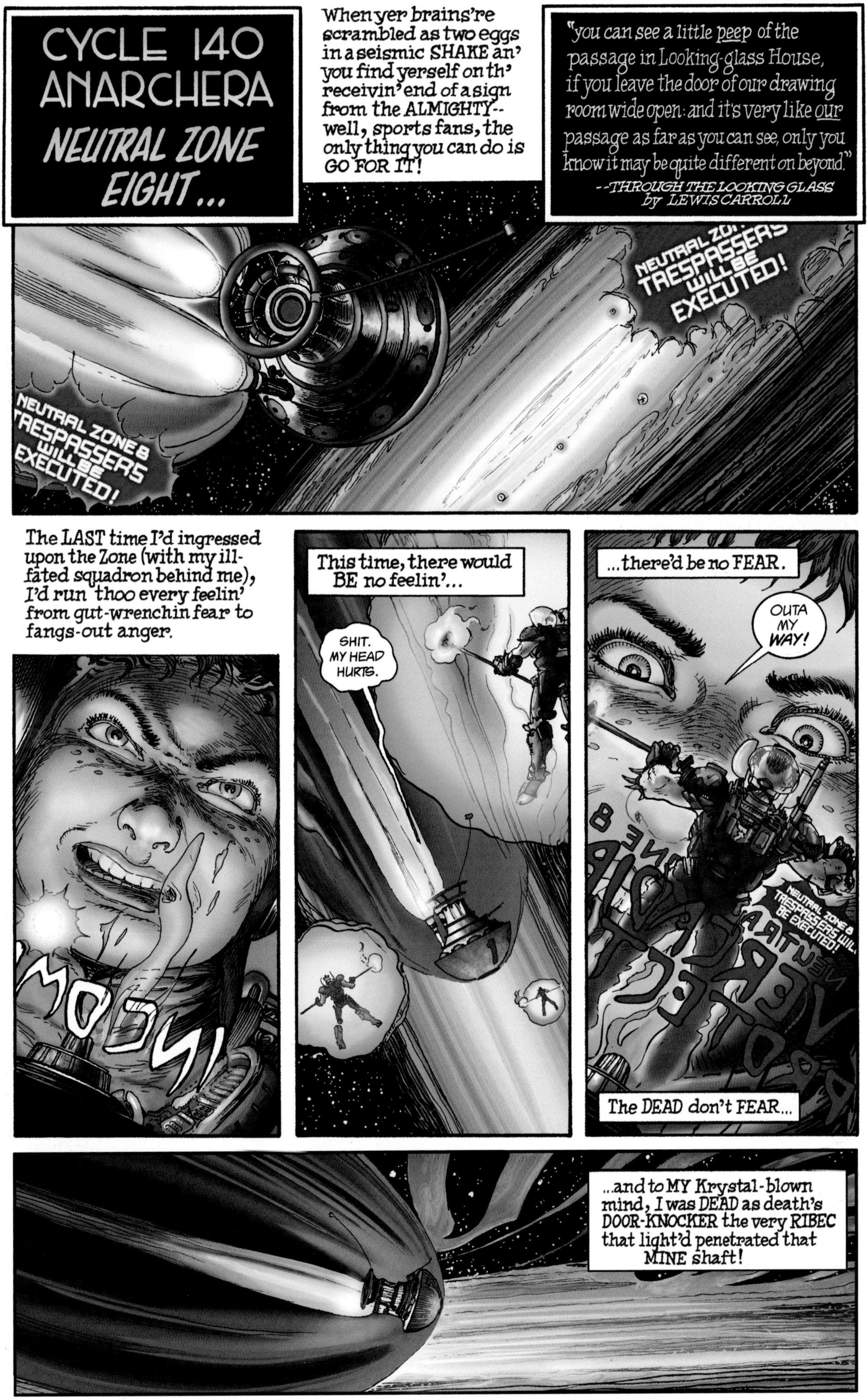
CYCLE 140 ANARCHERA
NEUTRAL ZONE EIGHT...
When yer brains're scrambled as two eggs in a seismic SHAKE an' you find yerself on th' receivin' end of a sign from the ALMIGHTY-- well, sports fans, the only thing you can do is GO FOR IT!
"you can see a little peep of the passage in Looking-glass House, if you leave the door of our drawing room wide open: and it's very like our passage as far as you can see, only you know it may be quite different on beyond."
--THROUGH THE LOOKING GLASS by LEWIS CARROLL
TRESPASSERS WILL BE EXECUTED!
NEUTRAL ZONE 8 TRESPASSERS WILL BE EXECUTED!
The LAST time I'd ingressed upon the Zone (with my ill-fated squadron behind me), I'd run 'thoo every feelin' from gut-wrenchin fear to fangs-out anger.
This time, there would BE no feelin'...
SHIT. MY HEAD HURTS.
...there'd be no FEAR.
OUTA MY WAY!
NEUTRAL ZONE 8 TRESPASSERS WILL BE EXECUTED!
The DEAD don't FEAR...
...and to MY Krystal-blown mind, I was DEAD as death's DOOR-KNOCKER the very RIBEC that light'd penetrated that MINE shaft!

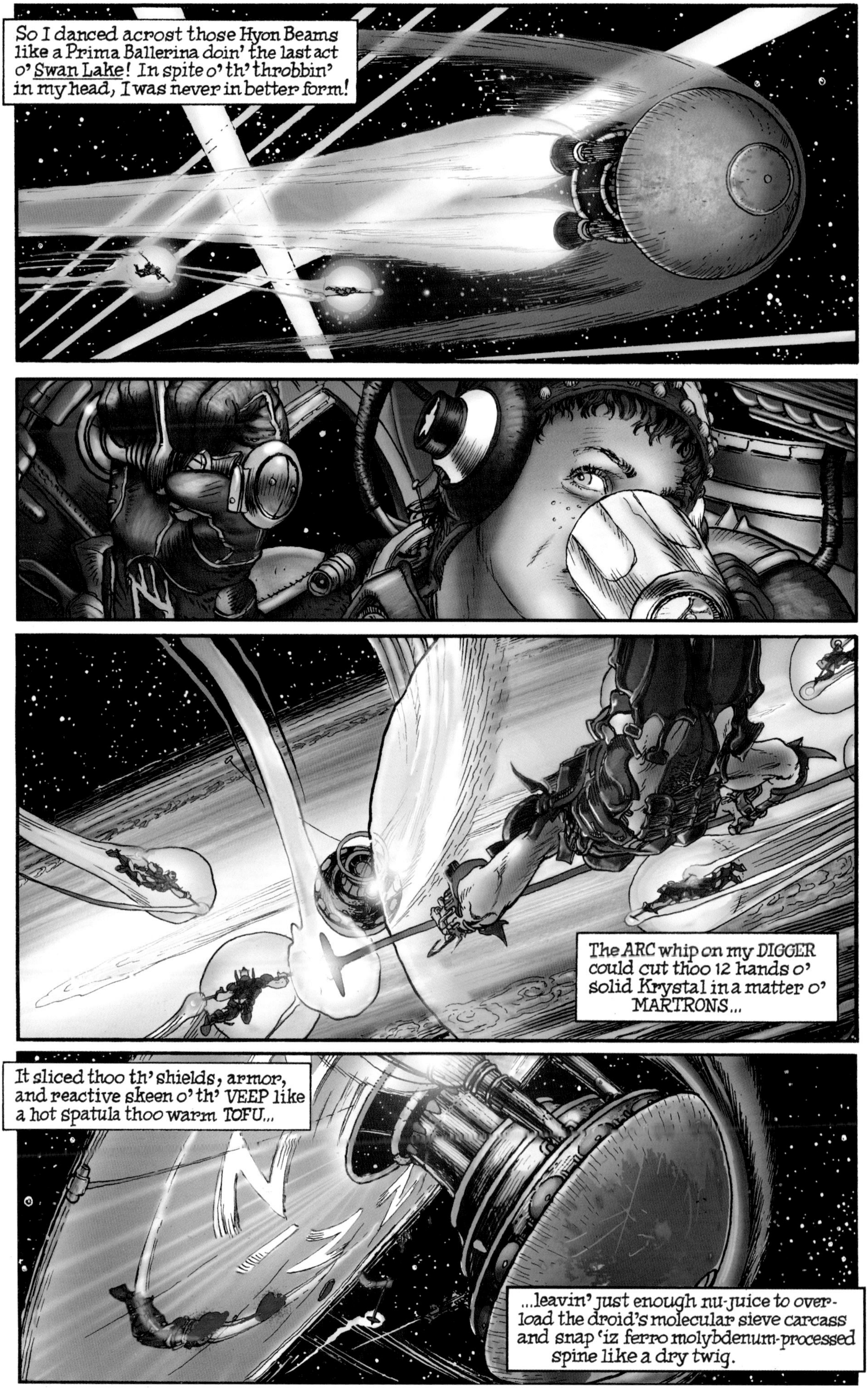
So I danced acrost those Hyon Beams like a Prima Ballerina doin' the last act o' Swan Lake! In spite o' th' throbbin' in my head, I was never in better form!
The ARC whip on my DIGGER could cut thoo 12 hands o' solid Krystal in a matter o' MARTRONS...
It sliced thoo th' shields, armor, and reactive skeen o' th' VEEP like a hot spatula thoo warm TOFU...
...leavin' just enough nu-juice to overload the droid's molecular sieve carcass and snap 'iz ferro molybdenum-processed spine like a dry twig.

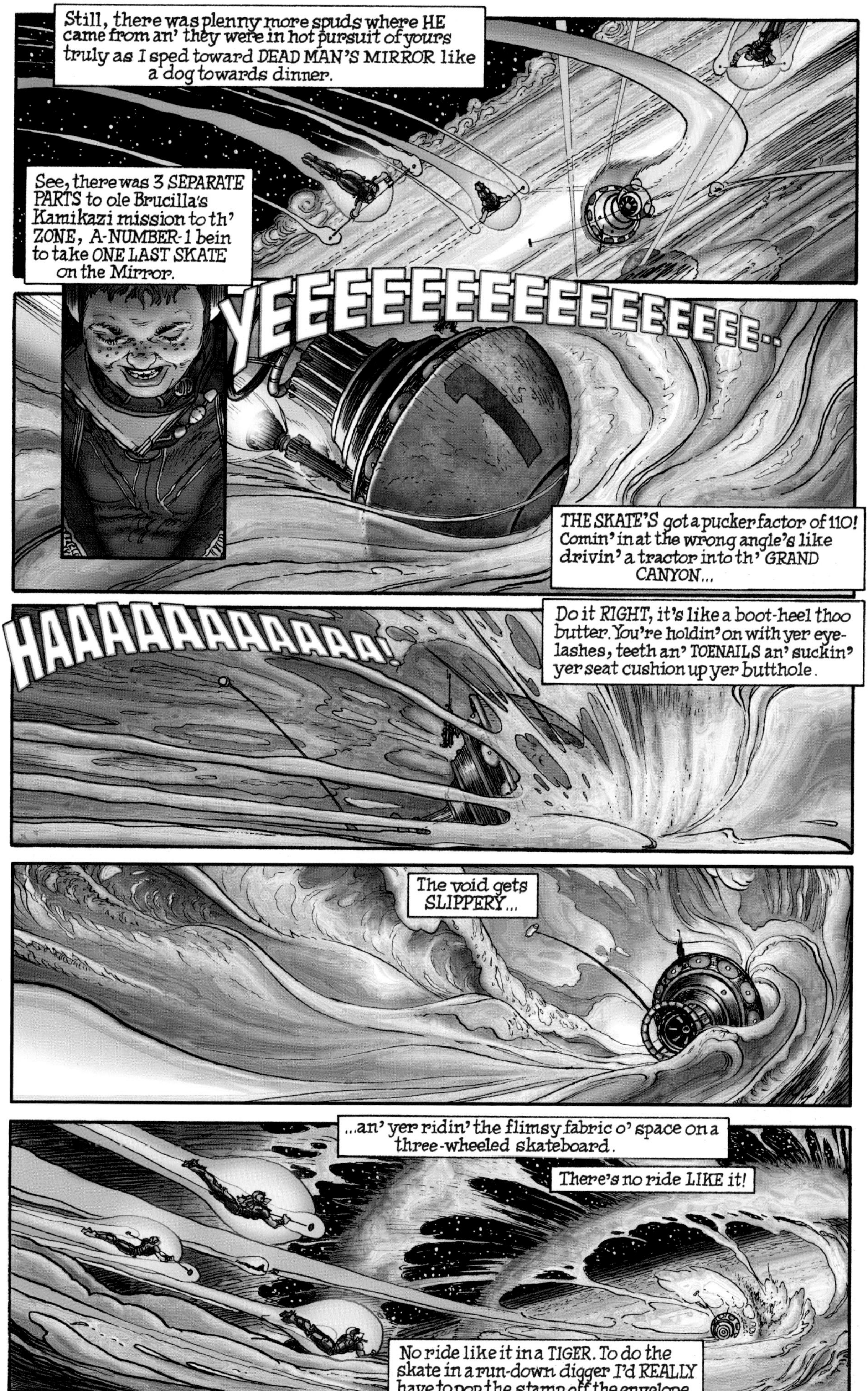
Still, there was plenny more spuds where HE came from an' they were in hot pursuit of yours truly as I sped toward DEAD MAN'S MIRROR like a dog towards dinner.
See, there was 3 SEPARATE PARTS to ole Brucilla's Kamikazi mission to th' ZONE, A-NUMBER-1 bein to take ONE LAST SKATE on the Mirror.
YEEEEEEEEEEEEEEE..
THE SKATE'S got a pucker factor of 110! Comin' in at the wrong angle's like drivin' a tractor into th' GRAND CANYON...
HAAAAAAAAAAAA!
Do it RIGHT, it's like a boot-heel thoo butter. You're holdin' on with yer eye-lashes, teeth an' TOENAILS an' suckin' yer seat cushion up yer butthole.
The void gets SLIPPERY...
...an' yer ridin' the flimsy fabric o' space on a three-wheeled skateboard.
There's no ride LIKE it!
No ride like it in a TIGER. To do the skate in a run-down digger I'd REALLY have to pop the stamp off the envelope.

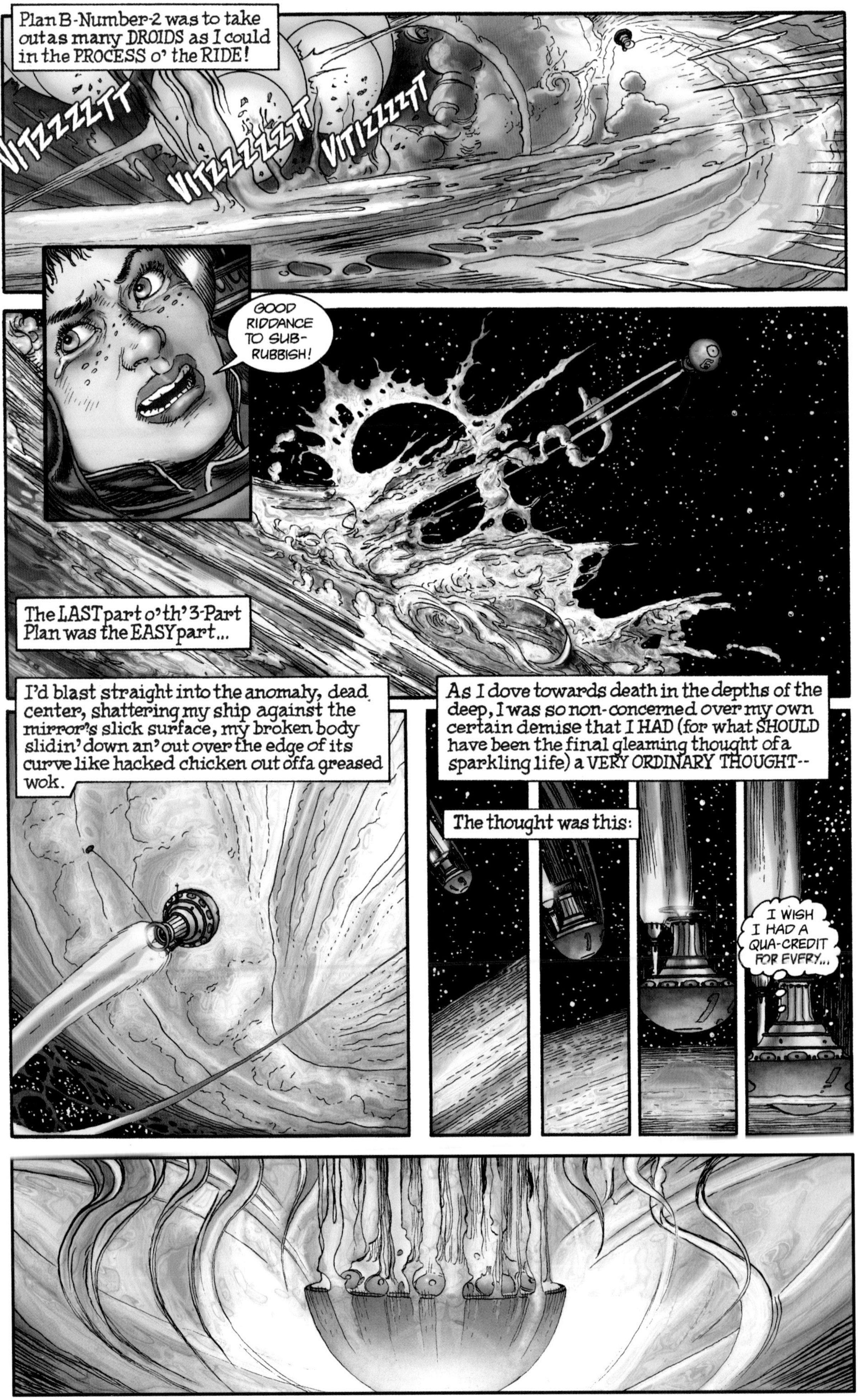

Plan B-Number-2 was to take out as many DROIDS as I could in the PROCESS o' the RIDE!
VITZZZZTT
VITZZZZZZTT
VITIZZZZTT
GOOD RIDDANCE TO SUB-RUBBISH!
The LAST part o'th' 3-Part Plan was the EASY part...
I'd blast straight into the anomaly, dead center, shattering my ship against the mirror's slick surface, my broken body slidin' down an' out over the edge of its curve like hacked chicken out offa greased wok.
As I dove towards death in the depths of the deep, I was so non-concerned over my own certain demise that I HAD (for what SHOULD have been the final gleaming thought of a sparkling life) a VERY ORDINARY THOUGHT--
The thought was this:
I WISH I HAD A QUA-CREDIT FOR EVERY...

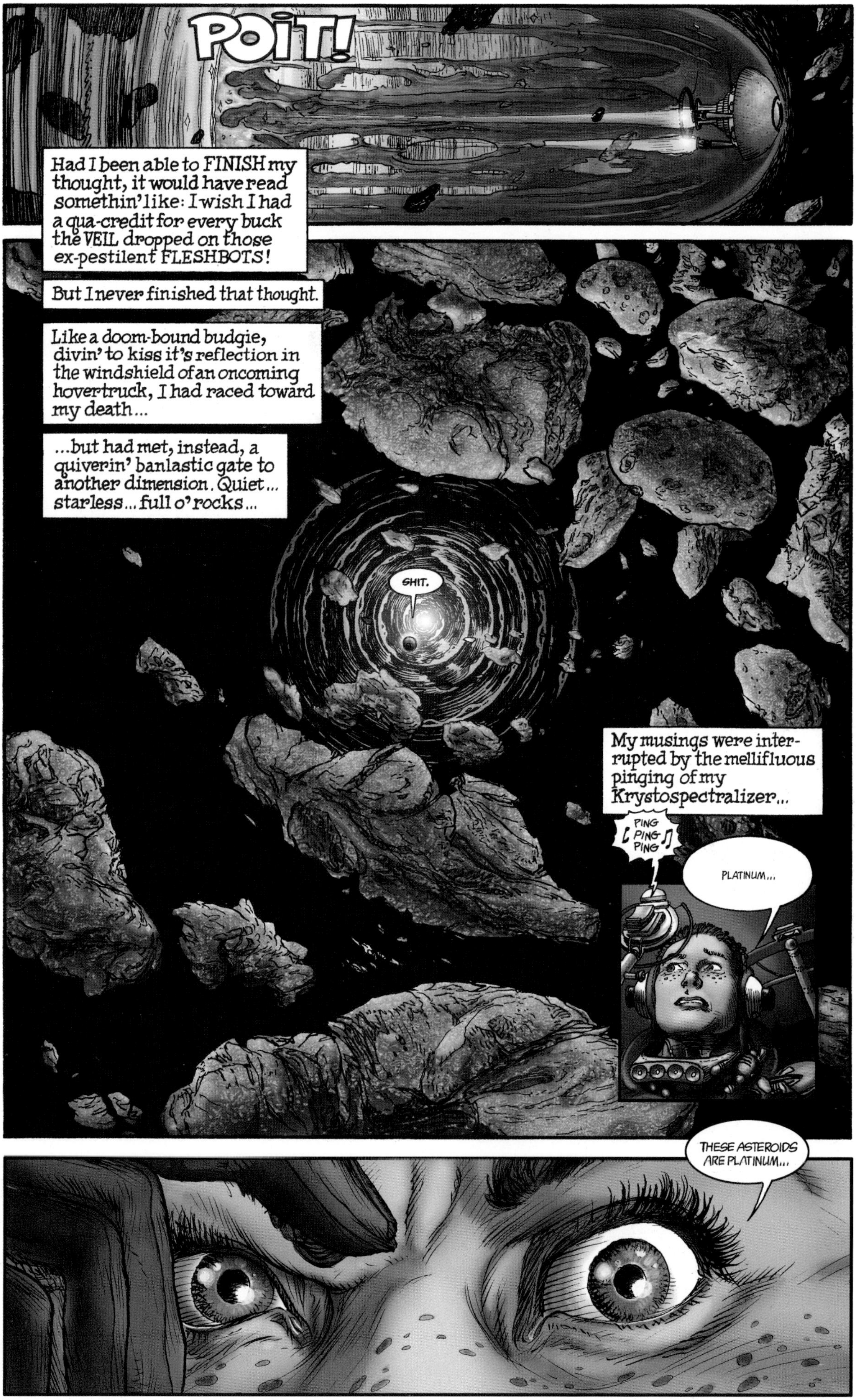
POIT!
Had I been able to FINISH my thought, it would have read somethin' like: I wish I had a qua-credit for every buck the VEIL dropped on those ex-pestilent FLESHBOTS!
But I never finished that thought.
Like a doom-bound budgie, divin' to kiss it's reflection in the windshield of an oncoming hovertruck, I had raced toward my death...
...but had met, instead, a quiverin' banlastic gate to another dimension. Quiet... starless... full o' rocks...
SHIT.
My musings were interrupted by the mellifluous pinging of my Krystospectralizer...
PING PING PING
PLATINUM...
THESE ASTEROIDS ARE PLATINUM...

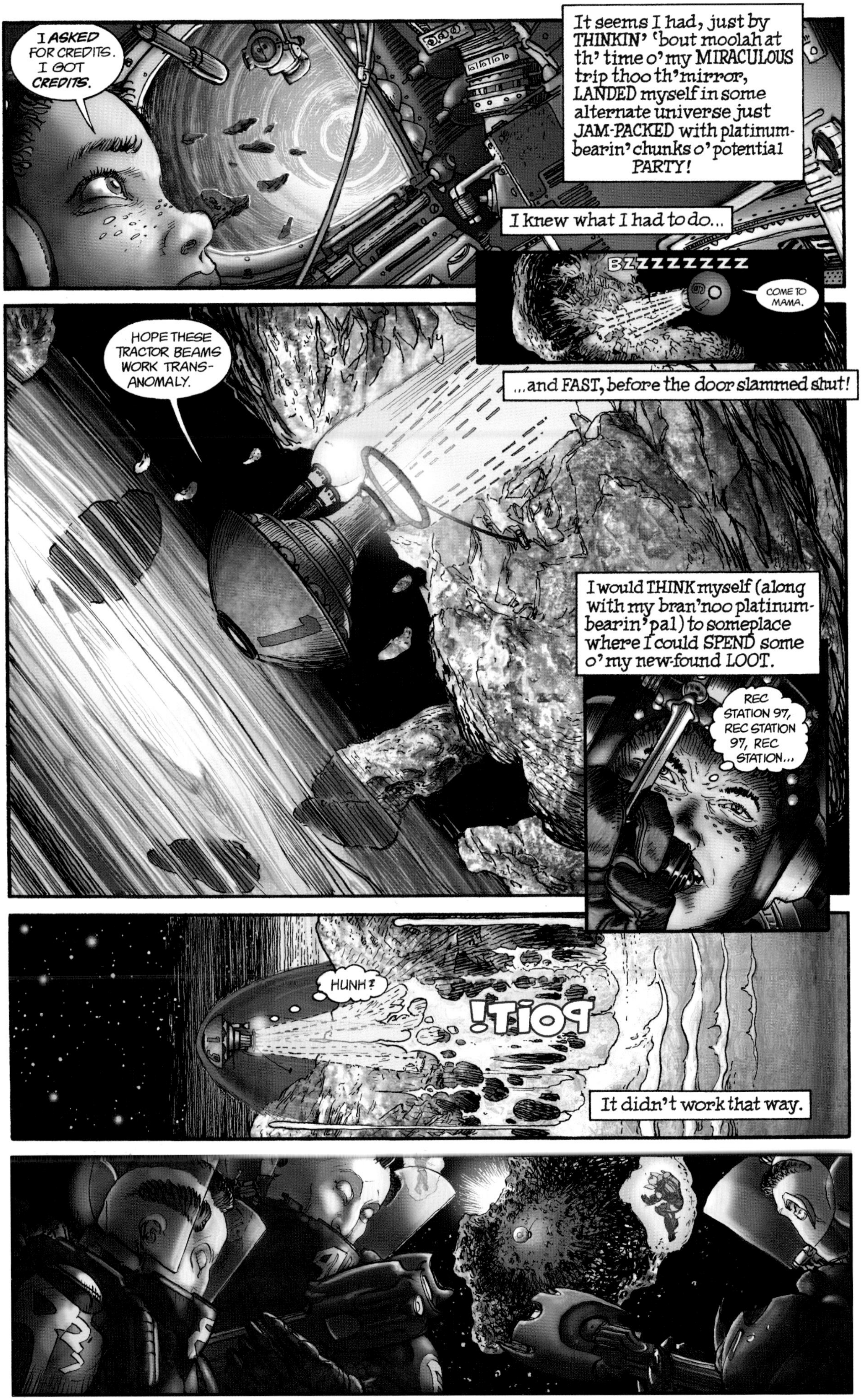

I ASKED FOR CREDITS. I GOT CREDITS.
It seems I had, just by THINKIN' 'bout moolah at th' time o' my MIRACULOUS trip thoo th' mirror, LANDED myself in some alternate universe just JAM-PACKED with platinum-bearin' chunks o' potential PARTY!
I knew what I had to do...
BZZZZZZZZ
COME TO MAMA.
HOPE THESE TRACTOR BEAMS WORK TRANS-ANOMALY.
...and FAST, before the door slammed shut!
I would THINK myself (along with my bran'noo platinum-bearin' pal) to someplace where I could SPEND some o' my new-found LOOT.
REC STATION 97, REC STATION 97, REC STATION...
HUNH?
POIT!
It didn't work that way.

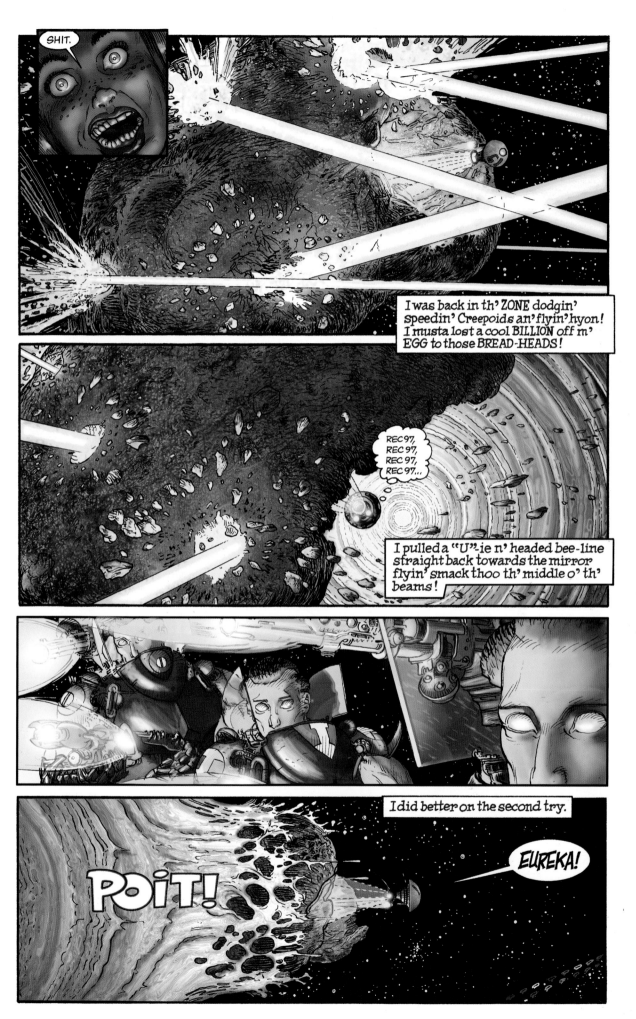

SHIT.

I was back in th' ZONE dodgin' speedin' Creepoids an' flyin' hyon! I musta lost a cool BILLION off m' EGG to those BREAD-HEADS!

REC 97, REC 97, REC 97, REC 97...

I pulled a "U"-ie n' headed bee-line straight back towards the mirror flyin' smack thoo th' middle o' th' beams!

I did better on the second try.

POIT!

EUREKA!

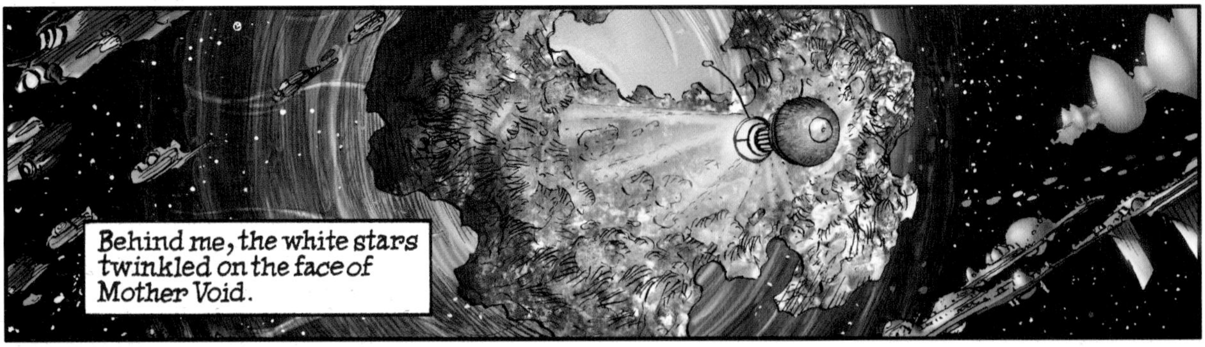
Behind me, the white stars twinkled on the face of Mother Void.

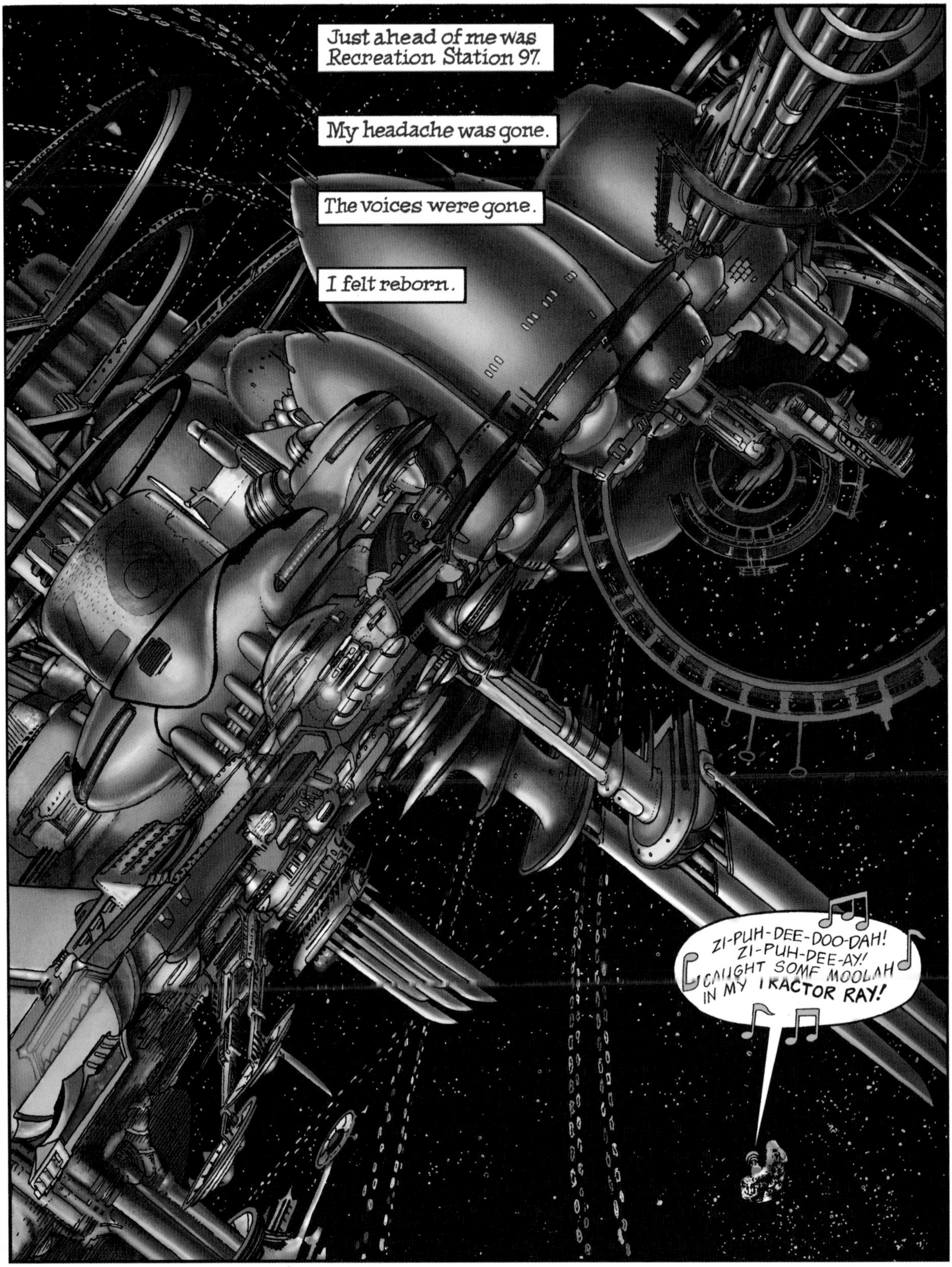
Just ahead of me was Recreation Station 97.
My headache was gone.
The voices were gone.
I felt reborn.
ZI-PUH-DEE-DOO-DAH! ZI-PUH-DEE-AY! CAUGHT SOME MOOLAH IN MY TRACTOR RAY!

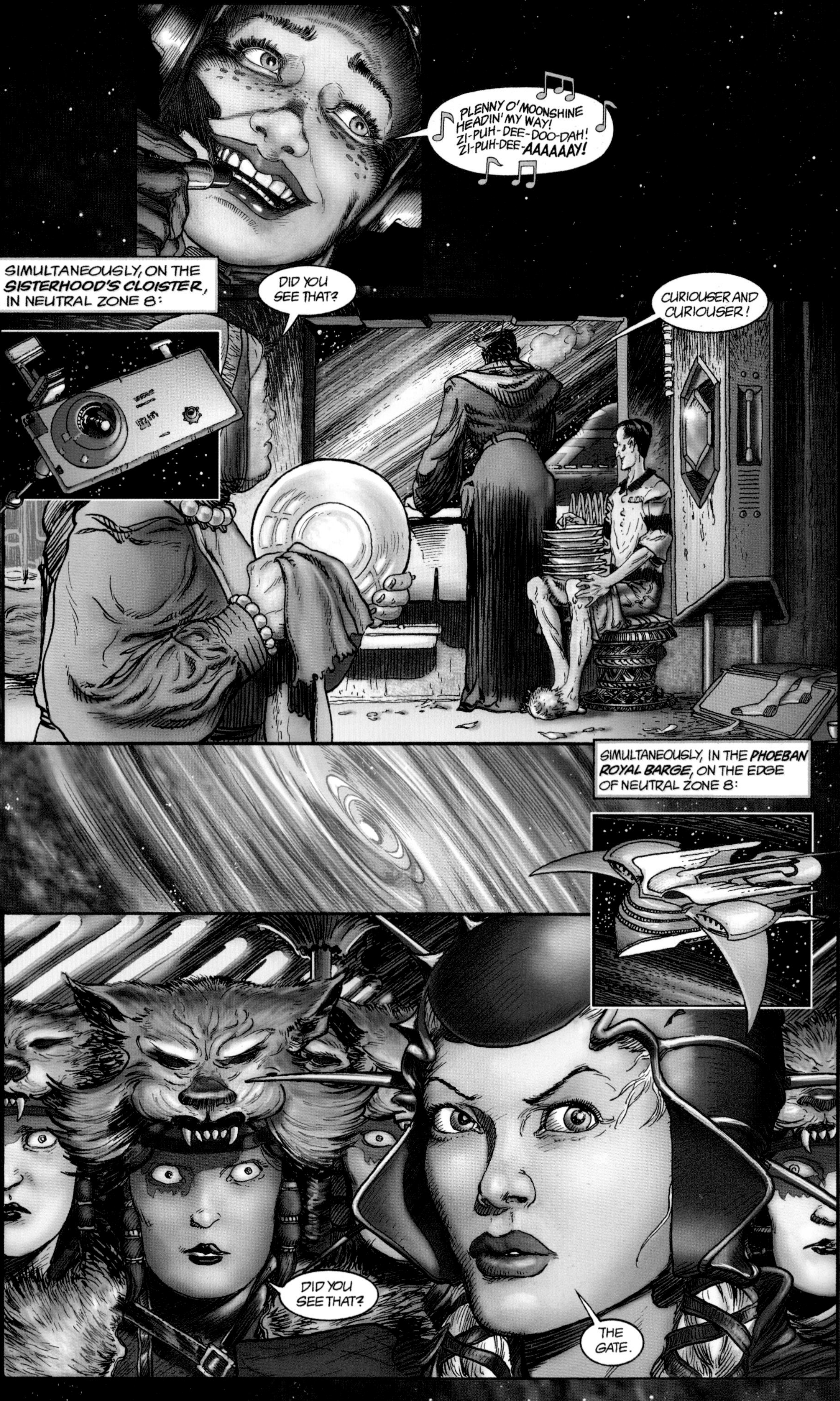
PLENNY O'MOONSHINE HEADIN' MY WAY! ZI-PUH-DEE-DOO-DAH! ZI-PUH-DEE-AAAAAAY!
SIMULTANEOUSLY, ON THE SISTERHOOD'S CLOISTER, IN NEUTRAL ZONE 8:
DID YOU SEE THAT?
CURIOUSER AND CURIOUSER!
SIMULTANEOUSLY, IN THE PHOEBAN ROYAL BARGE, ON THE EDGE OF NEUTRAL ZONE 8:
DID YOU SEE THAT?
THE GATE.

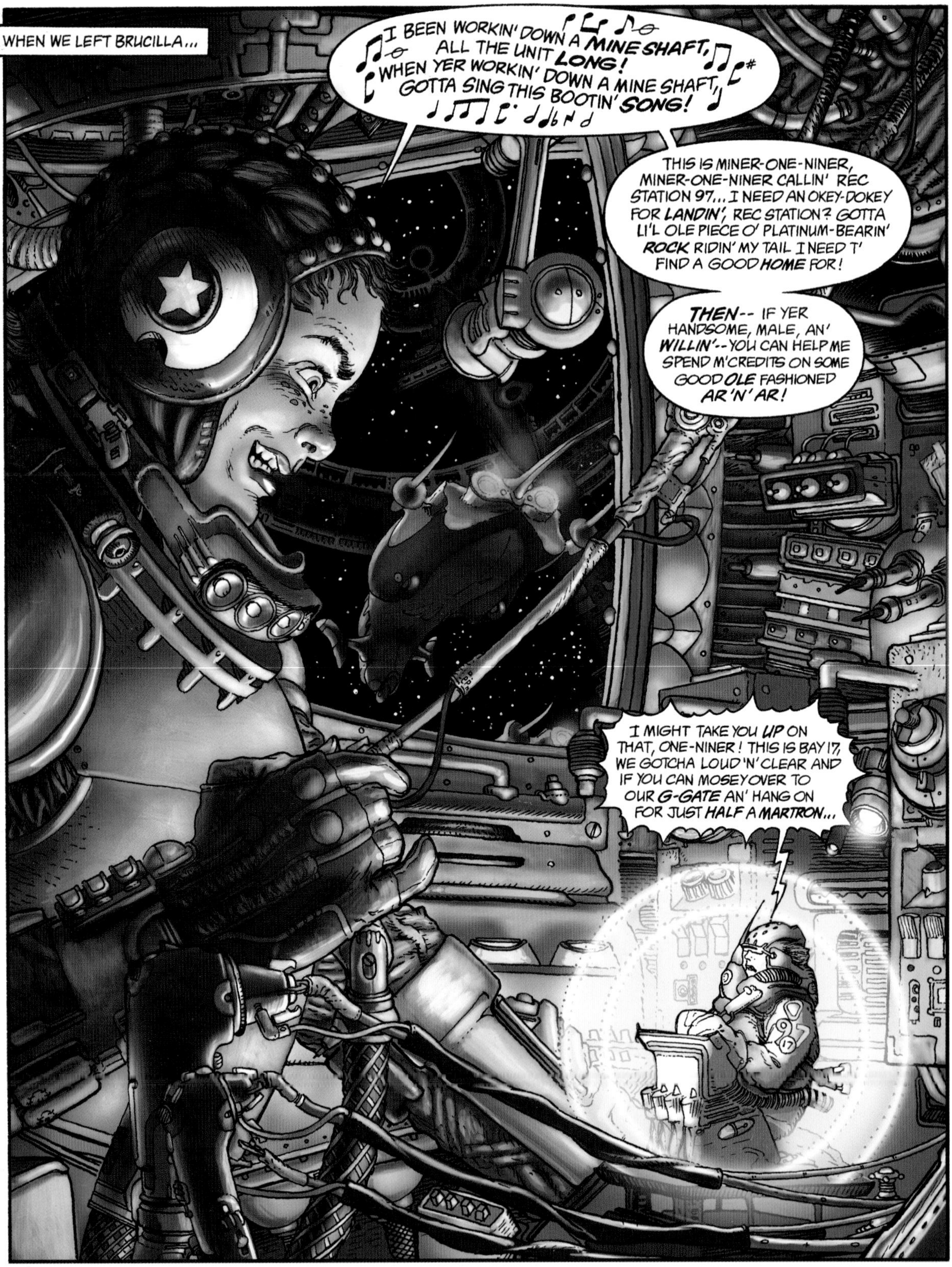
WHEN WE LEFT BRUCILLA...
I BEEN WORKIN' DOWN A MINE SHAFT, ALL THE UNIT LONG! WHEN YER WORKIN' DOWN A MINE SHAFT, GOTTA SING THIS BOOTIN' SONG!
THIS IS MINER-ONE-NINER, MINER-ONE-NINER CALLIN' REC STATION 97... I NEED AN OKEY-DOKEY FOR LANDIN', REC STATION? GOTTA LI'L OLE PIECE O' PLATINUM-BEARIN' ROCK RIDIN' MY TAIL I NEED T' FIND A GOOD HOME FOR!
THEN-- IF YER HANDSOME, MALE, AN' WILLIN'--YOU CAN HELP ME SPEND M'CREDITS ON SOME GOOD OLE FASHIONED AR'N'AR!
I MIGHT TAKE YOU UP ON THAT, ONE-NINER! THIS IS BAY 17, WE GOTCHA LOUD 'N' CLEAR AND IF YOU CAN MOSEY OVER TO OUR G-GATE AN' HANG ON FOR JUST HALF A MARTRON...

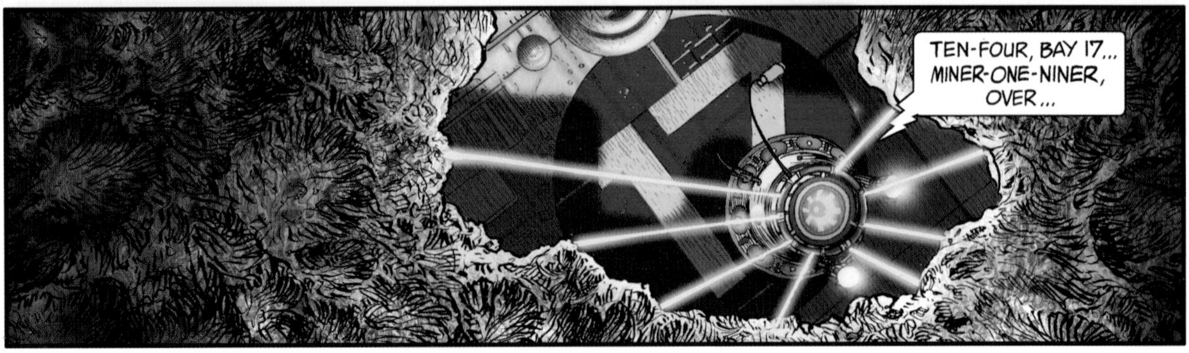
TEN-FOUR, BAY 17... MINER-ONE-NINER, OVER...

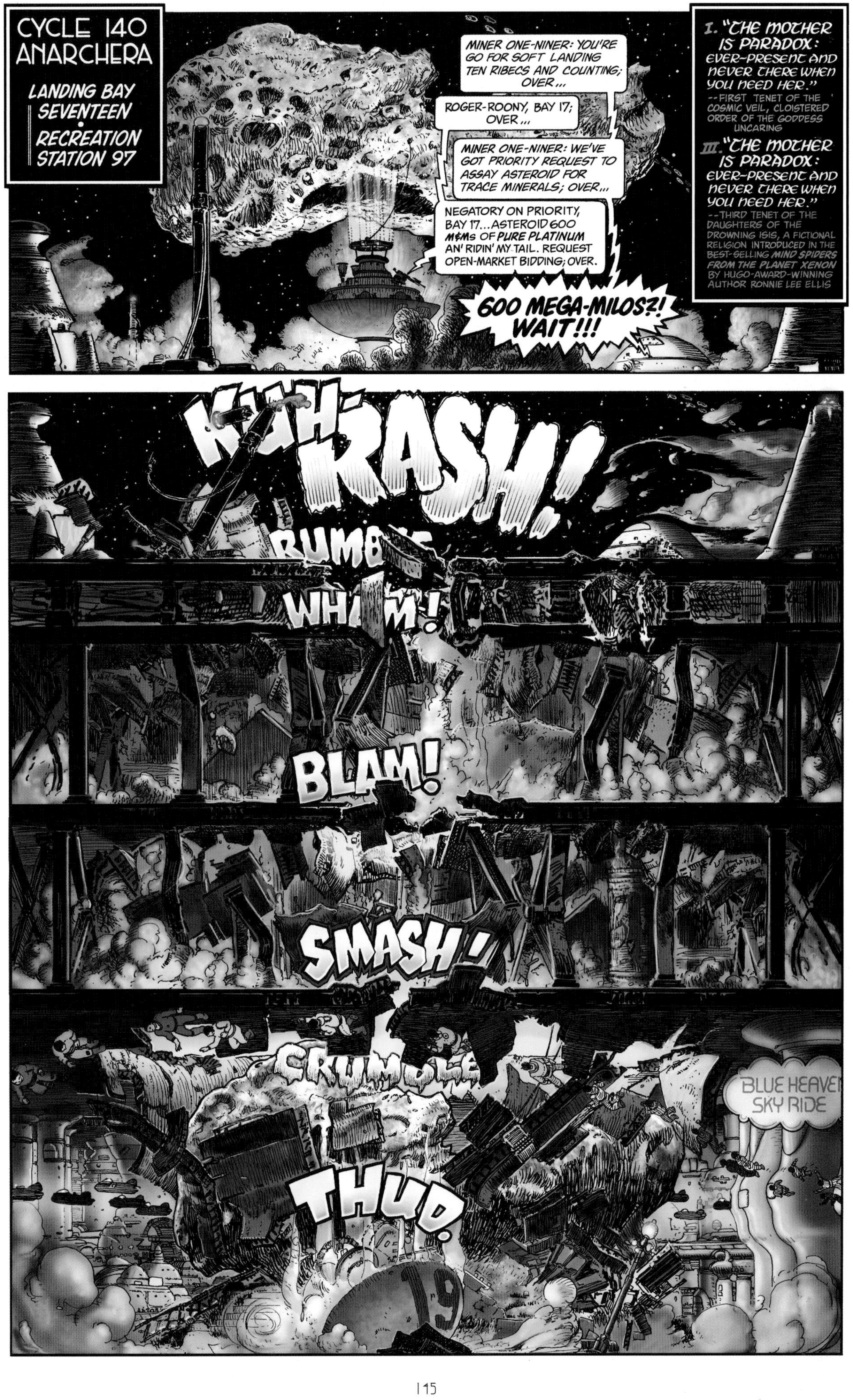
CYCLE 140
ANARCHERA
LANDING BAY SEVENTEEN • RECREATION STATION 97
MINER ONE-NINER: YOU'RE GO FOR SOFT LANDING TEN RIBECS AND COUNTING; OVER...
ROGER-ROONY, BAY 17; OVER...
MINER ONE-NINER: WE'VE GOT PRIORITY REQUEST TO ASSAY ASTEROID FOR TRACE MINERALS; OVER...
NEGATORY ON PRIORITY, BAY 17... ASTEROID 600 M$MS OF PURE PLATINUM AN' RIDIN' MY TAIL. REQUEST OPEN-MARKET BIDDING; OVER.
600 MEGA-MILOS?! WAIT!!!
I. "THE MOTHER IS PARADOX: EVER-PRESENT AND NEVER THERE WHEN YOU NEED HER."
--FIRST TENET OF THE COSMIC VEIL, CLOISTERED ORDER OF THE GODDESS UNCARING
III. "THE MOTHER IS PARADOX: EVER-PRESENT AND NEVER THERE WHEN YOU NEED HER."
--THIRD TENET OF THE DAUGHTERS OF THE DROWNING ISIS, A FICTIONAL RELIGION INTRODUCED IN THE BEST-SELLING MIND SPIDERS FROM THE PLANET XENON BY HUGO-AWARD-WINNING AUTHOR RONNIE LEE ELLIS
BLAM!
SMASH!
THUD!
BLUE HEAVEN SKY RIDE

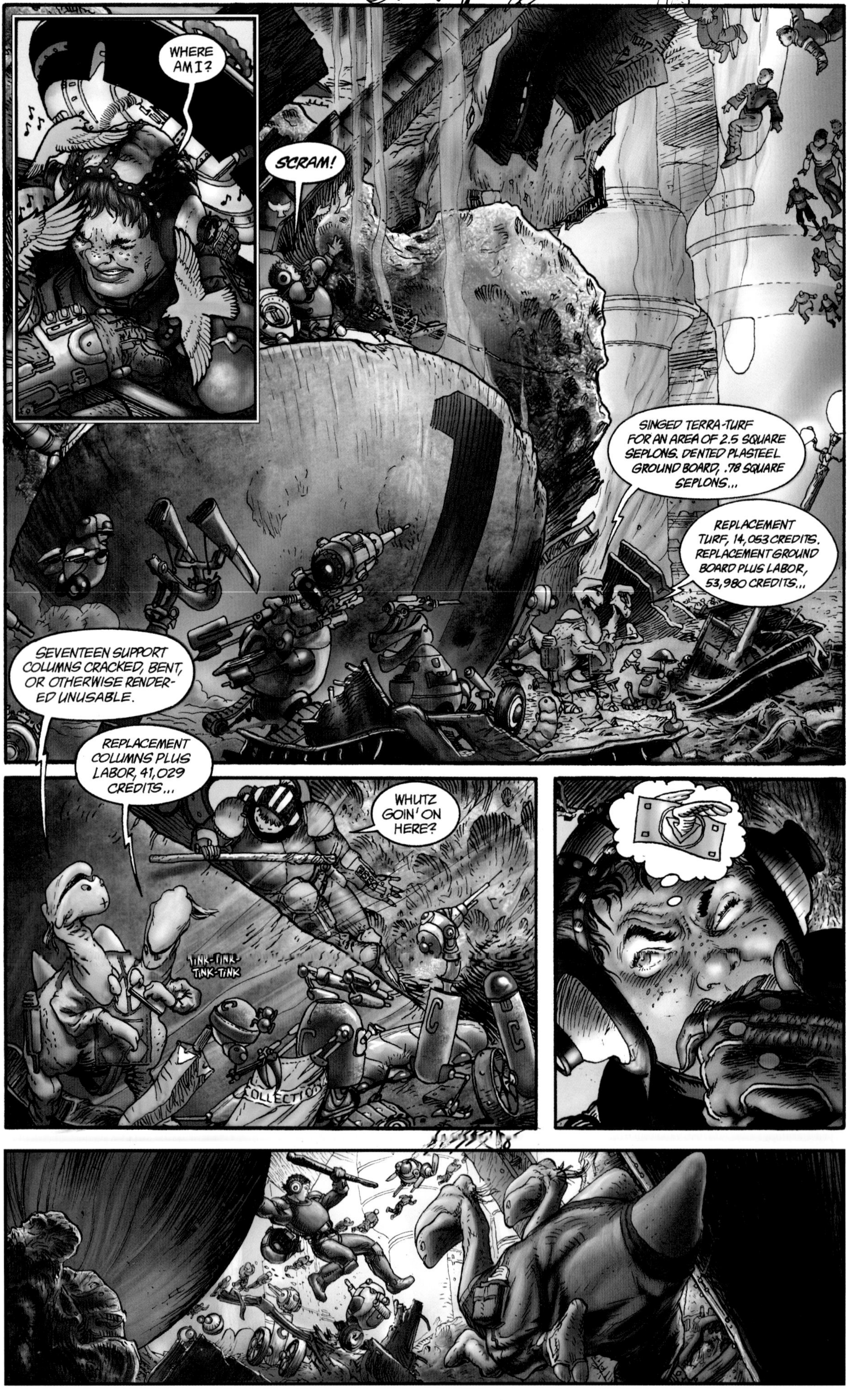
WHERE AM I?
SCRAM!
SINGED TERRA-TURF FOR AN AREA OF 2.5 SQUARE SEPLONS. DENTED PLASTEEL GROUND BOARD, .78 SQUARE SEPLONS...
REPLACEMENT TURF, 14,053 CREDITS. REPLACEMENT GROUND BOARD PLUS LABOR, 53,980 CREDITS...
SEVENTEEN SUPPORT COLUMNS CRACKED, BENT, OR OTHERWISE RENDERED UNUSABLE.
REPLACEMENT COLUMNS PLUS LABOR, 41,029 CREDITS...
WHUTZ GOIN' ON HERE?
TINK-TINK-TINK-TINK
COLLECTION

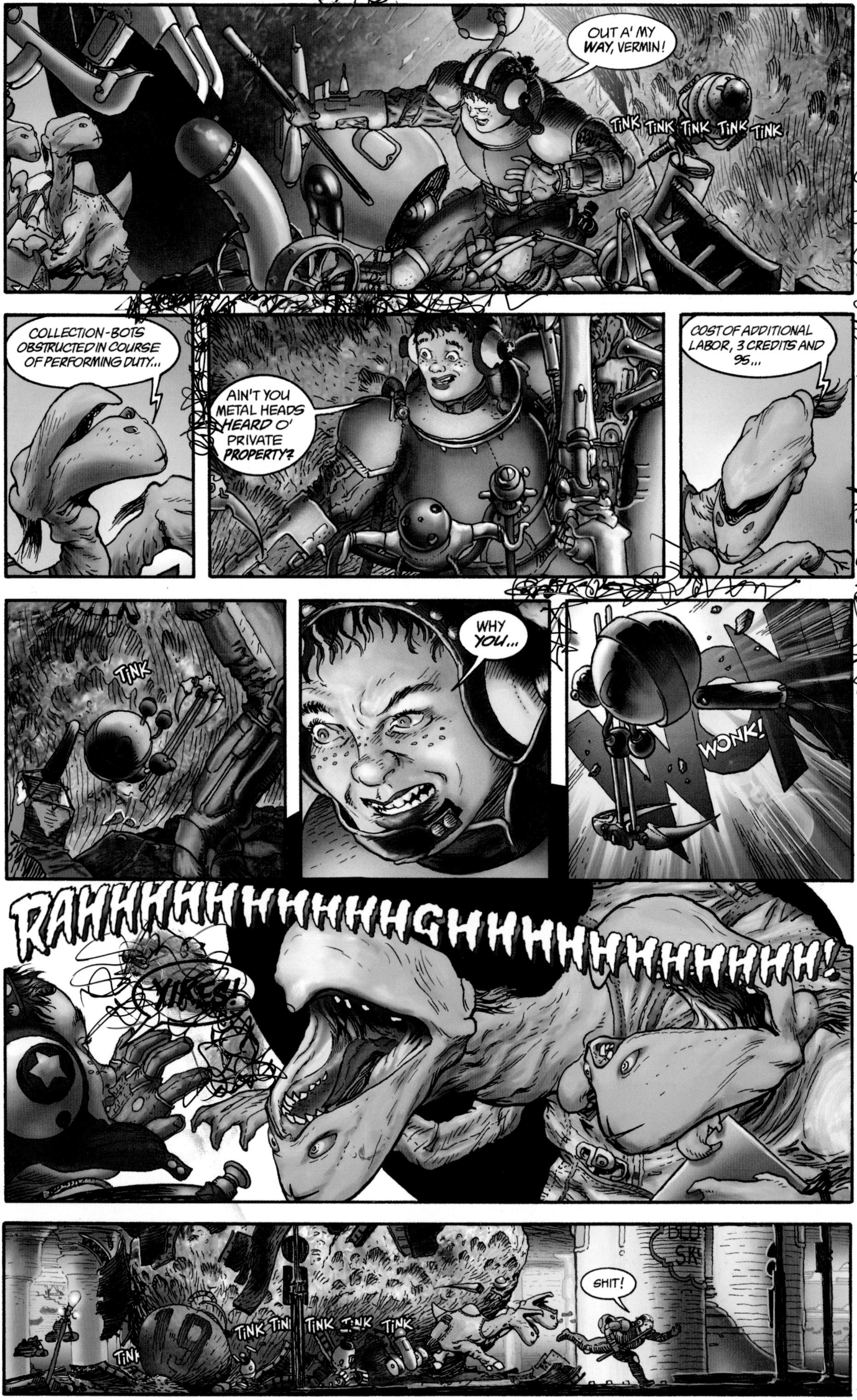
OUT A' MY WAY, VERMIN!
TINK TINK TINK TINK TINK
COLLECTION-BOTS OBSTRUCTED IN COURSE OF PERFORMING DUTY...
AIN'T YOU METAL HEADS HEARD O' PRIVATE PROPERTY?
COST OF ADDITIONAL LABOR, 3 CREDITS AND 95...
TINK
WHY YOU...
WONK!
RAHHHHHHHHHHHHGHHHHHHHHHHHHHH!
YIKES!
SHIT!
TINK TINK TINK TINK TINK TINK

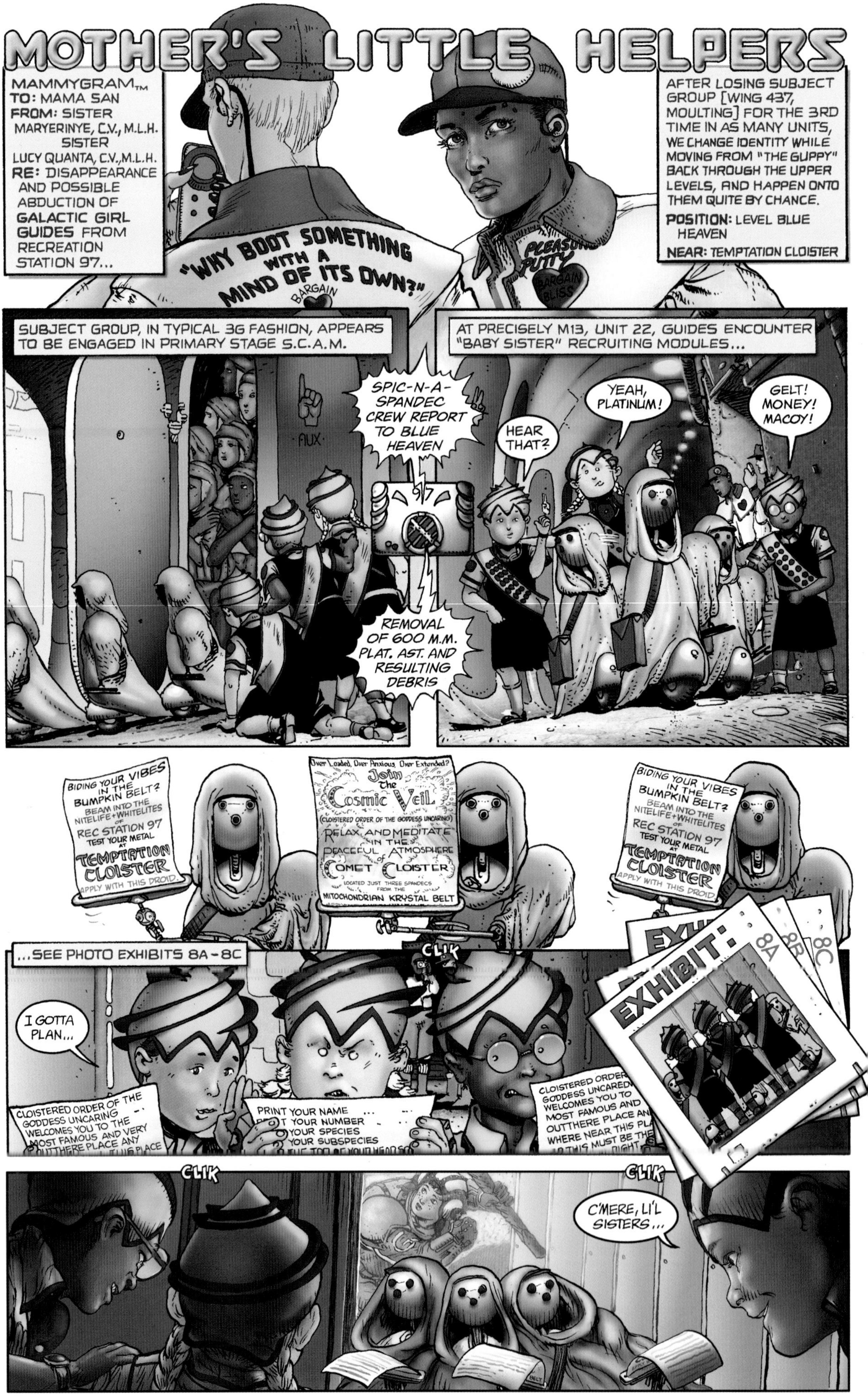
MOTHER'S LITTLE HELPERS
MAMMYGRAM™ TO: MAMA SAN FROM: SISTER MARYERINYE, C.V., M.L.H. SISTER LUCY QUANTA, C.V., M.L.H. RE: DISAPPEARANCE AND POSSIBLE ABDUCTION OF GALACTIC GIRL GUIDES FROM RECREATION STATION 97...
"WHY BOOT SOMETHING WITH A MIND OF ITS OWN?"
BARGAIN
PLEASURE PUTTY
BARGAIN BLISS
AFTER LOSING SUBJECT GROUP [WING 437, MOULTING] FOR THE 3RD TIME IN AS MANY UNITS, WE CHANGE IDENTITY WHILE MOVING FROM "THE GUPPY" BACK THROUGH THE UPPER LEVELS, AND HAPPEN ONTO THEM QUITE BY CHANCE.
POSITION: LEVEL BLUE HEAVEN
NEAR: TEMPTATION CLOISTER
SUBJECT GROUP, IN TYPICAL 3G FASHION, APPEARS TO BE ENGAGED IN PRIMARY STAGE S.C.A.M.
AUX
SPIC-N-A-SPANDEC CREW REPORT TO BLUE HEAVEN
REMOVAL OF 600 M.M. PLAT. AST. AND RESULTING DEBRIS
AT PRECISELY M13, UNIT 22, GUIDES ENCOUNTER "BABY SISTER" RECRUITING MODULES...
HEAR THAT?
YEAH, PLATINUM!
GELT! MONEY! MACOY!
BIDING YOUR VIBES IN THE BUMPKIN BELT? BEAM INTO THE NITELIFE + WHITELITES OF REC STATION 97 TEST YOUR METAL AT TEMPTATION CLOISTER APPLY WITH THIS DROID
Over Loaded, Over Anxious, Over Extended? Join the Cosmic Veil (CLOISTERED ORDER OF THE GODDESS UNCARING) RELAX AND MEDITATE IN THE PEACEFUL ATMOSPHERE OF COMET CLOISTER LOCATED JUST THREE SPANDECS FROM THE MITOCHONDRIAN KRYSTAL BELT
BIDING YOUR VIBES IN THE BUMPKIN BELT? BEAM INTO THE NITELIFE + WHITELITES OF REC STATION 97 TEST YOUR METAL AT TEMPTATION CLOISTER APPLY WITH THIS DROID
...SEE PHOTO EXHIBITS 8A - 8C
CLIK
I GOTTA PLAN...
CLOISTERED ORDER OF THE GODDESS UNCARING WELCOMES YOU TO THE MOST FAMOUS AND VERY OUTTHERE PLACE ANY
PRINT YOUR NAME ... YOUR NUMBER YOUR SPECIES YOUR SUBSPECIES
CLOISTERED ORDER GODDESS UNCARED WELCOMES YOU TO MOST FAMOUS AND OUTTHERE PLACE AN WHERE NEAR THIS PLA
EXHIBIT: 8A
8B
8C
CLIK
CLIK
C'MERE, LI'L SISTERS...

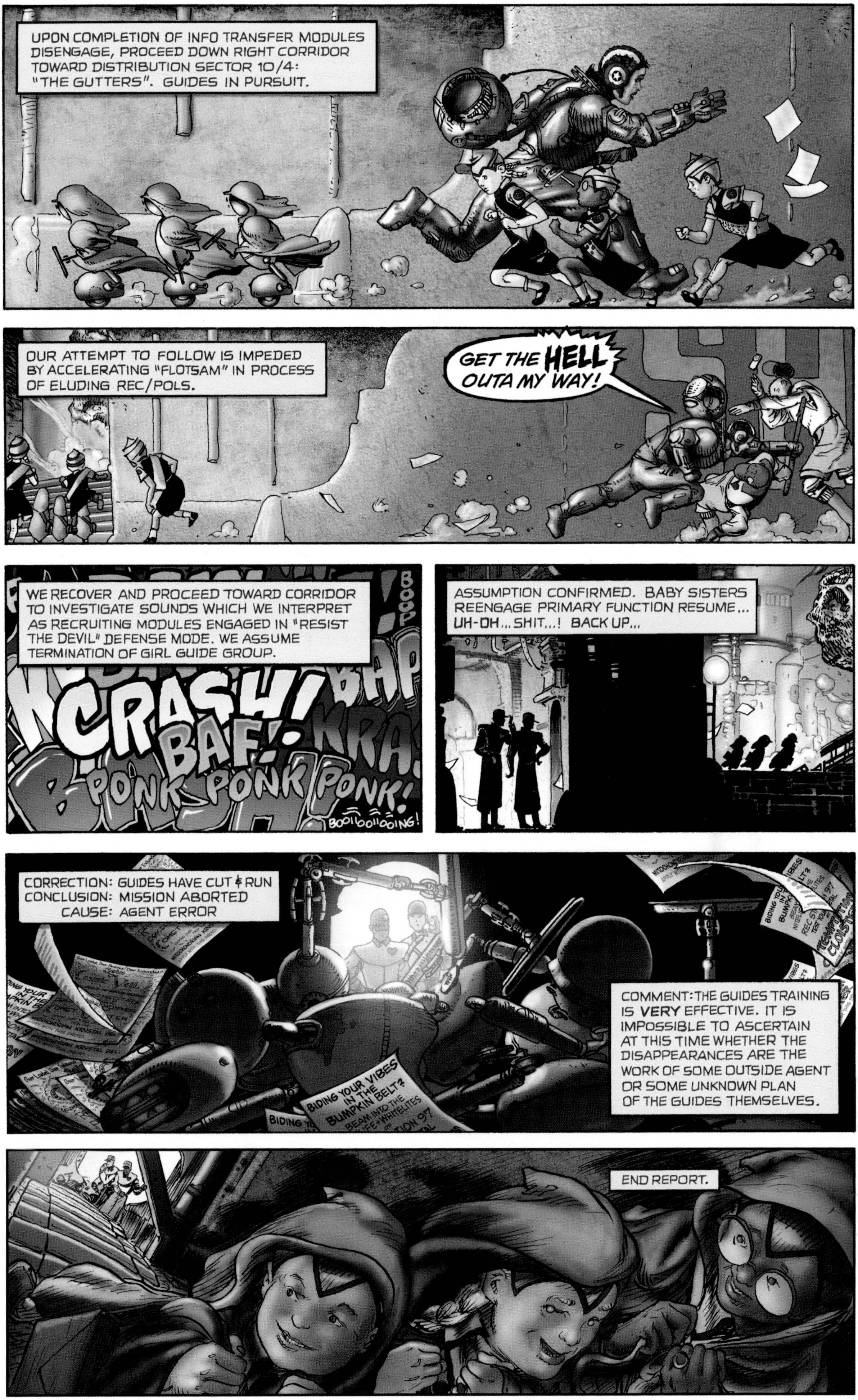
UPON COMPLETION OF INFO TRANSFER MODULES DISENGAGE, PROCEED DOWN RIGHT CORRIDOR TOWARD DISTRIBUTION SECTOR 10/4: "THE GUTTERS". GUIDES IN PURSUIT.
OUR ATTEMPT TO FOLLOW IS IMPEDED BY ACCELERATING "FLOTSAM" IN PROCESS OF ELUDING REC/POLS.
GET THE HELL OUTA MY WAY!
WE RECOVER AND PROCEED TOWARD CORRIDOR TO INVESTIGATE SOUNDS WHICH WE INTERPRET AS RECRUITING MODULES ENGAGED IN "RESIST THE DEVIL" DEFENSE MODE. WE ASSUME TERMINATION OF GIRL GUIDE GROUP.
BOOP
CRASH!
BAP
BAF!
KRAS
PONK PONK PONK!
BOOIIOOIIOOING!
ASSUMPTION CONFIRMED. BABY SISTERS REENGAGE PRIMARY FUNCTION RESUME... UH-OH... SHIT...! BACK UP...
CORRECTION: GUIDES HAVE CUT & RUN
CONCLUSION: MISSION ABORTED
CAUSE: AGENT ERROR
BIDING YOUR VIBES IN THE BUMPKIN BELT?
COMMENT: THE GUIDES TRAINING IS VERY EFFECTIVE. IT IS IMPOSSIBLE TO ASCERTAIN AT THIS TIME WHETHER THE DISAPPEARANCES ARE THE WORK OF SOME OUTSIDE AGENT OR SOME UNKNOWN PLAN OF THE GUIDES THEMSELVES.
END REPORT.

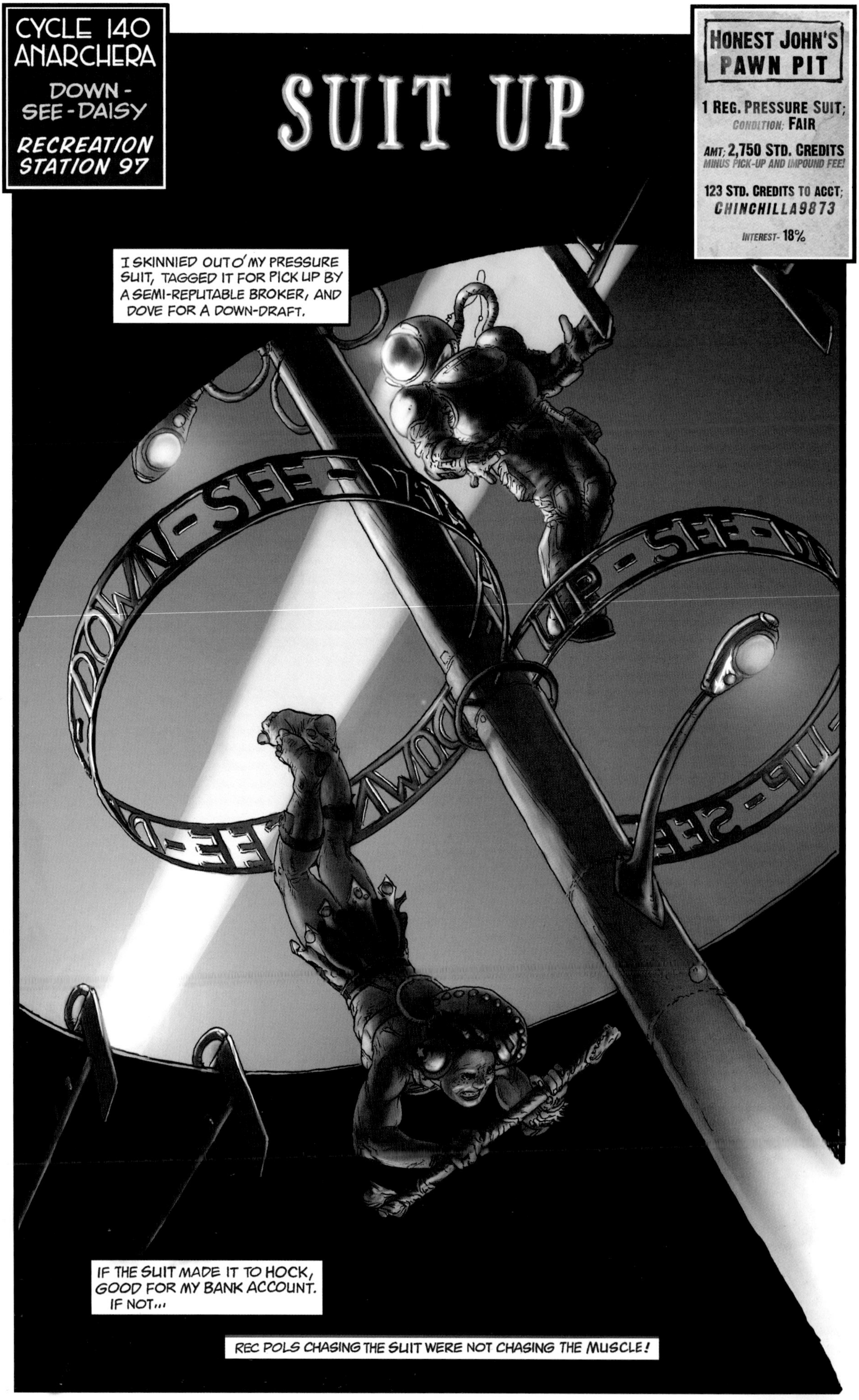
CYCLE 140
ANARCHERA
DOWN-SEE-DAISY
RECREATION STATION 97
SUIT UP
HONEST JOHN'S PAWN PIT
1 REG. PRESSURE SUIT; CONDITION; FAIR
AMT; 2,750 STD. CREDITS
MINUS PICK-UP AND IMPOUND FEE!
123 STD. CREDITS TO ACCT; CHINCHILLA9873
INTEREST- 18%
I SKINNIED OUT O' MY PRESSURE SUIT, TAGGED IT FOR PICK UP BY A SEMI-REPUTABLE BROKER, AND DOVE FOR A DOWN-DRAFT.
IF THE SUIT MADE IT TO HOCK, GOOD FOR MY BANK ACCOUNT. IF NOT...
REC POLS CHASING THE SUIT WERE NOT CHASING THE MUSCLE!

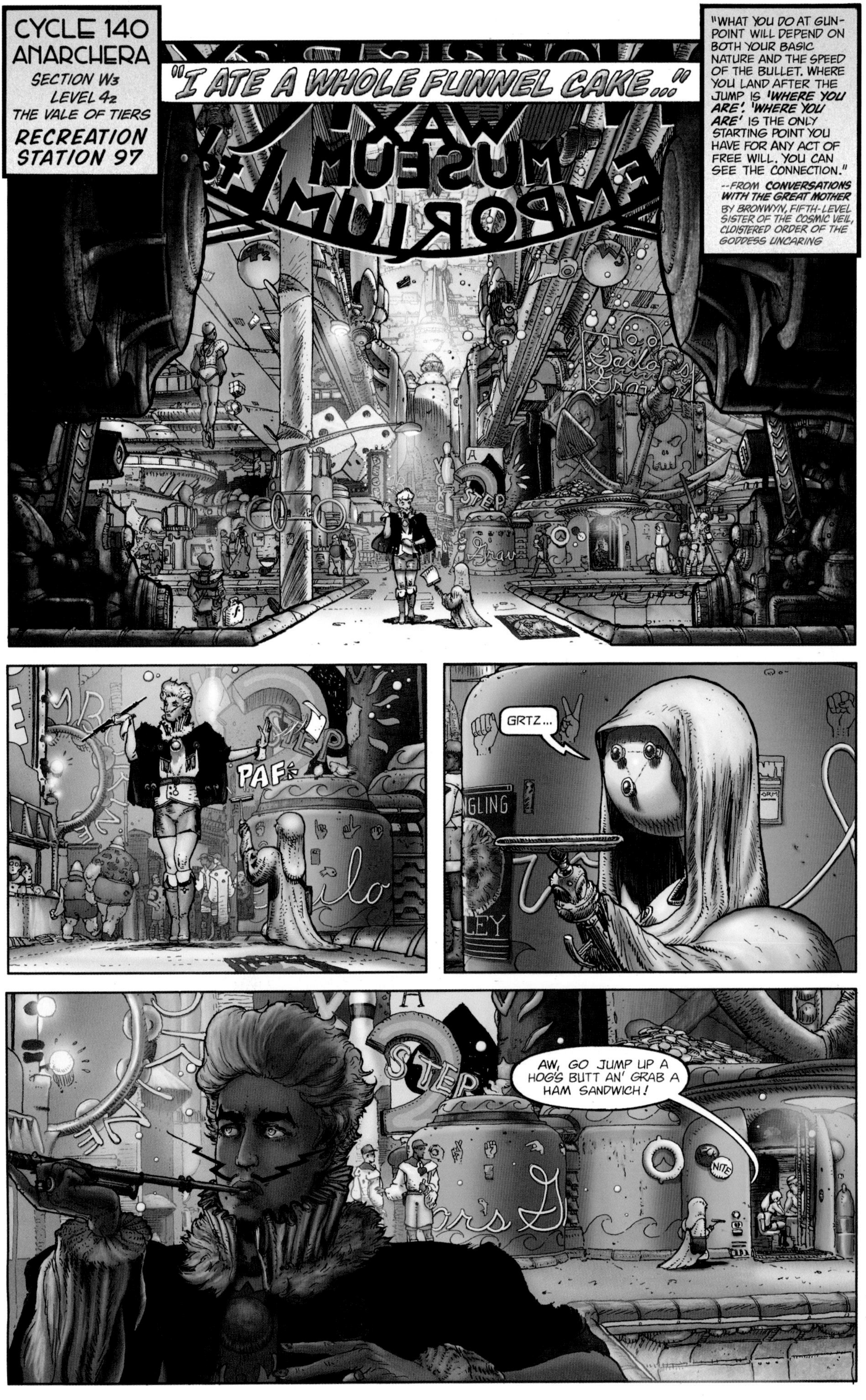
CYCLE 140
ANARCHERA
SECTION W3
LEVEL 42
THE VALE OF TIERS
RECREATION STATION 97
"I ATE A WHOLE FUNNEL CAKE..."
"WHAT YOU DO AT GUNPOINT WILL DEPEND ON BOTH YOUR BASIC NATURE AND THE SPEED OF THE BULLET. WHERE YOU LAND AFTER THE JUMP IS 'WHERE YOU ARE'. 'WHERE YOU ARE' IS THE ONLY STARTING POINT YOU HAVE FOR ANY ACT OF FREE WILL. YOU CAN SEE THE CONNECTION."
--FROM CONVERSATIONS WITH THE GREAT MOTHER BY BRONWYN, FIFTH-LEVEL SISTER OF THE COSMIC VEIL, CLOISTERED ORDER OF THE GODDESS UNCARING
STEP
PAF
GRTZ...
AW, GO JUMP UP A HOG'S BUTT AN' GRAB A HAM SANDWICH!

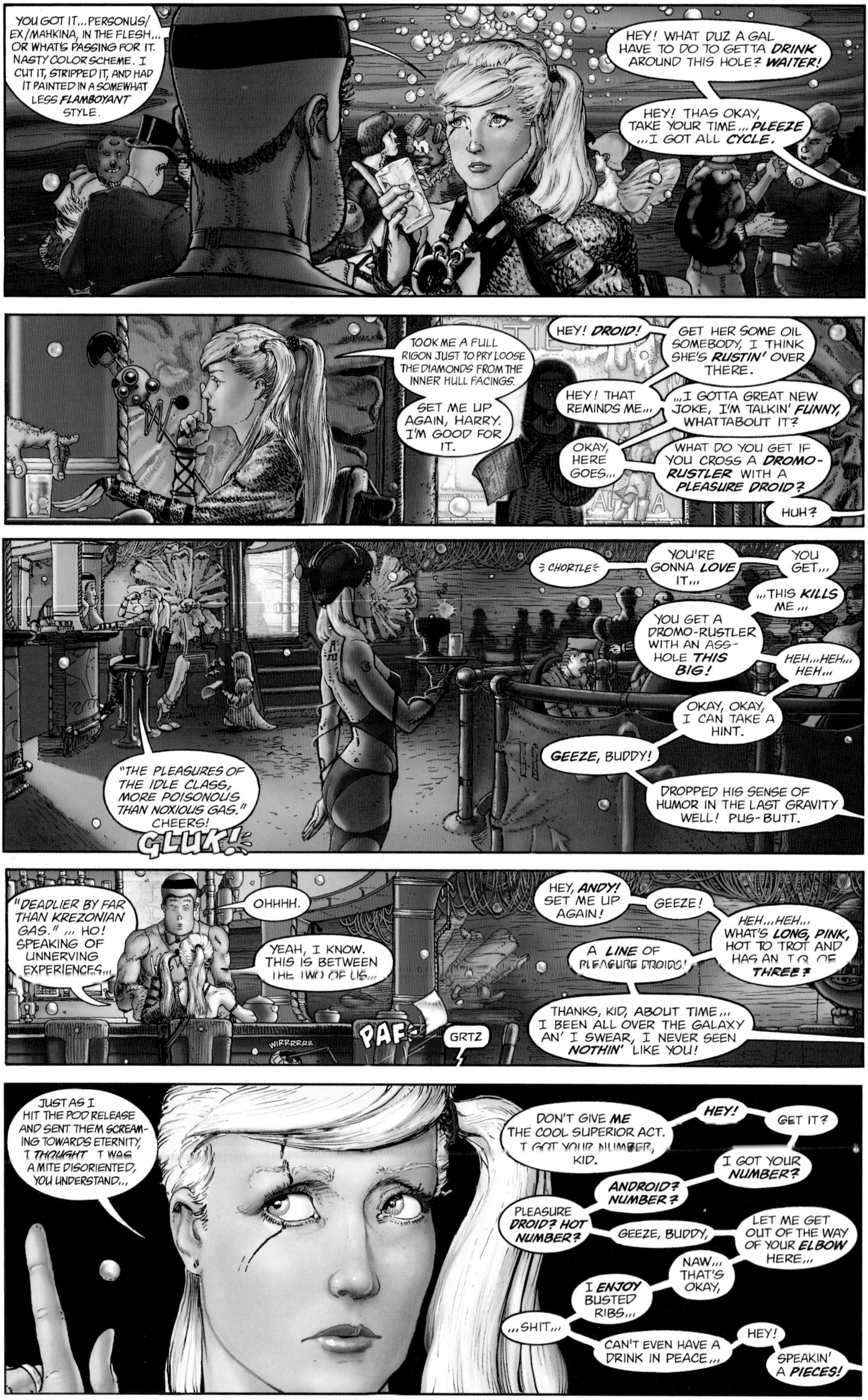
YOU GOT IT... PERSONUS/ EX/MAHKINA, IN THE FLESH... OR WHAT'S PASSING FOR IT. NASTY COLOR SCHEME. I CUT IT, STRIPPED IT, AND HAD IT PAINTED IN A SOMEWHAT LESS FLAMBOYANT STYLE.
HEY! WHAT DUZ A GAL HAVE TO DO TO GETTA DRINK AROUND THIS HOLE? WAITER!
HEY! THAS OKAY, TAKE YOUR TIME... PLEEZE ...I GOT ALL CYCLE.
TOOK ME A FULL RIGON JUST TO PRY LOOSE THE DIAMONDS FROM THE INNER HULL FACINGS.
SET ME UP AGAIN, HARRY. I'M GOOD FOR IT.
HEY! DROID!
GET HER SOME OIL SOMEBODY, I THINK SHE'S RUSTIN' OVER THERE.
HEY! THAT REMINDS ME...
...I GOTTA GREAT NEW JOKE, I'M TALKIN' FUNNY, WHATTABOUT IT?
OKAY, HERE GOES...
WHAT DO YOU GET IF YOU CROSS A DROMO-RUSTLER WITH A PLEASURE DROID?
HUH?
CHORTLE
YOU'RE GONNA LOVE IT...
YOU GET...
...THIS KILLS ME...
YOU GET A DROMO-RUSTLER WITH AN ASS-HOLE THIS BIG!
HEH...HEH... HEH...
OKAY, OKAY, I CAN TAKE A HINT.
GEEZE, BUDDY!
DROPPED HIS SENSE OF HUMOR IN THE LAST GRAVITY WELL! PUS-BUTT.
"THE PLEASURES OF THE IDLE CLASS, MORE POISONOUS THAN NOXIOUS GAS." CHEERS!
GLUK!
"DEADLIER BY FAR THAN KREZONIAN GAS." ... HO! SPEAKING OF UNNERVING EXPERIENCES...
OHHHH.
YEAH, I KNOW. THIS IS BETWEEN THE TWO OF US...
HEY, ANDY! SET ME UP AGAIN!
GEEZE!
HEH...HEH... WHAT'S LONG, PINK, HOT TO TROT AND HAS AN I.Q. OF THREE?
A LINE OF PLEASURE DROIDS!
THANKS, KID, ABOUT TIME... I BEEN ALL OVER THE GALAXY AN' I SWEAR, I NEVER SEEN NOTHIN' LIKE YOU!
WIRRRRRR
PAF
GRTZ
JUST AS I HIT THE POD RELEASE AND SENT THEM SCREAMING TOWARDS ETERNITY, I THOUGHT I WAS A MITE DISORIENTED, YOU UNDERSTAND...
DON'T GIVE ME THE COOL SUPERIOR ACT. I GOT YOUR NUMBER, KID.
HEY!
GET IT?
I GOT YOUR NUMBER?
ANDROID? NUMBER?
PLEASURE DROID? HOT NUMBER?
GEEZE, BUDDY,
LET ME GET OUT OF THE WAY OF YOUR ELBOW HERE...
NAW... THAT'S OKAY,
I ENJOY BUSTED RIBS...
...SHIT...
CAN'T EVEN HAVE A DRINK IN PEACE...
HEY!
SPEAKIN' A PIECES!

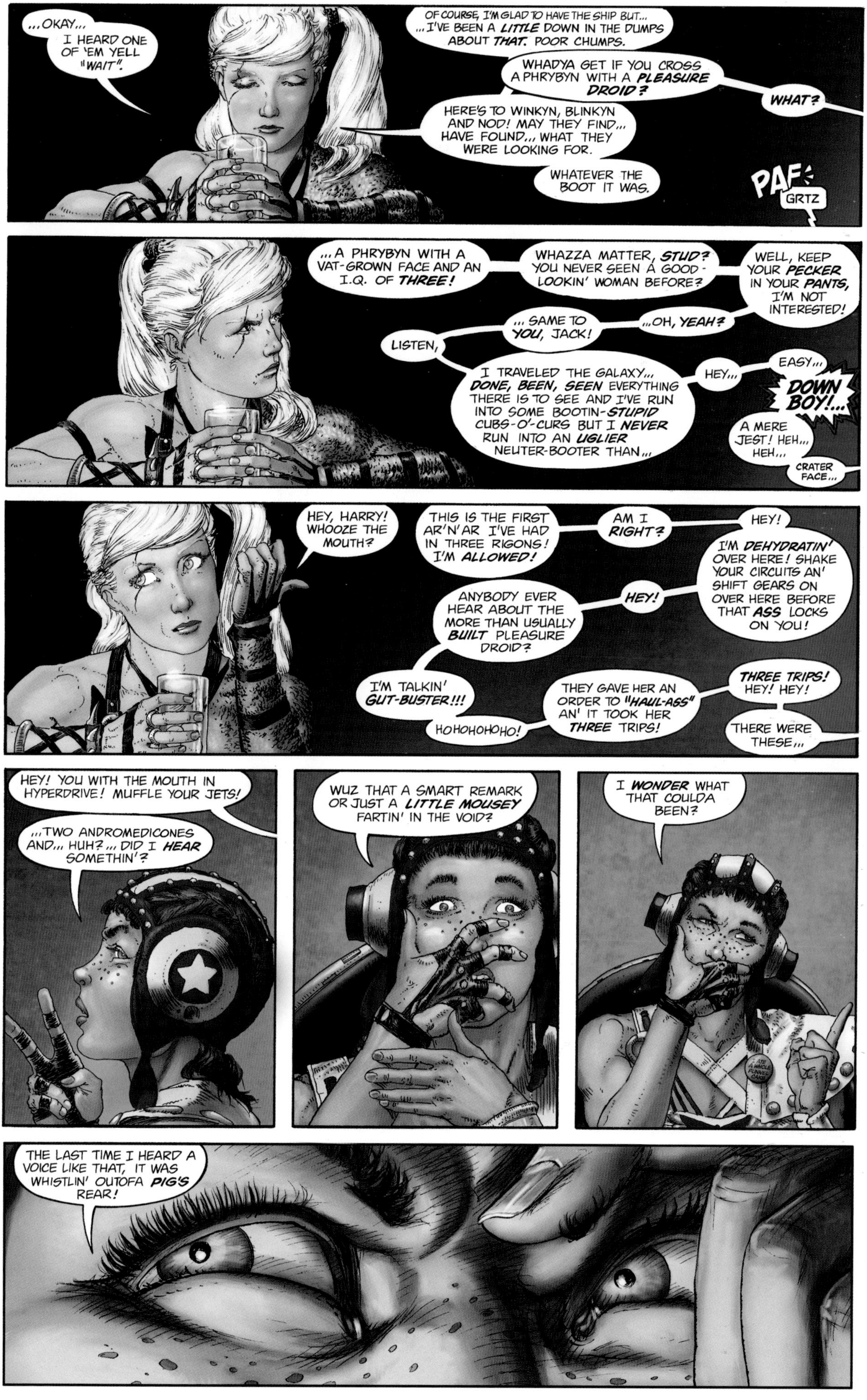
...OKAY... I HEARD ONE OF 'EM YELL "WAIT".
OF COURSE, I'M GLAD TO HAVE THE SHIP BUT... ...I'VE BEEN A LITTLE DOWN IN THE DUMPS ABOUT THAT. POOR CHUMPS.
WHADYA GET IF YOU CROSS A PHRYBYN WITH A PLEASURE DROID?
WHAT?
HERE'S TO WINKYN, BLINKYN AND NOD! MAY THEY FIND... HAVE FOUND... WHAT THEY WERE LOOKING FOR.
WHATEVER THE BOOT IT WAS.
PAF
GRTZ
...A PHRYBYN WITH A VAT-GROWN FACE AND AN I.Q. OF THREE!
WHAZZA MATTER, STUD? YOU NEVER SEEN A GOOD-LOOKIN' WOMAN BEFORE?
WELL, KEEP YOUR PECKER IN YOUR PANTS, I'M NOT INTERESTED!
...OH, YEAH?
...SAME TO YOU, JACK!
LISTEN,
I TRAVELED THE GALAXY... DONE, BEEN, SEEN EVERYTHING THERE IS TO SEE AND I'VE RUN INTO SOME BOOTIN-STUPID CUBS-O'-CURS BUT I NEVER RUN INTO AN UGLIER NEUTER-BOOTER THAN...
HEY...
EASY...
DOWN BOY!...
A MERE JEST! HEH... HEH...
CRATER FACE...
HEY, HARRY! WHOOZE THE MOUTH?
THIS IS THE FIRST AR'N'AR I'VE HAD IN THREE RIGONS! I'M ALLOWED!
AM I RIGHT?
HEY!
I'M DEHYDRATIN' OVER HERE! SHAKE YOUR CIRCUITS AN' SHIFT GEARS ON OVER HERE BEFORE THAT ASS LOCKS ON YOU!
HEY!
ANYBODY EVER HEAR ABOUT THE MORE THAN USUALLY BUILT PLEASURE DROID?
I'M TALKIN' GUT-BUSTER!!!
HOHOHOHOHO!
THEY GAVE HER AN ORDER TO "HAUL-ASS" AN' IT TOOK HER THREE TRIPS!
THREE TRIPS! HEY! HEY!
THERE WERE THESE...
HEY! YOU WITH THE MOUTH IN HYPERDRIVE! MUFFLE YOUR JETS!
...TWO ANDROMEDICONES AND... HUH? ...DID I HEAR SOMETHIN'?
WUZ THAT A SMART REMARK OR JUST A LITTLE MOUSEY FARTIN' IN THE VOID?
I WONDER WHAT THAT COULDA BEEN?
THE LAST TIME I HEARD A VOICE LIKE THAT, IT WAS WHISTLIN' OUTOFA PIG'S REAR!

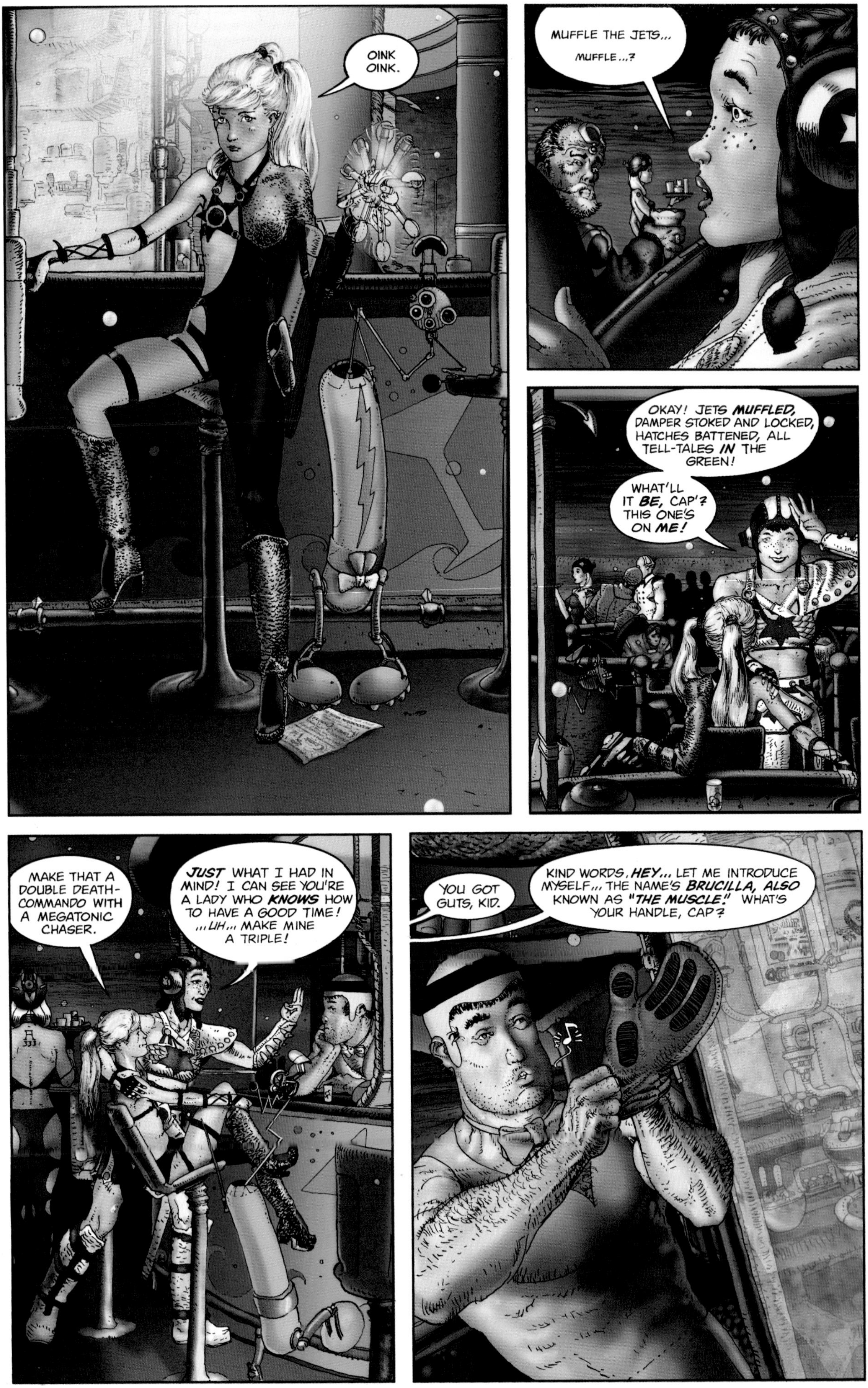
OINK OINK.
MUFFLE THE JETS...
MUFFLE...?
OKAY! JETS MUFFLED, DAMPER STOKED AND LOCKED, HATCHES BATTENED, ALL TELL-TALES IN THE GREEN!
WHAT'LL IT BE, CAP'? THIS ONE'S ON ME!
MAKE THAT A DOUBLE DEATH-COMMANDO WITH A MEGATONIC CHASER.
JUST WHAT I HAD IN MIND! I CAN SEE YOU'RE A LADY WHO KNOWS HOW TO HAVE A GOOD TIME! ...UH... MAKE MINE A TRIPLE!
YOU GOT GUTS, KID.
KIND WORDS, HEY... LET ME INTRODUCE MYSELF... THE NAME'S BRUCILLA, ALSO KNOWN AS "THE MUSCLE." WHAT'S YOUR HANDLE, CAP?

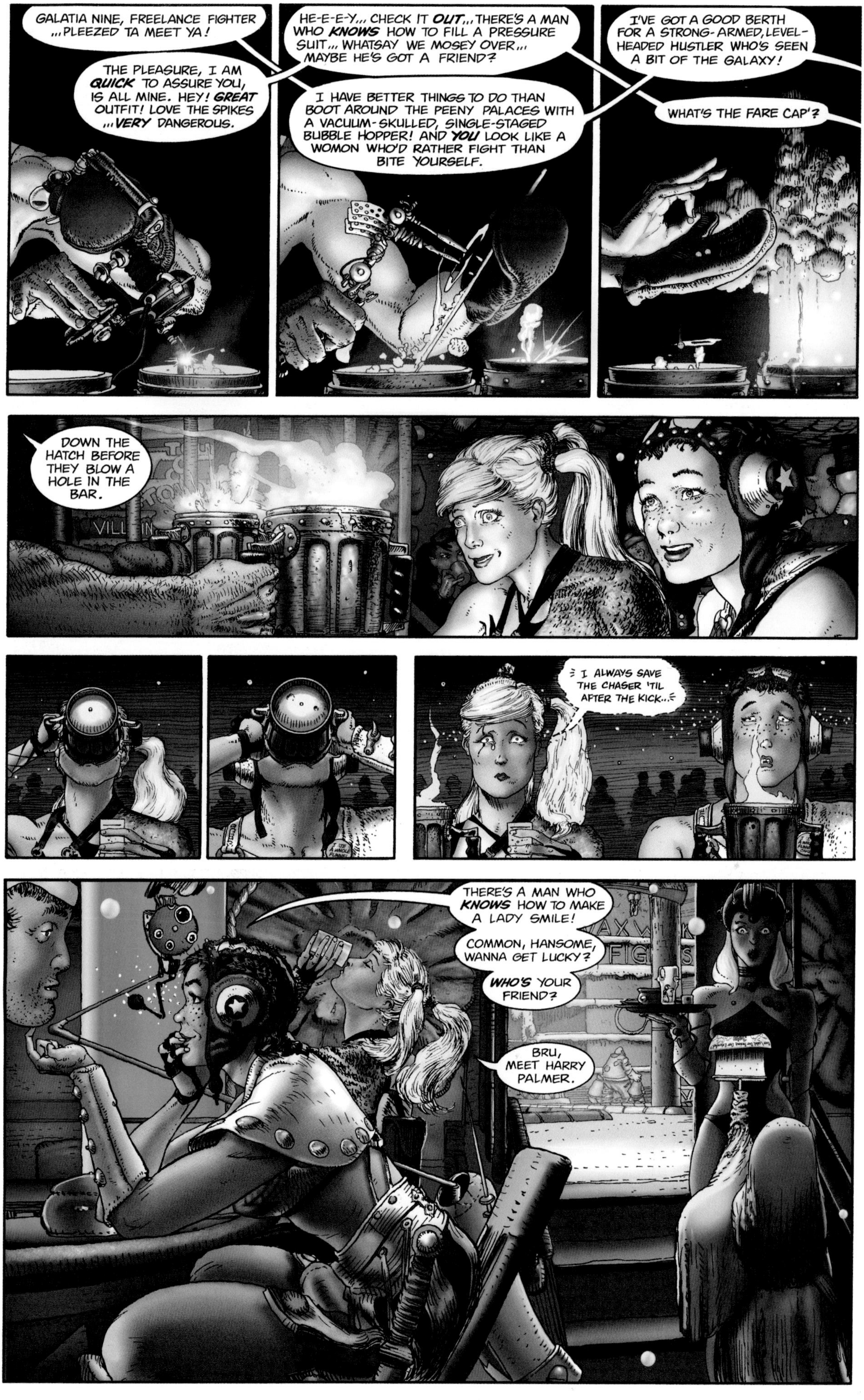
GALATIA NINE, FREELANCE FIGHTER ,,,PLEEZED TA MEET YA!
THE PLEASURE, I AM QUICK TO ASSURE YOU, IS ALL MINE. HEY! GREAT OUTFIT! LOVE THE SPIKES ,,,VERY DANGEROUS.
HE-E-E-Y,,, CHECK IT OUT,,, THERE'S A MAN WHO KNOWS HOW TO FILL A PRESSURE SUIT,,, WHATSAY WE MOSEY OVER,,, MAYBE HE'S GOT A FRIEND?
I HAVE BETTER THINGS TO DO THAN BOOT AROUND THE PEENY PALACES WITH A VACUUM-SKULLED, SINGLE-STAGED BUBBLE HOPPER! AND YOU LOOK LIKE A WOMON WHO'D RATHER FIGHT THAN BITE YOURSELF.
I'VE GOT A GOOD BERTH FOR A STRONG-ARMED, LEVEL-HEADED HUSTLER WHO'S SEEN A BIT OF THE GALAXY!
WHAT'S THE FARE CAP'?
DOWN THE HATCH BEFORE THEY BLOW A HOLE IN THE BAR.
I ALWAYS SAVE THE CHASER 'TIL AFTER THE KICK...
THERE'S A MAN WHO KNOWS HOW TO MAKE A LADY SMILE!
COMMON, HANSOME, WANNA GET LUCKY?
WHO'S YOUR FRIEND?
BRU, MEET HARRY PALMER.

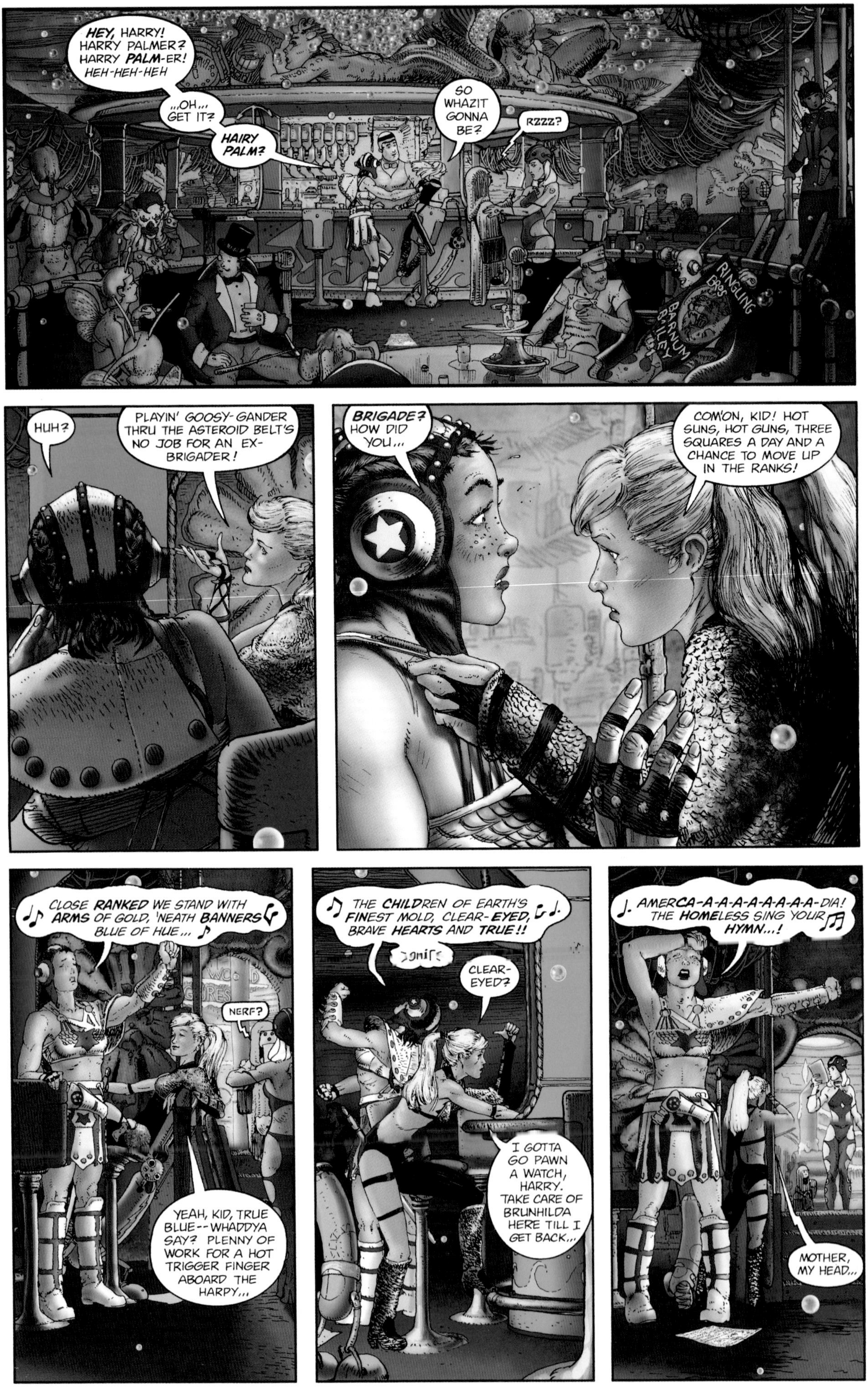
HEY, HARRY! HARRY PALMER? HARRY PALM-ER! HEH-HEH-HEH
...OH... GET IT?
HAIRY PALM?
SO WHAZIT GONNA BE?
RZZZ?
RINGLING BROS BARNUM & BAILEY
HUH?
PLAYIN' GOOSY-GANDER THRU THE ASTEROID BELT'S NO JOB FOR AN EX-BRIGADER!
BRIGADE? HOW DID YOU...
COM'ON, KID! HOT SUNS, HOT GUNS, THREE SQUARES A DAY AND A CHANCE TO MOVE UP IN THE RANKS!
CLOSE RANKED WE STAND WITH ARMS OF GOLD, 'NEATH BANNERS BLUE OF HUE...
NERF?
YEAH, KID, TRUE BLUE--WHADDYA SAY? PLENNY OF WORK FOR A HOT TRIGGER FINGER ABOARD THE HARPY...
THE CHILDREN OF EARTH'S FINEST MOLD, CLEAR-EYED, BRAVE HEARTS AND TRUE!!
CLEAR-EYED?
I GOTTA GO PAWN A WATCH, HARRY. TAKE CARE OF BRUNHILDA HERE TILL I GET BACK...
AMERCA-A-A-A-A-A-A-A-DIA! THE HOMELESS SING YOUR HYMN...!
MOTHER, MY HEAD...

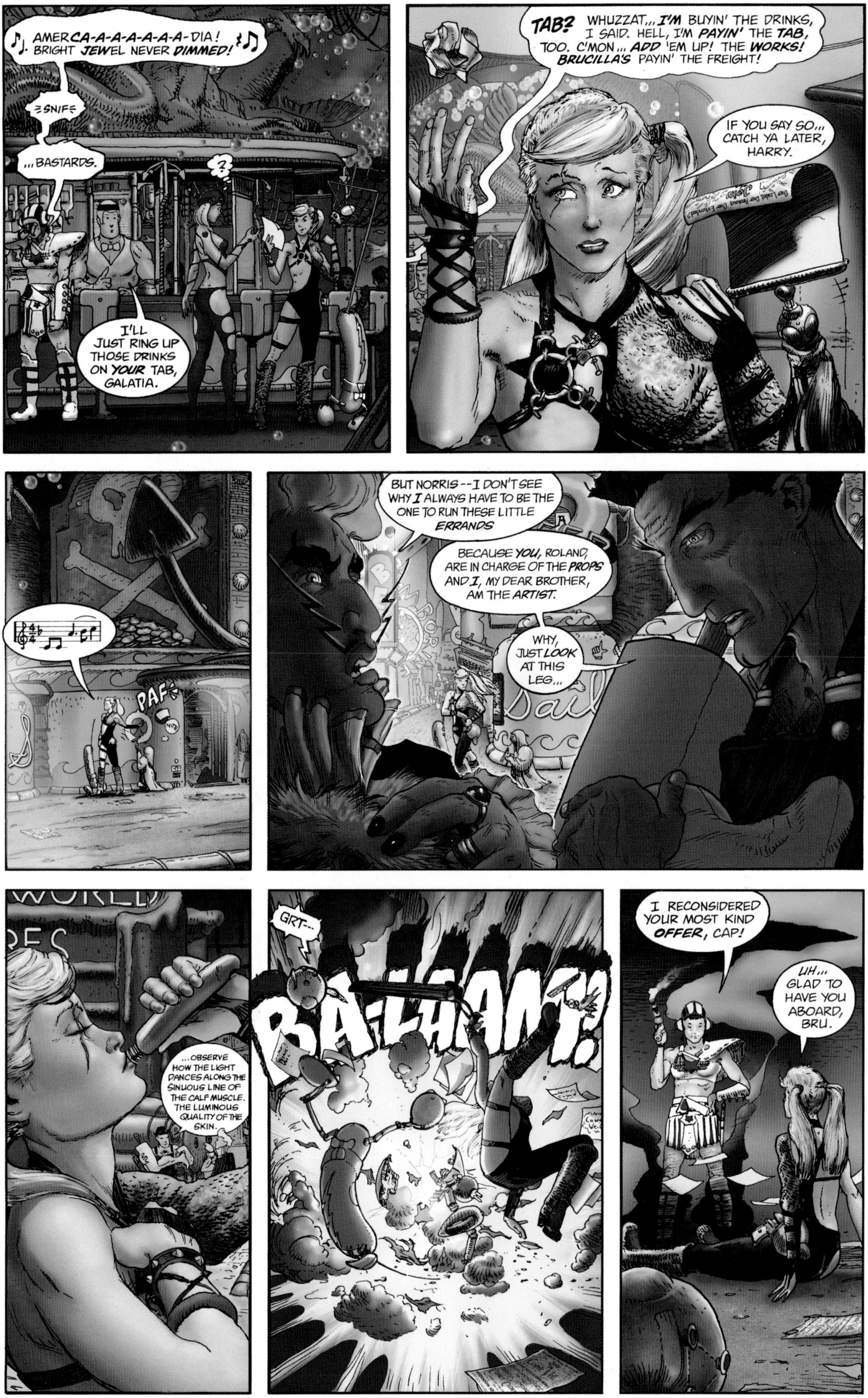
♪ AMERCA-A-A-A-A-A-A-DIA! BRIGHT JEWEL NEVER DIMMED! ♪
SNIF
...BASTARDS.
?
I'LL JUST RING UP THOSE DRINKS ON YOUR TAB, GALATIA.
TAB? WHUZZAT... I'M BUYIN' THE DRINKS, I SAID. HELL, I'M PAYIN' THE TAB, TOO. C'MON... ADD 'EM UP! THE WORKS! BRUCILLA'S PAYIN' THE FREIGHT!
IF YOU SAY SO... CATCH YA LATER, HARRY.
PAF
BUT NORRIS--I DON'T SEE WHY I ALWAYS HAVE TO BE THE ONE TO RUN THESE LITTLE ERRANDS
BECAUSE YOU, ROLAND, ARE IN CHARGE OF THE PROPS AND I, MY DEAR BROTHER, AM THE ARTIST.
WHY, JUST LOOK AT THIS LEG...
...OBSERVE HOW THE LIGHT DANCES ALONG THE SINUOUS LINE OF THE CALF MUSCLE. THE LUMINOUS QUALITY OF THE SKIN.
GRT--
BA-LLAAM!
I RECONSIDERED YOUR MOST KIND OFFER, CAP!
UH... GLAD TO HAVE YOU ABOARD, BRU.

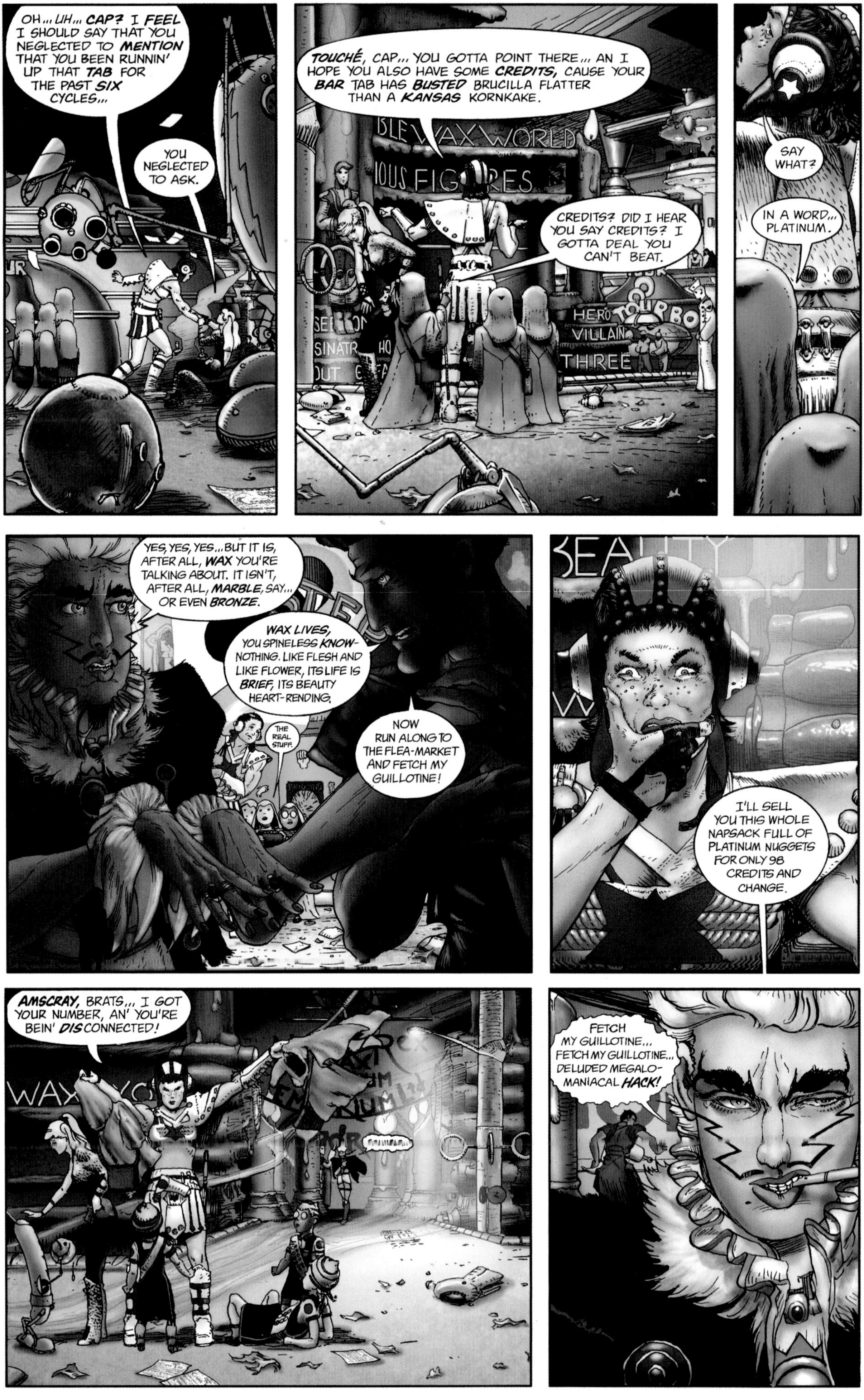
OH... UH... CAP? I FEEL I SHOULD SAY THAT YOU NEGLECTED TO MENTION THAT YOU BEEN RUNNIN' UP THAT TAB FOR THE PAST SIX CYCLES...
YOU NEGLECTED TO ASK.
TOUCHÉ, CAP... YOU GOTTA POINT THERE... AN I HOPE YOU ALSO HAVE SOME CREDITS, CAUSE YOUR BAR TAB HAS BUSTED BRUCILLA FLATTER THAN A KANSAS KORNKAKE.
BLE WAX WORLD
IOUS FIG RES
CREDITS? DID I HEAR YOU SAY CREDITS? I GOTTA DEAL YOU CAN'T BEAT.
HERO
VILLAIN
THREE
SAY WHAT?
IN A WORD... PLATINUM.
YES, YES, YES... BUT IT IS, AFTER ALL, WAX YOU'RE TALKING ABOUT. IT ISN'T, AFTER ALL, MARBLE, SAY... OR EVEN BRONZE.
WAX LIVES, YOU SPINELESS KNOW-NOTHING. LIKE FLESH AND LIKE FLOWER, ITS LIFE IS BRIEF, ITS BEAUTY HEART-RENDING.
THE REAL STUFF.
NOW RUN ALONG TO THE FLEA-MARKET AND FETCH MY GUILLOTINE!
I'LL SELL YOU THIS WHOLE NAPSACK FULL OF PLATINUM NUGGETS FOR ONLY 98 CREDITS AND CHANGE.
AMSCRAY, BRATS... I GOT YOUR NUMBER, AN' YOU'RE BEIN' DISCONNECTED!
WAX
FETCH MY GUILLOTINE... FETCH MY GUILLOTINE... DELUDED MEGALO-MANIACAL HACK!

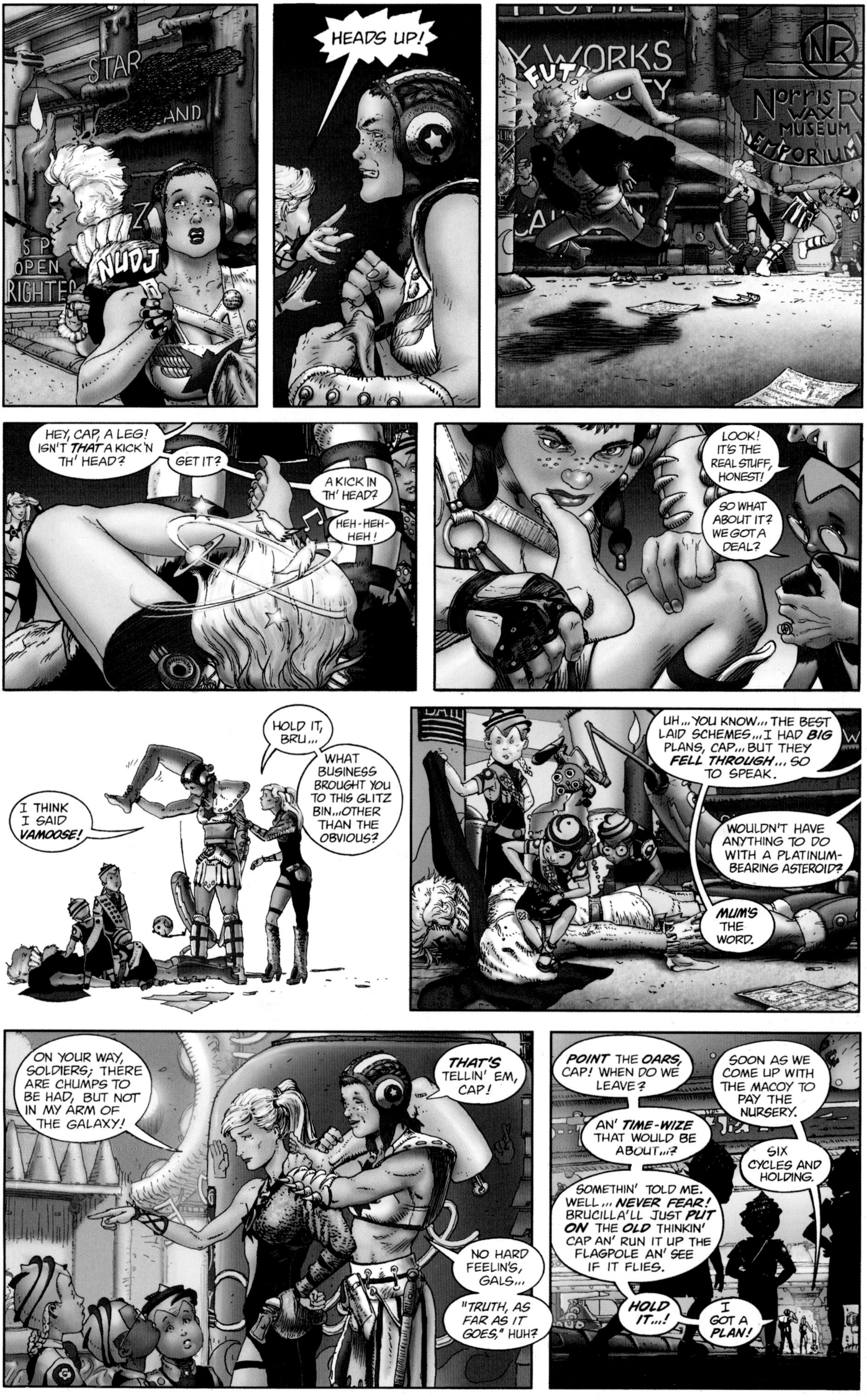
STAR
AND
OPEN
RIGHTE
NUDJ
HEADS UP!
X WORKS
FUT!
NR
Norris R
WAX
MUSEUM
EMPORIUM
HEY, CAP, A LEG! ISN'T THAT A KICK 'N TH' HEAD?
GET IT?
A KICK IN TH' HEAD?
HEH-HEH-HEH!
LOOK! IT'S THE REAL STUFF, HONEST!
SO WHAT ABOUT IT? WE GOT A DEAL?
I THINK I SAID VAMOOSE!
HOLD IT, BRU...
WHAT BUSINESS BROUGHT YOU TO THIS GLITZ BIN... OTHER THAN THE OBVIOUS?
UH... YOU KNOW... THE BEST LAID SCHEMES... I HAD BIG PLANS, CAP... BUT THEY FELL THROUGH... SO TO SPEAK.
WOULDN'T HAVE ANYTHING TO DO WITH A PLATINUM-BEARING ASTEROID?
MUM'S THE WORD.
ON YOUR WAY, SOLDIERS; THERE ARE CHUMPS TO BE HAD, BUT NOT IN MY ARM OF THE GALAXY!
THAT'S TELLIN' 'EM, CAP!
NO HARD FEELIN'S, GALS...
"TRUTH, AS FAR AS IT GOES," HUH?
POINT THE OARS, CAP! WHEN DO WE LEAVE?
SOON AS WE COME UP WITH THE MACOY TO PAY THE NURSERY.
AN' TIME-WIZE THAT WOULD BE ABOUT...?
SIX CYCLES AND HOLDING.
SOMETHIN' TOLD ME. WELL... NEVER FEAR! BRUCILLA'LL JUST PUT ON THE OLD THINKIN' CAP AN' RUN IT UP THE FLAGPOLE AN' SEE IF IT FLIES.
HOLD IT...!
I GOT A PLAN!

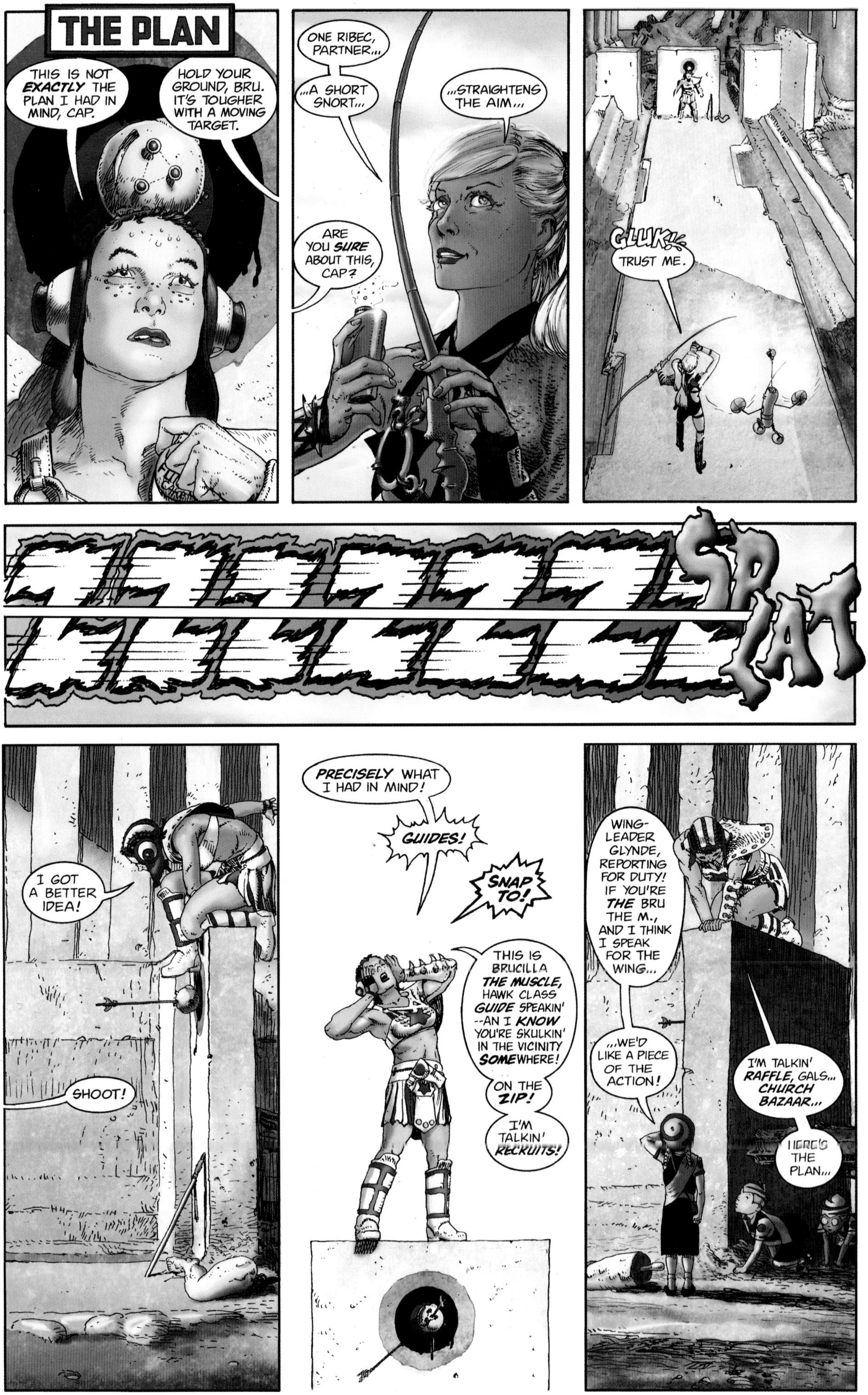
THE PLAN
THIS IS NOT EXACTLY THE PLAN I HAD IN MIND, CAP.
HOLD YOUR GROUND, BRU. IT'S TOUGHER WITH A MOVING TARGET.
ONE RIBEC, PARTNER...
...A SHORT SNORT...
...STRAIGHTENS THE AIM...
ARE YOU SURE ABOUT THIS, CAP?
GLUK!!
TRUST ME.
SPLAT
I GOT A BETTER IDEA!
SHOOT!
PRECISELY WHAT I HAD IN MIND!
GUIDES!
SNAP TO!
THIS IS BRUCILLA THE MUSCLE, HAWK CLASS GUIDE SPEAKIN' --AN I KNOW YOU'RE SKULKIN' IN THE VICINITY SOMEWHERE!
ON THE ZIP!
I'M TALKIN' RECKUITS!
WING-LEADER GLYNDE, REPORTING FOR DUTY! IF YOU'RE THE BRU THE M., AND I THINK I SPEAK FOR THE WING...
...WE'D LIKE A PIECE OF THE ACTION!
I'M TALKIN' RAFFLE, GALS... CHURCH BAZAAR...
HERE'S THE PLAN...

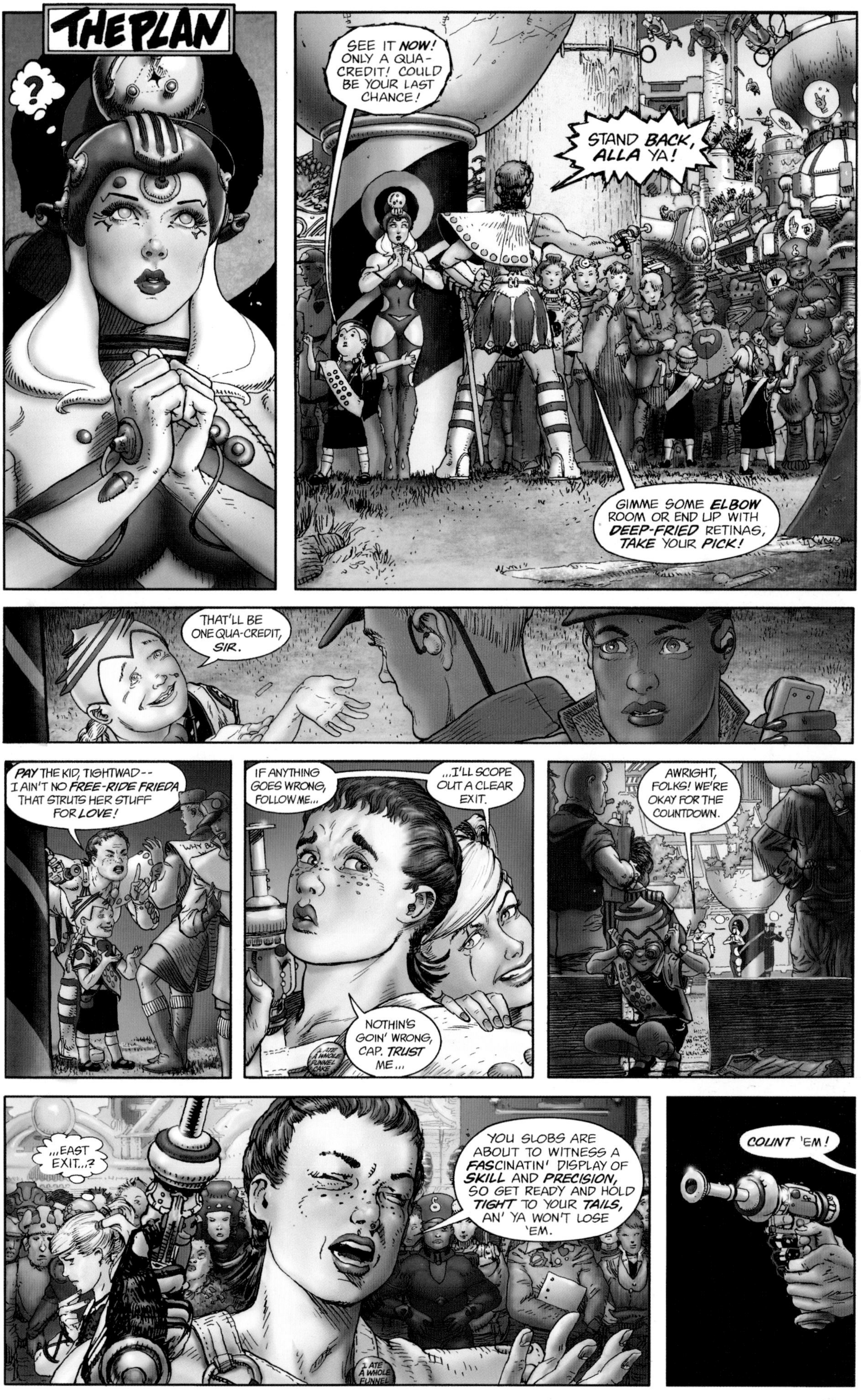
THE PLAN
?
SEE IT NOW! ONLY A QUA-CREDIT! COULD BE YOUR LAST CHANCE!
STAND BACK, ALLA YA!
GIMME SOME ELBOW ROOM OR END UP WITH DEEP-FRIED RETINAS, TAKE YOUR PICK!
THAT'LL BE ONE QUA-CREDIT, SIR.
PAY THE KID, TIGHTWAD-- I AIN'T NO FREE-RIDE FRIEDA THAT STRUTS HER STUFF FOR LOVE!
IF ANYTHING GOES WRONG, FOLLOW ME...
...I'LL SCOPE OUT A CLEAR EXIT.
NOTHIN'S GOIN' WRONG, CAP. TRUST ME...
I ATE A WHOLE FUNNEL CAKE
AWRIGHT, FOLKS! WE'RE OKAY FOR THE COUNTDOWN.
...EAST EXIT...?
YOU SLOBS ARE ABOUT TO WITNESS A FASCINATIN' DISPLAY OF SKILL AND PRECISION, SO GET READY AND HOLD TIGHT TO YOUR TAILS, AN' YA WON'T LOSE 'EM.
I ATE A WHOLE FUNNEL
COUNT 'EM!

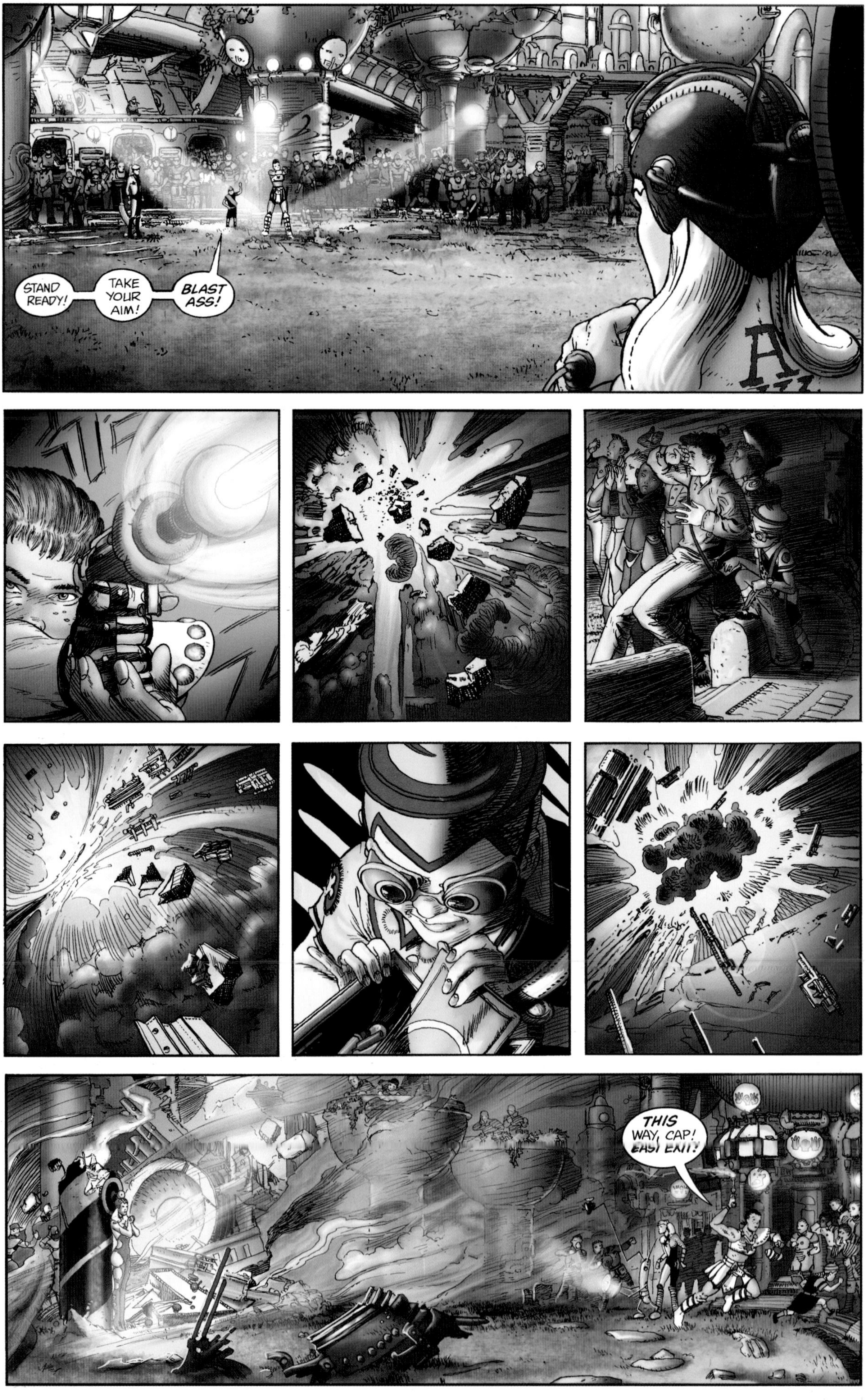
STAND READY!
TAKE YOUR AIM!
BLAST ASS!
THIS WAY, CAP! EAST EXIT!

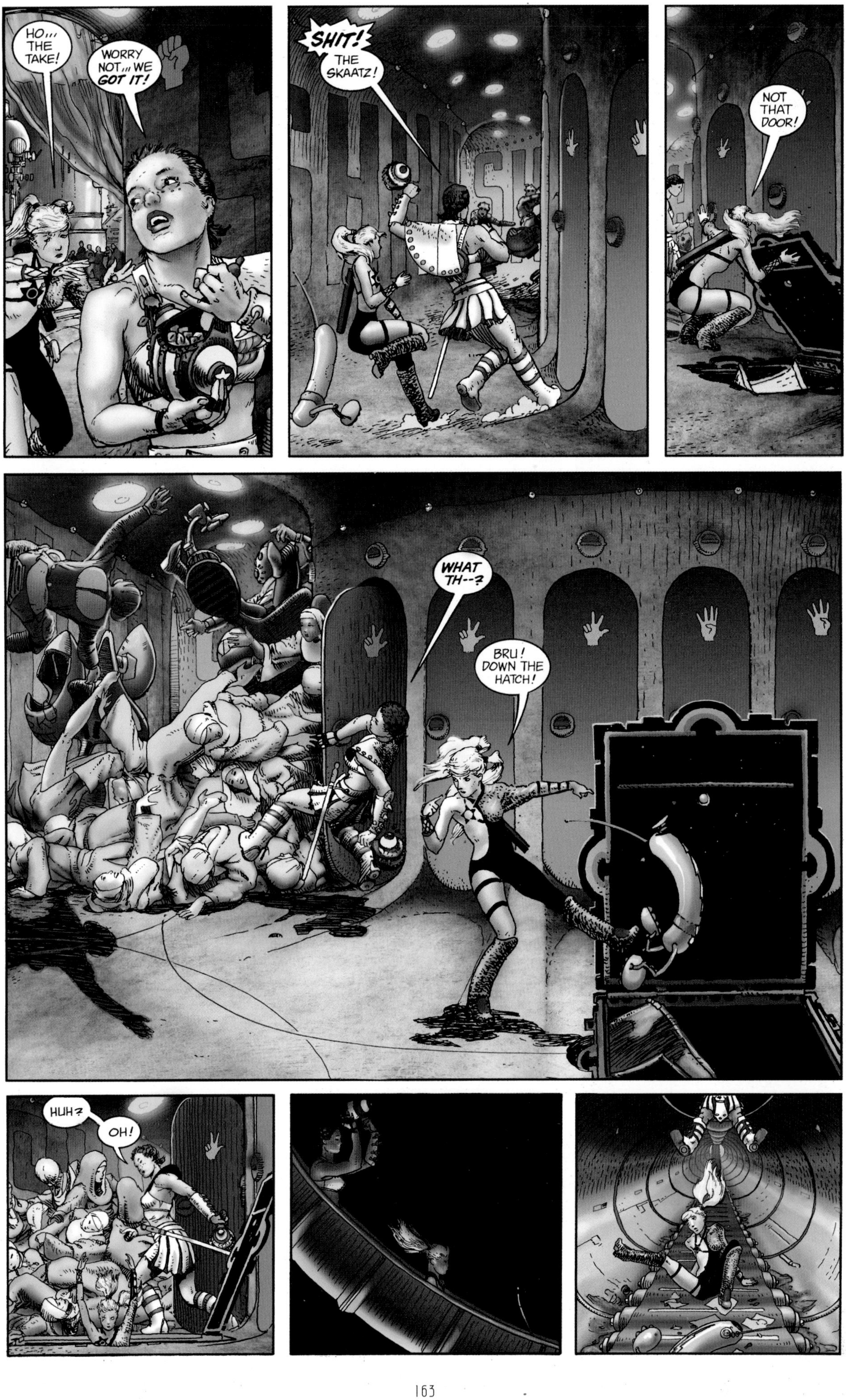
HO,,, THE TAKE!
WORRY NOT,,, WE GOT IT!
SHIT!
THE SKAATZ!
NOT THAT DOOR!
WHAT TH--?
BRU! DOWN THE HATCH!
HUH?
OH!

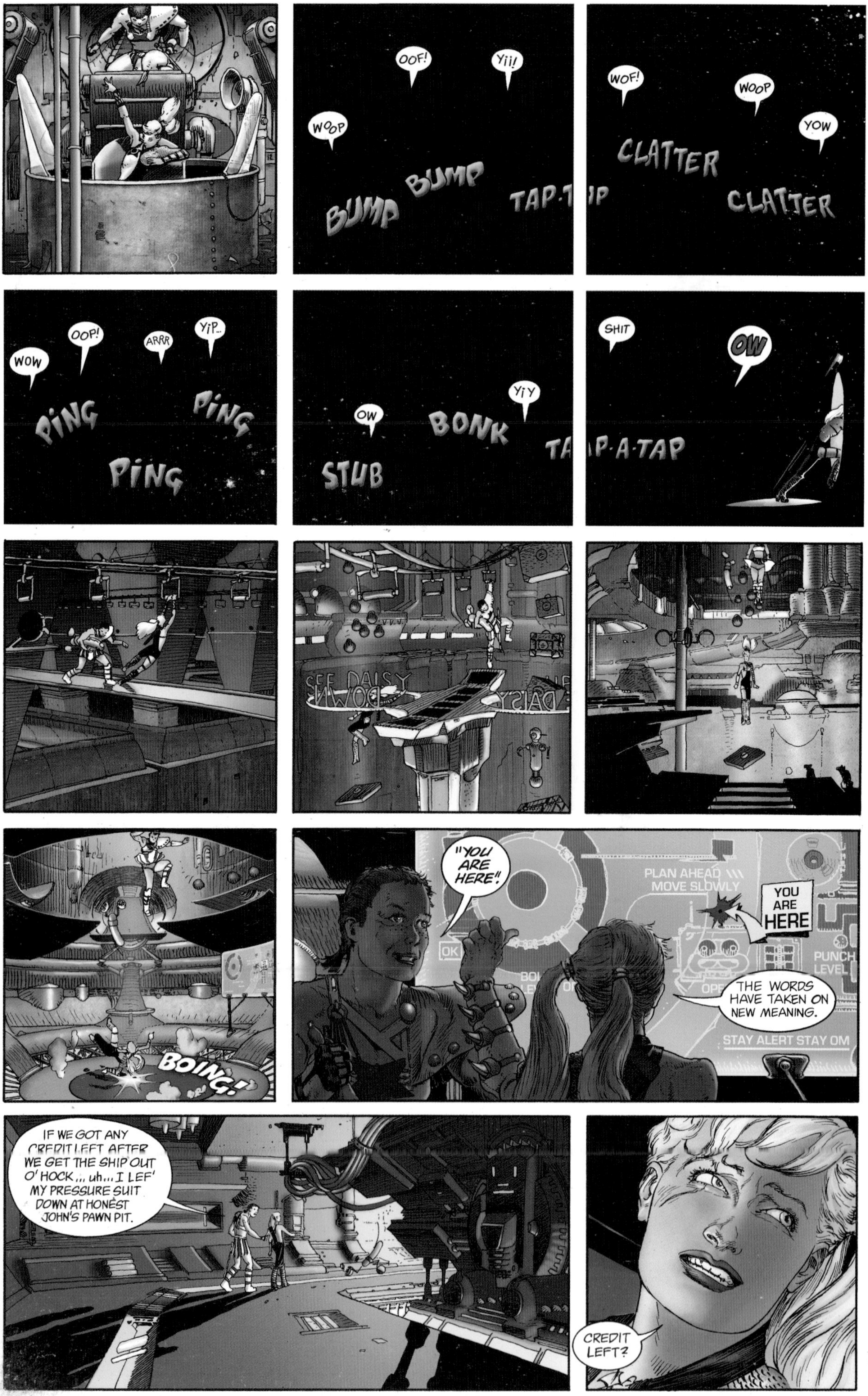
WOOP
OOF!
Yii!
BUMP
BUMP
TAP·T
WOF!
WOOP
YOW
CLATTER
CLATTER
WOW
OOP!
ARRR
YiP..
PiNG
PiNG
PiNG
OW
YiY
BONK
STUB
TA P-A-TAP
SHIT
OW
SEE DAISY
DAISY
BOING!
"YOU ARE HERE".
PLAN AHEAD
MOVE SLOWLY
YOU ARE HERE
OK
PUNCH LEVEL
THE WORDS HAVE TAKEN ON NEW MEANING.
STAY ALERT STAY OM
IF WE GOT ANY CREDIT LEFT AFTER WE GET THE SHIP OUT O' HOCK... uh... I LEF' MY PRESSURE SUIT DOWN AT HONEST JOHN'S PAWN PIT.
CREDIT LEFT?

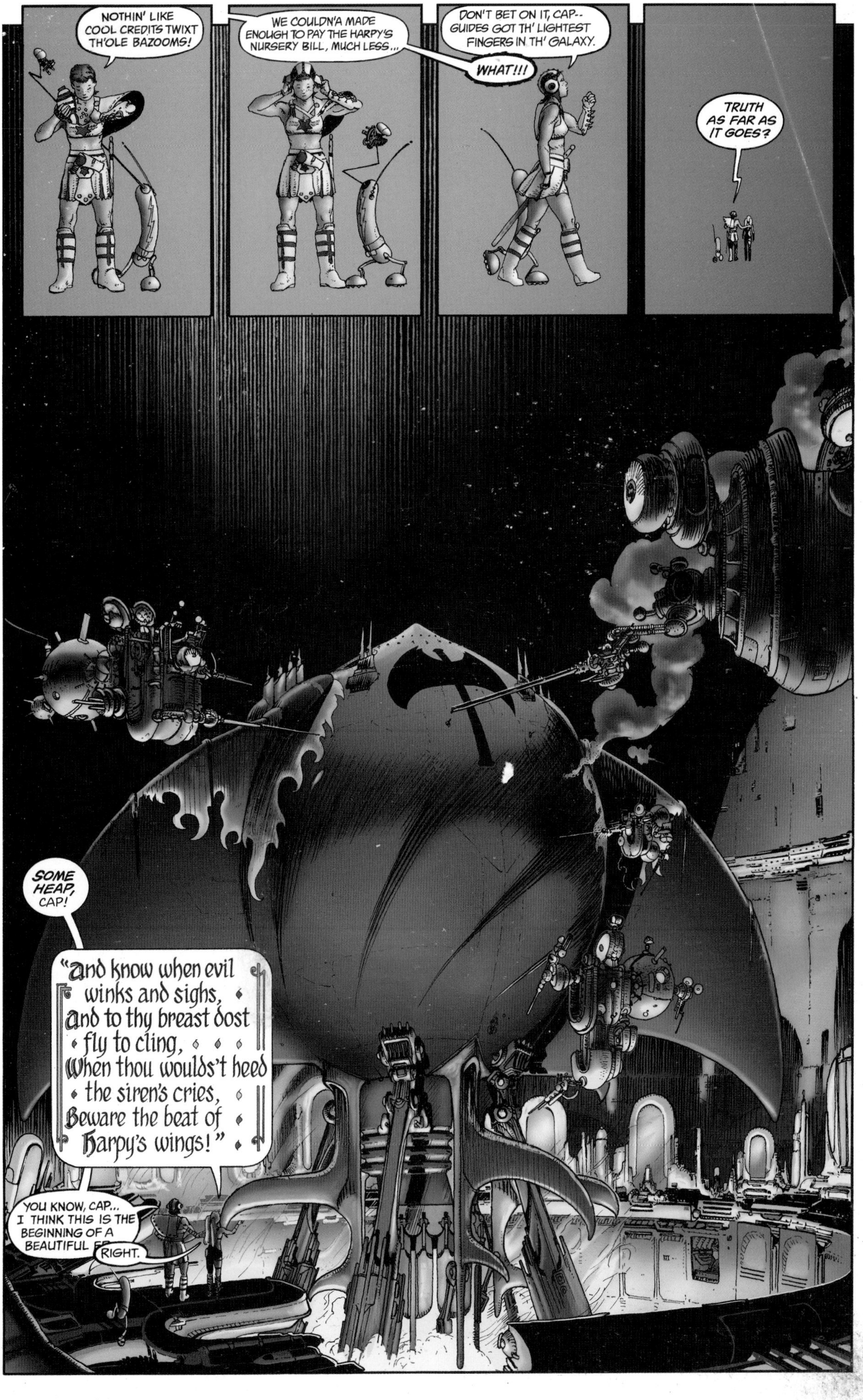
NOTHIN' LIKE COOL CREDITS TWIXT TH'OLE BAZOOMS!
WE COULDN'A MADE ENOUGH TO PAY THE HARPY'S NURSERY BILL, MUCH LESS...
DON'T BET ON IT, CAP-- GUIDES GOT TH' LIGHTEST FINGERS IN TH' GALAXY.
WHAT!!!
TRUTH AS FAR AS IT GOES?
SOME HEAP, CAP!
"And know when evil winks and sighs,
And to thy breast dost fly to cling,
When thou woulds't heed the siren's cries,
Beware the beat of Harpy's wings!"
YOU KNOW, CAP... I THINK THIS IS THE BEGINNING OF A BEAUTIFUL
RIGHT.

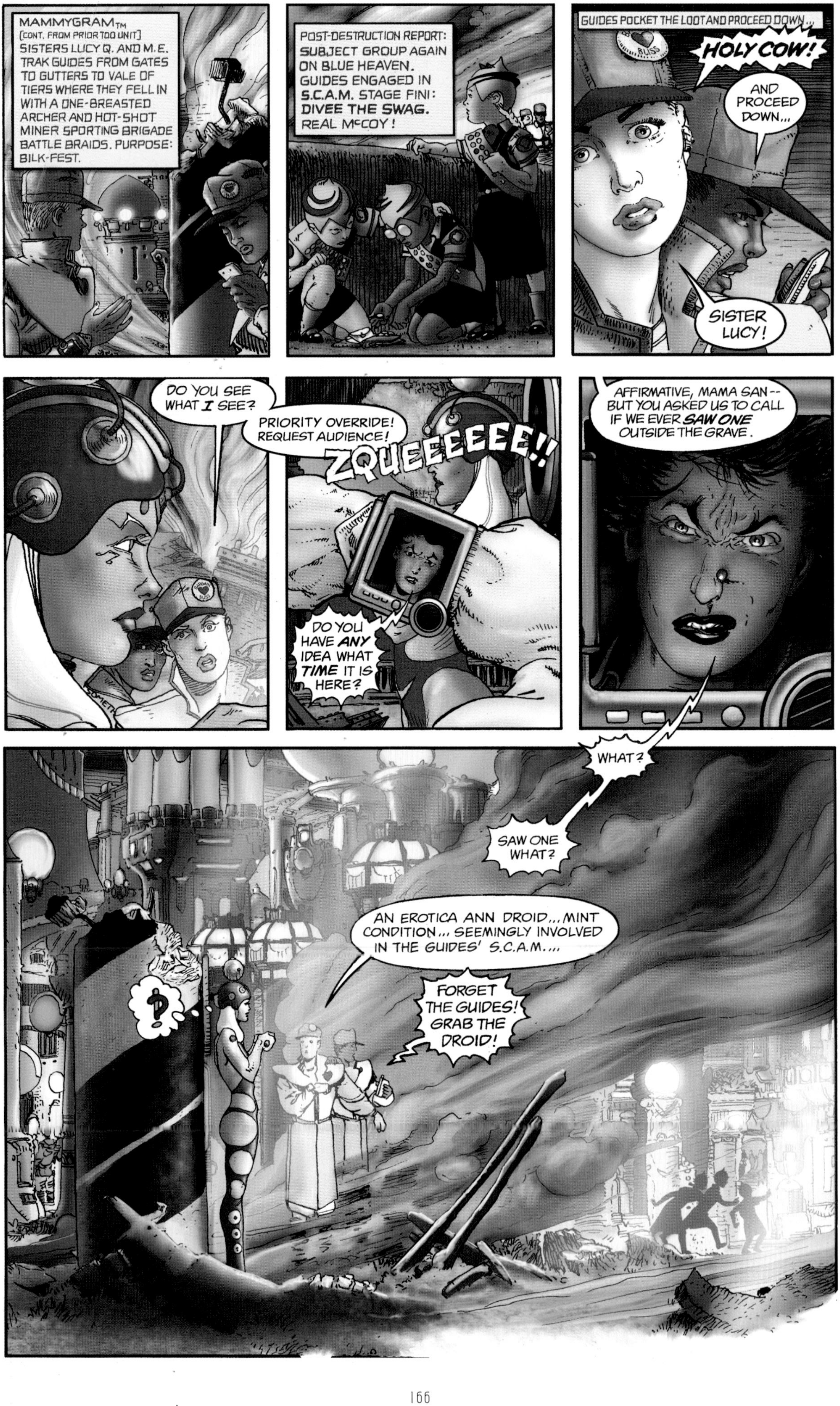
MAMMYGRAM TM
(CONT. FROM PRIOR TOO UNIT)
SISTERS LUCY Q. AND M.E. TRAK GUIDES FROM GATES TO GUTTERS TO VALE OF TIERS WHERE THEY FELL IN WITH A ONE-BREASTED ARCHER AND HOT-SHOT MINER SPORTING BRIGADE BATTLE BRAIDS. PURPOSE: BILK-FEST.
POST-DESTRUCTION REPORT: SUBJECT GROUP AGAIN ON BLUE HEAVEN. GUIDES ENGAGED IN S.C.A.M. STAGE FINI: DIVEE THE SWAG. REAL McCOY!
GUIDES POCKET THE LOOT AND PROCEED DOWN...
HOLY COW!
AND PROCEED DOWN...
SISTER LUCY!
DO YOU SEE WHAT I SEE?
PRIORITY OVERRIDE! REQUEST AUDIENCE!
ZQUEEEEEEE!!
DO YOU HAVE ANY IDEA WHAT TIME IT IS HERE?
AFFIRMATIVE, MAMA SAN-- BUT YOU ASKED US TO CALL IF WE EVER SAW ONE OUTSIDE THE GRAVE.
WHAT?
SAW ONE WHAT?
AN EROTICA ANN DROID... MINT CONDITION... SEEMINGLY INVOLVED IN THE GUIDES' S.C.A.M....
FORGET THE GUIDES! GRAB THE DROID!
?

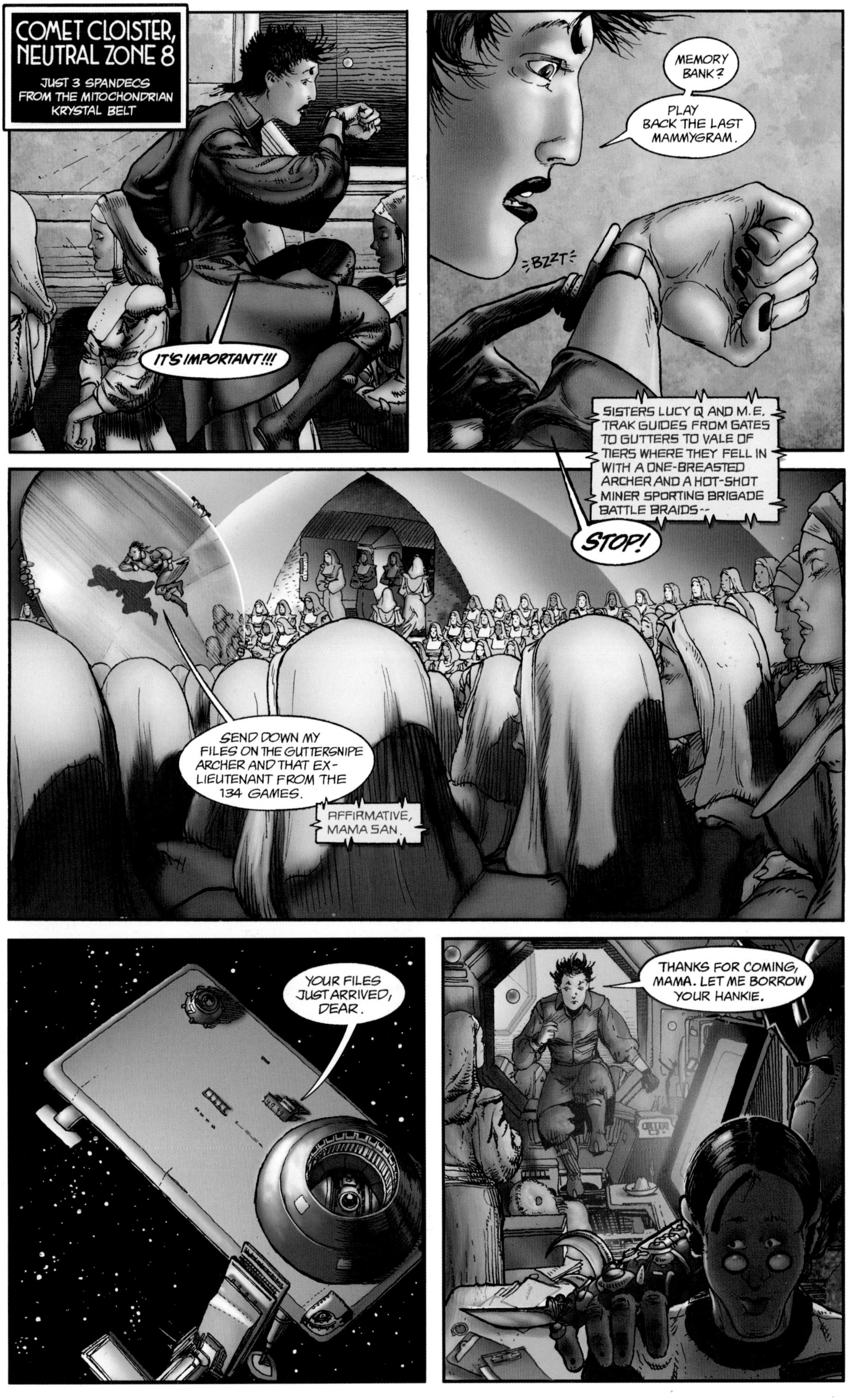
COMET CLOISTER, NEUTRAL ZONE 8
JUST 3 SPANDECS FROM THE MITOCHONDRIAN KRYSTAL BELT
IT'S IMPORTANT!!!
MEMORY BANK?
PLAY BACK THE LAST MAMMYGRAM.
BZZT
SISTERS LUCY Q AND M.E. TRAK GUIDES FROM GATES TO GUTTERS TO VALE OF TIERS WHERE THEY FELL IN WITH A ONE-BREASTED ARCHER AND A HOT-SHOT MINER SPORTING BRIGADE BATTLE BRAIDS--
STOP!
SEND DOWN MY FILES ON THE GUTTERSNIPE ARCHER AND THAT EX-LIEUTENANT FROM THE 134 GAMES.
AFFIRMATIVE, MAMA SAN.
YOUR FILES JUST ARRIVED, DEAR.
THANKS FOR COMING, MAMA. LET ME BORROW YOUR HANKIE.

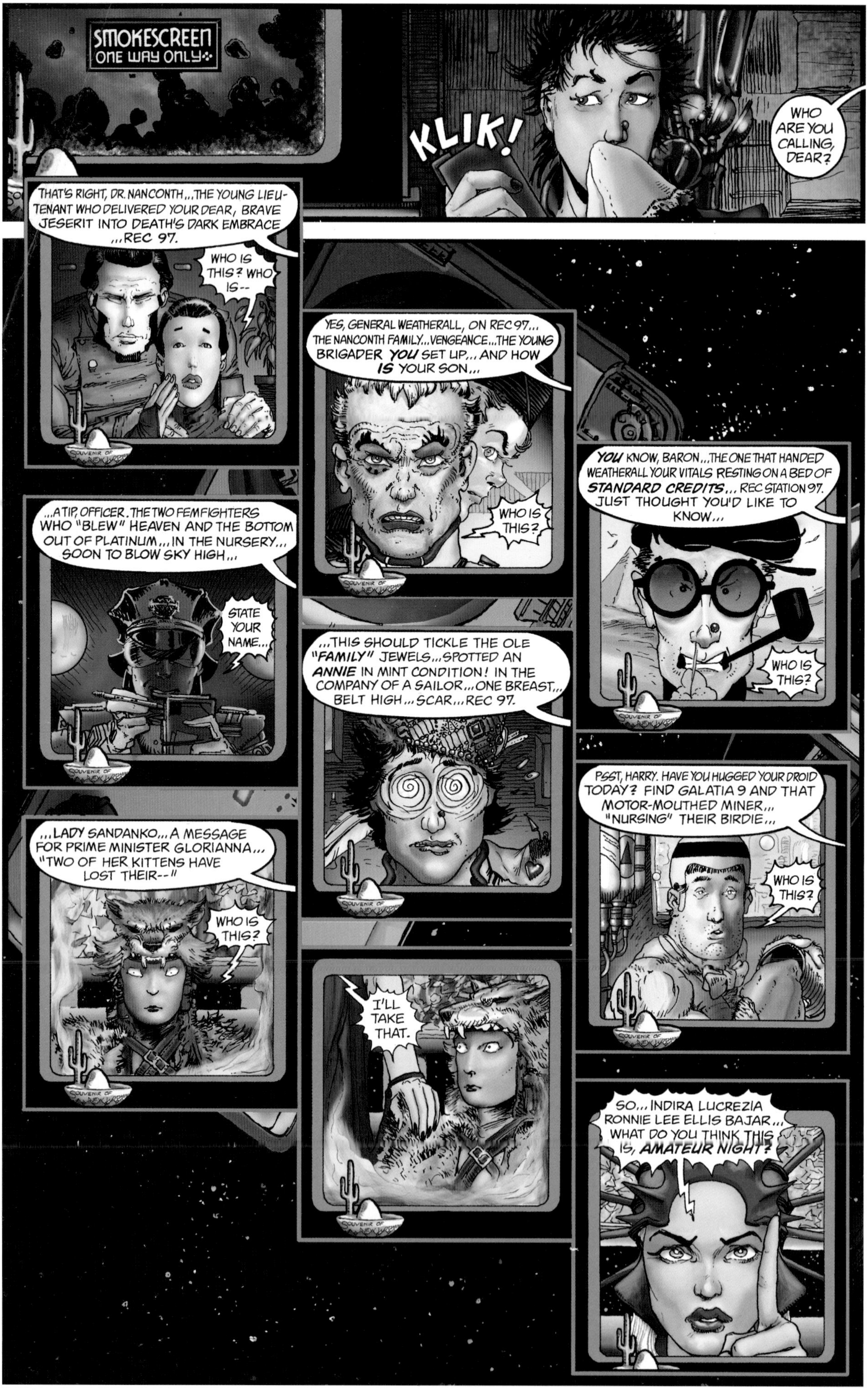
SMOKESCREEN
ONE WAY ONLY
KLIK!
WHO ARE YOU CALLING, DEAR?
THAT'S RIGHT, DR. NANCONTH... THE YOUNG LIEUTENANT WHO DELIVERED YOUR DEAR, BRAVE JESERIT INTO DEATH'S DARK EMBRACE ...REC 97.
WHO IS THIS? WHO IS--
YES, GENERAL WEATHERALL, ON REC 97... THE NANCONTH FAMILY... VENGEANCE... THE YOUNG BRIGADER YOU SET UP... AND HOW IS YOUR SON...
WHO IS THIS?
YOU KNOW, BARON... THE ONE THAT HANDED WEATHERALL YOUR VITALS RESTING ON A BED OF STANDARD CREDITS... REC STATION 97. JUST THOUGHT YOU'D LIKE TO KNOW...
WHO IS THIS?
...A TIP, OFFICER. THE TWO FEMFIGHTERS WHO "BLEW" HEAVEN AND THE BOTTOM OUT OF PLATINUM... IN THE NURSERY... SOON TO BLOW SKY HIGH...
STATE YOUR NAME...
...THIS SHOULD TICKLE THE OLE "FAMILY" JEWELS... SPOTTED AN ANNIE IN MINT CONDITION! IN THE COMPANY OF A SAILOR... ONE BREAST... BELT HIGH... SCAR... REC 97.
PSST, HARRY. HAVE YOU HUGGED YOUR DROID TODAY? FIND GALATIA 9 AND THAT MOTOR-MOUTHED MINER... "NURSING" THEIR BIRDIE...
WHO IS THIS?
...LADY SANDANKO... A MESSAGE FOR PRIME MINISTER GLORIANNA... "TWO OF HER KITTENS HAVE LOST THEIR--"
WHO IS THIS?
I'LL TAKE THAT.
SO... INDIRA LUCREZIA RONNIE LEE ELLIS BAJAR... WHAT DO YOU THINK THIS IS, AMATEUR NIGHT?

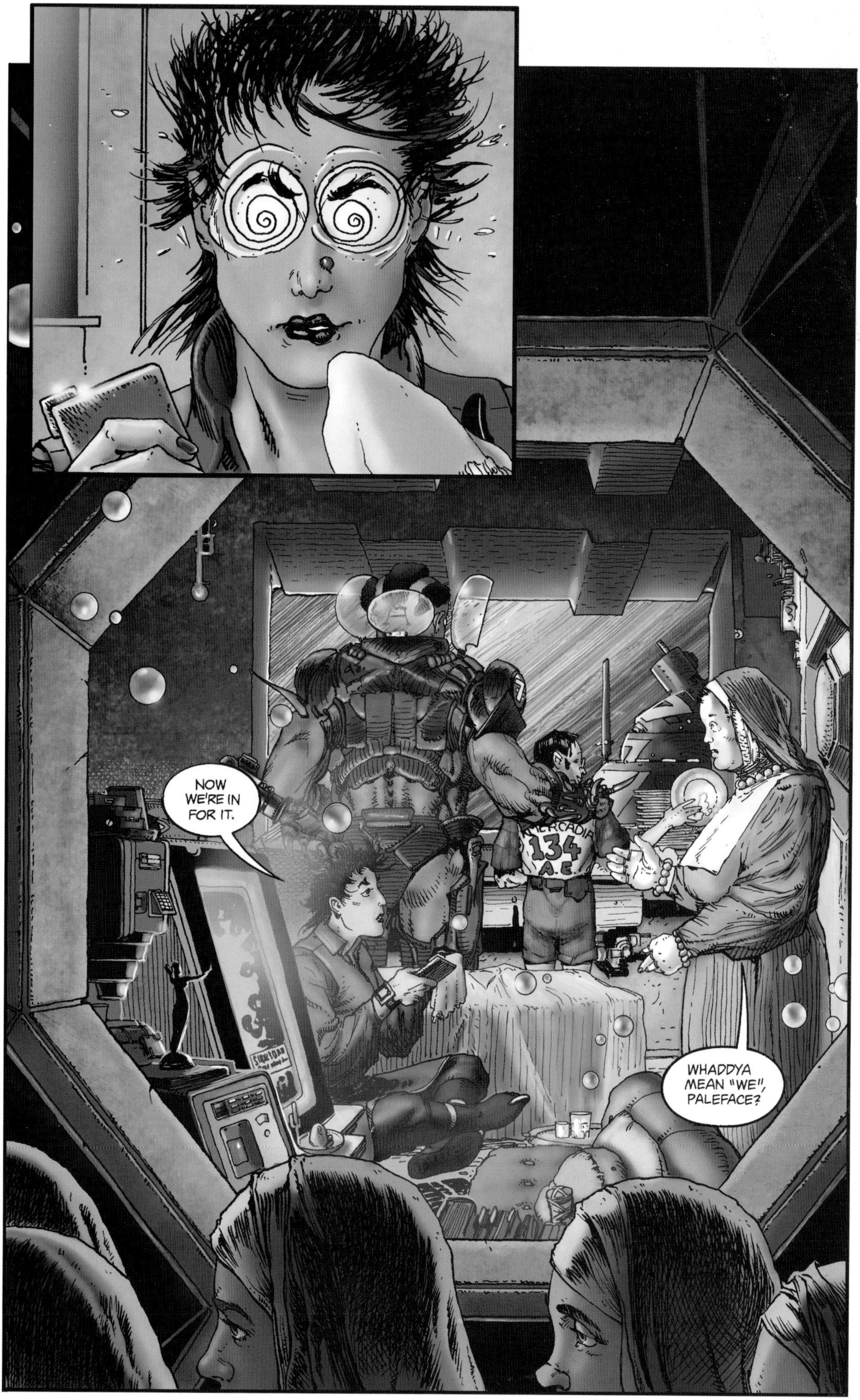
NOW WE'RE IN FOR IT.
WHADDYA MEAN "WE", PALEFACE?

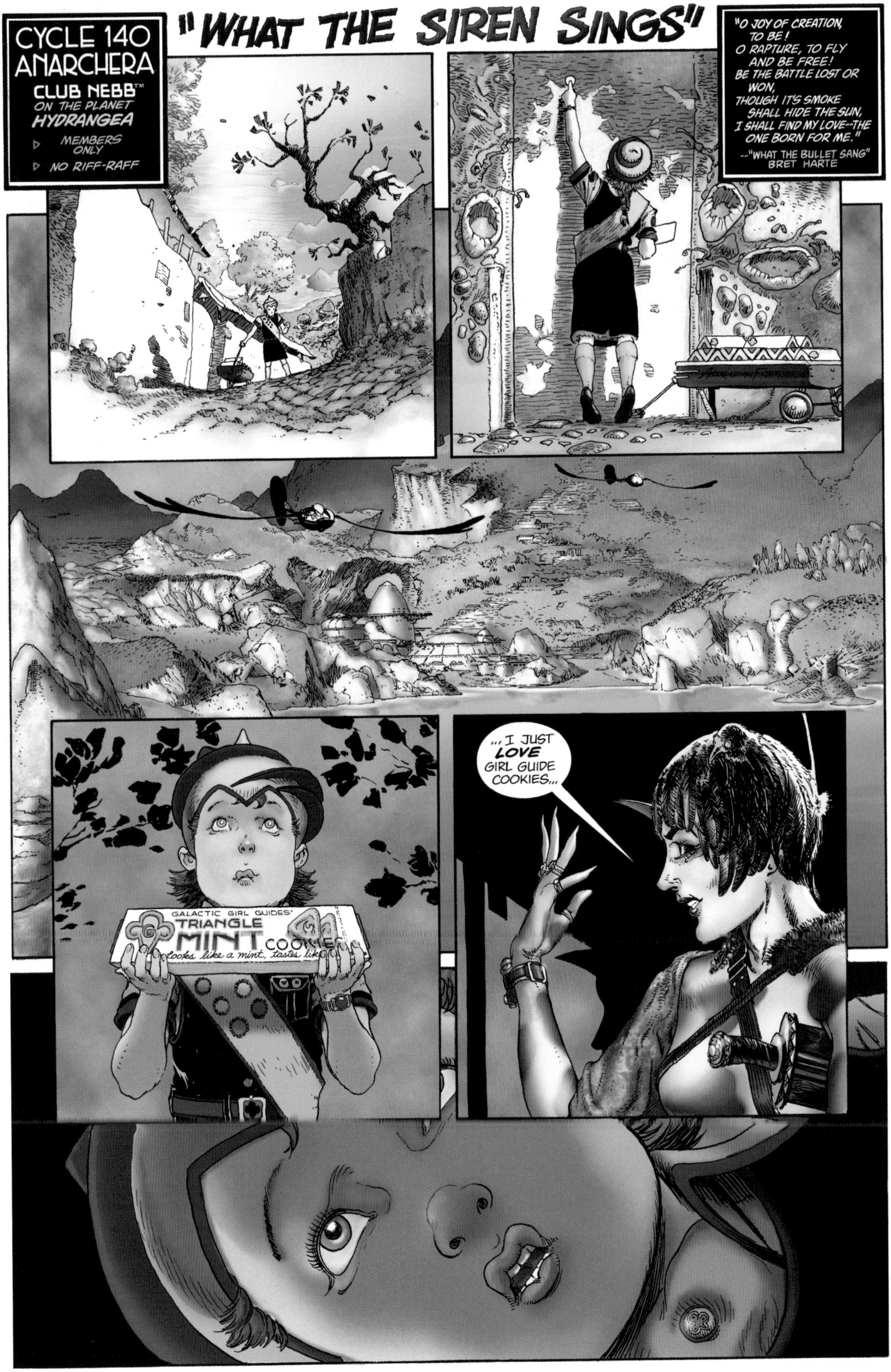
CYCLE 140
ANARCHERA
CLUB NEBB™
ON THE PLANET
HYDRANGEA
MEMBERS ONLY
NO RIFF-RAFF
"WHAT THE SIREN SINGS"
"O JOY OF CREATION, TO BE! O RAPTURE, TO FLY AND BE FREE! BE THE BATTLE LOST OR WON, THOUGH IT'S SMOKE SHALL HIDE THE SUN, I SHALL FIND MY LOVE--THE ONE BORN FOR ME."
--"WHAT THE BULLET SANG" BRET HARTE
GALACTIC GIRL GUIDES'
TRIANGLE MINT COOKIES
looks like a mint, tastes like
...I JUST LOVE GIRL GUIDE COOKIES...

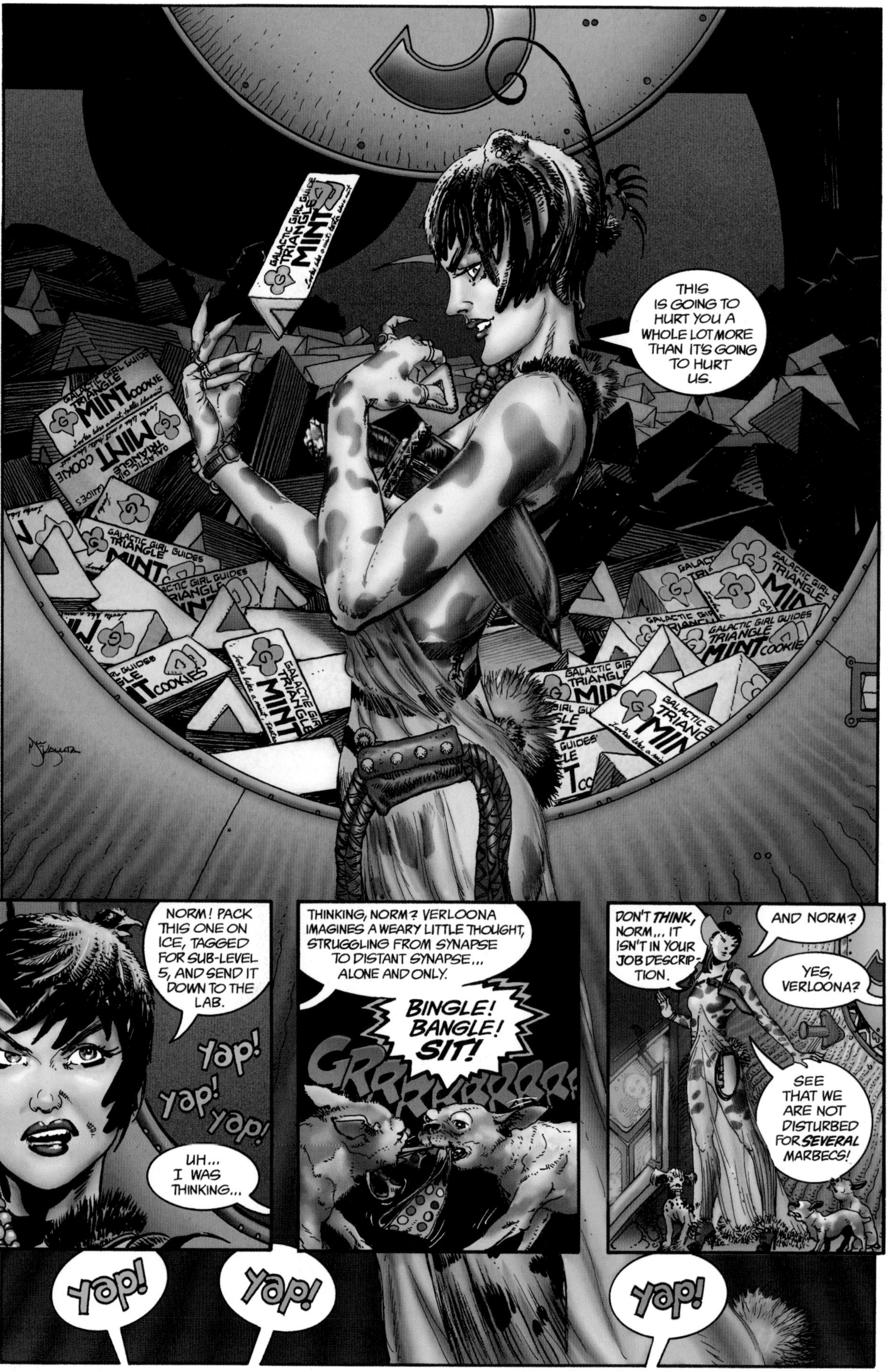
GALACTIC GIRL GUIDE TRIANGLE MINT
THIS IS GOING TO HURT YOU A WHOLE LOT MORE THAN IT'S GOING TO HURT US.
NORM! PACK THIS ONE ON ICE, TAGGED FOR SUB-LEVEL 5, AND SEND IT DOWN TO THE LAB.
YAP! YAP! YAP!
UH... I WAS THINKING...
THINKING, NORM? VERLOONA IMAGINES A WEARY LITTLE THOUGHT, STRUGGLING FROM SYNAPSE TO DISTANT SYNAPSE... ALONE AND ONLY.
BINGLE! BANGLE! SIT!
DON'T THINK, NORM... IT ISN'T IN YOUR JOB DESCRIPTION.
AND NORM?
YES, VERLOONA?
SEE THAT WE ARE NOT DISTURBED FOR SEVERAL MARBECS!
YAP!
YAP!
YAP!

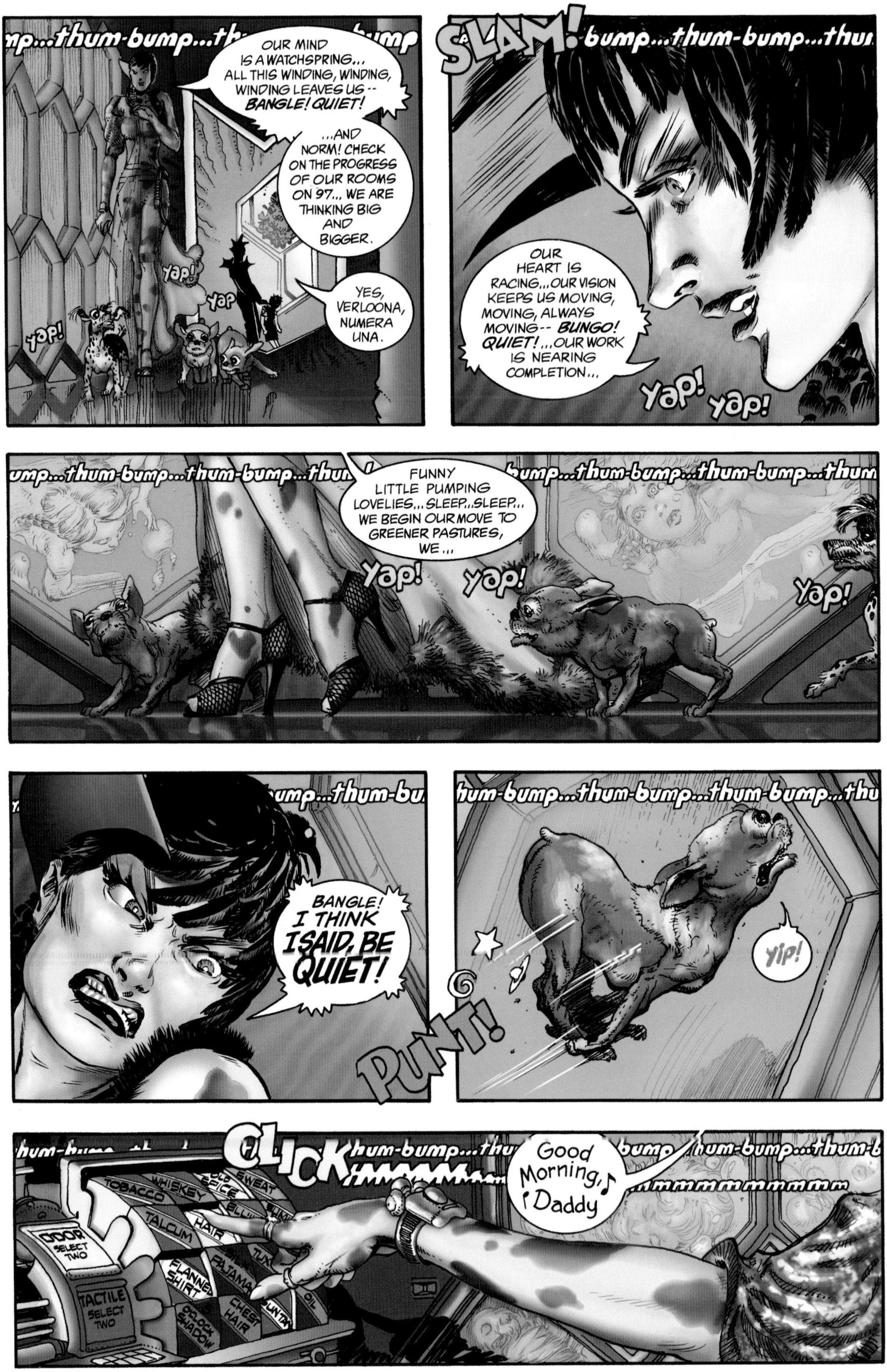

mp...thum-bump...th ...bump
OUR MIND IS A WATCHSPRING... ALL THIS WINDING, WINDING, WINDING LEAVES US -- BANGLE! QUIET!
...AND NORM! CHECK ON THE PROGRESS OF OUR ROOMS ON 97... WE ARE THINKING BIG AND BIGGER.
YAP!
YAP
YAP!
YES, VERLOONA, NUMERA UNA.
SLAM! bump...thum-bump...thu
OUR HEART IS RACING... OUR VISION KEEPS US MOVING, MOVING, ALWAYS MOVING-- BUNGO! QUIET! ... OUR WORK IS NEARING COMPLETION...
YAP! YAP!
ump...thum-bump...thum-bump...thum
FUNNY LITTLE PUMPING LOVELIES... SLEEP... SLEEP... WE BEGIN OUR MOVE TO GREENER PASTURES, WE...
bump...thum-bump...thum-bump...thum
YAP! YAP! YAP!
ump...thum-bu
BANGLE! I THINK I SAID, BE QUIET!
hum-bump...thum-bump...thum-bump...thu
YIP!
PUNT!
hum-bump
CLICK hum-bump...thu
Good Morning, Daddy
bump hum-bump...thum-b
mmmmmmmmmmm
TOBACCO
WHISKEY
OLD SPICE
SWEAT
TALCUM
HAIR
ODOR SELECT TWO
FLANNEL SHIRT
PAJAMA
TUX
TACTILE SELECT TWO
5 O'CLOCK SHADOW
CHEST HAIR
SUNTAN
OIL

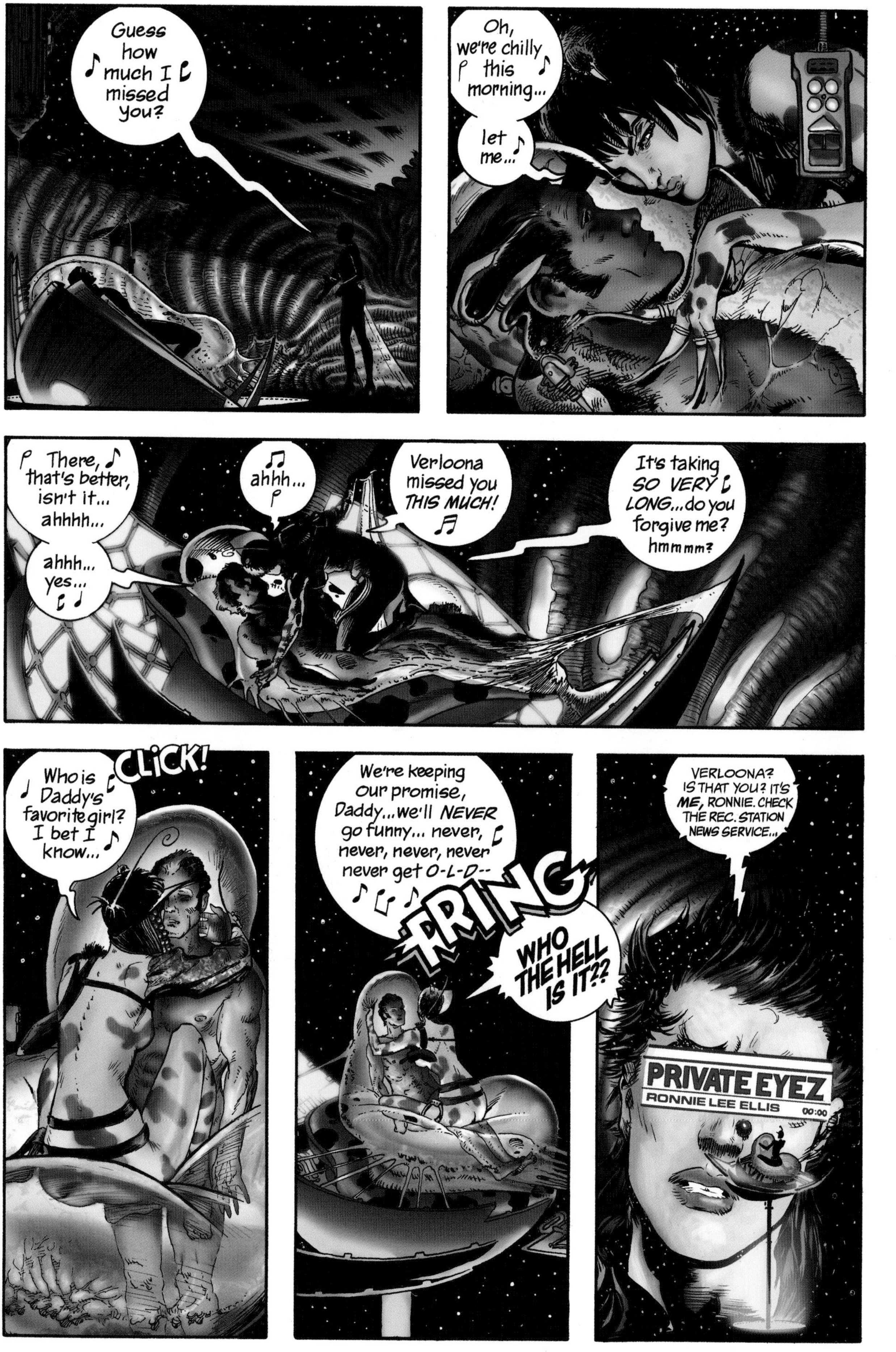
Guess how much I missed you?
Oh, we're chilly this morning...
let me...
There, that's better, isn't it... ahhhh...
ahhh... yes...
ahhh...
Verloona missed you THIS MUCH!
It's taking SO VERY LONG...do you forgive me? hmmmm?
Who is Daddy's favorite girl? I bet I know...
CLICK!
We're keeping our promise, Daddy...we'll NEVER go funny... never, never, never, never never get O-L-D--
FRING
WHO THE HELL IS IT??
VERLOONA? IS THAT YOU? IT'S ME, RONNIE. CHECK THE REC. STATION NEWS SERVICE...
PRIVATE EYEZ
RONNIE LEE ELLIS
00:00

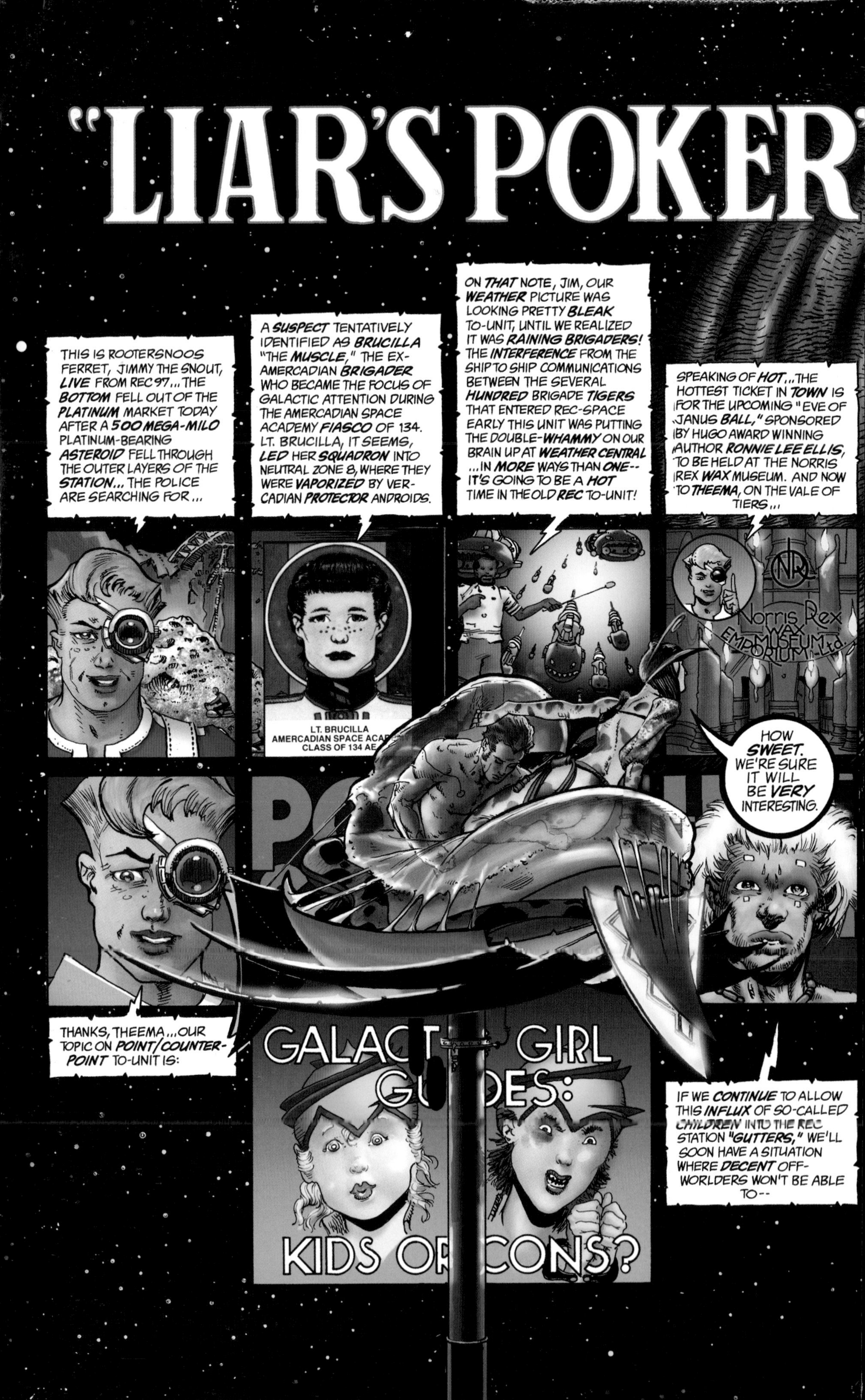
"LIAR'S POKER"
THIS IS ROOTERSNOOS FERRET, JIMMY THE SNOUT, LIVE FROM REC 97... THE BOTTOM FELL OUT OF THE PLATINUM MARKET TODAY AFTER A 500 MEGA-MILO PLATINUM-BEARING ASTEROID FELL THROUGH THE OUTER LAYERS OF THE STATION... THE POLICE ARE SEARCHING FOR...
A SUSPECT TENTATIVELY IDENTIFIED AS BRUCILLA "THE MUSCLE," THE EX-AMERCADIAN BRIGADER WHO BECAME THE FOCUS OF GALACTIC ATTENTION DURING THE AMERCADIAN SPACE ACADEMY FIASCO OF 134. LT. BRUCILLA, IT SEEMS, LED HER SQUADRON INTO NEUTRAL ZONE 8, WHERE THEY WERE VAPORIZED BY VER-CADIAN PROTECTOR ANDROIDS.
LT. BRUCILLA
AMERCADIAN SPACE ACA
CLASS OF 134 AE
ON THAT NOTE, JIM, OUR WEATHER PICTURE WAS LOOKING PRETTY BLEAK TO-UNIT, UNTIL WE REALIZED IT WAS RAINING BRIGADERS! THE INTERFERENCE FROM THE SHIP TO SHIP COMMUNICATIONS BETWEEN THE SEVERAL HUNDRED BRIGADE TIGERS THAT ENTERED REC-SPACE EARLY THIS UNIT WAS PUTTING THE DOUBLE-WHAMMY ON OUR BRAIN UP AT WEATHER CENTRAL ...IN MORE WAYS THAN ONE-- IT'S GOING TO BE A HOT TIME IN THE OLD REC TO-UNIT!
SPEAKING OF HOT... THE HOTTEST TICKET IN TOWN IS FOR THE UPCOMING "EVE OF JANUS BALL," SPONSORED BY HUGO AWARD WINNING AUTHOR RONNIE LEE ELLIS, TO BE HELD AT THE NORRIS REX WAX MUSEUM. AND NOW TO THEEMA, ON THE VALE OF TIERS...
NR
Norris Rex Wax Museum Emporium Ltd.
HOW SWEET. WE'RE SURE IT WILL BE VERY INTERESTING.
THANKS, THEEMA... OUR TOPIC ON POINT/COUNTER-POINT TO-UNIT IS:
GALACT GIRL
GU DES:
KIDS OR CONS?
IF WE CONTINUE TO ALLOW THIS INFLUX OF SO-CALLED CHILDREN INTO THE REC STATION "GUTTERS," WE'LL SOON HAVE A SITUATION WHERE DECENT OFF-WORLDERS WON'T BE ABLE TO--

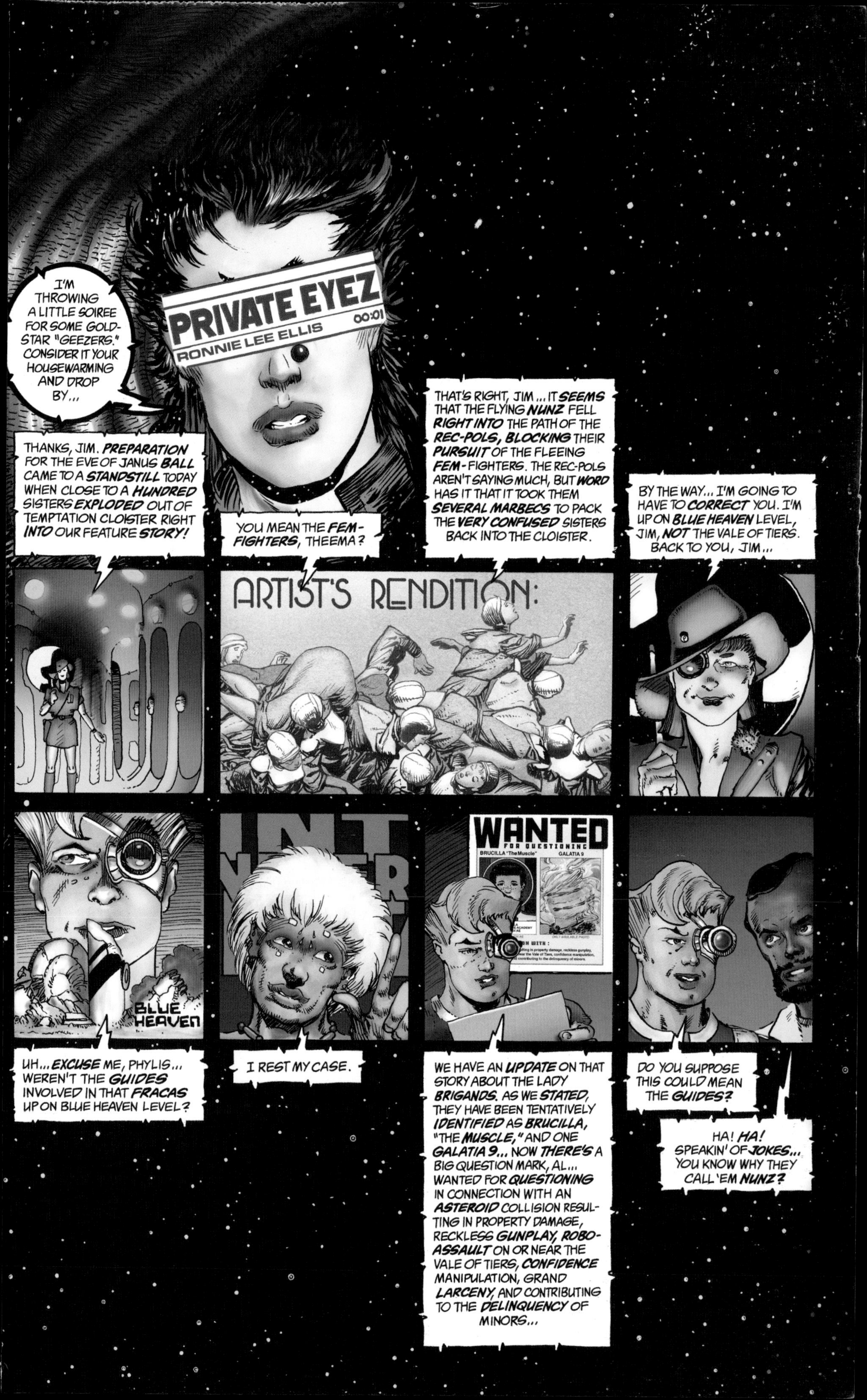

PRIVATE EYEZ
00:01
RONNIE LEE ELLIS
I'M THROWING A LITTLE SOIREE FOR SOME GOLD-STAR "GEEZERS." CONSIDER IT YOUR HOUSEWARMING AND DROP BY...
THANKS, JIM. PREPARATION FOR THE EVE OF JANUS BALL CAME TO A STANDSTILL TODAY WHEN CLOSE TO A HUNDRED SISTERS EXPLODED OUT OF TEMPTATION CLOISTER RIGHT INTO OUR FEATURE STORY!
YOU MEAN THE FEM-FIGHTERS, THEEMA?
THAT'S RIGHT, JIM... IT SEEMS THAT THE FLYING NUNZ FELL RIGHT INTO THE PATH OF THE REC-POLS, BLOCKING THEIR PURSUIT OF THE FLEEING FEM-FIGHTERS. THE REC-POLS AREN'T SAYING MUCH, BUT WORD HAS IT THAT IT TOOK THEM SEVERAL MARBECS TO PACK THE VERY CONFUSED SISTERS BACK INTO THE CLOISTER.
BY THE WAY... I'M GOING TO HAVE TO CORRECT YOU. I'M UP ON BLUE HEAVEN LEVEL, JIM, NOT THE VALE OF TIERS. BACK TO YOU, JIM...
ARTIST'S RENDITION:
BLUE HEAVEN
WANTED
FOR QUESTIONING
BRUCILLA "The Muscle"
GALATIA 9
UH... EXCUSE ME, PHYLIS... WEREN'T THE GUIDES INVOLVED IN THAT FRACAS UP ON BLUE HEAVEN LEVEL?
I REST MY CASE.
WE HAVE AN UPDATE ON THAT STORY ABOUT THE LADY BRIGANDS. AS WE STATED, THEY HAVE BEEN TENTATIVELY IDENTIFIED AS BRUCILLA, "THE MUSCLE," AND ONE GALATIA 9... NOW THERE'S A BIG QUESTION MARK, AL... WANTED FOR QUESTIONING IN CONNECTION WITH AN ASTEROID COLLISION RESULTING IN PROPERTY DAMAGE, RECKLESS GUNPLAY, ROBO-ASSAULT ON OR NEAR THE VALE OF TIERS, CONFIDENCE MANIPULATION, GRAND LARCENY, AND CONTRIBUTING TO THE DELINQUENCY OF MINORS...
DO YOU SUPPOSE THIS COULD MEAN THE GUIDES?
HA! HA! SPEAKIN' OF JOKES... YOU KNOW WHY THEY CALL 'EM NUNZ?

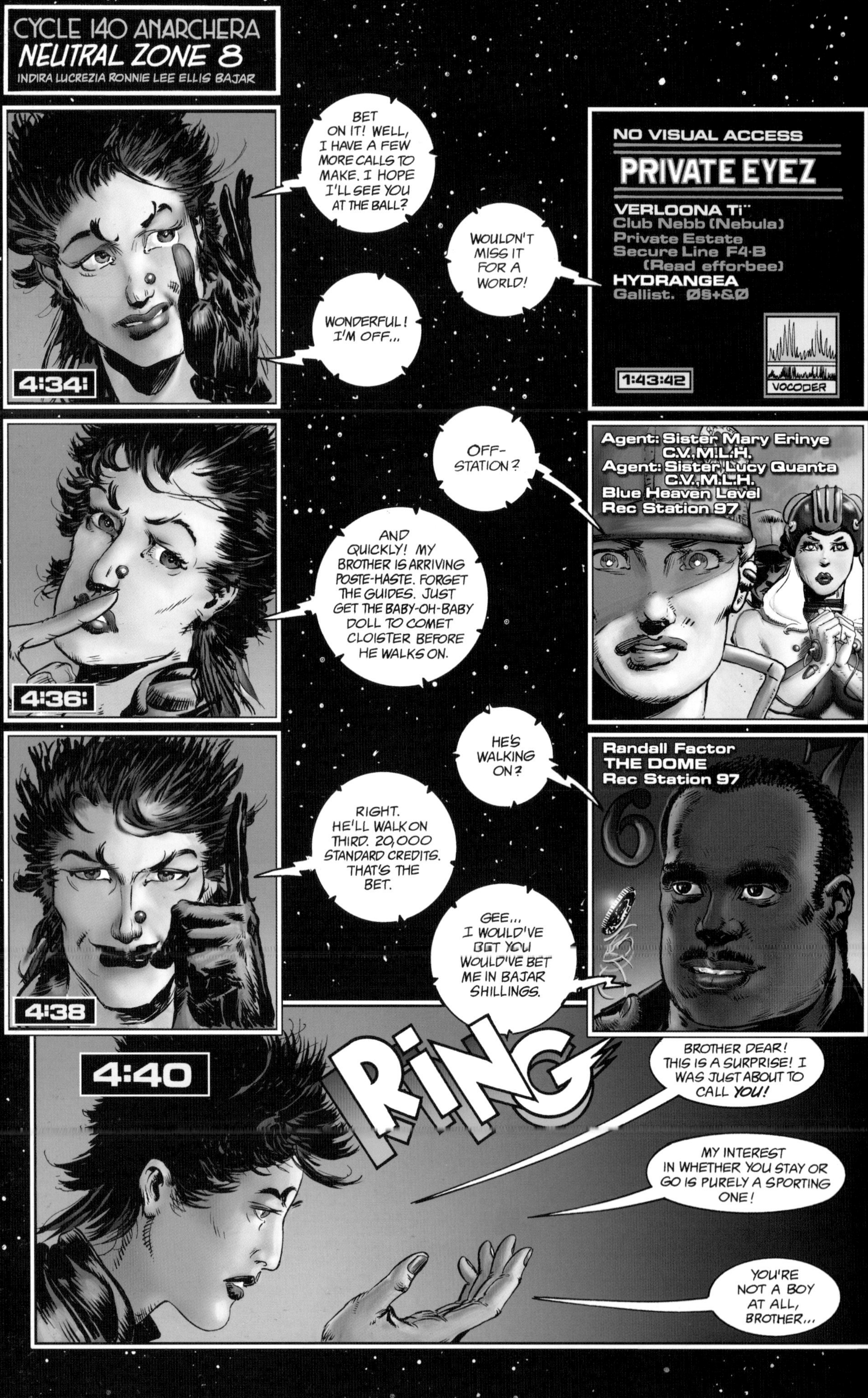
CYCLE 140 ANARCHERA
NEUTRAL ZONE 8
INDIRA LUCREZIA RONNIE LEE ELLIS BAJAR
BET ON IT! WELL, I HAVE A FEW MORE CALLS TO MAKE. I HOPE I'LL SEE YOU AT THE BALL?
NO VISUAL ACCESS
PRIVATE EYEZ
VERLOONA Ti''
Club Nebb (Nebula)
Private Estate
Secure Line F4-B
(Read efforbee)
HYDRANGEA
Gallist. ØS+&Ø
WOULDN'T MISS IT FOR A WORLD!
WONDERFUL! I'M OFF...
4:34:
1:43:42
VOCODER
Agent: Sister Mary Erinye
C.V.,M.L.H.
Agent: Sister Lucy Quanta
C.V.,M.L.H.
Blue Heaven Level
Rec Station 97
OFF-STATION?
AND QUICKLY! MY BROTHER IS ARRIVING POSTE-HASTE. FORGET THE GUIDES. JUST GET THE BABY-OH-BABY DOLL TO COMET CLOISTER BEFORE HE WALKS ON.
4:36:
Randall Factor
THE DOME
Rec Station 97
HE'S WALKING ON?
RIGHT. HE'LL WALK ON THIRD. 20,000 STANDARD CREDITS. THAT'S THE BET.
GEE... I WOULD'VE BET YOU WOULD'VE BET ME IN BAJAR SHILLINGS.
4:38
4:40
RiNG
BROTHER DEAR! THIS IS A SURPRISE! I WAS JUST ABOUT TO CALL YOU!
MY INTEREST IN WHETHER YOU STAY OR GO IS PURELY A SPORTING ONE!
YOU'RE NOT A BOY AT ALL, BROTHER...

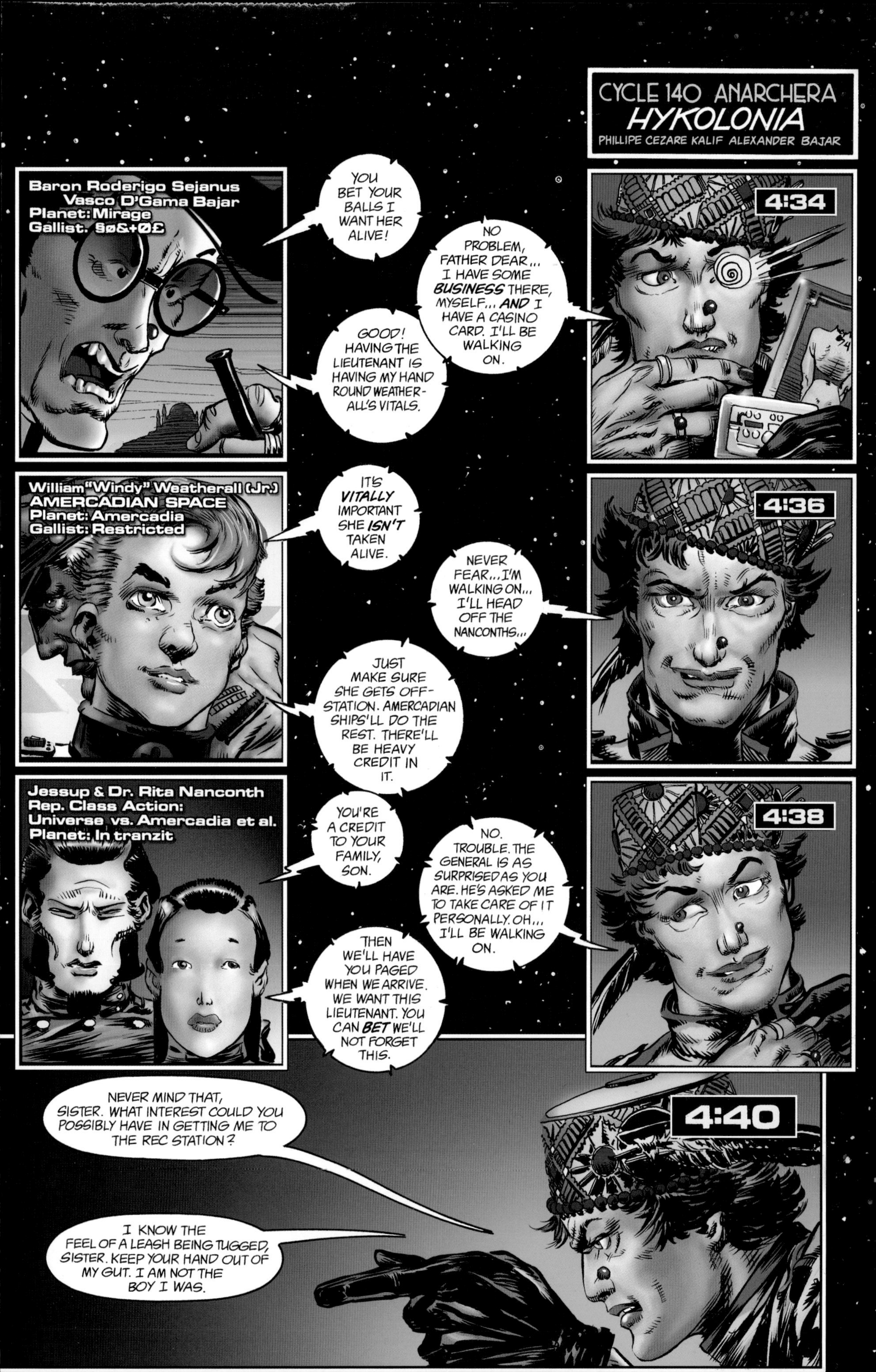
CYCLE 140 ANARCHERA
HYKOLONIA
PHILLIPE CEZARE KALIF ALEXANDER BAJAR
Baron Roderigo Sejanus Vasco D'Gama Bajar
Planet: Mirage
Gallist. §ø&+Ø£
4:34
YOU BET YOUR BALLS I WANT HER ALIVE!
NO PROBLEM, FATHER DEAR... I HAVE SOME BUSINESS THERE, MYSELF... AND I HAVE A CASINO CARD. I'LL BE WALKING ON.
GOOD! HAVING THE LIEUTENANT IS HAVING MY HAND ROUND WEATHER-ALL'S VITALS.
William "Windy" Weatherall (Jr.)
AMERCADIAN SPACE
Planet: Amercadia
Gallist: Restricted
4:36
IT'S VITALLY IMPORTANT SHE ISN'T TAKEN ALIVE.
NEVER FEAR... I'M WALKING ON... I'LL HEAD OFF THE NANCONTHS...
JUST MAKE SURE SHE GETS OFF-STATION. AMERCADIAN SHIPS'LL DO THE REST. THERE'LL BE HEAVY CREDIT IN IT.
Jessup & Dr. Rita Nanconth
Rep. Class Action:
Universe vs. Amercadia et al.
Planet: In tranzit
4:38
YOU'RE A CREDIT TO YOUR FAMILY, SON.
NO. TROUBLE. THE GENERAL IS AS SURPRISED AS YOU ARE. HE'S ASKED ME TO TAKE CARE OF IT PERSONALLY. OH... I'LL BE WALKING ON.
THEN WE'LL HAVE YOU PAGED WHEN WE ARRIVE. WE WANT THIS LIEUTENANT. YOU CAN BET WE'LL NOT FORGET THIS.
4:40
NEVER MIND THAT, SISTER. WHAT INTEREST COULD YOU POSSIBLY HAVE IN GETTING ME TO THE REC STATION?
I KNOW THE FEEL OF A LEASH BEING TUGGED, SISTER. KEEP YOUR HAND OUT OF MY GUT. I AM NOT THE BOY I WAS.

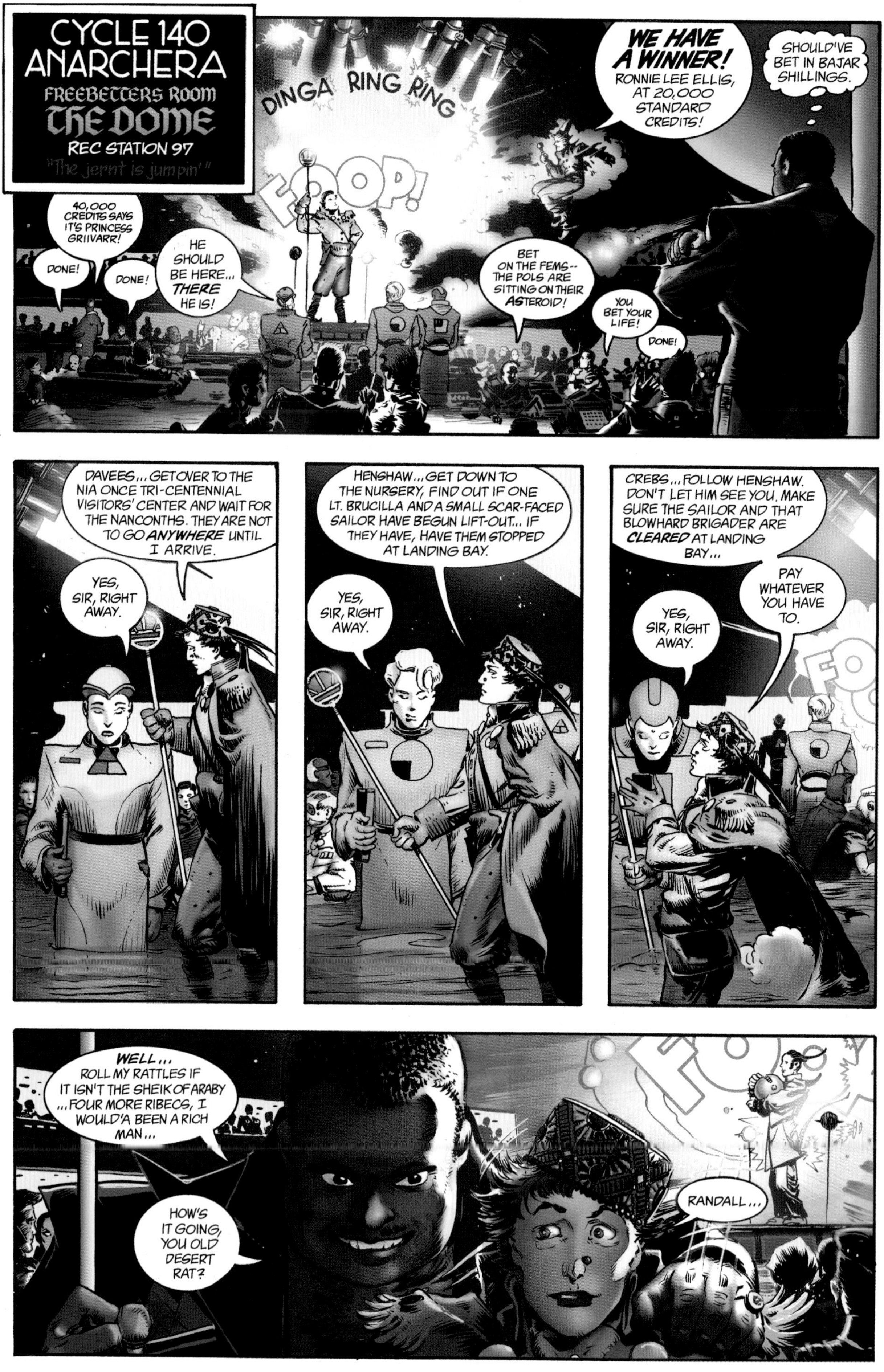
CYCLE 140
ANARCHERA
FREEBETTERS ROOM
THE DOME
REC STATION 97
"The jernt is jumpin'"
DINGA RING RING
FOOP!
WE HAVE A WINNER! RONNIE LEE ELLIS, AT 20,000 STANDARD CREDITS!
SHOULD'VE BET IN BAJAR SHILLINGS.
40,000 CREDITS SAYS IT'S PRINCESS GRIIVARR!
DONE!
DONE!
HE SHOULD BE HERE... THERE HE IS!
BET ON THE FEMS-- THE POLS ARE SITTING ON THEIR ASTEROID!
YOU BET YOUR LIFE!
DONE!
DAVEES... GET OVER TO THE NIA ONCE TRI-CENTENNIAL VISITORS' CENTER AND WAIT FOR THE NANCONTHS. THEY ARE NOT TO GO ANYWHERE UNTIL I ARRIVE.
YES, SIR, RIGHT AWAY.
HENSHAW... GET DOWN TO THE NURSERY, FIND OUT IF ONE LT. BRUCILLA AND A SMALL SCAR-FACED SAILOR HAVE BEGUN LIFT-OUT... IF THEY HAVE, HAVE THEM STOPPED AT LANDING BAY.
YES, SIR, RIGHT AWAY.
CREBS... FOLLOW HENSHAW. DON'T LET HIM SEE YOU. MAKE SURE THE SAILOR AND THAT BLOWHARD BRIGADER ARE CLEARED AT LANDING BAY...
PAY WHATEVER YOU HAVE TO.
YES, SIR, RIGHT AWAY.
WELL... ROLL MY RATTLES IF IT ISN'T THE SHEIK OF ARABY ...FOUR MORE RIBECS, I WOULD'A BEEN A RICH MAN...
HOW'S IT GOING, YOU OLD DESERT RAT?
RANDALL...

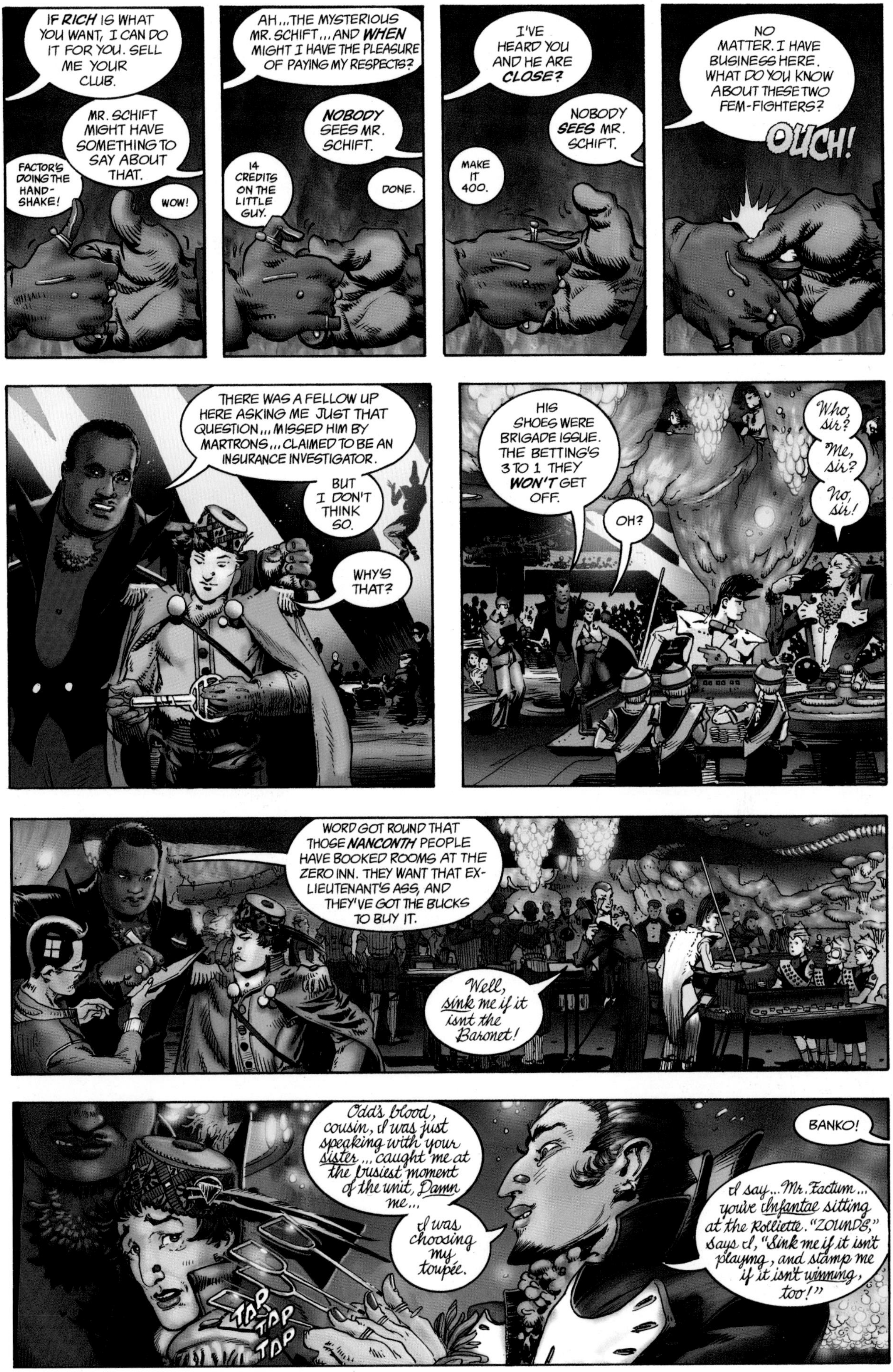
IF RICH IS WHAT YOU WANT, I CAN DO IT FOR YOU. SELL ME YOUR CLUB.
MR. SCHIFT MIGHT HAVE SOMETHING TO SAY ABOUT THAT.
FACTOR'S DOING THE HAND-SHAKE!
WOW!
AH... THE MYSTERIOUS MR. SCHIFT... AND WHEN MIGHT I HAVE THE PLEASURE OF PAYING MY RESPECTS?
NOBODY SEES MR. SCHIFT.
14 CREDITS ON THE LITTLE GUY.
DONE.
I'VE HEARD YOU AND HE ARE CLOSE?
NOBODY SEES MR. SCHIFT.
MAKE IT 400.
NO MATTER. I HAVE BUSINESS HERE. WHAT DO YOU KNOW ABOUT THESE TWO FEM-FIGHTERS?
OUCH!
THERE WAS A FELLOW UP HERE ASKING ME JUST THAT QUESTION... MISSED HIM BY MARTRONS... CLAIMED TO BE AN INSURANCE INVESTIGATOR.
BUT I DON'T THINK SO.
WHY'S THAT?
HIS SHOES WERE BRIGADE ISSUE. THE BETTING'S 3 TO 1 THEY WON'T GET OFF.
OH?
Who, sir?
Me, sir?
No, sir!
WORD GOT ROUND THAT THOSE NANCONTH PEOPLE HAVE BOOKED ROOMS AT THE ZERO INN. THEY WANT THAT EX-LIEUTENANT'S ASS, AND THEY'VE GOT THE BUCKS TO BUY IT.
Well, sink me if it isnt the Baronet!
Odd's blood, cousin, I was just speaking with your sister... caught me at the busiest moment of the unit, Damn me...
I was choosing my toupée.
BANKO!
I say... Mr. Factum... you've Infantae sitting at the Rolliette. "ZOUNDS," says I, "Sink me if it isn't playing, and stamp me if it isn't winning, too!"
TAP TAP TAP

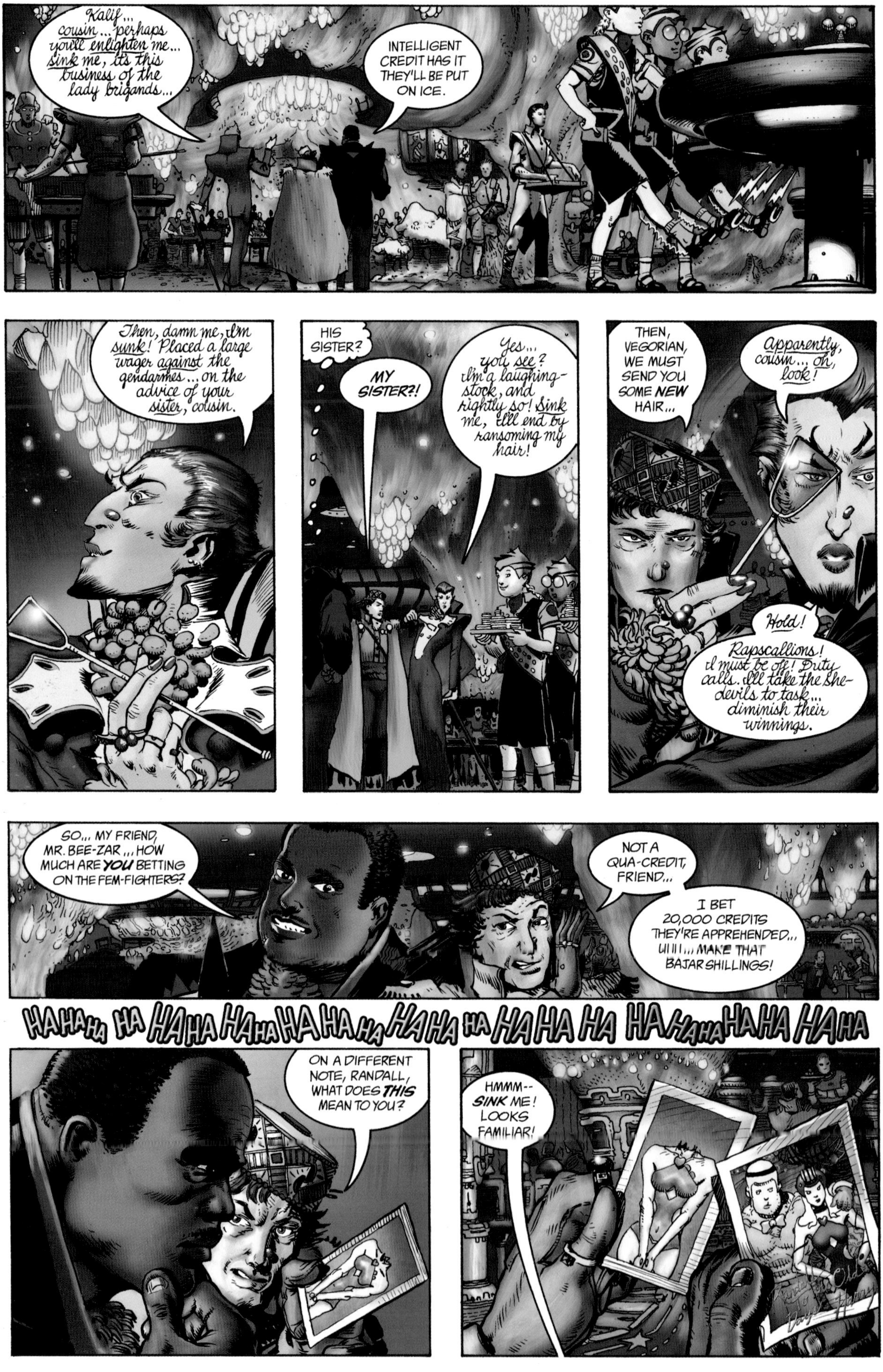

Kalif... cousin... perhaps you'll enlighten me... sink me, it's this business of the lady brigands...
INTELLIGENT CREDIT HAS IT THEY'LL BE PUT ON ICE.
Then, damn me, I'm sunk! Placed a large wager against the gendarmes... on the advice of your sister, cousin.
HIS SISTER?
MY SISTER?!
Yes... you see? I'm a laughing-stock, and rightly so! Sink me, I'll end by ransoming my hair!
THEN, VEGORIAN, WE MUST SEND YOU SOME NEW HAIR...
Apparently, cousin... oh, look!
Hold!
Rapscallions! I must be off! Duty calls. I'll take the she-devils to task... diminish their winnings.
SO... MY FRIEND, MR. BEE-ZAR... HOW MUCH ARE YOU BETTING ON THE FEM-FIGHTERS?
NOT A QUA-CREDIT, FRIEND...
I BET 20,000 CREDITS THEY'RE APPREHENDED... UH... MAKE THAT BAJAR SHILLINGS!
HAHAHA HA HAHA HAHAHAHA HA HA HAHA HA HAHA HA HA HA HAHAHA HAHA HAHA
ON A DIFFERENT NOTE, RANDALL, WHAT DOES THIS MEAN TO YOU?
HMMM-- SINK ME! LOOKS FAMILIAR!

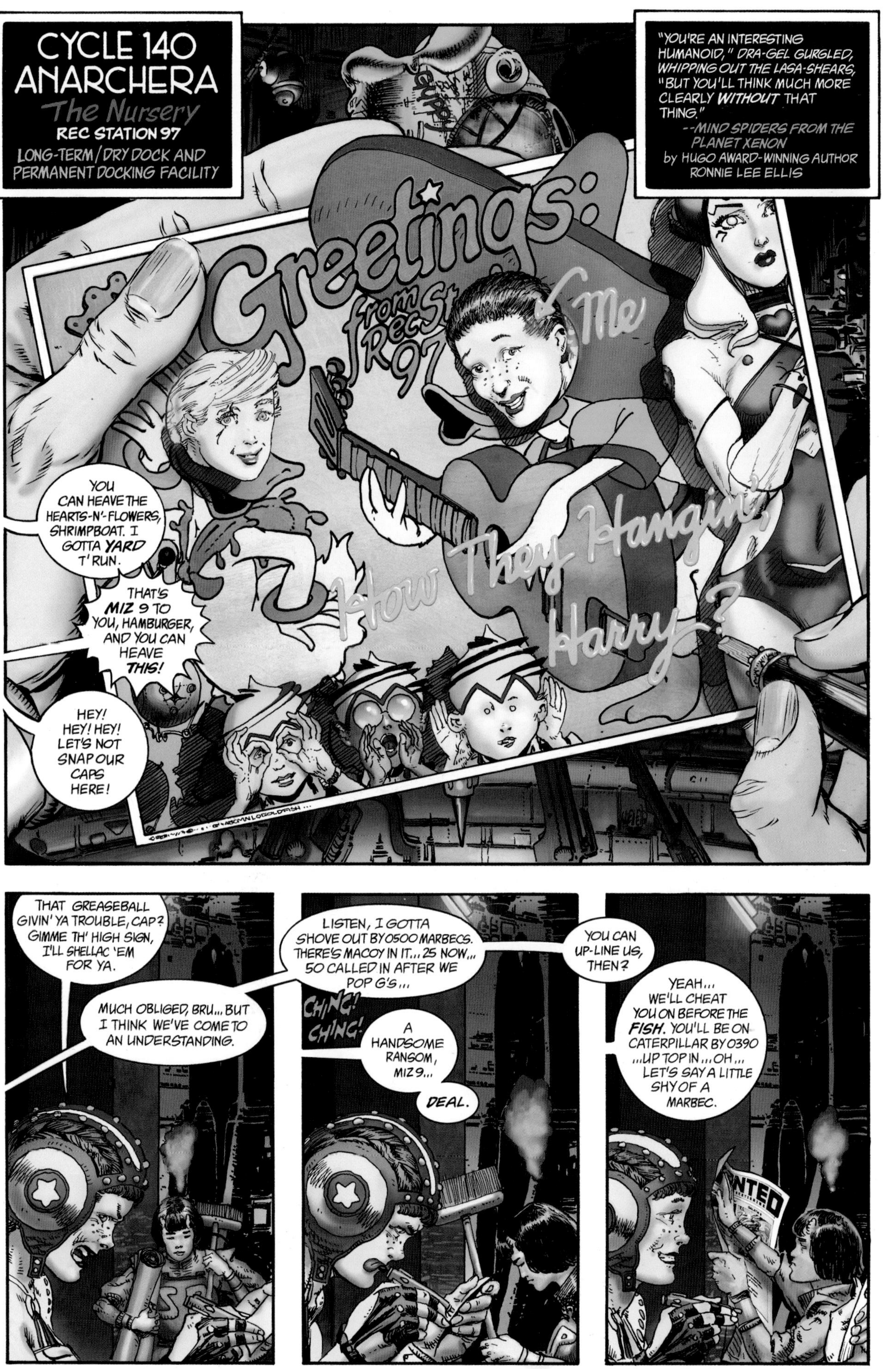
CYCLE 140
ANARCHERA
The Nursery
REC STATION 97
LONG-TERM/DRY DOCK AND PERMANENT DOCKING FACILITY
"YOU'RE AN INTERESTING HUMANOID," DRA-GEL GURGLED, WHIPPING OUT THE LASA-SHEARS, "BUT YOU'LL THINK MUCH MORE CLEARLY WITHOUT THAT THING."
--MIND SPIDERS FROM THE PLANET XENON
by HUGO AWARD-WINNING AUTHOR RONNIE LEE ELLIS
Greetings:
from Rec St 97
Me
How They Hangin', Harry?
YOU CAN HEAVE THE HEARTS-N'-FLOWERS, SHRIMPBOAT. I GOTTA YARD T'RUN.
THAT'S MIZ 9 TO YOU, HAMBURGER, AND YOU CAN HEAVE THIS!
HEY! HEY! HEY! LET'S NOT SNAP OUR CAPS HERE!
THAT GREASEBALL GIVIN' YA TROUBLE, CAP? GIMME TH' HIGH SIGN, I'LL SHELLAC 'EM FOR YA.
MUCH OBLIGED, BRU... BUT I THINK WE'VE COME TO AN UNDERSTANDING.
LISTEN, I GOTTA SHOVE OUT BY 0500 MARBECS. THERE'S MACOY IN IT... 25 NOW... 50 CALLED IN AFTER WE POP G'S...
CHING! CHING!
A HANDSOME RANSOM, MIZ 9...
DEAL.
YOU CAN UP-LINE US, THEN?
YEAH... WE'LL CHEAT YOU ON BEFORE THE FISH. YOU'LL BE ON CATERPILLAR BY 0390 ...UP TOP IN... OH... LET'S SAY A LITTLE SHY OF A MARBEC.

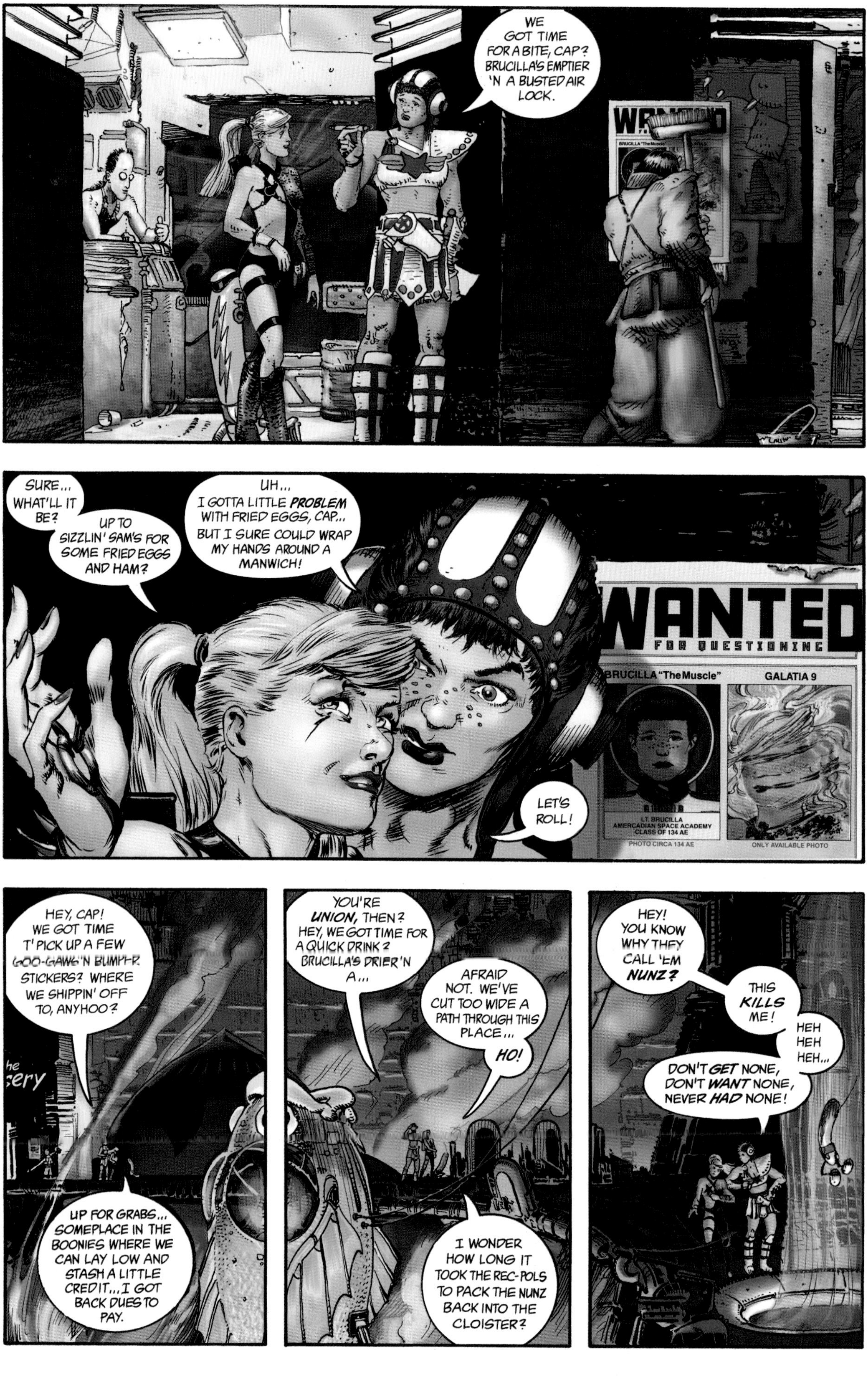

WE GOT TIME FOR A BITE, CAP? BRUCILLA'S EMPTIER 'N A BUSTED AIR LOCK.
SURE... WHAT'LL IT BE?
UP TO SIZZLIN' SAM'S FOR SOME FRIED EGGS AND HAM?
UH... I GOTTA LITTLE ***PROBLEM*** WITH FRIED EGGS, CAP... BUT I SURE COULD WRAP MY HANDS AROUND A MANWICH!
WANTED
FOR QUESTIONING
BRUCILLA "The Muscle"
GALATIA 9
LT. BRUCILLA
AMERCADIAN SPACE ACADEMY
CLASS OF 134 AE
PHOTO CIRCA 134 AE
ONLY AVAILABLE PHOTO
LET'S ROLL!
HEY, CAP! WE GOT TIME T' PICK UP A FEW GOO-GAWS 'N BUMPER STICKERS? WHERE WE SHIPPIN' OFF TO, ANYHOO?
UP FOR GRABS... SOMEPLACE IN THE BOONIES WHERE WE CAN LAY LOW AND STASH A LITTLE CREDIT... I GOT BACK DUES TO PAY.
YOU'RE ***UNION,*** THEN? HEY, WE GOT TIME FOR A QUICK DRINK? BRUCILLA'S DRIER 'N A...
AFRAID NOT. WE'VE CUT TOO WIDE A PATH THROUGH THIS PLACE... ***HO!***
I WONDER HOW LONG IT TOOK THE REC-POLS TO PACK THE NUNZ BACK INTO THE CLOISTER?
HEY! YOU KNOW WHY THEY CALL 'EM ***NUNZ?***
THIS ***KILLS*** ME!
HEH HEH HEH...
DON'T ***GET*** NONE, DON'T ***WANT*** NONE, NEVER ***HAD*** NONE!

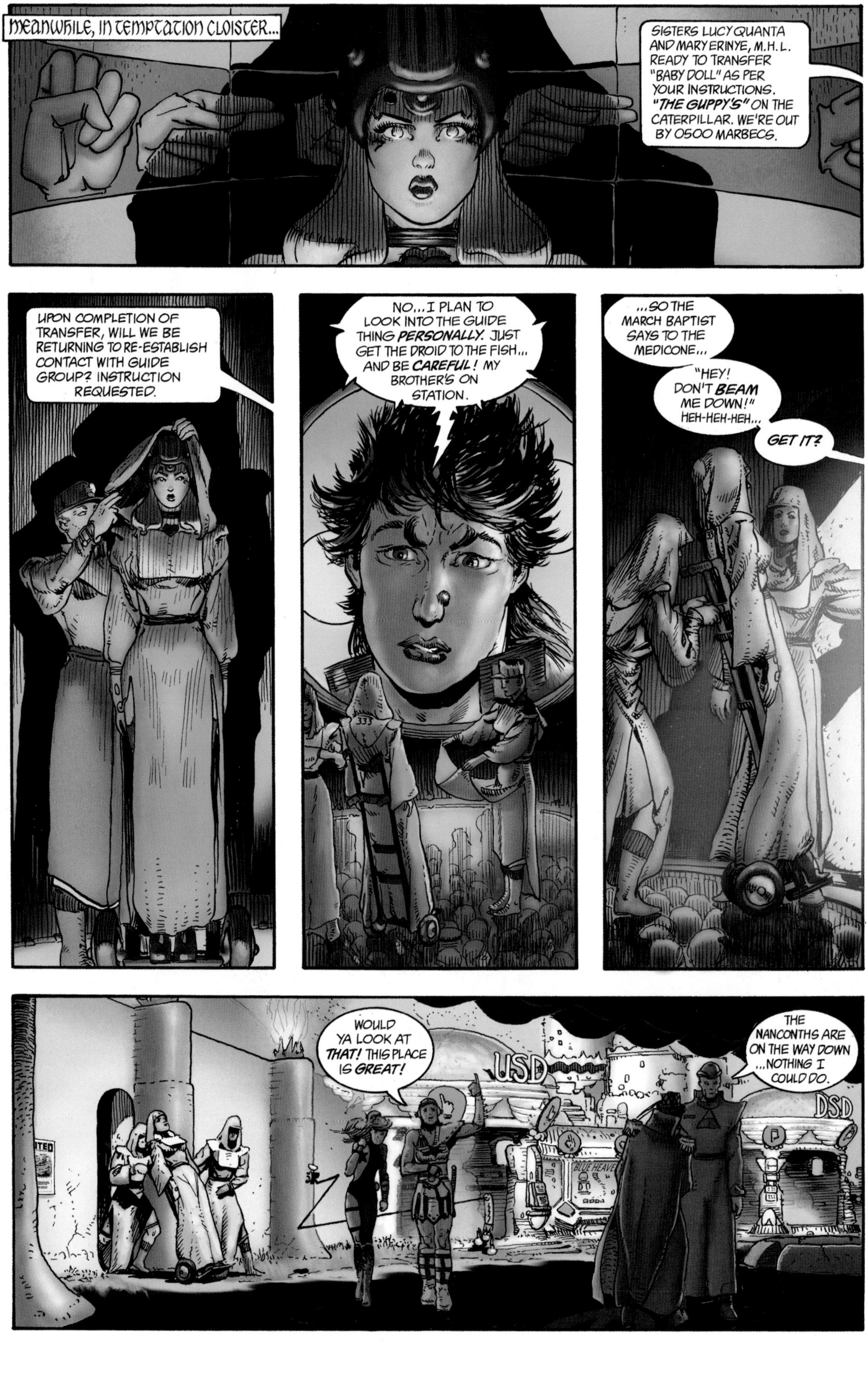
MEANWHILE, IN TEMPTATION CLOISTER...
SISTERS LUCY QUANTA AND MARY ERINYE, M.H.L. READY TO TRANSFER "BABY DOLL" AS PER YOUR INSTRUCTIONS. "THE GUPPY'S" ON THE CATERPILLAR. WE'RE OUT BY 0500 MARBECS.
UPON COMPLETION OF TRANSFER, WILL WE BE RETURNING TO RE-ESTABLISH CONTACT WITH GUIDE GROUP? INSTRUCTION REQUESTED.
NO...I PLAN TO LOOK INTO THE GUIDE THING PERSONALLY. JUST GET THE DROID TO THE FISH... AND BE CAREFUL! MY BROTHER'S ON STATION.
333
...SO THE MARCH BAPTIST SAYS TO THE MEDICONE...
"HEY! DON'T BEAM ME DOWN!" HEH-HEH-HEH...
GET IT?
WOULD YA LOOK AT THAT! THIS PLACE IS GREAT!
USD
THE NANCONTHS ARE ON THE WAY DOWN ...NOTHING I COULD DO.
DSD

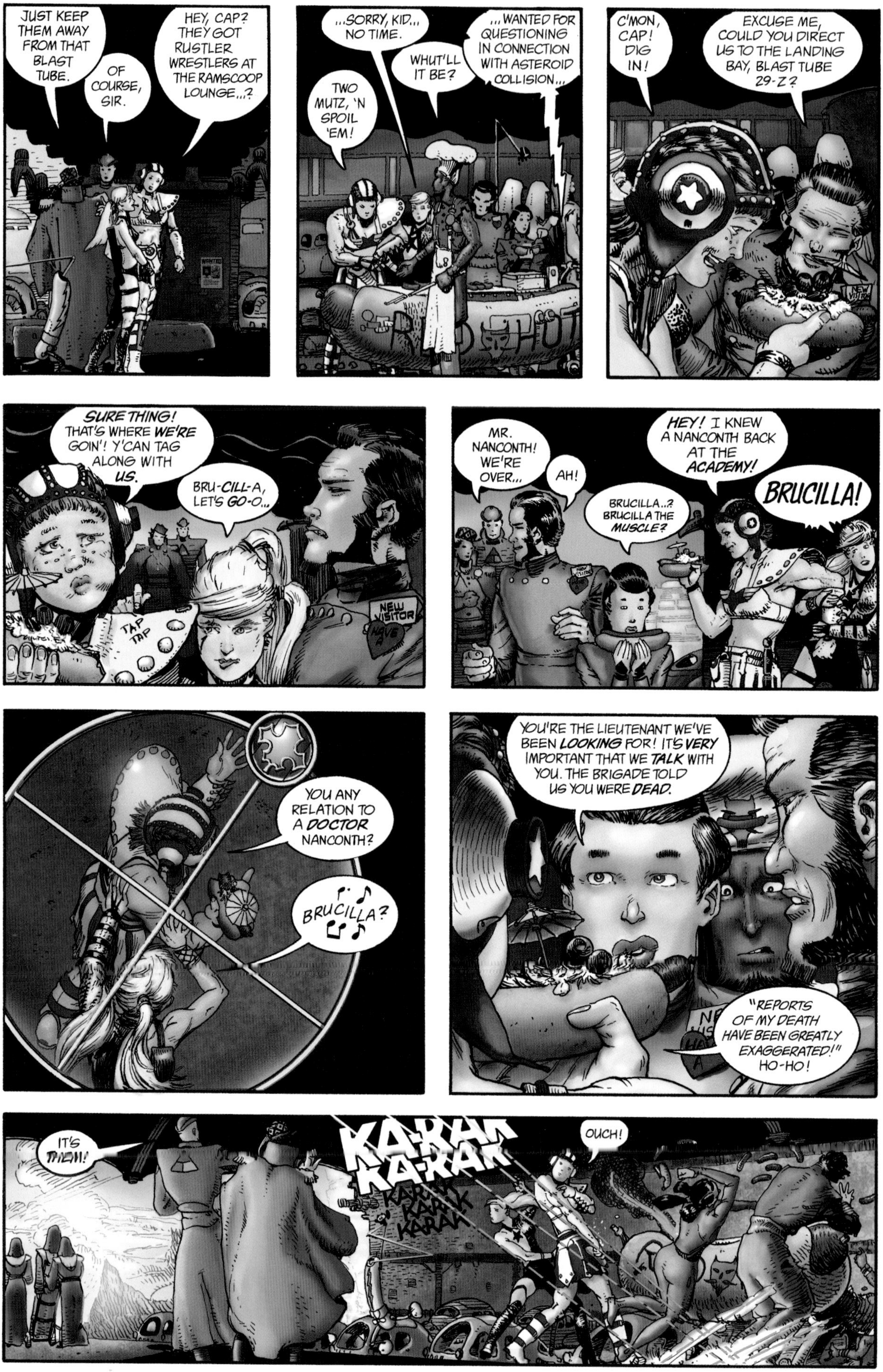
JUST KEEP THEM AWAY FROM THAT BLAST TUBE.
OF COURSE, SIR.
HEY, CAP? THEY GOT RUSTLER WRESTLERS AT THE RAMSCOOP LOUNGE...?
...SORRY, KID... NO TIME.
TWO MUTZ, 'N SPOIL 'EM!
WHUT'LL IT BE?
...WANTED FOR QUESTIONING IN CONNECTION WITH ASTEROID COLLISION...
C'MON, CAP! DIG IN!
EXCUSE ME, COULD YOU DIRECT US TO THE LANDING BAY, BLAST TUBE 29-Z?
SURE THING! THAT'S WHERE WE'RE GOIN'! Y'CAN TAG ALONG WITH US.
BRU-CILL-A, LET'S GO-O...
TAP TAP
NEW VISITOR
MR. NANCONTH! WE'RE OVER...
AH!
BRUCILLA...? BRUCILLA THE MUSCLE?
HEY! I KNEW A NANCONTH BACK AT THE ACADEMY!
BRUCILLA!
YOU ANY RELATION TO A DOCTOR NANCONTH?
BRUCILLA?
YOU'RE THE LIEUTENANT WE'VE BEEN LOOKING FOR! IT'S VERY IMPORTANT THAT WE TALK WITH YOU. THE BRIGADE TOLD US YOU WERE DEAD.
"REPORTS OF MY DEATH HAVE BEEN GREATLY EXAGGERATED!" HO-HO!
IT'S THEM!
KA-RAK KA-RAK
KA-RAK KA-RAK KA-RAK
OUCH!

GET 'EM!
JUMP!
DUCK!
HUNGRY, GUYS?
BONG
HATE TO EAT AND RUN! HOP IN, BRU, WE'RE OFF!
JUST SERVIN' DESSERT, CAP!
GOTTA SHAKE THIS GUY! WHERE'S TH' DAMN NUNZ WHEN Y'NEED 'EM?
I WISH YOU HADN'T SAID THAT...
HEADS UP!
groan
?
?
?

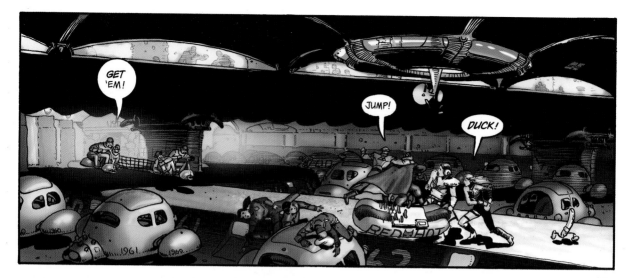

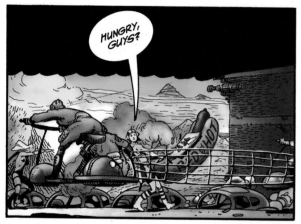

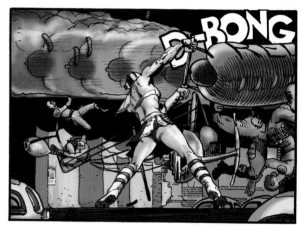

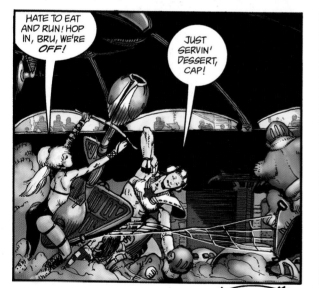

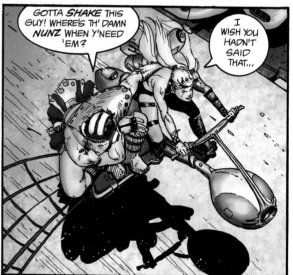

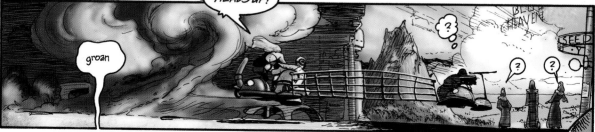

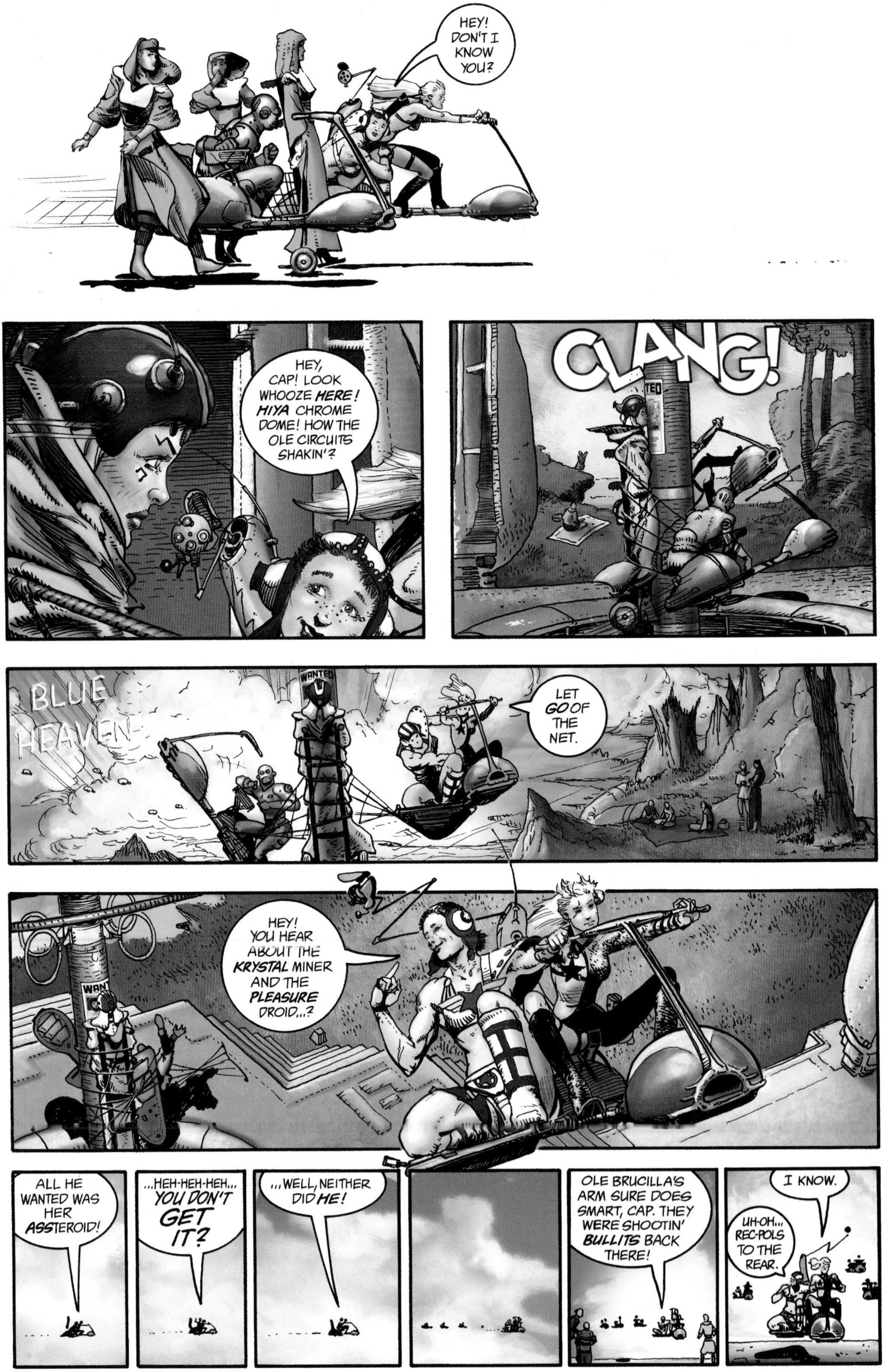

HEY! DON'T I KNOW YOU?
HEY, CAP! LOOK WHOOZE HERE! HIYA CHROME DOME! HOW THE OLE CIRCUITS SHAKIN'?
CLANG!
BLUE HEAVEN
LET GO OF THE NET.
HEY! YOU HEAR ABOUT THE KRYSTAL MINER AND THE PLEASURE DROID...?
ALL HE WANTED WAS HER ASSTEROID!
...HEH-HEH-HEH... YOU DON'T GET IT?
...WELL, NEITHER DID HE!
OLE BRUCILLA'S ARM SURE DOES SMART, CAP. THEY WERE SHOOTIN' BULLITS BACK THERE!
I KNOW.
UH-OH... REC-POLS TO THE REAR.

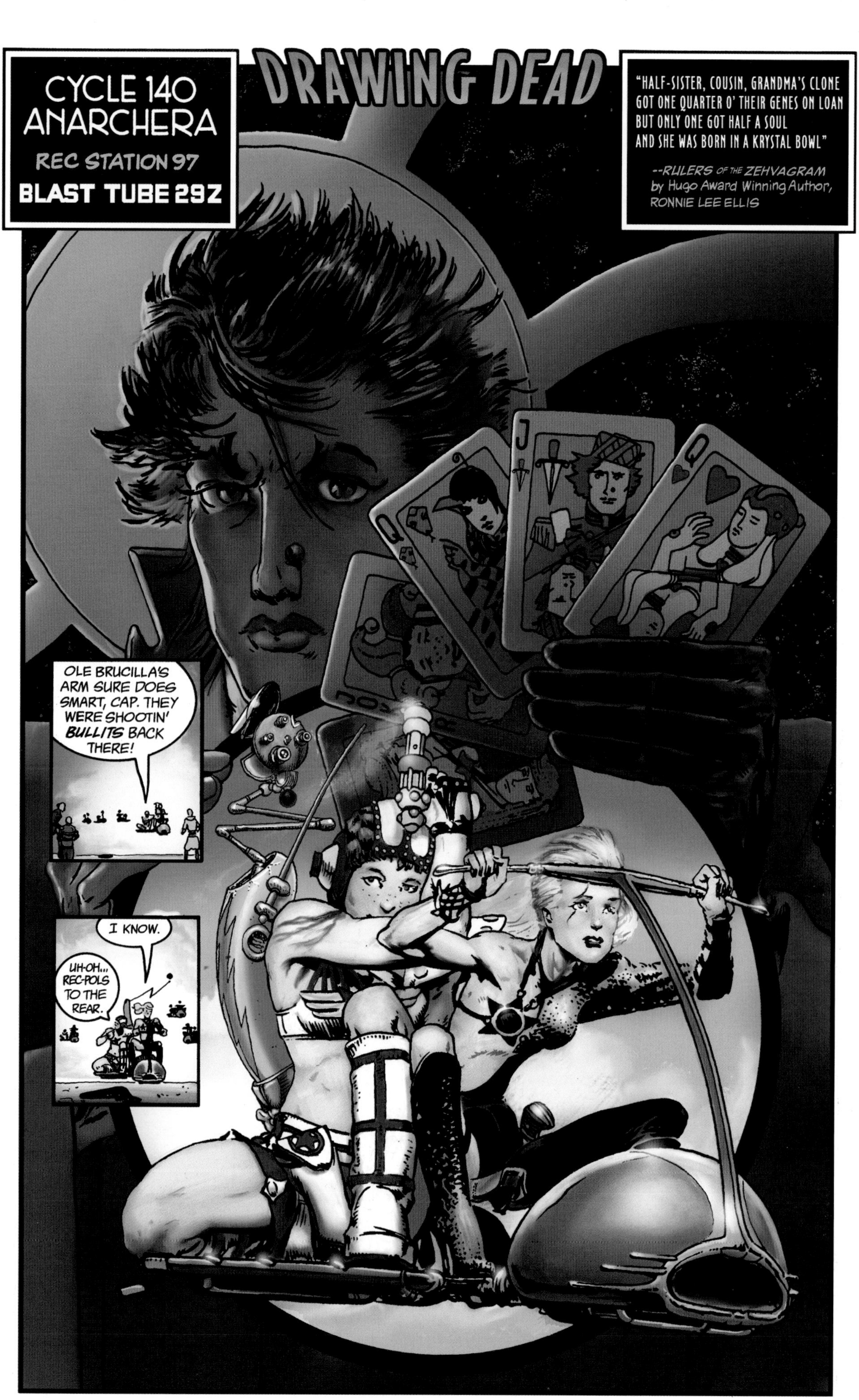
CYCLE 140
ANARCHERA
REC STATION 97
BLAST TUBE 29Z
DRAWING DEAD
"HALF-SISTER, COUSIN, GRANDMA'S CLONE
GOT ONE QUARTER O' THEIR GENES ON LOAN
BUT ONLY ONE GOT HALF A SOUL
AND SHE WAS BORN IN A KRYSTAL BOWL"
--RULERS OF THE ZEHVAGRAM
by Hugo Award Winning Author,
RONNIE LEE ELLIS
OLE BRUCILLA'S ARM SURE DOES SMART, CAP. THEY WERE SHOOTIN' BULLITS BACK THERE!
I KNOW.
UH-OH... REC-POLS TO THE REAR.

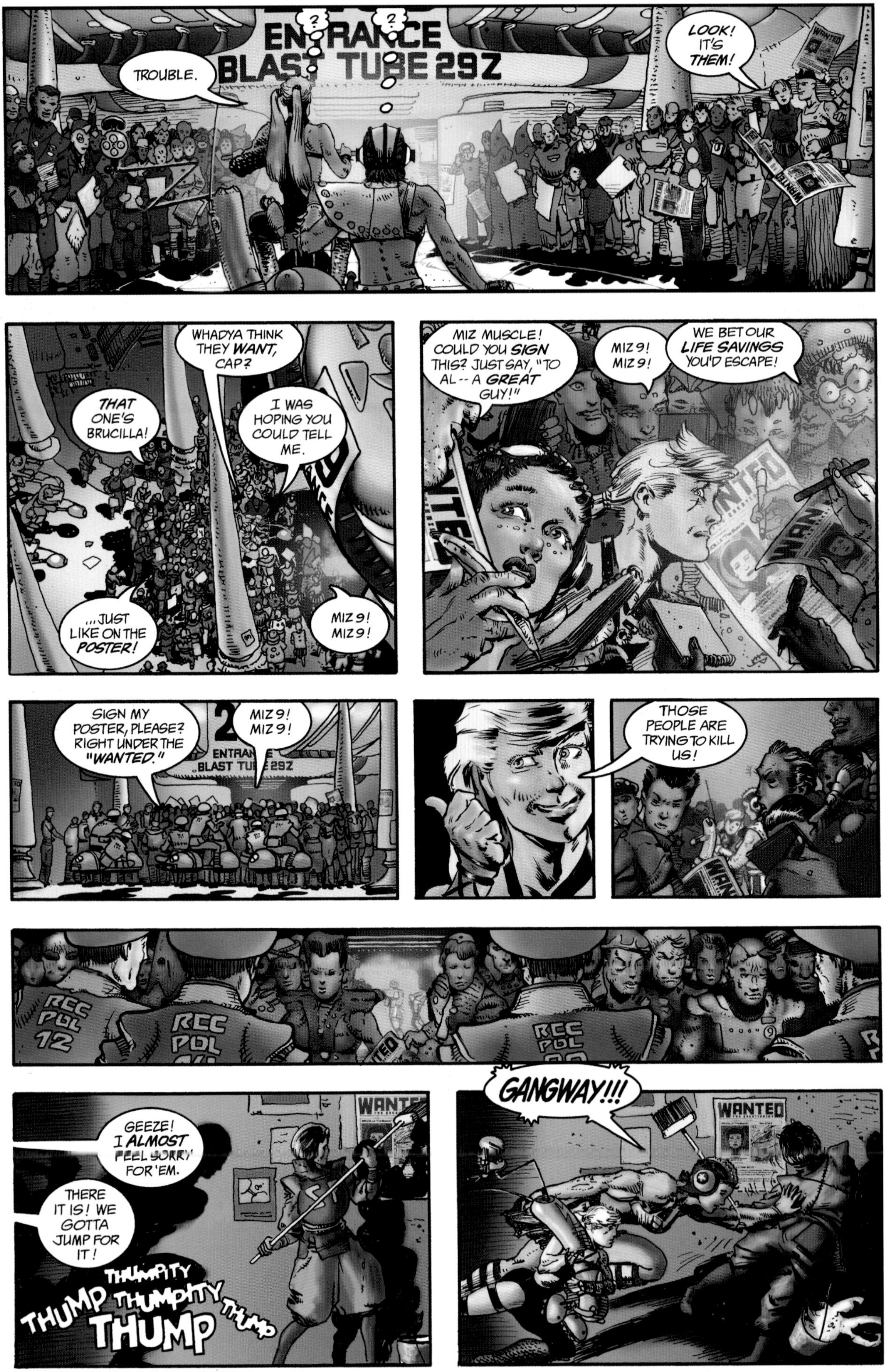
ENTRANCE
BLAST TUBE 29Z
TROUBLE.
LOOK! IT'S THEM!
WANTED
WHADYA THINK THEY WANT, CAP?
THAT ONE'S BRUCILLA!
I WAS HOPING YOU COULD TELL ME.
...JUST LIKE ON THE POSTER!
MIZ 9! MIZ 9!
MIZ MUSCLE! COULD YOU SIGN THIS? JUST SAY, "TO AL -- A GREAT GUY!"
MIZ 9! MIZ 9!
WE BET OUR LIFE SAVINGS YOU'D ESCAPE!
SIGN MY POSTER, PLEASE? RIGHT UNDER THE "WANTED."
MIZ 9! MIZ 9!
ENTRANCE
BLAST TUBE 29Z
THOSE PEOPLE ARE TRYING TO KILL US!
REC POL 12
REC POL
GEEZE! I ALMOST FEEL SORRY FOR 'EM.
THERE IT IS! WE GOTTA JUMP FOR IT!
THUMP THUMPITY THUMPITY THUMP THUMP
GANGWAY!!!
WANTED
WANTED

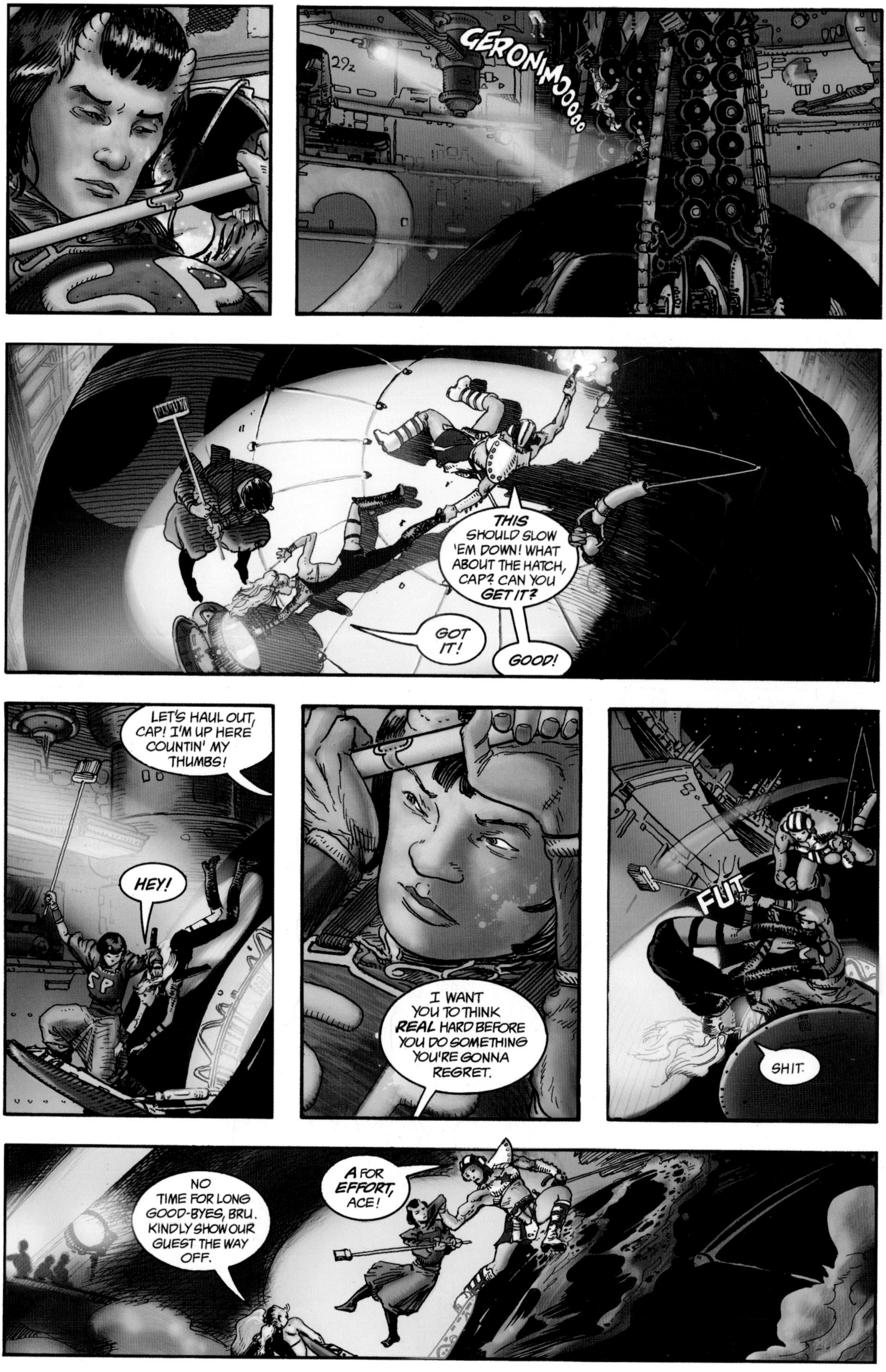
GERONIMOOOOO
THIS SHOULD SLOW 'EM DOWN! WHAT ABOUT THE HATCH, CAP? CAN YOU GET IT?
GOT IT!
GOOD!
LET'S HAUL OUT, CAP! I'M UP HERE COUNTIN' MY THUMBS!
HEY!
I WANT YOU TO THINK REAL HARD BEFORE YOU DO SOMETHING YOU'RE GONNA REGRET.
FUT
SHIT.
NO TIME FOR LONG GOOD-BYES, BRU. KINDLY SHOW OUR GUEST THE WAY OFF.
A FOR EFFORT, ACE!

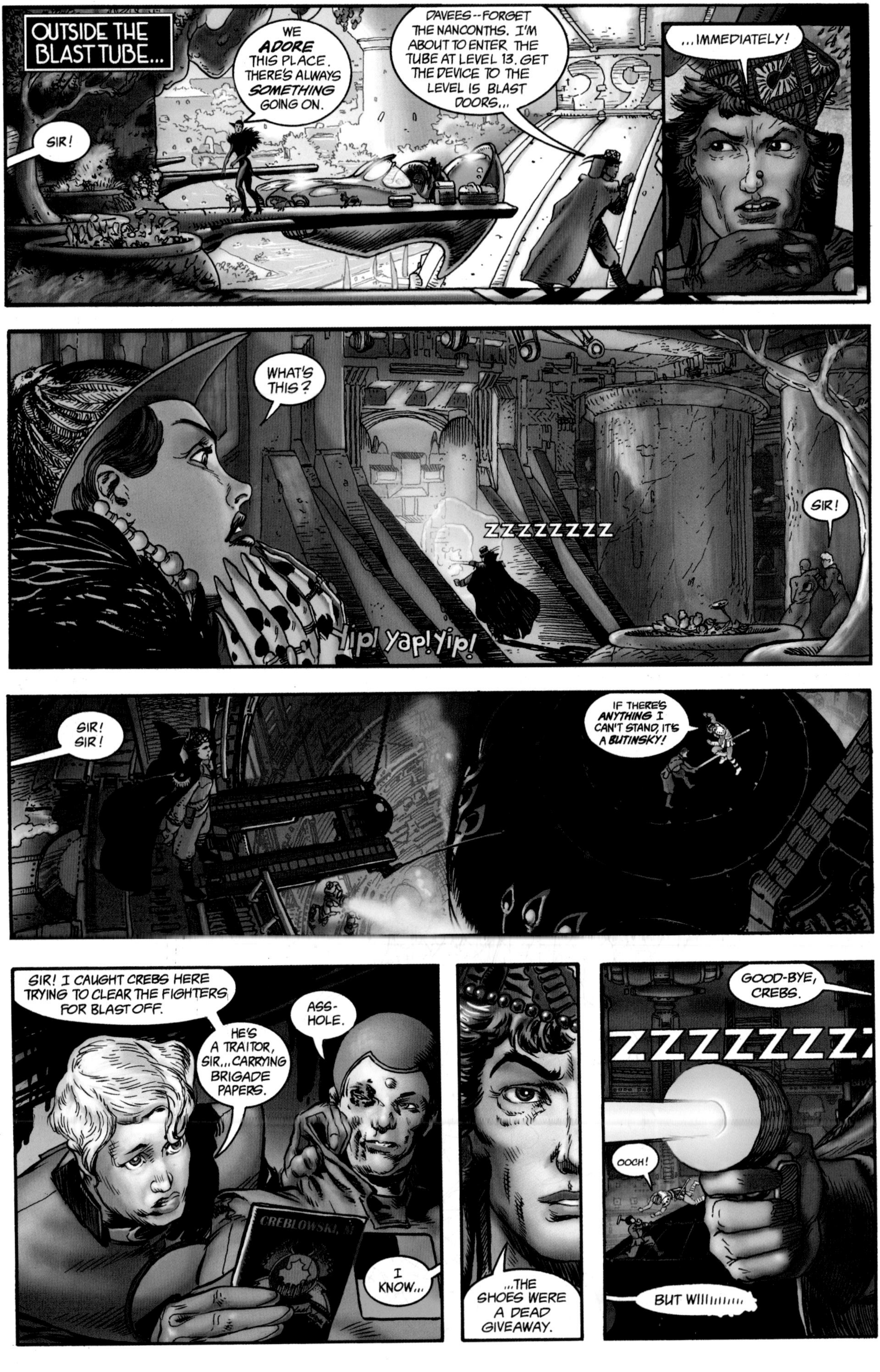
OUTSIDE THE BLAST TUBE...
WE ADORE THIS PLACE. THERE'S ALWAYS SOMETHING GOING ON.
SIR!
DAVEES--FORGET THE NANCONTHS. I'M ABOUT TO ENTER THE TUBE AT LEVEL 13. GET THE DEVICE TO THE LEVEL IS BLAST DOORS...
...IMMEDIATELY!
WHAT'S THIS?
ZZZZZZZZ
SIR!
YIP! YAP! YIP!
SIR! SIR!
IF THERE'S ANYTHING I CAN'T STAND, IT'S A BUTINSKY!
SIR! I CAUGHT CREBS HERE TRYING TO CLEAR THE FIGHTERS FOR BLAST OFF.
ASS-HOLE.
HE'S A TRAITOR, SIR,,, CARRYING BRIGADE PAPERS.
I KNOW...
...THE SHOES WERE A DEAD GIVEAWAY.
GOOD-BYE, CREBS.
ZZZZZZZZ
OOCH!
BUT WIIIIIIIII

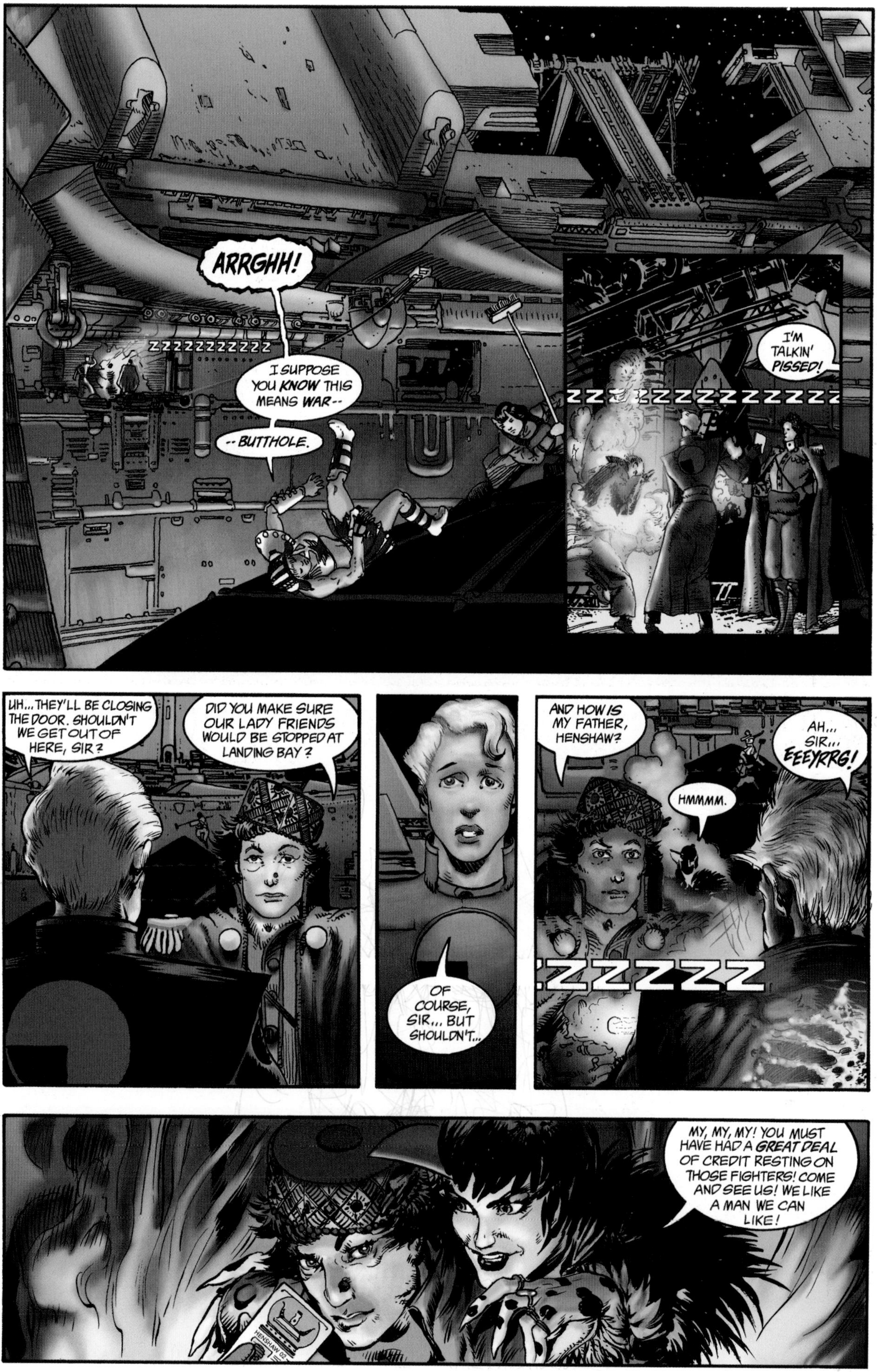
ARRGHH!
ZZZZZZZZZZ
I SUPPOSE YOU KNOW THIS MEANS WAR--
--BUTTHOLE.
I'M TALKIN' PISSED!
ZZZZZZZZZZZZZ
UH... THEY'LL BE CLOSING THE DOOR. SHOULDN'T WE GET OUT OF HERE, SIR?
DID YOU MAKE SURE OUR LADY FRIENDS WOULD BE STOPPED AT LANDING BAY?
OF COURSE, SIR... BUT SHOULDN'T...
AND HOW IS MY FATHER, HENSHAW?
HMMMM.
AH... SIR... EEEYRRG!
ZZZZZZ
MY, MY, MY! YOU MUST HAVE HAD A GREAT DEAL OF CREDIT RESTING ON THOSE FIGHTERS! COME AND SEE US! WE LIKE A MAN WE CAN LIKE!
HENSHAW 02

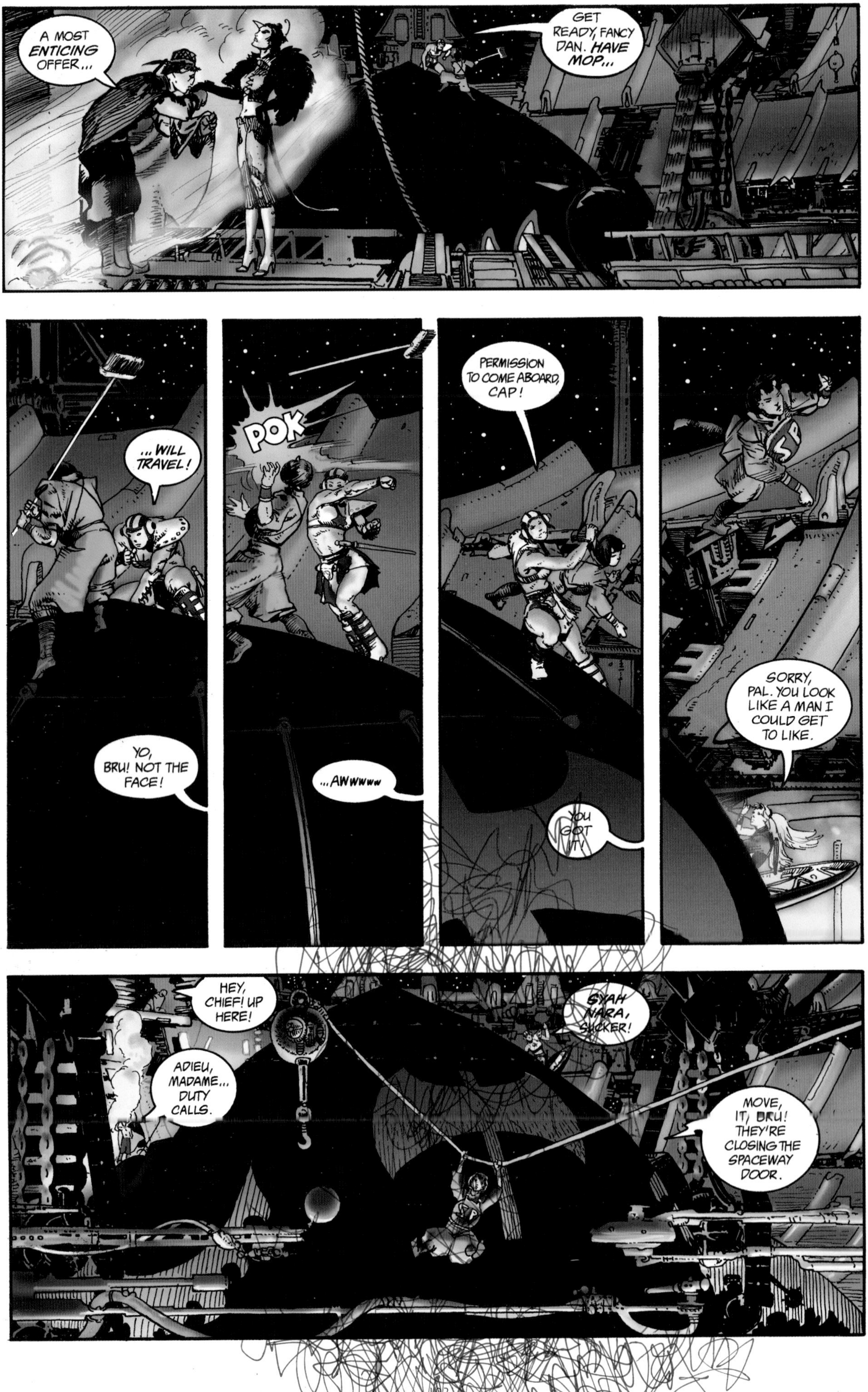
A MOST ENTICING OFFER...
GET READY, FANCY DAN. HAVE MOP...
...WILL TRAVEL!
YO, BRU! NOT THE FACE!
POK
...AWWWWW
PERMISSION TO COME ABOARD, CAP!
YOU GOT IT!
SORRY, PAL. YOU LOOK LIKE A MAN I COULD GET TO LIKE.
HEY, CHIEF! UP HERE!
ADIEU, MADAME... DUTY CALLS.
SYAH NARA, SUCKER!
MOVE IT, BRU! THEY'RE CLOSING THE SPACEWAY DOOR.

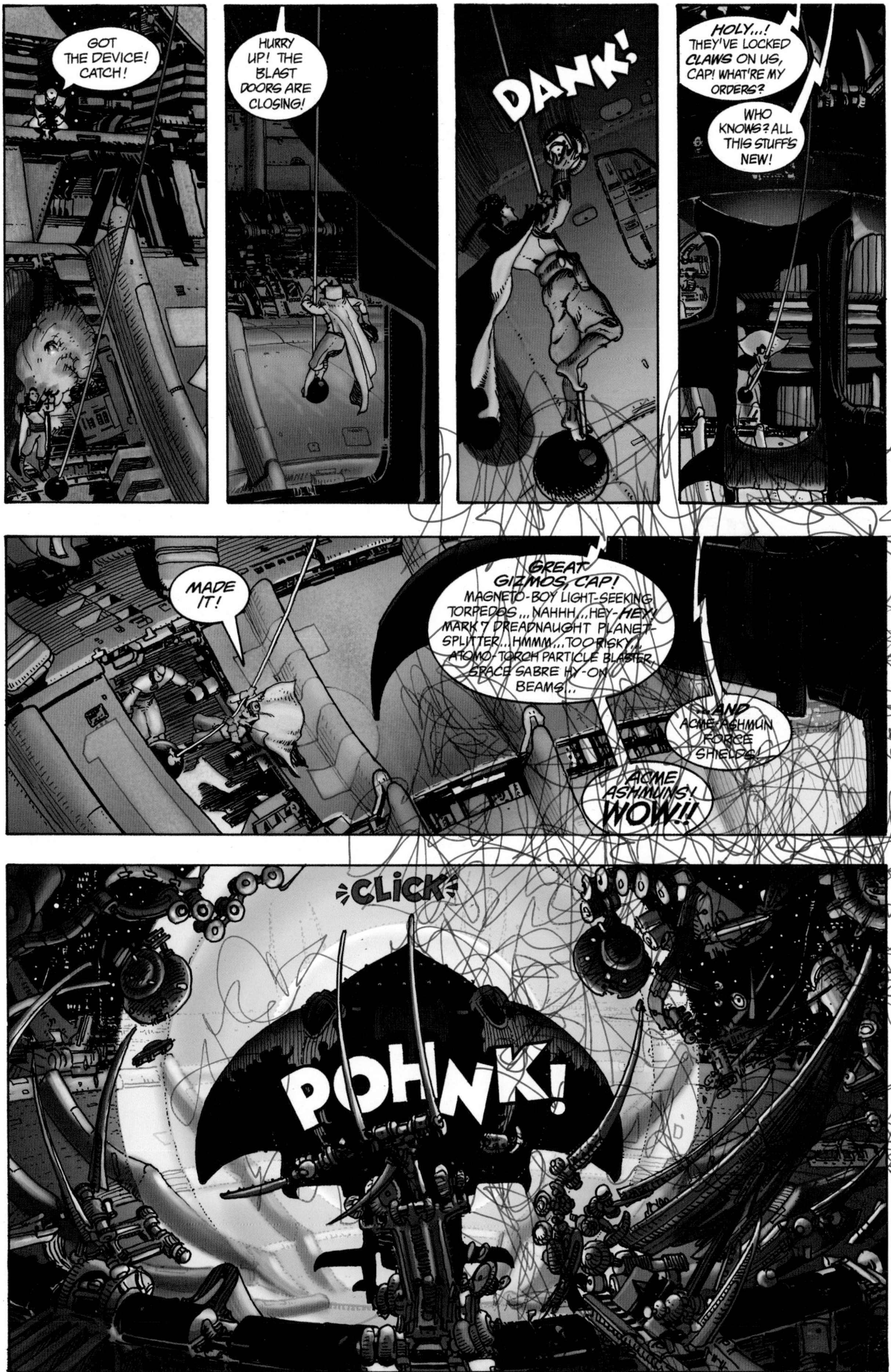
GOT THE DEVICE! CATCH!
HURRY UP! THE BLAST DOORS ARE CLOSING!
DANK!
HOLY...! THEY'VE LOCKED CLAWS ON US, CAP! WHAT'RE MY ORDERS?
WHO KNOWS? ALL THIS STUFF'S NEW!
MADE IT!
GREAT GIZMOS, CAP! MAGNETO-BOY LIGHT-SEEKING TORPEDOS... NAHHH... HEY-HEY! MARK 7 DREADNAUGHT PLANET-SPLITTER... HMMM... TOO RISKY... ATOMO-TORCH PARTICLE BLASTER, SPACE SABRE HY-ON BEAMS...
...AND ACME-ASHMUN FORCE SHIELDS!
ACME ASHMUNS! WOW!!
CLICK
POHNK!

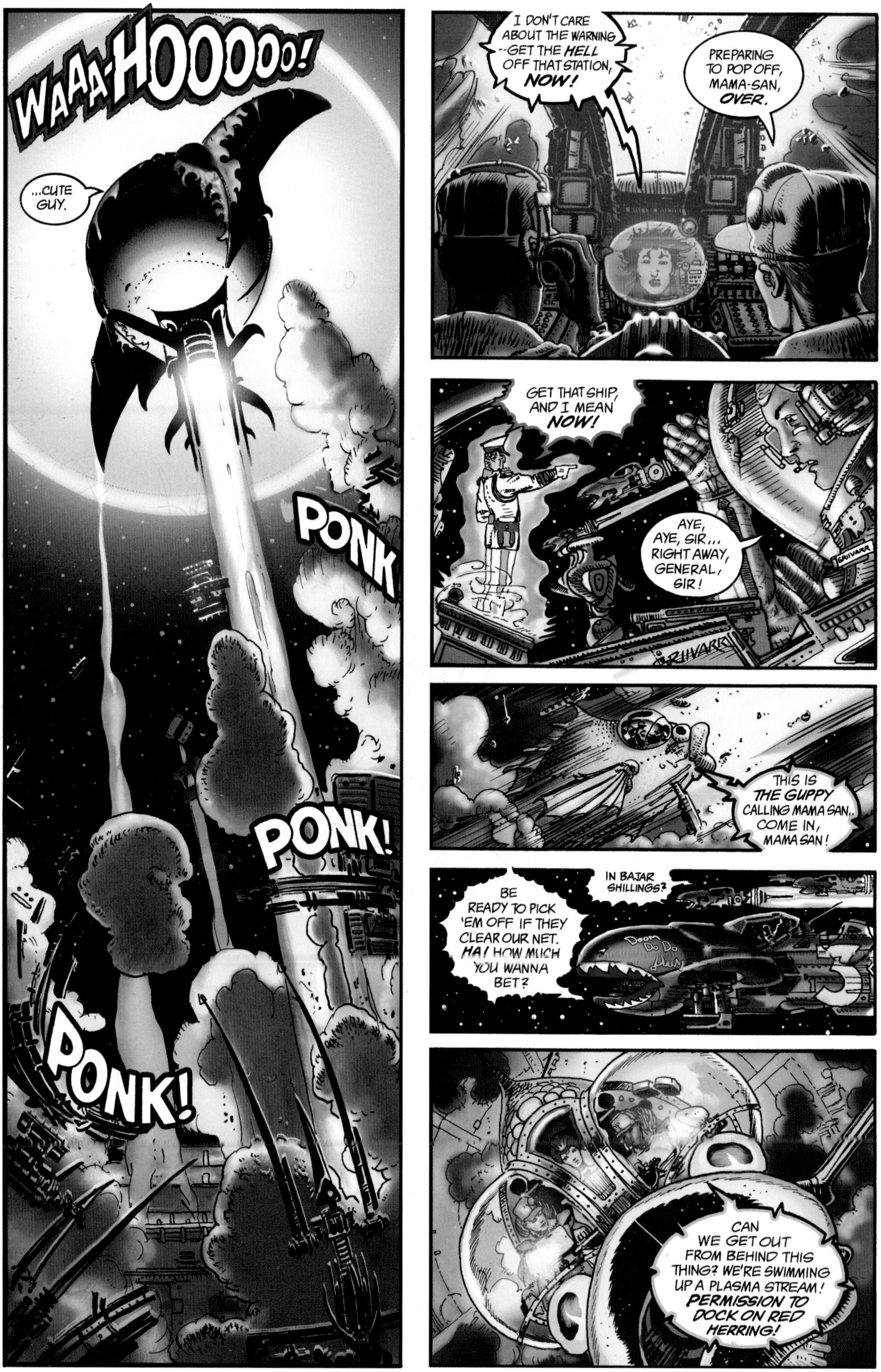
WAAA-HOOOOoo!
...CUTE GUY.
PONK
PONK!
PONK!
I DON'T CARE ABOUT THE WARNING --GET THE HELL OFF THAT STATION, NOW!
PREPARING TO POP OFF, MAMA-SAN, OVER.
GET THAT SHIP, AND I MEAN NOW!
AYE, AYE, SIR... RIGHT AWAY, GENERAL, SIR!
GRIVARR
THIS IS THE GUPPY CALLING MAMA SAN.. COME IN, MAMA SAN!
BE READY TO PICK 'EM OFF IF THEY CLEAR OUR NET. HA! HOW MUCH YOU WANNA BET?
IN BAJAR SHILLINGS?
CAN WE GET OUT FROM BEHIND THIS THING? WE'RE SWIMMING UP A PLASMA STREAM! PERMISSION TO DOCK ON RED HERRING!

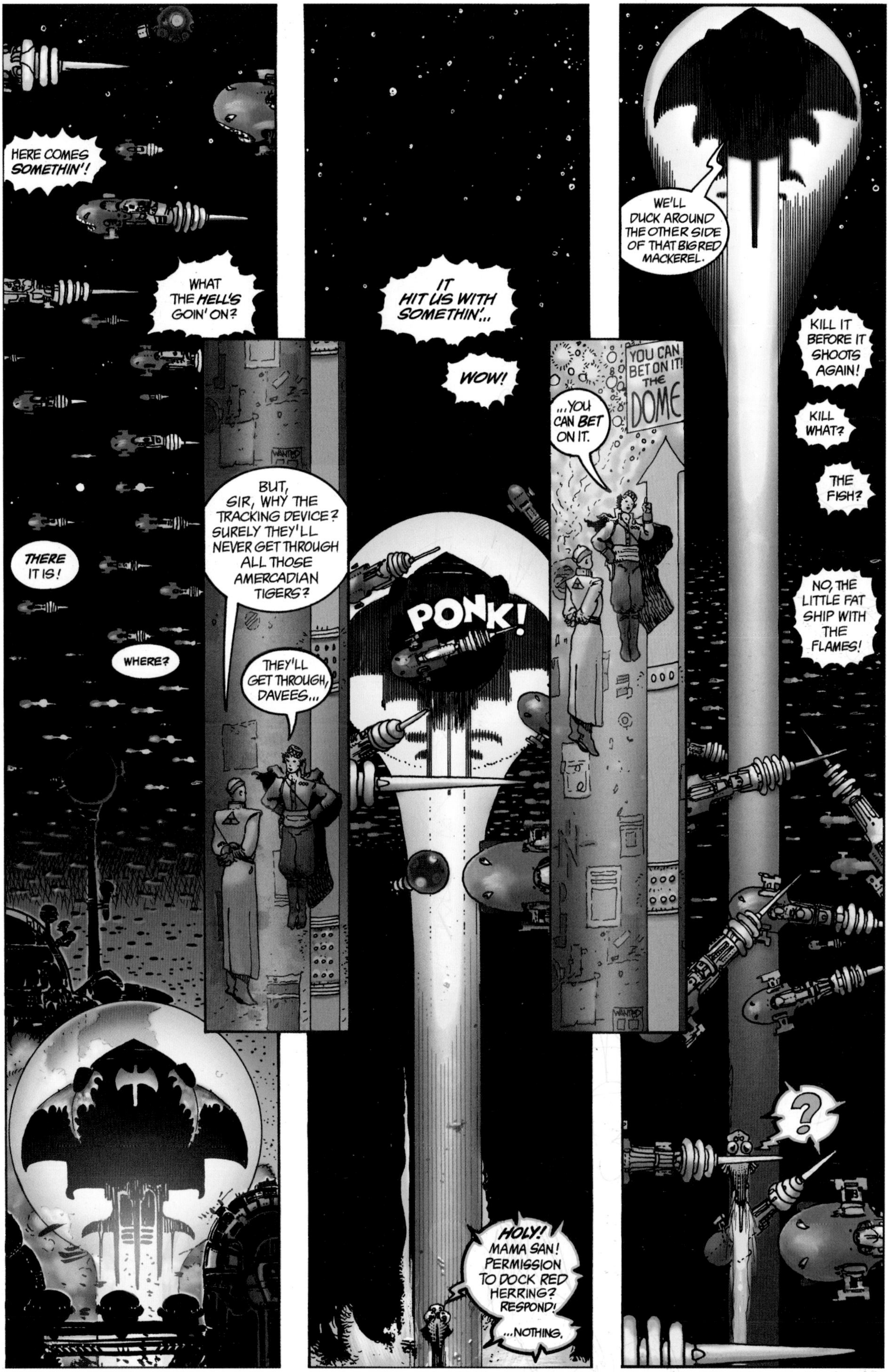
HERE COMES SOMETHIN'!
WHAT THE HELL'S GOIN' ON?
THERE IT IS!
WHERE?
BUT, SIR, WHY THE TRACKING DEVICE? SURELY THEY'LL NEVER GET THROUGH ALL THOSE AMERCADIAN TIGERS?
THEY'LL GET THROUGH, DAVEES...
IT HIT US WITH SOMETHIN'...
WOW!
PONK!
HOLY! MAMA SAN! PERMISSION TO DOCK RED HERRING? RESPOND!
...NOTHING.
YOU CAN BET ON IT! THE DOME
...YOU CAN BET ON IT.
WE'LL DUCK AROUND THE OTHER SIDE OF THAT BIG RED MACKEREL.
KILL IT BEFORE IT SHOOTS AGAIN!
KILL WHAT?
THE FISH?
NO, THE LITTLE FAT SHIP WITH THE FLAMES!
?

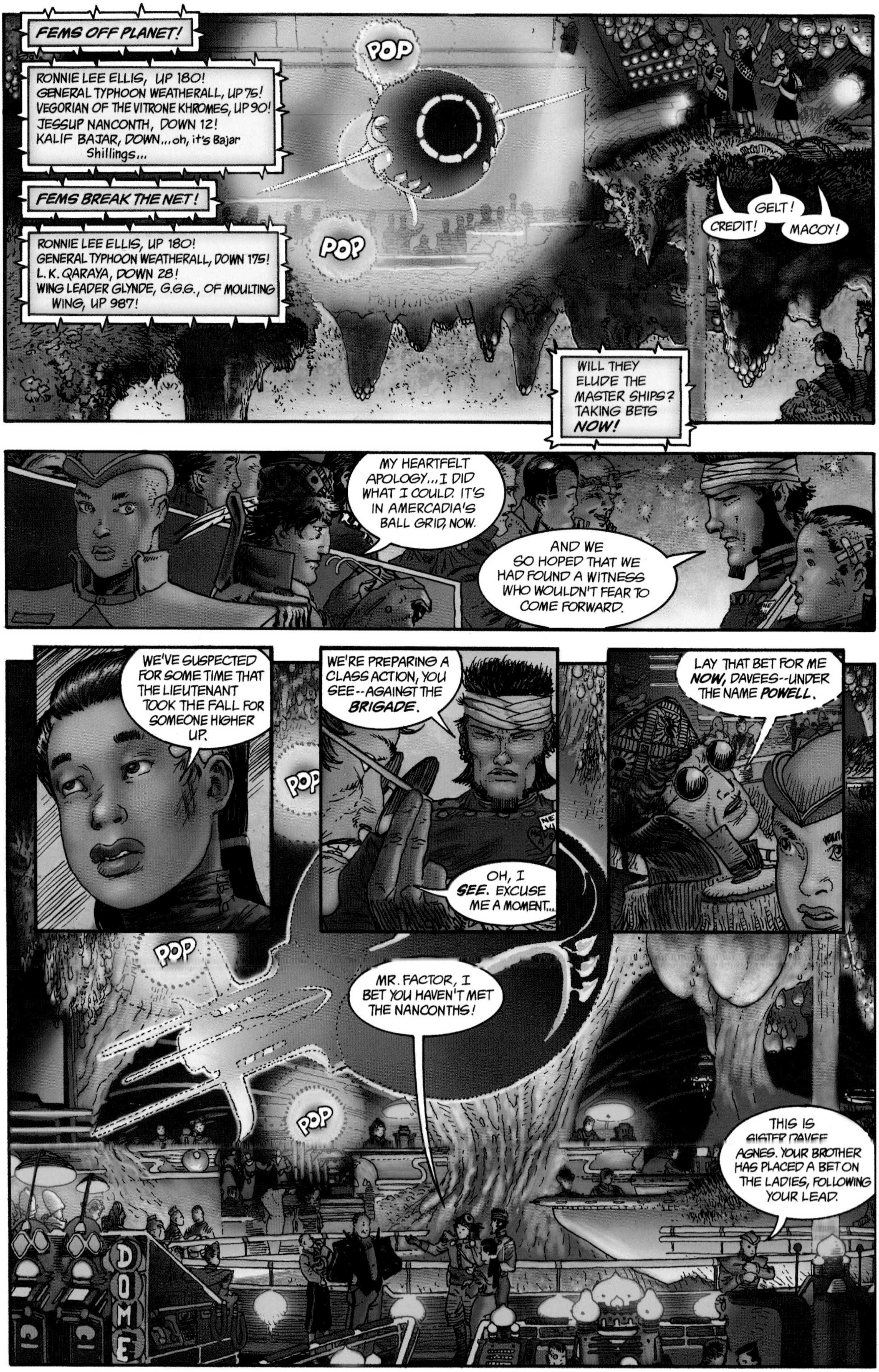
FEMS OFF PLANET!
RONNIE LEE ELLIS, UP 180! GENERAL TYPHOON WEATHERALL, UP 75! VEGORIAN OF THE VITRONE KHROMES, UP 90! JESSUP NANCONTH, DOWN 12! KALIF BAJAR, DOWN...oh, it's Bajar Shillings...
POP
FEMS BREAK THE NET!
RONNIE LEE ELLIS, UP 180! GENERAL TYPHOON WEATHERALL, DOWN 175! L.K. QARAYA, DOWN 28! WING LEADER GLYNDE, G.G.G., OF MOULTING WING, UP 987!
POP
CREDIT!
GELT!
MACOY!
WILL THEY ELUDE THE MASTER SHIPS? TAKING BETS NOW!
MY HEARTFELT APOLOGY...I DID WHAT I COULD. IT'S IN AMERCADIA'S BALL GRID, NOW.
AND WE SO HOPED THAT WE HAD FOUND A WITNESS WHO WOULDN'T FEAR TO COME FORWARD.
WE'VE SUSPECTED FOR SOME TIME THAT THE LIEUTENANT TOOK THE FALL FOR SOMEONE HIGHER UP.
POP
WE'RE PREPARING A CLASS ACTION, YOU SEE--AGAINST THE BRIGADE.
OH, I SEE. EXCUSE ME A MOMENT...
LAY THAT BET FOR ME NOW, DAVEES--UNDER THE NAME POWELL.
POP
MR. FACTOR, I BET YOU HAVEN'T MET THE NANCONTHS!
POP
THIS IS SISTER DAVEE AGNES. YOUR BROTHER HAS PLACED A BET ON THE LADIES, FOLLOWING YOUR LEAD.
DOME

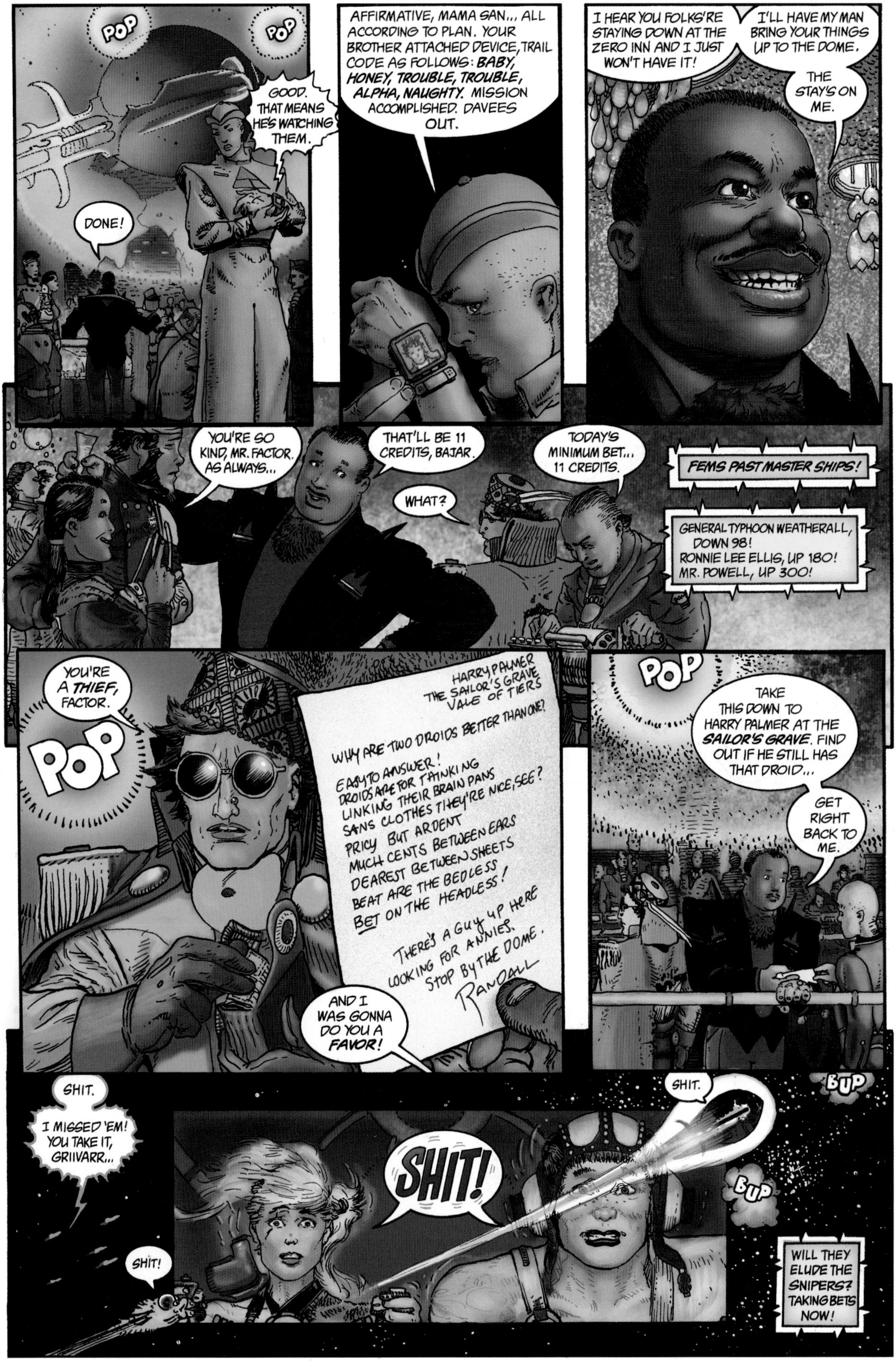
POP
POP
GOOD. THAT MEANS HE'S WATCHING THEM.
DONE!
AFFIRMATIVE, MAMA SAN... ALL ACCORDING TO PLAN. YOUR BROTHER ATTACHED DEVICE, TRAIL CODE AS FOLLOWS: BABY, HONEY, TROUBLE, TROUBLE, ALPHA, NAUGHTY. MISSION ACCOMPLISHED. DAVEES OUT.
I HEAR YOU FOLKS'RE STAYING DOWN AT THE ZERO INN AND I JUST WON'T HAVE IT!
I'LL HAVE MY MAN BRING YOUR THINGS UP TO THE DOME.
THE STAY'S ON ME.
YOU'RE SO KIND, MR. FACTOR. AS ALWAYS...
THAT'LL BE 11 CREDITS, BAJAR.
WHAT?
TODAY'S MINIMUM BET... 11 CREDITS.
FEMS PAST MASTER SHIPS!
GENERAL TYPHOON WEATHERALL, DOWN 98! RONNIE LEE ELLIS, UP 180! MR. POWELL, UP 300!
YOU'RE A THIEF, FACTOR.
POP
HARRY PALMER THE SAILOR'S GRAVE VALE OF TIERS
WHY ARE TWO DROIDS BETTER THAN ONE?
EASY TO ANSWER! DROIDS ARE FOR THINKING LINKING THEIR BRAIN PANS SANS CLOTHES THEY'RE NICE, SEE? PRICY BUT ARDENT MUCH CENTS BETWEEN EARS DEAREST BETWEEN SHEETS BEAT ARE THE BEDLESS BET ON THE HEADLESS!
THERE'S A GUY UP HERE LOOKING FOR ANNIES. STOP BY THE DOME. RANDALL
AND I WAS GONNA DO YOU A FAVOR!
POP
TAKE THIS DOWN TO HARRY PALMER AT THE SAILOR'S GRAVE. FIND OUT IF HE STILL HAS THAT DROID...
GET RIGHT BACK TO ME.
SHIT.
I MISSED 'EM! YOU TAKE IT, GRIIVARR...
SHIT!
SHIT!
SHIT.
BUP
BUP
WILL THEY ELUDE THE SNIPERS? TAKING BETS NOW!

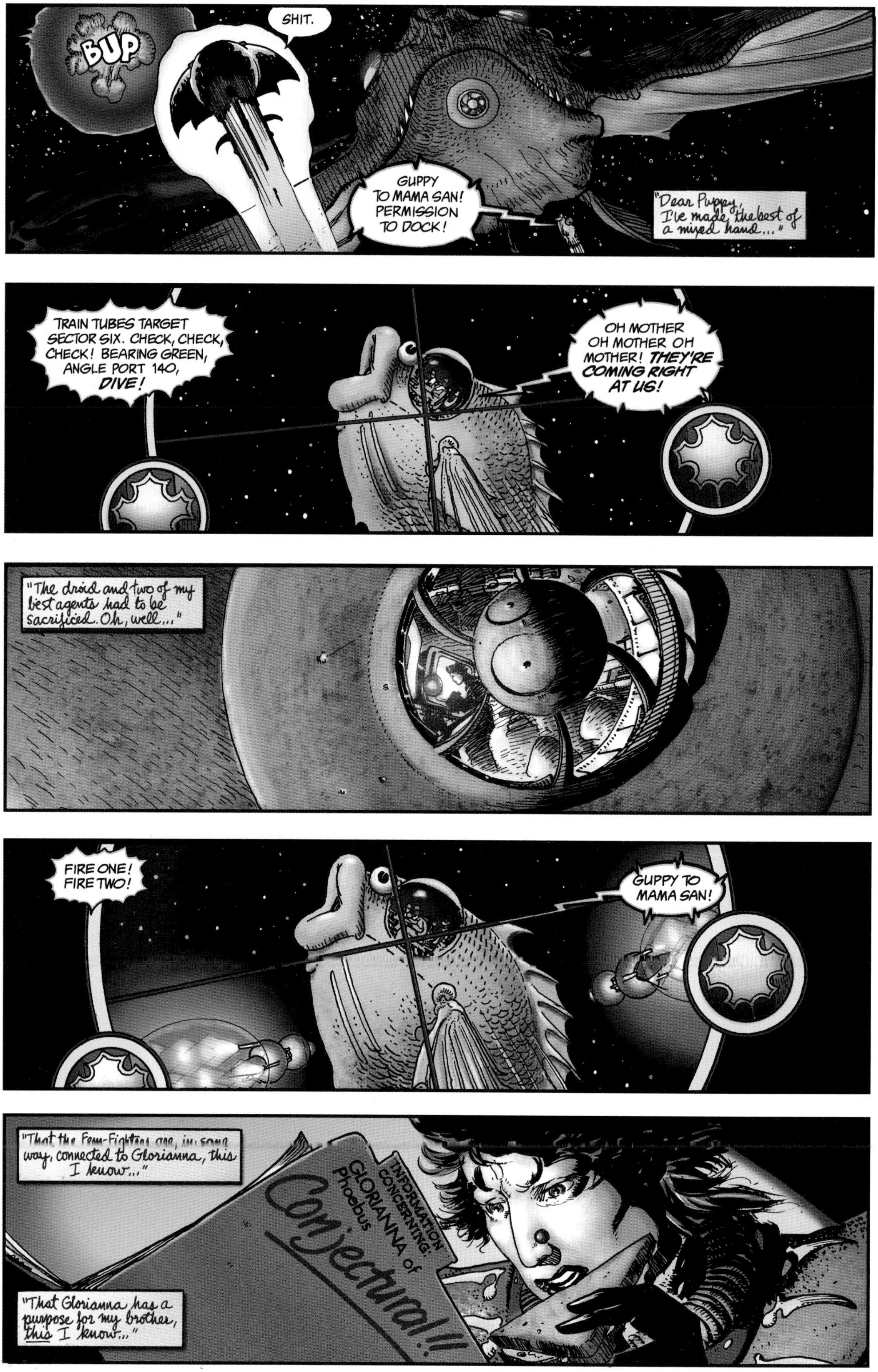

BUP
SHIT.
GUPPY TO MAMA SAN! PERMISSION TO DOCK!
"Dear Puppy, I've made the best of a mixed hand..."
TRAIN TUBES TARGET SECTOR SIX. CHECK, CHECK, CHECK! BEARING GREEN, ANGLE PORT 140, DIVE!
OH MOTHER OH MOTHER OH MOTHER! THEY'RE COMING RIGHT AT US!
"The droid and two of my best agents had to be sacrificed. Oh, well..."
FIRE ONE! FIRE TWO!
GUPPY TO MAMA SAN!
"That the Fem-Fighters are, in some way, connected to Glorianna, this I know..."
INFORMATION CONCERNING: GLORIANNA of Phoebus
Conjectural!!
"That Glorianna has a purpose for my brothers, this I know..."

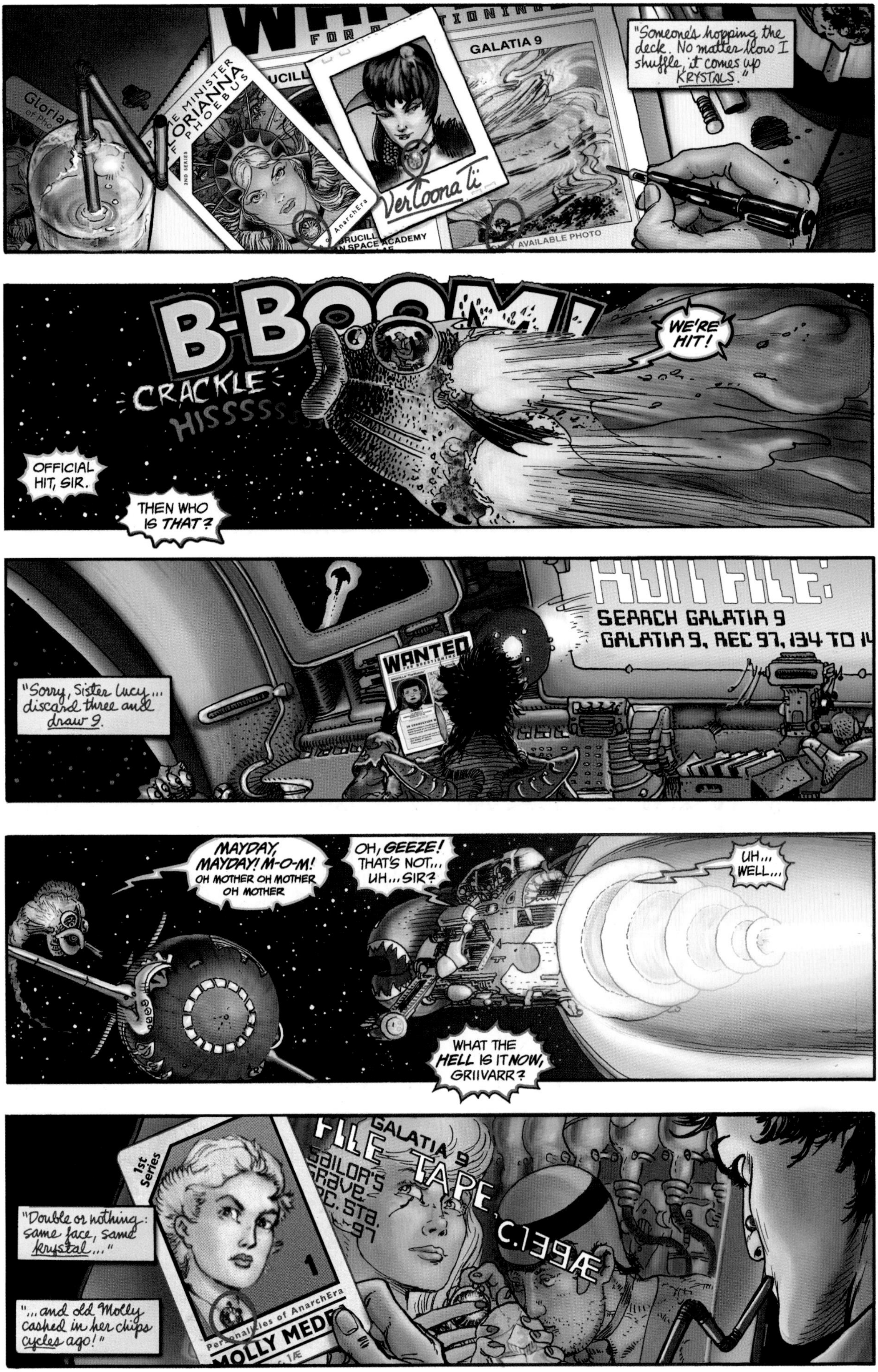
GALATIA 9
PRIME MINISTER
GLORIANNA
OF PHOEBUS
2ND SERIES
AnarchEra
VerCoona Ti
SPACE ACADEMY
AVAILABLE PHOTO
"Someone's hopping the deck. No matter how I shuffle, it comes up KRYSTALS."
B-BOOM!
WE'RE HIT!
CRACKLE
HISSSSS
OFFICIAL HIT, SIR.
THEN WHO IS THAT?
HOT FILE:
SEARCH GALATIA 9
GALATIA 9, REC 97, 134 TO 14
WANTED
"Sorry, Sister Lucy... discard three and draw 9."
MAYDAY, MAYDAY! M-O-M! OH MOTHER OH MOTHER OH MOTHER
OH, GEEZE! THAT'S NOT... UH... SIR?
UH... WELL...
WHAT THE HELL IS IT NOW, GRIIVARR?
1st Series
FILE TAPE
GALATIA 9
SAILOR'S GRAVE PC. STA. 97
C.139Æ
"Double or nothing: same face, same krystal..."
1
Personalities of AnarchEra
MOLLY MEDE
"...and old Molly cashed in her chips cycles ago!"

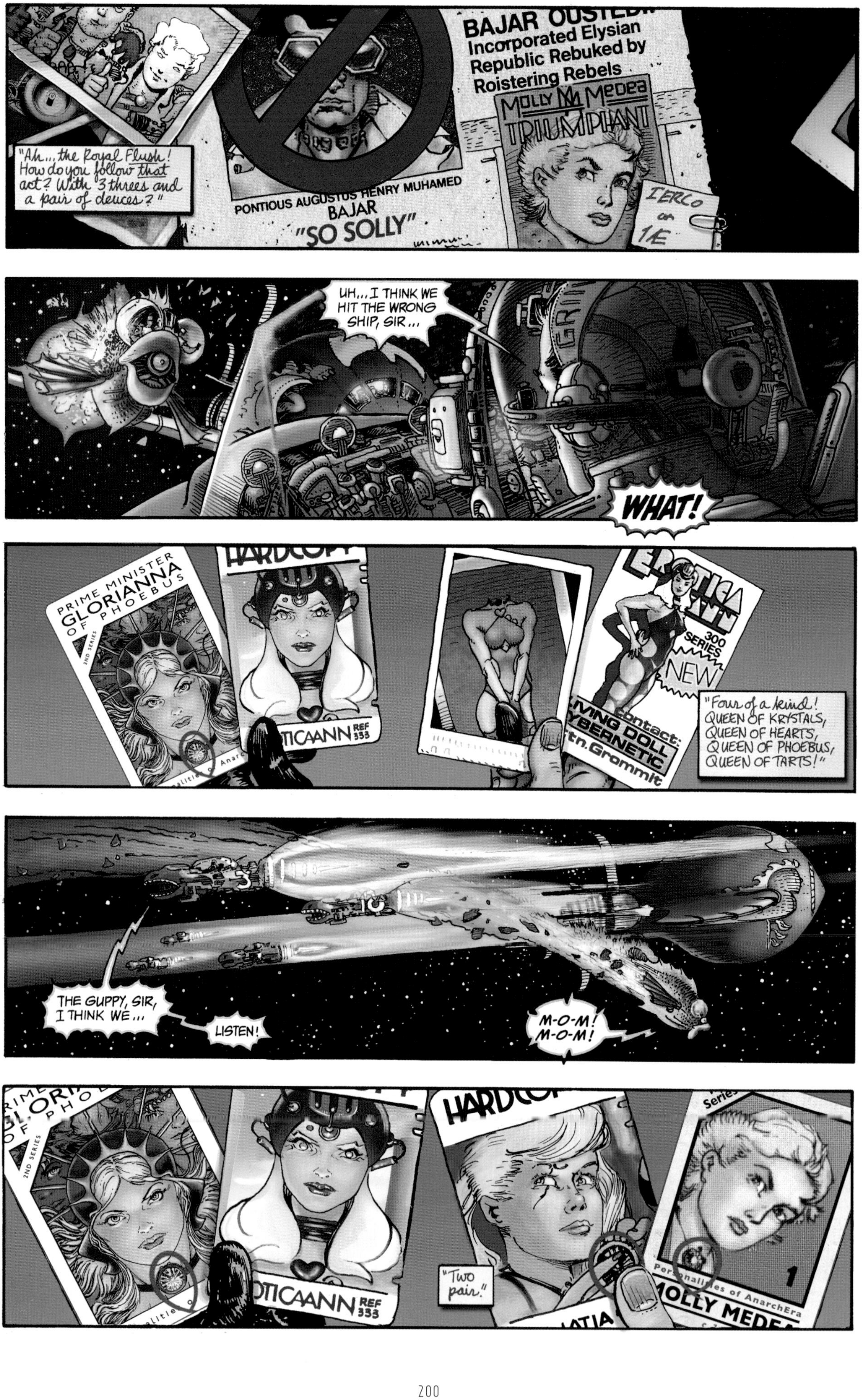

BAJAR OUSTED
Incorporated Elysian Republic Rebuked by Roistering Rebels
MOLLY M MEDEA
TRIUMPHANT
"Ah... the Royal Flush! How do you follow that act? With 3 threes and a pair of deuces?"
PONTIOUS AUGUSTUS HENRY MUHAMED
BAJAR
"SO SOLLY"
IERCO on 1/E
UH... I THINK WE HIT THE WRONG SHIP, SIR...
WHAT!
PRIME MINISTER GLORIANNA OF PHOEBUS
2ND SERIES
HARDCOPY
OTICAANN REF 333
300 SERIES
NEW
contact:
LIVING DOLL
CYBERNETIC
tn.Grommit
"Four of a kind! QUEEN OF KRYSTALS, QUEEN OF HEARTS, QUEEN OF PHOEBUS, QUEEN OF TARTS!"
THE GUPPY, SIR, I THINK WE...
LISTEN!
M-O-M! M-O-M!
2ND SERIES
OTICAANN REF 333
HARDCO
"Two pair."
Personalities of AnarchEra
MOLLY MEDEA
1

"Hm... interesting... I think they call this 'Shooting the Moon', but then, Hearts is my brother's game."

"Kalif is so predictable. Throw him a bone, he bites!"

The Erotic Ann 300 line was commissioned by M. Medea under auspices of Scream Corp. Inc.

LIVING DOLL
GROMMIT

MAY-DAY! MAY-DAY! M-O-M!

VERLOONA TI'' [aka Maggie Medea]
FILE TAPE c. 136 Æ
DEB NITE KRYSTO
7 OCHS

"This time I'll throw him a curve: enter the Queen of Vipers."

NEW WYOMING
UNEXPLAINED DISAPPEARANCES
GIRL GUIDES LOST!
1st Disappearance Unexplained

M-O-M!
≶SCRACKLE≶
↯POP!↯
HISSSSSSSSS
M-O-HSSMMMMM

CAN'T STOP! HEADED FOR STATION!

WAIT A MARTRON! THAT'S THE *SISTERHOOD'S* CODE! OH MOTHER OH MOTHER OH MOTHER *NOT AGAIN...*

NET THAT FISH, AND I MEAN *NOW!*

"And that Brigader again... turning up like a bad qua-credit."

BRUCILLA "The Muscle"
LT. BRUCILLA
AMERCADIAN SPACE ACADEMY
CLASS OF 134 ÆE

ROOTERS
AMERCADIA
SISTERHOOD STU

NEUTRAL ZONE FIASCO!!
Heads Roll as Prank Backfires
CIRCA 134 ÆE

AMY SIMPLE
Brigade Banned
Brigade flew, as Mot
Amy Simple, Mater
Sparks flew, as Mot
Supra of the Cosm
Cloistered Un

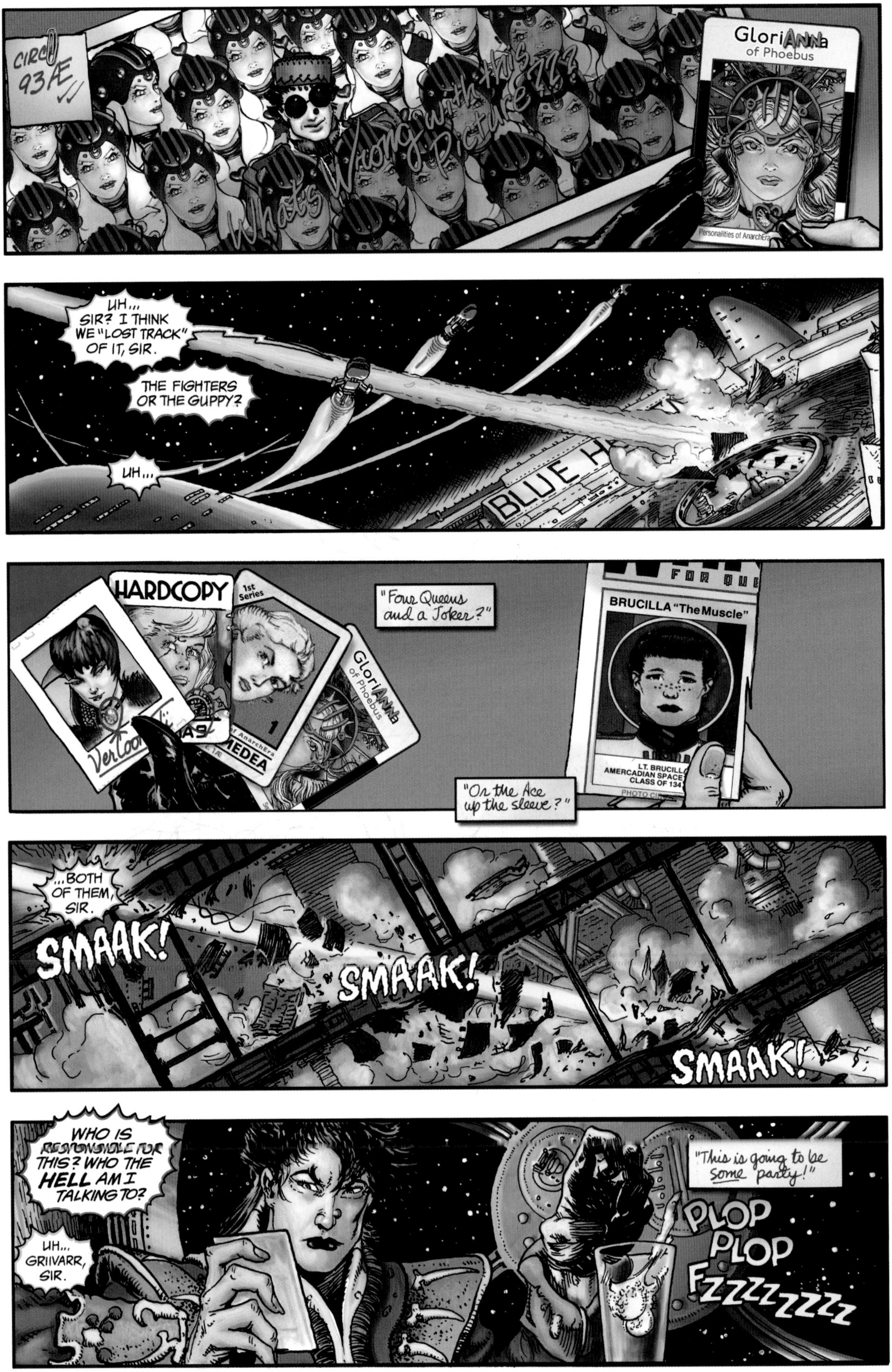
CIRCO 93Æ
What's Wrong with this Picture???
GloriANNa of Phoebus
Personalities of AnarchEra
UH... SIR? I THINK WE "LOST TRACK" OF IT, SIR.
THE FIGHTERS OR THE GUPPY?
UH...
BLUE H
HARDCOPY
1st Series
GloriANNa of Phoebus
MEDEA
"Four Queens and a Joker?"
BRUCILLA "The Muscle"
"Or the Ace up the sleeve?"
...BOTH OF THEM, SIR.
SMAAK!
SMAAK!
SMAAK!
WHO IS RESPONSIBLE FOR THIS? WHO THE HELL AM I TALKING TO?
UH... GRIIVARR, SIR.
"This is going to be some party!"
PLOP PLOP FZZZZZZZZ

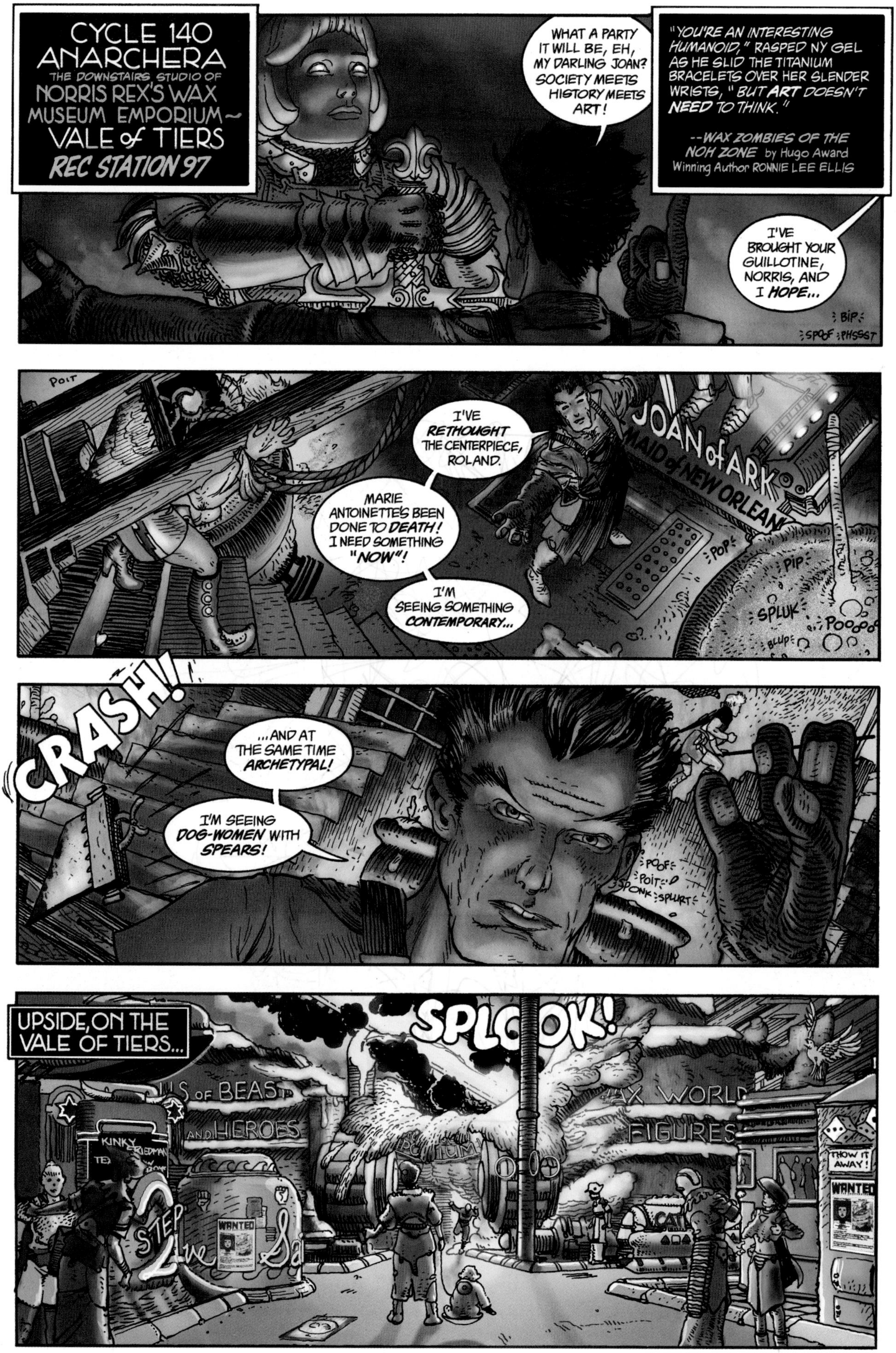

CYCLE 140
ANARCHERA
THE DOWNSTAIRS STUDIO OF
NORRIS REX'S WAX
MUSEUM EMPORIUM~
VALE of TIERS
REC STATION 97
WHAT A PARTY IT WILL BE, EH, MY DARLING JOAN? SOCIETY MEETS HISTORY MEETS ART!
"YOU'RE AN INTERESTING HUMANOID," RASPED NY GEL AS HE SLID THE TITANIUM BRACELETS OVER HER SLENDER WRISTS, "BUT ART DOESN'T NEED TO THINK."
--WAX ZOMBIES OF THE NOH ZONE by Hugo Award Winning Author RONNIE LEE ELLIS
I'VE BROUGHT YOUR GUILLOTINE, NORRIS, AND I HOPE...
BIP
SPOOF PHSSST
POIT
I'VE RETHOUGHT THE CENTERPIECE, ROLAND.
MARIE ANTOINETTE'S BEEN DONE TO DEATH! I NEED SOMETHING "NOW"!
I'M SEEING SOMETHING CONTEMPORARY...
JOAN of ARK
MAID of NEW ORLEAN
POP
PIP
SPLUK
BLUP
POOOOO
CRASH!
...AND AT THE SAME TIME ARCHETYPAL!
I'M SEEING DOG-WOMEN WITH SPEARS!
POOF
POIT
SPONK
SPLURT
UPSIDE, ON THE VALE OF TIERS...
SPLOOK!
AND HEROES
WAX WORLD
FIGURES
KINKY FRIEDMAN
WANTED
THOW IT AWAY!
WANTED

AH! PERFECT FOR MY GLORIANNA OF PHOEBUS!

SPOOT

BLOIK SPLORK

POIT PIP

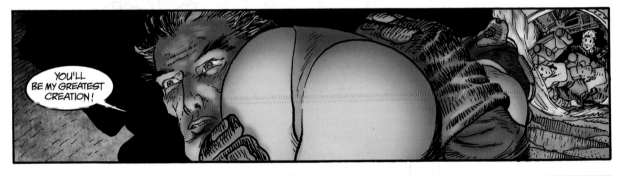

YOU'LL BE MY GREATEST CREATION!

MONEY.

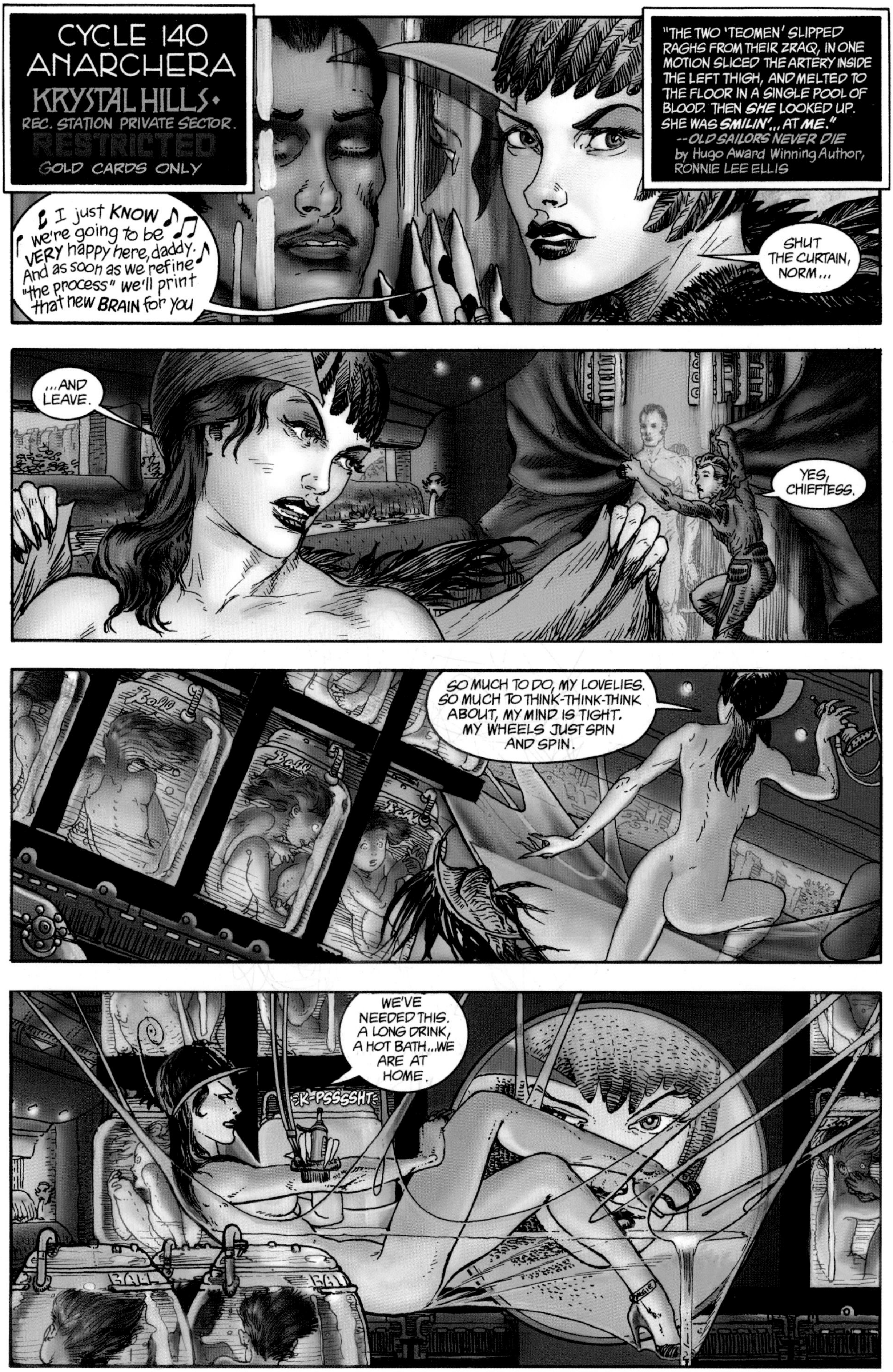
CYCLE 140
ANARCHERA
KRYSTAL HILLS
REC. STATION PRIVATE SECTOR.
RESTRICTED
GOLD CARDS ONLY
"THE TWO 'TEOMEN' SLIPPED RAGHS FROM THEIR ZRAQ, IN ONE MOTION SLICED THE ARTERY INSIDE THE LEFT THIGH, AND MELTED TO THE FLOOR IN A SINGLE POOL OF BLOOD. THEN SHE LOOKED UP. SHE WAS SMILIN'... AT ME."
--OLD SAILORS NEVER DIE
by Hugo Award Winning Author, RONNIE LEE ELLIS
I just KNOW we're going to be VERY happy here, daddy. And as soon as we refine "the process" we'll print that new BRAIN for you
SHUT THE CURTAIN, NORM...
...AND LEAVE.
YES, CHIEFTESS.
SO MUCH TO DO, MY LOVELIES. SO MUCH TO THINK-THINK-THINK ABOUT, MY MIND IS TIGHT. MY WHEELS JUST SPIN AND SPIN.
WE'VE NEEDED THIS. A LONG DRINK, A HOT BATH... WE ARE AT HOME.
K-PSSSSHT

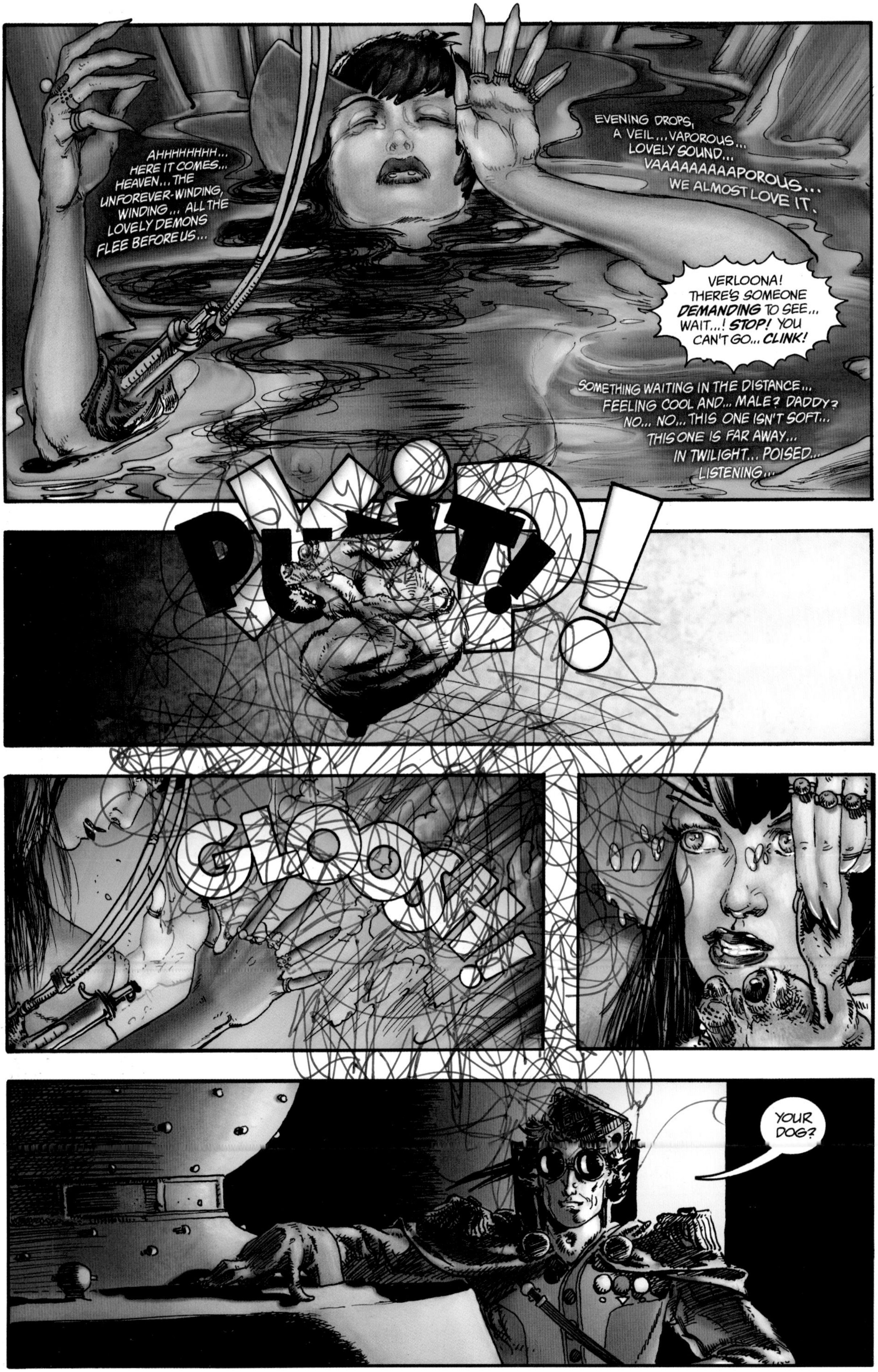
AHHHHHHHH... HERE IT COMES... HEAVEN... THE UNFOREVER-WINDING, WINDING... ALL THE LOVELY DEMONS FLEE BEFORE US...
EVENING DROPS, A VEIL... VAPOROUS... LOVELY SOUND... VAAAAAAAAAAPOROUS... WE ALMOST LOVE IT.
VERLOONA! THERE'S SOMEONE DEMANDING TO SEE... WAIT...! STOP! YOU CAN'T GO... CLINK!
SOMETHING WAITING IN THE DISTANCE... FEELING COOL AND... MALE? DADDY? NO... NO... THIS ONE ISN'T SOFT... THIS ONE IS FAR AWAY... IN TWILIGHT... POISED... LISTENING...
YOUR DOG?

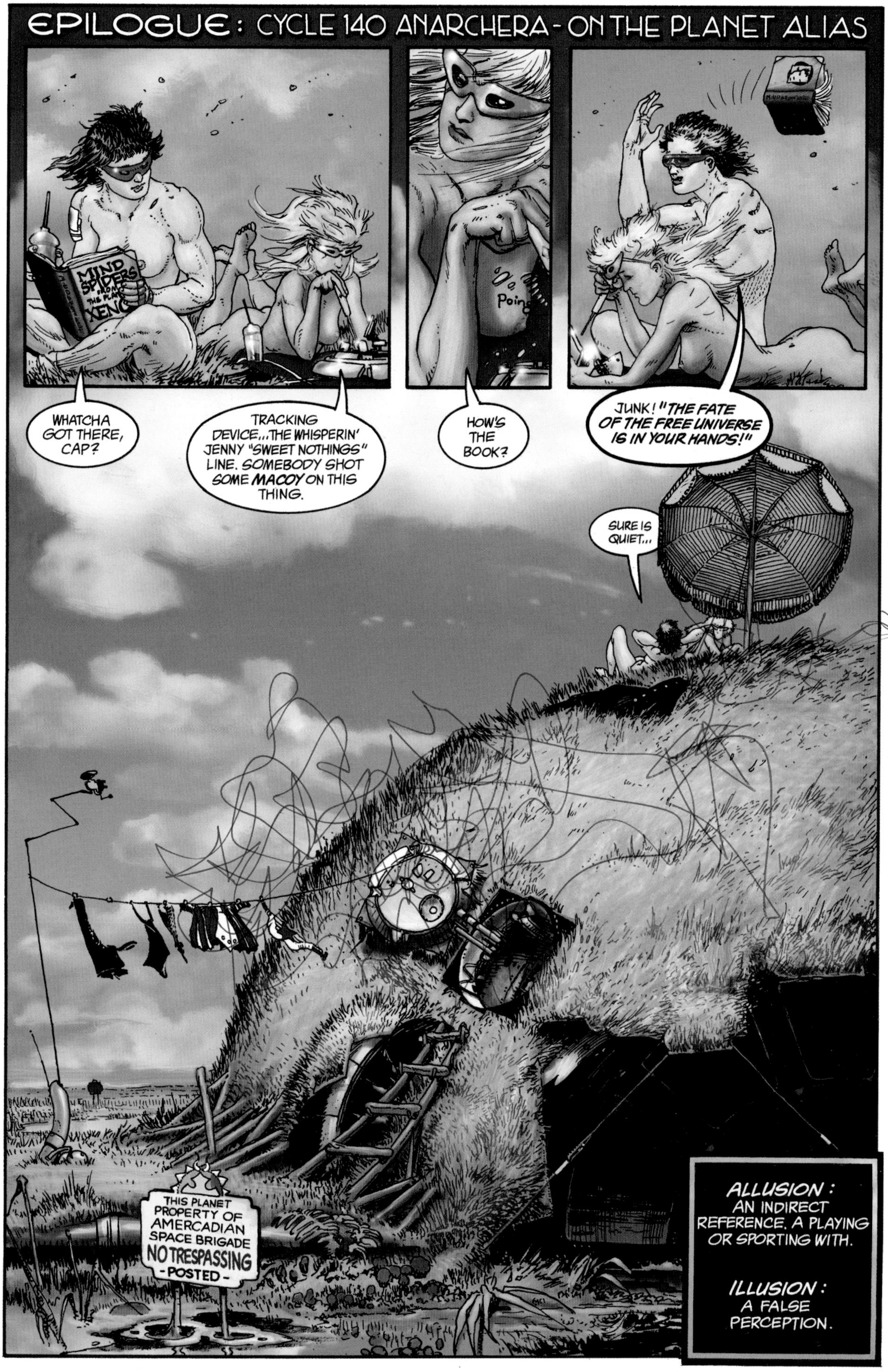
EPILOGUE: CYCLE 140 ANARCHERA - ON THE PLANET ALIAS
MIND SPIDERS FROM THE PLANET XENO
WHATCHA GOT THERE, CAP?
TRACKING DEVICE... THE WHISPERIN' JENNY "SWEET NOTHINGS" LINE. SOMEBODY SHOT SOME MACOY ON THIS THING.
Poing
HOW'S THE BOOK?
JUNK! "THE FATE OF THE FREE UNIVERSE IS IN YOUR HANDS!"
SURE IS QUIET...
THIS PLANET PROPERTY OF AMERCADIAN SPACE BRIGADE NO TRESPASSING -POSTED-
ALLUSION: AN INDIRECT REFERENCE. A PLAYING OR SPORTING WITH.
ILLUSION: A FALSE PERCEPTION.

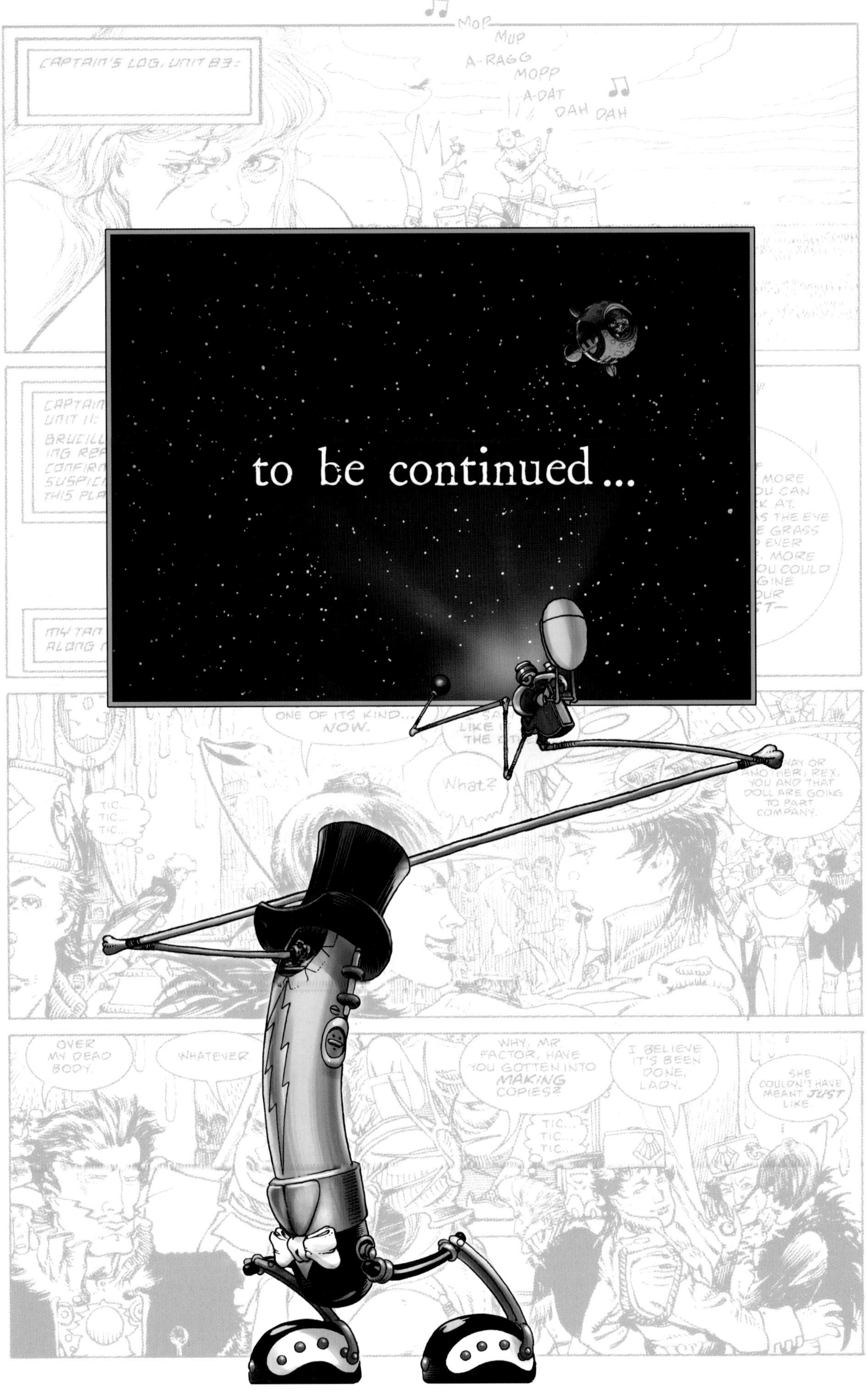

CAPTAIN'S LOG, UNIT 83:
MOP
MUP
A-RAGG
MOPP
A-DAT
DAH DAH
to be continued...
ONE OF ITS KIND... NOW.
What?
TIC... TIC... TIC...
OVER MY DEAD BODY.
WHATEVER.
WHY, MR. FACTOR, HAVE YOU GOTTEN INTO MAKING COPIES?
I BELIEVE IT'S BEEN DONE, LADY.
TIC... TIC... TIC...
SHE COULDN'T HAVE MEANT JUST LIKE.

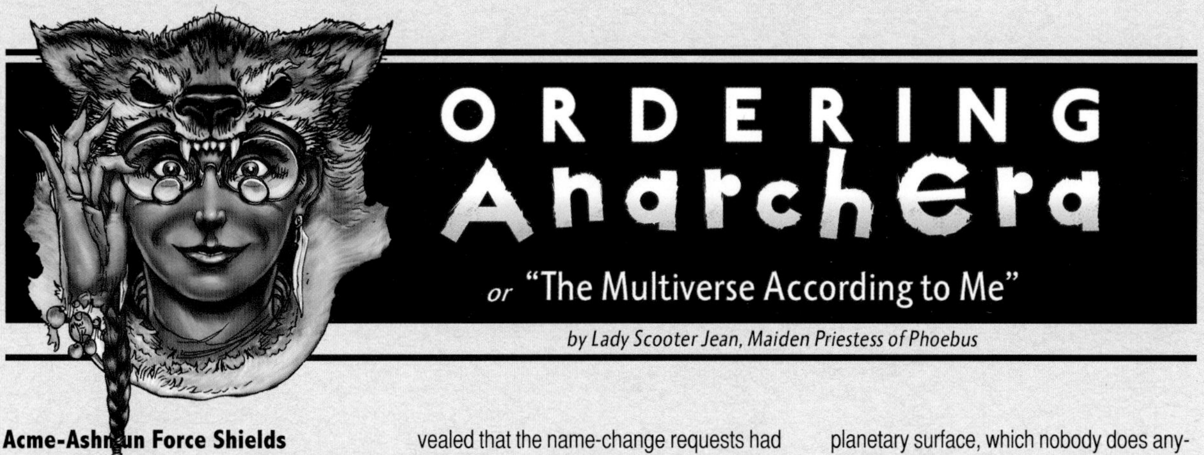

ORDERING AnarchEra

or "The Multiverse According to Me"

by Lady Scooter Jean, Maiden Priestess of Phoebus

Acme-Ashmun Force Shields
The bomb made calm. The beam's bad dream. The be-all-end-all of krystal-generated, charged-particle protection. The pinnacle, shield-wise. Acme-Ashmuns cost some real McCoy. They are, by all accounts, worth it.

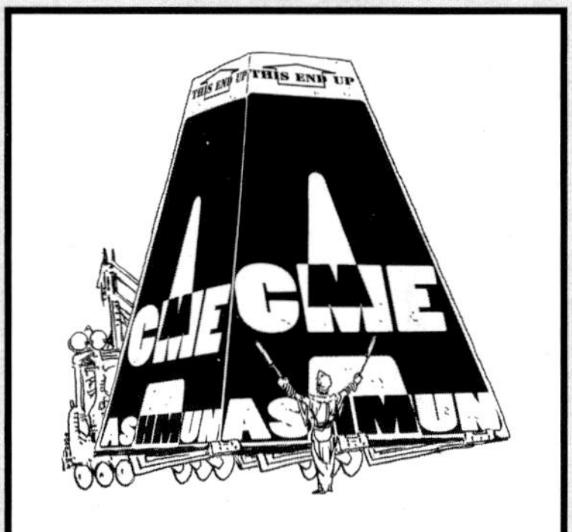

Acme-Ashmun Shield Generator

Alias
According to the latest data from the Galactic Registry of Planets, there are at least 927 inhabited planets named Alias, though use of the descriptor "inhabited" may be stretching a point. Most of these Alian Worlds could be described as marshy, muddy or swamp-like, though "grassy" and "greenish" are almost as frequently heard. There is wide agreement, however, that the most accurate word one might use, when referring to the physical features of the average Alias, is "nondescript." But how, we may ask, did this pan-galactic gaggle of nondescript Aliases come to be so named? During the time of the Incorporated Elysian Republic and into the early cycles of Anarchera, there were never more than a handful of planets named Alias registered under that name with the GRP. Then, in cycle 141 AE, the Registry experienced an unprecedented deluge of requests from previously registered planets, asking, for various undisclosed reasons, that their accepted planetary names be replaced with the name Alias. According to a juicy bit of investigative reporting by Rootersnoos ferret Jimmy the Snout, this multi-planet "bang de nom" was the work of Chuck and the Banana-Fanas, a division of the Guernican Art Squad calling themselves Post-Verbal Evictionalists. It was revealed that the name-change requests had been artistically forged, for the purpose of confusing the various governments and law-enforcement agencies, military and fringe groups, bounty hunters and celebrity stalkers who were, at the time, searching the Multiverse for the two lady brigands who had so recently laid waste to several levels of Rec Station 97; one Galatia 9 and disgraced former Lieutenant of the Amercadian Space Brigade, Brucilla the Muscle. After somehow stumbling upon the fact that the Mizzes 9 and Muscle had gone into hiding on a nondescript planet named Alias, Chuck and the Banana-Fanas decided there could be no such thing as too many Aliases, whereas, until that point in time, even one had been one too many. Still, thanks to the propensity of humanoids for mimicking the behavior of their fellow humanoids, the 90-odd Aliases spawned by the efforts of Chuck and his BFs were merely the snowball that started the avalanche. Like a virus, the Alian meme spread throughout the settled Multiverse. Flags were raised, wars fought, colonies on new worlds launched and, when the cosmic dust settled, Alias was by far the most popular planetary name known to humanoidkind.

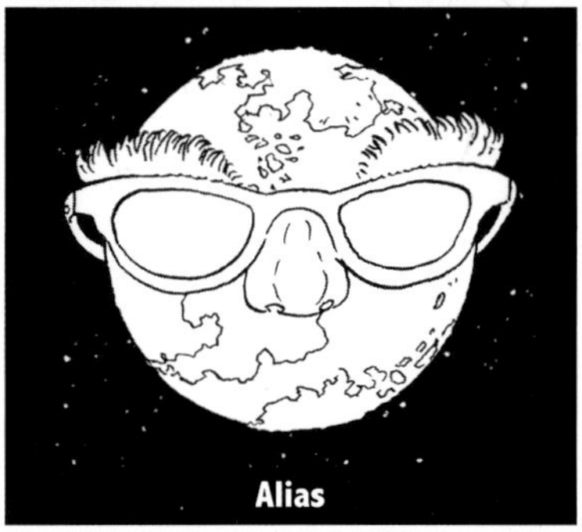

Alias

Alpha/Omega Time
Planet: Mirage. The division of the 60 marbec rotation of the planet Mirage into a 30 marbec period of light, or Alpha Time (A), and a 30 marbec period of darkness, or Omega Time (Ω). In the popular vernacular, Omega Time is referred to as "moovunit" and Alpha Time as "dontmoovunit," relating (obviously) to travel on the planetary surface, which nobody does anyway, so the reference is moot. The term "malton unit" is not used for either the Alpha or the Omega unit, because of the time disparity.

Amercadian Space Academy, The
An educational institution whose mission is threefold: 1) to supply the Amercadian Space Brigade with well-trained recruits (see: fodder, cannon), 2) to relieve the planet Amercadia of its surplus population, thus freeing up arable land, and 3) to provide exhausted parents from all corners of the known galaxy with a safe(ish) place to send their more "active" offspring.

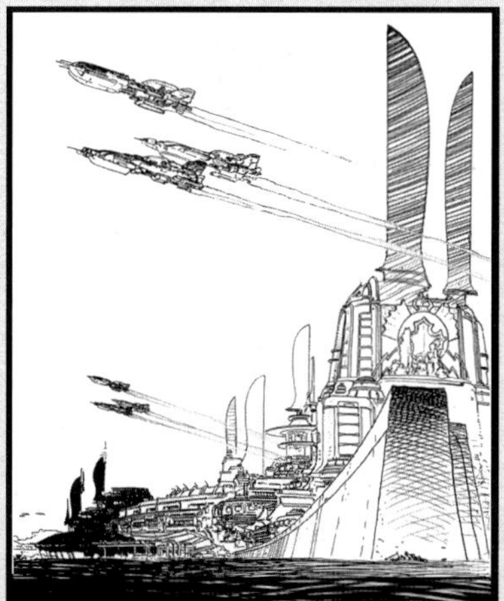

Amercadian Space Academy

"Dame Destiny has beckoned us
Into the starry blue
And all true hearts will reckon thus
To thine own class be true!
Academy! Academy!
Your spinning, G-less halls!
Good Amercadian girls and lads
Will ever heed your call!"
- from the Amercadian Space Academy School Song

Amercadian Space Academy Fight Song
Known to cadets simply as *Fight Fight Fight*, but originally titled *A Warning to Our Esteemed Adversaries*, this most recent of many Space Academy Fight Songs was

written in AE 12 by Cadet Amiable Goodwrench, of the planet Noo Mizoorah in the New Frontier. Critics have pointed to the line wherein Goodwrench suggests serving up Academy rivals in a "cheese fondu" as being proof of his sympathies with the goals of the Acadian Non-Brigade, though nothing in his history would support such a conclusion. The lyrics to Goodwrench's song are as follows:

Fight, fight, fight,
Turn the darkness into light!
Smash the night
With our terrible might!
Oh whatta oh whatta oh whatta sight!
Fight, fight, fight!

Give me a wall and I'll smash it down!
Stamp my foot and it shakes the ground!
Mash me a mountain into a mound!
Chew 'em up, spit 'em out!
If they want another bout,
We'll show 'em just who got the clout!
Grind 'em up and sell 'em by the quarter of a pound!

Fight, fight, fight,
Take a wrong and make it right!
Foes we'll smite
And our rivals afright!
Oh whatta oh whatta oh whatta sight!
Fight, fight, fight!

Show me a hoop and I'll jump right through!
Daze and amaze with my derring-do!
Nary a warrior that I can't unglue!
Knock 'em down, stomp 'em flat,
Give 'em several tits for tat!
Send 'em where the pain is at!
Slice 'em up and serve 'em in a cheese fondu!

Fight, fight, fight,
Turn the darkness into light!
Smash the night
With our terrible might!
Oh whatta oh whatta oh whatta sight!
Fight, fight, fight!

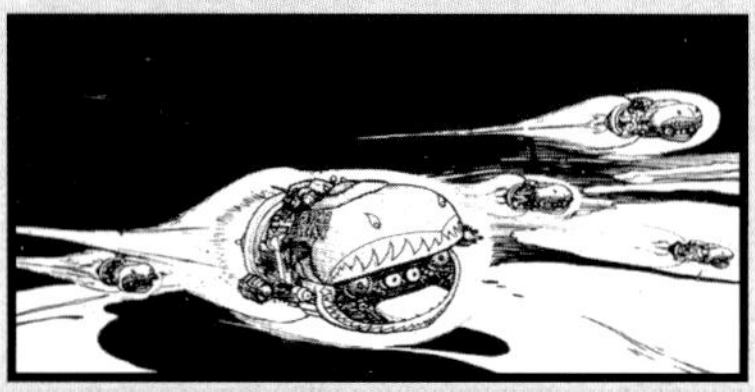

Amercadian Space Brigade, The

The military arm of Amercadia, whose motto is: "Good 'Til the Last Drops." Shortly after the Unification of Sovereign Townships ended the only longish period of peace in Old Terran History, the Associated Governments of the United States and Canada (now Amercadia) began to wonder what THEY were up to. All the little home guards were made into one big HOME GUARD. Its chief function was to protect Amercadia from THOSE PEOPLE OVER THERE. When nobody came, Amercadia began to have bigger worries. If THEY weren't coming from the other side of the globe, there was a good chance THEY were planning an attack from the inside. Thus began a rather dark period of Amercadian history (see: National Delusion, the) that only ended when Amercadians believed they had located an even more powerful enemy. After all, if THEY weren't coming from the other side of the globe, and THEY weren't planning an attack from the inside, THEY must be coming from OUT THERE. Amercadia mobilized a great space fleet. Brave lads and lasses were "recruited" into the new Amercadian Space Brigade and prepared to go OUT THERE. The Brigade's chief function was to protect Amercadia from THOSE BEINGS OUT THERE. Once they got OUT THERE, they discovered that no one in the wider multiverse had even the slightest interest in Amercadia. Having been robbed of their raison d'etre, they pondered the alternatives. They adapted. Their chief functions became PRESERVE AND SUSTAIN THE BRIGADE. The brigade prospered and grew, trading its military might to an ally HERE for... oh let's say Borinyum Krystals... becoming involved in a small conflict THERE and being repaid by an oh-so-grateful government with a tiny shipment of monopoles. Amercadia itself became less and less a real place and more and more an ideal of the Brigade. Amercadia's chief function became FEED THE BRIGADE.

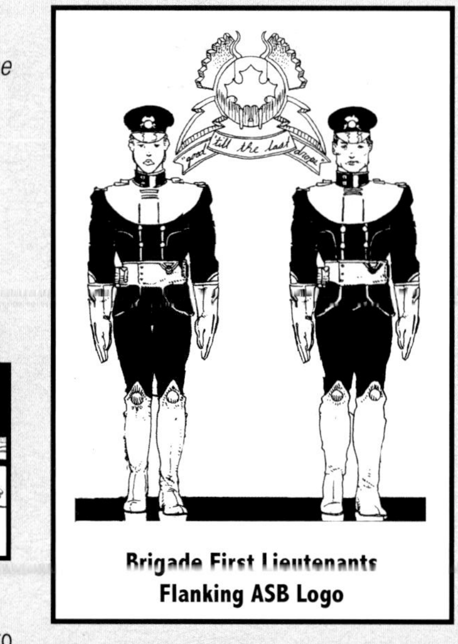

Good 'Til the Last Drops

Brigade First Lieutenants Flanking ASB Logo

AnarchEra

The accepted designation for the current time period, which began shortly after the fall of IER-CO, or the Incorporated Elysian Republic (which was neither heavenly, nor a republic), on the heels of the historic proclamation of the First Galactic Council for Deciding What to Do Next. The name is descriptive of a certain, shall we say, dismissive attitude toward the rule of law. Those who suffered under IER-CO rule might say appropriately dismissive.

Andromedicones

A self-propagating race of androids, capable of independent thought. Each Andromedicone serves a tour of duty in order to repay her or his builders for the expense of building him or her. S/he may be leased out for the 20-cycle term, or spend the time on Medi-18 building more Andromedicones. In Cycle 3 (SET), a peevish Mediconian faction with beady little eyes set on dreams of empire, emigrated to Vercadia and began the manufacture of the incredibly dangerous and incredibly expensive Vercadian Protector Androids, thus giving the Mediconian race a name less than MUDD ®. (See: MUDD ®)

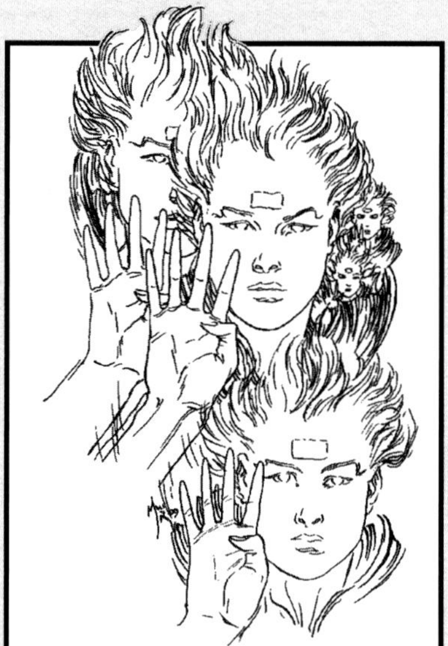

AL Series Andromedicones

According to some sources, the participation of Andromedicones in the Droid Wars, though they served only as medics and support to human allies, was a deciding factor in its positive outcome. To this molten unit, each and every Andromedicone devotes one of its seven communication frequencies to the repetitive chanting of a verse honoring the humans who fought for Cyberforms in the wars.

Anti-Baptists

1) The disparaging name given to the Pro-Labor Party on the planet Onolo Dos, part of the Seven Planets system, which is, in turn, part of United Free Trade Planets, Inc. During the religious wars that raged from Cycle 92 to Cycle 111 AE (but which some say began as a secular rebellion against the rule of UFTP several cycles earlier), the label Anti-Baptist came to apply to anyone, human or cyberform, who sympathized with the Labor cause on that, or on any, world. 2) Any sentient being whose innate sense of fashion precludes the wearing of brown shoes.

ArcheOrganaApocolypsla

By all accounts the worst play ever produced, *ArcheOrganaApocolypsia* traces the humanoid race from its humble beginnings to its predicted destruction (see: Brand New Testament). Each performance lasted a full nargon and was presented in three acts: The Creation, The Duration, and The Devastation. The play was written by playboy theologian Brother Anthony Quantis, ex-member of the Brothers of the Dangling Zed, a heretical Christo Zedian sect. It was rewritten and staged by well-known director Sambo Thrace-Smythe. In the words of Onus Wren, renowned theatre critic "A futile exercise in intellectual autoeroticism. Better by far had he (Thrace-Smythe) inserted a trisone injectable into his left ear." *ArcheOrganaApocolypsia* resulted in the financial devastation of anyone even slightly involved with the production and, less directly, the deaths of the Troikani actors, Personus/Ex/Mahkina, and the well-known director Sambo Thrace-Smythe.

Assessaur

Playful slang name given to members of the Ootoud race of the Lotus Root System and based on the Amercadian word assessor, defined as one who values property, or the damage to property, this due to the Ootouds' outstanding ability in this line of work. Once thought to have reproduced sexually, the two sexes of the two-headed Ootouds are now believed to have somehow merged, at some point in their evolution, into single beings that reproduce asexually. Both heads are equally officious, each sporting a generous mouth, perched atop its brow and ringed with razor-sharp teeth.

Assessaur

Atomo-Torch Particle Blaster

When the Mark 7 Dreadnaught Planet-Splitter is overkill and the dependable old Hyon Beam lacks the pinpoint precision to accomplish the job at hand, the Atomo-Torch Particle Blaster is just what the doctor ordered (assuming the doctor is a sadistic old bastard). It can cut an adversary's titanium- alloy hull into a string of tinfoil dollies, while blasting through thruspace at near light speed. Mucho dineros, but worth every qua-credit!

Baby Sisters

Nickname for the small, gold-toned, blue-clad recruiting droids commissioned by the Cloistered Order of the Cosmic Veil and built by the Handi-Andi® Corporation, though calling them droids is stretching a point, as they are actually robots, albeit with limited memories imprinted on thin sections of vat-grown brain tissue, then coupled with an electronic brain, mainly concerned with the recording and storage of images. Though the nickname was inspired by the size of the droids, as well as the fact that they are dressed in the same clothing as Comet Cloister Nunz, it also points to the fact that most sentient beings find them to be more than slightly annoying. They are ubiquitous on the galaxy's many Rec Stations.

Baby Sister Droids

Bajar, Roderigo Sejanus Vasco d'Gama

(6531 IET – 174 AE) A brilliant and ruthless businessman, the Baron RSVdG Bajar built a mighty empire from the tiny desert planet, Mirage, where he had, as a boy, been exiled with the remains of his family, after the fall of the Incorporated Elysian Republic, which was neither heavenly, nor a republic. His first business, the enormously successful Crown and Sceptor, was a shipping enterprise. It soon began to gobble up the smaller businesses it dealt with and United Free Trade Planets, Ltd., was born. This company/kingdom includes Seven Planets, its satellites and mining belts, Hydrangea and several other resort planets scattered about the galaxy, the Onolos, and a number of uninhabited worlds that were stripped of their resources and left drifting like pockmarks on the face of Mother Void. The Baron's strange and violent death is still a mystery. He was found early one Alpha, sitting in his courtroom on Mirage. A sprig of rosemary had been potted in the bowl of his pipe. A child's report card with every subject marked "failed" had been pinned to his jacket. Certain of his vital organs had been removed, individually wrapped in birthday paper, and placed in a krystal box on the Baron's desk. Bajar was survived by a son, Kalif, and a daughter, Lucrezia. He left the two of them his huge estate, to be in shared equally and run jointly, "in the hopes that they will destroy itself like the monster they is."

The Baron RSVdG Bajar

Bajar Shilling

A small, octagonal, titanium alloy coin. The head of the Baron RSVdG Bajar, in profile, and the words "WREDDE AD CAESAREM QUOD CAESARIEST," are stamped on one side of the coin. On the other, a steel taloned shreeguh clutches a crown and scepter. The Baron Roderigo Bajar (under the auspices of the United Free Trade Planets) had these coins minted in cycle AE 78, hence the phrase, "Not worth a Bajar Shilling."

The ubiquitous jar of Bajar Shillings

Banlastic

1) When referring to a certain "place" in space/time, banlastic is that quality of elas-

ticity that, in some cases, allows for near-instantaneous travel from wherever it is you are to various distant corners of the Multiverse. 2) When referring to the waistlines of yo-yo dieters of the type disposed to periodically visit certain Rec Station eating establishments, banlastic is a quality of elasticity in one's skin and clothing that is required by a continually expanding and contracting circumference of the belly.

Banlon

1) An elastic or expandable unit of space. 2) A subjective measure of space, always longer than "right over here," never as long as "way over yonder," and just wide enough for an average humanoid to rest on it comfortably.

Bargain Bliss®

A division of Living Doll Cybernetics® specializing in the development and marketing of nonsentient "love toys." Bargain Bliss only came into being after the departure of LDC co-founder Mary Medea and was a special project of her former business partner, Mr. Anderson Grommit.

Beastie

1) Any member of the elite guard of Prime Minister Glorianna of Pheobus. 2) Any devotee of the religion practiced by the Krystal Miners of the Mitochondrian Belt in the Pheobus System. 3) Any bad tempered, ill-mannered individual. 4) Any individual existing in an altered state of consciousness whether chemically, hypnotically, or Krystal-induced. In its religious sense, the word "beastie" implies a state of union with the Natural Multiverse. In its drunken sense, the word denotes a period of release from the strictures of rational thought and civilized society, hence the phrase, "walking his (or her) beastie."

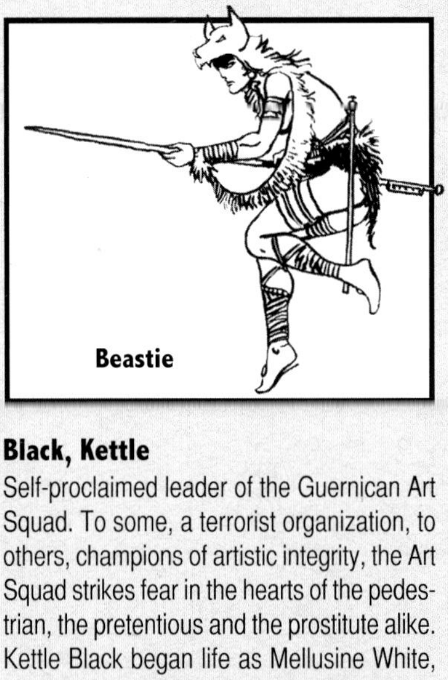

Beastie

Black, Kettle

Self-proclaimed leader of the Guernican Art Squad. To some, a terrorist organization, to others, champions of artistic integrity, the Art Squad strikes fear in the hearts of the pedestrian, the pretentious and the prostitute alike. Kettle Black began life as Mellusine White, the daughter of IER-CO-era krystal miners, and (after the fall of the Incorporated Elysian Republic) studied art at the Stellavista Conservatory, graduating with a double major in quantum sculpture and light-weaving. Though her first professional gallery show, Private Particles, was a popular success, with 2/3rds of her pieces selling to an enthusiastic crowd, (then) Miz White's work received mixed reviews. Subsequent shows sold less well, hurt no doubt by the bad press, and Mellusine White disappeared from the scene, to emerge cycles later as Kettle Black. Her first act as self-appointed leader of the Art Squad was to purge the civilized Multiverse of the very critics who had wounded her pride and ended her career, painfully reducing them to their constituent particles and putting them to use in various objets d'art. Over the cycles, she seems to have spent less and less time as an artist and more and more time as an artistic activist. Current critics claim that, lacking a successful career, Kettle Black has made her life her art. That they claim this anonymously is completely understandable.

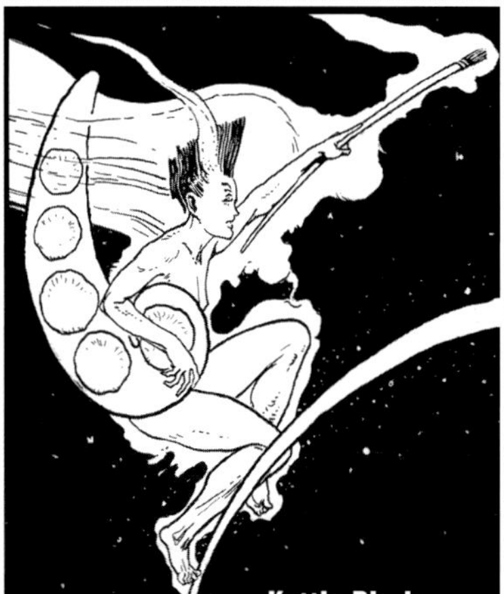

Kettle Black

Boot

1) To engage in copulation, 2) to copulate with a being or substance for which one has little regard, 3) to harm, confuse or destroy someone or something, 4) to express surprise at a turn of events while simultaneously castigating oneself, as in "Boot me!"

Bread-Heads

A derogatory name for Cybernetic Lifeforms, alluding to the importance of yeast in the formation or "baking" of Android cultures or lines. The term, however, is a misnomer. Though android bodies are vat-grown, yeast has very little to do with the process.

Bumpkinville in the Zero Zone

A mythical village on an unnamed planet in a zone so far removed from the civilized universe that it has not rated a number. A person said to be from Bumpkinville is usually an untutored naïf who lacks the sense to come in out of a meteor shower, though it can be used simply to describe an extremely distant location.

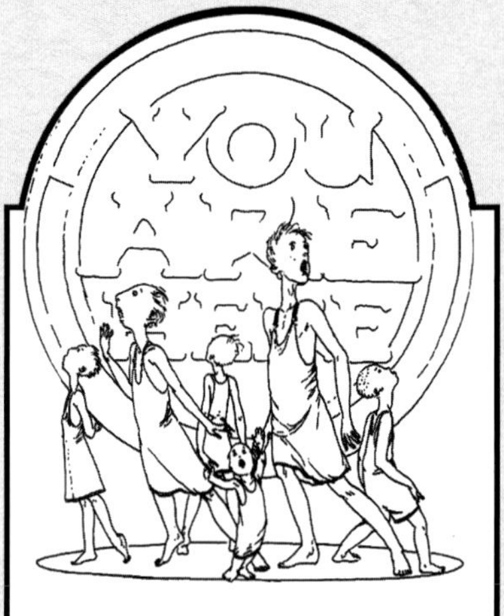

Bumpkins from Bumpkinville

Byzon Galaxy

A mythical galaxy that is always farther away than anything else, no matter where you happen to be in the known universe. Hence the expression: "I'm gonna kick your tail from here to the Byzon Galaxy." A person said to be from the Byzon Galaxy is almost always said to be from "Bum-Boot, Egypt, in the Byzon Galaxy." Translation: "You are a person (or person equivalent) from a town no one wants to visit, much less live in, in a country that no longer exists, if indeed it ever existed, in a Galaxy that is farther away than anything else in the known universe." (see: Bumpkinville in the Zero Zone)

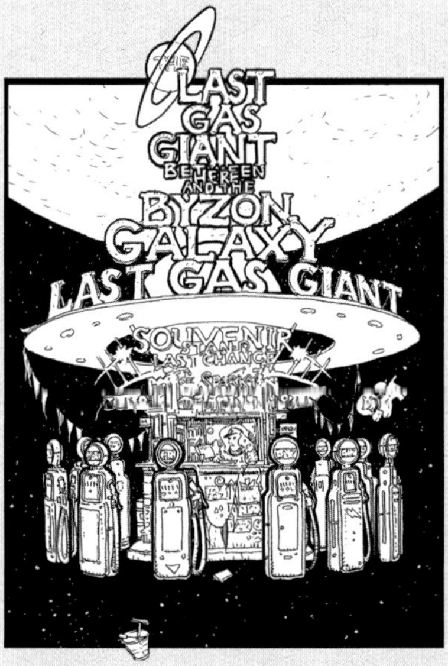
LAST GAS GIANT
BYZON GALAXY
LAST GAS GIANT
SOUVENIR

Casino Cards

Yet another version of the Gold Card® used by very wealthy patrons of the 483 (at this printing) Recreation Stations in our Galaxy, for the purpose of Walking On®. Casino Cards® were first issued by The Dome, Recreation Station 97, as a perk for their High Rollers. The cards are leased by The Dome from Swell's Bells®, the company that developed this mode of transport and has guarded the technology fiercely for the last

89 cycles. The Dome defrays part of the tremendous cost of this service by placing their Walking On Depot® in the club's Free-betters' Room and allowing their customers to place bets on "who'll materialize next." It is doubtful that Walking On® will ever replace Krystal-driven starships as the primary means of transportation in the galaxy, as the cost is prohibitive.

Chub Sprouts

1) A chubby toddler or young child, 2) an innocent, 3) a newbie, 4) a "green" kid, one who, due either to age or inexperience, doesn't know boots from banlons.

Comet Cloister

Possibly the most famous of all the Cosmic Veil's cloisters, due to its part in the Amercadian Space Brigade Neutral Zone Fiasco of AE 134, Comet Cloister is reported to be the quietest of the Sisterhood's many cloisters scattered about the more densely populated regions of the settled Multiverse. Unlike its sister cloisters, which are round in shape and small in size, Comet Cloister is quite spacious and houses the Veil's Galactic Offices and the living quarters of Mother Amy Simple, Prime Mother of the religious order, as well as quarters of other Veil notables and well-appointed visitors' rooms for honored guests. ILRLE Bajar is said to visit quite often.

Over Loaded, Over Anxious, Over Extended?
Join the
Cosmic Veil
(CLOISTERED ORDER OF THE GODDESS UNCARING)
RELAX AND MEDITATE IN THE PEACEFUL ATMOSPHERE of COMET CLOISTER
LOCATED JUST THREE SPANDECS FROM THE
MITOCHONDRIAN KRYSTAL BELT
APPLY WITH THIS DROID.
®COGU

Cosmic Veil, Cloistered Order of the

Of the myriad religions in the known Universe, the Cloistered Order of the Cosmic Veil is the only one with no splinter factions, hence, it is easily definable by its own tenets which are as follows: 1) The Mother is Paradox; Ever present and never there when you need Her, 2) Non-participation is the better part of action, 3) If the pond is illusion, then what are the ripples? 4) All things come to she who waits... and waits...and waits, 5) Confuse Karma; stand quite still and think of nothing. The Cosmic Veil's cloisters, which are scattered about the more densely populated regions of the settled Multiverse, are round in shape, small in size, and packed full-to-bursting with pious sisters meditating in blissful union with the Void. Or so they say. The fact that novices are asked to donate all (or at least a good chunk) of their worldly possessions to the order has caused some critics to claim that the Cosmic Veil is simply a very lucrative business venture.

Sister of the Cosmic Veil

Others call it a front for various criminal activities, though this has never been proven. Certain socioarcheologists have pointed to the similarities between the tenets of the Cosmic Veil and the tenets of the Daughters of the Drowning Isis, a fictional religion introduced in the best-selling *Mind Spiders from the Planet Xenon*, by the Hugo Award-winning author Ronnie Lee Ellis.

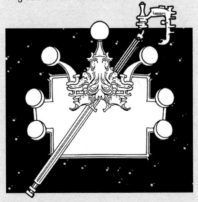

Crown and Scepter, Ltd.

The incorporated Family Bajar (descended from PAHM Bajar), its planets, palaces and holdings, as well as its several divisions and offshoots, including United Free Trade Planets, Inc., which is both an import/export business and the government of Seven Planets and its various colonies, outer territories, satellite worlds and mining operations. Ostensibly founded by GHMM Bajar, son of PAHM (see: Dictator, the Dread), but only on paper, the brain behind Crown and Scepter was that of RSVdG Bajar, a minor child at the time. The fact that GHMM Bajar met his death in an "iffy" boating accident less than a week after his son and successor came of age made headlines in the interglax noos and was a hot topic for holochats and docudramas of the day. RSVdG Bajar was subsequently cleared of any wrongdoing by the High Court of Seven Planets, a division of United Free Trade Planets, which was, in turn, a division of Crown and Scepter.

Dead Man's Mirror

An anomaly in Neutral Zone 8 that seems to change its physical attributes depending on the angle and velocity at which a spacecraft approaches, sometimes becoming a slippery, wok-shaped slide, at other times manifesting as rock-like, diamond-hard "lumps" of space, beneath a deceptive, watery, mirror-like surface, or even, it has been said, becoming a portal to other destinations in the Multiverse (see: Gate, the). Though Neutral Zone 8 is officially off-limits to members of the Amercadian Space Brigade, taking a skate on the mirror is a challenge that has proved irresistible to generations of Amercadian Space Academy Cadets, even since the infamous Amercadian Space Brigade Neutral Zone Fiasco of AE 134. For hotdogs and heroes of every stripe, Dead Man's Mirror is the pinnacle, risk-wise.

D.O.G. Years

An acronym for Dubious Orbits of Gem, D.O.G. Years, as a measure of time, are used on New Wyoming and several other inhabited planets of the Last Frontier. Gem, as you no doubt know, was the popular name for Vaikuntha, the Krystal-rich planet used as a base and center of mining operations by IER CO forces during the latter days of the Stagnation (see: Stagnation, the Great). During the Revolution, it was shattered by Rebel forces hoping to deprive P.A.H.M. Baiar {see: Dictator, the Dread) of the only fuel capable of powering the Krystal-driven thruships used by his IER CO Cherubim. The strategy succeeded and the Revolution ended. The remains of Vaikuntha became part of the Mitochondrian Krystal Belt of the Phoebus System, which was owned and mined primarily by the Medea family of New Wyoming until AE 93, when it was willed to the Krystal miners and their families by one Mary Medea, eldest daughter of Krystals 'n Things magnate Margaret Medea. After the Revolution, New Wyoming and several nearby planets dropped the Standard Cycle as their official "year" and adopted D.O.G. Years, as a tribute to the planet whose Krystal deposits had made the families of the Last Frontier rich beyond their wildest dreams. Since Vaikuntha/Gem no longer exists, an exact measure of the length of its orbits is dubious.

Doll Maker, The

A Hugo award-nominated book by Hugo Award-winning author Ronnie Lee Ellis. First released and marketed as a work of nonfiction under its original title, *Slave Trader: An Unauthorized Biography of Mary Medea*, the book tanked big time, ignored by the media and Miz Ellis's fans alike. According to sources close to the Bajar family, Miz Ellis attributed the failure to the fact that, after Mary Medea's death, the galactic citizenry lost interest in the descendants of revolutionary hera Molly Medea. A second attempt to sell the book as a nonfiction title (some cycles later and with several added chapters) under the name, *Cult Leader: An Unauthorized Biography of Glorianna of Phoebus*, achieved similar results. With this publication, Miz Ellis seemed to be trying to attach her work to the unsubstantiated rumor that Mary Medea and Glorianna of Phoebus were one and the same person, as G-of-P had only risen to prominence in the Phoebus System after Medea's death.

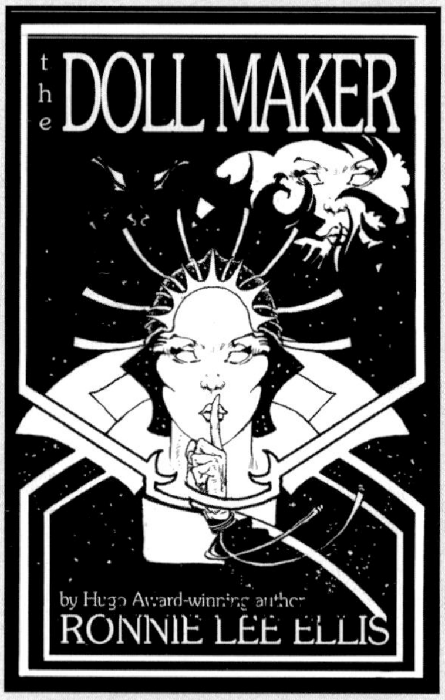
the DOLL MAKER
by Hugo Award-winning author
RONNIE LEE ELLIS

Conspiracy theorist loners aside, the public did not appear ready to jump on this particular bandwagon and rejected the book, en masse. Not to be deterred, Miz Ellis went back to the drawing board and began to turn her book into a work of fiction (though some say this wasn't a great leap). She changed the names of the characters, added some plot and description, then published *The Doll Maker* to wide acclaim. The following is a brief synopsis of the plot of *The Doll Maker* from *The Galactic Encyclopedia of Literature and Literature-Equivalents*: *"Wealthy krystal heiress and pan-galactic busybody Ariadne Josephs forms a company called Baby-Oh-Baby Dolls for the purpose of producing pleasure droids, which are then sent to destroy the children of her rival, ruthless business tycoon Vercingetorix Moses Hannibal Rajab McPhee. Through an overlong series of events, McPhee's children, the brilliant Lucrezia and her mentally challenged brother Phaleef, turn the tables on Josephs, annihilating the sex droids and taking down the religious cult Ariadne has maintained to mask her various nefarious plots."*

Double Death Commando

A specialty of Harry Palmer, Bartender-Owner of the SAILOR'S GRAVE, Recreation Station 97. The Double Death Commando consists of two scoops of vanilla ice cream, High Colonian Vodka, menthol de menthe, extracts from certain poisonous tubers, a two-ribec zap of semi-inert positrons, and a one-quarter dose of pharmaceutical Kublacaine. The explosive reaction of the Kublacaine neutralizes the deadly effects of the organic poisons. Must be imbibed within 30 ribecs.

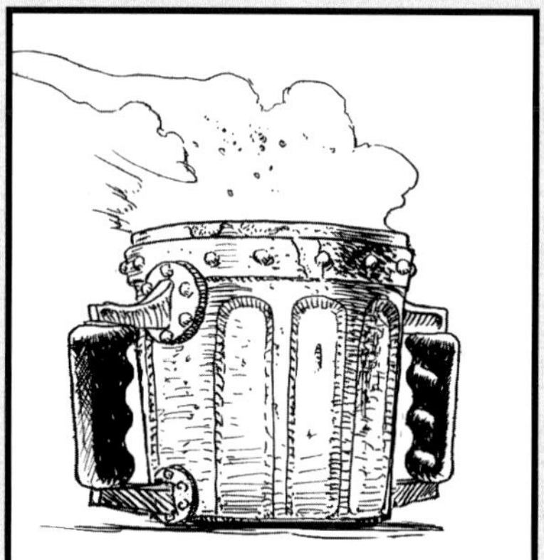

Double Death Commando

Dream Enhancement Games

A generic term for any number of personal and multi-player adventure games, designed for the Land-o-Nod ® gaming system, which allows players to enter, armed and conscious, into their own dreams, in order to do battle with their personal demons. For some, a pleasurable way to waste a few martrons, for others, a crippling addiction, but for the spiritually advanced, an exciting and inexpensive substitute for traditional psychotherapies. DEGs are (next to games of chance) the most popular games going.

E-V Series Record-o-Droid

Though not precisely a droid, the E-V series, released by Handi-Andi in Cycle 130 AnarchEra, was the top of the line in personal PR-Bots. Its combo-brain, built from slices of cloned canine brain enhanced with electronics, offered its owner a unique blend of loyalty and serviceability. Equipped with three lasaround cameras, two still cameras and several boom mikes on extendable arms, the wiener-shaped E-V happily padded, ran, rolled or blasted after its owner, recording any and all events in said owner's life. A favorite with celebrities and wannabes alike (and, indeed, the E-V often helped turn the one into the other), the little cyberbot with the lightening bolt logo was the next best thing to a fully humanoid publicist and PR team and was certainly more reasonably priced!

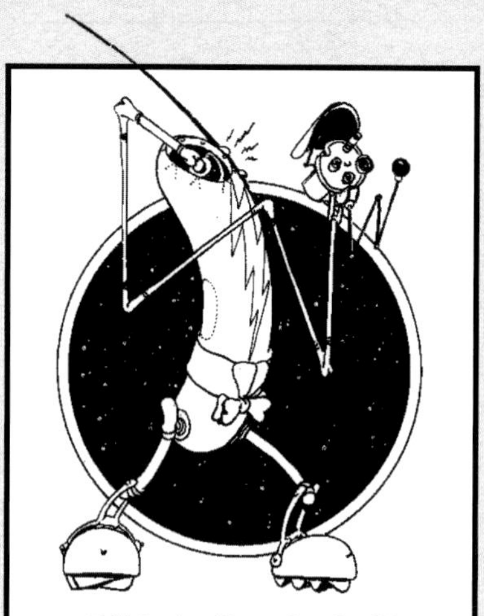

E-V Series Record-o-Droid

Freebetters Room

The VIP room of VIP rooms, part of the very upscale casino in The Dome, Rec Station 97, where Star-Hoppers, High Muckety-Mucks, and big-spending members of the Gold Card Class bet freely on the outcome of whatever war, skirmish, sporting event, chance meeting or random happening may be taking place in their vicinity or beyond. Fortunes have been lost, lives ruined, deals sealed and strange bedfellows made, as the dice keep rolling on and the chips continue to fall where they may. The Freebetters' Room was built around The Dome's WALKING ON DEPOT® and the club allows their customers to place bets on "who'll materialize next" as a means to defray part of the tremendous cost of that service.

Galactic Girl Guide Manual, Official

Along with Ordering AnarchEra, the go-to guide (as opposed to Guide) for the discriminating spacer who wants to know what's what and who's who in the inhabited zones of the multiverse, though the 3G Manual may be a touch more cynical (realistic, according to Guide Leadership) than the reference you are currently browsing. Aside from its sections on Guide Badges, Rank Climbing and Soup Can Derby rules, which are (for the most part) important only to active Guides, the Manual includes chapters on basic survival on the various planets and artificial worlds, tips on bribing officials, maps to the homes of suckers (kind supporters, according to Guide Leadership), How-To instructions on topics from lock-picking to negotiating with pawn brokers and winning at craps, and a Galactic Bestiary, containing descriptions of the fighting, mating and feeding habits of creatures from numerous worlds, both sentient and non. The Bestiary alone has saved innumerable lives. Needless to say, the Official Galactic Girl Manual is an extremely valuable commodity. If you manage to run across a copy, you should obtain it by any means and guard it with your life.

Galactic Girl Guide with Manual

Galactic Girl Guide Mobile Campground and Headquarters

A huge Krystal-driven station-ship that houses the offices of the 3G Rotating Leadership, as well as a fully functioning campground, built by Griivarr Interprises, Inc., and paid for with annual dues from the 5,300,487 Galactic Girl Guide wings. The acquisition of the 3GMCH at a discounted price (see: Griivarr Interprises Stock Slump of AE 96) was a real coup for the organization, as having a camp and headquarters that is also a station-ship allows the Guides to schedule events in different parts of the known universe, while avoiding the related (some might say, "inevitable") legal difficulties, somewhat like a moving craps game. Sporting a very realistic simulated sky, tuned to old Terran day/night sequence, the campground includes seven large lakes, 37 water slides, archery and blaster ranges, five NATURE ® trails, 53 Guide-knotted rope bridges, 18 go-can tracks, and a state-of-the-art obstacle course that rivals that of the Amercadian Space Academy (see: Mysterious Course Looting of AE 99, the). There is a camp canteen where the practice of filching skills is encouraged, an Indoor Games Lodge where three-card monty and other games of chance may be played, and a Motorpool where campers learn the invaluable art of hotwiring "abandoned" ships. The seven million and some odd scenic campsites are decorated with attractive and long-lasting Plant-y-Pals, a premium foliage substitute designed, manufactured and supplied by GII. All maintenance and repairs on the 3GMCH are done through Merry Mechs, a repair service company founded and run by former Guides. It is rumored that all parts and upgrades

used on the 3GMCH "fell from the holds" of Merry Mechs ships on their way to other jobs, allowing Merry Mechs to service the campground for an extremely reasonable price. The 3G Mobile Campground is the preferred site for the annual Guide/Ranger Camporee (see: Guide/Ranger Camporee, the Annual) and Soup-Can Derby.

3G Mobile Campground and Headquarters

Galactic Girl Guides

"On my honor I will do my best to do my duty to the Mother and to my Universe, to help other Girl Guides, whenever doing so does not conflict with my own best interest, and to obey, if possible, the Girl Guide Law" - *Galactic Girl Guide Pledge*. An organization dedicated to the schooling of young girls in survival tactics on a galactic scale, the Galactic Girl Guides trace their roots to Pre-Unification Amercadia. They began as the Junior Girl Guard, a branch of the Home Guard of the Sovereign Township of Kansas. The Girl Guard served as a training ground for future Kansan patriots (see: Rocket Rangers) and, according to tounit's Official Galactic Girl Guide Handbook, was "probably okay, if you fancy being bullet bait for a bunch of blowhard big shots who could care less if you got your tail kicked forty ways from Sunday." The Guard was immensely popular and spread to other Sovereign Townships in what was soon to become Amercadia. Their popularity dwindled during The Unification and the nationalization of the Home Guard. This was due, in part, to a lack of funding, as well as to the fact that most of the J.G.G.'s leadership had been drafted into the new Amercadian Home Guard. Their common-

sense outlook and grassroots ideals remained close to the hearts of Amercadians, however, and during the early Expansion, they resurfaced. They broke their ties with what had been the Home Guard (now the Amercadian Space Brigade) and advertised themselves as a "school of hard knocks" that prepared young girls to cut the mustard in a tough galaxy. "It's a TOUGH GALAXY," read the recruiting posters, "but SOMEBODY'S gotta live in it. It might as well be YOU!" And from the official Galactic Girl Guide Handbook, "A Girl Guide is wary, cunning, clever, assertive, flexible, patient, inventive and brave, but not stupidly so." Guides belong to a small group or "wing" and are classified by age as Chickadees, Jaybirds, Blackbirds and Senior Guides, or Voidettes. The coveted title Hawk Class Guide is an earned-only position. Today's Guides are part of a Galaxy-wide net of 5,300,487 wings. The Guides are very loosely connected to each other through the 3G Mobile Galactic Headquarters and Campground. They work their way up in the ranks by acquiring merit badges. Some examples are: The "Do Yo Stuff" badge, awarded for escaping punishment when caught in the act. This badge is sometimes accompanied by the "Silver Tongued Sister" badge, if the guide manages to turn the situation entirely around in her favor so that she escapes with honor and awards. There are shark badges (card, pool, darkbone mark), a stowaway badge, and the highly prized "Sign of the Nova" badge, which is awarded for deceiving the Girl Guide staff into awarding you at least 52 badges you haven't earned. This very useful education has created a great demand for Guide-trained women. They make terrific corporate spies, professional gamblers and hostess/ bouncers at some of the rougher leisure spots. Finally, the spirit of the Galactic Girl Guides is summed up in their motto: "TRUTH AS FAR AS IT GOES."

Galactic Girl Guides

Gate, The

A concept quite common in the lexicons of many of our galaxy's more sensible religions. Also known as the Portal, the Passage, and the Strong Door (because no amount of physical strength will open it), the Gate is the opening (or openings, as all openings are the one opening) between our Universe (Multiverse, Omniverse, All) and every other possible Universe. According to experts in these matters, not just anyone can pass through The Gate. The odds are weighted heavily in favor of the Natural Man (Woman) and the Spiritual Adept and are, likewise, weighted against the overcivilized and the uninitiated. These same experts disagree as to whether The Gate is a physical reality or a fact of the psyche. They do, however, agree that the best way to pass through The Gate is to think (or unthink) your way through.

The Gate

Geezer

1) A senile old fool. 2) A stuffed shirt, stick in the mud, or joy-stifling bore. 3) Any sentient being who spends the majority of his, her or its time on-world and thus, in the eyes of spacers, ages quickly. 4) Any sentient being with too much credit in the holding bay.

Griivarr, Bob

Born on Brown's World in 167 I.E.T. and dubbed Brzzt Oomph Burble by his doting parents, Bob Griivarr grew to manhood without once giving any indication of possessing any quality that might raise him above the masses of the mediocre from whence he'd sprung. He stood head and shoulders above his torso and that was about it. But in AE 53, after a short apprenticeship to a spot welder, Bob joined the Collected Galactic Sheet Metal and Mine Workers and began work as a Marginal Shaft Safety Inspector (or Guinea Bird) on the Rec Station 85 project. While shinnying down an inactive shaft on Ficus II, Bob stumbled upon a time capsule packed in the type of coffin capsule so popular during pre wasting times on Amercadia (then Earth) due to the lack of pre-wasting burial sites (see: Over-Population, Terran). No one

knows what was in that capsule, but it certainly changed the course of Bob Griivarr's rather mundane life. He emerged from the Fican mine shaft, some three rigons later, holding the first draft of his galaxy-shattering tome, Bob Griivarr's Simple Recipe for Happiness. The recipe included ingredients such as, "a generous measure of meaningful work, sweetened with companionship and affection, and leavened with familial duty." The book was a huge success. With it's proceeds, he purchased his first planet and named it Nyren Varr. This was the first of eight planets that would soon be known as the Griivarr Worlds, their culture and government based upon Bob Griivarr's Simple Recipe for Happiness. (for more information see, Griivarr Worlds, the) The most famous of the Griivarr worlds is Hon Ober, thanks to the galaxy class amusement park in its capitol, Hon Grii. The park, Uncle Bob's Fantanimalland, features exhibits of creatures, both sentient and non, from every corner of the known multiverse. Countless holorounds of Bob Griivarr, in his well-known persona, Uncle Bob, give instructions to visitors and bark for the parks numerous sideshows. After establishiing himself as a power in the universe, Bob Griivarr went on to father four famous children: Dwannyun "Bulldog" Griivarr (the semi-famous historian), Grunnyun "Buddy" Griivarr (the famous talkshow host), Bud Younger "Bud" Griivarr (the incredibly famous March Baptist Evangelist, Brother Bud) and Elizbut "Princess" Griivarr (the brilliant businesswoman).

Bob Grivarr as Uncle Bob®

Griivarr T-Vyou

The ever-present, blandly comforting countenance of Brzzzt Oomph Burble "You can call me BOB" Griivarr, as seen and heard in every household, restaurant, park and public facility on each and every Griivarr World. Uncle Bob, as GW residents call him, is a virtual droid, programmed with the personality

and memories of its prototype. Uncle Bob interacts with "his" citizens on a very personal level, providing companionship, giving aid, and offering advice.

Griivarr Worlds, The

Eight planets in the Tevalt, Grubsteak, and Yesteryear Systems, on the edge of the Last Frontier. These planets were bought, developed and are now managed by Brzzzt Oomph Burble "You can call me BOB" Griivarr, under the auspices of Griivarr Interprises, Inc. and their government and culture is based on the philosophy put forward in the galaxy-shattering tome Bob Griivarr's Simple Recipe for Happiness. Griivarr's joy-producing recipe included "ingredients" such as meaningful work, membership in a cohesive community and opportunity for displaying unselfish concern for one's neighbors.The Griivarr Worlds and their capital cities are as follows: Hon Grii (Hon Ober), Nyren Var (Varr Enov), Un D' Varr (Varr Aut), Ve D' Varr (Varr Niss), Tu Varr (Hao Varr), Grii Dii (Neer Enov), Varr Var (Yaway) and D' Varrthest (Varr Anaway).

Guernica

Standard name for the fourth planet in the Guernican System; chosen home of the Guernican Art Squad, a cultural organization dedicated to the eradication of ill-conceived or poorly exectuted works of art. The planet's original name (from expansionist times) is lost in obscurity. Every aspect of the planet, environment, geography, size, inclination on axis, et cetera, is in constant flux for various artistic reasons, except for its gorgeous (one could almost say "gaudy") ring system, constructed by the "Return to Forever" Neo-Pre-Expansionist Movement (Cycle 6 AE) from the second, sixth and 12th planets of the same system. The rings are quite large and unstable, nudging into orbits of the third and fifth planets. The remaining planets of the system have been variously carved, reassembled, or vaporized into gaseous statements, except for the fifth planet which doesn't actually exist except as a concept in the mind of Ann Ominous, a nonverbal conceptual constructionalist and gun runner. A 13th planet was comissioned in Cyce 142 AE, by Kettle Black, the Art Squad's self-proclaimed leader, but work was abandoned when the artist, after a particularly bad week, sunk into an 18-cycle slough of despond with accompanying creative block. The planet name, as well as the name of its sun and various orbiting objets d'art, is constantly changing according to the whim of the inhabitants; names like "Red" or "Spike" or "Crystal Palette of the Aethric Plane." The name Guernica is used in this definition and all major star charts, since it was the first post-IER planetary name. You will find other names for the Guernican System on star charts designed on Guernica, but the editors strongly suggest such charts be used strictly as conversation pieces, as they have absolutely no reference to reality as we know it. Pretty, though!

Guide/Ranger Camporee, the Annual
A week of camping, contests and camaraderie for active members of the Galactic Girl Guides and (Boy) Rocket Rangers, the 3GRR Camporee is the ultimate in "girls versus boys" competition. The event is almost always held on the Galactic Girl Guide Mobile Campground and Headquarters, as this allows the Camporee to serve those Guides and Rangers hailing from "Bumpkinville in the Zero Zone" or even as far away as "Bum-Boot, Egypt, in the Byzon Galaxy." Campers must register for the event through their respective organizations and are sent invitations with the Campground's coordinates just units before the Camporee's opening ceremonies, in order to keep the spoilsports guessing! Camporee games include the usual sack racing, knot tying, swimming and blaster-tag competitions, as well as sing-a-longs and tall tales around the campfire. The highlight of the 7-Unit event is the Soup-Can Derby, in which Guide and Ranger teams race kid-made airships made of cannibalized parts and thrown together with the proverbial "duct tape, gum and baling wire," the first step to building something space-worthy! The three exciting units leading up to the Derby are spent souping up cans, developing an arsenal of dirty tricks, and trying to find and destroy the opponents' entries

Soup Can Derby Trophy

Heart Knox
A prison for women on planet 007 in the heart of the Xychromo Zone, Heart Knox purportedly houses an unusual number of political prisoners, which is not so unusual, if you know anything about the Xychromo Zone. While classified as a maximum-security correctional facility, Heart Knox is, for many of the more troublesome prisoners, merely a stopover on their way to much harder time, usually served on an Omega Disque.

I Can't Wait Until Tomorrow 'Cause I Get Better-Lookin' Every Malton Unit
Subtitled *The Life and Times of Brucilla the Muscle: Woman of War, Lucky in Love*, this autobiography of the infamous ex-brigader from Kansas, Amercadia, the original manuscript recorded on a Galactic Girl Guide *How I Spent My Summer Vacation* recording myd, became a Galactic Best Seller, when first published in AE 78

Jimmy the Snout
A well-known Rootersnoos Ferret, famous for his reports on the Rec Station News service, his news magazine show *48 Marbecs* (a production of Rootersnoos, in conjunction with Rec Station Infotainment), his shock of wavy reddish hair and his boyish good looks. Jimmy burst onto the galactic scene in AE 122, as the tap-dancing teen "Cubby" on *Uncle Bob's Fantanimals*, the long-running children's show produced by Griivarr Worlds Funtasm. Rumored to be a RIP zoner (person addicted to Running In Place, the popular means of life-extension), the Snout's physical appearance has changed remarkably little since his days of hoofing it with his four-, six- and nine-legged pals.

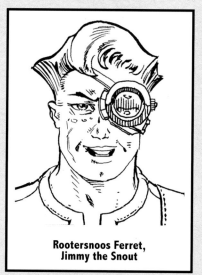

Rootersnoos Ferret, Jimmy the Snout

Keengdum Kuhm
The land to which Dromo Rustlers expect to repair upon death. The streets are paved with gold. The beer flows like wine and the wine flows like beer. Great ham hocks grow on trees. All a rustler has to do is snap his fin-

gers and ZAP! - a steak THIS BIG sizzling on a golden platter. He snaps his fingers again and ZAP! - a beautiful woman with breasts THIS BIG... sizzling on a golden platter. A Rustler's passage to Keengdum Kuhm is usually booked by another Rustler.

Gone to Keengdum Kuhm

Kinder Brut ®
Manufactured and marketed by the Kinder Brut Anstalt, the Kinder Brut ® is a mechanical crèche, sold for the purpose of fertilizing a human egg, making genetic modifications on the resulting embryo (if so desired by the parent), gestating the fetus (providing womb-like protection and nutrition during those first nine months of its life), and monitoring the child's health and wellbeing until age two (standard cycles), after which time it is up to the parent to keep it from killing itself before reaching adulthood. Translated from the extinct ancient Terran language known as Deutsches, its name means "Children Brood," which pretty much says it all. In the Institute's advertising holos, inventor of the Kinder Brut, Maximo Edmunds, explains that he was trying to fill a void (and the wombs of sterile humanoids) by giving the aging galactic population a better way to reproduce.

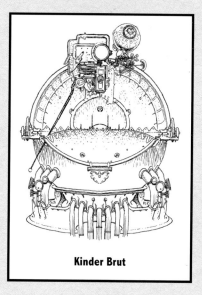

Kinder Brut

It seems that, after the Krystal Drive revolutionized space travel and more average Joes and Janes were spending more of their time blasting around the multiverse at near light speed (see: Thought Speed), their planetbound pals and loved ones needed a way to level the playing field age-wise. No one wanted Mom to jet off to the system next door and return looking like his or her granddaughter! Once the term "Geezers" came into popular usage, referring to those who chose to remain in a "gravity-rich" environment, great minds began working on the problem of life extension and great pocketbooks funded them. And with great success! But while most popular means of life extension, such as the controversial *Running In Place* ®, could keep bodies youthful-looking and healthy indefinitely, they could not give a humanoid female any more than her natural allotment of eggs, or keep a tri-century-old male's sperm swimming. And it was soon discovered that the use of artificial life-extension in a pregnant mother was dangerous to a developing fetus. The Kinder Brut, which could either incubate the parent's own frozen embryos, or splice their genetic information into a donor egg, was just what the doctor ordered... literally.

Krabian Slavegirls

The leading credit export of the Xychromo Zone, Krabian Slavegirls are spliced and bred to be "The 'Insignificant Other' for the Man Who Can't Commit." What this means is this: 1) They are built like the proverbial brick pagoda, 2) they have brains the size of pinto beans, and 3) though they live to mate, they only mate once and then immediately lay their eggs and die. (This is, according to one ad campaign, "The kind of planned obsolescence a guy can learn to love!") Krabian young hatch quickly, but remain in the larval stage for 427 standard cycles. Krabians are spliced from a mix of human and Lacertian stock. Their sale has been banned in most of the civilized Multiverse (see: Multiverse, Civilized), though the ban has done little to slow the trade in Krabians and, in at least one case, was even used as a sales pitch: "Our Krabians Are So Darned *Bad*, They're Banned in the Civilized Multiverse!"

Krabian Slavegirl

Krystal-Blown

A slang term for a psychotic state brought on by many marbecs spent in close proximity to a large, naturally occuring deposit of Borinyum Krystals. The term came into popular usage among Krystal miners of the Mitochondrian Krystal belt, during the early cycles of IER-CO. (see: Light Deprivation)

Krystals, Borinyum

To some a source of great wealth, to most a source of power, to still others, an inspiring bit of the manifest divine worthy of the most religious awe (see: Mood Rings), the Borinyum Crystal or Krystal is the pinnacle, rockwise. Borinyum Krystals differ from all other known types of crystal in that, whereas all other crystals are as different, one from the other, as the zillion and three snowflakes in a blizzard, Borinyum Krystals duplicate themselves exactly and come in only 47 flavors or varieties. They also differ in the fact that they don't behave the way crystals are supposed to behave. Example: The first Borinyum Krystal to be marketed commercially was the well known Tone Kone Krystal ®.

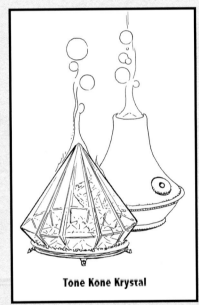

Tone Kone Krystal

The small, faceted cone, nestled in a tiny bed of its native soil (see: Mitochondrian Krystal Belt), was first packaged and sold as a paperweight by the capsule industry, Krystals 'n Things ®. Shortly thereafter (thanks to the propensity of small sentients for putting shiny objects into their mouths), it was found that licking the top of a Tone Kone Krystal caused it to emit small, iridescent bubbles that rose contentedly ceilingward and, upon reaching their destination, popped with a pleasant-sounding "bip" that had a tranquilizing effect on the nervous systems of most carbon-based creatures. Another history-making Krystal is the Star of Ziham; named for marketing genius, Ziham Geħ Furtz, the man who set the small, star-shaped gems in pen-

dants, diadems, and the infamous Mood Rings. Star of Ziham Krystals are now known to feed back emotions, intensifying whatever mood the wearer may be in. They are very dangerous and were much sought after during the Stagnation (peak experiences being somewhat rare during those cycles). In Cycle 143 IET, Ziham Geħ Furtz presented the Dread Dictator (see: Bajar, Ponious Augustus Henry Mohammed) with a platinum Mood Ring in the shape of a steel-taloned shreeguh clutching a Star of Ziham. It is said that when the Dread Dictator slipped the ring on his finger, the Krystal shrieked, turned dull brown and died. Bajar ordered Furtz executed and Mood Rings banned, the result being the nearly 12,000 religious cults built around Mood Rings and surviving to this malton unit. Finally, the K Krystal ®; In Cycle 150 IET, a maintenance worker at New Eden Multi Tech Labs, who went by the name of Lotti Bo Sugar, waddled into a laboratory where, only that up unit, Dr. Proserpina K. Dowd had been experimenting with a new type of Krystal, and changed, inadvertently, the course of our lives. Sugar (having the type of mind that becomes confused and disoriented in the presence of objects that are not positioned either in straight lines or at right angles to each other) picked up eight of the octagonal, fist-sized Krystals and placed them face-to-face in a small dish-drying rack at the back of the laboratory. Then, as if putting the period to the end of her Krystal statement, she switched on the radio at the end of the rack and "BOOM!" Hearing of the accident, Dowd shouted, "EUREKA!" and ran off to invent the Proserpina K Krystal Dowd Drive. After much digging and delving, Dowd found that, at the time of the explosion, channel 46 Valhala Beacon had been broadcasting the Amercadian Space Brigade Drum and Bugle Corps' version of the Brigade Anthem, "Us Against the Void." It would seem that this particular version of this particular anthem, when played into one end of a line of exactly eight K-Krystals, is converted by the Krystals into energy, which is then blown from the far end of the line. Dowd used the eight small crystals and a continuous loop recording of "Us Against the Void" to create the Krystal Drive, which replaced the standard plasma and ion drives in a matter of cycles and resulted in a fortune in royalties for the Brigade's Drum and Bugle Corps.

Krystals, K

One of the two most important of the 47 varieties of Borinyum Krystals, so named for the middle initial of Dr. Proserpina K. Dowd, inventor of the Krystal Drive (though the right to this title is still in litigation). It is thanks to the "K" in K Krystal that all varieties of what were formerly known as Borinyum crystals began to be referred to as Krystals.

Kublacaine

An ego enhancing drug that takes hold of a normal (or hyper-normal) ego, foundering in the umbra of rational thought, id ridden, fumbling, and unaware of it or idself, and transforms it into a forged titanium fortress, housing a crystalline consciousness just dripping with highlights and bristling with juicily dangerous sharp edges. Upon consumption of the drug, the consumer remains calm, outwardly, while within burgeons a much larger and Oh-So-Very-Calmer calm... a waveless calm... a serene reposeful, halcyonian calm... a calm based on the sudden and irrefutable knowledge that one is really quite a nice guy... no, a great guy... a prince, in fact... Nay, a Lord! A GREAT LORD, STARK AND TERRIBLE, WHOSE NAME OR INTIMATION OF ONE'S NAME CONJURES OVERAWE AND SOLEMN VENERATION IN EACH MERE AND MORTAL CONSCIOUSNESS WITHIN THE VAST BREADTH OF ONES OMNISCIENT GAZE! FAINT HEARTS QUAIL! ALL BOW - NAY, GENUFLECT - BEFORE THE ALL-KNOWING, ALL-SEEING, ALL-BEING BEING! Outwardly, as we've stated, one remains calm. One tipples a beverage, disturbs the nap of the rug with a languorous toe, flicks a speck of mortal coil from one's cuff, sighs, stifles a well deserved yawn of nascent ennui, while one's golden thoughts caress the dulcifluous knowledge that one's oafish acquaintances, ne'er do well relatives, interfering in laws, insensible siblings, impaired parents, gross supplicants and servile hangers-on, the family dog and the whole famdamnily of humanoid kind, along with their wives, husbands, sisters, cousins, drones, droids, pets and parasites and the countless rat-like embryos of the cosmos at large and their crawling, toady alien counterparts exist ONLY AT ONE'S WHIM, craving only a nod, a wink, a kick to feel elevated for but an instant above the meaningless morass of their own near lives. Kublacaine is the pinnacle, headwise. Needless to say, it comes in mighty handy on an interstellar jaunt of any great distance. Puts it all in its proper perspective.

Light Deprivation

A mental state somewhat akin to schizophrenia, though usually temporary in duration, and brought about by prolonged exposure to Borinyum Krystals. Light-deprived humanoids may exhibit any combination of the following symptoms: confusion, lightheadedness, auditory hallucinations, visual hallucinations, paranoia, dry mouth, numbness in the extremities, headaches and a physical sensation some describe as repeating full-body energy waves. The term Light Deprivation is a theological construct that came into use after Glorianna of Phoebus introduced the Krystal Light religion to the long-suffering miners of the Mitochondrian Krystal Belt. While not alleviating all of its symptoms, the new religion and its practices gave context to the manifestations of Light Deprivation, so that its adherents, or Beasties, might view the hallucinations as collective revelation, rather than personal hell. Viewed in this manner, the plague becomes a gift.

Lycon

The Galactic Survey lists Lycon as a level 8 swamp planet that, in the words of Uvulesian Missionary Bloit Plunkett, looks "lahk unto a globular great mass o' putrifyin' chocolit chock full o' tee-nine-see bobbin' marshmellers." The appearance of intelligent life on the planet Lycon is concurrent with the Uvulesian planetfall. Indigenous life forms ("them thangs innuh mud") were affected by the telepathic spill from interUvulesian communication, causing a stirring of intelligence (?), a need to replicate and aspirations toward Godhead (see: Keengdum Kuhm). In short, the incredibly mean, incredibly stupid Lyconian Dromo Rustlers were heaved up, gasping, from the primal ooze.

Lyconian Dromo Rustlers

They gave new meaning to the lives of Uvulesian Missionaries. To the majority of the Uvulesian populace, however, they gave new meaning to the word "disgusting." Disgusting was their habit of beating, booting, eating or looting anything in sight. Disgusting was the fact that they could mate with anything. Disgusting was the fact that anything they mated with immediately became gravid with their young, who issued forth in great litters, often numbering 18 or more. The ravenous pups would then devour the host-mother in a sickening display of near-adult behavior. They multiplied like maggots in a mass grave. The Uvulese found it fairly simple to ward off the amorous advances of the rustlers by telepathically implanting the message, "We are angil thangs frum Keengdum Kuhm. Don't boot wid us," in the dim reaches of the creatures' minds. A word concerning the off-planet exportation of Lyconian Dromo Rustlers, a last-ditch effort to save the crumbling economy of Uvulesian Lycon: Due to the Dromo Rustlers' habit of impregnating and devouring Lyconian Dromo cows (hence the name, Lyconian Dromo Rustlers), the Lyconian Better Business Bureau implemented a plan to send breeding pairs of Dromo Rustlers (two males) to off-planet zoos (as exhibits) and circuses (as mud wrestlers), suggesting very strongly to the new owners that they sterilize the brood after first mating (TRUST US!). By denuding the planet Lycon of Dromo Rustlers, the Dromo Cows could breed happily in their natural bovine way, without the worry of wild rustlers grabbing them from behind. It is said that the Galactic Mud Wrestling Management Association has bred a rustler whose love life is less extreme. They are said to make up for this lack in the beating, eating, and looting departments.

Magneto Boy Light-Seeking Torpedoes

What it says. The Magneto Boy Light-Seeking Torpedo homes in on any light-emitting target, hauls ass after it, attaches itself and clings onto either its force shield or hull, absorbs the target's energy until it builds sufficient force, then explodes, destroying either the target or its force shield. Mmm-mmm good!

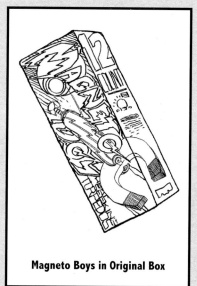

Magneto Boys in Original Box

March Baptist

Probably the wealthiest Christo-Zedian Denomination in the inhabited universe, the proselytizing March Baptists can be traced back to Pre-Expansion Amercadia (then Earth). Their faith rests on the belief that Jesus (see: Terran Religions, Early) did indeed come again, as predicted in scripture, this time as a fellow named Zed. Zed was so dismayed at the condition of the planet (Earth) that he hung himself by his left foot from a fig tree for forty days and forty nights (see: Zed, The Dangling) and then wasted the planet (see: Wasting, The Great). He did, however (and this is where the Baptists differ from their fellow Zedians), relent and send his gospel, The Brand New Testament, to the survivors (The Faithful) through his prophet, Jim the Baptist. In the book of South Carolinians 1:35, Zed gives to his followers his famous 27 AMENDMENTS to the 10 COMMANDMENTS of Moses (Old Testament). The first seven of these are: 1) Thou shalt wear brown shoes, 2) Thou shalt purport thyself in commodious and seemly ways at all times, 3) Thou shalt talk louder than anyone else in the room, 4) Thou shalt leaveth thy door open by six inches and keep thy best foot on the floor at all times, 5) Thou shalt not be surprised by anything the Lord Thy Zed doeth unto thee, 6) Thou shalt button thy top button in the presence of thy neighbors, 7) Thou shalt March faithfully and without hesitation into the Heavens. The March Baptists took the Seventh Amendment quite literally. After the Unification, the March Baptists did more for the push into space than any other Amercadians. March Baptists researchers developed ships and weapons, March Baptist workers built them, wealthy March Baptists financed the work. They poured credits and human fodder into the new Amercadian Space Brigade. They were not among the first to go into space, however. During simulated flights it was found that non-Baptist crewmembers (the majority) developed a tendency to repeatedly bash the heads of the March Baptists into large metal objects after only a few marbecs' confinement in the small (by our standards) ships. Only after they began to build and launch their own mission-ships were March Baptists able to realize their god's commandment. As of this writing, the March Baptists have missions on 938 planets and free-floating temples EVERYWHERE.

Straight-Backed March Baptists in Straight-Backed Chairs

Their Galactic Headquarters, the Peace Free Will Missionary Tabernacle of the Stars, is a wonder to behold. They have been responsible for a goodly number of civil wars and religious revolutions (including the Onolo Dos Actions of AE 101 that effectively put an end to the planet's rebellion against the rule of Seven Planets). Their most Charismatic evangelist, Brother Bud, has the distinction of being the most often misquoted being in the inhabited universe. The following is his most misquoted quote: "Self-sacrifice, unless it's God-Almighty motivated, is like plasma-powered poot. A lot of energy goes into it, but what do you get out of it in the long run?"

Mark 7 Dreadnaught Planet-Splitter
Not your run-of-the-mill ray and oh-so-much-more blast power than the average Hyon Beam, the Mark 7 Dreadnaught Planet-Splitter is the ultimate in ass coverage, its name

meaning, literally, "to fear not." The M7DP-S is the love-child of the IER-CO-era SMITE System, standard on all Seraphim Flyers, and the lethal yet energy-efficient Hull-Gutters favored by U4F Freelance Fighters. It can gut, slice, dice, fry or frappe an enemy vessel, before you can say "Up the Brigade's!"

Mastering Dream Enhancement Games
Written by Intersolar Protoarchetypal Id-Imex Level Touchémento Champion Virgil H, the three-volume tome *Mastering Dream Enhancement Games* is not only the go-to reference for all things DEG, but is valued throughout the civilized Multiverse as a how-to manual for would-be heroes, despots and captains of Interprise.

Mind Spiders from the Planet Xenon
A hugely popular Hugo Award-winning book from author Ronnie Lee Ellis, *Mind Spiders from the Planet Zenon* changed the course of many, many lives. Trust us on this.

Mitochondria
1) A membrane-enclosed organelle, found in most eukaryotic cells, that generates adenosine triphosphate, a source of chemical energy. 2) One of two inhabited planets in the Phoebus System, on the inner edge of the Last Frontier, the other being New Wyoming, though the name "Mitochondria" is sometimes used to refer to both the planet and the nearby Krystal-rich asteroid belt. For most of its history an unpleasant ball of rock and ice, this fifth planet of the Phoebus System rates a "must see" from the Starhopper Tours Traveler's Companion. After its neighboring planet, Vaikuntha, was blown to smithereens (or at least into many Krystal-bearing asteroids) at the end of the Revolution, Mitochondria became the base of mining operations for the new Mitochondrian Krystal Belt, though the planet itself could hardly be called hospitable.

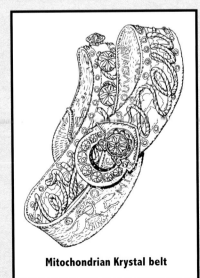

Mitochondrian Krystal belt

The planet stayed inhospitable for the next 90-odd cycles. Once the Krystal miners were united under the new Glorianan religion, the planet became the seat of their new government. Needless to say, the government has spent a pretty penny spiffing the place up. Tourists visiting any planet in the Phoebus System should be sure to pick up at least one of the redundantly named, but absolutely fabulous Mitochondrian Krystal Belts.

Montreal
1) A township in Acadian Amercadia (or Acadia, if you self-identify as Acadian), on the site of what is said to have been a great city of the same name, during the later centuries of pre-wasting Terra. 2) A mythical city, similar to Atlantis, Atlanta or Ys. 3) A revolving city-sphere in orbit around the planet Toulouse, the third planet of the Guernican System. 4) A subdivision of the La Belle Level of Recreation Station 34. Citizens of all the Montreals, whether mythic or actual, speak a form of the ancient language Français, the speaking of which has been shown to lead to nicotine addiction, sexual excess and an emotional state that could be best described as chronic ennui, a condition that is somewhat mitigated by the fact that these same citizens seem to imbibe an inordinate amount of sparkling wine.

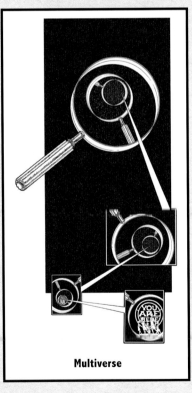

Multiverse

Multiverse
1) Everything there is. 2) The whole shebang. 3) In spiritual terms (see: Mumbo Jumbo), the whole She-Bang, or everything born of the Great Mother at the beginning of Time. The word Multiverse is sometimes used interchangeably with the word Universe, some-

times to differentiate between our own finite universe and the collective ALL, in which an infinite number of universes - existing beside, above, beneath, beyond and through our own – are connected, one to all others, in an eternal web of existence.

Multiverse, Civilized

Any part of the multiverse that you, yourself, live in, as opposed to that part of the Mutiverse that "they" live in. Sometimes used interchangably with the term "settled Multiverse."

Myd

An information storage unit made of Borinyum Krystal, Type 23, and so named due to its shape; that of a pyramid.

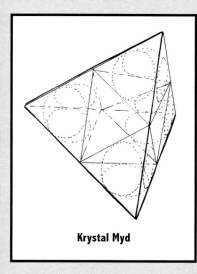

Krystal Myd

Myd-Cap

The encapsulated consciousness of a member of any number of Android Lines, as programmed into Borinyum Krystal, Type 23, and either attached through a connection in the head or headgear of the Droid, or (as is the case with Andromedicones) implanted into its skull. After connection or implantation, the Type 23 Krystal in the Myd-Cap continues to be written on by the life experience of the individual Droid and, some say, by the collective experience of the Droid's entire line.

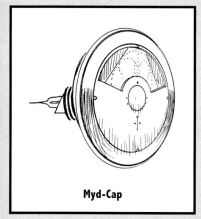

Myd-Cap

Mystic Nyts of the Sea

A stage name used by certain theatrically inclined Aguatunesian empaths, Mystic Nyts of the Sea is a registered trademark of Uncle Bob's Fantanimalland, a hugely popular theme park in Hon Ober, on Hon Grii, Grivarr Worlds.

Mystic Nÿts

Visitors to the park's Aguacade are invited to feed the Nyts with processed food pellets, which must be won by catching a hard-to-grasp floating ring, after which they may "think a question" to the performing Nyts. The Nyts then swim into patterns that spell out the words of the answer. As the park's humanoid patrons tend to think the same five or ten questions over and over again, ad nauseum, this miraculous feat of mind-reading is somewhat less remarkable than it would seem to the casual viewer. If traveling to Aguatunesia, it is important to note that Mystic Nyts of the Sea is not an Aguatunesian self-name recognized by any governing school of Aguatunesia. Most natives of the water world find the name slightly insulting.

Nargon

A Standard Galactic Unit of Time, the Nargon is roughly (usually just a tad more than) 1/6th of a Standard Cycle and is comprised of 30(ish) Malton Units.

Neuter Booter

One who copulates or would enjoy copulating with a non-sentient and/or genderless creature or substance. The expression came into vogue, early this Era, shortly after Pleasure Putty®, a product of Bargain Bliss® (a division of Living Doll Cybernetics®, a company specializing in the development and marketing of non-sentient "love toys"), appeared on the market. The spearhead of the ad campaign that launched Pleasure Putty® onto the Galactic Scene was the slogan, "Why boot something with a mind of its own?" The derogatory term "neuter booter" was, for those who thought they had better things to boot, a way of lashing back at those who kept Bargain Bliss in business and the slogan on the airwaves.

Neutral Zones

During the Expansionist Era, the first Neutral Zone was declared shortly after two Amercadian Scouts were lost in the vicinity of Barnard's Star. The last recorded communication from the ship (the Beaver) still echoes, echoes, echoes down the hollow arm of Father Time...

Rongschilde: Sure is quiet...?
Jones: Yeah...too quiet.

By the early days of IER-CO, any slice, hunk, wedge or space of space deemed responsible for three verified disappearances of sentient beings became a lawfully designated Neutral Zone. Verification Recordings, Neutral Zone 8:

1) "It's amazing! It's FANTASTIC!!! It's... it's..." (static)
2) "I see a... I see... I..." (static)
3) "These reports musta been fakes. This place is as safe as a..." (static)

As the concept of Neutral Zones caught on, some beings found it convenient to augment the ruling to fit other situations. Areas of dispute plagued by border wars (where there was no real profit motive) soon became Neutral Zones, saving wear and tear on the Borderees. This ruling was enforced by Expansionist and, later, IER-CO authorities, in an effort to quiet troubled trade areas. Toward the end of the Stagnation, PAHM Bajar began an experiment using Vercadian Protector Androids to defend the Zones. During the early AnarchEra cycles (when, for all practical purposes, there were no authorities), the incredibly expensive Vercadian Protector Androids became the chief means of enforcing Neutral Zones. If you were rich enough to have a droid, you could have a Zone.

THE LAST GREAT NOVEL BY HUGO AWARD WINNER
RONNIE LEE ELLIS
more than 200 billion books in print
NEWNIVERSE
WITH NEW INTRODUCTION BY JIMMY THE SNOUT

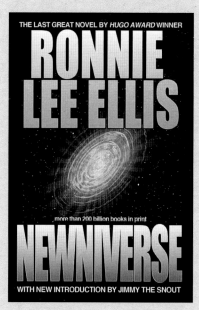

Newniverse

A late, unfinished and unpublished (or, at least, never *officially* published) novel of Hugo Award-winning author Ronnie Lee

Ellis, *Newniverse* tracks the adventures of conjoined twins Phaleef and Elron as they attempt to create a new universe (see: Multiverse, Minor Divisions of the) by finding and entering an anomaly called Looking Glass, which legend asserts is a portal to previously unclaimed Multiversal real estate. Early chapters of the book were unearthed (or devoided) by Rootersnoos ferret Jimmy the Snout, with portions made public in his well-received docudrama, *Where in the Multiverse is Ronnie Lee Ellis?* Shortly after Miz Ellis's unexplained departure from Everywhere, a book entitled *Newniverse*, with introduction by Jimmy the Snout, became a pan-galactic bestseller. The estate of Ronnie Lee Ellis and the Cloistered Order of the Cosmic Veil (who received the bulk of the estate, when Miz Ellis was declared dead by the Writers Guild of Amercadia North) filed suit against the publisher, Mindz Eye Books, claiming that neither they nor Miz Ellis had ever given Mindz Eye the rights to publish the work. Furthermore, they claimed the later chapters of the book had been written by an uncredited ghost that had not been vetted by the estate. Called as a witness in the resulting civil trial, Jimmy the Snout testified that he had, in fact, never written the introduction credited to him at the beginning of the book. The court found in favor of the plaintiffs and required the publisher to pay the sum of 560,000,000 standard galactic credits.

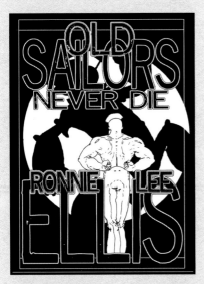

OLD
SAILORS
NEVER DIE
RONNIE LEE
ELLIS

Old Sailors Never Die

A lesser-known work of speculative fiction by Hugo Award-winning author Ronnie Lee Ellis. *Old Sailors Never Die* chronicles the adventures of Barry Soul, ex-sailor, ex-hero of the Cyberform Conflict and sometime detective who runs afoul of self-centered heiress Sedona My while searching for a lost android. The novel's important themes are 1) forbidden human/android love, 2) the very mixed blessings of inherited titles and/or fortunes, and 3) the power of the random factor to eclipse both destiny and free will. Reviews of the novel were mixed. That the novel ends as our hero Barry Soul simply finds himself in the wrong place at the wrong time, and so dies a cruel and meaningless death, seems to have been a main reason for the novel's less than enthusiastic reception, especially considering the book's title.

Omegazon Priestess

Omegazons

Omegan Amazons. It is commonly believed that women prisoners banded together on the automated farming disque and penal colony, Omega 6, after it was abandoned at the overthrow of the Incorporated Elysian Republic, in order to protect themselves from certain undesirable elements on the colony. Many such prisoner bands were formed, the stronger growing into tribes. The Omegazons grew to be one of the strongest tribes due, so they claim, to their religious beliefs. These warrior women, led by a Priestess-Queen, worshipped the Star Mother, a triple Goddess strikingly similar to Orakian and Old Terran lunar deities (or deity, as they are claimed to be aspects of the same One Goddess). This is more than a little strange, as the Omega Disque has no moon. Legend has it that Trivia, Priestess of the Mother, walked down to Omega 6 on a tiny beam of starlight, bringing word of the Star Mother's love to her women. Young girls were trained in the way of the sword and, later, the bow. They were topnotch fighters. Male tribe members were often strays, or ex-slaves, won during raids on other tribes. They were offered protection in exchange for performing certain domestic and child-rearing duties. Often, the Omegazons raided enemy tribes (such as that of the unusually mean and incredibly stupid Lyconian Dromo Rustlers) in order to free their female captives. Women who had spent any time at all with the Dromo Rustlers were not good for fighting and were brought into the tribe on the same basis as the men.

Rec Pols

Recreation Station Police. Due to the large volume of criminal activity on the Rec Stations, the duties of the Rec Pols are kept confined to 1) the prevention of destruction of Rec Station property, 2) apprehension of vandals responsible for the destruction of Rec Station property, 3) the surveillance of Rec Station visitors even thought to be considering the destruction of Rec Station Property and 4) any post-destruction investigations required by Rec Station owners or proprietors of Rec Station business establishments. Visitor-on-visitor crimes have no place in the Rec Station Police job description.

SK
VIII

Rec Pol

Rec Station News

A news organization that serves those members of the space-going public who frequent the 483 (as of this printing) Recreation Stations sprinkled about the settled Multiverse. The name Rec Station News refers to both the umbrella organization and to the 483 affiliate Channels that broadcast its content, as well as their own local programming.

97NEWS97

Red Herring

1) A rather tasty reddish-colored fish, 2) a deliberate attempt to redirect attention, 3) a deliberate attempt to change the subject or deflect an argument, 4) the private, Krystal-driven yacht of Hugo Award-winning author Ronnie Lee Ellis, formerly ILRLE Bajar.

Rigon

A Standard Galactic Unit of Time, the Rigon is roughly 1/3rd of a Standard Cycle and is equal to two(ish) Nargons, 60(ish) Malton Units, approximately 1,500 Marbecs, or 90,000 Ribecs, give or take a few. The Standard Galactic Units are based (again, roughly) on the New Terran Units that were adopted soon after the expulsion of Amercadia's Eastern Hemisphere, once the implementation of the Eastern Matrix (see: Only Possible Recourse, Our) had added the extra marbec to the planet's rotation and increased (almost doubled, in fact) the time it took for the moon to revolve around the planet. Only after Amercadia had gained sufficient control of its planetary climate was the Rigon (then called "a Fortmoonth") added to the table of units, dividing the planet's cycle around its sun into three growing seasons of two Nargons each. Why the Rigon became a standard unit on planets whose growing seasons (or lack of them) had little or nothing in common with those of Amercadia is a matter of debate, though most would agree with the well-known saying that a Rigon is "too long for a start, too short for a finish, long enough to get boring."

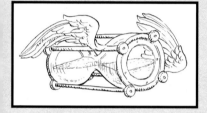

Rocket Rangers

An organization that, according to its own recruiting literature, "builds character and encourages assertiveness in young Amercadians," though whether or not character can actually be built remains unproven. (see: Free Will, Theory of) As to how this is to be accomplished, there seems to be a lot of camping, knot tying and the walking of geezers across busy intersections involved. (see: Geezers)

Rocket Ranger

Most thinking sentients take the whole character-building claim with a large grain of salt. According to more reputable sources, the Rangers exist primarily to funnel semi-trained recruits directly into the Amercadian Space Brigade's Academy, which (by extension) exists primarily to funnel fully trained recruits directly into the Amercadian Space Brigade. With membership at first open only to Amercadians, the organization eventually welcomed humanoid males from other galactic races. In 113 AE, the Rocket Rangers even opened their doors to Teoman who, while arguably humanoid, are not precisely male. (see: Teoman) Many famous (and infamous) humanoid (and other) males claim membership to the Rangers, including Typhoon Weatherall, PCKA Bajar, and semi-famous historian, Dwanyun of Griivarr. Griivarr's memoir of his childhood Ranger experience, Of Playgrounds and Pecking Orders, inspired the WWHAMMY winning lasaround, Rocket Rangers of the Omniverse, and its many sequels.

Rootersnoos

An intergalactic news and infotainment (or "noos") agency owned cooperatively by member news services scattered about the settled Multiverse, but operating independently. Rootersnoos both supplies content, written and broadcast by its huge full-time staff, and distributes stories submitted by reporters from its member services and stations. Non-owning broadcasters may become Rootersnoos subscribers, purchasing content from the agency for a hefty cyclical fee. A number of Rootersnoos Ferrets (their clever designation for reporters) have become inextricably linked to the primary outlets for their work, most notably tap-dancing ferret Jimmy the Snout and Rec Station News.

Shreeguh

A small flying mammal native to the now nonexistent planet, Shangri-La (see: Incorporated Elysian Republic). The average shreeguh weighs about 8 mili-milos, is about 11 nihlons tall, and looks something like an Amercadian Spaniel with wings. The wings themselves are strong, leathery and covered with tough, grayish scales that resemble human toenails. Shreegae make wonderful pets. The most ferocious member of the Shreeguh family, the Steel-Taloned Shreeguh, has retractable talons in its forepaws. These talons are razor sharp and serve to make the Steel-Taloned Shreeguh a formidable opponent. They are highly prized as watch animals and intensely loyal to their owners. The Steel-Taloned Shreeguh was the official animal of the Incorporated Elysian Republic (which was neither heavenly, nor a republic) and still appears on the family crest of The Bajars of Seven Planets. The Galactic Survey lists the Shreeguh on the endan-

gered species list. There are only about 2,500 of them in existence, most on the planet Mirage.

Steel-Taloned Shreeguh

Siegfriedson, Siegfried "McMauMau"

A freedom fighter and hero of the Rebellion, first husband to Krystals 'n Things magnate Margaret Medea, and protégé of his wife's mother, Molly Medea, one of the Rebellion's most famous leaders. After the overthrow of Pontius Augustus Henry Mohammed Bajar (see: Dictator, the Dread), Siegfriedson, not being the type to stay home by the fire, became involved in a number of smaller planetary and system-wide skirmishes, always siding with the disadvantaged over the Powers that Be. His marriage to Margaret Medea produced two daughters. The eldest, Mary, followed in Daddy's footsteps, becoming first a fighter in the Rebellion, then a freelance freedom fighter, most notably in the Droid Wars and various battles for Cyberform rights, and is credited as the mind behind the Tri-Clone invasion. Upon her death, Cycle 93 AE, Mary famously left her interest in the Phoebus System's Mitochondrian Krystal Belt to the Belt's Miners, a decision that must have made Siegfried proud. Siegfried and Margaret's second daughter, Molly Younger (AKA Galatia 9), seems to have been a late bloomer (by all accounts deeply affected by her father's death in 99 AE), but eventually went into the family "business" as a member of the U4F (see: United Federation of Female Freedom Fighters, the). Less famous than the women of this powerful matriarchal clan, Siegfried was, nevertheless, the lynchpin of the family. According to biographer Oriona Pei (see: Rebellion's Son), his relationships with the contentious Medea females often cast Siegfried as the peaceful eye of the family storm.

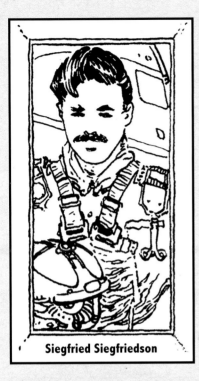

Siegfried Siegfriedson

Sore Chum

1) Archaic (pre-Amercadian). Live Bait. From Chum: small fish thrown into the water by fishermen to attract larger fish. And Sore: To become colorful and stick out. 2) Any green and very innocent individual. Aggressively naive. 3) Hick, nubie, noobie, neck, drome-dome, pie kicker, hayseed, possum-eater, bohunk, homebilly, herkimer, "Just Plain Folks." 4) Rabbit buyer, ump chay, pigeon, patsy, sucker, mark, blockhead, bonehead, meat-head, dimwit, "Dead from the Neck Up." 5) Geezer. Any first-time visitor (newly arrived) to Recreation Station 97, the most challenging of the 483 (at this printing) Recreation Stations in our Galaxy.

Rec Station Sore Chum

Upon arrival, each new visitor to the station is given an I.D. brooch printed with the words: "New Visitor, Have a Heart." This printed entreaty, designed and distributed by Rec Station P.R., serves to identify the Sore Chum to those inhabitants of the Rec who might make best use of him or her. To any of our readers considering a visit to Recreation Station 97, we remind you that the station motto is: "If You Can Dodge it Here, You'll Dodge it Anywhere!"

Soul Sharing

The idea that all members of an android line share the same field of selfness, or soul. This would mean that, even though each individual unit is capable of moving independently of the others, it is, in truth, only a mobile bit of the greater being. An android, or so it is said, cannot conceive of an individual death, so long as others of its line continue to live. The loss of a few units would have no more importance to the line than, say, the sloughing off of a few skin cells would have for most sentients. In her best selling novel, The Prince and the Pleasure Droid, Hugo Award winning author, Ronnie Lee Ellis, has her young hero melt down all but one member in a line of pleasure droids. According to Miz Ellis, as each individual unit is terminated, its (partial) soul or field of selfness does not disperse, but is passed along to the surviving members, thus making each fraction or "slice" of the group soul larger. If only one member survives, this unit becomes "Holder of Souls" for the line, an awesome thing indeed.

In the novel by Miz Ellis, the Soul Holder becomes capable of autonomous action, escapes her life of slavery, is made leader of a powerful religious movement, and has a hand in deciding the Fate of the Free Universe. The Prince and the Pleasure Droid is, of course, purely speculative. However, its release in Cycle 99 AE caused an unprecedented furor in the android community. It seems that, prior to the publication of the novel, no android had ever seriously considered the possibility that every other member of its line would be destroyed and, android communication being what it is, every droid in the galaxy shared what amounted to a collective moment of clarity. They thought, "I could cease to exist." They thought it for the first time, at the same time. Then they put all of their communications channels to work analyzing the problem. Droid performance was impaired all over the galaxy for nearly a rigon. The result of all this talking was

summed up by philosopher rogue, A1 10 (see: Stark Verse), in his famous essay, The Free Universe: Is it? ...

> Rise
> we
> die,
> we die,
> he said.
> Who cares?
> Cares who?

Space Sabre Hyon Beams

The "meat and potatoes" of the vacuum-based warfare arsenal, Space Sabre Hyon Beams come standard on Brigade Tigers and starter-fighters of every model and make. While there certainly are more powerful beams (see: Mark 7 Dreadnaught Planet-Splitter), and beams that allow you to target with greater precision (see: Atomo-Torch Particle Blaster), when you're not sure what to fire, you're fairly safe firing a space sabre.

Spandec

1) An elastic or expandable unit of time. 2) A measure of subjective time, always longer than a moment and never longer than three malton units.

Sweet Nothings ®

A top-of-the-line tracking device, part of the Whispering Jenny ® line from Spybot Gadgets, Ltd. Until recently, the Sweet Nothings ® was said to have been best described by its very first advertising campaign: "We shot it into the heart of a star, we pounded it with a plasma hammer, we dropped it down a mini-black hole! Nothing, no, nothing, can stop Sweet Nothings from whispering into your ear!" And it was true, for the most part. None of the things listed in the ad could keep a Sweet Nothings device from whispering into its owner's ear. But any humanoid with a will, an average IQ and a screwdriver could.

Temple of Beauty

A school of beauty and modelng, originally owned and operated by Verlloona Ti (born Maggie Medea), with branches scattered across the galaxy. Their motto: Be a Krabian or Only Look Like One!

Teomen

A humanoid (barely) race that hails from Teo Parda, Barok, in the Xychromo Zone, known for the ease with which its members suicide. Even the slightest embarrassment will cause a Teoman to do itself in, usually slitting the several arteries inside the left thigh with its Ragh, a ceremonial dagger. Gifted with a highly developed sense of smell, Teomen are much valued as bounty hunters, though failure to capture its prey may result in a hunter's untimely (and self-inflicted) death. And as a Teoman's sense of justice very

221

nearly rivals its sense of shame, they often go into the field of law, becoming first-rate barristers and judges. It is not, in fact, possible for a Teoman to become anything other than a first-rate barrister or judge, as achieving any rate other than first would result in immediate self-termination. Though culturally male, a Teoman reproduces asexually, with the offspring (or bud) growing from the parent's shoulder and only freeing itself when its sense of shame has developed sufficiently. Should the parent be killed (or, more likely, kill itself) before the bud has detached, the conscienceless bud will attack, viciously, the being that either killed the parent, or shamed the parent into killing itself. The bud will keep attacking, anything and everything, until it is itself killed. In 113 AE, the Rocket Rangers, an organization for young, humanoid males, stretched their rules to allow young Teomen to join the organization, though Teomen, while arguably humanoid, are not precisely male. The pride that the Teoman race took in being admitted to the Rangers resulted in a dramatic drop in suicides throughout the remaining cycles of the decade.

Teoman and Bud

Thrace-Smythe, Sambo

Well-known director famous for producing very big works, with very big names, and of a quasi-religious nature. Little is known of his early life. He left the Boones Dock Academy of Speech and Drama in AE 23 after having lost his scholarship to an unknown performance artist. With the aid of an obsolete Miz Fix It droid (see: Handy Andi) and a Thialine Drone, he captured a Rootersnoos Beacon in the Noh Zone and began broadcasting the cult classic audio series, *WHY?* "WHY," the voice echoed electronically down the back streets of the galaxy, "...or Blown from the Ass of God! The continuing adventures of Perplexus Eqs Youth! (dramatic music) Jour-

ney with me to the thrilling daze of yestercycle, when magic was real and every new beginning had a new name. (more dramatic music) My name? (ditto) Just call me...(echo effect) A CRY IN THE NOTHINGNESS!" By the time Rootersnoos discovered what was going on and sent someone to check it out, the voidspace surrounding the beacon was packed out to 58 sparlons with the ships and stellercopters of loyal fans that looked, from a distance, like a school of Aguatunesian tuna. *WHY?* was syndicated, Thrace-Smythe an overunit success. Between AE 29 and 92, he would write, produce, and direct more than 50 plays including *Paraplegia*, *Metamorphica*, *Metaphorica* and the enormously successful *Aeriopagitica*. Between Cycles 93 and 120 he became disillusioned and depressed and did his famous "blue period" work, the eternally running soap opera, *Cycles Infinitum* and the silly but financially rewarding musical, *Let Go and Let God!* In Cycle 128, Thrace-Smythe staged what was, by all accounts, the worst play ever produced: *ArcheorganaApocolypsia*. Due to the public humiliation and the outcry at the ritual deaths of the Troikani actors Personus/Ex/Mahkina, Thrace-Smythe went underground for 9 cycles and emerged in AE 137 as a director of lasarounds. He directed 13 lasarounds and then disappeared mysteriously at the opening of his 14th, *Phoenixflowerotica* (based on Lotti Bo Sugar's best-selling autobiography, *How I Inadvertently Stumbled Into a Scientific Breakthrough and Was Blinded*. He was never seen again. One explanation of his disappearance can be found in Kettle Black's controversial play, *The Persecution and Assassination of Sambo Thrace-Smythe, as Performed by the Members of the Guernican Art Squad, Under the Direction of Teronia Ta* (or *Thrace-Smythe/Ta*). During the course of the play, Black (playing herself) recreates the scene in which she and two other members of the squad capture Thrace-Smythe. He is murdered horribly and his emotional essence, preserved at the last milirebec of his life, is bottled by Brush and Blaster ® (the Art Squad's mercenary division) and sold as their famous "Emotional Colors #3, Angst and Agony." Emotional Colors are mixed with any pigment and add to a finished painting a palpable aura of feeling.

Emotional Colors #3: Angst and Agony

Tiger, Brigade

One of the small, two-person ships that began as standard Brigade-issue systemships, but evolved over time into state-of-the-art, multi-mission, thruspace fighters.

Brigade Tiger

Depending upon the nature and duration of its mission, an extensive range of life support, weapons and powerplant components may be fixed to the standard, Brigade-issue, two-person, fighter frame, wed to one of three progressively larger, mission-specific cargo hoppers. The hoppers may be fitted with any number of cargo packs, and are the delivery casement of choice for both Dumb-Chuck and Brainy-Boy minibombs. Once the mission augmentations have been mounted on the frame, the iconic Tiger hull is fitted over it and locked, the explosive bolts armed and the one-way permeable shield engaged. The shield can withstand Hyon beam attacks of up to 34,000 bamps, impact-point assaults to 18,000 and, in some cases, is enhanced with an array of pilot and/or gunner-manipulated Geisha Guard fan shields. As has been demonstrated under a variety of extreme circumstances, any of the Tiger's cargo hoppers can double as an escape pod when crewmembers find they must eject into surroundings deemed something less than life-friendly. The powerplant combines a Proserpina K-Krystal Rack Matrix, common in thru-space vessels, with the articulated photon hoop surrounding a guidance stinger that gives the Brigade Tiger its oh-so-recognizable tail assembly. The powerplant is fed with the same sonic fuel that keeps the Brigade Chorus and Drum Corps swimming in royalty checks (See: Us Against the Void).

Triangle Mints

Inarguably the most popular Galactic Girl Guide cookie of all time and the pinnacle, sweet-wise, Triangle Mints are known for their crisp mint-flavored centers, their dark chocolate-like coating and their advertising slogan, "Looks like a Mint, Tastes like a Dream!" It is rumored that the recipe for Triangle Mints was lifted from André Vaniteux, the famous Acadian chef at Stargazers, the hottest restaurant at Club Nebb, on the planet Hydrangea, though Guides maintain it was won from the chef in an honest game of chance. However it was obtained, the recipe has been a krystal-mine for the Galactic Girl Guides. In the interest of full disclosure, this writer, having spent some time as a Jaybird Class Guide from Moulting Wing, is in the position to know that some boxes of Triangle Mints may not contain the promised number of Triangle Mint Cookies. It is not, in fact, unusual for a purchaser to find that five or even ten of the cookies have been eaten and replaced with a wad of paper, or even an old sock. Nevertheless, thanks to the satisfying experience of chowing down on (however many) of these tasty delights, the buying public remains the buying public.

GALACTIC GIRL GUIDES'
TRIANGLE
MINT COOKIES
Looks like a mint, tastes like a Dream

Troikani

The people of Troika (both singular and plural). A Troikani has an extremely flexible persona, a very shallow id, and almost no sense of self. It takes the hearts, minds and souls of at least three Troikani to make even one respectable psyche. Even so, they can quickly adapt to the most extreme environment, melt quietly into the strangest of cultures and mimic ANYTHING, creature or concept, in the known universe. They make excellent actors. When left alone, without the company of others of its species, a Troikani will have one of three reactions: 1) It will pine away and die, 2) It will run through its entire repertoire of roles (these collected over a lifetime) at a speed incredible to behold until dead from exhaustion, 3) It will call the actors' union every marbec on the marbec to complain about everything in the known universe until the union sends someone to put it out of its misery.

Troikani Actors

United Federation of Female Freedom Fighters, The

"How ya gonna keep 'em down on the farm, after they've seen the war?" read the recruiting poster - the very first recruiting poster for the U4F. Formed in Cycle 1 AE by rebel leaders Nia Once, Molly Medea and Leilani Qa'Kuraya, the stated purpose of the U4F was "to secure employment for the millions of female fighters who distinguished themselves in the great battle," and "to bring, if we can, a halt to the senseless destruction of property that has marked, indeed marred, the first cycle of a new era" and "to make sure we don't wind up back in the same soup we just crawled out of." The patriarchal regime of Henry Mohammed Pontious Augustus Bajar (see: Dictator, The Dread) during the incorporated Elysian Republic had not been a good time for women. During the revolution, many young fighting women found that, when compared to their previous lives of boredom and drudgery, war was a piece of cake. Many were loathe to give it up after the glorious conclusion. Many didn't. After the First Galactic Council for Deciding What to Do Next reached its history-making decision, hordes of female fighters surged, unimpeded, through the IER-CO armories and shipyards on Shangrila. They appropriated IER-CO Thunderbolts® and weapons and K Krystals by the podful. Then, they began, or rather, continued to blow things up.

UNITED FEDERATION OF FEMALE FREEDOM FIGHTERS

U4F Logo

Dr. A. Sherwyn Xyn, the distinguished psychiatrist who has made his life's work the study of these women, tells us, in his brilliant volume, *The Tendency to Senseless Violence in Female Ex Rebels During Early Anarchera*: "They were really pissed. Most had spent their entire pre-war existence involved in the exhausting and meaningless labor, the fruits of which were being reaped by some fat-tailed Mr. Big, sitting in his palace in the Comfort Zone. For these women, life had boiled down to the simple equation, 'Blow up or be blown.' When seen in this light, the violence is completely sensible." Today, the U4F is a vital, growing union of mercenary fighters, with a membership of more than 3 million. The employment rate of its members is the highest in the galaxy and it offers a very generous pension plan. The union entry examination is tougher than that for officers of the Amercadian Space Brigade. Ninety-five percent of their missions are completed successfully and their rates are extremely reasonable. "We're females fighting for the little gal." A note of warning to prospective employers: Pay your bill on time.

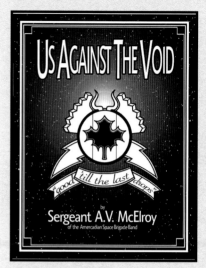

Us Against The Void
"good 'till the last drops"
by
Sergeant A.V. McElroy
of the Amercadian Space Brigade Band

Us Against The Void

Written in early Expansionist times by Sargeant A. V. McElroy, a bassoon player in the newly-formed Amercadian Space Brigade Band, *Us Against The Void* (The Amercadian Space Brigade Anthem) became both a source of inspiration and a source of power for Amercadia and the Universe at large. The lyrics are as follows:

Close-ranked we stand,
With arms of gold,
'Neath banners blue of hue.
The children of
Earth's finest mold,
Clear-eyed, brave hearts
And true.
Our occupation, soldiering.
Against the Void
Our voices ring!
Our long lost home,
Of thee we sing!
To thee we sing of you!

Amerca-a-dia!
So distant and so brown!
Amerca-a-dia!
The homeless sing your hymn!
Amerca-a-dia!
'Tis true you once were round!
Amerca-a-dia!
Bright jewel ne'er dimmed!

If there's a battle,
You can bet,
Though fun we love 'tis true,
We love our fighting
Better yet!
We love our freedom, too!
And through the course
Of history,
There was but one society,
That stood for might

And liberty,
The old Red, Green and Blue!

Amerca-a-dia!
Sweet old terrestrial ball!
Amerca-a-dia!
Our Mother's finest whim!
Amerca-a-dia!
For you we give our all!
Amerca-a-dia!
Bright jewel ne'er dimmed!

(drums)

We stand and raise
Our voices high,
For those in peril in the sky,
Who love their lives,
Yet live to die,
And never give a damn!
So off we go,
When there's a threat,
We love our home,
We owe a debt,
If we've not said it,
You can bet,
Her name begins with Am!

(tenors)

Amerca-a-dia!
The glory and the gall!
Amerca-a-dia!
The hopeful and the grim!
Amerca-a-dia!
We die who heed your call!
Amerca-a-dia!
Bright jewel ne'er dimmed!

We turn our faces
Toward the sun.
Most any sun will do!
It's might for all
And all for one;
The old Red, Green and Blue!
So, off we blast to victory,
In courage and humility!
We ever strive
For piety,
The soul's eternal glue!

Amerca-a-dia! (ta-ta-ta-tum)
So distant and so brown!
Amerca-(ta-ta-ta-tum)-dia! (ta-ta-ta-tum)
The homeless sing your hymn!
Amerca-a-dia! (ta-ta-ta-tum)
'Tis true you once were round!
Amerca-(ta-ta-ta-tum)-dia! (ta-ta-ta-tum)
Bright Jewel n'ere -
Our foes beware!
Bright jewel n'ere dimmed!
(ta-ta-ta-tum-BOOM)

As of this writing, the Brigade still receives royalties on each and every Krystal Drive sold by New Eden Multi-Tech Labs for the continuous-loop recording of the Amercadian Space Brigade Drum and Bugle Corps' version (Cycle 149 ET) of *Us Against The Void* that is used as fuel by the now standard drive. (See: Krystals, Borinyum)

Vale of Tiers

The 17 central levels of Recreation Station 97, with spoke-like avenues converging on a central hub of terraced balconies, offering a stunning view of adjacent tiers. The various levels are accessed by a system of Up-and-Down-See-Daisys®, running through the hub. Restaurants, bars, theatres, casinos and clubs dotting the spoke-like avenues and winding cross-streets cater to middle-income and working-caste spacers. Entertainers and asteroid miners, backwater bumpkins and professional gamblers, vacationing Teoman and off-duty Brigaders, mercenary proldiers and adventurous families looking for something new, all mix and mingle on the Vale of Tiers. A warning printed in the official *Guide to the Galaxy's 467 Rec Stations* states, "When visiting the Vale of Tiers on Rec 97, walk in a determined manner. Try to look as though you know where you are going. Don't look up. Don't look down." Sound advice, indeed! For those thinking of starting or moving a business to the Vale, lot prices on the hub, where one is likely to get the most walk-ins, are quite high. On the outer wheel, where views look out onto nearby (relatively speaking) stars, they are astronomical.

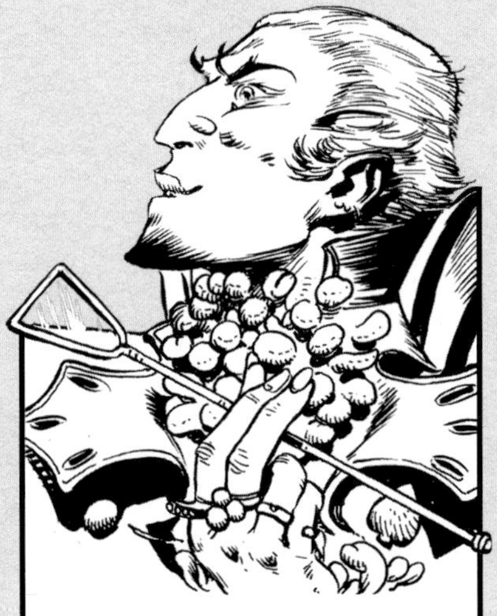

Vegorian Vitronus Khrome

Vegorian the Vain

The descriptive and more than usually accurate nickname for Vegorian Vitronus Khrome, wealthy space-hopper and ne'er-do-well nephew of RSVdG Bajar through his wife, Ambrosia Vitronia Khrome, Vegorian being the son of her twin brother, Ambrosius Vitronus Khrome. (Twins do seem to run in that family!) A notorious gossip and inveterate gambler, Vegorian had the dubious honor of having parted with more credit at the Rouliette tables of The Dome, Recreation Station 97, than had any other humanoid in the galaxy, before or since. Vegorian died mysteriously in Cycle 151 AE, having mistaken a Wrenchin face-eater for his favorite toupee, following a large gathering of friends and family to celebrate the anniversary of his birth. That one of the gathered had purposely made the old switcheroo, substituting the face-eater for the hairpiece, was something that could never be proved, owing to the large amounts of Kublacaine and other mind-altering substances imbibed at the fête. Vegorian's was the first of a slew of similar deaths, the victims related in one way or another to the family Bajar, following the public disowning of the Baron RSVdG Bajar's two adult children, during the trial of Brucilla the Muscle, 142 AE. One must surmise that the events were related.

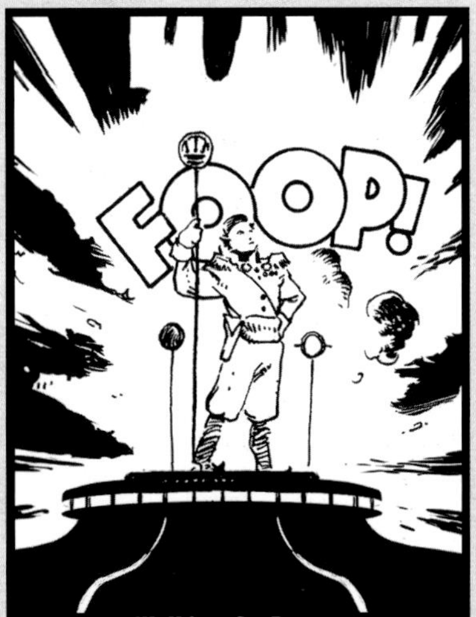
FOOP!

Walking On Depot

Walking On

A mode of transport, developed by Swells' Bells®, that allows wealthy Gold Card® owners to travel over short (by Multiversal standards) distances without the use of a space-going craft. Swells' Bells® leases their Walking On Depot® to various upscale venues around and about the settled Multiverse, then offers its Gold Card®, or the card's niche-market cousins, the Casino and Boardroom cards, to the venue's wealthy patrons. In order to protect their exorbitant service fees, the company guards their technology fiercely, though some of their customers have found their way around the wallet-rending expense. For example, The Dome, a posh nightclub on Rec Station 97, defrays part of the tremendous cost of this service by placing their Walking On Depot® in the club's Freebetters Room and allowing their customers to place bets on "who'll materialize next." Even so, it is doubtful that

Walking On® will ever replace Krystal driven starships as the primary means of transportation in the galaxy, as the cost is prohibitive and the distance one can travel in a single walk is limited.

Wax Zombies of the Noh Zone

Described as more of a "futuristic horror movie" than a work of speculative fiction, this best-selling novel by Hugo Award-winning author Ronnie Lee Ellis tracks the nefarious comings and goings of waxmeister Boris Hex and his mad sister Raquel, as they transform various galactic luminaries into mindless, wax-covered slaves, for the purposes of employing them in strange theatrical performances. Major themes include 1) the price of a life dedicated to art, 2) sibling rivalry, its costs and rewards, and 3) the madness that inevitably arises from the thwarted creative impulse. Not that the readers noticed any of that. The popularity of the novel has often been attributed to the public fascination with seeing their leaders and celebrities transformed into shambling monstrosities that are forced to "strut and fret" their marbec upon the stage in a very odd corner of the Multiverse. *Wax Zombies of the Noh Zone* was later made into the highly successful lasaround, *WaxWorx*, which spawned numerous (though less inspired) sequels.

General Typhoon Weatherall

Weatherall, General Typhoon

A general in the Amercadian Space Brigade and administrative head of the Amercadian Space Academy, who famously turned a blind eye to incursions by Academy cadets into the Cosmic Veil's territory in Neutral Zone 8, resulting in the Amercadian Space Brigade Neutral Zone Fiasco of AE 134.

Commander Windy Weatherall

Weatherall, Commander Windy

Eldest son of General Typhoon Weatherall. As a young lieutenant in the graduating class of the Amercadian Space Academy, Windy's misguided sense of honor played a part in the events surrounding the ASB Neutral Zone Fiasco of AE 134, which resulted in the deaths of an entire Brigade squadron and the Brigade's banishment from Neutral Zone 8.

Vercadian Protector Android

The only android culture (or batch) capable of premeditated assault on a sentient being... the Cyberphobe's nightmare. They are incredibly expensive and incredibly dangerous. Vercadian Protector Androids were built in the early Cycles of IER-CO by the Vercadian Andromedicones in an effort to 1) fulfill their programming by providing a nearly indestructible protector for its human owners, 2) scratch an old itch, by providing humankind

with yet another means of destroying itself, and 3) bring home the bacon. Lots and lots of bacon. Standard features include Atomo-Torch Power Gauntlets, thought-activated body shield, Pec-Flex Implosion-Head Destructo-Dart System, Rear Guard atomic cannon, Boot Up disemboweling horns, adjustable vanity mirror, Chakra Rocket Id-Seeking Quasar Bullets, and Switz Armsy Guards with gutting, slicing, and filleting knives (tweezers optional). The two best known and most feared of all Vercadian Protector Androids were Veep 7, the warrior poet, and 785, the gold-plated bodyguard of the Mayor of Casterbridge. An old children's tale tells of Veep 7, the masterless droid, that he was once stared down by a chinchilla from the Yndokrin Mining Belts and so lost his arm guard.

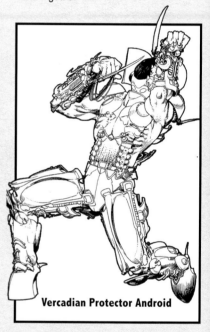

Vercadian Protector Android

Xychromo Zone

A zone comprised of several systems in which, as noted historian Dwannyun of Griivarr has written, the "bullies run the school." No place for a relaxing holiday!

About the Author

Born in the low Acadian parishes of central Amercadia, Scooter Jean Spivey, now Lady Scooter Jean, Maiden Priestess of Phoebus, began life inauspiciously as a fish wrangler's kid. At about age 5, she joined a local Wing of the Chickadee Guides and then, at age 7, blasted off into the wider Multiverse as a member of Moulting Wing.

When the usual series of random and/or ill-fated events (depending on your point of view) took the wing to Rec Station 97, landing them there smack-in-the-middle of the terrifying Guide-Nappings of AE 140, Scooter's wing-mates, Glynde and Sneaker, were "disappeared" by a mysterious woman in green.

- YOU KNOW WHO YOU ARE! -

Rescued from a similar fate by none other than Glorianna of Phoebus, Scooter started happily down the path to Priesstesshood. The wildly successful Ordering AnarchEra is her second book, the first being her memoir, *Snatched into the Light*.

Glynde

Scooter Jean

Sneaker

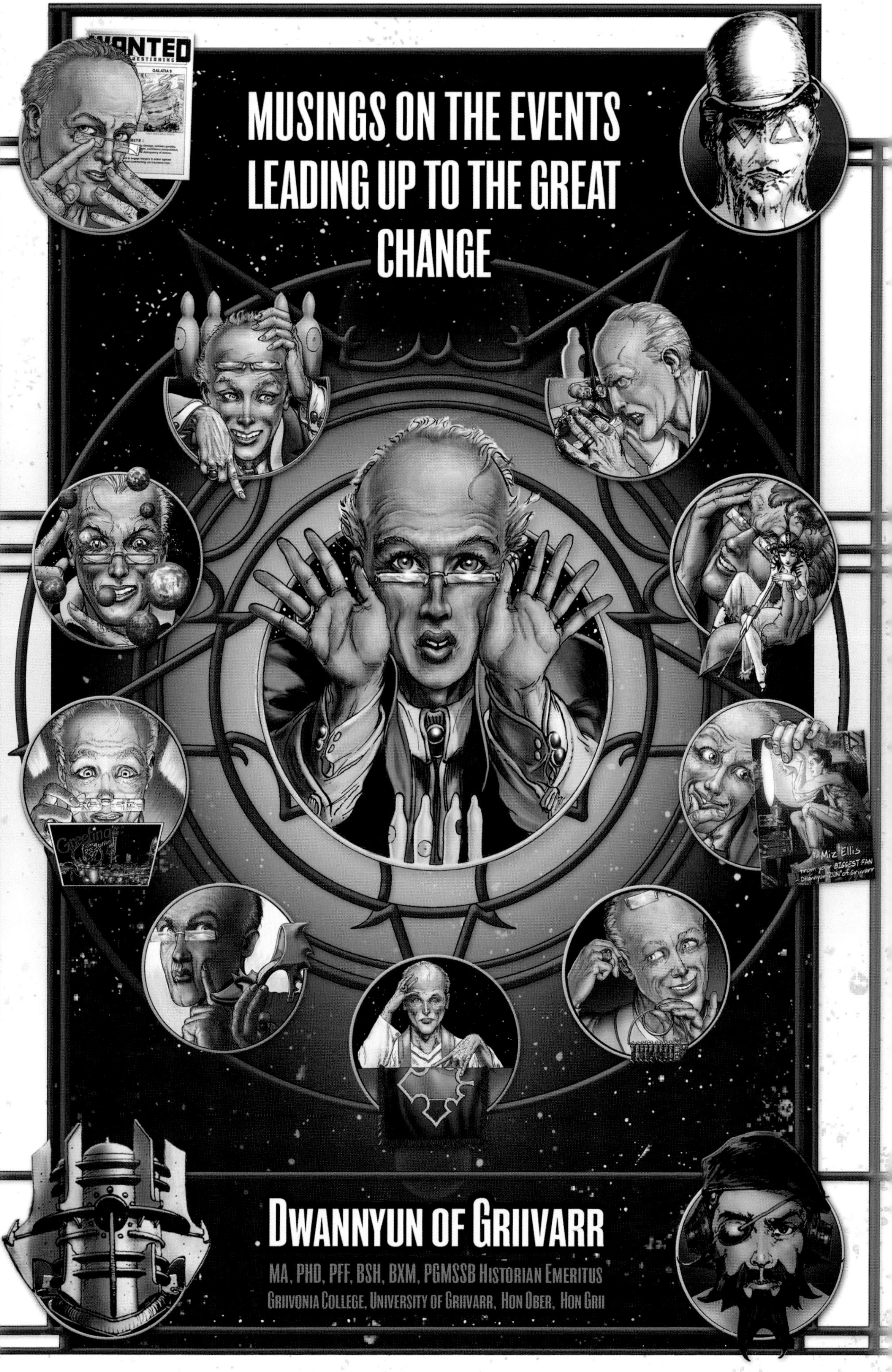
MUSINGS ON THE EVENTS LEADING UP TO THE GREAT CHANGE
WANTED
GALATIA 9
To Miz Ellis
from your BIGGEST FAN
— Dwannyun "ZUN" of Griivarr
DWANNYUN OF GRIIVARR
MA, PHD, PFF, BSH, BXM, PGMSSB HISTORIAN EMERITUS
GRIIVONIA COLLEGE, UNIVERSITY OF GRIIVARR, HON OBER, HON GRII

YOU ARE HERE or "THE END OF THE BEGINNING"
(excerpted from his Introduction)

There are many versions of the The Truth ®. We are all of us, each and every one, the center of our own universe and each individual tends to look at things from the perspective of that singular perch. Like the old sign says, "You Are Here," wherever the heck here is.

With this in mind, I have taken it upon myself to describe events that I may have taken a small part in, if mainly as an observer, often at a distance, sometimes from the hurricane's eye, always as if through a glass, darkly. While many historians have traced the Great Change from the happenings of 157 Anarchera, my "truth" is far stranger and more interesting, if only because it is told from the viewpoint of a well-placed fly on the wall. And my "truth" begins much earlier.

It all has to do with two dynastic families whose offspring found themselves on opposite sides of the rebellion that toppled the Incorporated Elysian Republic (which was neither heavenly, nor a republic), then went on to struggle for supremacy in the chaotic cycles of the aptly named Anarchera. The Griivarr Clan (in answer to those calling the Griivarrs a third dynasty, I must demur) became entangled in the various plots and passions of members of these squabbling dynasties and their allies, in the cycles from 92 AE, through the early units of the Change. My self, my father and my siblings, Bud and Princess (and to a lesser extent, Buddy), would, unbeknownst to ourselves, serve the interests of the Bajar and Medea families in numerous ways.

In the following pages, I will attempt to fill in some gaps, as it were, in the accepted story, as presented in both the "official" histories and in the deliberately heightened lasarounds, holoshows and nooscasts of popular galactic culture. Please bear with me should I wax nostalgic once in awhile, and forgive me if I wander too far away from the path to focus on some tangential point or "shiny object" in my all-too-imperfect memory. So, with all ten fingers gripping my seat cushion, I begin.

I remember it like it was, if not quite yesterday, then certainly no more than a rigon or two ago...

Concerning Margaret Medea, I think it is safe to say that she never fully recovered from the loss of her eldest daughter, Mary. Sources close to the family say that she experienced some amount of guilt associated with the death*, though what her part in it could have been is impossible to say. As Mary Medea died* on Onolo Dos, while on a mission she had undertaken with her father, Siegfried "McMauMau" Siegfriedson, and her mother had spurned the life of a freedom fighter in favor of a career in business, it is difficult to believe that Margaret could've played a significant role.

By all reports, Margaret was never close to her second daughter, Molly Younger, who left the family home on New Wyoming at age 16 (though there is some disagreement as to whether her years were counted in standard cycles or D.O.G. years), and it is true that Molly was not mentioned in her Mother's will.

Much has been written about the so-called "missing years" of Molly Younger (AKA Galatia 9), though much of this is pure speculation.

What is known is that Molly, for some years after leaving home, attached herself to one lost cause after another, often running into problems with the authorities in whichever arm of the galaxy she happened to be stirring up trouble. She "fell off the map" for some cycles, disappearing sometime around Cycle 131 AE, only to resurface on Rec Station 97, circa 138, about the time of the publication of her book of political poetry, entitled **Rhymes Time Nine** and written under the name, Galatia 9, "Freelance Fighter and Poet Militant."

In the interest of full disclosure, this poor writer owes his life to Captain Galatia 9 (later of the U4F) and served as a member of her crew on the Freelance Freedom Fighter Harpy, cycles 156-158 AnarchEra, though working in close proximity to the Captain gave me little insight into her early life.

* Conspiracy theorists, throughout the settled Multiverse, claim that Mary Medea never met her death on Onolo Dos, but instead:

1) was secretly an android and so did not officially die (see: Souls, Holder of),

2) faked her own death and reappeared as any one of a number of powerful rulers and/or leaders, or

3) lives "amongst the angel-thangs in Keengduhm Kuhm." (see: Keengduhm Kuhm)

Much has been written about the **Last Will + Testament of Mary Medea** and it is generally agreed that this document was the catalyst (along with the establishment of the Glorianan religion) that spurred the Miners of the Mitochondrian Krystal Belt to create a permanent government that would unify the belt.

The will was witnessed by Mary Medea's personal assistant, an andromedicone droid of the AL line. This is interesting, as it was the participation of Miz Medea and the other human allies who fought alongside cyberforms in the Droid Wars, that led to legal rights being extended to independent thinking androids (thus making the aforementioned witnessing possible).

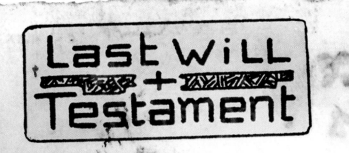

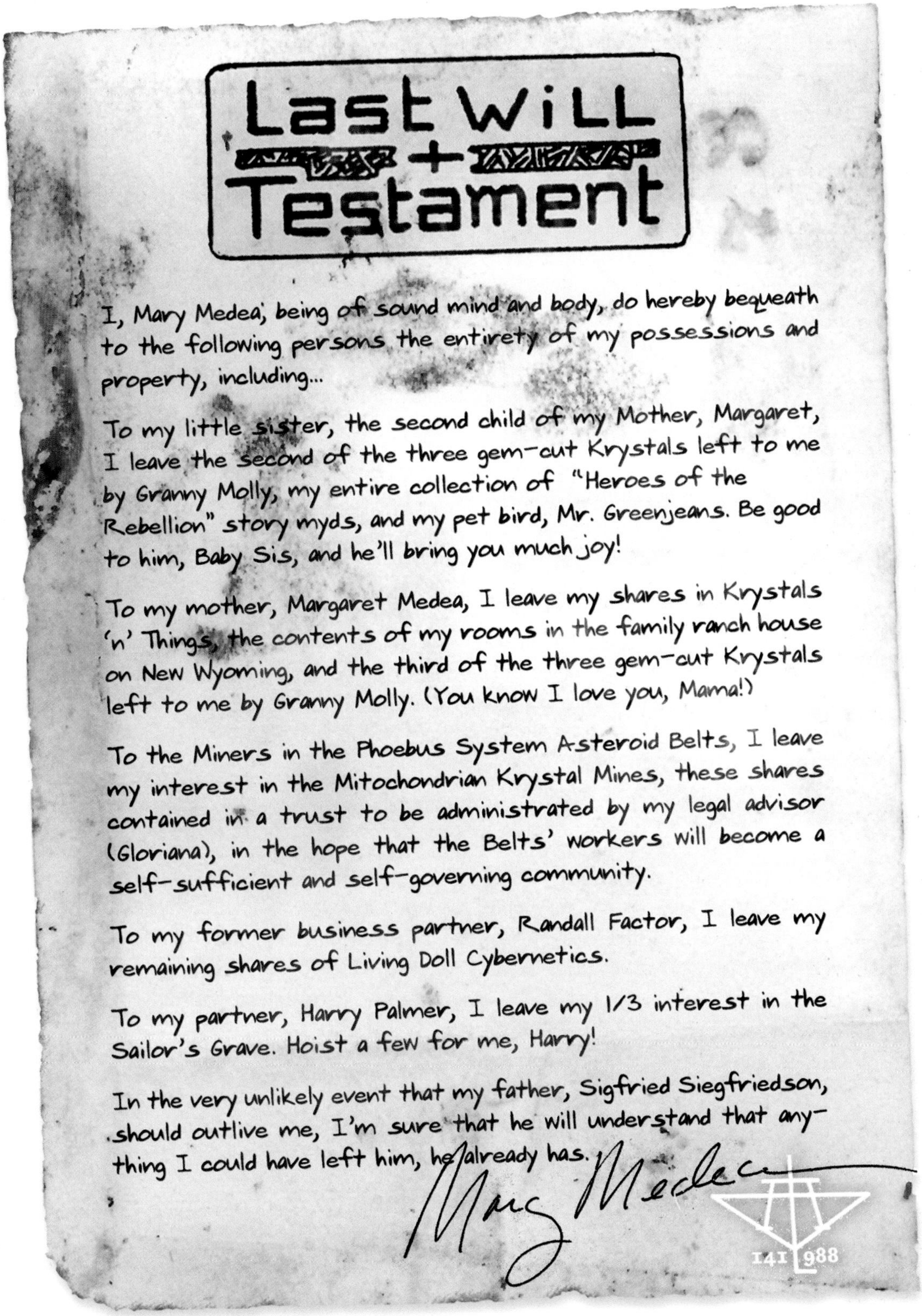

I, Mary Medea, being of sound mind and body, do hereby bequeath to the following persons the entirety of my possessions and property, including...

To my little sister, the second child of my Mother, Margaret, I leave the second of the three gem-cut Krystals left to me by Granny Molly, my entire collection of "Heroes of the Rebellion" story myds, and my pet bird, Mr. Greenjeans. Be good to him, Baby Sis, and he'll bring you much joy!

To my mother, Margaret Medea, I leave my shares in Krystals 'n' Things, the contents of my rooms in the family ranch house on New Wyoming, and the third of the three gem-cut Krystals left to me by Granny Molly. (You know I love you, Mama!)

To the Miners in the Phoebus System Asteroid Belts, I leave my interest in the Mitochondrian Krystal Mines, these shares contained in a trust to be administrated by my legal advisor (Gloriana), in the hope that the Belts' workers will become a self-sufficient and self-governing community.

To my former business partner, Randall Factor, I leave my remaining shares of Living Doll Cybernetics.

To my partner, Harry Palmer, I leave my 1/3 interest in the Sailor's Grave. Hoist a few for me, Harry!

In the very unlikely event that my father, Sigfried Siegfriedson, should outlive me, I'm sure that he will understand that anything I could have left him, he already has.

Mary Medea

141 988

THE SPIDERLINGS HATCH *or "When Fiction Births Fact"* (excerpted from Chapter 5)

How often is it that a genre novel truly changes the course of history?

I read Miz Ellis's prophetic tome *Mind Spiders From the Planet Xenon*, back when I was a marmot-class Ranger. To say it caught my imagination would be an understatement. It was as though the aptly named *Mind Spiders* had planted its egg case in my brain, where, cycles later, it would hatch ravenous spiderlings that would slowly devour my gray matter, turning me into its zombie slave and, ultimately, sending me on a doomed quest to find my evil twin. But, more on that later!

The enormously successful *Mind Spiders* and its various spin-off lasarounds and holoshows, trading cards and action figures, gave Miz Ellis the wherewithal to do whatever she pleased. And what she pleased was to interfere in the lives of certain powerful members of the Medea and Bajar clans, much as a wayward child might influence a battle between clans of red and black ants, using a magnifying lens and sunlight. That this seems to have been an experiment sparked by curiosity, as much as anything, made very little difference to the "ants" involved. (But now I'm mixing metaphors; insects and arthropods, as it were!)

Miz Ellis's deleterious effect on the life of her brother, the Baronette PCKA Bajar, has been well established and is supported by her own published diaries, as is her involvement with certain of the Medeas. But it is her influence (through the Cosmic Veil) on many thousands of lost souls in search of meaning with which this chapter is concerned.

In my own case, I don't think it would be stretching a point to say that *Mind Spiders from the Planet Xenon* changed the course of my life.

IN THE ZONE *or "Where Bullies Run the School"* (excerpted from Chapter 9)

Close your eyes and imagine a world where there is no boredom, no crime, basic needs are taken care of and every citizen is blessed with a sense of purpose.

Can such a place exist?

With good planning, based on a very good plan, yes, it can. In fact, this humble writer grew up in such a place. And I am more than proud to say that it was my own father, Brzzt Oomph Burble "Bob" Griivarr, who envisioned such a world(s), planned such a plan, and who was, through his own ingenuity and hard work (and, okay, a modicum of luck), able to purchase his first planet and go on to establish a collective of eight worlds, governed by the most beneficent of governments.

My father's "Simple Recipe for Happiness" provided the basis for this government, assuring our citizens of the right to health, happiness and meaningful work, with the understanding that such rights must be paid for with a sufficient measure of good citizenship and familial duty. It seems to have been a good trade-off. In our world(s), mothers are wise and loving, children are curious and well behaved, and fathers really do know best.

Were it not for a confusing over-abundance of youngsters with the given names of Princess and Bud, life on the Griivarr Worlds would be near-perfection. (In my father's defense, one could certainly imagine the appeal such simple names would have to one saddled with the handle Brzzt Oomph Burble!)

But I digress.

Suffice it to say that, from the standpoint of any humanoid raised on the Griivarr Worlds, there is no more different (one might easily say "repugnant") place in the known Multiverse than any one of the several planets of the Xychromo Zone.

As an exercise, close your eyes and imagine an entire section of the Multiverse, run by the worst of schoolyard bullies. No, really… go ahead, close your eyes and imagine. Good…

Feel that tightening knot of fear and loathing in your churning gut?

You will never have to hop a transport to the Xychromo Zone.

IN THESE HEELS? or "From Socialite to Sociopath to Sociogenatrix" (excerpted from Chapter 11)

Any chapter on the life and career of Verloona Ti, born Maggie Medea, would have to begin with A) her early life on New Wyoming, B) go on to talk about her effect on the life of her sister, Molly (better known as Galatia 9), C) would include her "dark" years and, finally D) would speculate on the reasons for her inclusion in the "Fortunate Conjoining" that led to the Change.

To say Verloona Ti was a celebrity would be understating the fact. She was a space-hopping celebutant, famous for being famous, and left a trail of broken hearts (sometimes literally) wherever she went. And she went everywhere. To understand the hold Miz Ti had on the AnarchEran pre-Change consciousness, you would have to understand the place that the system of 483 Rec Stations and their PR & Infotainment wing, Rootersnoos, held in the lives of the space-going public.

Plopped into the dead space between, say, a popular planet and the nearest wormhole portal, a Rec Station provided weary travelers with one-stop shopping for entertainment and companionship, mind-altering beverages and comestibles, gambling and life-extension services, cosmetic interventions and much-needed R&R. The Rec Station Noos Service, broadcast on the Recs and across numerous worlds, and with much time and many channels to fill, provided Verloona with an endless supply of publicity. She was a star before the age of 15 (D.O.G. years).

Parlaying this fame into a business opportunity, she sunk most of the family credit into her Temple of Beauty® venture, which capitalized on the galactic fascination with Krabian females (the ultimate in no-strings dating - slaves with benefits!), their company motto stating: "Be a Krabian, or Just Look Like One!"

The Temple-Spas took off. Franchises sold like Kansas Korncakes®* in all corners of the settled Multiverse. Females of nearly every race and species decided they wanted to look like a Krabian.

* The expression, "sold like Kansas Korncakes" is actually a misnomer, as the sale of said Korncakes was never dependent on a free market. Korncakes were "sold" to the Amercadian Space Brigade, who in turn "resold" them to any person, planet, nation, race or cyberform who owed them a favor. A gazillion of them changed hands, hence the expression.

CRUEL SISTER or "The Third Medea's Murdered Children" (excerpted from Chapter 10)

How do you solve a problem like Verloona?

Born into an up-by-their-bootstraps Last Frontier family that included both titans of business and heroes of the revolution, Maggie Medea (AKA Verloona Ti) began life as the spoiled "little princess" of Krystals 'n Things magnate Margaret Medea and her second husband Geron Ti. She had everything; beauty, credit, smarts. She started and ran a successful business and was a minor celebrity among the star-hopping public.

So, what led her to commit the monstrous acts that formed the core of her infamous beauty regimen? There are several schools of thought.

1) Her pathological fear of aging and the entrepreneurial spirit that inspired her Temple of Beauty Franchises combined to create in her an obsession with finding a means of age-prevention that would remain completely under her control, while competing with Running In Place, thereby adding to her already significant bank account.

2) Easy pickings. Polluted water runs downhill, taking the path of least resistance.
Need youth? Steal someone else's. Make sure the "someone" is a person who a) won't be missed, or b) whose own habits make them difficult to track. Only logical.

3) Because she could. She had the wherewithal, as well as the requisite beauty and charisma, to enlist the help of a brilliant bioengineer who might normally have found the idea repellent.

4) She was broken, a sociopath, and was born that way.

If one accepts the information on Miz Ti provided in earlier chapters of this book, one must come to the conclusion that all four of these explanations are part of the truth. But why was she born that way?

Perhaps the Multiverse needed her to be. She was, after all, one third of the sisterly triad who gave language, memory and soul (in her case, inadvertently) to the Prime Krystal, thereby helping to trigger events that led to the Change.

ON REC 97 or "THE RECREATION STATION AS EVENT FACTORY" (excerpted from Chapter 38)

It was the Playground of Gots and Geezers, or salvation for burnt-out spacers in need of a little humanoid contact. It was the Brigader's port of choice for R&R and the Galactic Girl Guide's favorite spot for chump fishing. More to the point, Rec 97 was the magnetic field at the center of the space-hopper's Multiverse, where Up-and-Comers and Down-and-Outers, mingled with the Has-Beens, Wannabes and Now-and-Forever-Ares. Things happened here. Important things.

Rec Station 97 served as launch pad for Nick the Geezer Pico's ubiquitous Running-In-Place Parlors, where those in need of credit could sell years of life to those who felt they needed it worse (and had the cold, hard McCoy to back them up).

On the Vale of Tiers, the moderately-priced midlevels of the Rec, you could have Warrior of the Revolution (or facsimile) Harry Palmer pour you a tall, cool one in his popular drinking establishment, The Sailor's Grave. Or you could visit the Norris Rex Emporium/Wax Museum, where you might run into Rex's patroness, Ronnie Lee Ellis of *Mind Spiders* fame.

You could hop an Up-See-Daisy to the outer rings and visit Blue Heaven Level and The Dome, to watch Randall Factor, Hero of the Droid Wars, rub platinum- plated elbows with Bajars and Medeas. Have a game of Dark-Bone-Mark with a deposed noble from the days of the Incorporated Elysian Republic (neither heavenly, nor a republic). Or get away from it all in the quiet confines of the Veil's Temptation Cloister.

For more adventurous souls, the Station Gutters offered a dip into the scummy end of the pond. Have your droid rogued at a body shop, buy yourself some cybernetic protection, or purchase a very short-term lease on a used pleasure model. In the Gutters, you could buy, rent, pawn, sample or steal almost any controlled, illegal or impossible-to-come-by item or substance known to humanoid kind.

On the opposite end of the spectrum, Krystal Hills was the home-away-from-palace for the galaxy's upper crust. Verloona Ti kept rooms there, as did several Bajars and a certain Phoeban Prime Minister.

Movers and Shakers tended to make their way here and, once here, to bump into others of their ilk. Introductions were wangled, plans were made, schemes hatched, drinks drunk. Love affairs began or concluded. Surprises, good and bad, altered or ended lives.

Yes, things happened here. Important things.

SHIPWRECKED or "THE LAW OF UNINTENDED CONSEQUENCES" (excerpted from Chapter 77)

Nothing prepares a young Brigader for shooting down the wrong ship. No amount of training, no amount of mental conditioning, no amount of gung-ho-atta-boy-can-do spirit.

Likewise, no amount of therapy, self-flagellation or conversation with deity can expunge the horrifying deed, after the fact.

That the void around the Rec Station was chock-full of Brigade Tigers, packed nose to tail, in stacks from the voidfront up to banlons past the G-Gates, causing confusion and miscommunication among the ranks, does not ease the pain of having committed such a deed, inadvertent though it may have been.

The facts are these. I was in a Tiger. Two ships exited Blast Tube 29Z. There was confusion. I was ordered to fire and I did. I hit the wrong ship, which crashed into the Rec Station, instantly killing two occupants. Then, before I could even register what exactly had happened, I heard the terrible words: *"That's the Sisterhood's code!"*

Thus ended my career in the Brigade.

Two things did finally help me recover my equilibrium: the subjective passage of time and the eventual understanding that, had I hit the correct target, I would've terminated two very different sterling humanoids, both of whom came to mean a lot to me and everything to the Multiverse at large.

In this case, my pain was the worlds' gain.

THE MOVERS AND THE SHAKERS (excerpted from Appendix 1)

The official family trees of the Medea and Bajar families, as listed in *Who's Who in the Spiral Arm*, can be found in figures 1 and 2, though there is now evidence that the information contained therein is only partial, at best.

FIGURE 1 THE MEDEA FAMILY

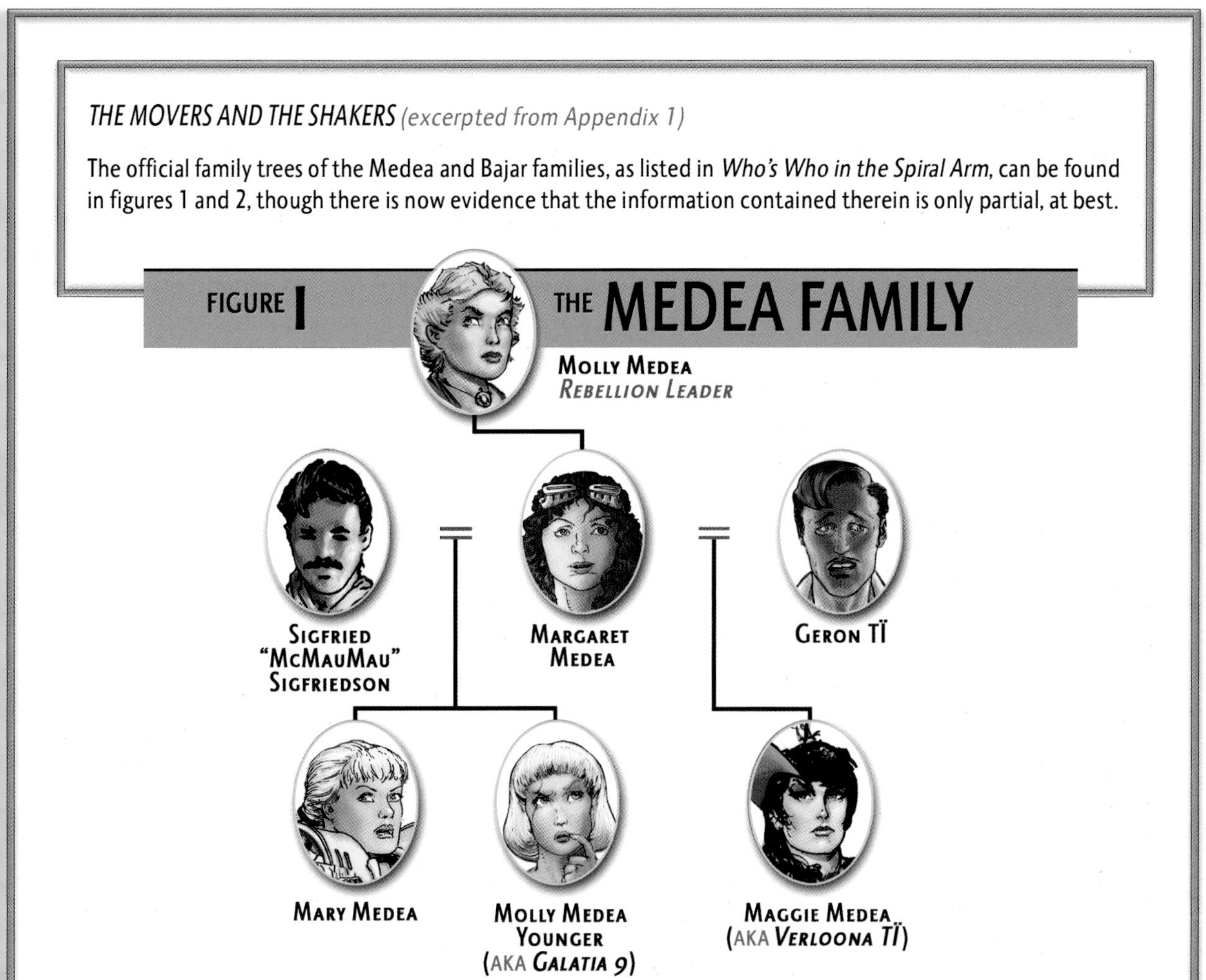

Molly Medea
Rebellion Leader
Sigfried "McMauMau" Sigfriedson
Margaret Medea
Geron Tï
Mary Medea
Molly Medea Younger (aka Galatia 9)
Maggie Medea (aka Verloona Tï)

FIGURE 2 THE BAJAR FAMILY

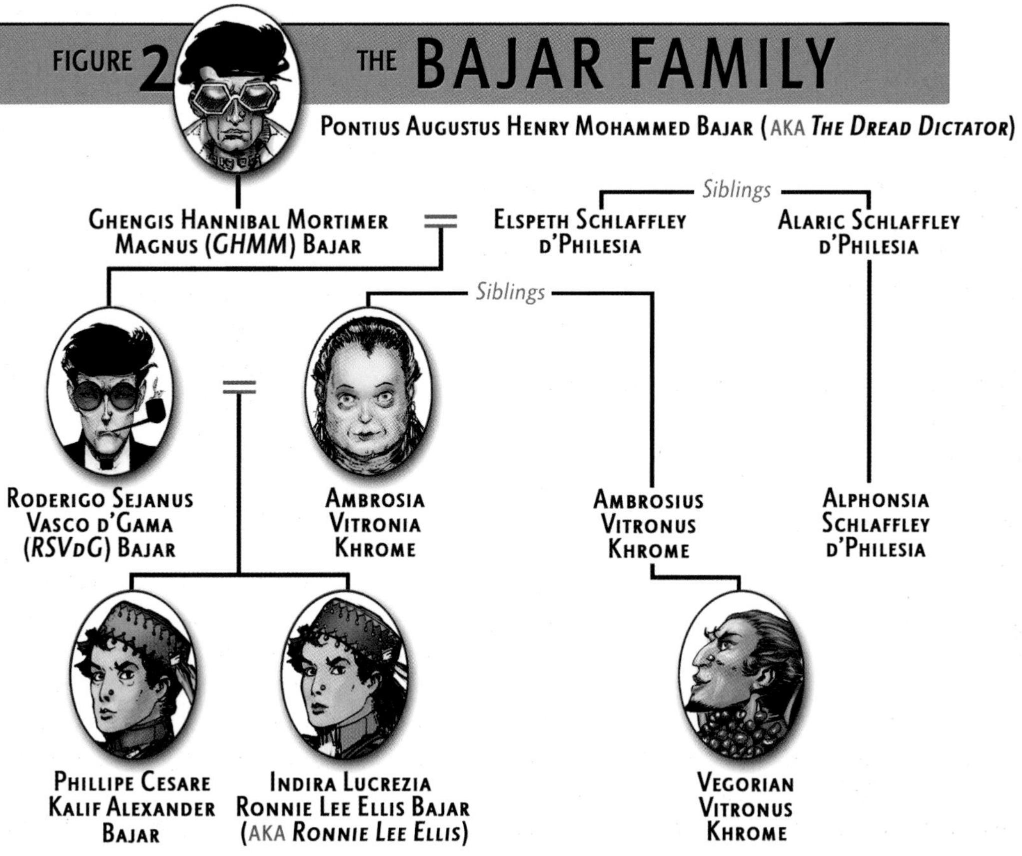

Pontius Augustus Henry Mohammed Bajar (aka The Dread Dictator)
Ghengis Hannibal Mortimer Magnus (GHMM) Bajar
Siblings
Elspeth Schlaffley d'Philesia
Alaric Schlaffley d'Philesia
Siblings
Roderigo Sejanus Vasco d'Gama (RSVdG) Bajar
Ambrosia Vitronia Khrome
Ambrosius Vitronus Khrome
Alphonsia Schlaffley d'Philesia
Phillipe Cesare Kalif Alexander Bajar
Indira Lucrezia Ronnie Lee Ellis Bajar (aka Ronnie Lee Ellis)
Vegorian Vitronus Khrome

THE NINE MOST IMPORTANT BOOKS OF ANARCHERA
(excerpted from Appendix 4 of the 3rd Edition)

Of Mice and Movers: Ripples in the Cosmic Pond
by Glorianna of Phoebus

Discusses the lives and obsessions of central figures of the pre-Change Multiverse, including ILRLE Bajar, Randal Factor, Galatia 9 and Verloona Ti. But the prime mover, the queen who kicked all the other pieces around the cosmic chessboard, was the author herself.

The Free Universe: Is it?
by Al 10

Along with **Who Cares? - Conversations with Myselves in Stark Verse**, these ponderings (on multiple channels) of famous rogue droid AL 10 allowed humanoids a sneak peek into the workings of the Cyberform Mind. Without this foundation-building exercise in consciousness expansion, it is doubtful "thinking meat" mortals would've been ready for the Change to come.

Dear Puppy: The Diary of ILRLE Bajar
by Indira Lucrezia Ronnie Lee Ellis Bajar

Published posthumously, the 38-volume diary of ILRLE Bajar takes us into the mind of one who inadvertently triggered events leading to the Change, while actually trying to manipulate the manipulator supreme, Glorianna of Phoebus.

Mind Spiders from the Planet Xenon *and* The Prince and the Pleasure Droid
by Ronnie Lee Ellis

Really volumes 1 and 3 of a tetralogy, **Mind Spiders** and **P&P** introduce us to the Daughters of the Drowning Isis, a fictional religion that closely resembles the Cosmic Veil, then go on to explore the relationship of androids to others of their line, speculating that they share a common soul.

Ordering AnarchEra -or- The Multiverse According to Me
by Scooter Jean, Maiden Priestess of Phoebus

This book by Glorianna's young protégée is, for the most part, an encyclopedia of AnarchEra, though it contains hints and foreshadowing of the age destined to follow.

Conversations with the Great Mother
by Bronwyn, Fifth Level Sister of the Cosmic Veil

Whether or not one believes in the existence of the Great Mother, one must come to the conclusion that Sister Bronwyn was hooked into some higher power (touching the Krystaline Consciousness, perhaps?), as she foresaw many hidden truths that would soon become common knowledge.

Mastering Dream Enhancement Games
by Virgil H.

As Machiavelli was to his Prince, Virgil H. was to Ms. Ellis-Bajar. Though she claimed never to have played Touchémento® or any other Dream Enhancement game, she frequently credited Mr. H. as having provided the underlying structure to her worldview.

I Can't Wait Until Tomorrow 'Cause I Get Better Lookin' Every Malton-Unit
by Brucilla the Muscle

Though this 6-volume autobiography must be taken with several grains of salt, as Miz Muscle's tendency to engage in hyperbole cannot be overestimated, it is valuable as a first-hand account of pre-Change events, as seen through the eyes of the innocent destined to become bodyguard to the Krystal Bearer.

The Annotated Rhymes Times Nine
Galatia 9, with notes by Dwannyun of Griivarr

While Galatia 9 was not, by any stretch of the imagination, a poet, her efforts in this slim volume of verse do shed a tiny beam on some of the key figures in events surrounding the Great Change.

The two rhymes dealing with her sisters, MARY WENT A'WARRING and MAGGIE KILLED A LITTLE BIRD, are especially poignant in light of recent history.

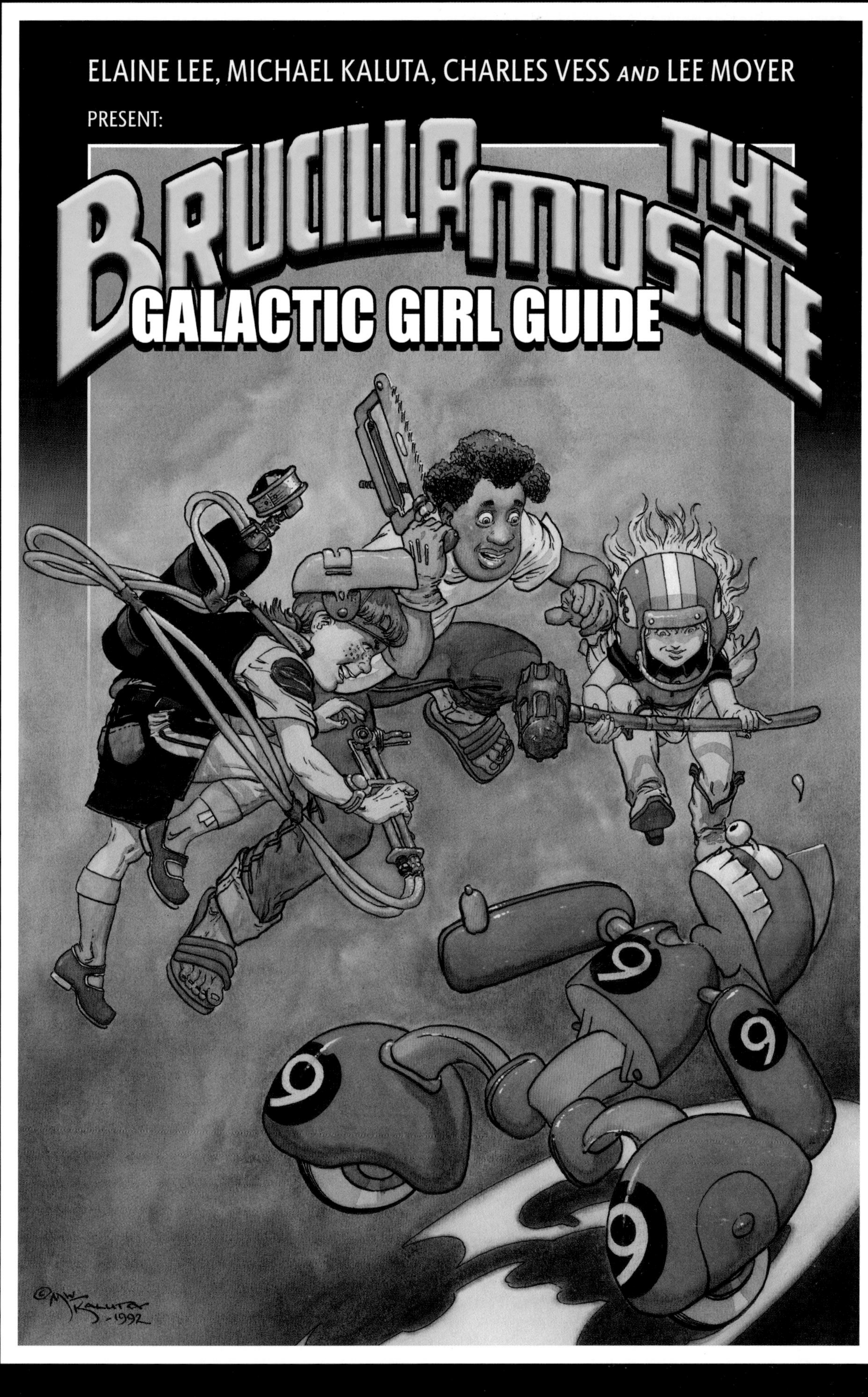
ELAINE LEE, MICHAEL KALUTA, CHARLES VESS AND LEE MOYER
PRESENT:
BRUCILLA THE MUSCLE
GALACTIC GIRL GUIDE
©MW Kaluta 1992

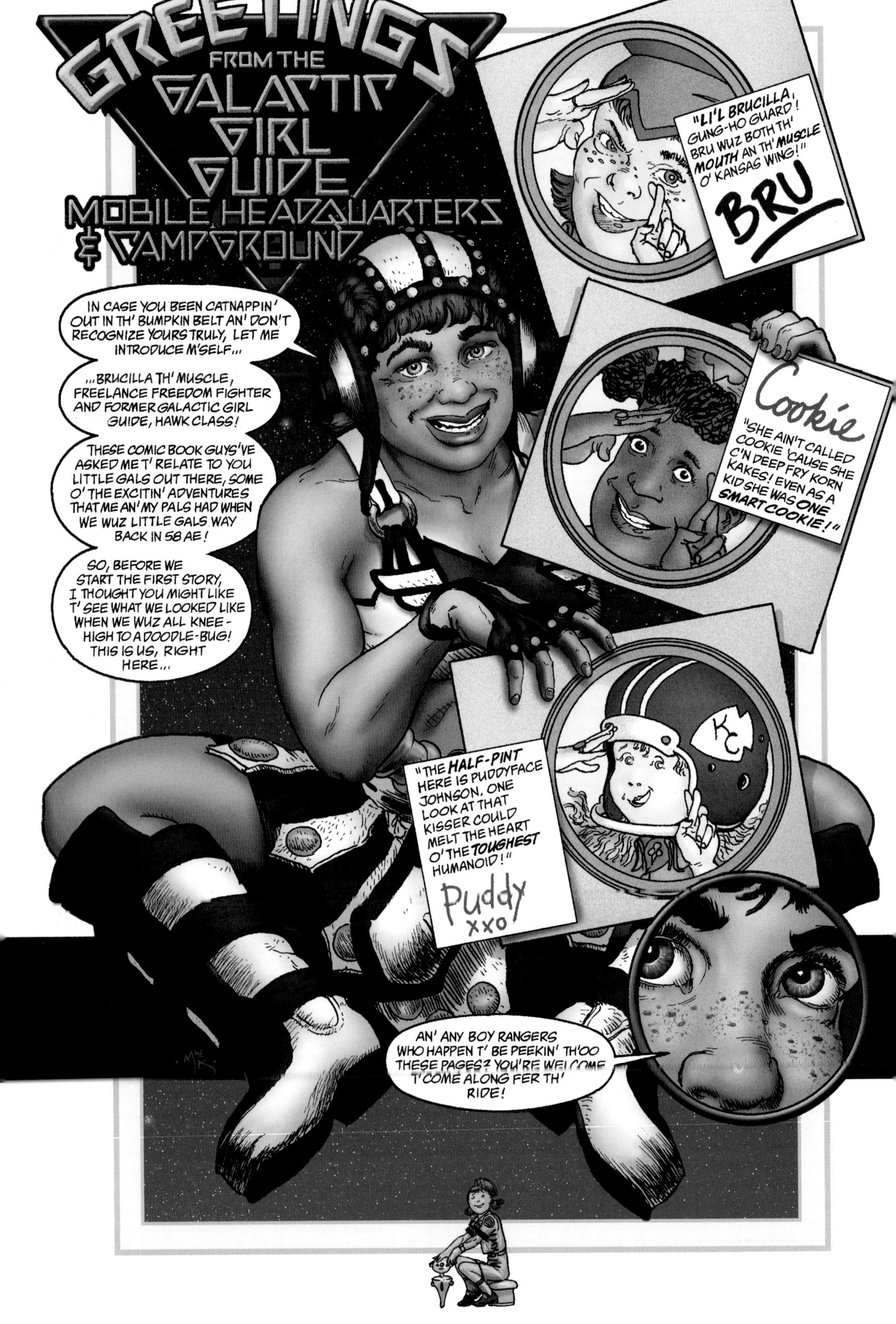
GREETINGS FROM THE GALACTIC GIRL GUIDE MOBILE HEADQUARTERS & CAMPGROUND
IN CASE YOU BEEN CATNAPPIN' OUT IN TH' BUMPKIN BELT AN' DON'T RECOGNIZE YOURS TRULY, LET ME INTRODUCE M'SELF...
...BRUCILLA TH' MUSCLE, FREELANCE FREEDOM FIGHTER AND FORMER GALACTIC GIRL GUIDE, HAWK CLASS!
THESE COMIC BOOK GUYS'VE ASKED ME T' RELATE TO YOU LITTLE GALS OUT THERE, SOME O' THE EXCITIN' ADVENTURES THAT ME AN' MY PALS HAD WHEN WE WUZ LITTLE GALS WAY BACK IN 58 AE!
SO, BEFORE WE START THE FIRST STORY, I THOUGHT YOU MIGHT LIKE T' SEE WHAT WE LOOKED LIKE WHEN WE WUZ ALL KNEE-HIGH TO A DOODLE-BUG! THIS IS US, RIGHT HERE...
"LI'L BRUCILLA, GUNG-HO GUARD! BRU WUZ BOTH TH' MUSCLE MOUTH AN TH' O' KANSAS WING!"
BRU
Cookie
"SHE AIN'T CALLED COOKIE 'CAUSE SHE C'N DEEP FRY KORN KAKES! EVEN AS A KID SHE WAS ONE SMART COOKIE!"
KC
"THE HALF-PINT HERE IS PUDDYFACE JOHNSON. ONE LOOK AT THAT KISSER COULD MELT THE HEART O' THE TOUGHEST HUMANOID!"
Puddy
XXO
AN' ANY BOY RANGERS WHO HAPPEN T' BE PEEKIN' TH'OO THESE PAGES? YOU'RE WELCOME T' COME ALONG FER TH' RIDE!

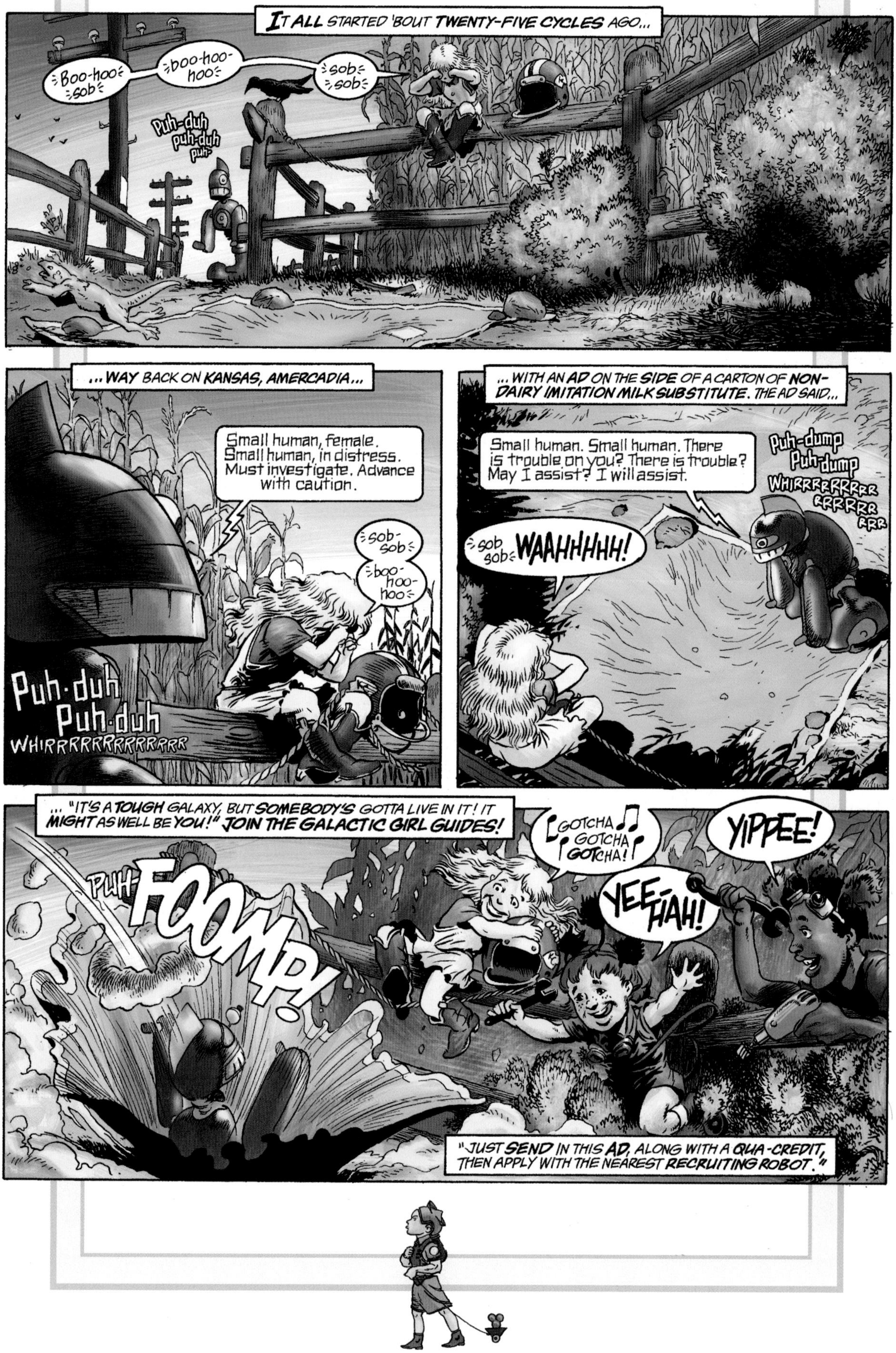
IT ALL STARTED 'BOUT TWENTY-FIVE CYCLES AGO...
Boo-hoo sob
boo-hoo-hoo
sob sob
Puh-duh puh-duh puh-
...WAY BACK ON KANSAS, AMERCADIA...
Small human, female. Small human, in distress. Must investigate. Advance with caution.
sob-sob
boo-hoo-hoo
Puh-duh Puh-duh WHIRRRRRRRRRRRRR
...WITH AN AD ON THE SIDE OF A CARTON OF NON-DAIRY IMITATION MILK SUBSTITUTE. THE AD SAID...
Small human. Small human. There is trouble on you? There is trouble? May I assist? I will assist.
Puh-dump Puh-dump WHIRRRRRRRRRRRRRRR
sob sob WAAHHHHH!
..."IT'S A TOUGH GALAXY, BUT SOMEBODY'S GOTTA LIVE IN IT! IT MIGHT AS WELL BE YOU!" JOIN THE GALACTIC GIRL GUIDES!
GOTCHA GOTCHA GOTCHA!
YIPPEE!
YEE-HAH!
PUH-FOOMP!
"JUST SEND IN THIS AD, ALONG WITH A QUA-CREDIT, THEN APPLY WITH THE NEAREST RECRUITING ROBOT."

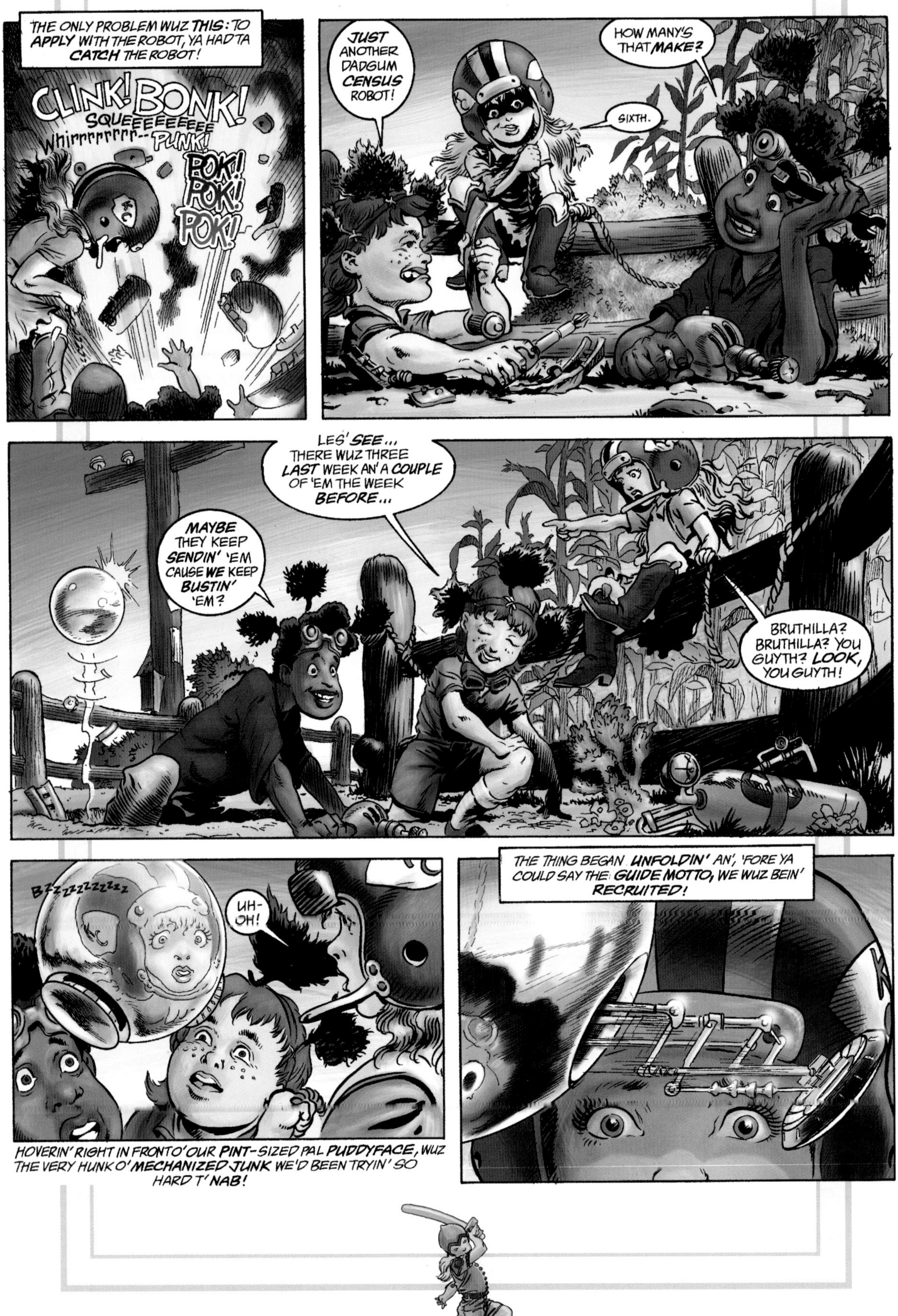
THE ONLY PROBLEM WUZ THIS: TO APPLY WITH THE ROBOT, YA HAD'TA CATCH THE ROBOT!
CLINK! BONK!
SQUEEEEEEEEE
Whirrrrrrrr--PUNK!
POK! POK! POK!
JUST ANOTHER DADGUM CENSUS ROBOT!
HOW MANY'S THAT MAKE?
SIXTH.
LES' SEE... THERE WUZ THREE LAST WEEK AN' A COUPLE OF 'EM THE WEEK BEFORE...
MAYBE THEY KEEP SENDIN' 'EM CAUSE WE KEEP BUSTIN' 'EM?
BRUTHILLA? BRUTHILLA? YOU GUYTH? LOOK, YOU GUYTH!
BZZZZZZZZZZZ
UH-OH!
HOVERIN' RIGHT IN FRONT O' OUR PINT-SIZED PAL PUDDYFACE, WUZ THE VERY HUNK O' MECHANIZED JUNK WE'D BEEN TRYIN' SO HARD T' NAB!
THE THING BEGAN UNFOLDIN' AN', 'FORE YA COULD SAY THE GUIDE MOTTO, WE WUZ BEIN' RECRUITED!

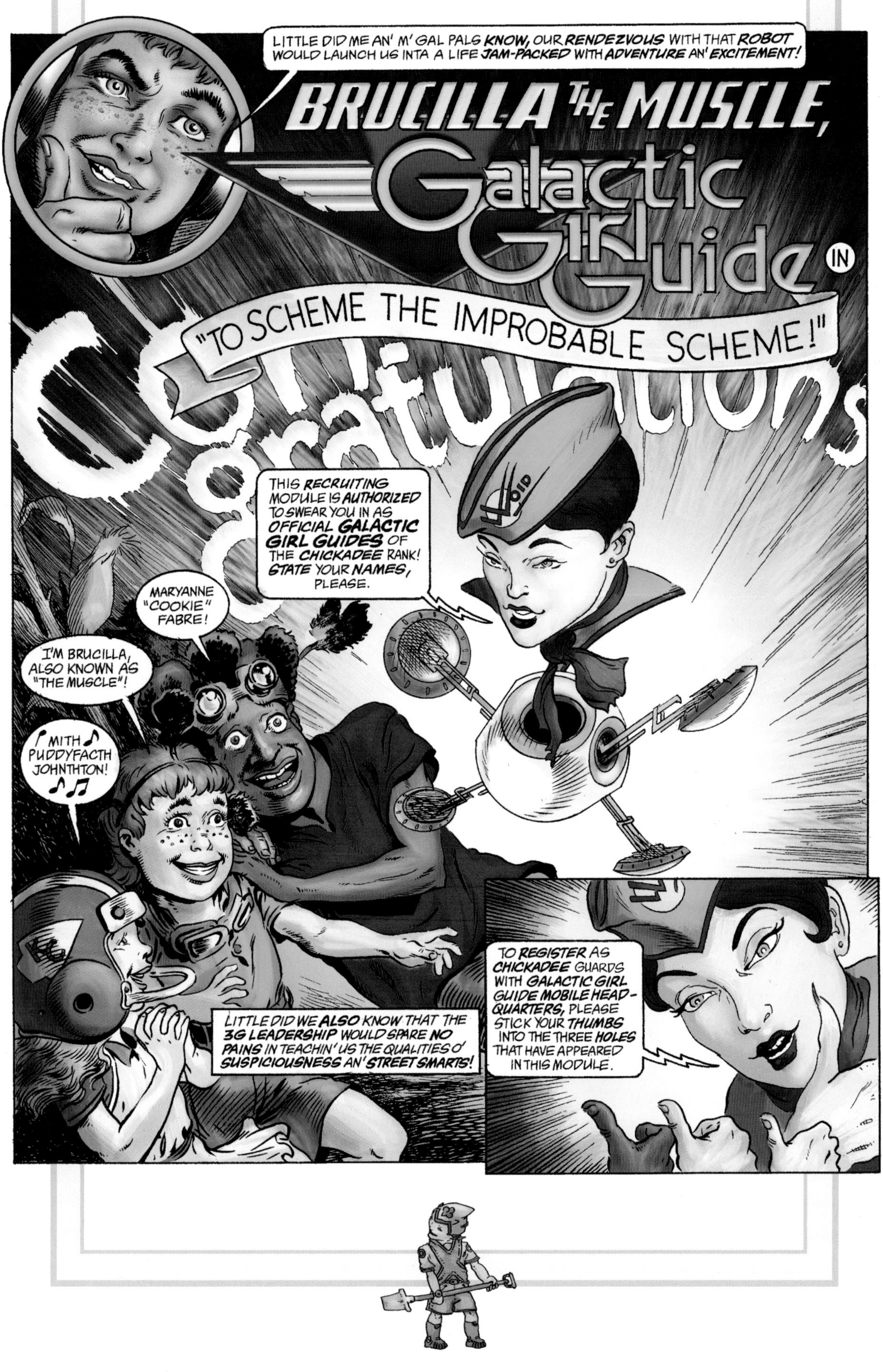
LITTLE DID ME AN' M' GAL PALS KNOW, OUR RENDEZVOUS WITH THAT ROBOT WOULD LAUNCH US INTA A LIFE JAM-PACKED WITH ADVENTURE AN' EXCITEMENT!
BRUCILLA THE MUSCLE, Galactic Girl Guide IN
"TO SCHEME THE IMPROBABLE SCHEME!"
Congratulations
THIS RECRUITING MODULE IS AUTHORIZED TO SWEAR YOU IN AS OFFICIAL GALACTIC GIRL GUIDES OF THE CHICKADEE RANK! STATE YOUR NAMES, PLEASE.
MARYANNE "COOKIE" FABRE!
I'M BRUCILLA, ALSO KNOWN AS "THE MUSCLE"!
MITH PUDDYFACTH JOHNTHTON!
TO REGISTER AS CHICKADEE GUARDS WITH GALACTIC GIRL GUIDE MOBILE HEAD-QUARTERS, PLEASE STICK YOUR THUMBS INTO THE THREE HOLES THAT HAVE APPEARED IN THIS MODULE.
LITTLE DID WE ALSO KNOW THAT THE 3G LEADERSHIP WOULD SPARE NO PAINS IN TEACHIN' US THE QUALITIES O' SUSPICIOUSNESS AN' STREET SMARTS!

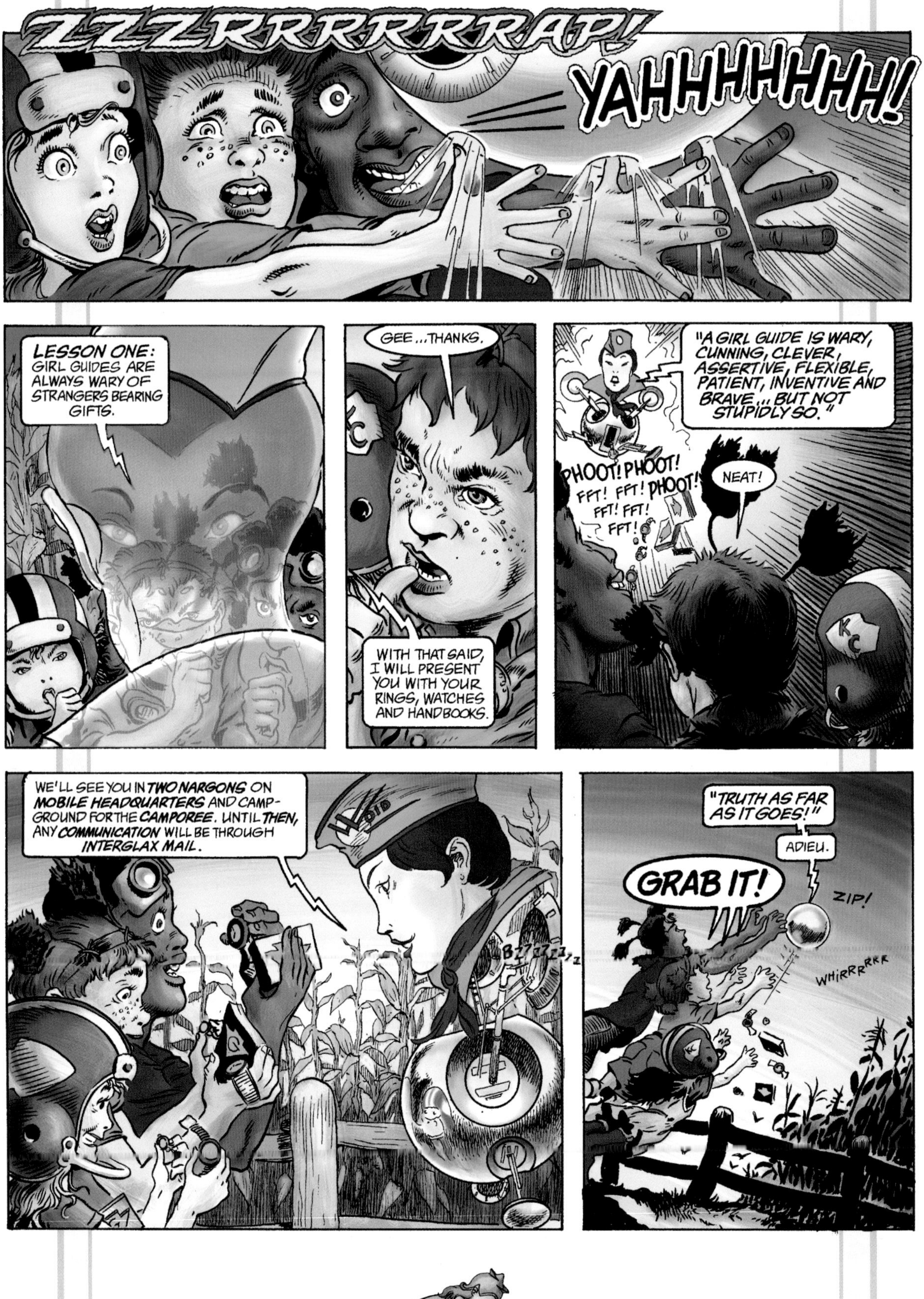
ZZZZRRRRRRRRAP!
YAHHHHHHH!
LESSON ONE: GIRL GUIDES ARE ALWAYS WARY OF STRANGERS BEARING GIFTS.
GEE... THANKS.
WITH THAT SAID, I WILL PRESENT YOU WITH YOUR RINGS, WATCHES AND HANDBOOKS.
"A GIRL GUIDE IS WARY, CUNNING, CLEVER, ASSERTIVE, FLEXIBLE, PATIENT, INVENTIVE AND BRAVE... BUT NOT STUPIDLY SO."
PHOOT! PHOOT! PHOOT!
FFT! FFT! FFT! FFT! FFT!
NEAT!
WE'LL SEE YOU IN TWO NARGONS ON MOBILE HEADQUARTERS AND CAMPGROUND FOR THE CAMPOREE. UNTIL THEN, ANY COMMUNICATION WILL BE THROUGH INTERGLAX MAIL.
"TRUTH AS FAR AS IT GOES!"
ADIEU.
GRAB IT!
ZIP!
WHIRRRRRR

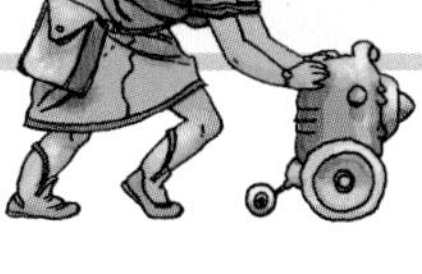

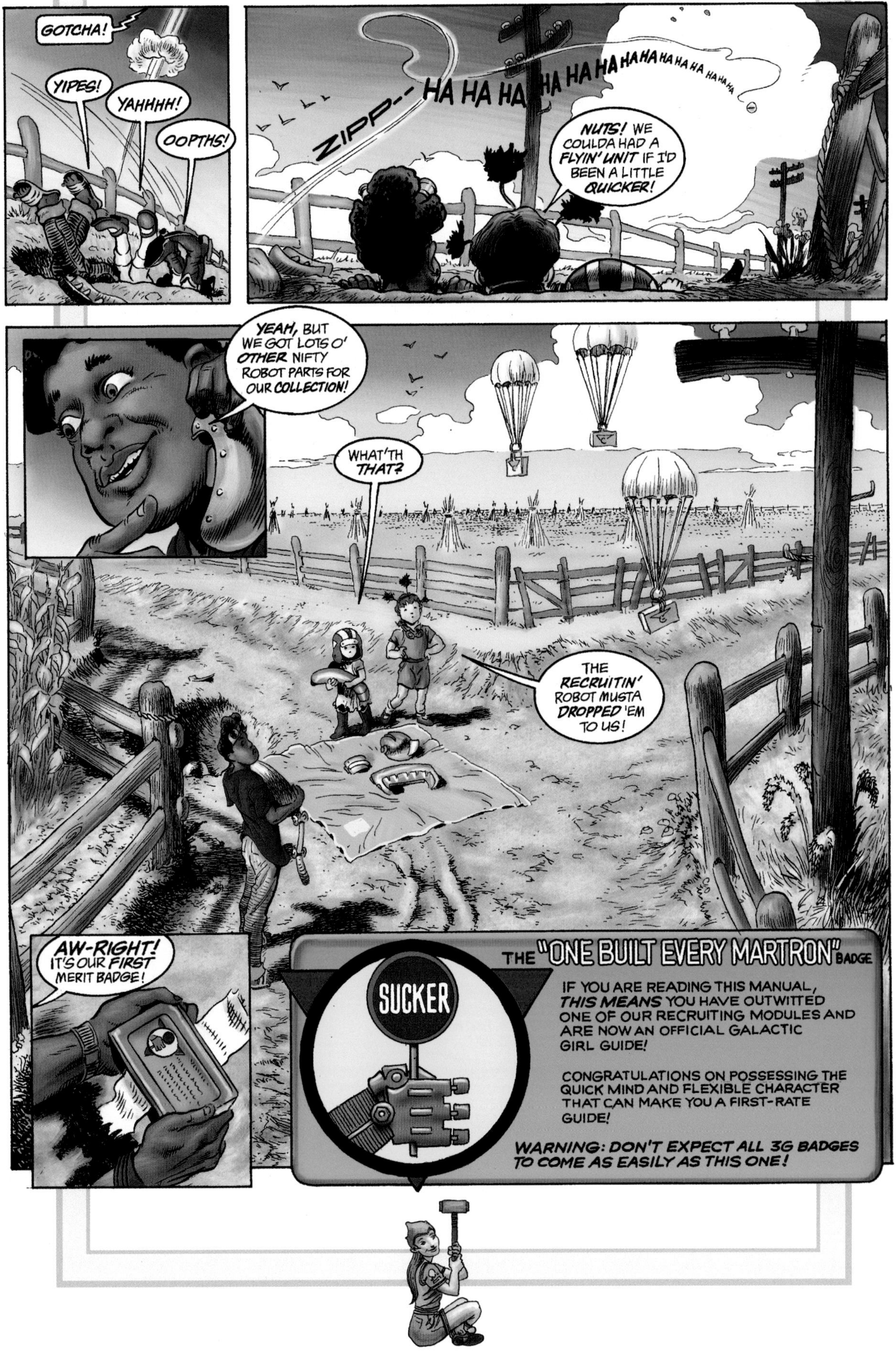
GOTCHA!
YIPES!
YAHHHH!
OOPTHS!
ZIPP-- HA HA HA HA HA HA HA HA HA HA HA HA HA HA HA
NUTS! WE COULDA HAD A FLYIN' UNIT IF I'D BEEN A LITTLE QUICKER!
YEAH, BUT WE GOT LOTS O' OTHER NIFTY ROBOT PARTS FOR OUR COLLECTION!
WHAT'TH THAT?
THE RECRUITIN' ROBOT MUSTA DROPPED 'EM TO US!
AW-RIGHT! IT'S OUR FIRST MERIT BADGE!
THE "ONE BUILT EVERY MARTRON" BADGE
SUCKER
IF YOU ARE READING THIS MANUAL, THIS MEANS YOU HAVE OUTWITTED ONE OF OUR RECRUITING MODULES AND ARE NOW AN OFFICIAL GALACTIC GIRL GUIDE!
CONGRATULATIONS ON POSSESSING THE QUICK MIND AND FLEXIBLE CHARACTER THAT CAN MAKE YOU A FIRST-RATE GUIDE!
WARNING: DON'T EXPECT ALL 3G BADGES TO COME AS EASILY AS THIS ONE!

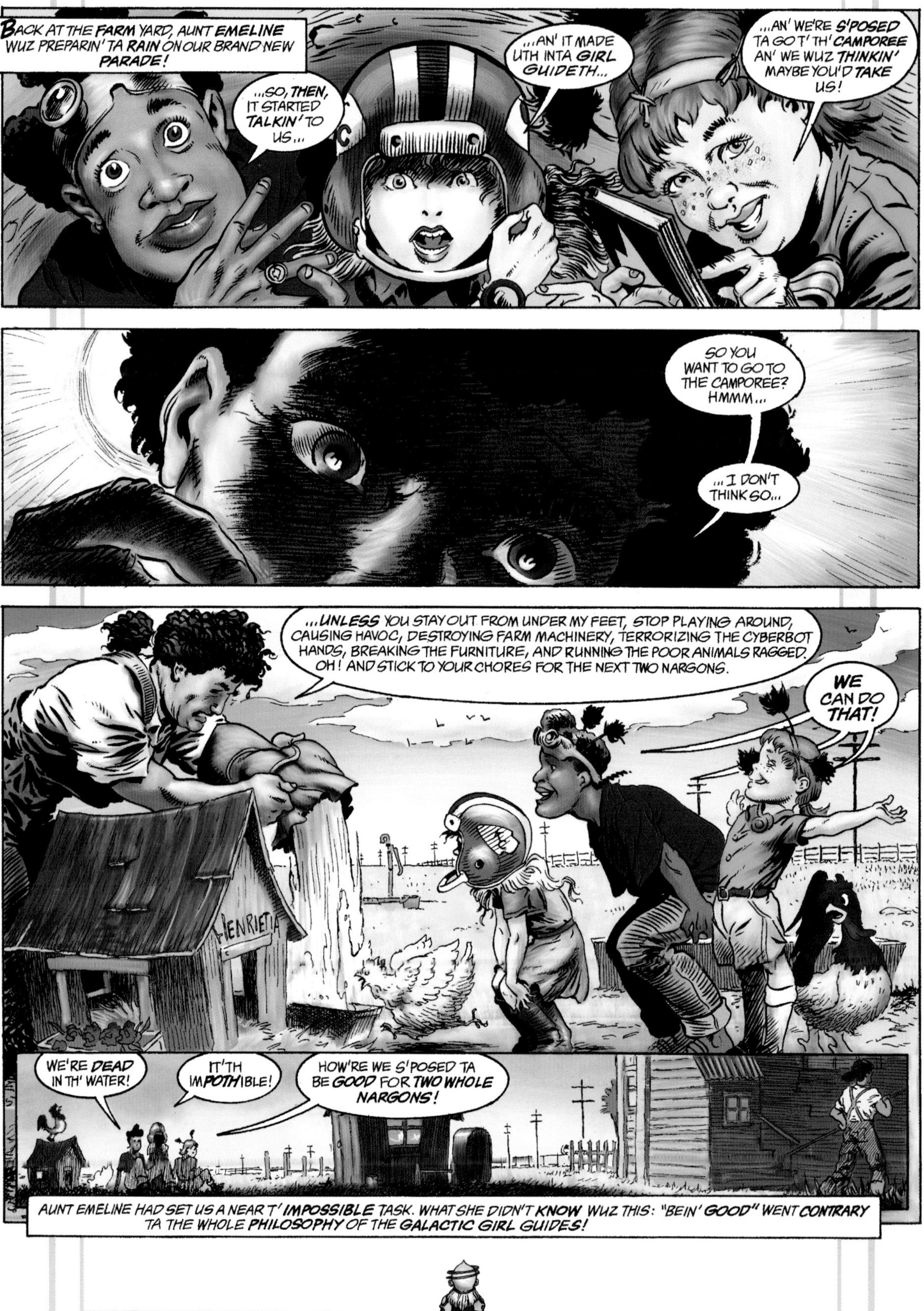
BACK AT THE FARM YARD, AUNT EMELINE WUZ PREPARIN' TA RAIN ON OUR BRAND NEW PARADE!
...SO, THEN, IT STARTED TALKIN' TO US...
...AN' IT MADE UTH INTA GIRL GUIDETH...
...AN' WE'RE S'POSED TA GO T' TH' CAMPOREE AN' WE WUZ THINKIN' MAYBE YOU'D TAKE US!
SO YOU WANT TO GO TO THE CAMPOREE? HMMM...
...I DON'T THINK SO...
...UNLESS YOU STAY OUT FROM UNDER MY FEET, STOP PLAYING AROUND, CAUSING HAVOC, DESTROYING FARM MACHINERY, TERRORIZING THE CYBERBOT HANDS, BREAKING THE FURNITURE, AND RUNNING THE POOR ANIMALS RAGGED. OH! AND STICK TO YOUR CHORES FOR THE NEXT TWO NARGONS.
WE CAN DO THAT!
HENRIETTA
WE'RE DEAD IN TH' WATER!
IT'TH IMPOTHIBLE!
HOW'RE WE S'POSED TA BE GOOD FOR TWO WHOLE NARGONS!
AUNT EMELINE HAD SET US A NEAR T' IMPOSSIBLE TASK. WHAT SHE DIDN'T KNOW WUZ THIS: "BEIN' GOOD" WENT CONTRARY TA THE WHOLE PHILOSOPHY OF THE GALACTIC GIRL GUIDES!

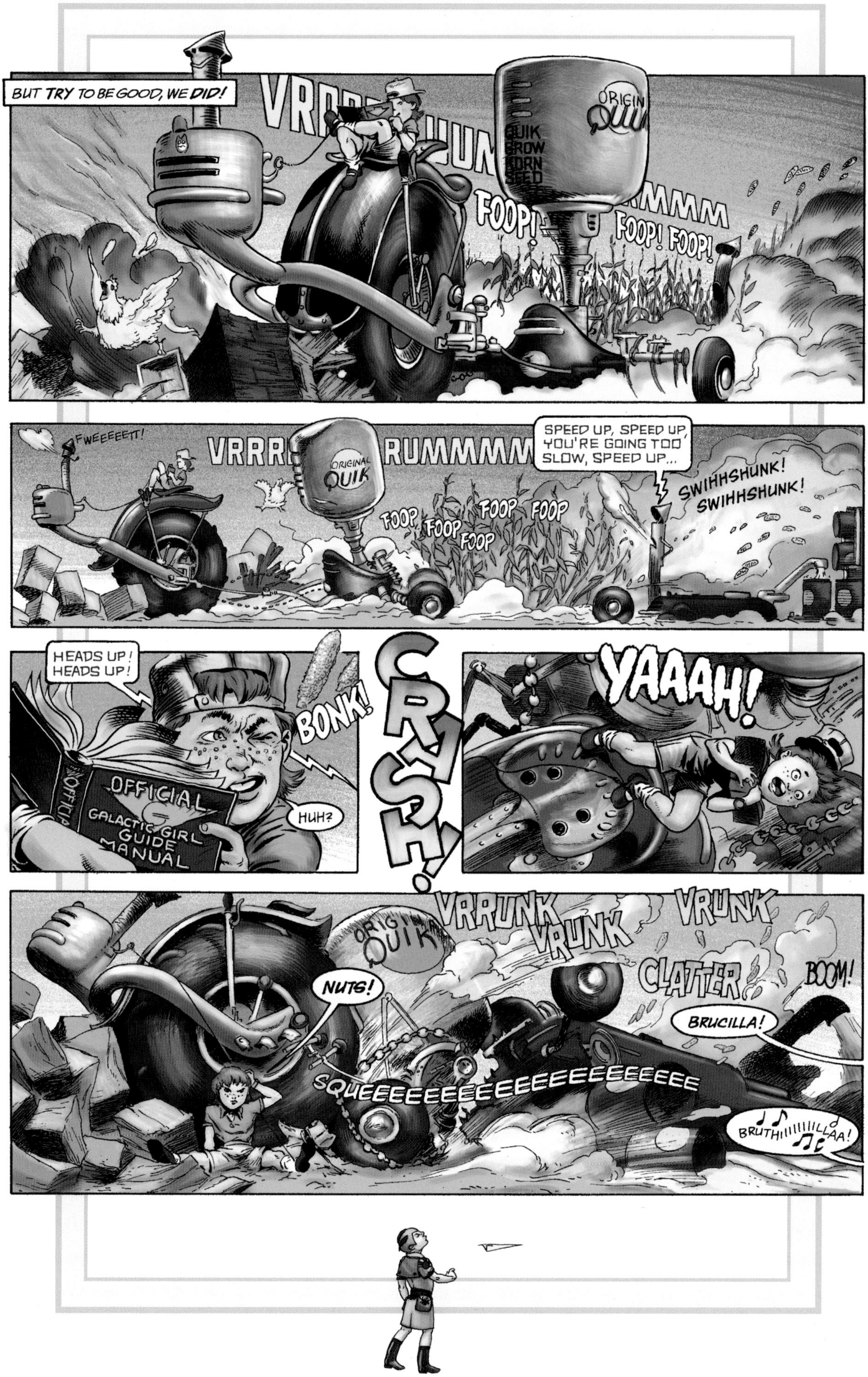

BUT TRY TO BE GOOD, WE DID!
QUIK GROW KORN SEED
FOOP!
FOOP! FOOP!
FWEEEEETT!
VRRR
RUMMMM
ORIGINAL QUIK
FOOP FOOP FOOP FOOP FOOP
SPEED UP, SPEED UP, YOU'RE GOING TOO SLOW, SPEED UP...
SWIHHSHUNK! SWIHHSHUNK!
HEADS UP! HEADS UP!
BONK!
OFFICIAL GALACTIC GIRL GUIDE MANUAL
HUH?
CRASH!
YAAAH!
VRRUNK VRUNK VRUNK
CLATTER
BOOM!
NUTS!
BRUCILLA!
SQUEEEEEEEEEEEEEEEEEEEEEE
BRUTHIIIIIIILLAA!

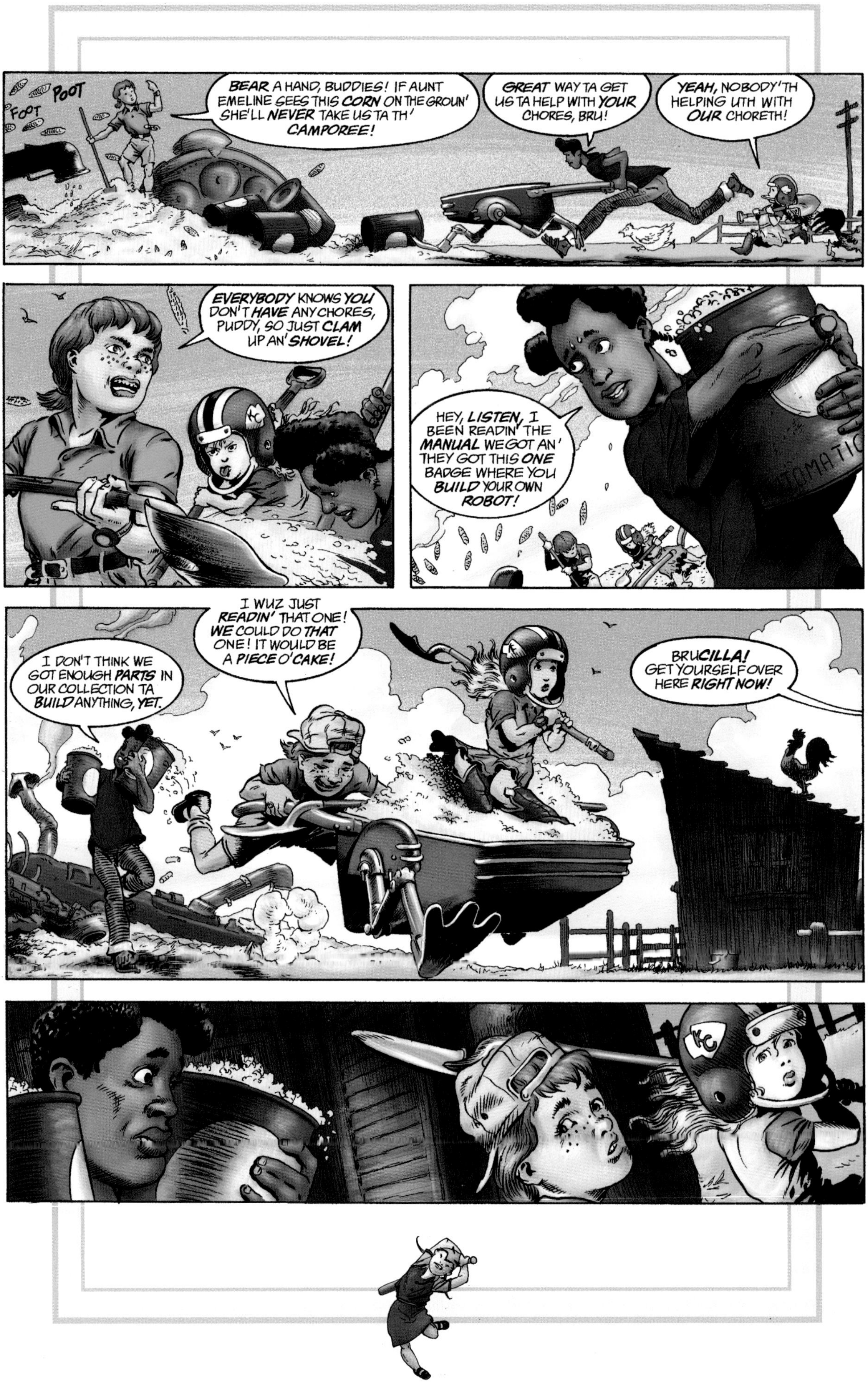
POOT
FOOT
BEAR A HAND, BUDDIES! IF AUNT EMELINE SEES THIS CORN ON THE GROUN' SHE'LL NEVER TAKE US TA TH' CAMPOREE!
GREAT WAY TA GET US TA HELP WITH YOUR CHORES, BRU!
YEAH, NOBODY'TH HELPING UTH WITH OUR CHORETH!
EVERYBODY KNOWS YOU DON'T HAVE ANY CHORES, PUDDY, SO JUST CLAM UP AN' SHOVEL!
HEY, LISTEN, I BEEN READIN' THE MANUAL WE GOT AN' THEY GOT THIS ONE BADGE WHERE YOU BUILD YOUR OWN ROBOT!
I DON'T THINK WE GOT ENOUGH PARTS IN OUR COLLECTION TA BUILD ANYTHING, YET.
I WUZ JUST READIN' THAT ONE! WE COULD DO THAT ONE! IT WOULD BE A PIECE O'CAKE!
BRUCILLA! GET YOURSELF OVER HERE RIGHT NOW!

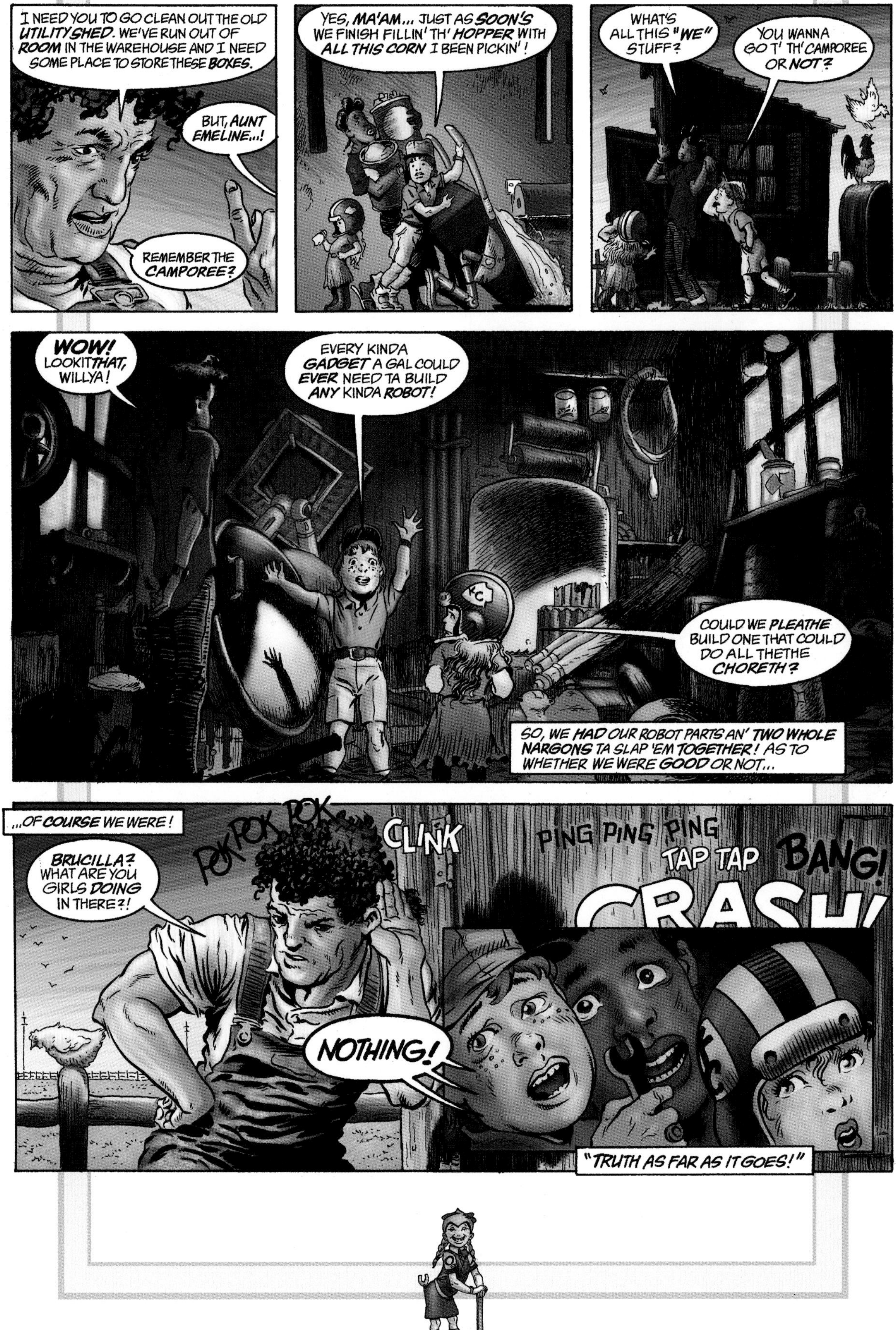
I NEED YOU TO GO CLEAN OUT THE OLD UTILITY SHED. WE'VE RUN OUT OF ROOM IN THE WAREHOUSE AND I NEED SOME PLACE TO STORE THESE BOXES.
BUT, AUNT EMELINE...!
REMEMBER THE CAMPOREE?
YES, MA'AM... JUST AS SOON'S WE FINISH FILLIN' TH' HOPPER WITH ALL THIS CORN I BEEN PICKIN'!
WHAT'S ALL THIS "WE" STUFF?
YOU WANNA GO T' TH' CAMPOREE OR NOT?
WOW! LOOKIT THAT, WILLYA!
EVERY KINDA GADGET A GAL COULD EVER NEED TA BUILD ANY KINDA ROBOT!
COULD WE PLEATHE BUILD ONE THAT COULD DO ALL THETHE CHORETH?
SO, WE HAD OUR ROBOT PARTS AN' TWO WHOLE NARGONS TA SLAP 'EM TOGETHER! AS TO WHETHER WE WERE GOOD OR NOT...
...OF COURSE WE WERE!
POK POK POK
CLINK
PING PING PING
TAP TAP
BANG!
CRASH!
BRUCILLA? WHAT ARE YOU GIRLS DOING IN THERE?!
NOTHING!
"TRUTH AS FAR AS IT GOES!"

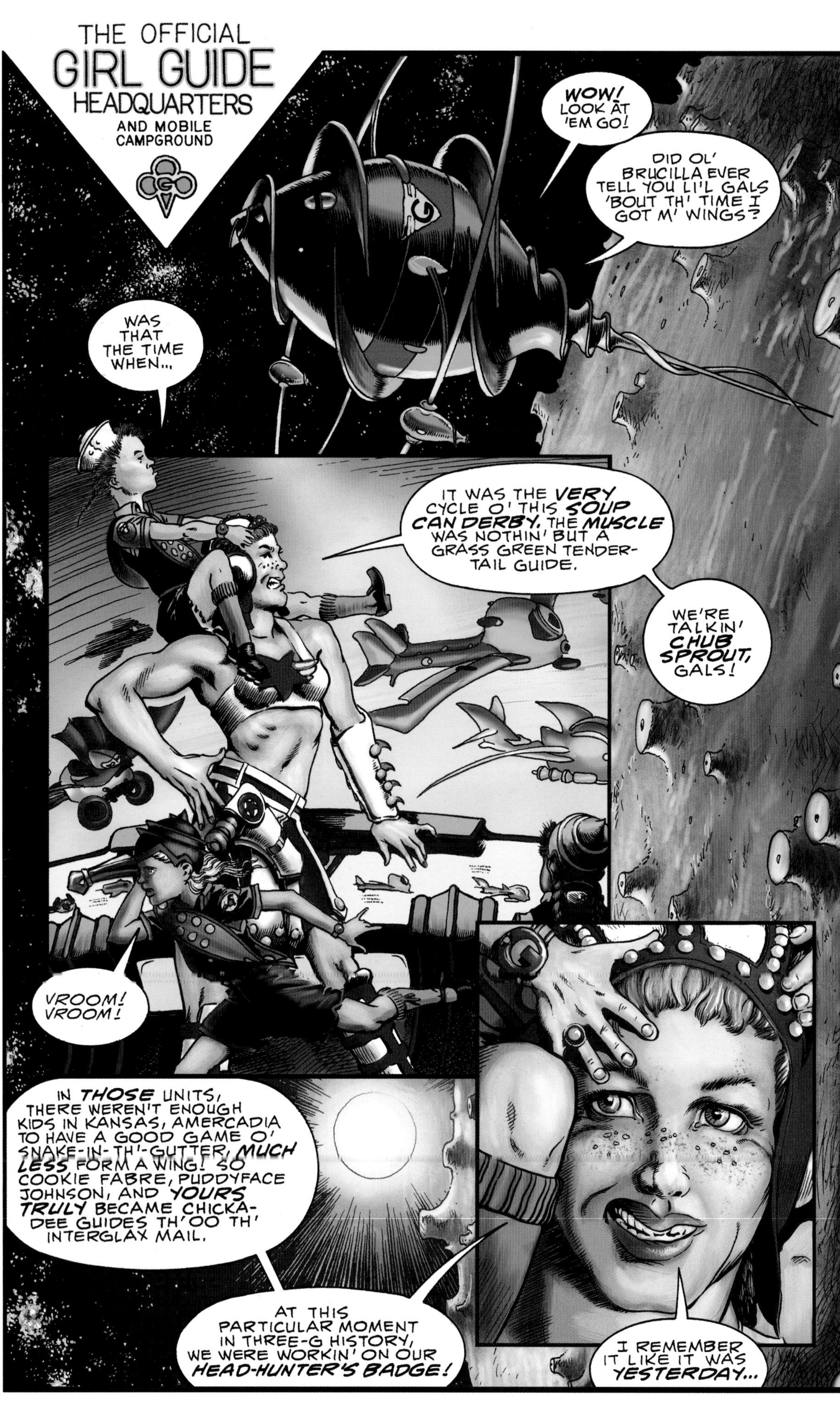
THE OFFICIAL GIRL GUIDE HEADQUARTERS AND MOBILE CAMPGROUND
WOW! LOOK AT 'EM GO!
DID OL' BRUCILLA EVER TELL YOU LI'L GALS 'BOUT TH' TIME I GOT M' WINGS?
WAS THAT THE TIME WHEN...
IT WAS THE VERY CYCLE O' THIS SOUP CAN DERBY. THE MUSCLE WAS NOTHIN' BUT A GRASS GREEN TENDER-TAIL GUIDE.
WE'RE TALKIN' CHUB SPROUT, GALS!
VROOM! VROOM!
IN THOSE UNITS, THERE WEREN'T ENOUGH KIDS IN KANSAS, AMERCADIA TO HAVE A GOOD GAME O' SNAKE-IN-TH'-GUTTER, MUCH LESS FORM A WING! SO COOKIE FABRE, PUDDYFACE JOHNSON, AND YOURS TRULY BECAME CHICKA-DEE GUIDES TH'OO TH' INTERGLAX MAIL.
AT THIS PARTICULAR MOMENT IN THREE-G HISTORY, WE WERE WORKIN' ON OUR HEAD-HUNTER'S BADGE!
I REMEMBER IT LIKE IT WAS YESTERDAY...

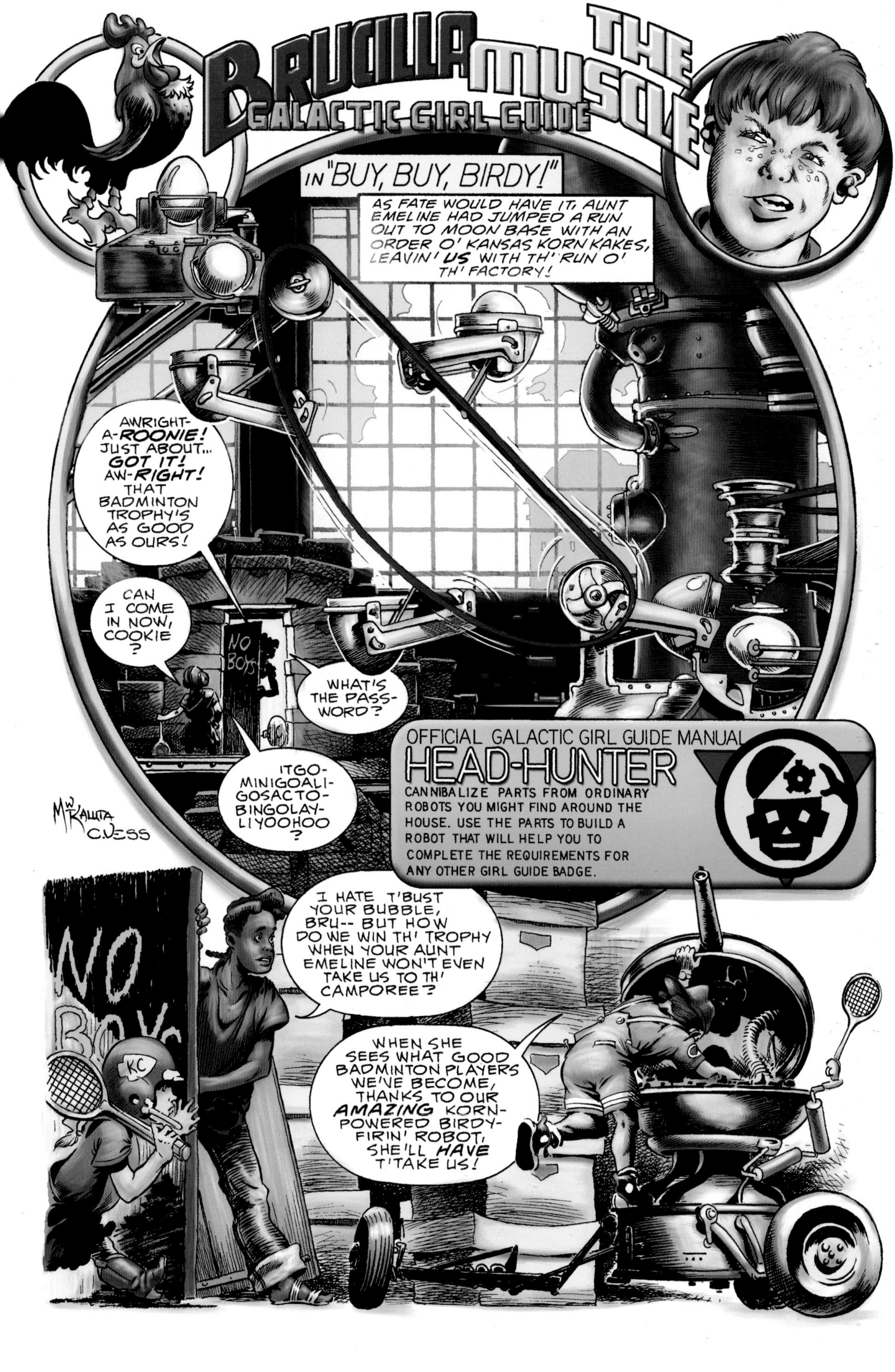

BRUCILLA THE MUSCLE
GALACTIC GIRL GUIDE
IN "BUY, BUY, BIRDY!"
AS FATE WOULD HAVE IT, AUNT EMELINE HAD JUMPED A RUN OUT TO MOON BASE WITH AN ORDER O' KANSAS KORN KAKES, LEAVIN' US WITH TH' RUN O' TH' FACTORY!
AWRIGHT-A-ROONIE! JUST ABOUT... GOT IT! AW-RIGHT! THAT BADMINTON TROPHY'S AS GOOD AS OURS!
CAN I COME IN NOW, COOKIE?
NO BOYS
WHAT'S THE PASS-WORD?
ITGO-MINIGOALI-GOSACTO-BINGOLAY-LIYOOHOO?
M.W. KALUTA
C.VESS
OFFICIAL GALACTIC GIRL GUIDE MANUAL
HEAD-HUNTER
CANNIBALIZE PARTS FROM ORDINARY ROBOTS YOU MIGHT FIND AROUND THE HOUSE. USE THE PARTS TO BUILD A ROBOT THAT WILL HELP YOU TO COMPLETE THE REQUIREMENTS FOR ANY OTHER GIRL GUIDE BADGE.
I HATE T'BUST YOUR BUBBLE, BRU-- BUT HOW DO WE WIN TH' TROPHY WHEN YOUR AUNT EMELINE WON'T EVEN TAKE US TO TH' CAMPOREE?
NO BOYS
KC
WHEN SHE SEES WHAT GOOD BADMINTON PLAYERS WE'VE BECOME, THANKS TO OUR AMAZING KORN-POWERED BIRDY-FIRIN' ROBOT, SHE'LL HAVE T'TAKE US!

HEY, PUDDY! TAKE TH' RACKET AN' STAND BY TH' DART BOARD!

PT-OOP!

SPONG!

uh-oh.

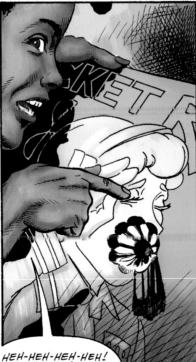

HEH-HEH-HEH-HEH! LOOK, BRU! TEN POINTS FOR TH' BOY RANGER!

THIS IS GREAT! BRUCILLA'S ALL NEW KORN-POWERED BIRDY-FIRIN' RANGER-ROASTIN' ROBOT! HEY! WE C'N FILL 'ER UP WITH EGGS 'N' WHEN TH' RANGERS HEAD FOR TH' TOONAMENT WE'LL BUSHWACK TH' GOODY-TWO-BOOTS BIF-BAP-BAM! RANGER OMELET!

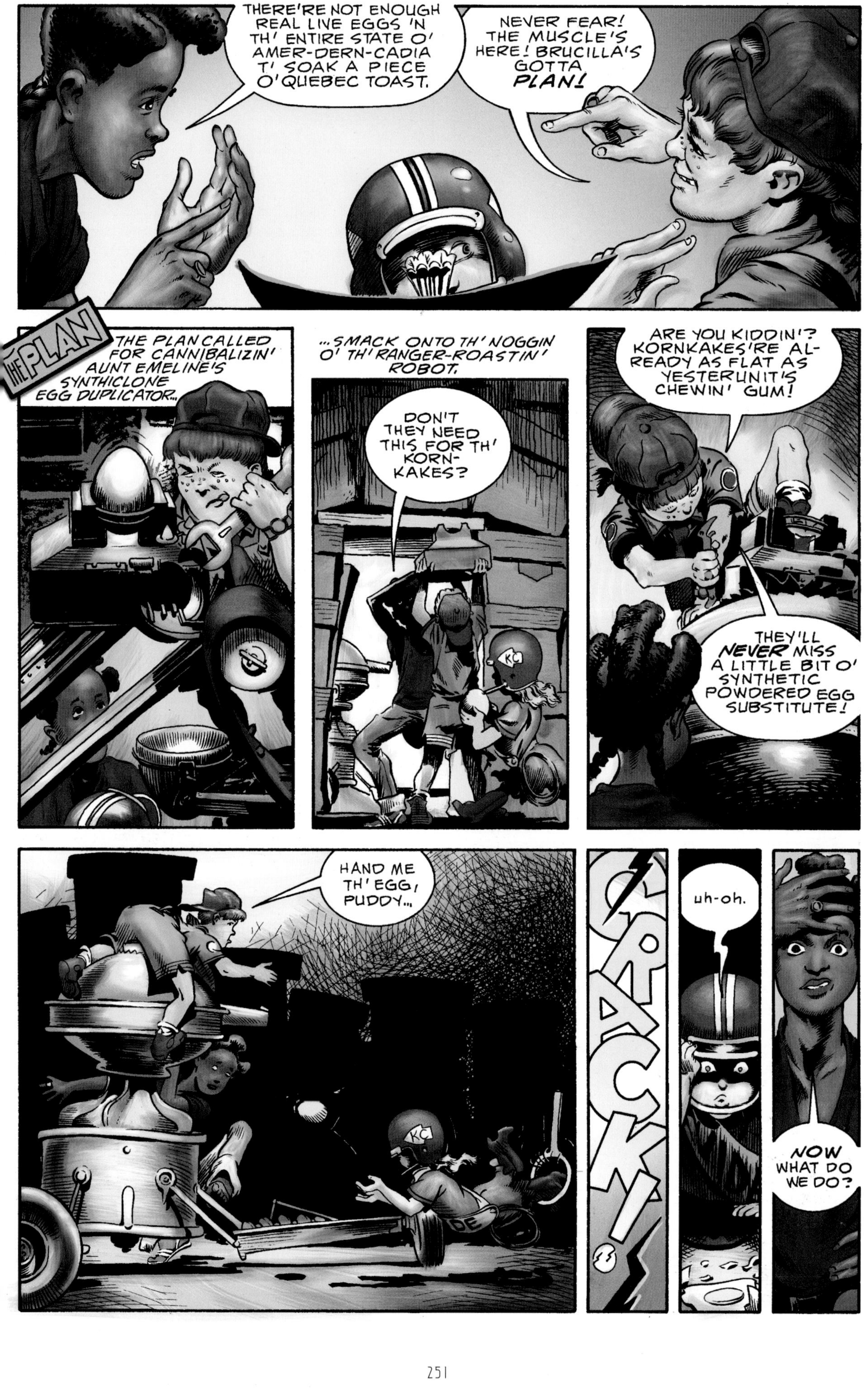

THERE'RE NOT ENOUGH REAL LIVE EGGS 'N TH' ENTIRE STATE O' AMER-DERN-CADIA T' SOAK A PIECE O'QUEBEC TOAST.
NEVER FEAR! THE MUSCLE'S HERE! BRUCILLA'S GOTTA PLAN!
THE PLAN
THE PLAN CALLED FOR CANNIBALIZIN' AUNT EMELINE'S SYNTHICLONE EGG DUPLICATOR...
...SMACK ONTO TH' NOGGIN O' TH' RANGER-ROASTIN' ROBOT.
DON'T THEY NEED THIS FOR TH' KORN-KAKES?
ARE YOU KIDDIN'? KORNKAKES'RE AL-READY AS FLAT AS YESTERUNIT'S CHEWIN' GUM!
THEY'LL NEVER MISS A LITTLE BIT O' SYNTHETIC POWDERED EGG SUBSTITUTE!
HAND ME TH' EGG, PUDDY...
CRACK!
uh-oh.
NOW WHAT DO WE DO?

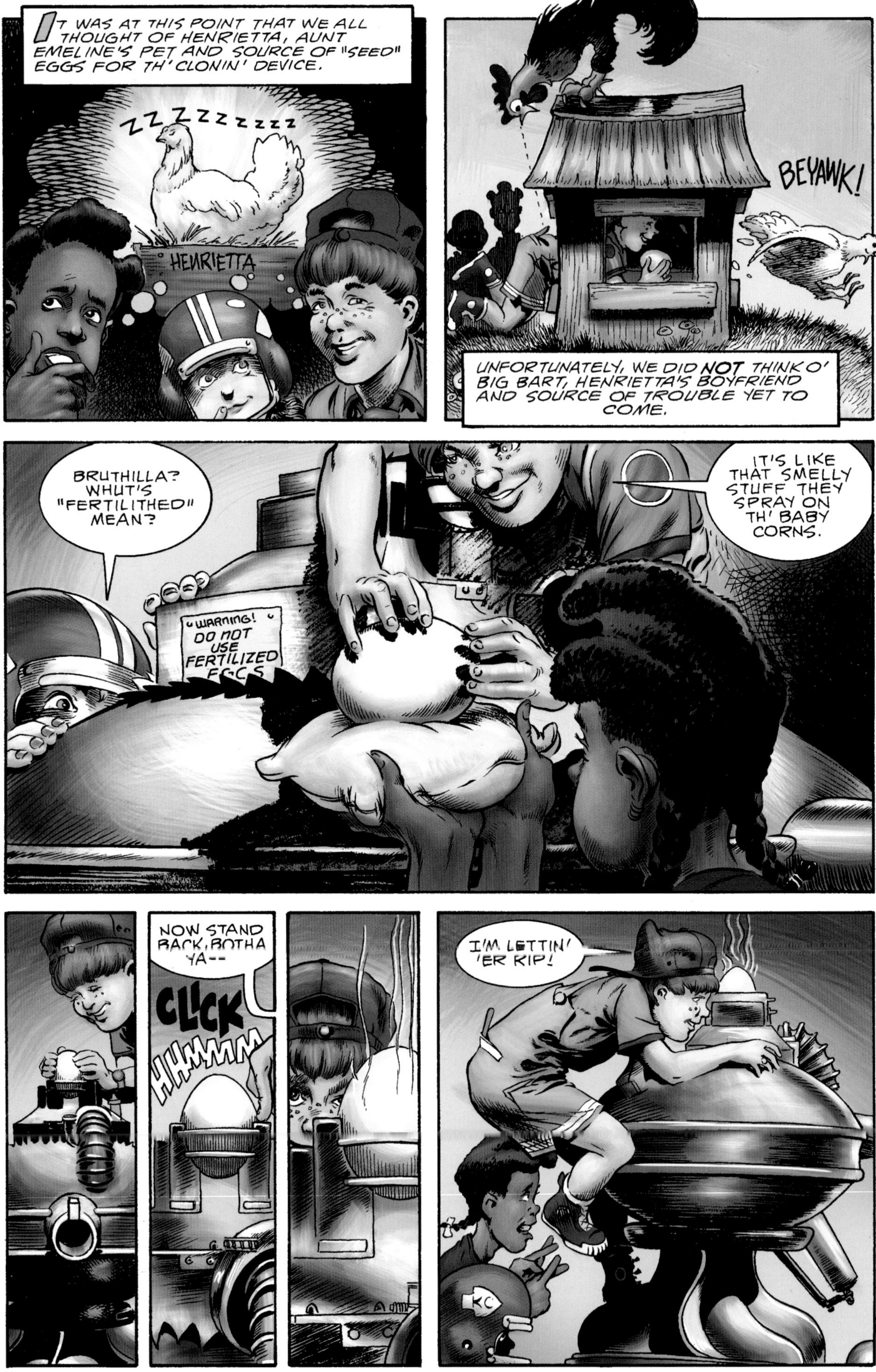
IT WAS AT THIS POINT THAT WE ALL THOUGHT OF HENRIETTA, AUNT EMELINE'S PET AND SOURCE OF "SEED" EGGS FOR TH' CLONIN' DEVICE.
ZZZZZZZZZ
HENRIETTA
BEYAWK!
UNFORTUNATELY, WE DID NOT THINK O' BIG BART, HENRIETTA'S BOYFRIEND AND SOURCE OF TROUBLE YET TO COME.
BRUTHILLA? WHUT'S "FERTILITHED" MEAN?
IT'S LIKE THAT SMELLY STUFF THEY SPRAY ON TH' BABY CORNS.
WARNING! DO NOT USE FERTILIZED EGGS
NOW STAND BACK, BOTHA YA--
CLICK
HHMMMM
I'M LETTIN' 'ER RIP!
KC

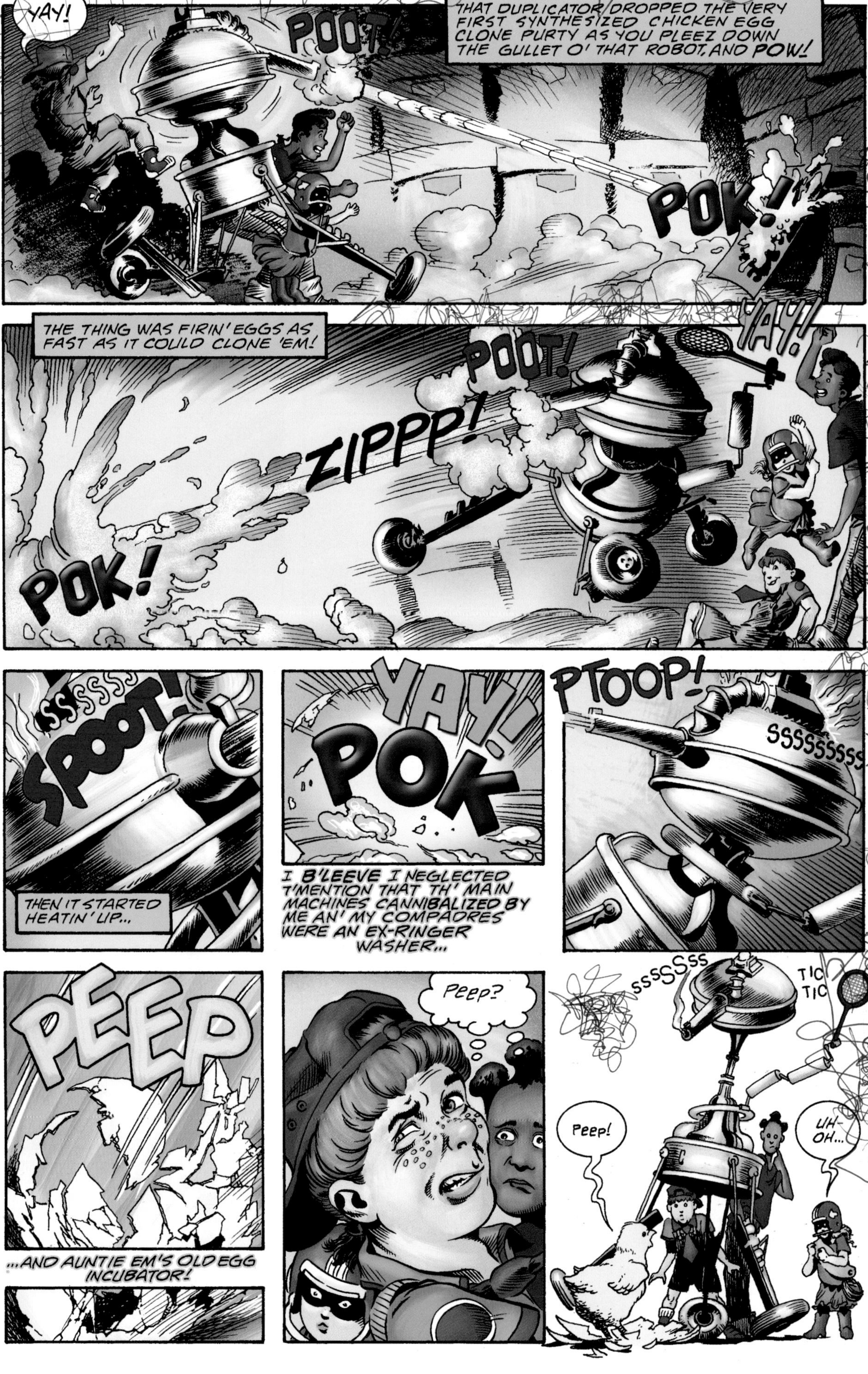
YAY!
POOT!
THAT DUPLICATOR DROPPED THE VERY FIRST SYNTHESIZED CHICKEN EGG CLONE PURTY AS YOU PLEEZ DOWN THE GULLET O' THAT ROBOT, AND POW!
POK!
THE THING WAS FIRIN' EGGS AS FAST AS IT COULD CLONE 'EM!
YAY!
POOT!
ZIPPPP!
POK!
SSSSSS
SPOOT!
THEN IT STARTED HEATIN' UP...
YAY!
POK
I B'LEEVE I NEGLECTED T'MENTION THAT TH' MAIN MACHINES CANNIBALIZED BY ME AN' MY COMPADRES WERE AN EX-RINGER WASHER...
PTOOP!
SSSSSSSSS
PEEP
...AND AUNTIE EM'S OLD EGG INCUBATOR!
Peep?
SSSSSSS
TIC TIC
Peep!
UH-OH...

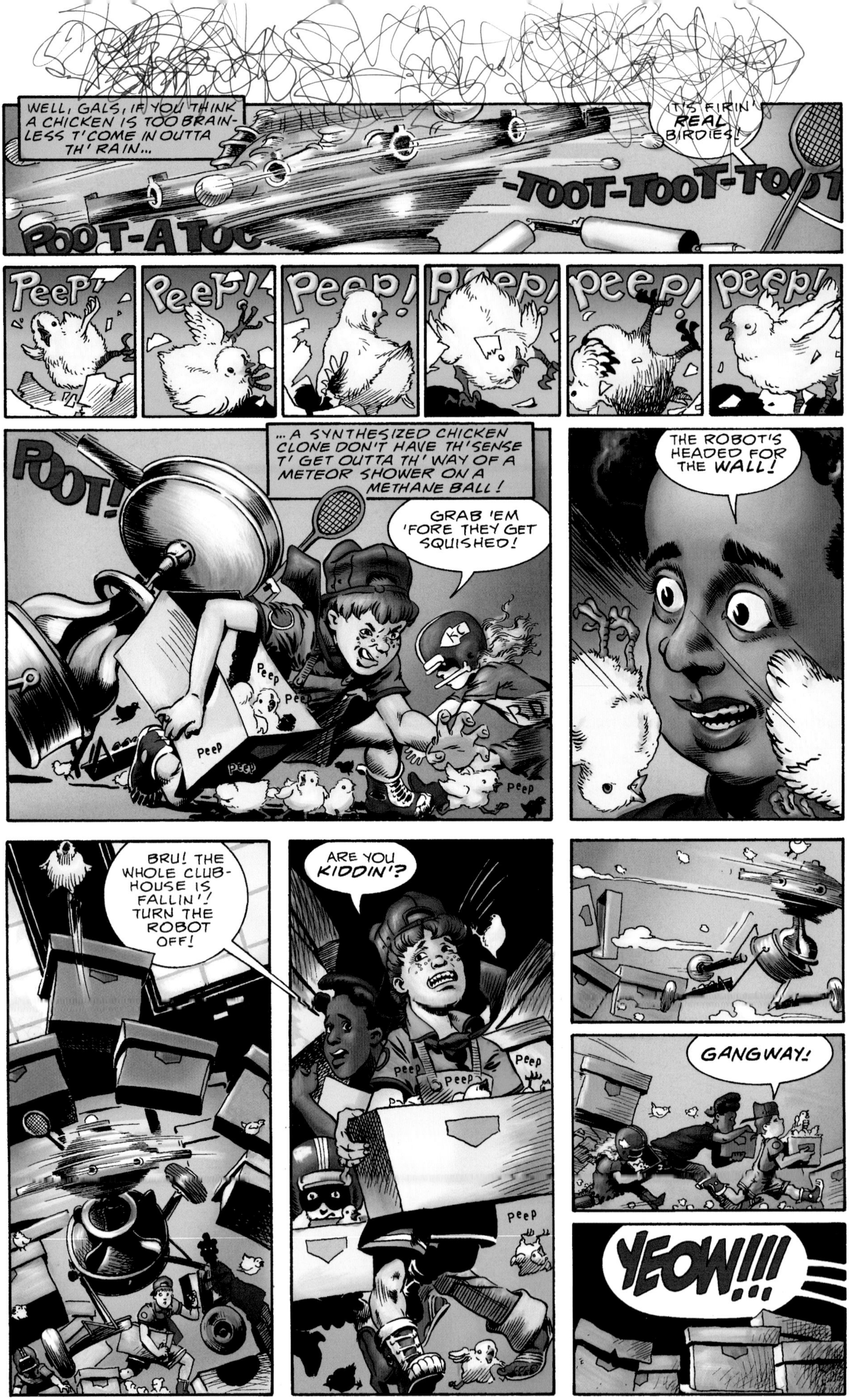

WELL, GALS, IF YOU THINK A CHICKEN IS TOO BRAIN-LESS T'COME IN OUTTA TH' RAIN...
IT'S FIRIN' REAL BIRDIES!
-TOOT-TOOT-TOOT
POOT-A TOO
Peep!
Peep!
Peep!
Peep!
peep!
peep!
...A SYNTHESIZED CHICKEN CLONE DON'T HAVE TH' SENSE T' GET OUTTA TH' WAY OF A METEOR SHOWER ON A METHANE BALL!
POOT!
GRAB 'EM 'FORE THEY GET SQUISHED!
Peep
peep
peep
THE ROBOT'S HEADED FOR THE WALL!
BRU! THE WHOLE CLUB-HOUSE IS FALLIN'! TURN THE ROBOT OFF!
ARE YOU KIDDIN'?
peep
peep
peep
GANGWAY!
YEOW!!!

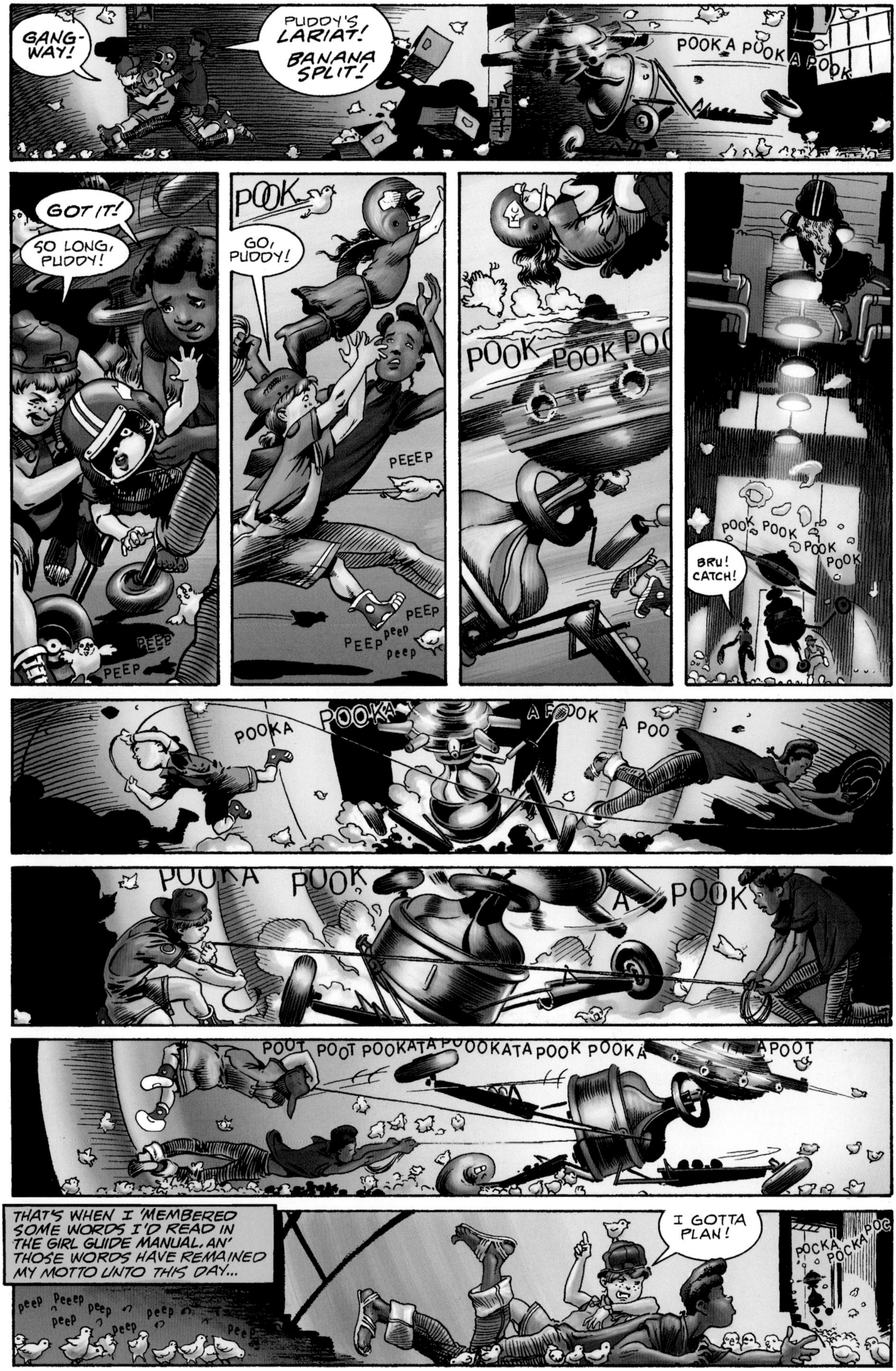
GANG-WAY!
PUDDY'S LARIAT! BANANA SPLIT!
POOK A POOK A POOK
GOT IT!
SO LONG, PUDDY!
PEEP
PEEP
POOK
GO, PUDDY!
PEEEP
PEEP
PEEP peep peep
POOK POOK POO
POOK POOK POOK POOK
BRU! CATCH!
POOKA POOKA POOK A POO
POOKA POOK A POOK
POOT POOT POOKATA POOOKATA POOK POOKA APOOT
THAT'S WHEN I 'MEMBERED SOME WORDS I'D READ IN THE GIRL GUIDE MANUAL, AN' THOSE WORDS HAVE REMAINED MY MOTTO UNTO THIS DAY...
I GOTTA PLAN!
POCKA POCKA POC
peep Peeep peep peep peep peep

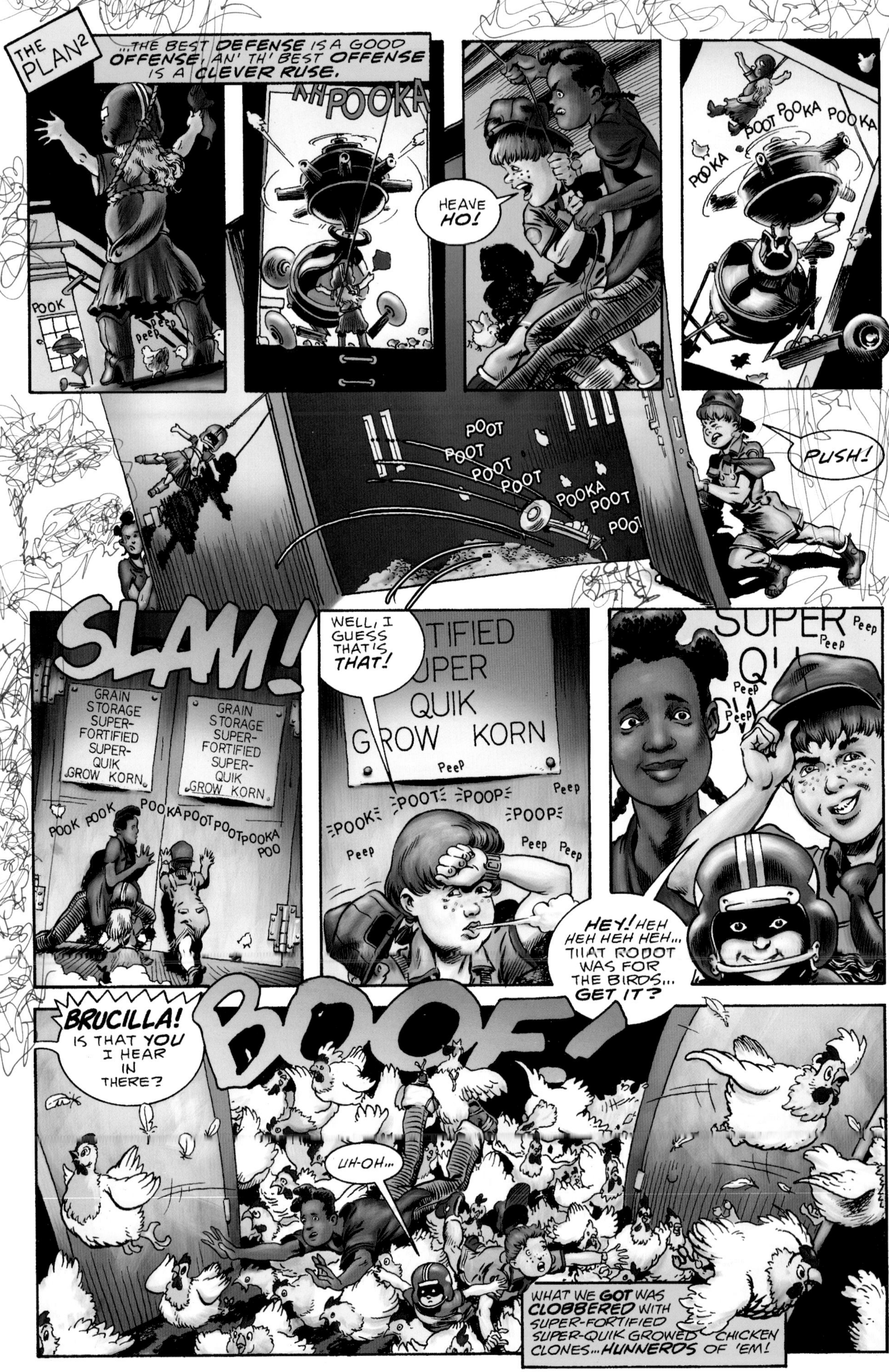
THE PLAN²
...THE BEST DEFENSE IS A GOOD OFFENSE, AN' TH' BEST OFFENSE IS A CLEVER RUSE.
POOK
Peep Peep
NH POOKA
HEAVE HO!
POOKA POOT POOKA POOKA
POOT POOT POOT POOT POOKA POOT POO
PUSH!
SLAM!
GRAIN STORAGE SUPER-FORTIFIED SUPER-QUIK GROW KORN
GRAIN STORAGE SUPER-FORTIFIED SUPER-QUIK GROW KORN
POOK POOK POOKA POOT POOT POOKA POO
WELL, I GUESS THAT'S THAT!
TIFIED UPER QUIK GROW KORN
POOT POOP POOK POOP Peep
SUPER Peep
HEY! HEH HEH HEH HEH... THAT ROBOT WAS FOR THE BIRDS... GET IT?
BRUCILLA! IS THAT YOU I HEAR IN THERE?
BOOF!
UH-OH...
WHAT WE GOT WAS CLOBBERED WITH SUPER-FORTIFIED SUPER-QUIK GROWED CHICKEN CLONES... HUNNERDS OF 'EM!

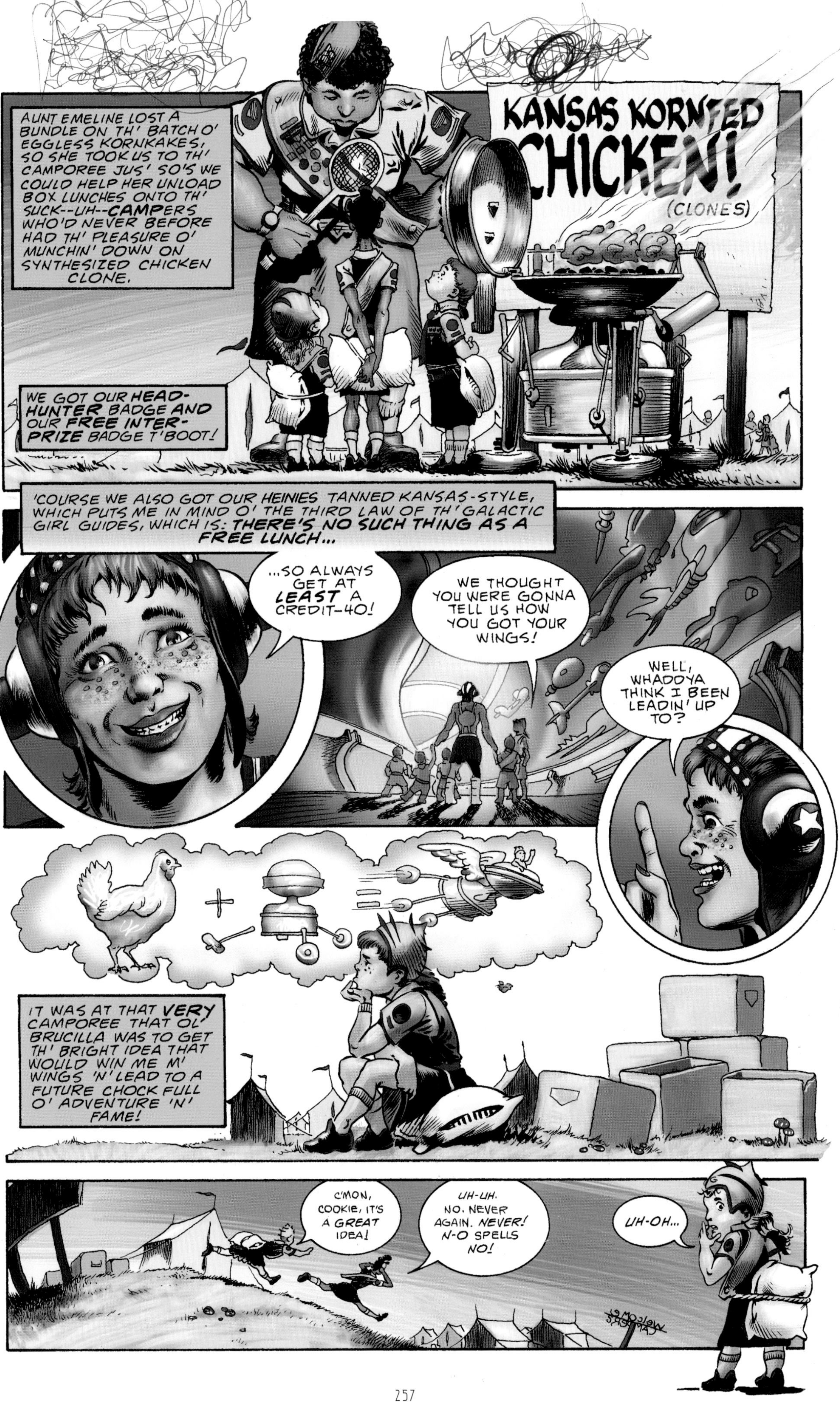

AUNT EMELINE LOST A BUNDLE ON TH' BATCH O' EGGLESS KORNKAKES, SO SHE TOOK US TO TH' CAMPOREE JUS' SO'S WE COULD HELP HER UNLOAD BOX LUNCHES ONTO TH' SUCK--UH--CAMPERS WHO'D NEVER BEFORE HAD TH' PLEASURE O' MUNCHIN' DOWN ON SYNTHESIZED CHICKEN CLONE.
KANSAS KORNFED CHICKEN!
(CLONES)
WE GOT OUR HEAD-HUNTER BADGE AND OUR FREE INTER-PRIZE BADGE T'BOOT!
'COURSE WE ALSO GOT OUR HEINIES TANNED KANSAS-STYLE, WHICH PUTS ME IN MIND O' THE THIRD LAW OF TH' GALACTIC GIRL GUIDES, WHICH IS: THERE'S NO SUCH THING AS A FREE LUNCH...
...SO ALWAYS GET AT LEAST A CREDIT-40!
WE THOUGHT YOU WERE GONNA TELL US HOW YOU GOT YOUR WINGS!
WELL, WHADDYA THINK I BEEN LEADIN' UP TO?
IT WAS AT THAT VERY CAMPOREE THAT OL' BRUCILLA WAS TO GET TH' BRIGHT IDEA THAT WOULD WIN ME M' WINGS 'N' LEAD TO A FUTURE CHOCK FULL O' ADVENTURE 'N' FAME!
C'MON, COOKIE, IT'S A GREAT IDEA!
UH-UH. NO. NEVER AGAIN. NEVER! N-O SPELLS NO!
UH-OH...

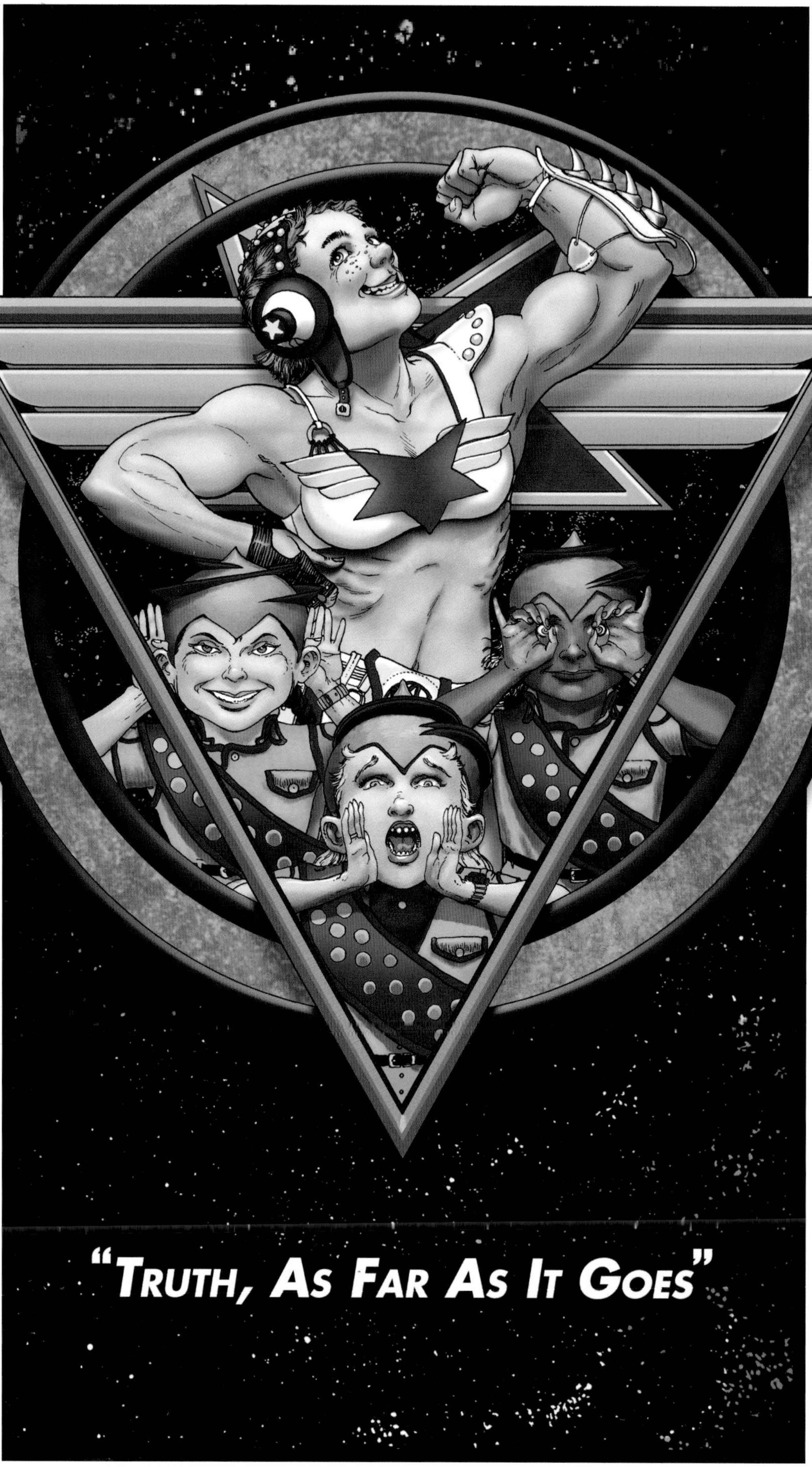
"Truth, As Far As It Goes"

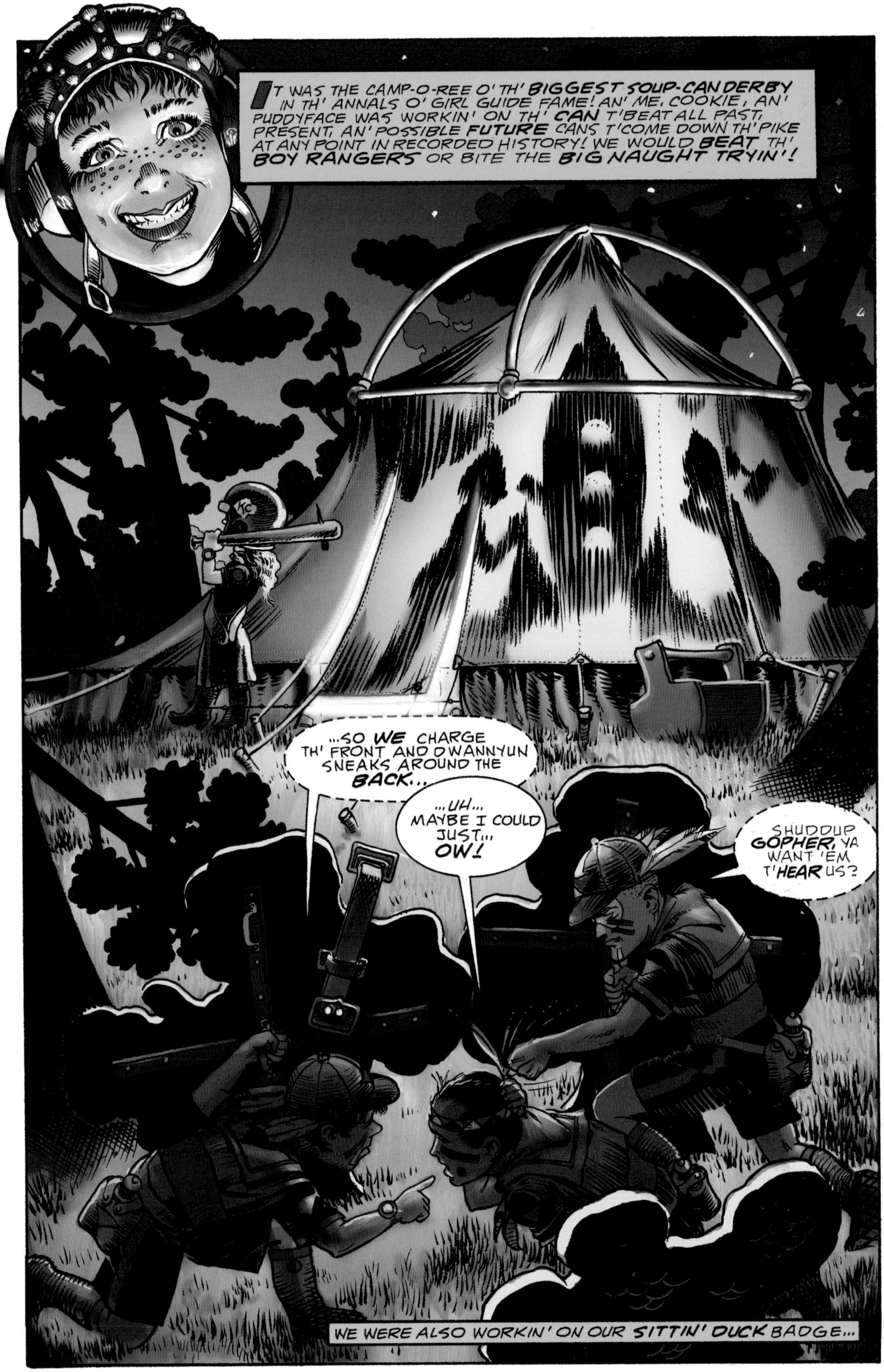
IT WAS THE CAMP-O-REE O' TH' BIGGEST SOUP-CAN DERBY IN TH' ANNALS O' GIRL GUIDE FAME! AN' ME, COOKIE, AN' PUDDYFACE WAS WORKIN' ON TH' CAN T'BEAT ALL PAST, PRESENT, AN' POSSIBLE FUTURE CANS T'COME DOWN TH' PIKE AT ANY POINT IN RECORDED HISTORY! WE WOULD BEAT TH' BOY RANGERS OR BITE THE BIG NAUGHT TRYIN'!
...SO WE CHARGE TH' FRONT AND DWANNYUN SNEAKS AROUND THE BACK...
...UH... MAYBE I COULD JUST... OW!
SHUDDUP GOPHER, YA WANT 'EM T'HEAR US?
WE WERE ALSO WORKIN' ON OUR SITTIN' DUCK BADGE...

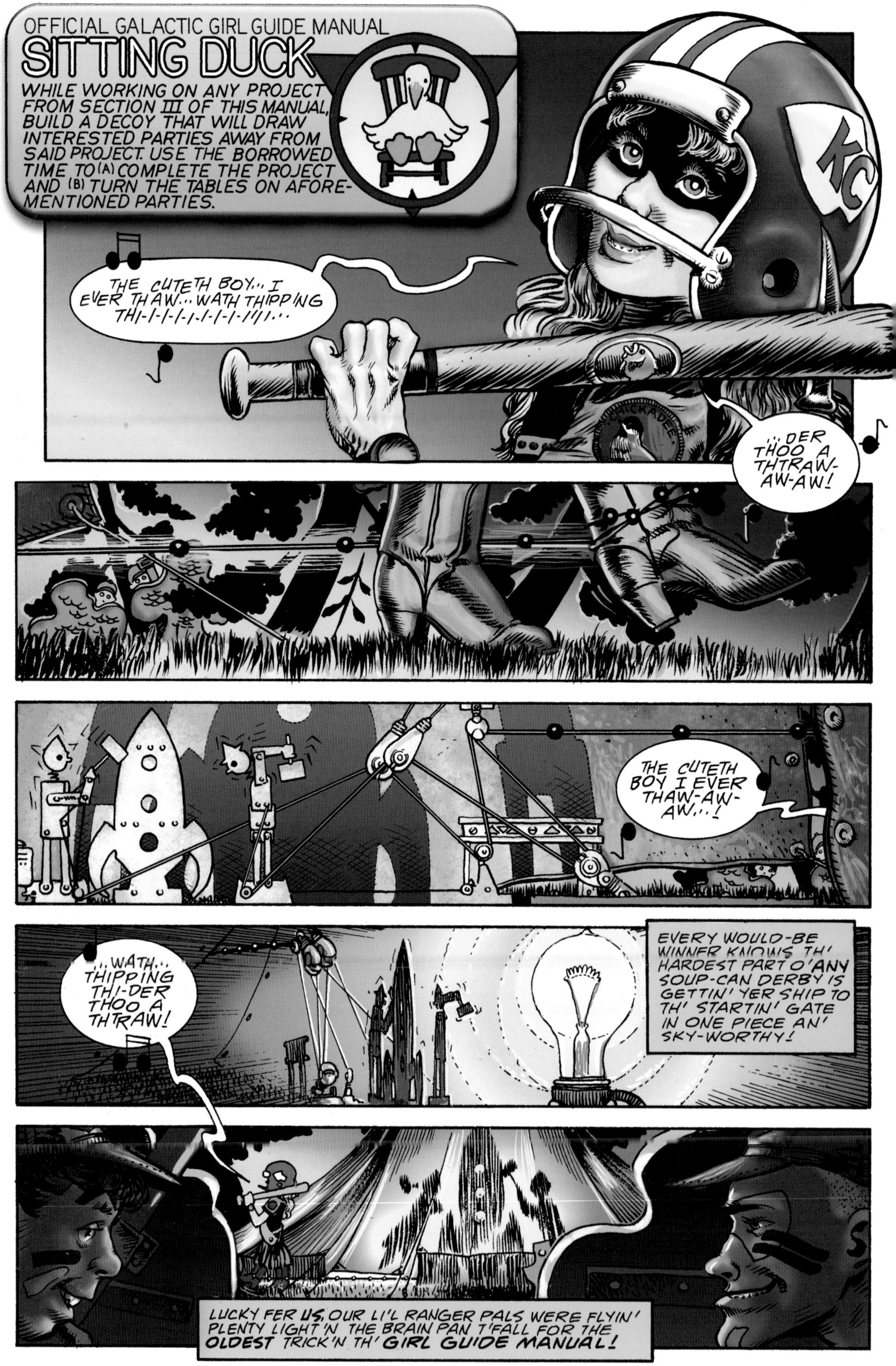

OFFICIAL GALACTIC GIRL GUIDE MANUAL
SITTING DUCK
WHILE WORKING ON ANY PROJECT FROM SECTION III OF THIS MANUAL, BUILD A DECOY THAT WILL DRAW INTERESTED PARTIES AWAY FROM SAID PROJECT. USE THE BORROWED TIME TO (A) COMPLETE THE PROJECT AND (B) TURN THE TABLES ON AFORE-MENTIONED PARTIES.
THE CUTETH BOY... I EVER THAW... WATH THIPPING THI-I-I-I-I-I-I-I-III...
...DER THOO A THRAW-AW-AW!
THE CUTETH BOY I EVER THAW-AW-AW...!
...WATH... THIPPING THI-DER THOO A THRAW!
EVERY WOULD-BE WINNER KNOWS TH' HARDEST PART O' ANY SOUP-CAN DERBY IS GETTIN' YER SHIP TO TH' STARTIN' GATE IN ONE PIECE AN' SKY-WORTHY!
LUCKY FER US, OUR LI'L RANGER PALS WERE FLYIN' PLENTY LIGHT 'N THE BRAIN PAN T'FALL FOR THE OLDEST TRICK 'N TH' GIRL GUIDE MANUAL!

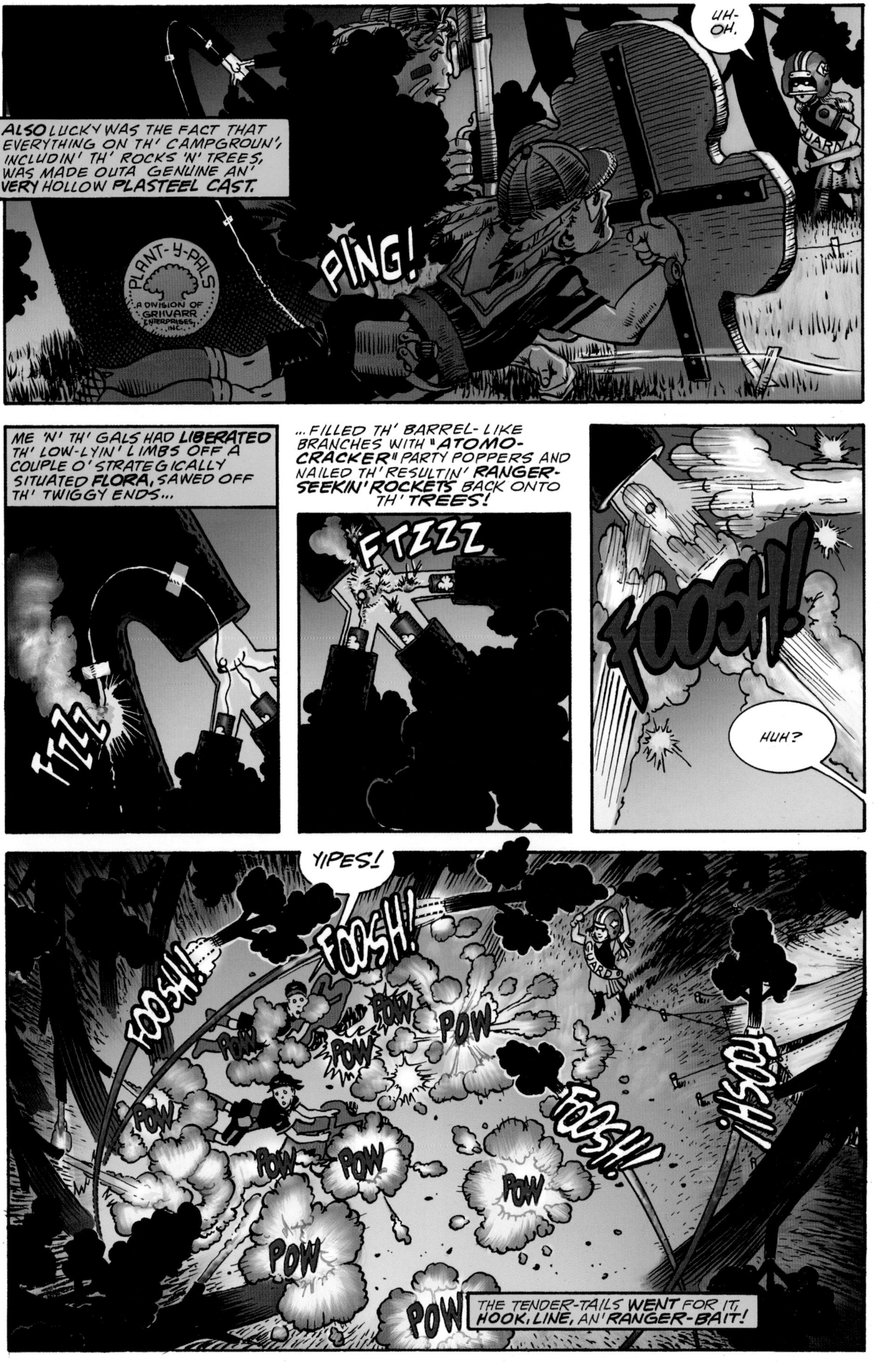
UH-OH.
ALSO LUCKY WAS THE FACT THAT EVERYTHING ON TH' CAMPGROUN', INCLUDIN' TH' ROCKS 'N' TREES, WAS MADE OUTA GENUINE AN' VERY HOLLOW PLASTEEL CAST.
GUARD
PLANT-Y-PALS
A DIVISION OF GRIIVARR ENTERPRISES, INC.
PING!
ME 'N' TH' GALS HAD LIBERATED TH' LOW-LYIN' LIMBS OFF A COUPLE O' STRATEGICALLY SITUATED FLORA, SAWED OFF TH' TWIGGY ENDS...
FTZZZ
...FILLED TH' BARREL-LIKE BRANCHES WITH "ATOMO-CRACKER" PARTY POPPERS AND NAILED TH' RESULTIN' RANGER-SEEKIN' ROCKETS BACK ONTO TH' TREES!
FTZZZ
FOOSH!
HUH?
YIPES!
FOOSH!
FOOSH!
GUARD
POW
POW
POW
POW
FOOSH!
FOOSH!
POW
POW
POW
POW
POW
POW
THE TENDER-TAILS WENT FOR IT, HOOK, LINE, AN' RANGER-BAIT!

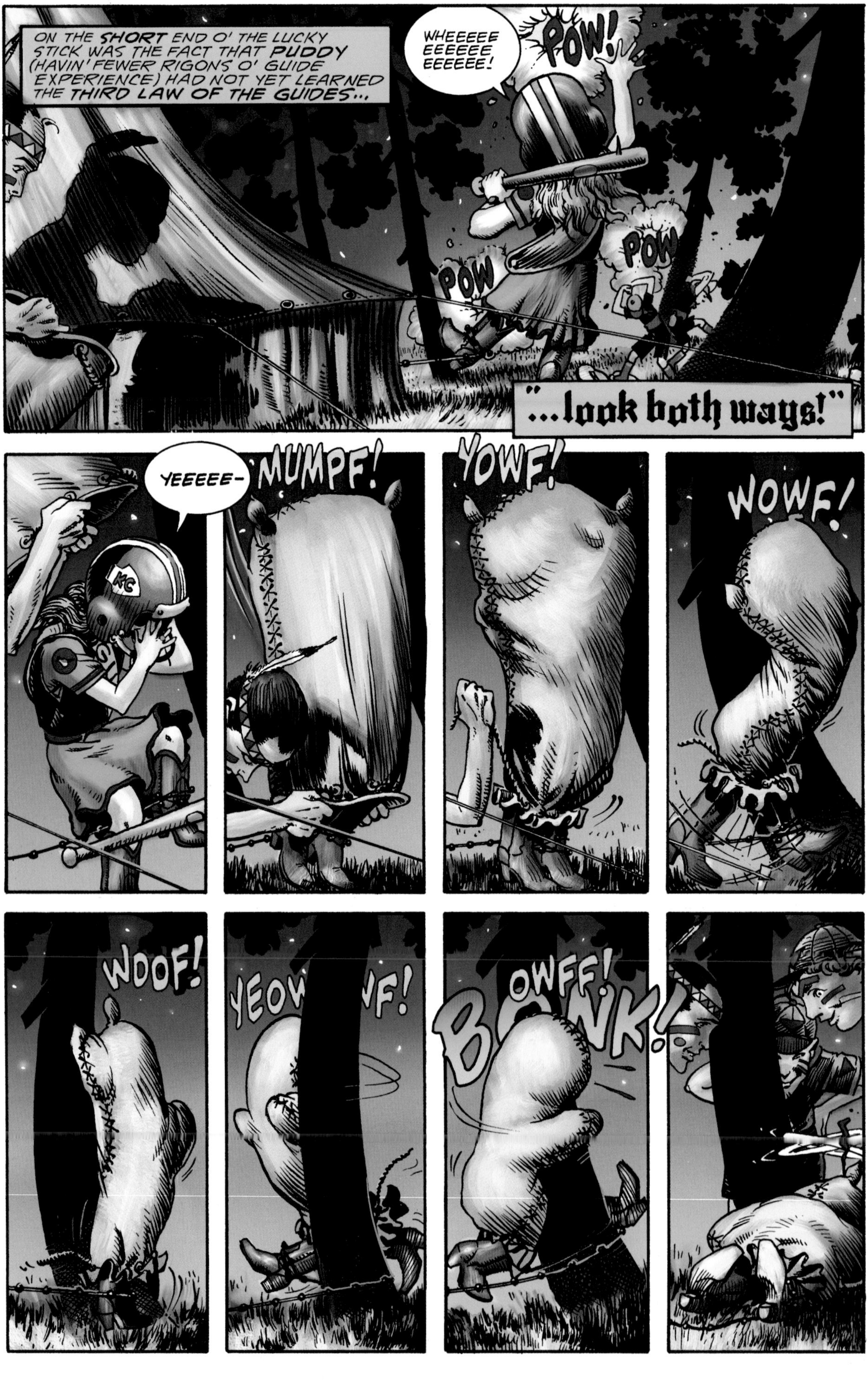
ON THE SHORT END O' THE LUCKY STICK WAS THE FACT THAT PUDDY (HAVIN' FEWER RIGONS O' GUIDE EXPERIENCE) HAD NOT YET LEARNED THE THIRD LAW OF THE GUIDES...
WHEEEEE EEEEEE EEEEEE!
POW!
POW
POW
"...look both ways!"
YEEEEE-
MUMPF!
YOWF!
WOWF!
WOOF!
YEOW
NF!
OWFF!
BONK!

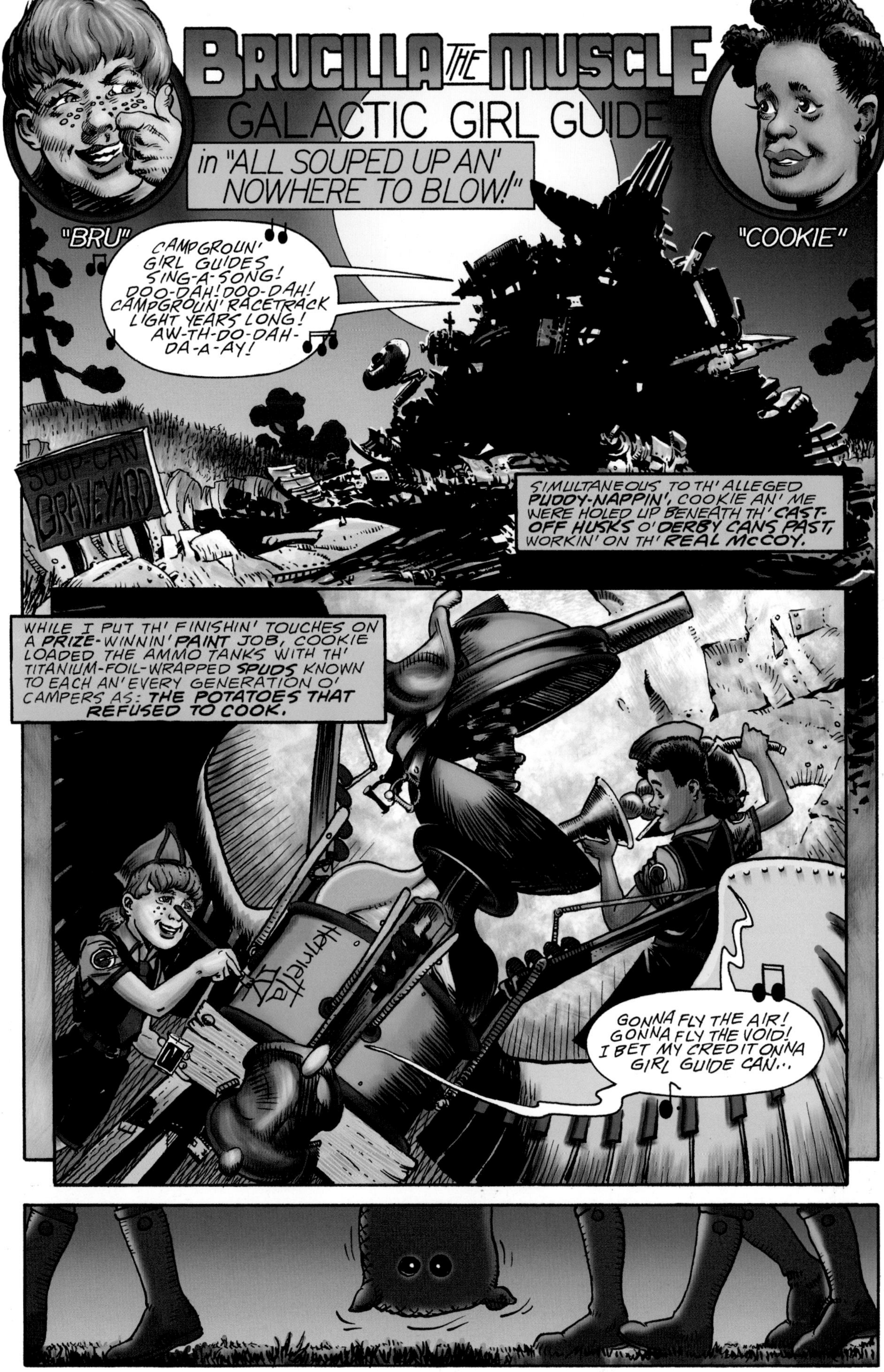
BRUCILLA THE MUSCLE
GALACTIC GIRL GUIDE
in "ALL SOUPED UP AN' NOWHERE TO BLOW!"
"BRU"
"COOKIE"
CAMPGROUN' GIRL GUIDES SING-A-SONG! DOO-DAH! DOO-DAH! CAMPGROUN' RACETRACK LIGHT YEARS LONG! AW-TH-DO-DAH-DA-A-AY!
SOUP-CAN GRAVEYARD
SIMULTANEOUS TO TH' ALLEGED PUDDY-NAPPIN', COOKIE AN' ME WERE HOLED UP BENEATH TH' CAST-OFF HUSKS O' DERBY CANS PAST, WORKIN' ON TH' REAL McCOY.
WHILE I PUT TH' FINISHIN' TOUCHES ON A PRIZE-WINNIN' PAINT JOB, COOKIE LOADED THE AMMO TANKS WITH TH' TITANIUM-FOIL-WRAPPED SPUDS KNOWN TO EACH AN' EVERY GENERATION O' CAMPERS AS: THE POTATOES THAT REFUSED TO COOK.
Henrietta
GONNA FLY THE AIR! GONNA FLY THE VOID! I BET MY CREDIT ONNA GIRL GUIDE CAN...

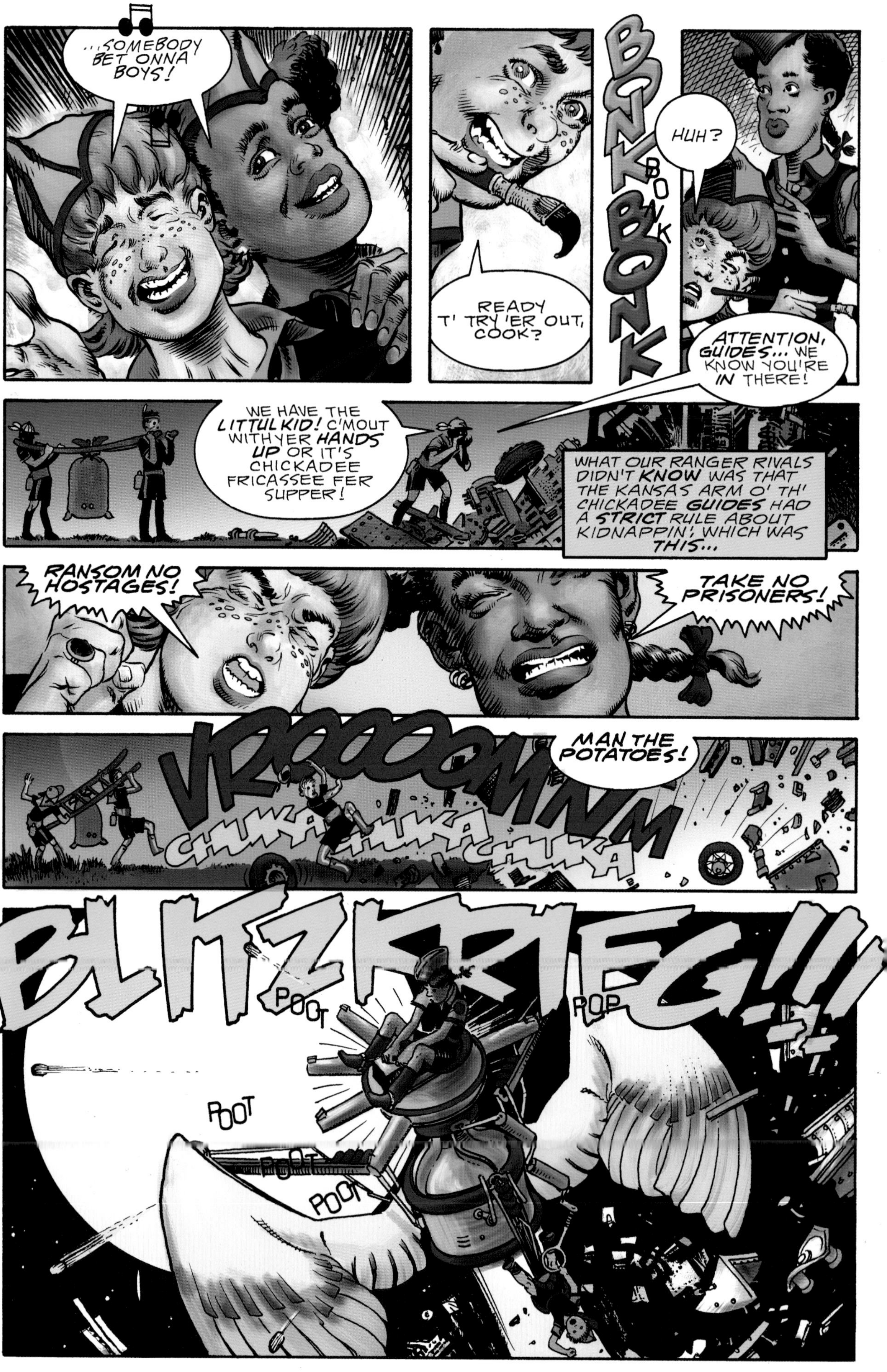
...SOMEBODY BET ONNA BOYS!
READY T' TRY 'ER OUT, COOK?
BONK BONK BONK BONK
HUH?
ATTENTION, GUIDES... WE KNOW YOU'RE IN THERE!
WE HAVE THE LITTUL KID! C'MOUT WITH YER HANDS UP OR IT'S CHICKADEE FRICASSEE FER SUPPER!
WHAT OUR RANGER RIVALS DIDN'T KNOW WAS THAT THE KANSAS ARM O' TH' CHICKADEE GUIDES HAD A STRICT RULE ABOUT KIDNAPPIN', WHICH WAS THIS...
RANSOM NO HOSTAGES!
TAKE NO PRISONERS!
VROOOOOMMM
MAN THE POTATOES!
CHUKA CHUKA CHUKA
BLITZKRIEG!!!
POOT
POP
POOT
POOT
POOT

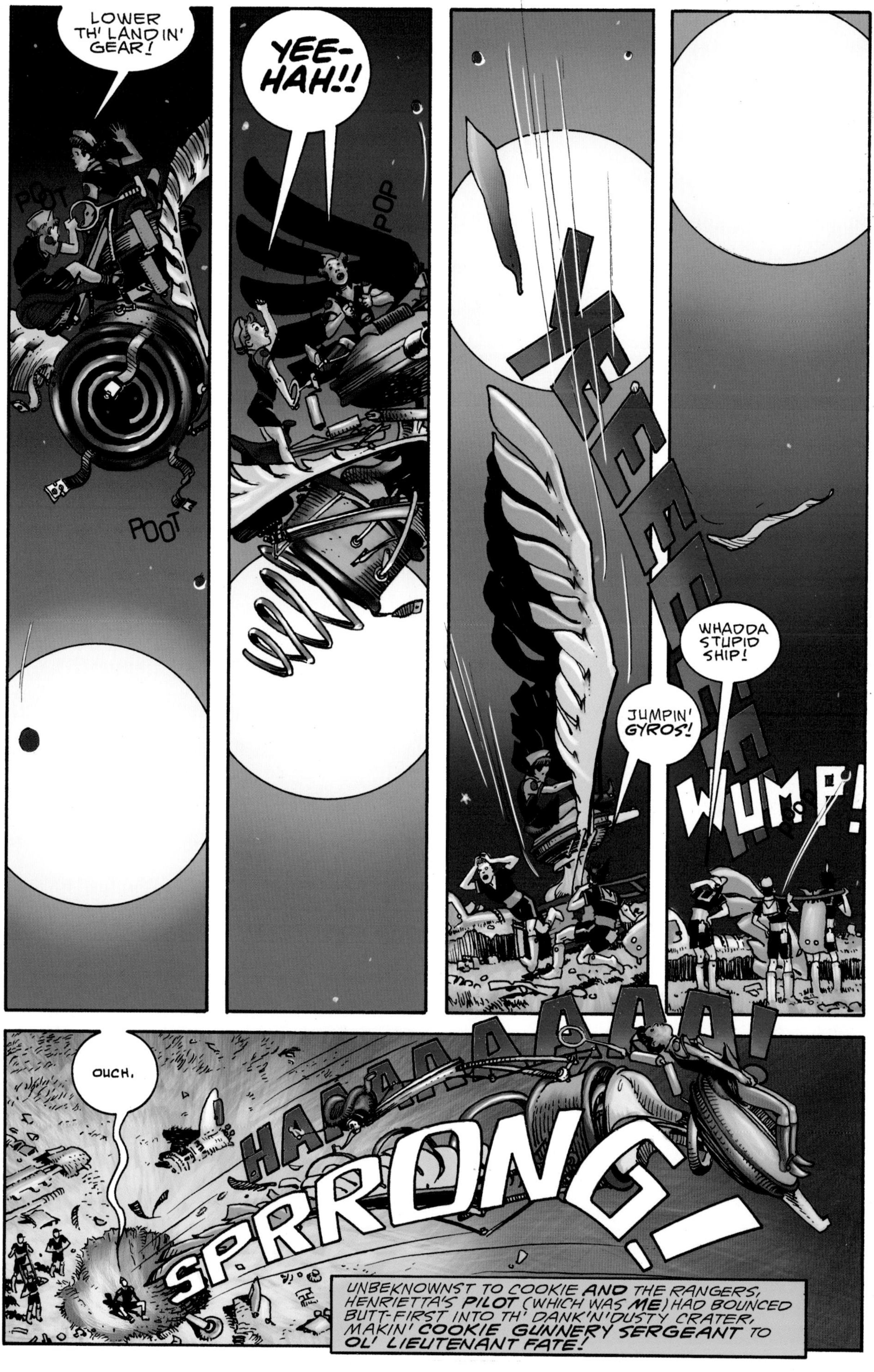
LOWER TH' LANDIN' GEAR!
POOT
POOT
YEE-HAH!!
POP
WHADDA STUPID SHIP!
JUMPIN' GYROS!
WUMP!
OUCH.
HAAAAAAAA!
SPRRONG!
UNBEKNOWNST TO COOKIE AND THE RANGERS, HENRIETTA'S PILOT (WHICH WAS ME) HAD BOUNCED BUTT-FIRST INTO TH' DANK'N'DUSTY CRATER, MAKIN' COOKIE GUNNERY SERGEANT TO OL' LIEUTENANT FATE!

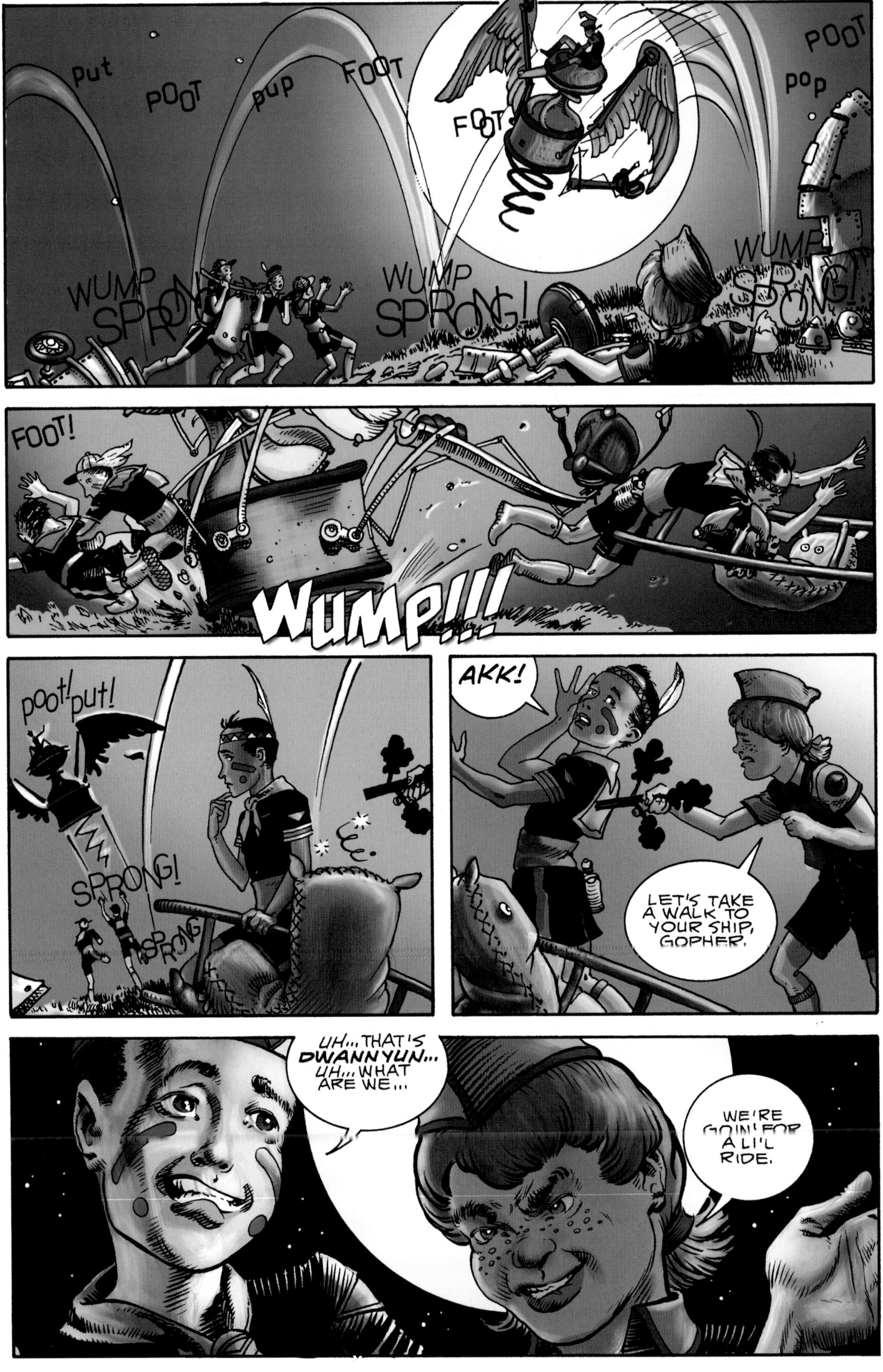

Put
POOT
pup
FOOT
FOOT
POOT
pop
WUMP
SPRONG
WUMP
SPRONG!
WUMP
SPRONG!
FOOT!
WUMP!!!
poot! put!
SPRONG!
SPRONG
AKK!
LET'S TAKE A WALK TO YOUR SHIP, GOPHER.
UH... THAT'S DWANNYUN... UH... WHAT ARE WE...
WE'RE GOIN' FOR A LI'L RIDE.

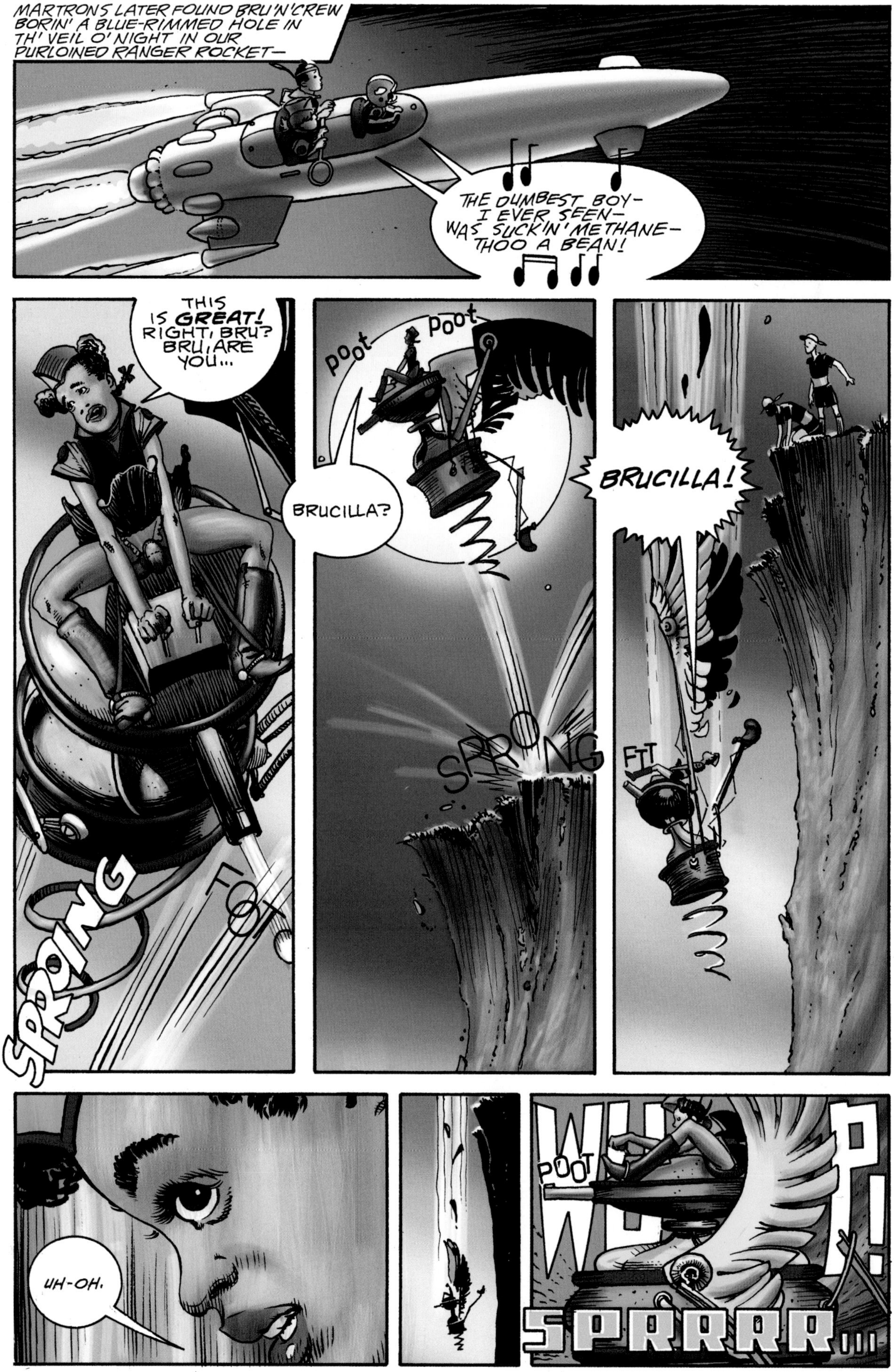
MARTRONS LATER FOUND BRU'N'CREW BORIN' A BLUE-RIMMED HOLE IN TH' VEIL O' NIGHT IN OUR PURLOINED RANGER ROCKET—
THE DUMBEST BOY— I EVER SEEN— WAS SUCKIN' METHANE— THOO A BEAN!
THIS IS GREAT! RIGHT, BRU? BRU, ARE YOU...
SPRING
FOT
POOT POOT
BRUCILLA?
SPRING
BRUCILLA!
FIT
UH-OH.
POOT
WHUMP!
SPRRRR...

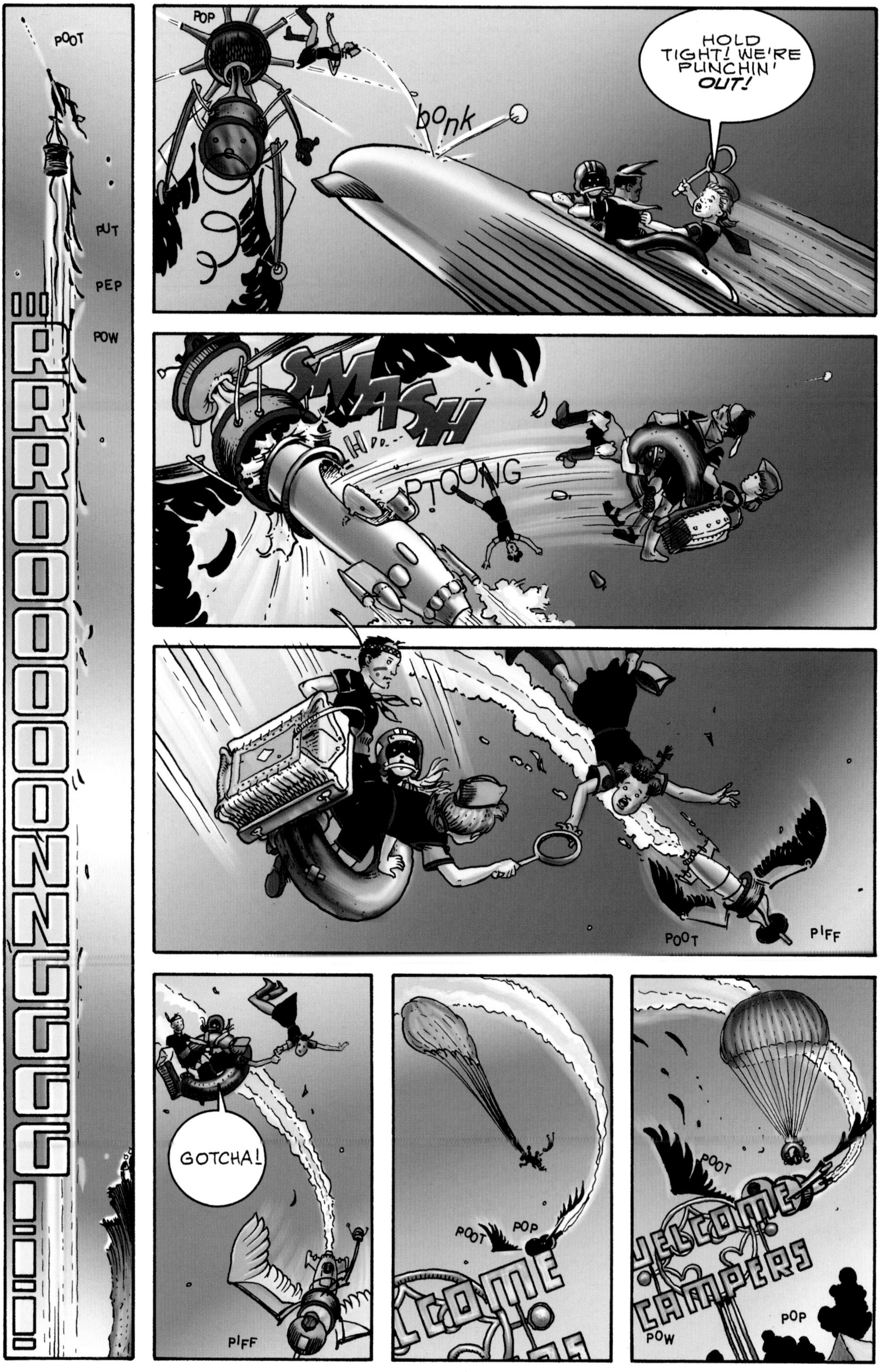
POOT
PUT
PEP
POW
!!!RRROOOOOONNGGG!!!
POP
bonk
HOLD TIGHT! WE'RE PUNCHIN' *OUT!*
SMASH
PTOONG
POOT
PIFF
GOTCHA!
PIFF
POOT
POP
POOT
POP
WELCOME CAMPERS
POW
POP

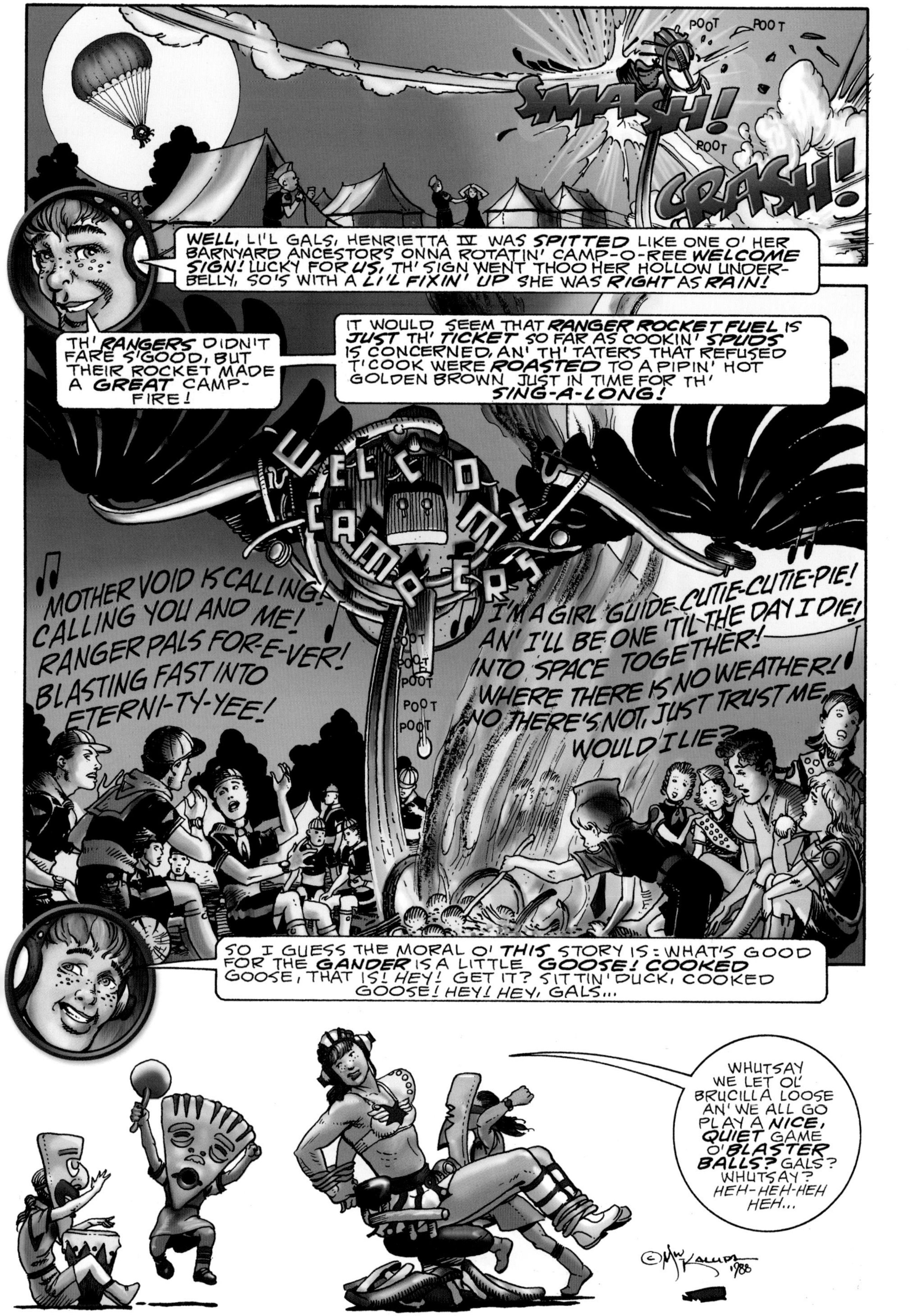

POOT POOT
SMASH!
POOT
CRASH!
WELL, LI'L GALS, HENRIETTA IV WAS SPITTED LIKE ONE O' HER BARNYARD ANCESTORS ONNA ROTATIN' CAMP-O-REE WELCOME SIGN! LUCKY FOR US, TH' SIGN WENT THOO HER HOLLOW UNDER-BELLY, SO'S WITH A LI'L FIXIN' UP SHE WAS RIGHT AS RAIN!
TH' RANGERS DIDN'T FARE S'GOOD, BUT THEIR ROCKET MADE A GREAT CAMP-FIRE!
IT WOULD SEEM THAT RANGER ROCKET FUEL IS JUST TH' TICKET SO FAR AS COOKIN' SPUDS IS CONCERNED, AN' TH' TATERS THAT REFUSED T'COOK WERE ROASTED TO A PIPIN' HOT GOLDEN BROWN JUST IN TIME FOR TH' SING-A-LONG!
WELCOME CAMPERS
MOTHER VOID IS CALLING! CALLING YOU AND ME! RANGER PALS FOR-E-VER! BLASTING FAST INTO ETERNI-TY-YEE!
POOT POOT POOT POOT POOT
I'M A GIRL GUIDE CUTIE-CUTIE-PIE! AN' I'LL BE ONE 'TIL THE DAY I DIE! INTO SPACE TOGETHER! WHERE THERE IS NO WEATHER! NO THERE'S NOT, JUST TRUST ME, WOULD I LIE?
SO I GUESS THE MORAL O' THIS STORY IS: WHAT'S GOOD FOR THE GANDER IS A LITTLE GOOSE! COOKED GOOSE, THAT IS! HEY! GET IT? SITTIN' DUCK, COOKED GOOSE! HEY! HEY, GALS...
WHUTSAY WE LET OL' BRUCILLA LOOSE AN' WE ALL GO PLAY A NICE, QUIET GAME O' BLASTER BALLS? GALS? WHUTSAY? HEH-HEH-HEH HEH...
©MW KALUTA 1988

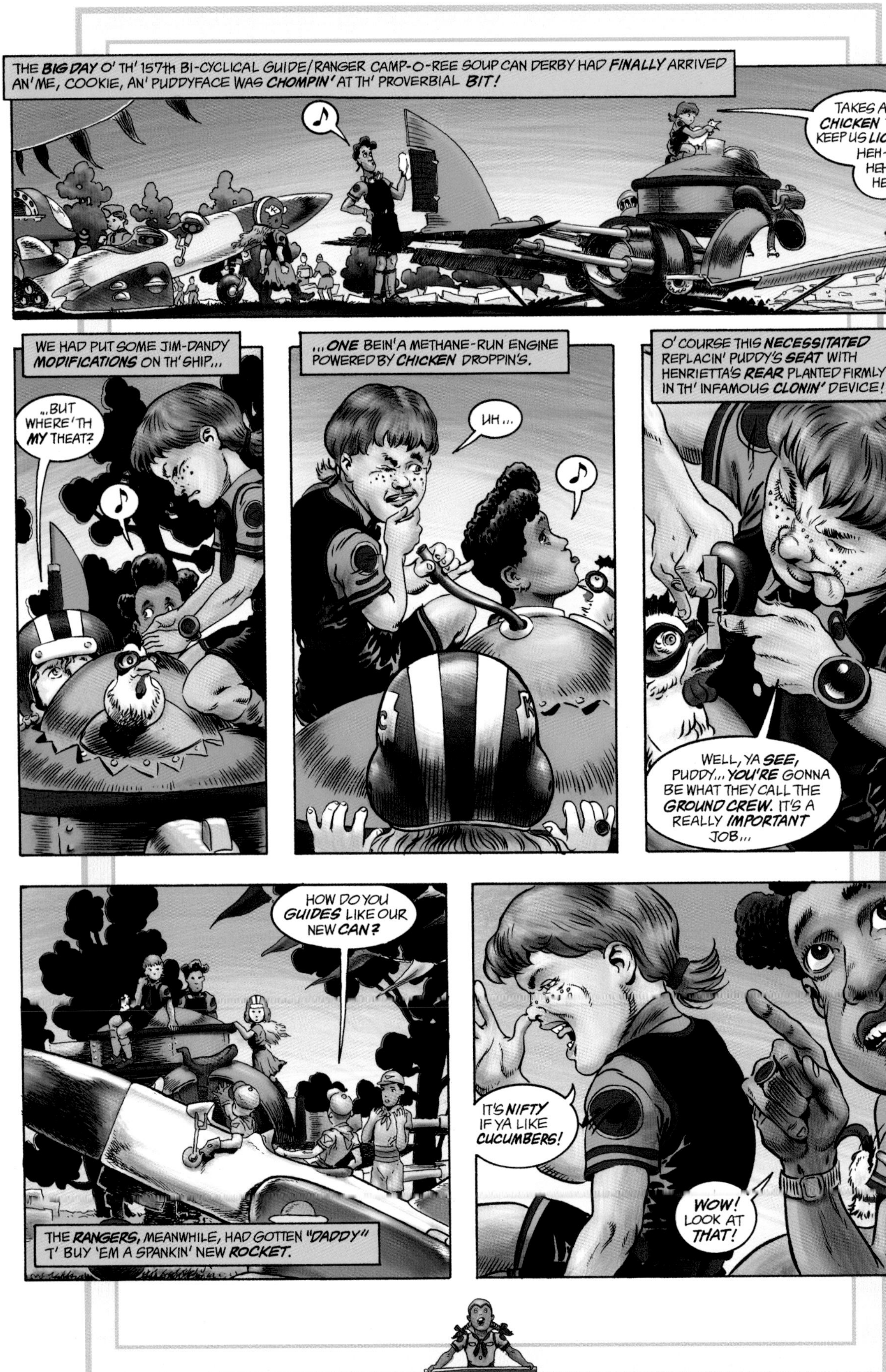
THE BIG DAY O' TH' 157th BI-CYCLICAL GUIDE/RANGER CAMP-O-REE SOUP CAN DERBY HAD FINALLY ARRIVED AN' ME, COOKIE, AN' PUDDYFACE WAS CHOMPIN' AT TH' PROVERBIAL BIT!
♪
TAKES A CHICKEN TA KEEP US LICKIN'! HEH-HEH-HEH!
WE HAD PUT SOME JIM-DANDY MODIFICATIONS ON TH' SHIP...
...BUT WHERE'TH MY THEAT?
♪
...ONE BEIN' A METHANE-RUN ENGINE POWERED BY CHICKEN DROPPIN'S.
UH...
♪
O' COURSE THIS NECESSITATED REPLACIN' PUDDY'S SEAT WITH HENRIETTA'S REAR PLANTED FIRMLY IN TH' INFAMOUS CLONIN' DEVICE!
WELL, YA SEE, PUDDY... YOU'RE GONNA BE WHAT THEY CALL THE GROUND CREW. IT'S A REALLY IMPORTANT JOB...
HOW DO YOU GUIDES LIKE OUR NEW CAN?
THE RANGERS, MEANWHILE, HAD GOTTEN "DADDY" T' BUY 'EM A SPANKIN' NEW ROCKET.
IT'S NIFTY IF YA LIKE CUCUMBERS!
WOW! LOOK AT THAT!

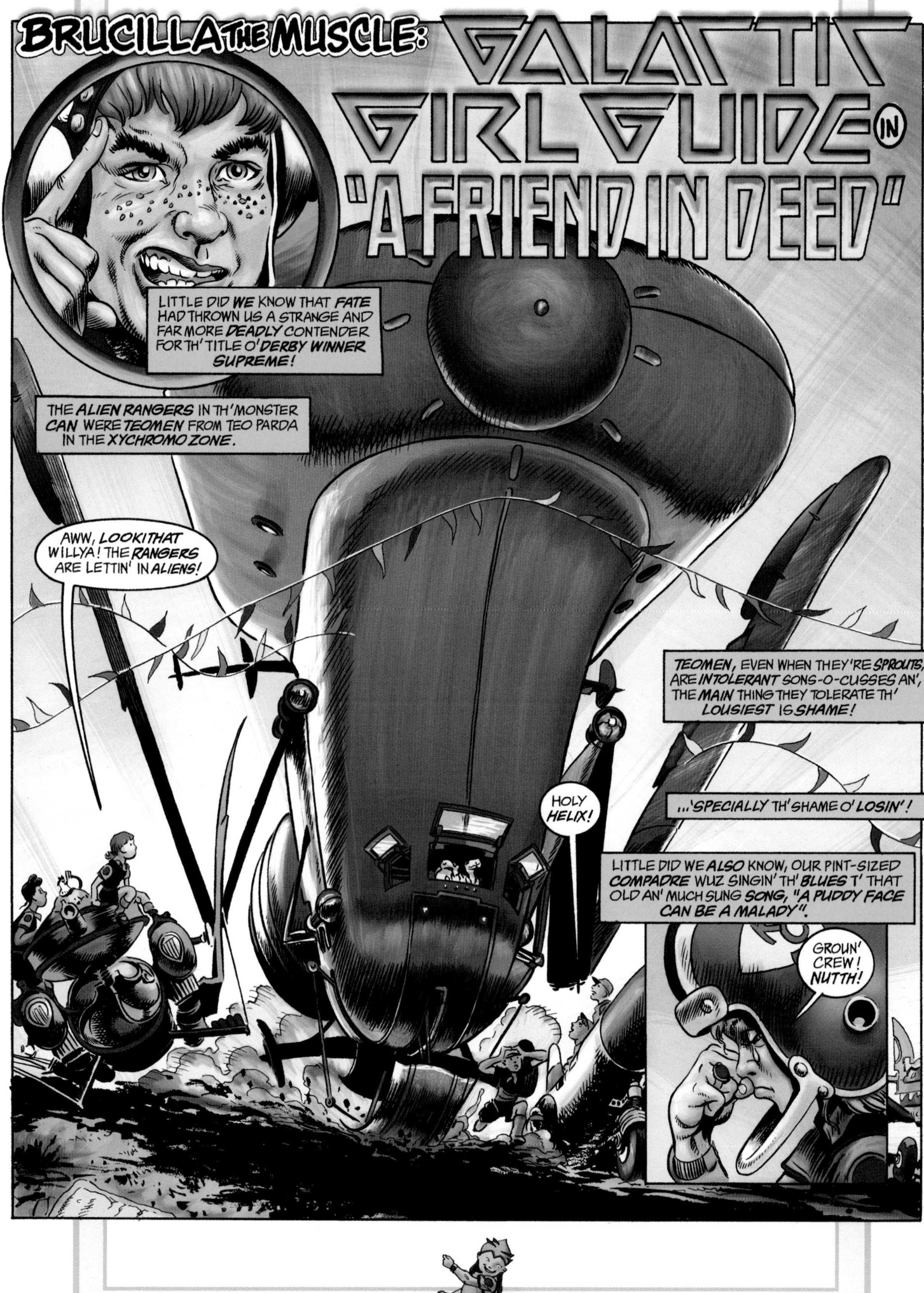
BRUCILLA THE MUSCLE: GALACTIC GIRL GUIDE IN "A FRIEND IN DEED"
LITTLE DID WE KNOW THAT FATE HAD THROWN US A STRANGE AND FAR MORE DEADLY CONTENDER FOR TH' TITLE O' DERBY WINNER SUPREME!
THE ALIEN RANGERS IN TH' MONSTER CAN WERE TEOMEN FROM TEO PARDA IN THE XYCHROMO ZONE.
AWW, LOOKITHAT WILLYA! THE RANGERS ARE LETTIN' IN ALIENS!
TEOMEN, EVEN WHEN THEY'RE SPROUTS, ARE INTOLERANT SONS-O-CUSSES AN', THE MAIN THING THEY TOLERATE TH' LOUSIEST IS SHAME!
...'SPECIALLY TH' SHAME O' LOSIN'!
HOLY HELIX!
LITTLE DID WE ALSO KNOW, OUR PINT-SIZED COMPADRE WUZ SINGIN' TH' BLUES T' THAT OLD AN' MUCH SUNG SONG, "A PUDDY FACE CAN BE A MALADY".
GROUN' CREW! NUTTH!

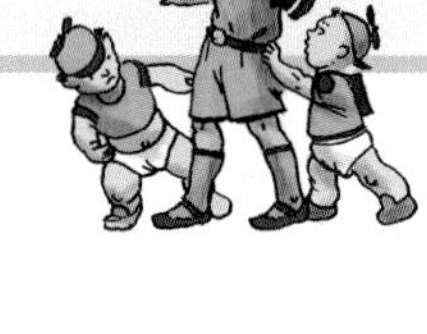

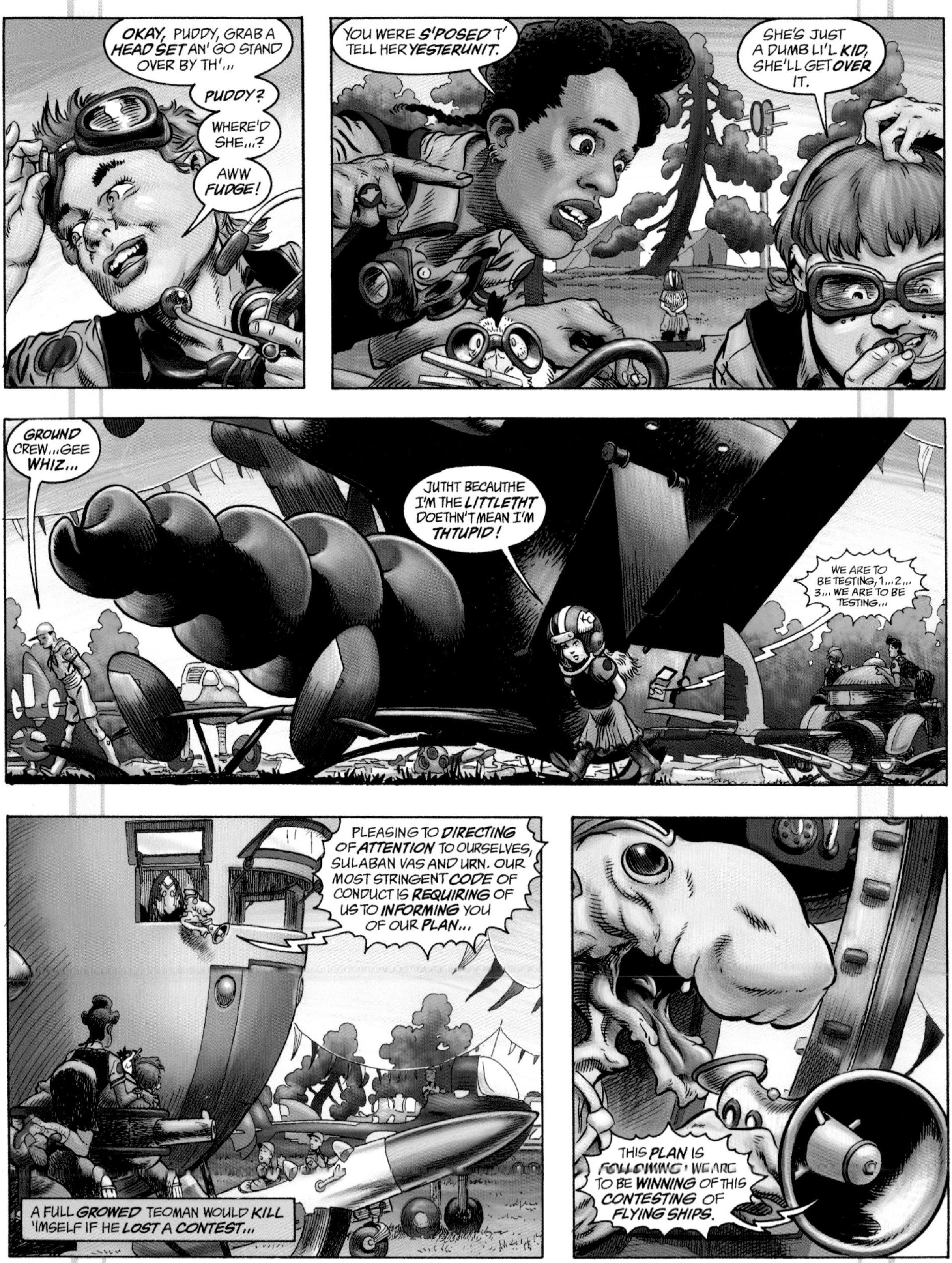
OKAY, PUDDY, GRAB A HEAD SET AN' GO STAND OVER BY TH'...
PUDDY?
WHERE'D SHE...?
AWW FUDGE!
YOU WERE S'POSED T' TELL HER YESTERUNIT.
SHE'S JUST A DUMB LI'L KID, SHE'LL GET OVER IT.
GROUND CREW... GEE WHIZ...
JUTHT BECAUTHE I'M THE LITTLETHT DOETHN'T MEAN I'M THTUPID!
WE ARE TO BE TESTING, 1... 2... 3... WE ARE TO BE TESTING...
PLEASING TO DIRECTING OF ATTENTION TO OURSELVES, SULABAN VAS AND URN. OUR MOST STRINGENT CODE OF CONDUCT IS REQUIRING OF US TO INFORMING YOU OF OUR PLAN...
A FULL GROWED TEOMAN WOULD KILL 'IMSELF IF HE LOST A CONTEST...
THIS PLAN IS FOLLOWING: WE ARE TO BE WINNING OF THIS CONTESTING OF FLYING SHIPS.

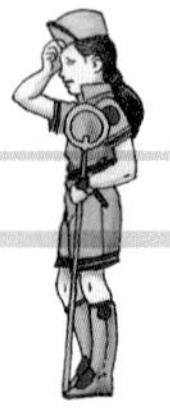

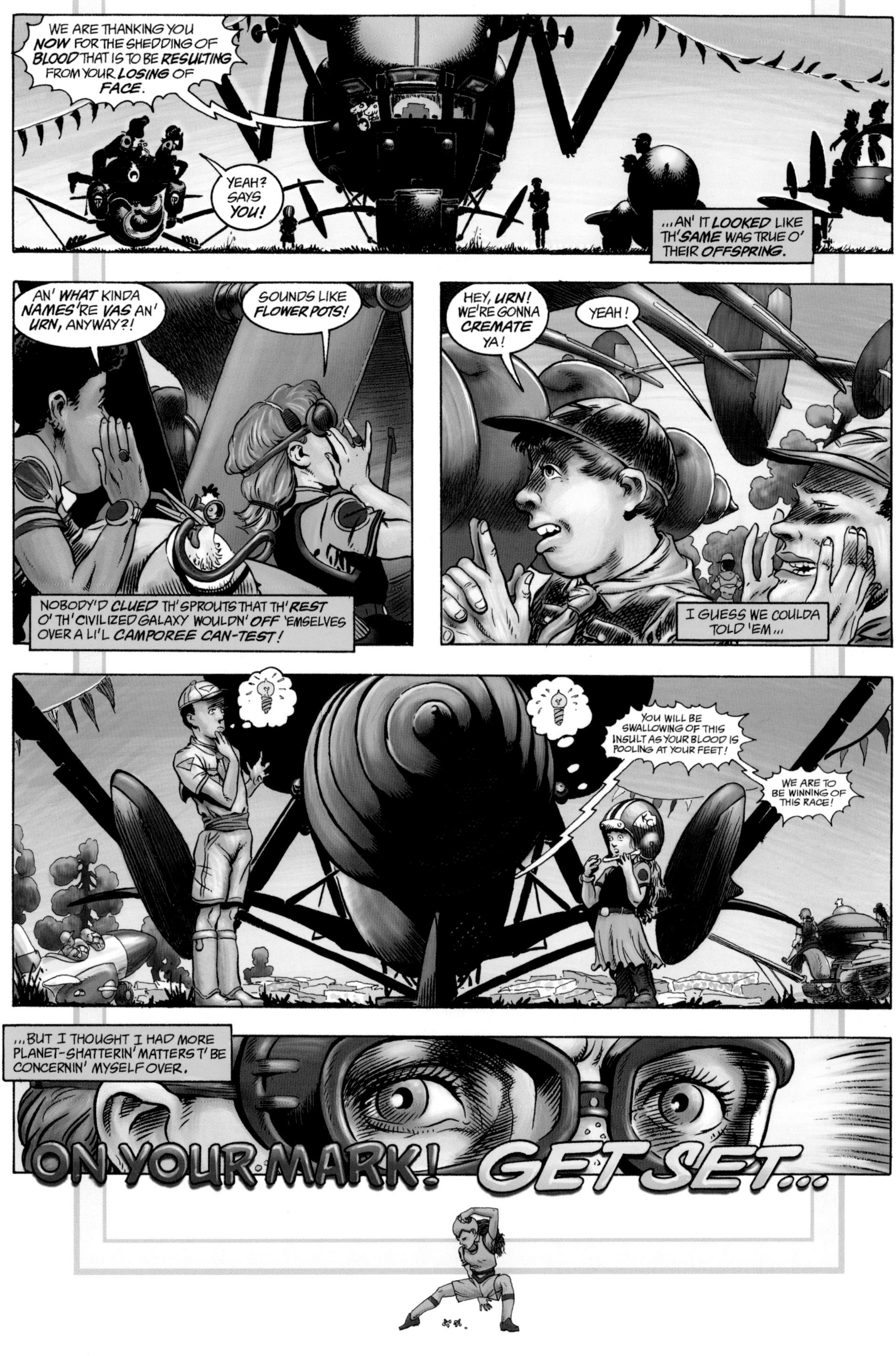
WE ARE THANKING YOU NOW FOR THE SHEDDING OF BLOOD THAT IS TO BE RESULTING FROM YOUR LOSING OF FACE.
YEAH? SAYS YOU!
...AN' IT LOOKED LIKE TH' SAME WAS TRUE O' THEIR OFFSPRING.
AN' WHAT KINDA NAMES'RE VAS AN' URN, ANYWAY?!
SOUNDS LIKE FLOWER POTS!
NOBODY'D CLUED TH' SPROUTS THAT TH' REST O' TH' CIVILIZED GALAXY WOULDN' OFF 'EMSELVES OVER A LI'L CAMPOREE CAN-TEST!
HEY, URN! WE'RE GONNA CREMATE YA!
YEAH!
I GUESS WE COULDA TOLD 'EM...
YOU WILL BE SWALLOWING OF THIS INSULT AS YOUR BLOOD IS POOLING AT YOUR FEET!
WE ARE TO BE WINNING OF THIS RACE!
...BUT I THOUGHT I HAD MORE PLANET-SHATTERIN' MATTERS T' BE CONCERNIN' MYSELF OVER.
ON YOUR MARK! GET SET...

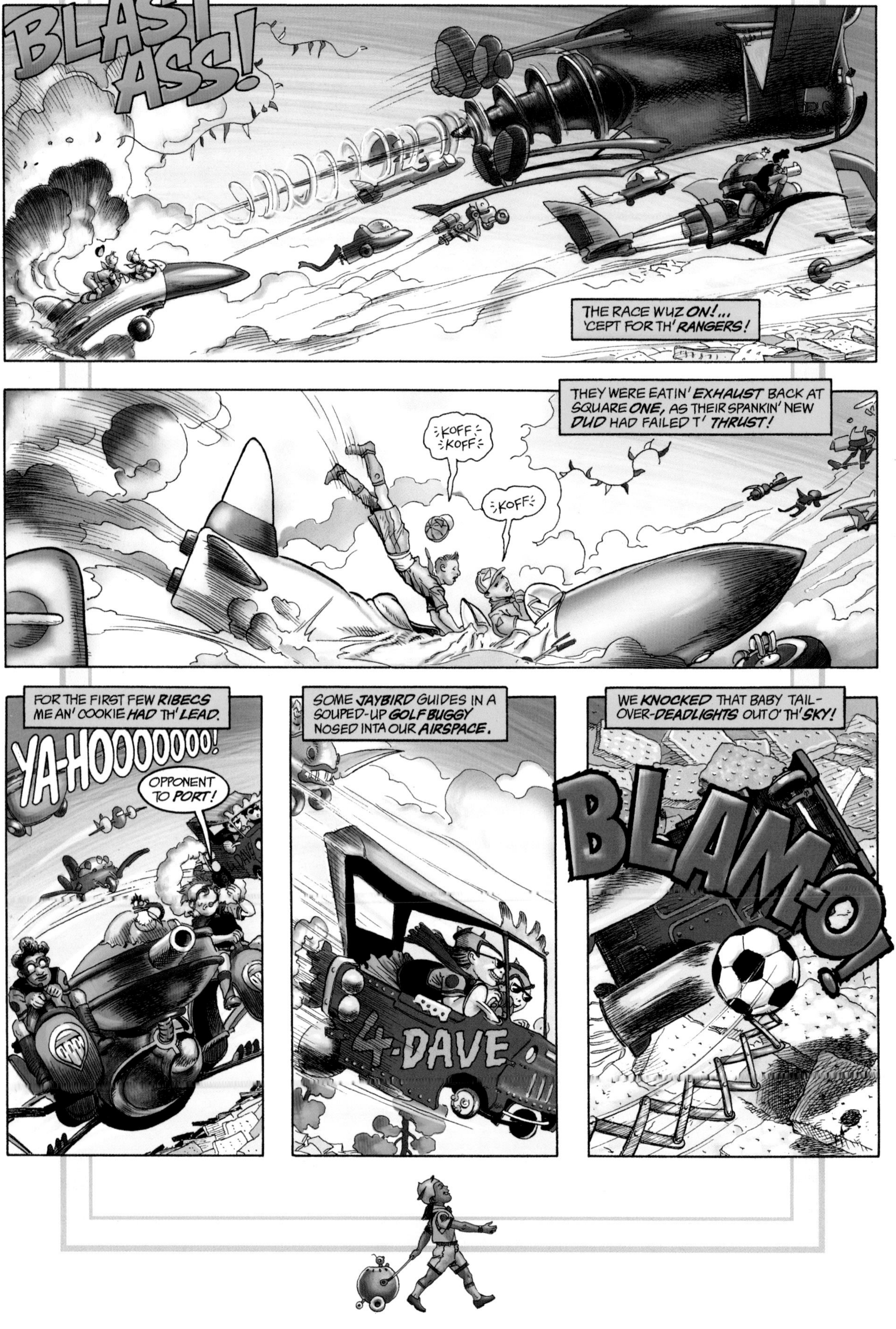
BLAST ASS!
THE RACE WUZ ON!... 'CEPT FOR TH' RANGERS!
THEY WERE EATIN' EXHAUST BACK AT SQUARE ONE, AS THEIR SPANKIN' NEW DUD HAD FAILED T' THRUST!
KOFF KOFF
KOFF
FOR THE FIRST FEW RIBECS ME AN' COOKIE HAD TH' LEAD.
YA-HOOOOOOO!
OPPONENT TO PORT!
SOME JAYBIRD GUIDES IN A SOUPED-UP GOLF BUGGY NOSED INTA OUR AIRSPACE.
4-DAVE
WE KNOCKED THAT BABY TAIL-OVER-DEADLIGHTS OUT O' TH' SKY!
BLAM-O!

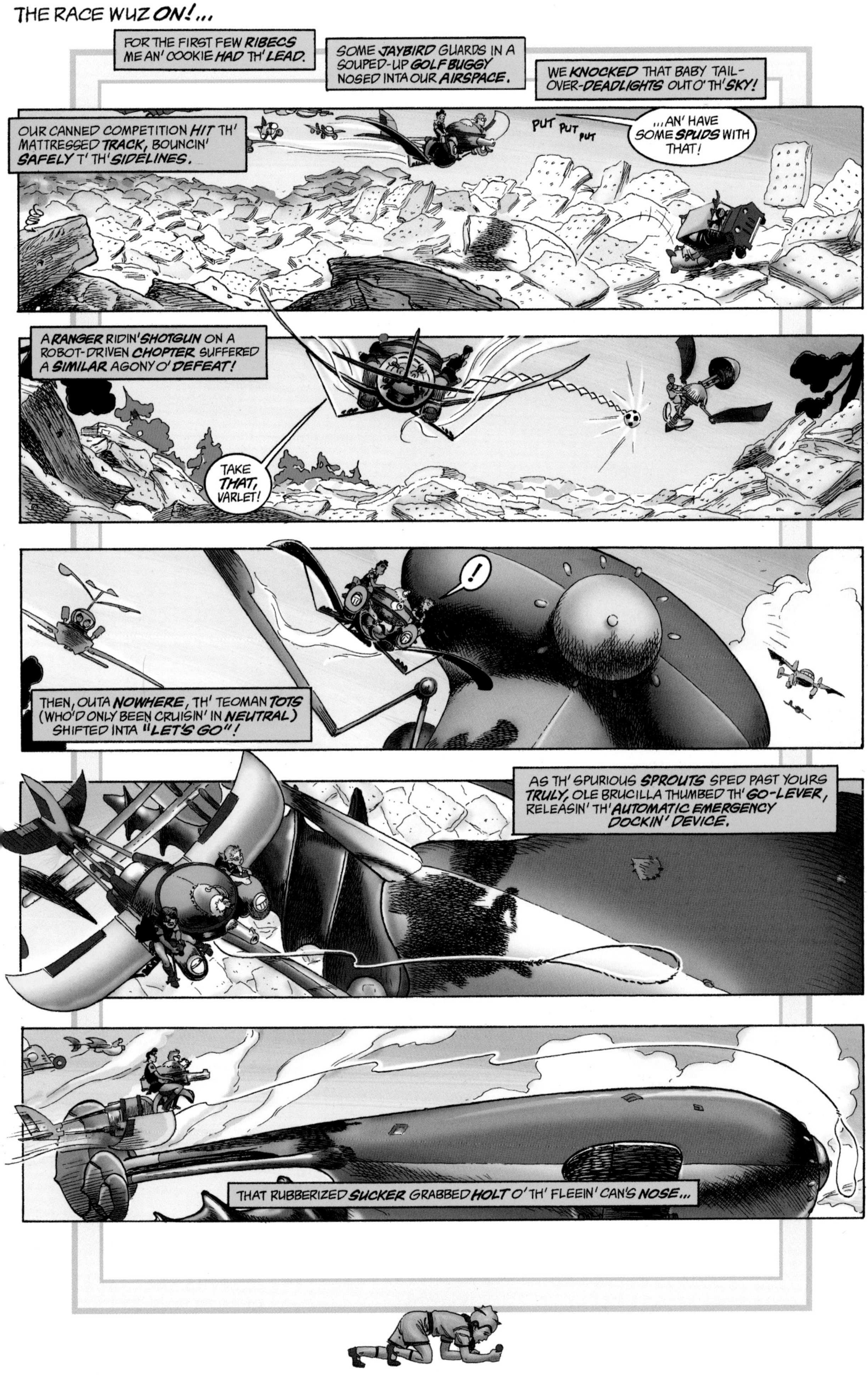
THE RACE WUZ ON!...
FOR THE FIRST FEW RIBECS ME AN' COOKIE HAD TH' LEAD.
SOME JAYBIRD GUARDS IN A SOUPED-UP GOLF BUGGY NOSED INTA OUR AIRSPACE.
WE KNOCKED THAT BABY TAIL-OVER-DEADLIGHTS OUT O' TH' SKY!
OUR CANNED COMPETITION HIT TH' MATTRESSED TRACK, BOUNCIN' SAFELY T' TH' SIDELINES.
PUT PUT PUT
...AN' HAVE SOME SPUDS WITH THAT!
A RANGER RIDIN' SHOTGUN ON A ROBOT-DRIVEN CHOPTER SUFFERED A SIMILAR AGONY O' DEFEAT!
TAKE THAT, VARLET!
!
THEN, OUTA NOWHERE, TH' TEOMAN TOTS (WHO'D ONLY BEEN CRUISIN' IN NEUTRAL) SHIFTED INTA "LET'S GO"!
AS TH' SPURIOUS SPROUTS SPED PAST YOURS TRULY, OLE BRUCILLA THUMBED TH' GO-LEVER, RELEASIN' TH' AUTOMATIC EMERGENCY DOCKIN' DEVICE.
THAT RUBBERIZED SUCKER GRABBED HOLT O' TH' FLEEIN' CAN'S NOSE...

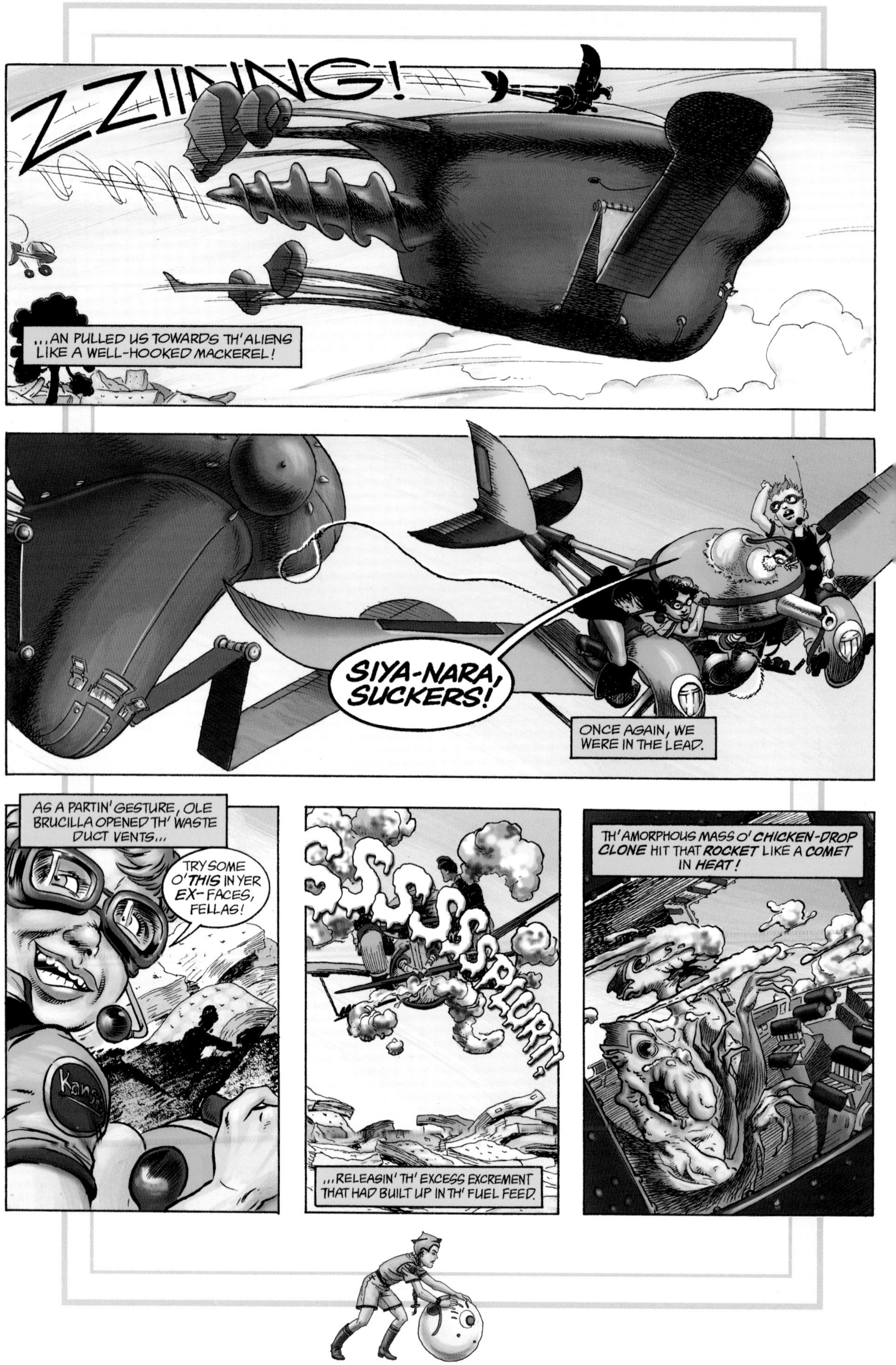
ZZIING!
...AN PULLED US TOWARDS TH' ALIENS LIKE A WELL-HOOKED MACKEREL!
SIYA-NARA, SUCKERS!
ONCE AGAIN, WE WERE IN THE LEAD.
AS A PARTIN' GESTURE, OLE BRUCILLA OPENED TH' WASTE DUCT VENTS...
TRY SOME O' THIS IN YER EX-FACES, FELLAS!
SSSSSPLURT!
...RELEASIN' TH' EXCESS EXCREMENT THAT HAD BUILT UP IN TH' FUEL FEED.
TH' AMORPHOUS MASS O' CHICKEN-DROP CLONE HIT THAT ROCKET LIKE A COMET IN HEAT!

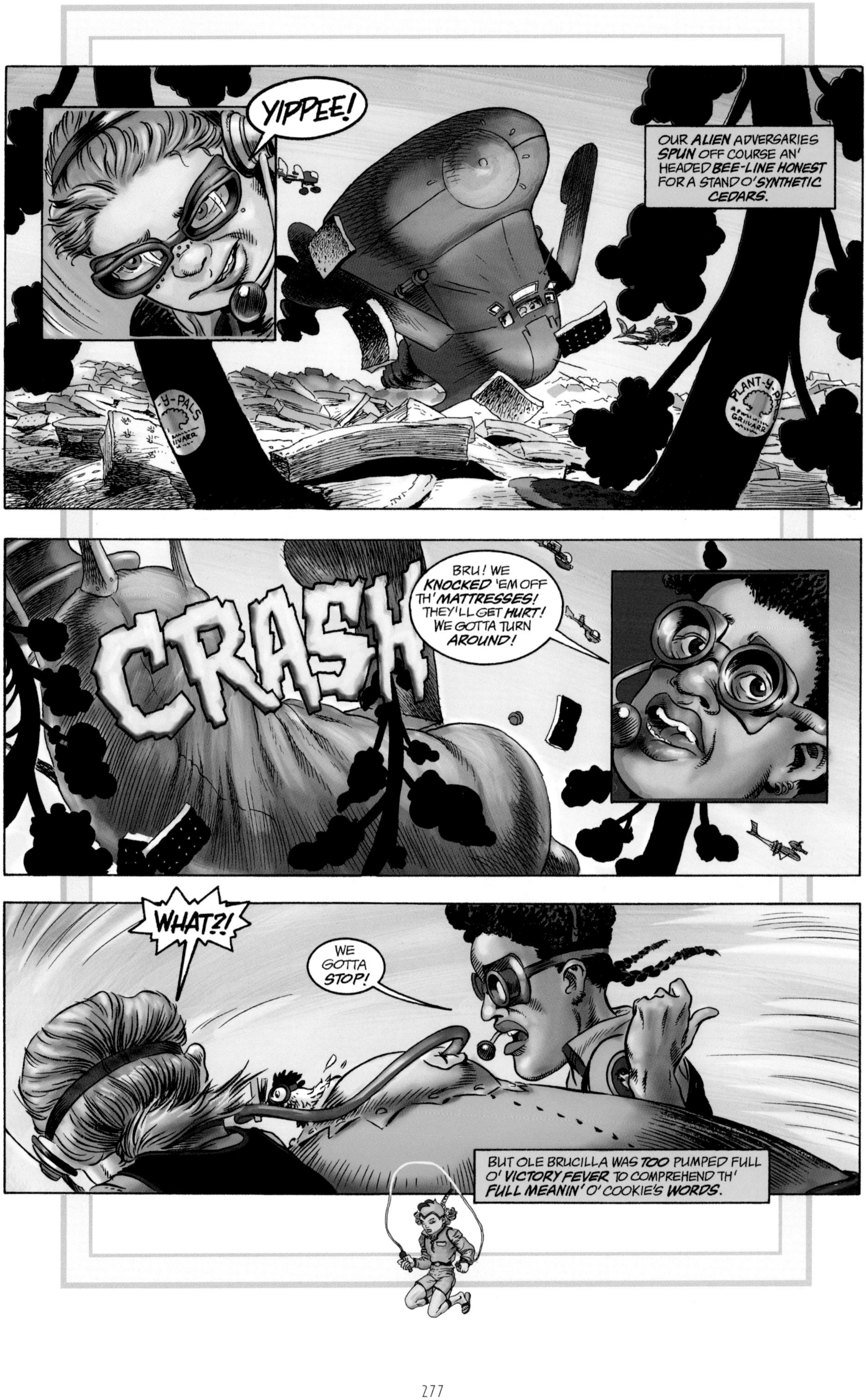
YIPPEE!
OUR ALIEN ADVERSARIES SPUN OFF COURSE AN' HEADED BEE-LINE HONEST FOR A STAND O' SYNTHETIC CEDARS.
CRASH
BRU! WE KNOCKED 'EM OFF TH' MATTRESSES! THEY'LL GET HURT! WE GOTTA TURN AROUND!
WHAT?!
WE GOTTA STOP!
BUT OLE BRUCILLA WAS TOO PUMPED FULL O' VICTORY FEVER TO COMPREHEND TH' FULL MEANIN' O' COOKIE'S WORDS.

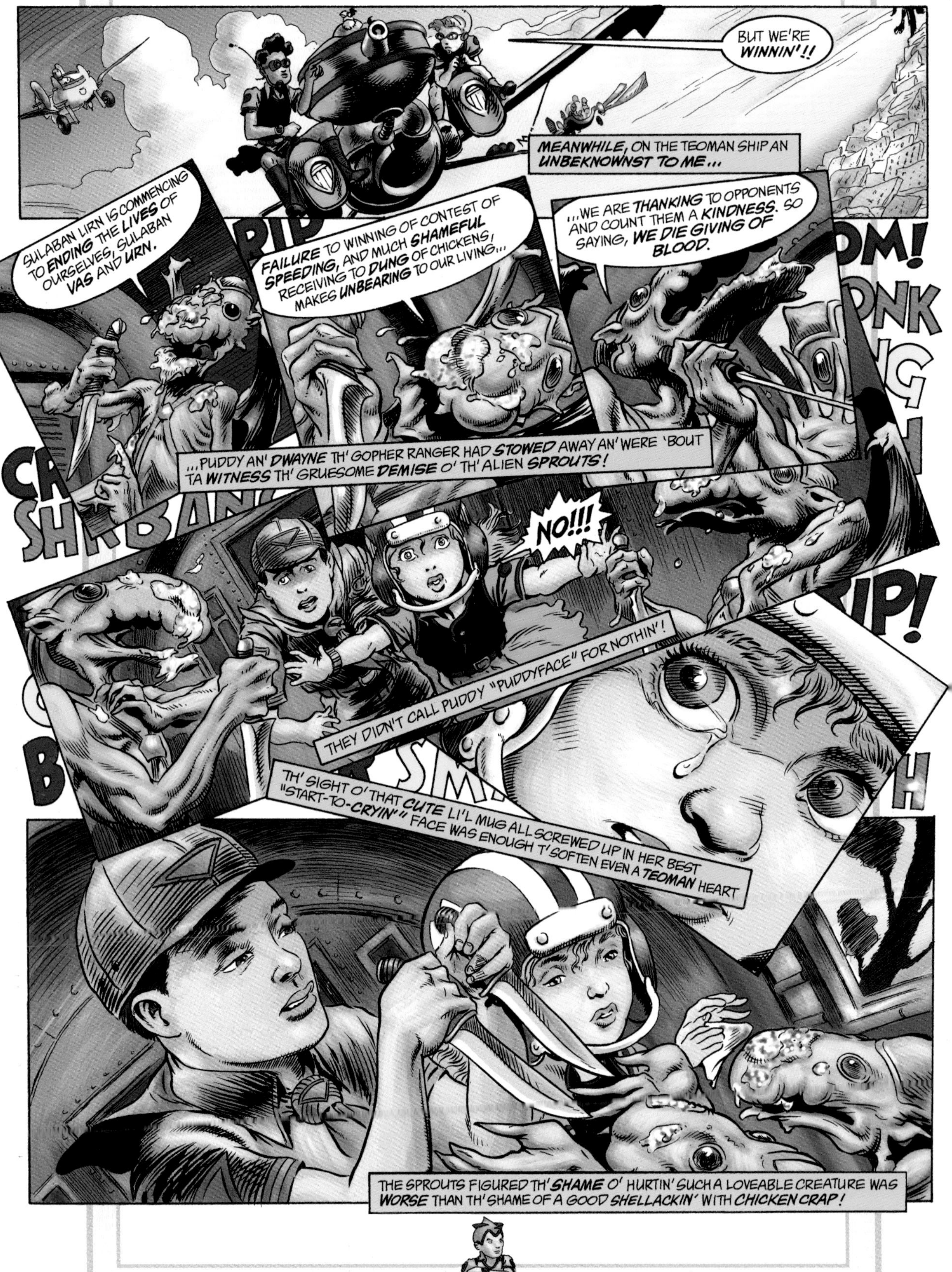
BUT WE'RE WINNIN'!!
MEANWHILE, ON THE TEOMAN SHIP AN UNBEKNOWNST TO ME...
SULABAN LIRN IS COMMENCING TO ENDING THE LIVES OF OURSELVES, SULABAN VAS AND URN.
FAILURE TO WINNING OF CONTEST OF SPEEDING, AND MUCH SHAMEFUL RECEIVING TO DUNG OF CHICKENS, MAKES UNBEARING TO OUR LIVING...
...WE ARE THANKING TO OPPONENTS AND COUNT THEM A KINDNESS. SO SAYING, WE DIE GIVING OF BLOOD.
...PUDDY AN' DWAYNE TH' GOPHER RANGER HAD STOWED AWAY AN' WERE 'BOUT TA WITNESS TH' GRUESOME DEMISE O' TH' ALIEN SPROUTS!
NO!!!
RIP!
THEY DIDN'T CALL PUDDY "PUDDYFACE" FOR NOTHIN'!
TH' SIGHT O' THAT CUTE LI'L MUG ALL SCREWED UP IN HER BEST "START-TO-CRYIN'" FACE WAS ENOUGH T'SOFTEN EVEN A TEOMAN HEART
THE SPROUTS FIGURED TH' SHAME O' HURTIN' SUCH A LOVEABLE CREATURE WAS WORSE THAN TH' SHAME OF A GOOD SHELLACKIN' WITH CHICKEN CRAP!
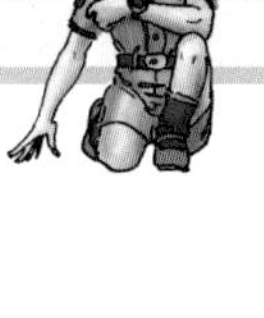

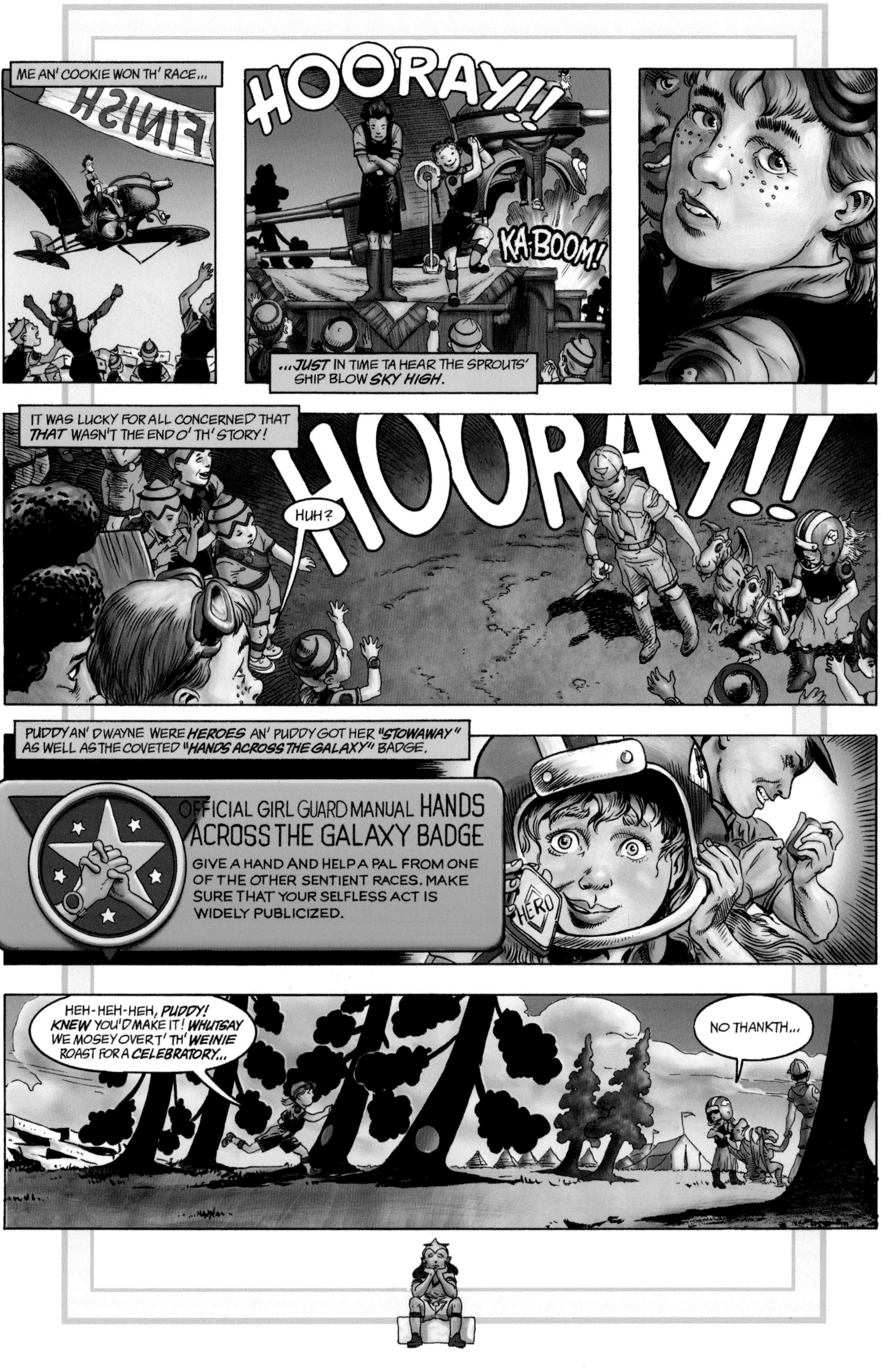
ME AN' COOKIE WON TH' RACE...
FINISH
HOORAY!!
KA-BOOM!
...JUST IN TIME TA HEAR THE SPROUTS' SHIP BLOW SKY HIGH.
IT WAS LUCKY FOR ALL CONCERNED THAT THAT WASN'T THE END O' TH' STORY!
HOORAY!!
HUH?
PUDDY AN' DWAYNE WERE HEROES AN' PUDDY GOT HER "STOWAWAY" AS WELL AS THE COVETED "HANDS ACROSS THE GALAXY" BADGE.
OFFICIAL GIRL GUARD MANUAL HANDS ACROSS THE GALAXY BADGE
GIVE A HAND AND HELP A PAL FROM ONE OF THE OTHER SENTIENT RACES. MAKE SURE THAT YOUR SELFLESS ACT IS WIDELY PUBLICIZED.
HERO
HEH-HEH-HEH, PUDDY! KNEW YOU'D MAKE IT! WHUTSAY WE MOSEY OVER T' TH' WEINIE ROAST FOR A CELEBRATORY...
NO THANKTH...

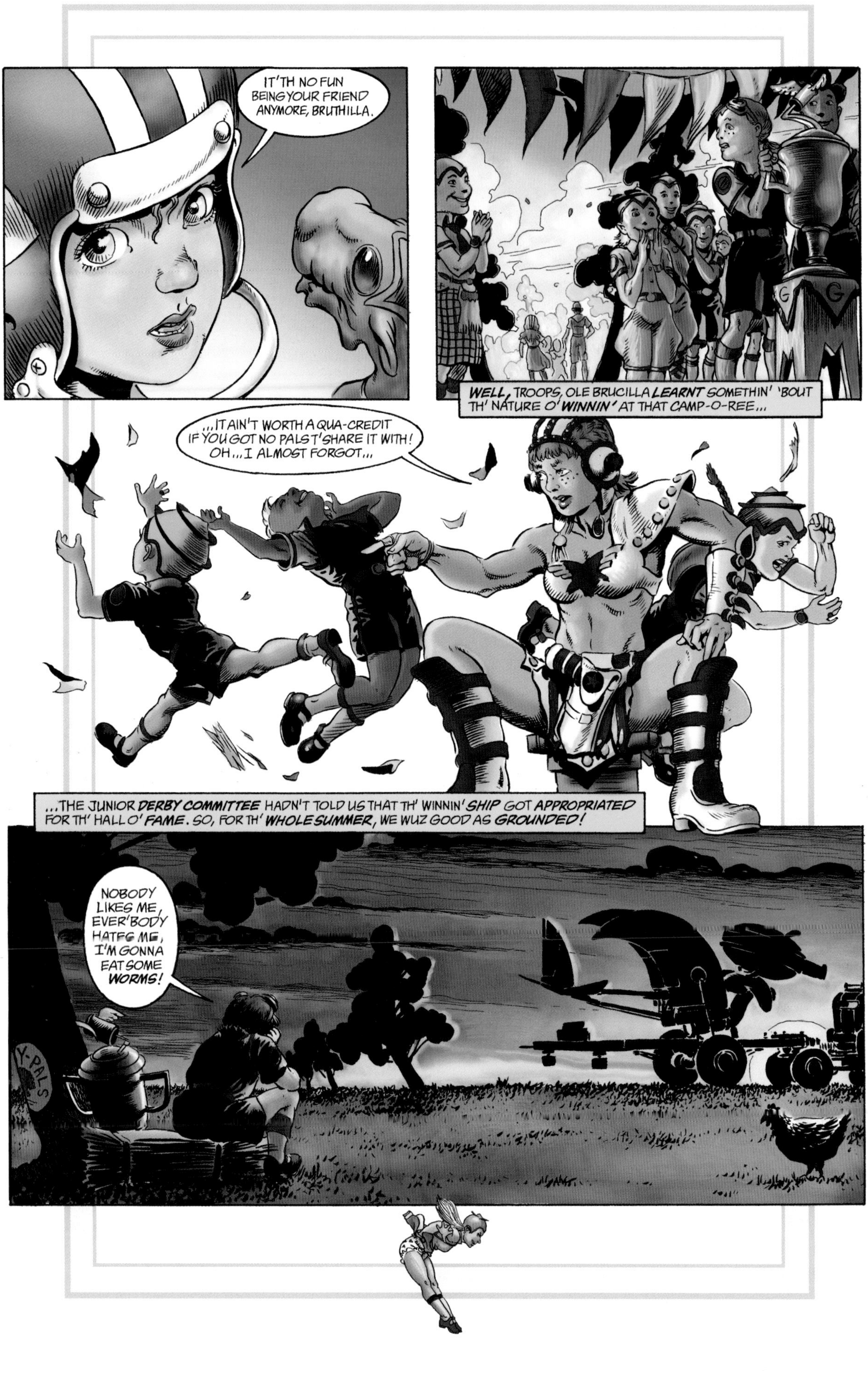
IT'TH NO FUN BEING YOUR FRIEND ANYMORE, BRUTHILLA.
WELL, TROOPS, OLE BRUCILLA LEARNT SOMETHIN' 'BOUT TH' NATURE O' WINNIN' AT THAT CAMP-O-REE...
...IT AIN'T WORTH A QUA-CREDIT IF YOU GOT NO PALS T'SHARE IT WITH! OH... I ALMOST FORGOT...
...THE JUNIOR DERBY COMMITTEE HADN'T TOLD US THAT TH' WINNIN' SHIP GOT APPROPRIATED FOR TH' HALL O' FAME. SO, FOR TH' WHOLE SUMMER, WE WUZ GOOD AS GROUNDED!
NOBODY LIKES ME, EVER'BODY HATES ME, I'M GONNA EAT SOME WORMS!
Y-PALS

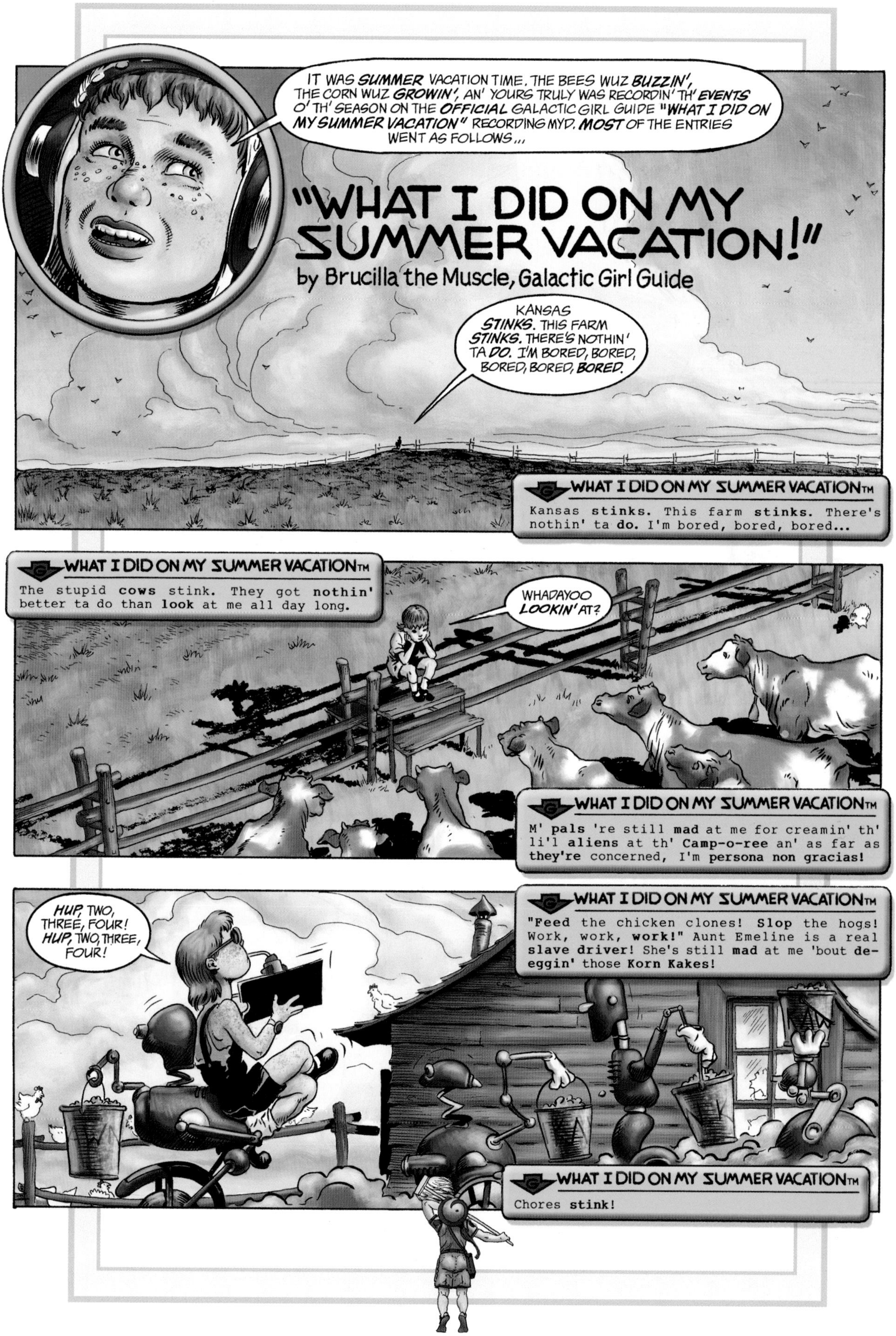
IT WAS SUMMER VACATION TIME. THE BEES WUZ BUZZIN', THE CORN WUZ GROWIN', AN' YOURS TRULY WAS RECORDIN' TH' EVENTS O' TH' SEASON ON THE OFFICIAL GALACTIC GIRL GUIDE "WHAT I DID ON MY SUMMER VACATION" RECORDING MYD. MOST OF THE ENTRIES WENT AS FOLLOWS...
"WHAT I DID ON MY SUMMER VACATION!"
by Brucilla the Muscle, Galactic Girl Guide
KANSAS STINKS. THIS FARM STINKS. THERE'S NOTHIN' TA DO. I'M BORED, BORED, BORED, BORED, BORED.
WHAT I DID ON MY SUMMER VACATION™
Kansas stinks. This farm stinks. There's nothin' ta do. I'm bored, bored, bored...
WHAT I DID ON MY SUMMER VACATION™
The stupid cows stink. They got nothin' better ta do than look at me all day long.
WHADAYOO LOOKIN' AT?
WHAT I DID ON MY SUMMER VACATION™
M' pals 're still mad at me for creamin' th' li'l aliens at th' Camp-o-ree an' as far as they're concerned, I'm persona non gracias!
HUP, TWO, THREE, FOUR! HUP, TWO, THREE, FOUR!
WHAT I DID ON MY SUMMER VACATION™
"Feed the chicken clones! Slop the hogs! Work, work, work!" Aunt Emeline is a real slave driver! She's still mad at me 'bout de-eggin' those Korn Kakes!
WHAT I DID ON MY SUMMER VACATION™
Chores stink!

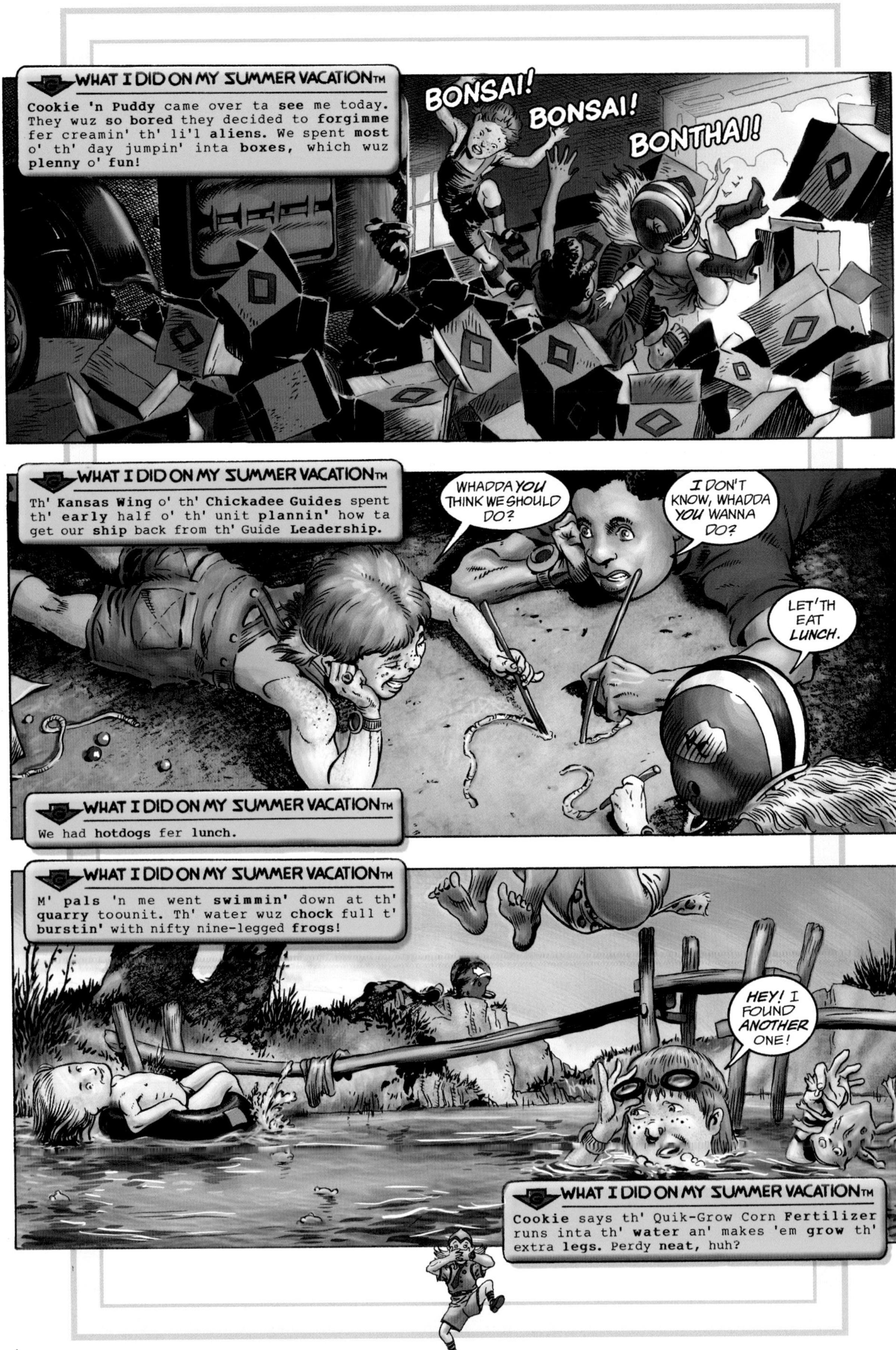
WHAT I DID ON MY SUMMER VACATION™
Cookie 'n Puddy came over ta see me today. They wuz so bored they decided to forgimme fer creamin' th' li'l aliens. We spent most o' th' day jumpin' inta boxes, which wuz plenny o' fun!
BONSAI!
BONSAI!
BONTHAI!
WHAT I DID ON MY SUMMER VACATION™
Th' Kansas Wing o' th' Chickadee Guides spent th' early half o' th' unit plannin' how ta get our ship back from th' Guide Leadership.
WHADDA YOU THINK WE SHOULD DO?
I DON'T KNOW, WHADDA YOU WANNA DO?
LET'TH EAT LUNCH.
WHAT I DID ON MY SUMMER VACATION™
We had hotdogs fer lunch.
WHAT I DID ON MY SUMMER VACATION™
M' pals 'n me went swimmin' down at th' quarry toounit. Th' water wuz chock full t' burstin' with nifty nine-legged frogs!
HEY! I FOUND ANOTHER ONE!
WHAT I DID ON MY SUMMER VACATION™
Cookie says th' Quik-Grow Corn Fertilizer runs inta th' water an' makes 'em grow th' extra legs. Perdy neat, huh?

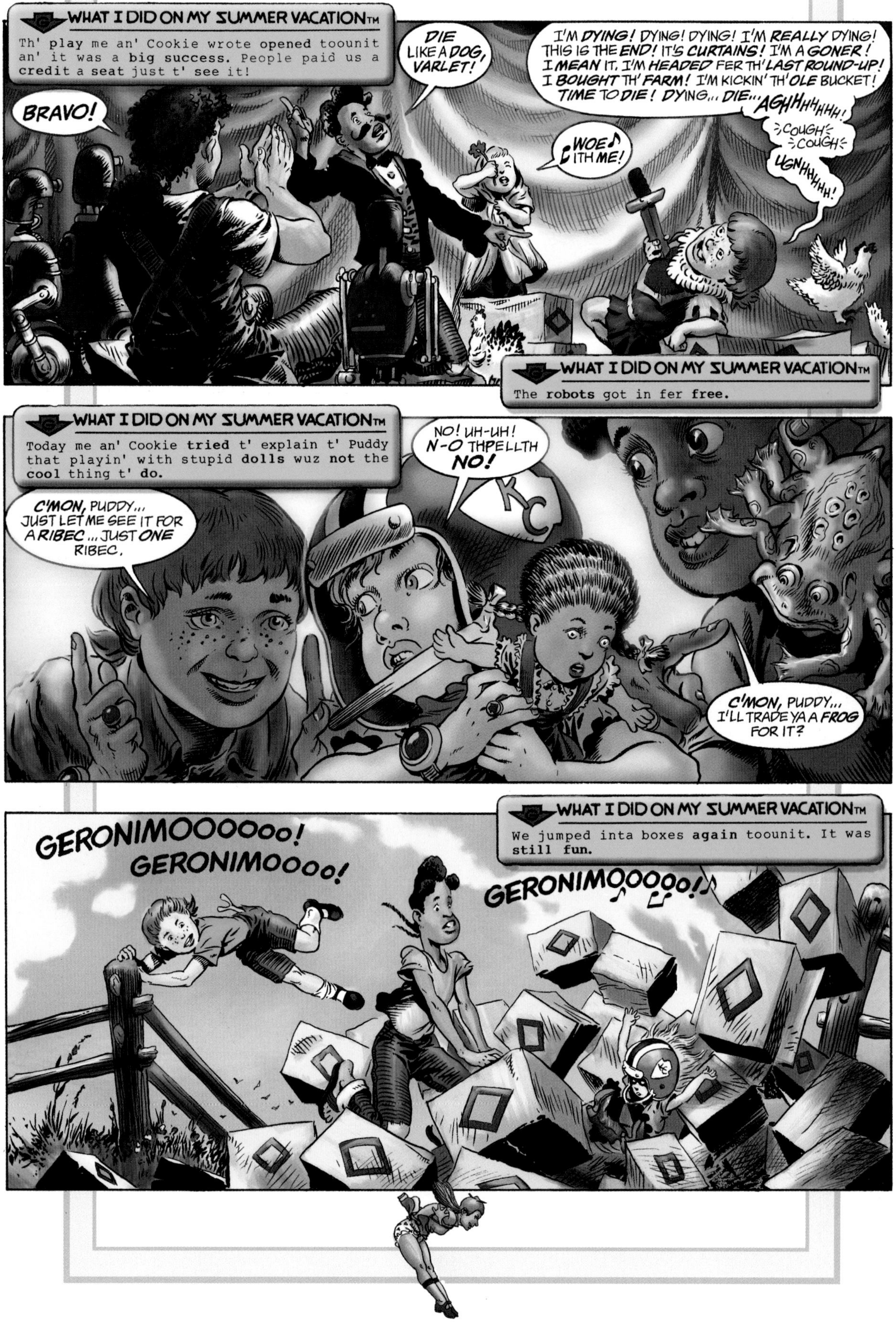
WHAT I DID ON MY SUMMER VACATION™
Th' play me an' Cookie wrote opened toounit an' it was a big success. People paid us a credit a seat just t' see it!
BRAVO!
DIE LIKE A DOG, VARLET!
I'M DYING! DYING! DYING! I'M REALLY DYING! THIS IS THE END! IT'S CURTAINS! I'M A GONER! I MEAN IT. I'M HEADED FER TH' LAST ROUND-UP! I BOUGHT TH' FARM! I'M KICKIN' TH' OLE BUCKET! TIME TO DIE! DYING... DIE... AGHHHHHHH!
COUGH COUGH
UGNHHHHHH!
WOE ITH ME!
WHAT I DID ON MY SUMMER VACATION™
The robots got in fer free.
WHAT I DID ON MY SUMMER VACATION™
Today me an' Cookie tried t' explain t' Puddy that playin' with stupid dolls wuz not the cool thing t' do.
NO! UH-UH! N-O THPELLTH NO!
C'MON, PUDDY... JUST LET ME SEE IT FOR A RIBEC... JUST ONE RIBEC.
C'MON, PUDDY... I'LL TRADE YA A FROG FOR IT?
WHAT I DID ON MY SUMMER VACATION™
We jumped inta boxes again toounit. It was still fun.
GERONIMOOOOOoo!
GERONIMOoooo!
GERONIMOOOOO!

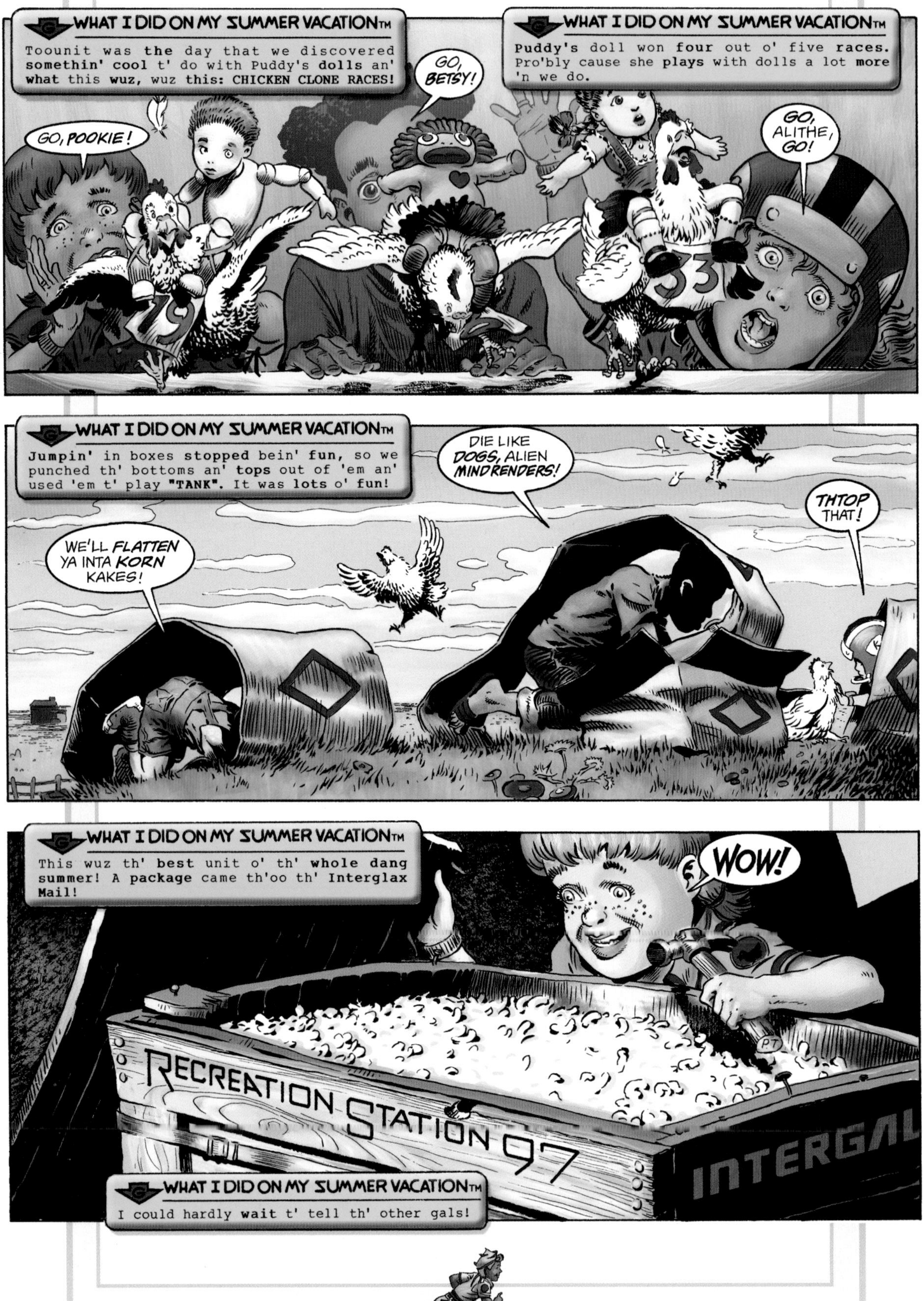
WHAT I DID ON MY SUMMER VACATION™
Toounit was the day that we discovered somethin' cool t' do with Puddy's dolls an' what this wuz, wuz this: CHICKEN CLONE RACES!
GO, POOKIE!
GO, BETSY!
WHAT I DID ON MY SUMMER VACATION™
Puddy's doll won four out o' five races. Pro'bly cause she plays with dolls a lot more 'n we do.
GO, ALITHE, GO!
33
19
WHAT I DID ON MY SUMMER VACATION™
Jumpin' in boxes stopped bein' fun, so we punched th' bottoms an' tops out of 'em an' used 'em t' play "TANK". It was lots o' fun!
DIE LIKE DOGS, ALIEN MINDRENDERS!
WE'LL FLATTEN YA INTA KORN KAKES!
THTOP THAT!
WHAT I DID ON MY SUMMER VACATION™
This wuz th' best unit o' th' whole dang summer! A package came th'oo th' Interglax Mail!
WOW!
RECREATION STATION 97
INTERGAL
WHAT I DID ON MY SUMMER VACATION™
I could hardly wait t' tell th' other gals!

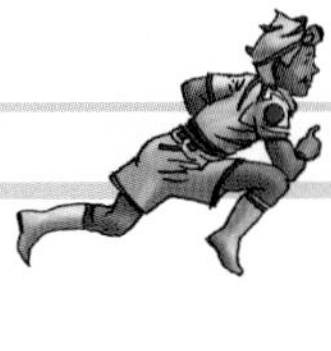

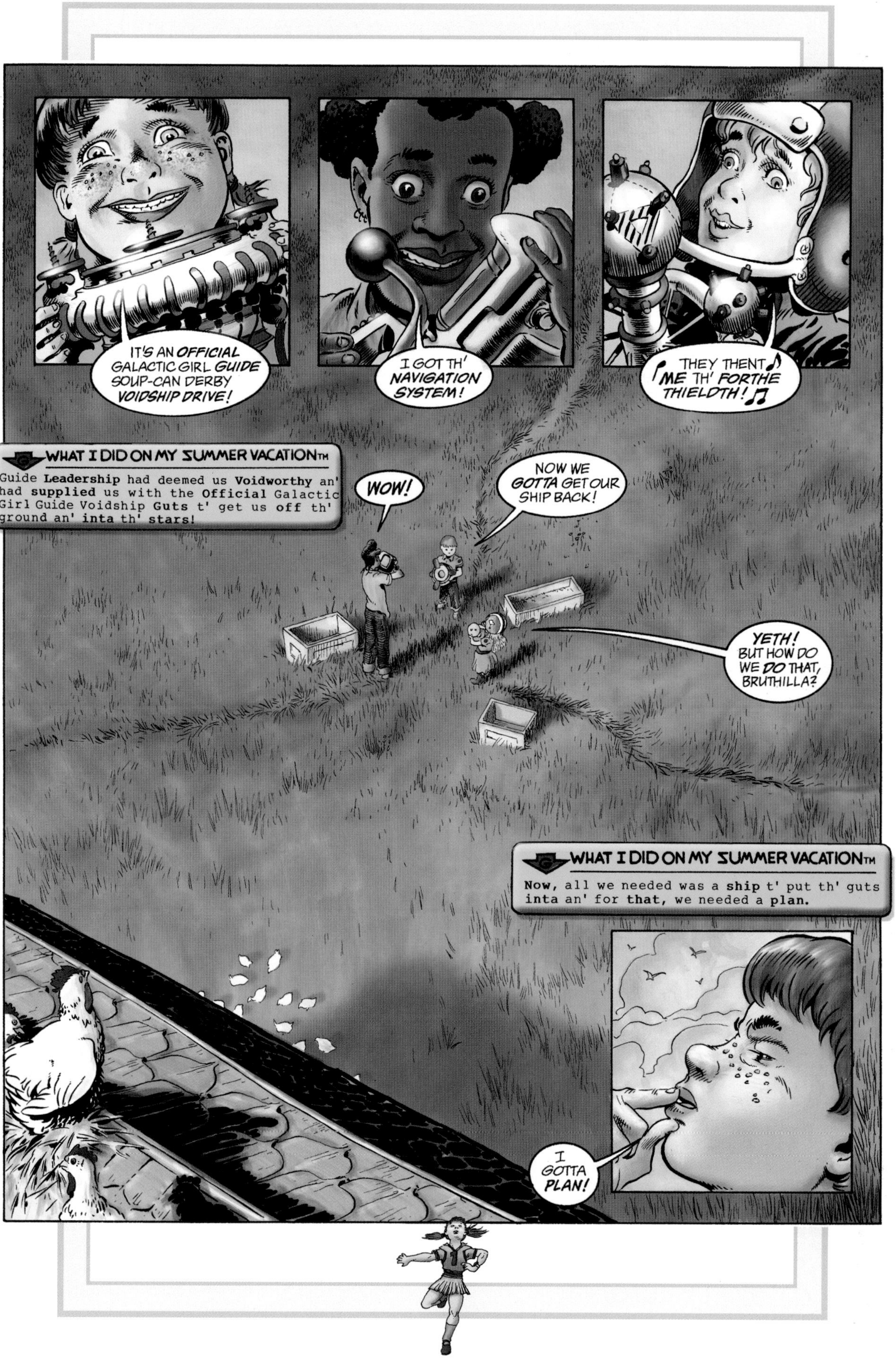
IT'S AN OFFICIAL GALACTIC GIRL GUIDE SOUP-CAN DERBY VOIDSHIP DRIVE!
I GOT TH' NAVIGATION SYSTEM!
THEY THENT ME TH' FORTHE THIELDTH!
WHAT I DID ON MY SUMMER VACATION™
Guide Leadership had deemed us Voidworthy an' had supplied us with the Official Galactic Girl Guide Voidship Guts t' get us off th' ground an' inta th' stars!
WOW!
NOW WE GOTTA GET OUR SHIP BACK!
YETH! BUT HOW DO WE DO THAT, BRUTHILLA?
WHAT I DID ON MY SUMMER VACATION™
Now, all we needed was a ship t' put th' guts inta an' for that, we needed a plan.
I GOTTA PLAN!

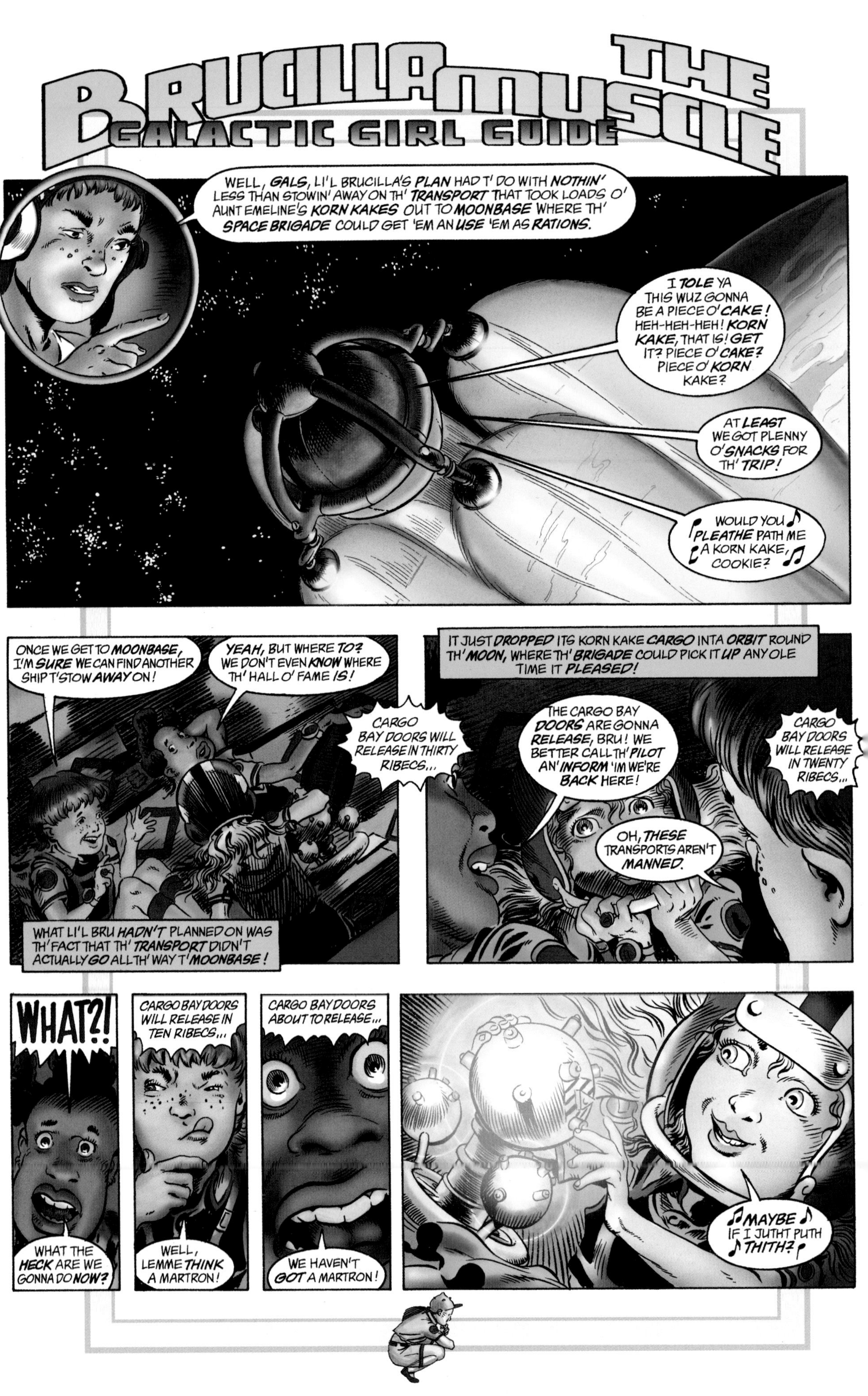
BRUCILLA THE MUSCLE
GALACTIC GIRL GUIDE
WELL, GALS, LI'L BRUCILLA'S PLAN HAD T' DO WITH NOTHIN' LESS THAN STOWIN' AWAY ON TH' TRANSPORT THAT TOOK LOADS O' AUNT EMELINE'S KORN KAKES OUT TO MOONBASE WHERE TH' SPACE BRIGADE COULD GET 'EM AN USE 'EM AS RATIONS.
I TOLE YA THIS WUZ GONNA BE A PIECE O' CAKE! HEH-HEH-HEH! KORN KAKE, THAT IS! GET IT? PIECE O' CAKE? PIECE O' KORN KAKE?
AT LEAST WE GOT PLENNY O' SNACKS FOR TH' TRIP!
WOULD YOU PLEATHE PATH ME A KORN KAKE, COOKIE?
ONCE WE GET TO MOONBASE, I'M SURE WE CAN FIND ANOTHER SHIP T' STOW AWAY ON!
YEAH, BUT WHERE TO? WE DON'T EVEN KNOW WHERE TH' HALL O' FAME IS!
CARGO BAY DOORS WILL RELEASE IN THIRTY RIBECS...
WHAT LI'L BRU HADN'T PLANNED ON WAS TH' FACT THAT TH' TRANSPORT DIDN'T ACTUALLY GO ALL TH' WAY T' MOONBASE!
IT JUST DROPPED ITS KORN KAKE CARGO INTA ORBIT ROUND TH' MOON, WHERE TH' BRIGADE COULD PICK IT UP ANY OLE TIME IT PLEASED!
THE CARGO BAY DOORS ARE GONNA RELEASE, BRU! WE BETTER CALL TH' PILOT AN' INFORM 'IM WE'RE BACK HERE!
CARGO BAY DOORS WILL RELEASE IN TWENTY RIBECS...
OH, THESE TRANSPORTS AREN'T MANNED.
WHAT?!
WHAT THE HECK ARE WE GONNA DO NOW?
CARGO BAY DOORS WILL RELEASE IN TEN RIBECS...
WELL, LEMME THINK A MARTRON!
CARGO BAY DOORS ABOUT TO RELEASE...
WE HAVEN'T GOT A MARTRON!
MAYBE IF I JUTHT PUTH THITH?

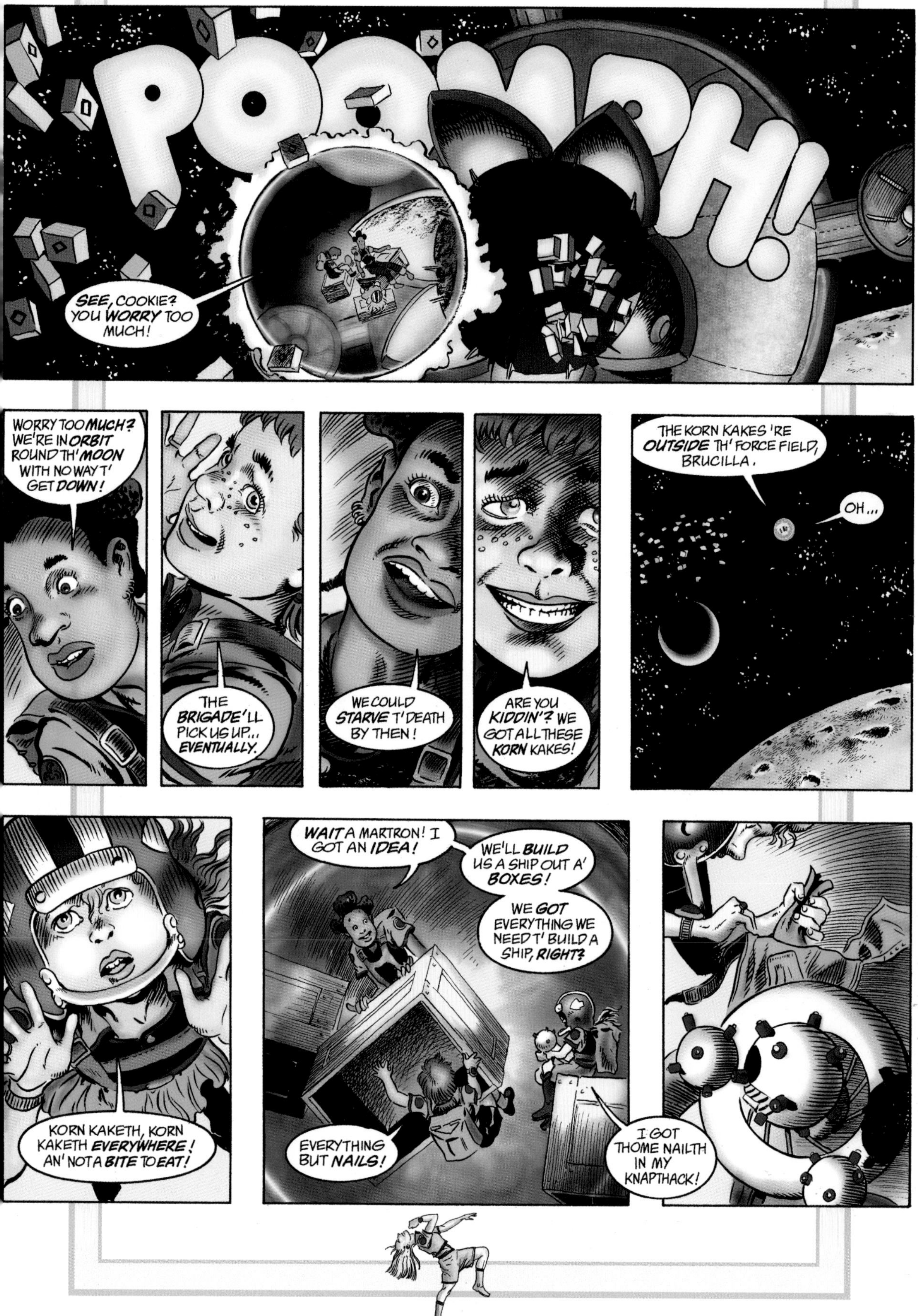
POOMPH!
SEE, COOKIE? YOU WORRY TOO MUCH!
WORRY TOO MUCH? WE'RE IN ORBIT ROUND TH' MOON WITH NO WAY T' GET DOWN!
THE BRIGADE'LL PICK US UP... EVENTUALLY.
WE COULD STARVE T' DEATH BY THEN!
ARE YOU KIDDIN'? WE GOT ALL THESE KORN KAKES!
THE KORN KAKES 'RE OUTSIDE TH' FORCE FIELD, BRUCILLA.
OH...
KORN KAKETH, KORN KAKETH EVERYWHERE! AN' NOT A BITE TO EAT!
WAIT A MARTRON! I GOT AN IDEA!
WE'LL BUILD US A SHIP OUT A' BOXES!
WE GOT EVERYTHING WE NEED T' BUILD A SHIP, RIGHT?
EVERYTHING BUT NAILS!
I GOT THOME NAILTH IN MY KNAPTHACK!

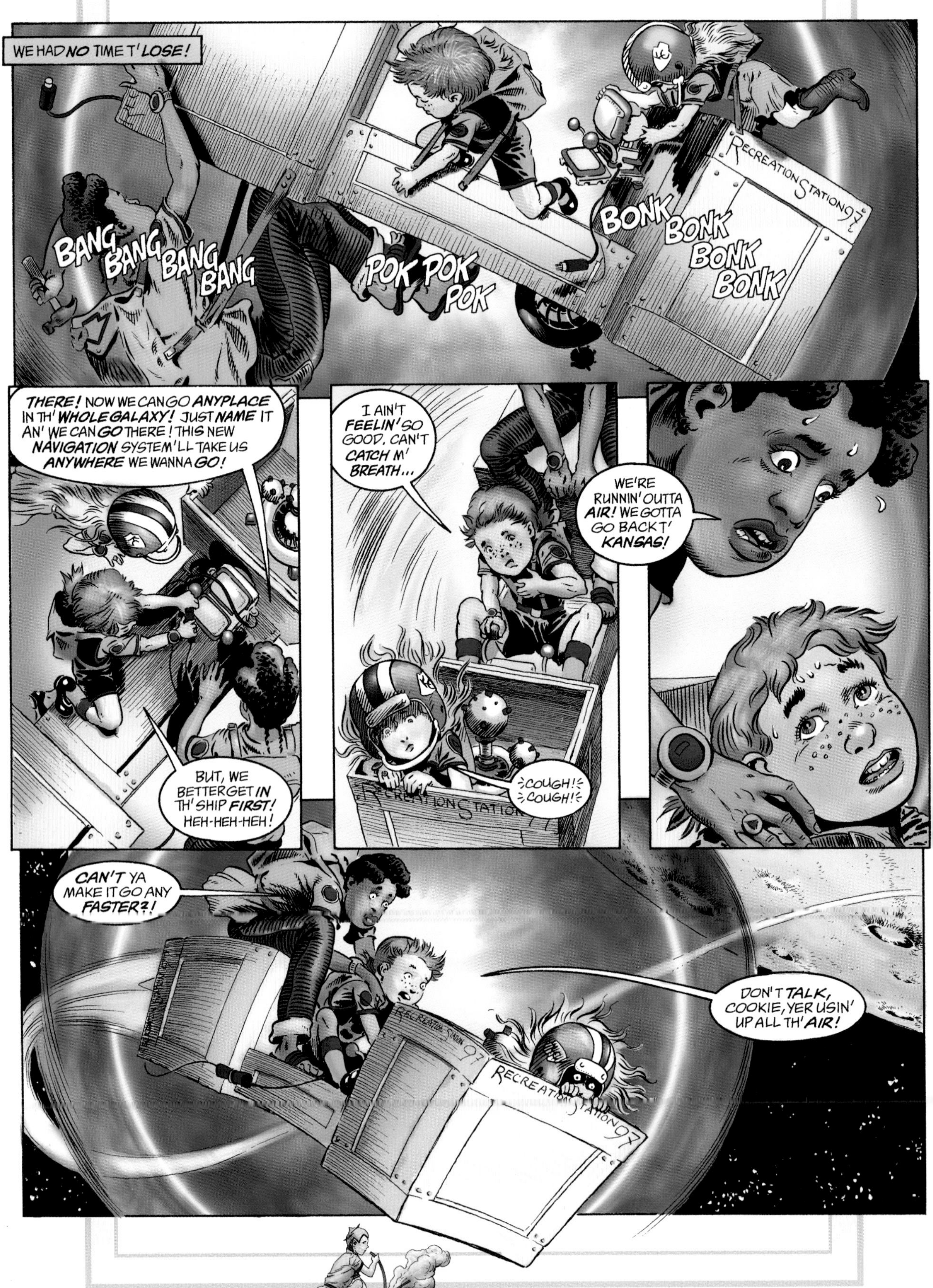
WE HAD NO TIME T' LOSE!
BANG BANG BANG BANG
POK POK POK
BONK BONK BONK BONK
RECREATION STATION 97
THERE! NOW WE CAN GO ANYPLACE IN TH' WHOLE GALAXY! JUST NAME IT AN' WE CAN GO THERE! THIS NEW NAVIGATION SYSTEM'LL TAKE US ANYWHERE WE WANNA GO!
BUT, WE BETTER GET IN TH' SHIP FIRST! HEH-HEH-HEH!
I AIN'T FEELIN' SO GOOD. CAN'T CATCH M' BREATH...
COUGH! COUGH!
WE'RE RUNNIN' OUTTA AIR! WE GOTTA GO BACK T' KANSAS!
CAN'T YA MAKE IT GO ANY FASTER?!
DON'T TALK, COOKIE, YER USIN' UP ALL TH' AIR!

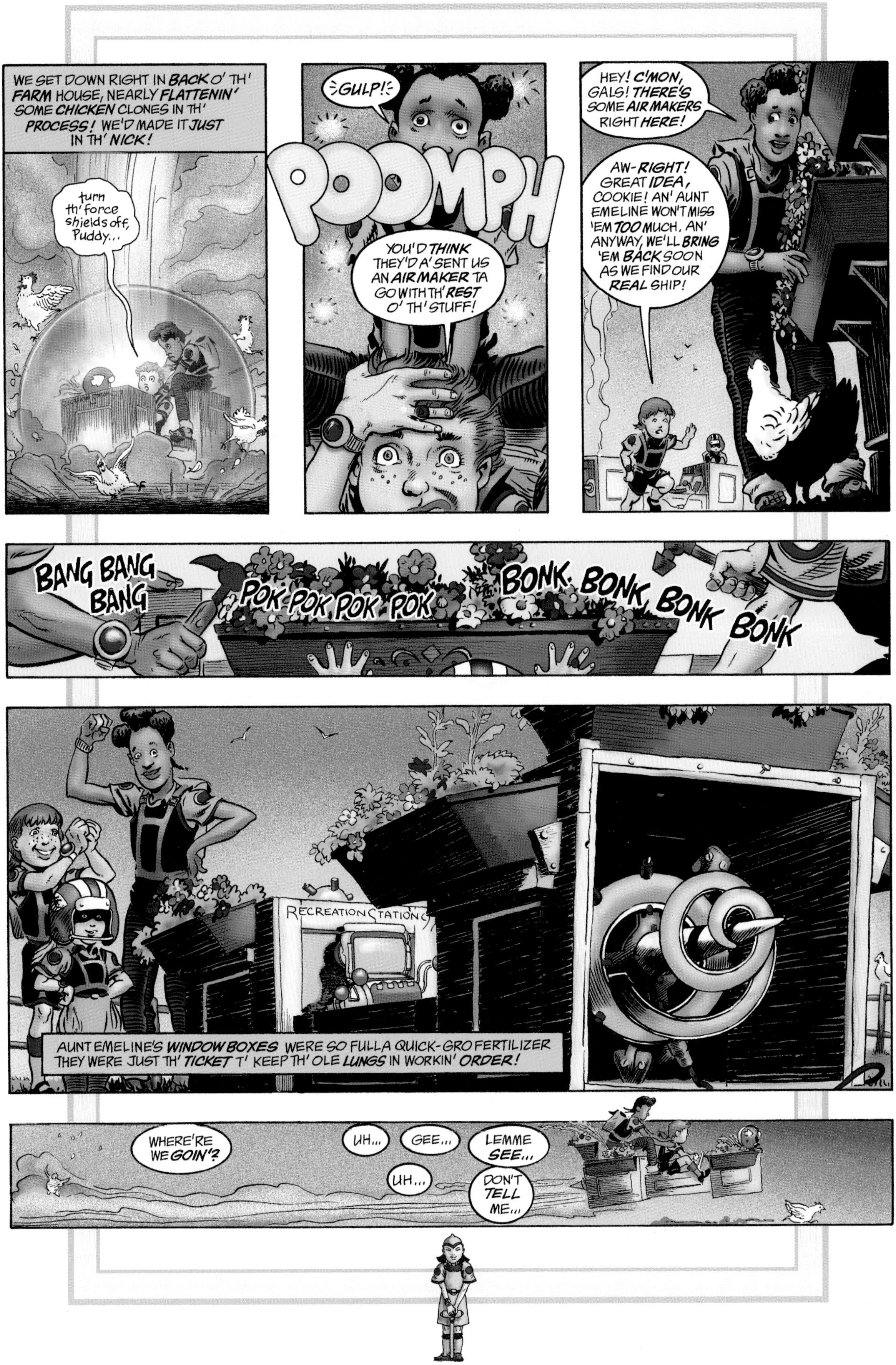
WE SET DOWN RIGHT IN BACK O' TH' FARM HOUSE, NEARLY FLATTENIN' SOME CHICKEN CLONES IN TH' PROCESS! WE'D MADE IT JUST IN TH' NICK!
turn th' force shields off, Puddy...
GULP!
POOMPH
YOU'D THINK THEY'D A' SENT US AN AIR MAKER TA GO WITH TH' REST O' TH' STUFF!
HEY! C'MON, GALS! THERE'S SOME AIR MAKERS RIGHT HERE!
AW-RIGHT! GREAT IDEA, COOKIE! AN' AUNT EMELINE WON'T MISS 'EM TOO MUCH. AN' ANYWAY, WE'LL BRING 'EM BACK SOON AS WE FIND OUR REAL SHIP!
BANG BANG BANG
POK POK POK POK
BONK BONK BONK BONK
RECREATION STATION
AUNT EMELINE'S WINDOW BOXES WERE SO FULLA QUICK-GRO FERTILIZER THEY WERE JUST TH' TICKET T' KEEP TH' OLE LUNGS IN WORKIN' ORDER!
WHERE'RE WE GOIN'?
UH...
GEE...
UH...
LEMME SEE...
DON'T TELL ME...

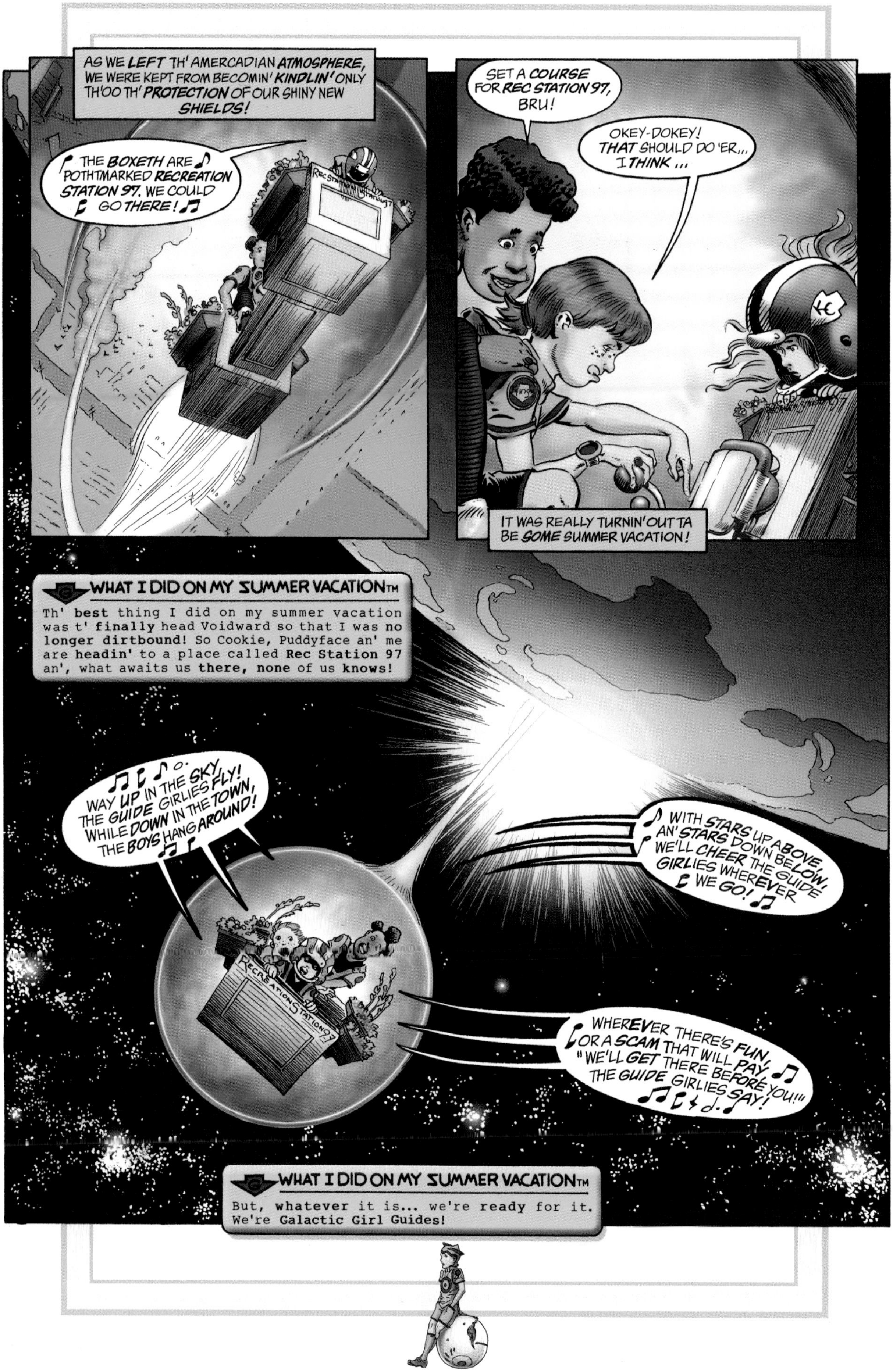
AS WE LEFT TH' AMERCADIAN ATMOSPHERE, WE WERE KEPT FROM BECOMIN' KINDLIN' ONLY TH'OO TH' PROTECTION OF OUR SHINY NEW SHIELDS!
THE BOXETH ARE POTHTMARKED RECREATION STATION 97. WE COULD GO THERE!
REC STATION 97
SET A COURSE FOR REC STATION 97, BRU!
OKEY-DOKEY! THAT SHOULD DO 'ER... I THINK...
IT WAS REALLY TURNIN' OUT TA BE SOME SUMMER VACATION!
WHAT I DID ON MY SUMMER VACATION™
Th' best thing I did on my summer vacation was t' finally head Voidward so that I was no longer dirtbound! So Cookie, Puddyface an' me are headin' to a place called Rec Station 97 an', what awaits us there, none of us knows!
WAY UP IN THE SKY, THE GUIDE GIRLIES FLY! WHILE DOWN IN THE TOWN, THE BOYS HANG AROUND!
WITH STARS UP ABOVE, AN' STARS DOWN BELOW, WE'LL CHEER THE GUIDE GIRLIES WHEREVER WE GO!
RECREATION STATION 97
WHEREVER THERE'S FUN, OR A SCAM THAT WILL PAY, "WE'LL GET THERE BEFORE YOU!" THE GUIDE GIRLIES SAY!
WHAT I DID ON MY SUMMER VACATION™
But, whatever it is... we're ready for it. We're Galactic Girl Guides!

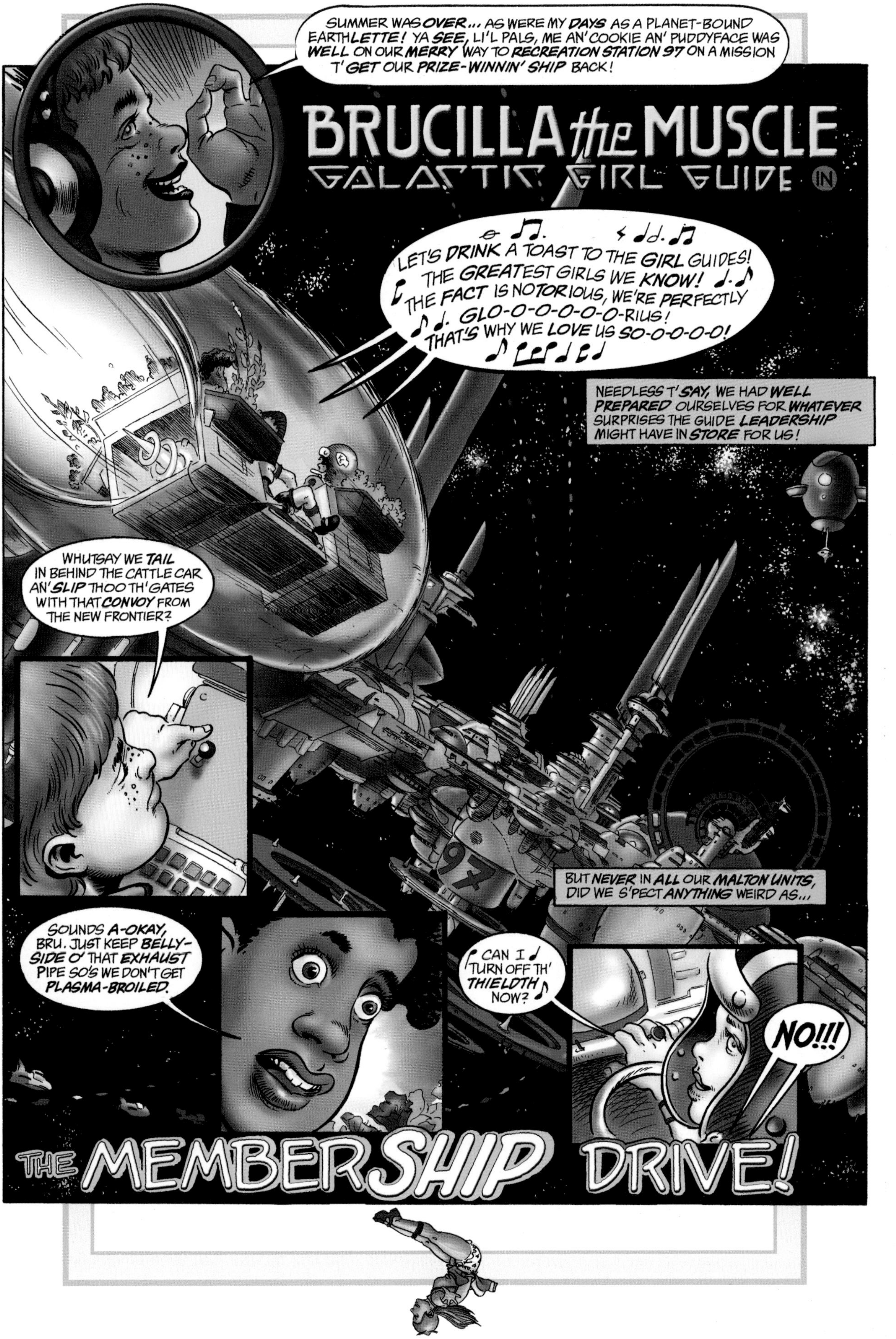
SUMMER WAS OVER... AS WERE MY DAYS AS A PLANET-BOUND EARTHLETTE! YA SEE, LI'L PALS, ME AN' COOKIE AN' PUDDYFACE WAS WELL ON OUR MERRY WAY TO RECREATION STATION 97 ON A MISSION T'GET OUR PRIZE-WINNIN' SHIP BACK!
BRUCILLA the MUSCLE
GALACTIC GIRL GUIDE IN
LET'S DRINK A TOAST TO THE GIRL GUIDES! THE GREATEST GIRLS WE KNOW! THE FACT IS NOTORIOUS, WE'RE PERFECTLY GLO-O-O-O-O-O-O-RIUS! THAT'S WHY WE LOVE US SO-O-O-O-O!
NEEDLESS T'SAY, WE HAD WELL PREPARED OURSELVES FOR WHATEVER SURPRISES THE GUIDE LEADERSHIP MIGHT HAVE IN STORE FOR US!
WHUTSAY WE TAIL IN BEHIND THE CATTLE CAR AN' SLIP THOO TH'GATES WITH THAT CONVOY FROM THE NEW FRONTIER?
BUT NEVER IN ALL OUR MALTON UNITS, DID WE S'PECT ANYTHING WEIRD AS...
SOUNDS A-OKAY, BRU. JUST KEEP BELLY-SIDE O' THAT EXHAUST PIPE SO'S WE DON'T GET PLASMA-BROILED.
CAN I TURN OFF TH' THIELDTH NOW?
NO!!!
THE MEMBERSHIP DRIVE!

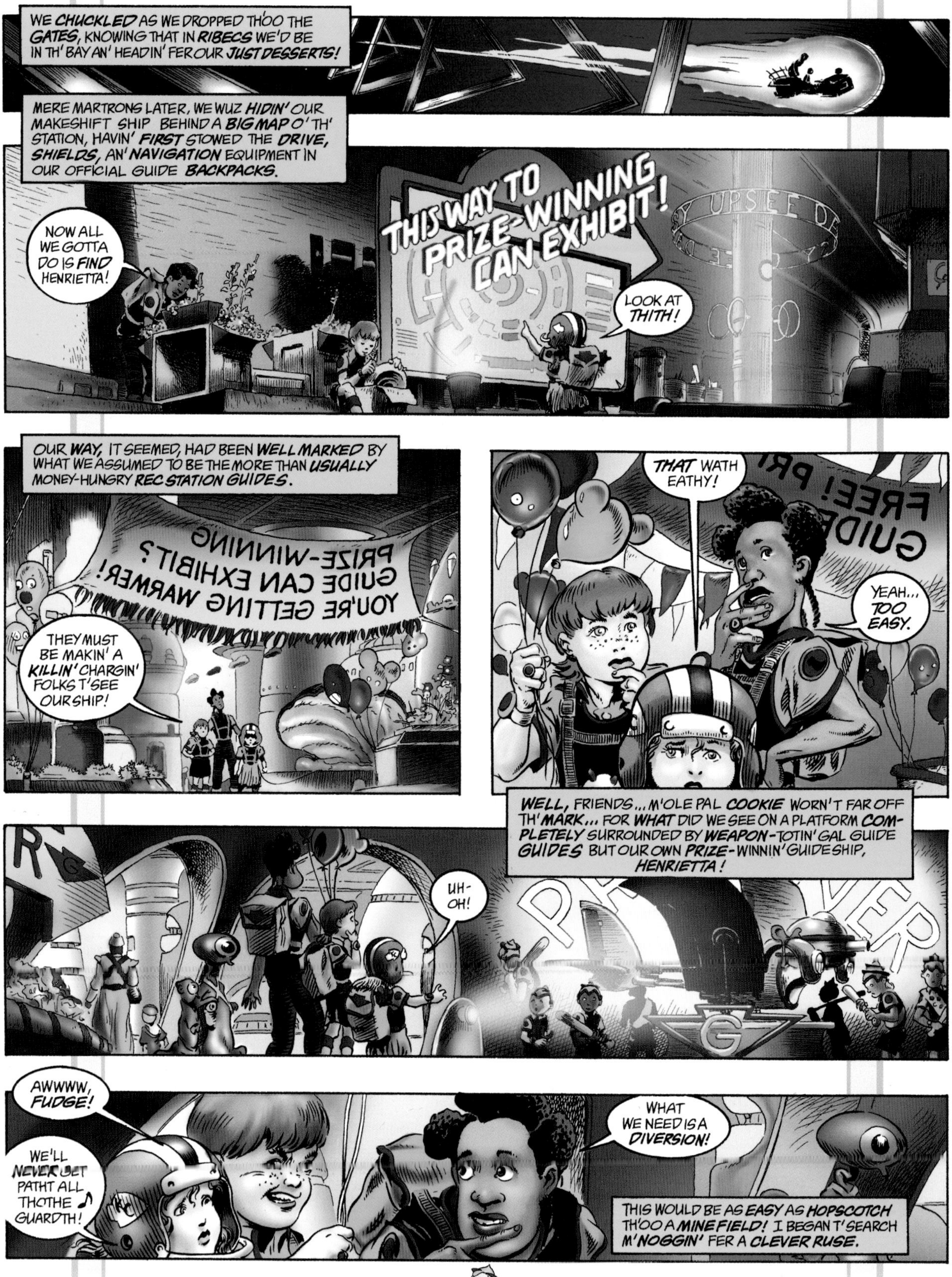

WE CHUCKLED AS WE DROPPED TH'OO THE GATES, KNOWING THAT IN RIBECS WE'D BE IN TH' BAY AN' HEADIN' FER OUR JUST DESSERTS!
MERE MARTRONS LATER, WE WUZ HIDIN' OUR MAKESHIFT SHIP BEHIND A BIG MAP O' TH' STATION, HAVIN' FIRST STOWED THE DRIVE, SHIELDS, AN' NAVIGATION EQUIPMENT IN OUR OFFICIAL GUIDE BACKPACKS.
THIS WAY TO PRIZE-WINNING CAN EXHIBIT!
NOW ALL WE GOTTA DO IS FIND HENRIETTA!
LOOK AT THITH!
OUR WAY, IT SEEMED, HAD BEEN WELL MARKED BY WHAT WE ASSUMED TO BE THE MORE THAN USUALLY MONEY-HUNGRY REC STATION GUIDES.
PRIZE-WINNING GUIDE CAN EXHIBIT? YOU'RE GETTING WARMER!
THEY MUST BE MAKIN' A KILLIN' CHARGIN' FOLKS T'SEE OUR SHIP!
THAT WATH EATHY!
YEAH... TOO EASY.
WELL, FRIENDS... M'OLE PAL COOKIE WORN'T FAR OFF TH' MARK... FOR WHAT DID WE SEE ON A PLATFORM COMPLETELY SURROUNDED BY WEAPON-TOTIN' GAL GUIDE GUIDES BUT OUR OWN PRIZE-WINNIN' GUIDESHIP, HENRIETTA!
UH-OH!
AWWWW, FUDGE!
WE'LL NEVER GET PATHT ALL THOTHE ♪ GUARDTH!
WHAT WE NEED IS A DIVERSION!
THIS WOULD BE AS EASY AS HOPSCOTCH TH'OO A MINE FIELD! I BEGAN T' SEARCH M' NOGGIN' FER A CLEVER RUSE.

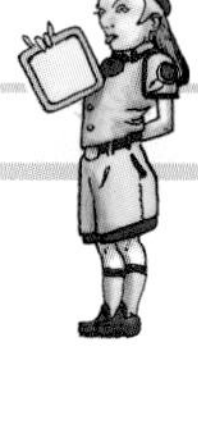

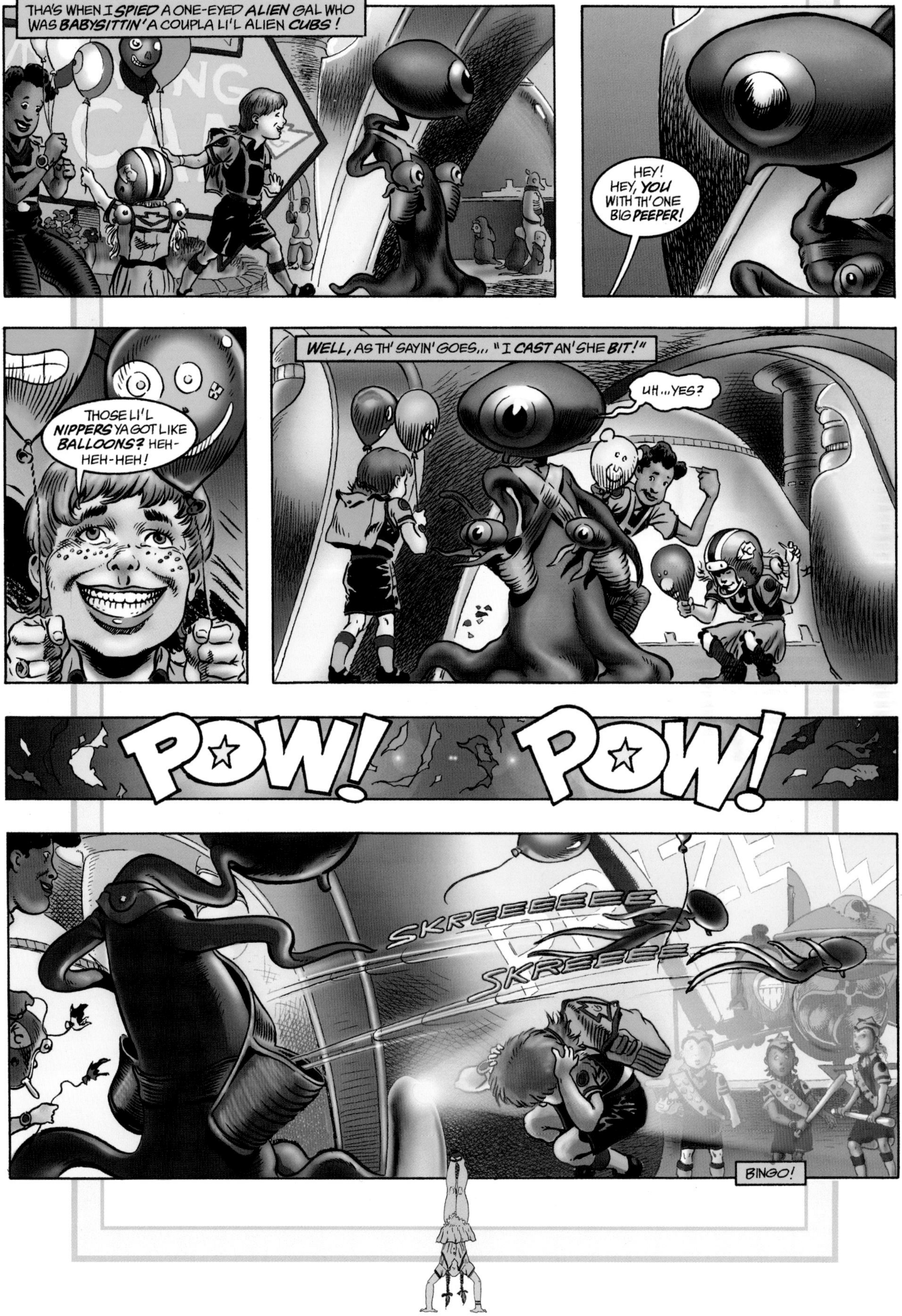
THA'S WHEN I SPIED A ONE-EYED ALIEN GAL WHO WAS BABYSITTIN' A COUPLA LI'L ALIEN CUBS!
HEY! HEY, YOU WITH TH' ONE BIG PEEPER!
THOSE LI'L NIPPERS YA GOT LIKE BALLOONS? HEH-HEH-HEH!
WELL, AS TH' SAYIN' GOES... "I CAST AN' SHE BIT!"
UH...YES?
POW! POW!
SKREEEEEEE
SKREEEEE
BINGO!

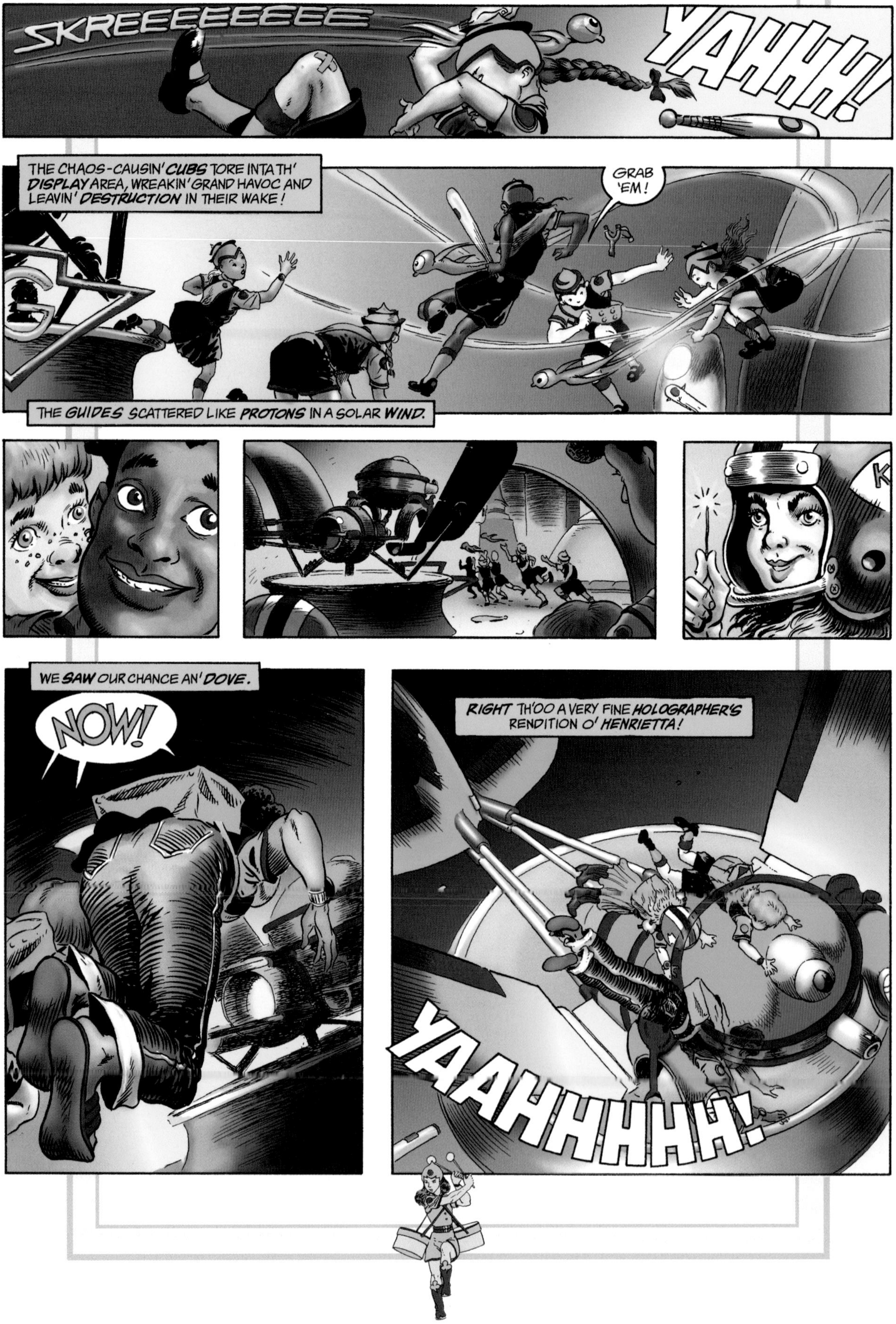
SKREEEEEEEEE
YAHHH!
THE CHAOS-CAUSIN' CUBS TORE INTA TH' DISPLAY AREA, WREAKIN' GRAND HAVOC AND LEAVIN' DESTRUCTION IN THEIR WAKE!
GRAB 'EM!
THE GUIDES SCATTERED LIKE PROTONS IN A SOLAR WIND.
WE SAW OUR CHANCE AN' DOVE.
NOW!
RIGHT TH'OO A VERY FINE HOLOGRAPHER'S RENDITION O' HENRIETTA!
YAAHHHHH!

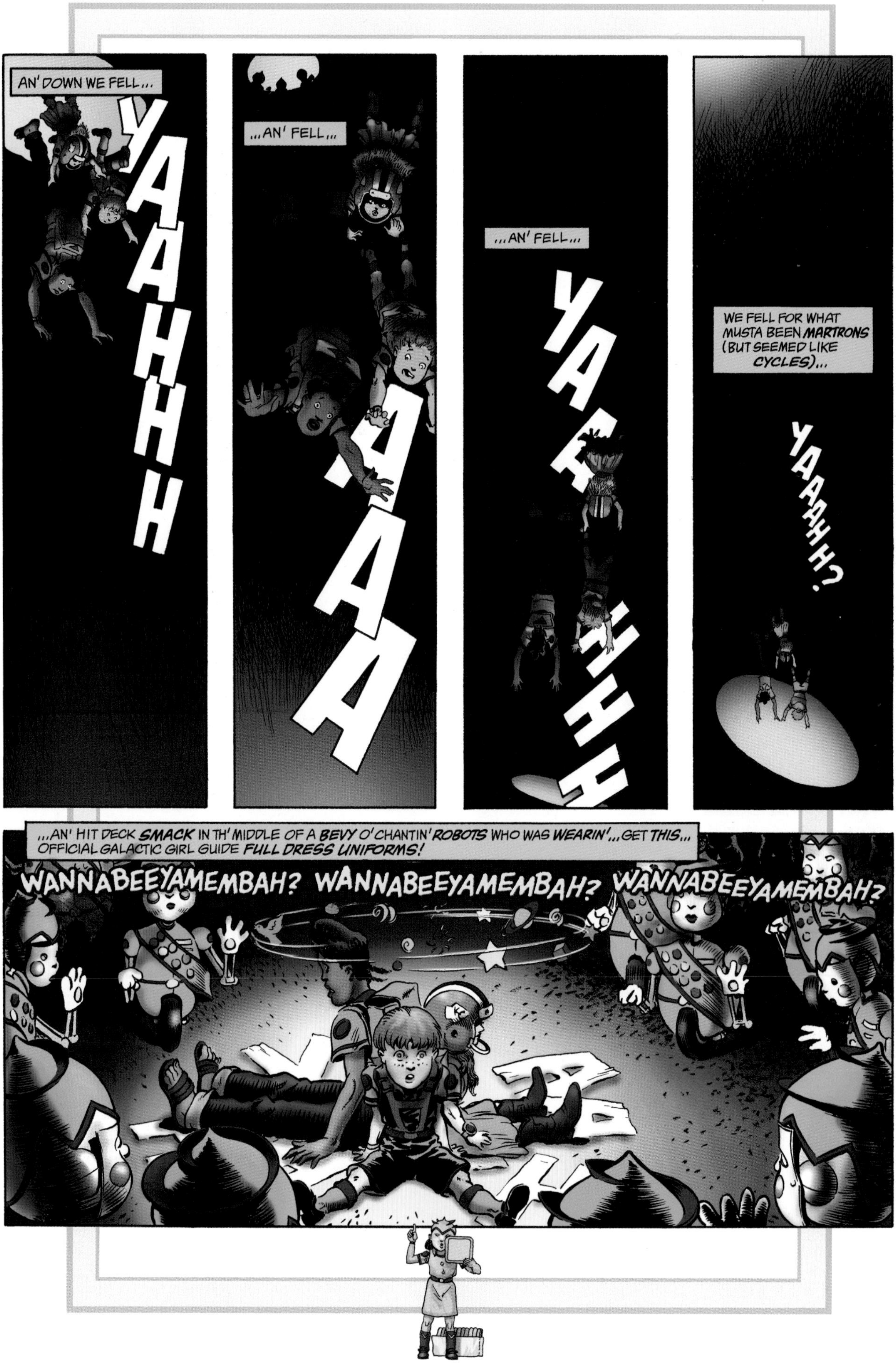

AN' DOWN WE FELL...
YAAHHH
...AN' FELL...
AAAA
...AN' FELL...
YAAAHHH
WE FELL FOR WHAT MUSTA BEEN MARTRONS (BUT SEEMED LIKE CYCLES)...
YAAAHH?
...AN' HIT DECK SMACK IN TH' MIDDLE OF A BEVY O' CHANTIN' ROBOTS WHO WAS WEARIN'... GET THIS... OFFICIAL GALACTIC GIRL GUIDE FULL DRESS UNIFORMS!
WANNABEEYAMEMBAH? WANNABEEYAMEMBAH? WANNABEEYAMEMBAH?

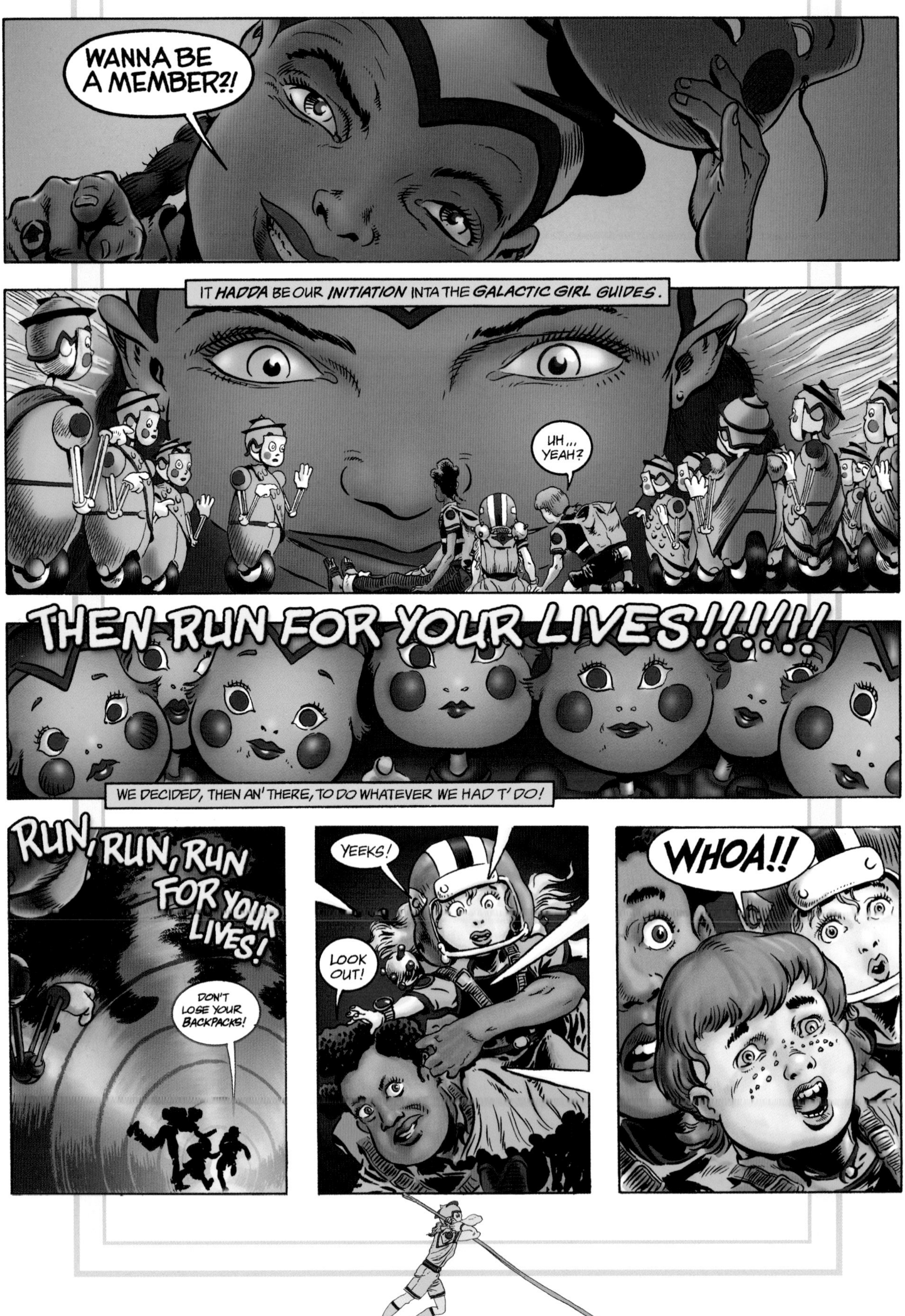
WANNA BE A MEMBER?!
IT HADDA BE OUR INITIATION INTA THE GALACTIC GIRL GUIDES.
UH... YEAH?
THEN RUN FOR YOUR LIVES!!!!!!
WE DECIDED, THEN AN' THERE, TO DO WHATEVER WE HAD T' DO!
RUN, RUN, RUN FOR YOUR LIVES!
DON'T LOSE YOUR BACKPACKS!
YEEKS!
LOOK OUT!
WHOA!!

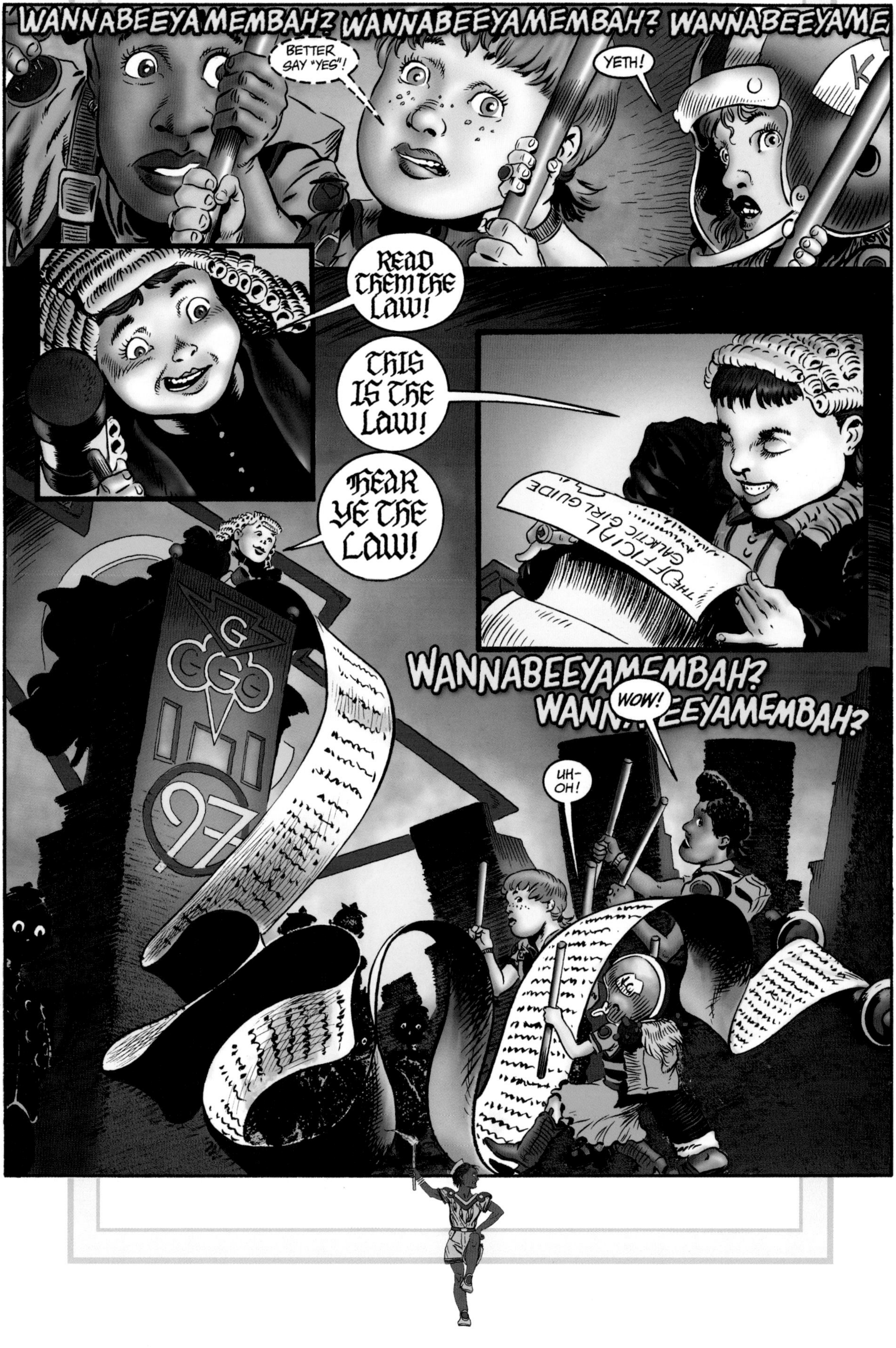
WANNABEEYAMEMBAH? WANNABEEYAMEMBAH? WANNABEEYAME
BETTER SAY "YES"!
YETH!
READ THEM THE LAW!
THIS IS THE LAW!
HEAR YE THE LAW!
THE OFFICIAL GALACTIC GIRL GUIDE
WANNABEEYAMEMBAH?
WANNABEEYAMEMBAH?
WOW!
UH-OH!

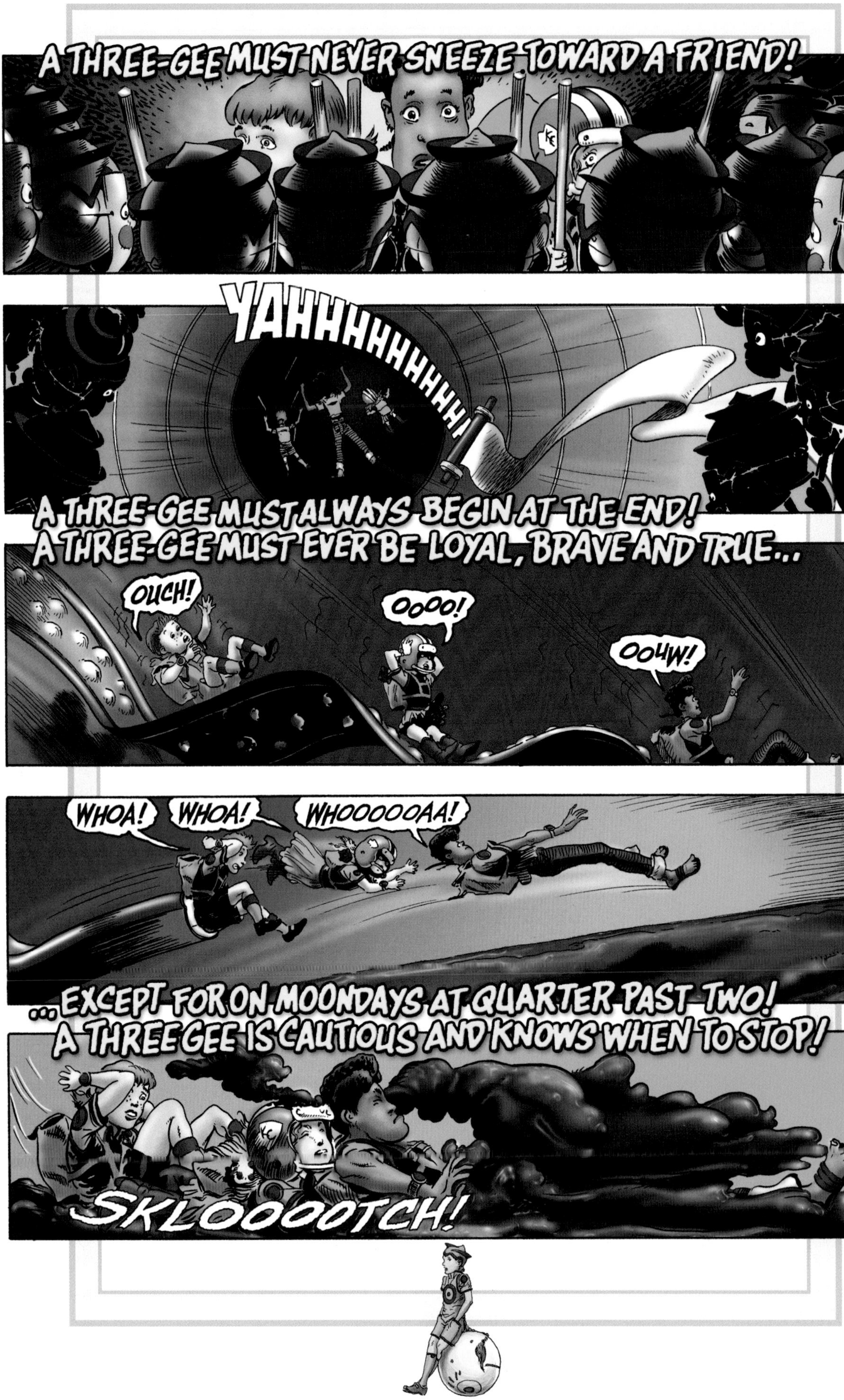
A THREE-GEE MUST NEVER SNEEZE TOWARD A FRIEND!
YAHHHHHHHHHH
A THREE-GEE MUST ALWAYS BEGIN AT THE END!
A THREE-GEE MUST EVER BE LOYAL, BRAVE AND TRUE...
OUCH!
OOOO!
OOUW!
WHOA!
WHOA!
WHOOOOOAA!
...EXCEPT FOR ON MOONDAYS AT QUARTER PAST TWO!
A THREE GEE IS CAUTIOUS AND KNOWS WHEN TO STOP!
SKLOOOOTCH!

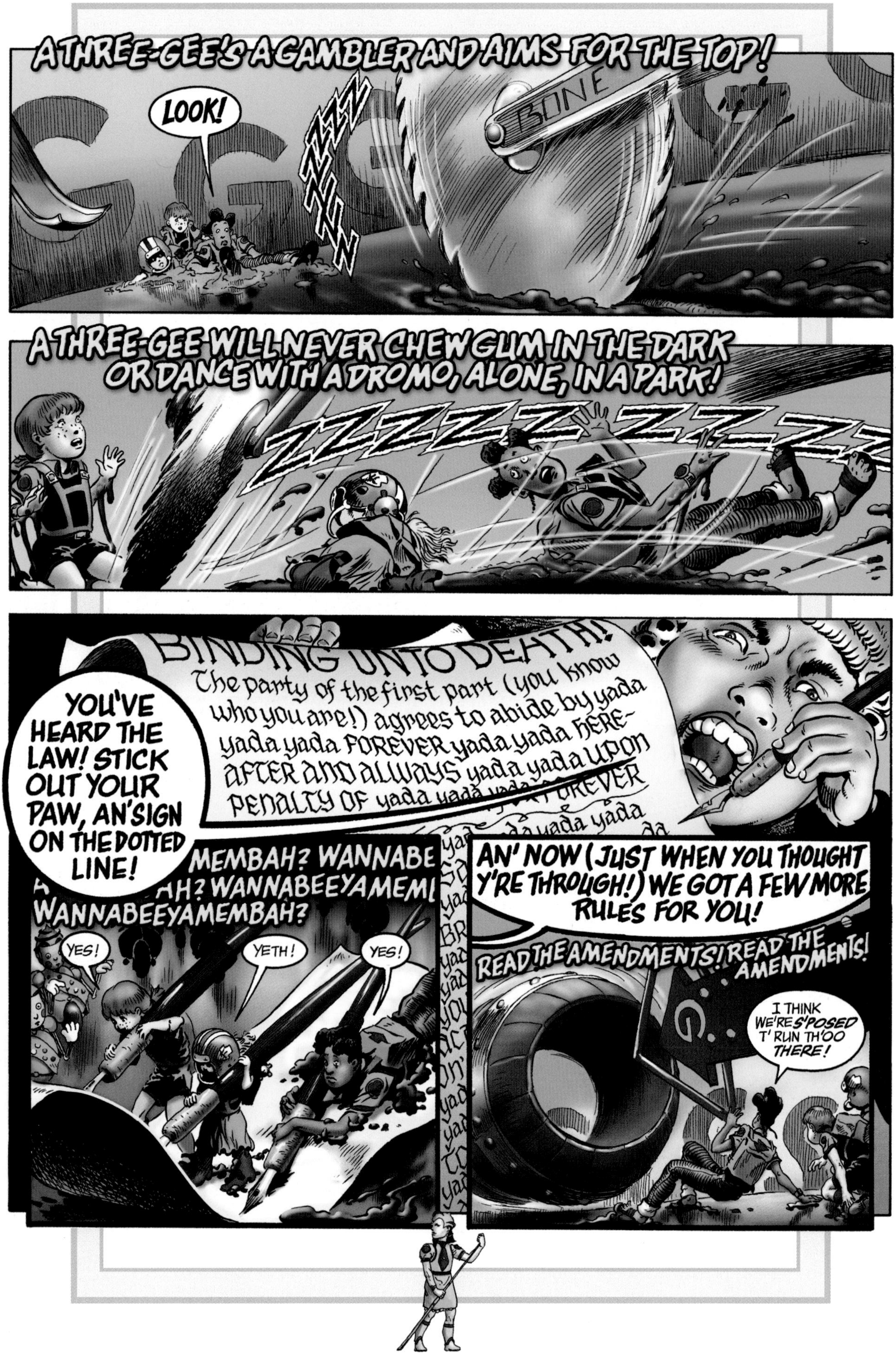

A THREE-GEE'S A GAMBLER AND AIMS FOR THE TOP!
LOOK!
BONE
A THREE-GEE WILL NEVER CHEW GUM IN THE DARK
OR DANCE WITH A DROMO, ALONE, IN A PARK!
YOU'VE HEARD THE LAW! STICK OUT YOUR PAW, AN' SIGN ON THE DOTTED LINE!
BINDING UNTO DEATH!
The party of the first part (you know who you are!) agrees to abide by yada yada yada FOREVER yada yada HERE-AFTER AND ALWAYS yada yada UPON PENALTY OF yada yada yada FOREVER
yada yada
WANNABEEYAMEMBAH?
YES!
YETH!
YES!
AN' NOW (JUST WHEN YOU THOUGHT Y'RE THROUGH!) WE GOT A FEW MORE RULES FOR YOU!
READ THE AMENDMENTS! READ THE AMENDMENTS!
I THINK WE'RE S'POSED T' RUN TH'OO THERE!

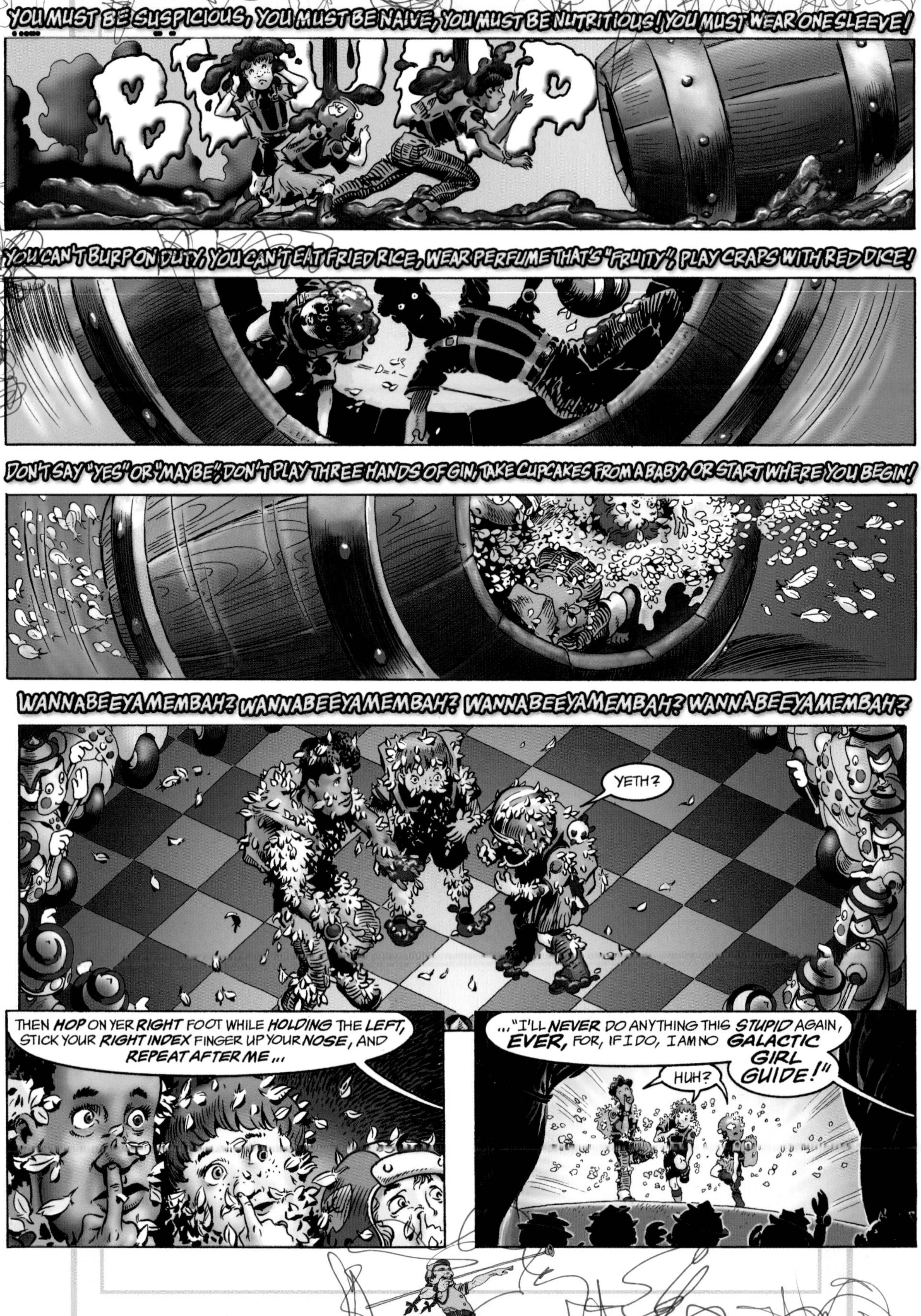
YOU MUST BE SUSPICIOUS, YOU MUST BE NAIVE, YOU MUST BE NUTRITIOUS! YOU MUST WEAR ONE SLEEVE!
YOU CAN'T BURP ON DUTY, YOU CAN'T EAT FRIED RICE, WEAR PERFUME THAT'S "FRUITY", PLAY CRAPS WITH RED DICE!
DON'T SAY "YES" OR "MAYBE", DON'T PLAY THREE HANDS OF GIN, TAKE CUPCAKES FROM A BABY, OR START WHERE YOU BEGIN!
WANNABEEYAMEMBAH? WANNABEEYAMEMBAH? WANNABEEYAMEMBAH? WANNABEEYAMEMBAH?
YETH?
THEN HOP ON YER RIGHT FOOT WHILE HOLDING THE LEFT, STICK YOUR RIGHT INDEX FINGER UP YOUR NOSE, AND REPEAT AFTER ME...
..."I'LL NEVER DO ANYTHING THIS STUPID AGAIN, EVER, FOR, IF I DO, I AM NO GALACTIC GIRL GUIDE!"
HUH?

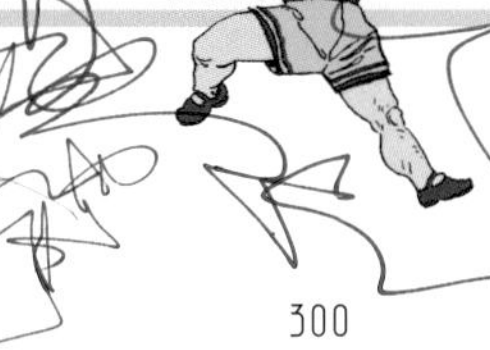

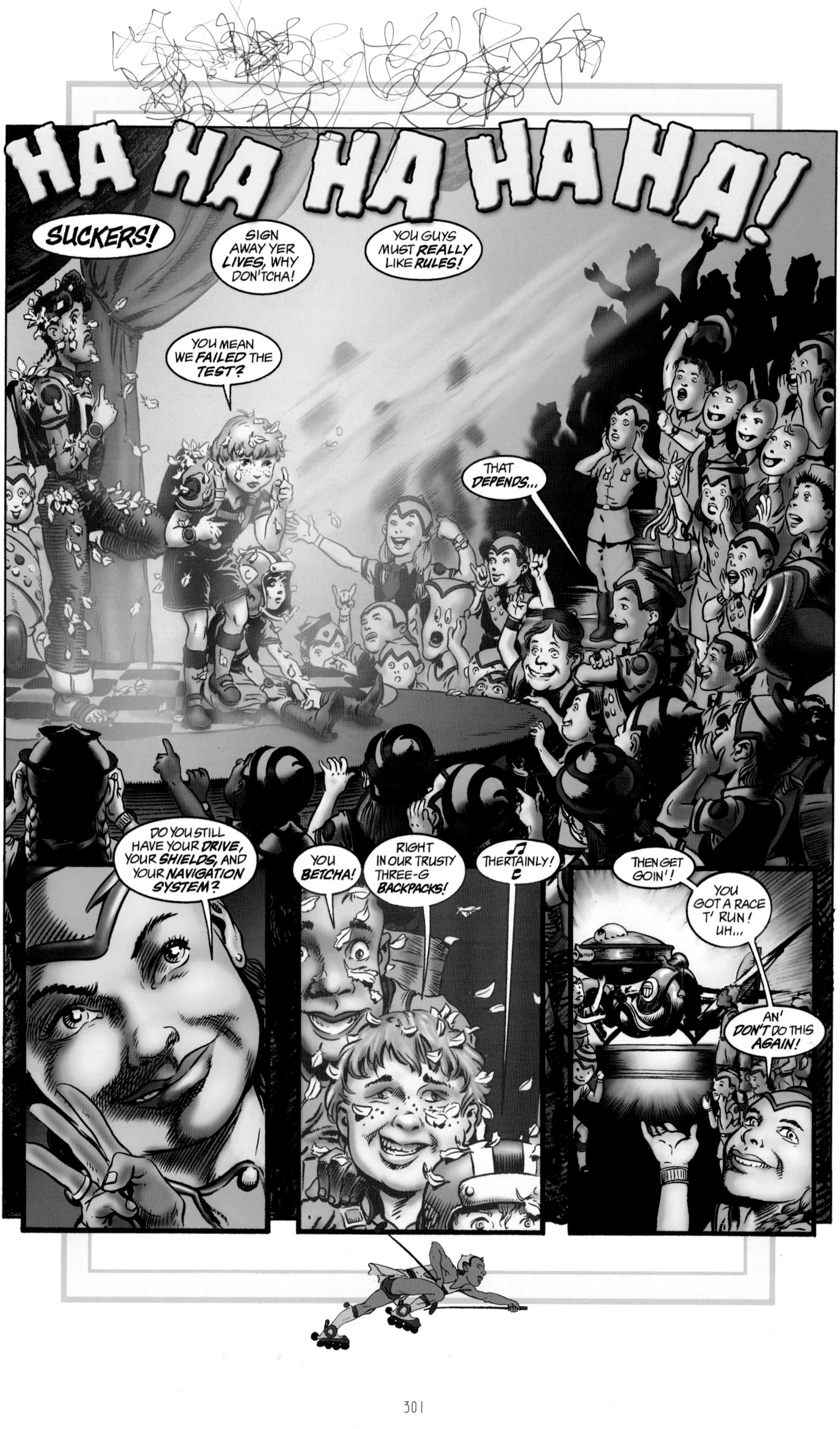

HA HA HA HA HA HA!
SUCKERS!
SIGN AWAY YER LIVES, WHY DON'TCHA!
YOU GUYS MUST REALLY LIKE RULES!
YOU MEAN WE FAILED THE TEST?
THAT DEPENDS...
DO YOU STILL HAVE YOUR DRIVE, YOUR SHIELDS, AND YOUR NAVIGATION SYSTEM?
YOU BETCHA!
RIGHT IN OUR TRUSTY THREE-G BACKPACKS!
THERTAINLY!
THEN GET GOIN'!
YOU GOT A RACE T' RUN! UH...
AN' DON'T DO THIS AGAIN!

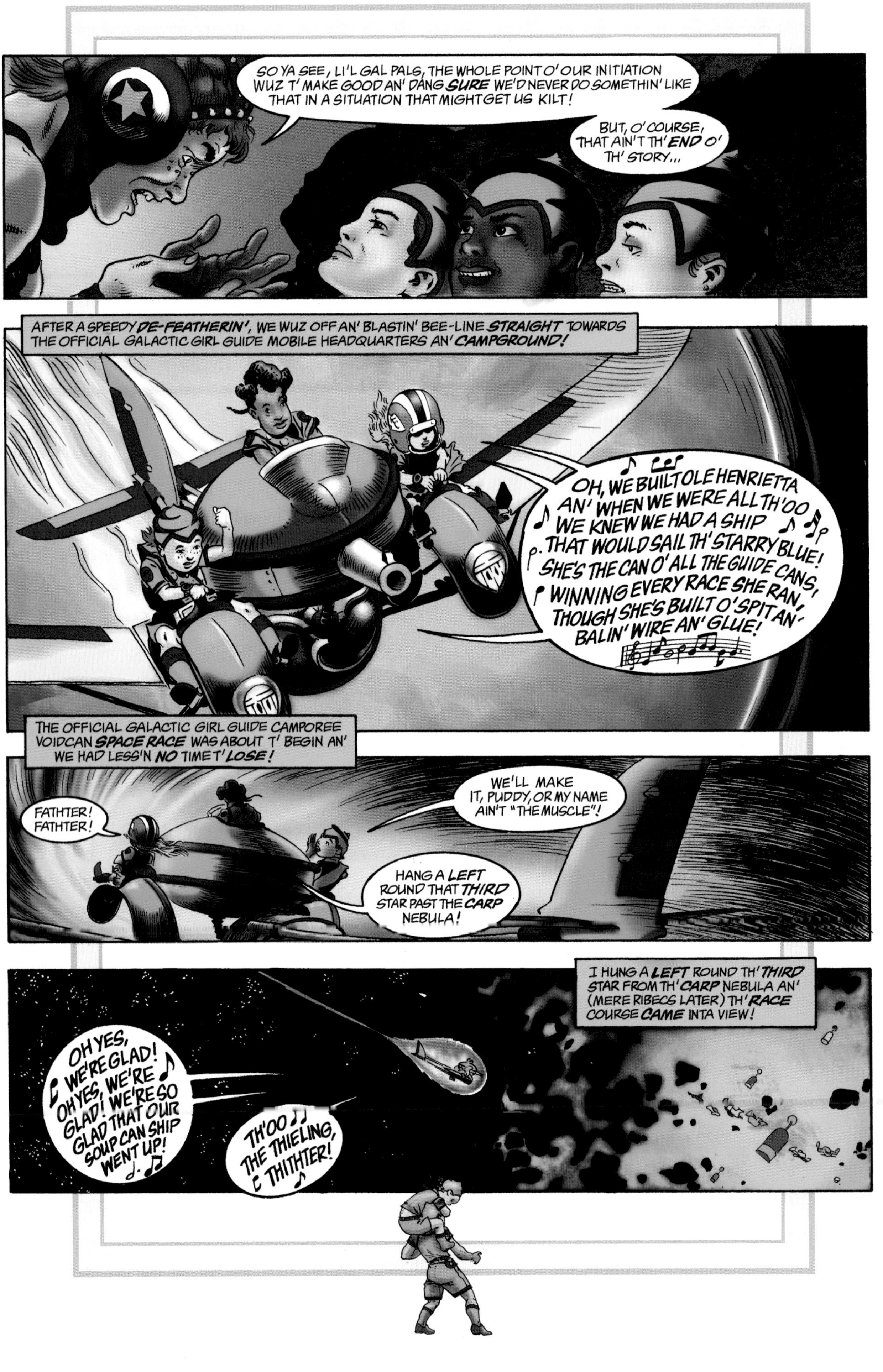

SO YA SEE, LI'L GAL PALS, THE WHOLE POINT O' OUR INITIATION WUZ T' MAKE GOOD AN' DANG SURE WE'D NEVER DO SOMETHIN' LIKE THAT IN A SITUATION THAT MIGHT GET US KILT!
BUT, O' COURSE, THAT AIN'T TH' END O' TH' STORY...
AFTER A SPEEDY DE-FEATHERIN', WE WUZ OFF AN' BLASTIN' BEE-LINE STRAIGHT TOWARDS THE OFFICIAL GALACTIC GIRL GUIDE MOBILE HEADQUARTERS AN' CAMPGROUND!
OH, WE BUILT OLE HENRIETTA AN' WHEN WE WERE ALL TH'OO WE KNEW WE HAD A SHIP THAT WOULD SAIL TH' STARRY BLUE! SHE'S THE CAN O' ALL THE GUIDE CANS, WINNING EVERY RACE SHE RAN, THOUGH SHE'S BUILT O' SPIT AN' BALIN' WIRE AN' GLUE!
THE OFFICIAL GALACTIC GIRL GUIDE CAMPOREE VOIDCAN SPACE RACE WAS ABOUT T' BEGIN AN' WE HAD LESS'N NO TIME T' LOSE!
FATHTER! FATHTER!
WE'LL MAKE IT, PUDDY, OR MY NAME AIN'T "THE MUSCLE"!
HANG A LEFT ROUND THAT THIRD STAR PAST THE CARP NEBULA!
I HUNG A LEFT ROUND TH' THIRD STAR FROM TH' CARP NEBULA AN' (MERE RIBECS LATER) TH' RACE COURSE CAME INTA VIEW!
OH YES, WE'RE GLAD! OH YES, WE'RE GLAD! WE'RE SO GLAD THAT OUR SOUP CAN SHIP WENT UP!
TH'OO THE THIELING, THITHTER!

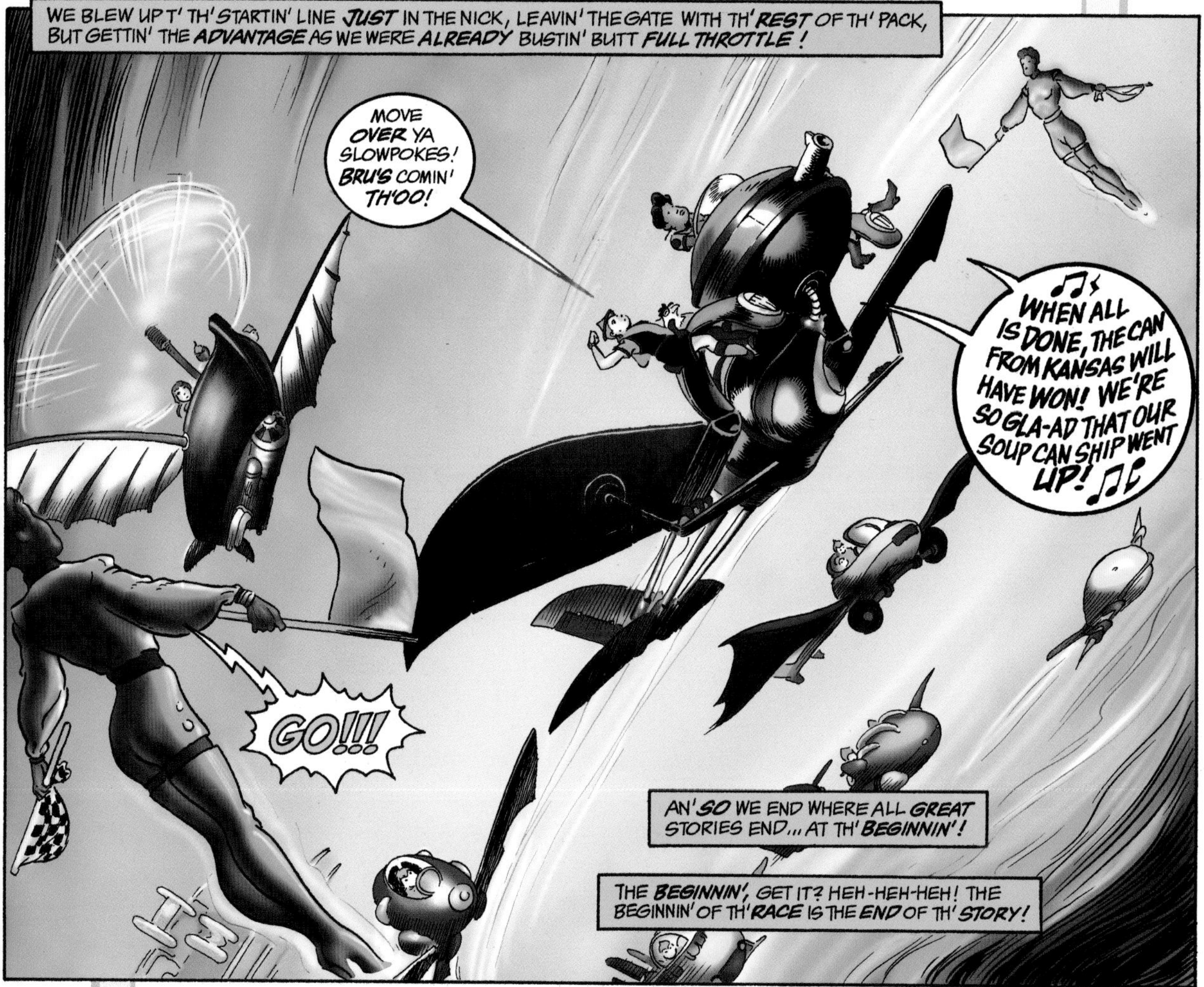
WE BLEW UP T' TH' STARTIN' LINE JUST IN THE NICK, LEAVIN' THE GATE WITH TH' REST OF TH' PACK, BUT GETTIN' THE ADVANTAGE AS WE WERE ALREADY BUSTIN' BUTT FULL THROTTLE!
MOVE OVER YA SLOWPOKES! BRU'S COMIN' TH'OO!
♫ WHEN ALL IS DONE, THE CAN FROM KANSAS WILL HAVE WON! WE'RE SO GLA-AD THAT OUR SOUP CAN SHIP WENT UP! ♫
GO!!!
AN' SO WE END WHERE ALL GREAT STORIES END... AT TH' BEGINNIN'!
THE BEGINNIN', GET IT? HEH-HEH-HEH! THE BEGINNIN' OF TH' RACE IS THE END OF TH' STORY!

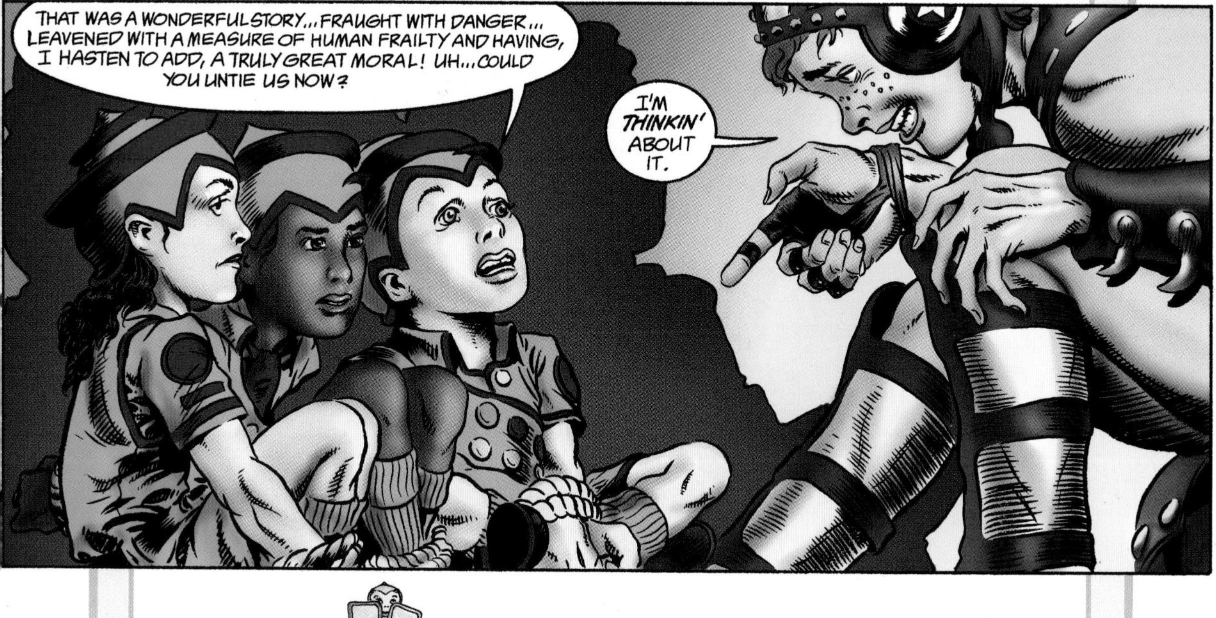
THAT WAS A WONDERFUL STORY... FRAUGHT WITH DANGER... LEAVENED WITH A MEASURE OF HUMAN FRAILTY AND HAVING, I HASTEN TO ADD, A TRULY GREAT MORAL! UH... COULD YOU UNTIE US NOW?
I'M THINKIN' ABOUT IT.

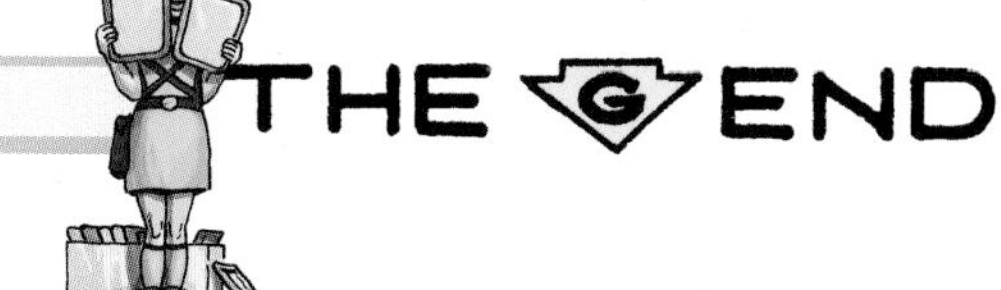
THE END

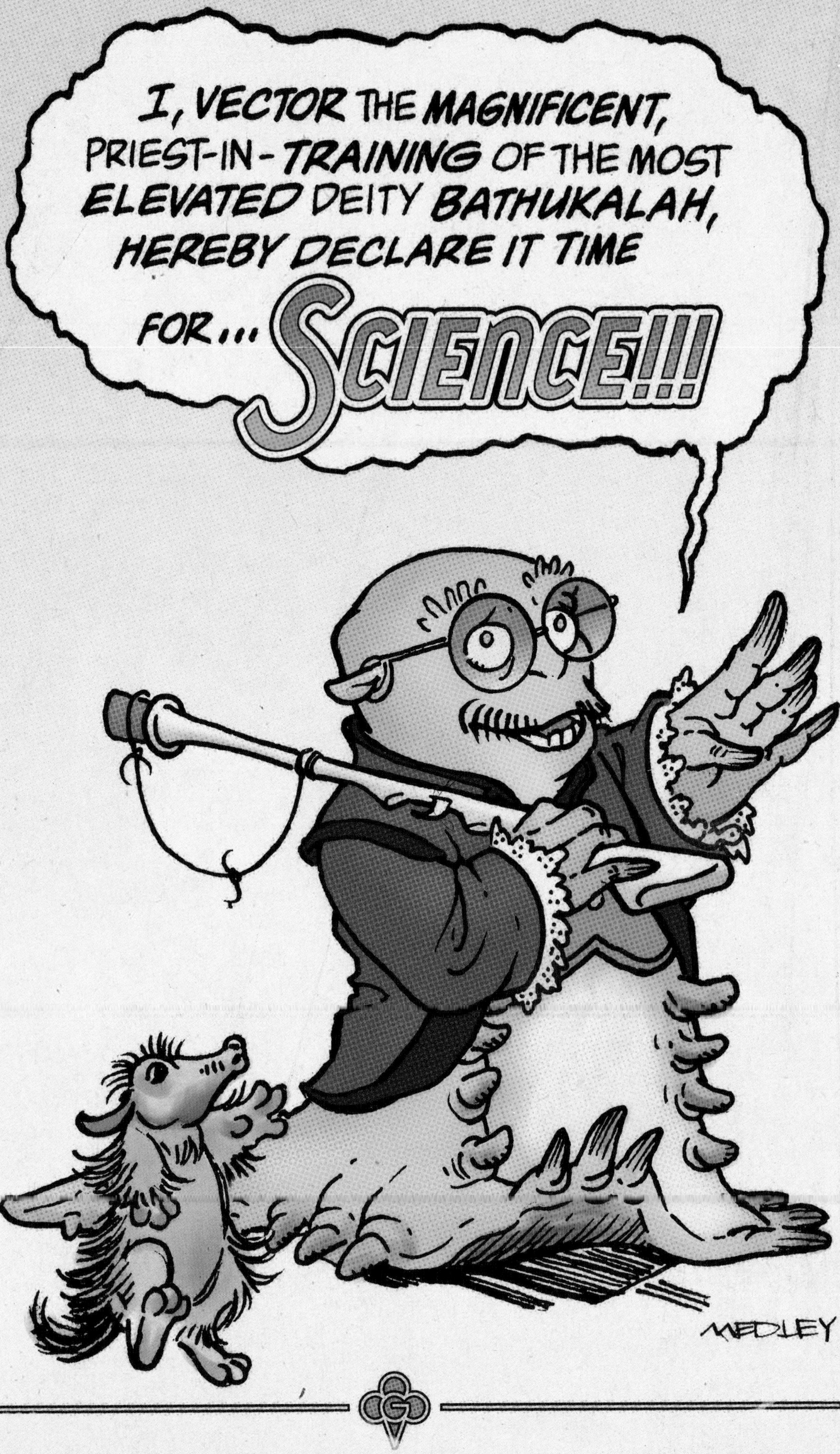
I, VECTOR THE MAGNIFICENT, PRIEST-IN-TRAINING OF THE MOST ELEVATED DEITY BATHUKALAH, HEREBY DECLARE IT TIME FOR... SCIENCE!!!
MEDLEY

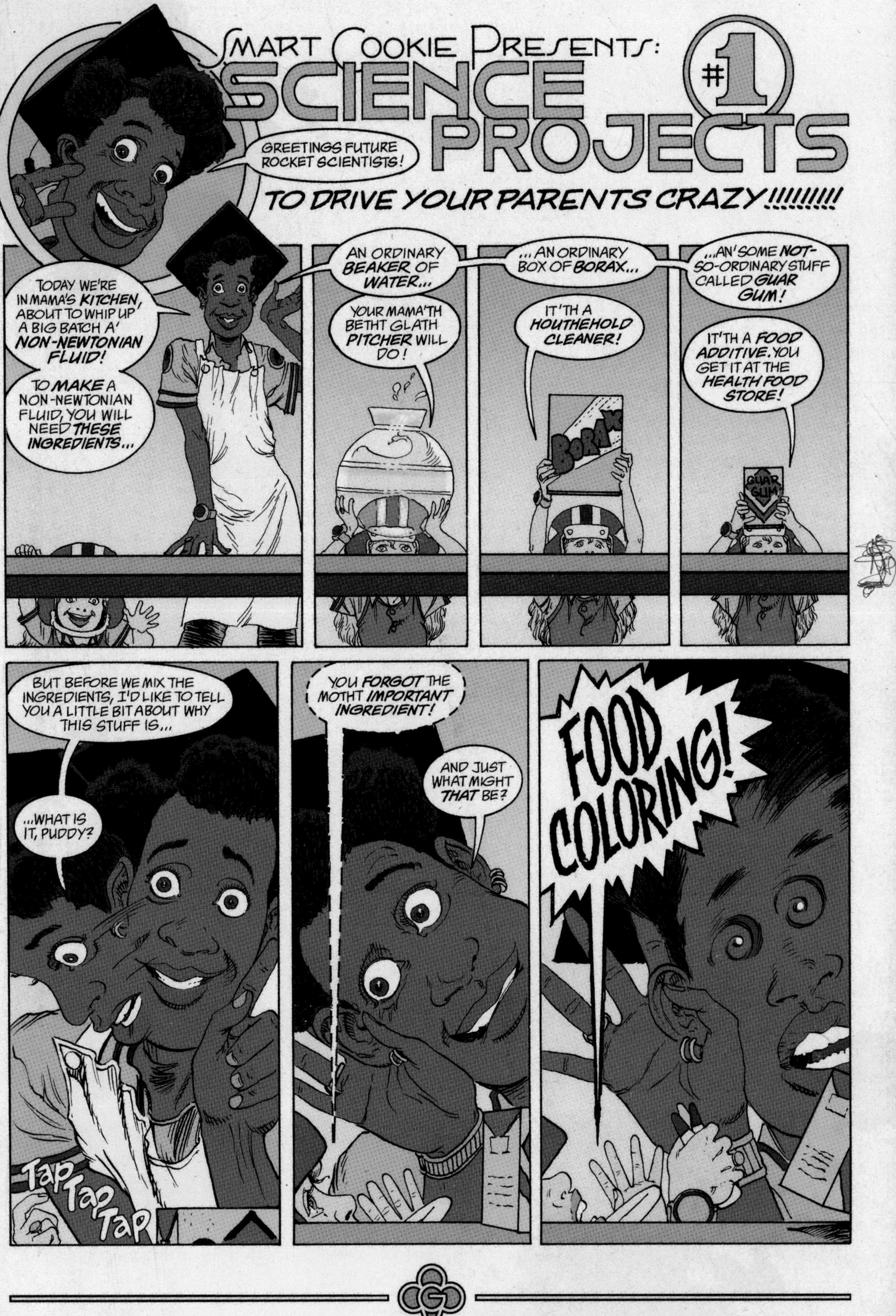
SMART COOKIE PRESENTS:
SCIENCE PROJECTS
#1
GREETINGS FUTURE ROCKET SCIENTISTS!
TO DRIVE YOUR PARENTS CRAZY!!!!!!!!!
TODAY WE'RE IN MAMA'S KITCHEN, ABOUT TO WHIP UP A BIG BATCH A' NON-NEWTONIAN FLUID!
TO MAKE A NON-NEWTONIAN FLUID, YOU WILL NEED THESE INGREDIENTS...
AN ORDINARY BEAKER OF WATER...
YOUR MAMA'TH BETHT GLATH PITCHER WILL DO!
...AN ORDINARY BOX OF BORAX...
IT'TH A HOUTHEHOLD CLEANER!
BORAX
...AN' SOME NOT-SO-ORDINARY STUFF CALLED GUAR GUM!
IT'TH A FOOD ADDITIVE. YOU GET IT AT THE HEALTH FOOD STORE!
GUAR GUM
BUT BEFORE WE MIX THE INGREDIENTS, I'D LIKE TO TELL YOU A LITTLE BIT ABOUT WHY THIS STUFF IS...
...WHAT IS IT, PUDDY?
TAP TAP TAP
YOU FORGOT THE MOTHT IMPORTANT INGREDIENT!
AND JUST WHAT MIGHT THAT BE?
FOOD COLORING!

SMART COOKIE PRESENTS:

SCIENCE PROJECTS *TO DRIVE YOUR PARENTS CRAZY!!!!!!!!*

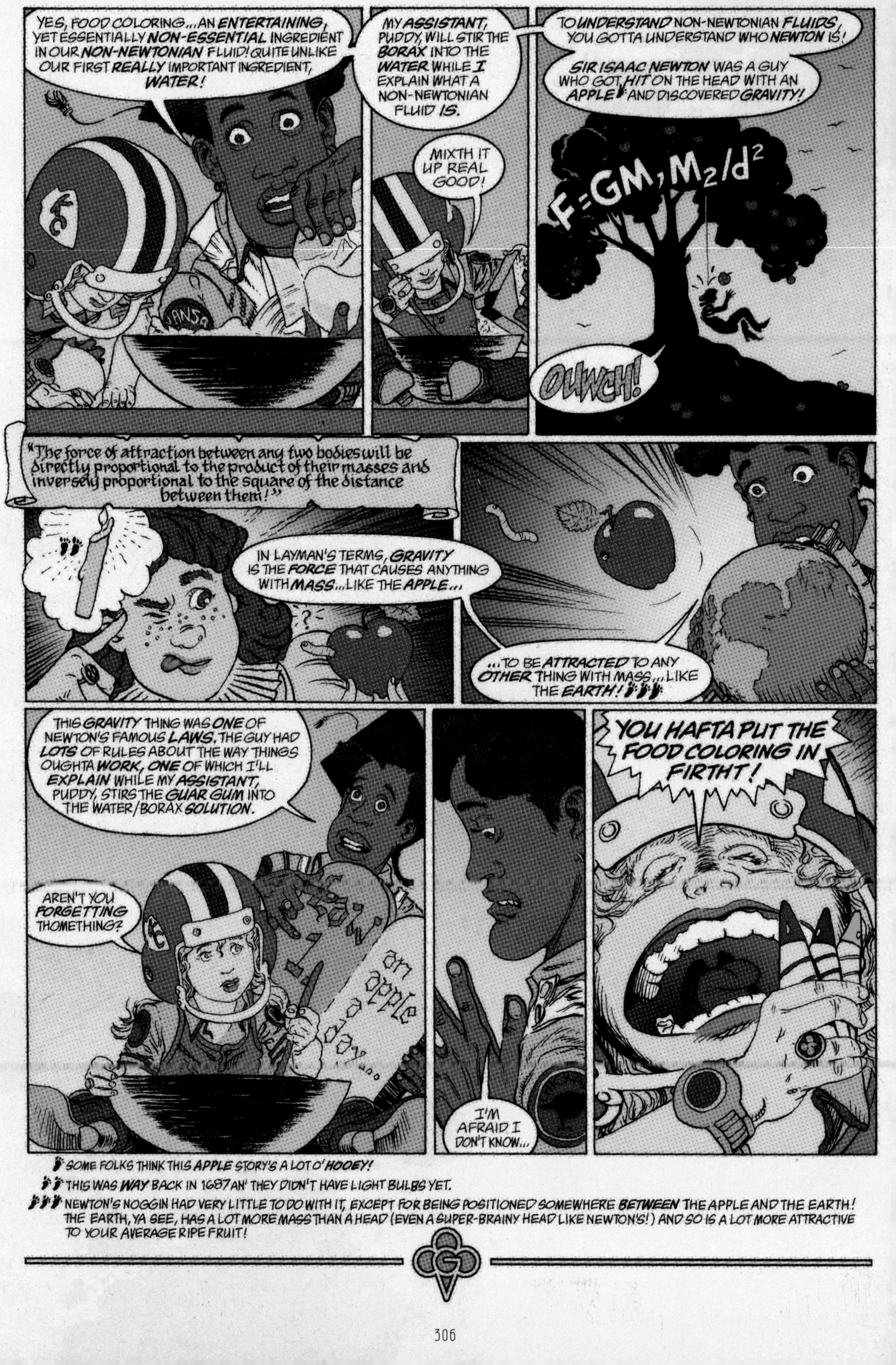

YES, FOOD COLORING... AN ENTERTAINING, YET ESSENTIALLY NON-ESSENTIAL INGREDIENT IN OUR NON-NEWTONIAN FLUID! QUITE UNLIKE OUR FIRST REALLY IMPORTANT INGREDIENT, WATER!
MY ASSISTANT, PUDDY, WILL STIR THE BORAX INTO THE WATER WHILE I EXPLAIN WHAT A NON-NEWTONIAN FLUID IS.
MIXTH IT UP REAL GOOD!
TO UNDERSTAND NON-NEWTONIAN FLUIDS, YOU GOTTA UNDERSTAND WHO NEWTON IS!
SIR ISAAC NEWTON WAS A GUY WHO GOT HIT ON THE HEAD WITH AN APPLE AND DISCOVERED GRAVITY!
F=GM₁M₂/d²
OUWCH!
"The force of attraction between any two bodies will be directly proportional to the product of their masses and inversely proportional to the square of the distance between them!"
IN LAYMAN'S TERMS, GRAVITY IS THE FORCE THAT CAUSES ANYTHING WITH MASS... LIKE THE APPLE...
?
...TO BE ATTRACTED TO ANY OTHER THING WITH MASS... LIKE THE EARTH!
THIS GRAVITY THING WAS ONE OF NEWTON'S FAMOUS LAWS. THE GUY HAD LOTS OF RULES ABOUT THE WAY THINGS OUGHTA WORK, ONE OF WHICH I'LL EXPLAIN WHILE MY ASSISTANT, PUDDY, STIRS THE GUAR GUM INTO THE WATER/BORAX SOLUTION.
AREN'T YOU FORGETTING THOMETHING?
an apple a day...
I'M AFRAID I DON'T KNOW...
YOU HAFTA PUT THE FOOD COLORING IN FIRTHT!

* SOME FOLKS THINK THIS *APPLE* STORY'S A LOT O' *HOOEY!*

** THIS WAS *WAY* BACK IN 1687 AN' THEY DIDN'T HAVE LIGHT BULBS YET.

*** NEWTON'S NOGGIN HAD VERY LITTLE TO DO WITH IT, EXCEPT FOR BEING POSITIONED SOMEWHERE *BETWEEN* THE APPLE AND THE EARTH! THE EARTH, YA SEE, HAS A LOT MORE MASS THAN A HEAD (EVEN A SUPER-BRAINY HEAD LIKE NEWTON'S!) AND SO IS A LOT MORE ATTRACTIVE TO YOUR AVERAGE RIPE FRUIT!

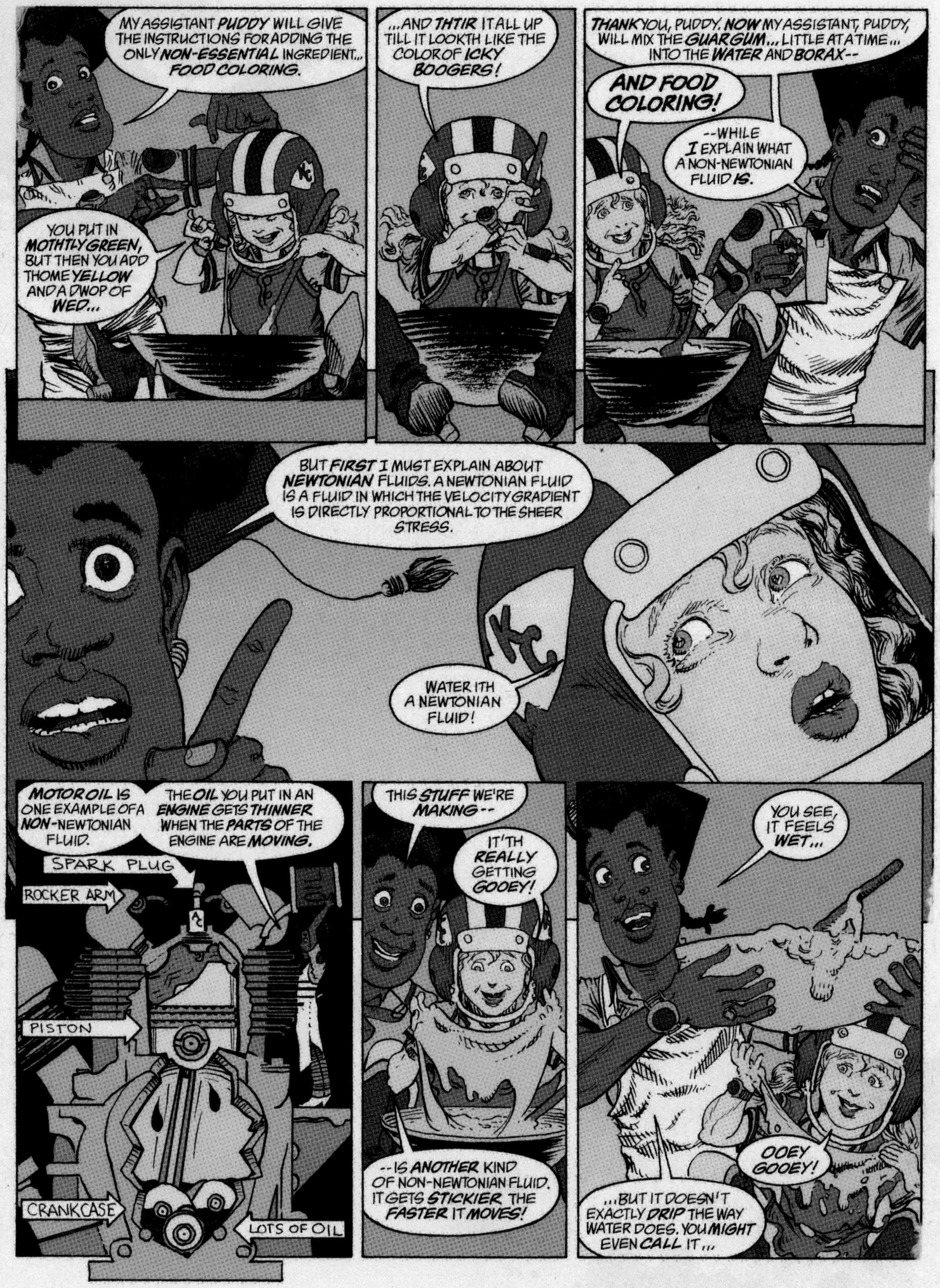
MY ASSISTANT PUDDY WILL GIVE THE INSTRUCTIONS FOR ADDING THE ONLY NON-ESSENTIAL INGREDIENT... FOOD COLORING.
YOU PUT IN MOTHTLY GREEN, BUT THEN YOU ADD THOME YELLOW AND A DWOP OF WED...
...AND THTIR IT ALL UP TILL IT LOOKTH LIKE THE COLOR OF ICKY BOOGERS!
THANK YOU, PUDDY. NOW MY ASSISTANT, PUDDY, WILL MIX THE GUAR GUM... LITTLE AT A TIME... INTO THE WATER AND BORAX--
AND FOOD COLORING!
--WHILE I EXPLAIN WHAT A NON-NEWTONIAN FLUID IS.
BUT FIRST I MUST EXPLAIN ABOUT NEWTONIAN FLUIDS. A NEWTONIAN FLUID IS A FLUID IN WHICH THE VELOCITY GRADIENT IS DIRECTLY PROPORTIONAL TO THE SHEER STRESS.
WATER ITH A NEWTONIAN FLUID!
MOTOR OIL IS ONE EXAMPLE OF A NON-NEWTONIAN FLUID.
THE OIL YOU PUT IN AN ENGINE GETS THINNER WHEN THE PARTS OF THE ENGINE ARE MOVING.
SPARK PLUG
ROCKER ARM
PISTON
CRANKCASE
LOTS OF OIL
THIS STUFF WE'RE MAKING--
IT'TH REALLY GETTING GOOEY!
--IS ANOTHER KIND OF NON-NEWTONIAN FLUID. IT GETS STICKIER THE FASTER IT MOVES!
YOU SEE, IT FEELS WET...
OOEY GOOEY!
...BUT IT DOESN'T EXACTLY DRIP THE WAY WATER DOES. YOU MIGHT EVEN CALL IT...

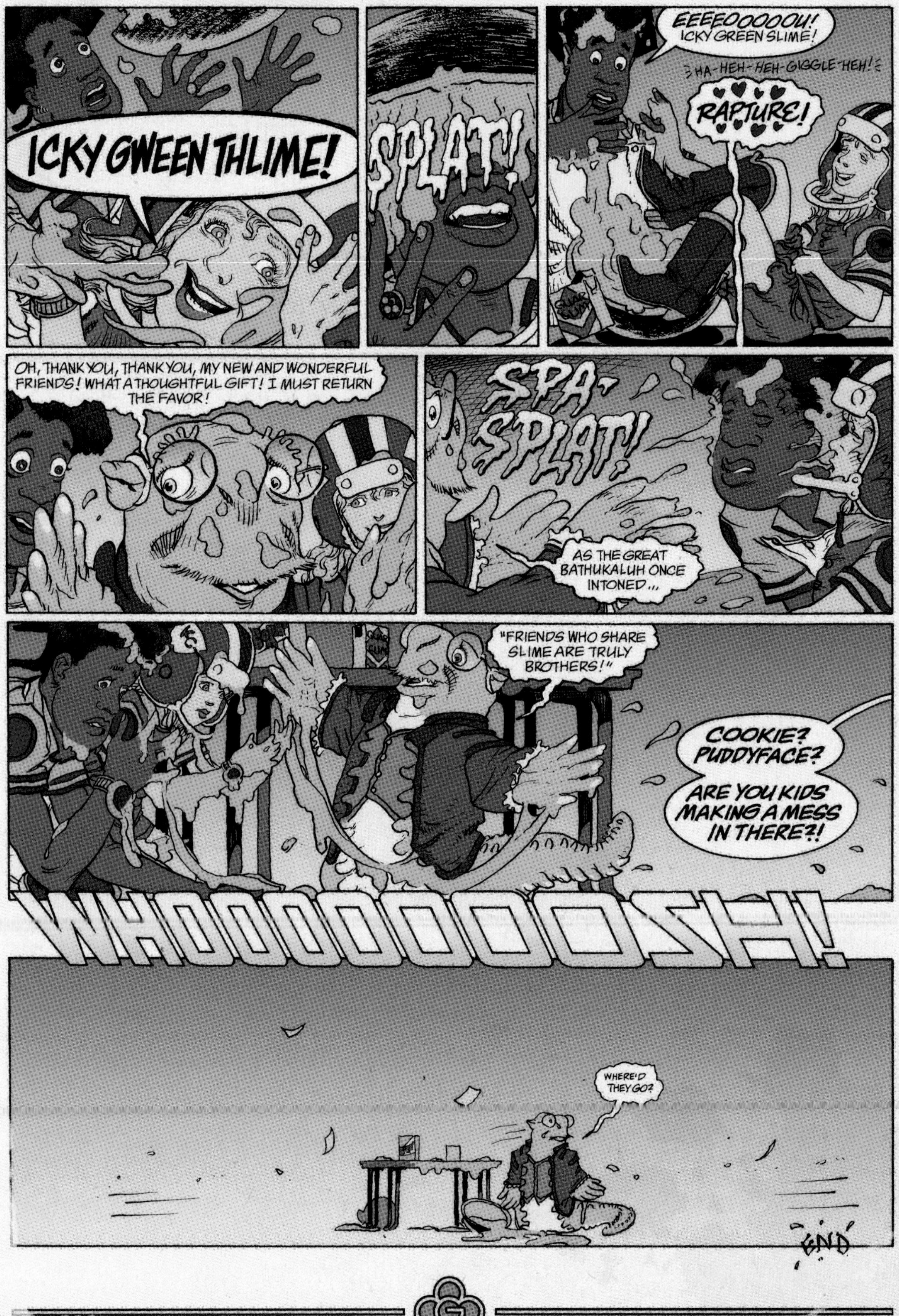
ICKY GWEEN THLIME!
SPLAT!
EEEEOOOOOU! ICKY GREEN SLIME!
HA-HEH-HEH-GIGGLE-HEH!
RAPTURE!
OH, THANK YOU, THANK YOU, MY NEW AND WONDERFUL FRIENDS! WHAT A THOUGHTFUL GIFT! I MUST RETURN THE FAVOR!
SPA-SPLAT!
AS THE GREAT BATHUKALUH ONCE INTONED...
"FRIENDS WHO SHARE SLIME ARE TRULY BROTHERS!"
COOKIE? PUDDYFACE?
ARE YOU KIDS MAKING A MESS IN THERE?!
WHOOOOOOOSH!
WHERE'D THEY GO?
END

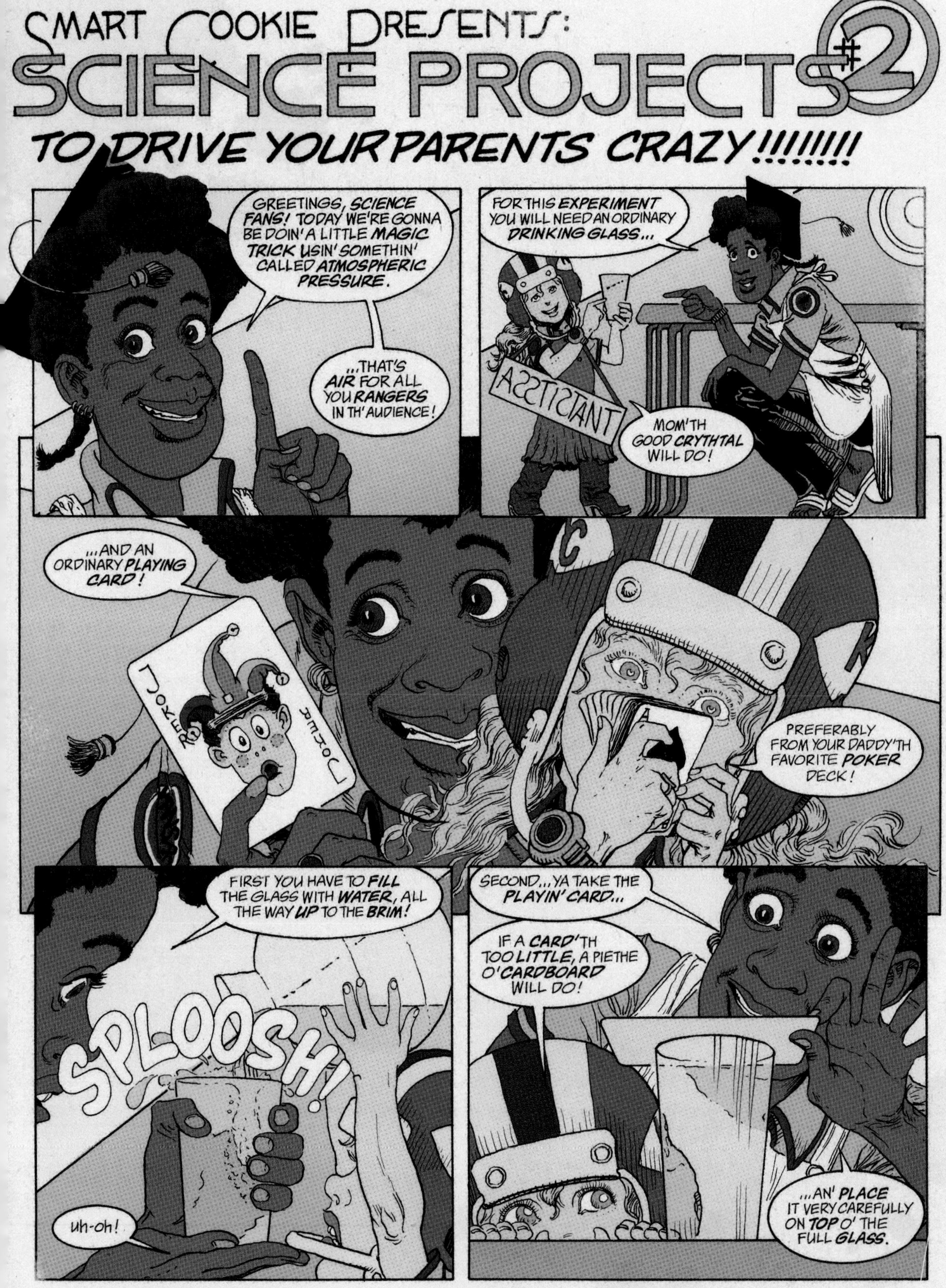
SMART COOKIE PRESENTS:
SCIENCE PROJECTS #2
TO DRIVE YOUR PARENTS CRAZY!!!!!!!!
GREETINGS, SCIENCE FANS! TODAY WE'RE GONNA BE DOIN' A LITTLE MAGIC TRICK USIN' SOMETHIN' CALLED ATMOSPHERIC PRESSURE.
...THAT'S AIR FOR ALL YOU RANGERS IN TH' AUDIENCE!
FOR THIS EXPERIMENT YOU WILL NEED AN ORDINARY DRINKING GLASS...
ASSISTANT
MOM'TH GOOD CRYTHTAL WILL DO!
...AND AN ORDINARY PLAYING CARD!
JOKER
JOKER
PREFERABLY FROM YOUR DADDY'TH FAVORITE POKER DECK!
FIRST YOU HAVE TO FILL THE GLASS WITH WATER, ALL THE WAY UP TO THE BRIM!
SPLOOSH!
uh-oh!
SECOND... YA TAKE THE PLAYIN' CARD...
IF A CARD'TH TOO LITTLE, A PIETHE O'CARDBOARD WILL DO!
...AN' PLACE IT VERY CAREFULLY ON TOP O' THE FULL GLASS.

Smart Cookie Presents:

SCIENCE PROJECTS TO DRIVE YOUR PARENTS CRAZY!!!!!!!!

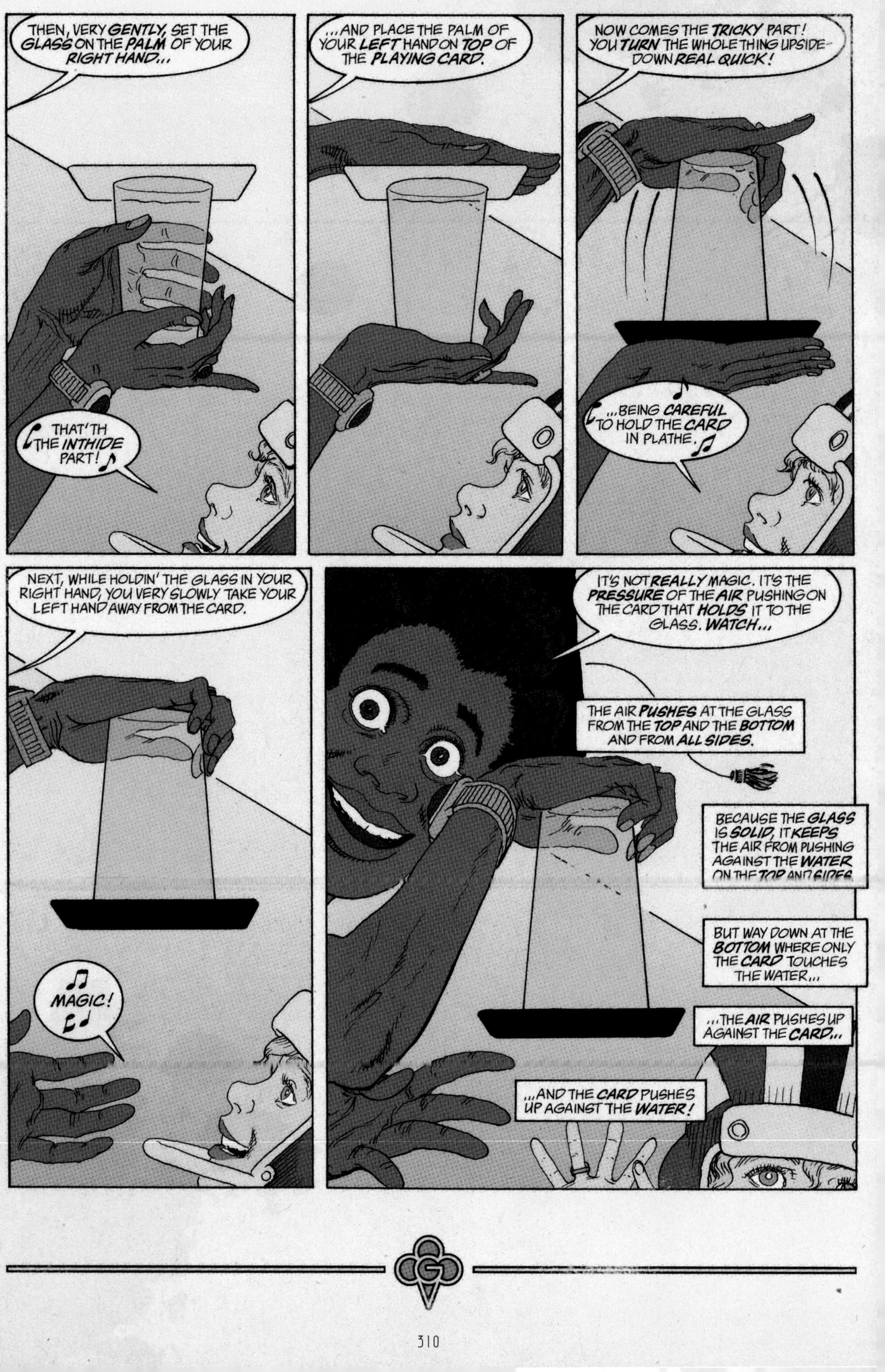

THEN, VERY GENTLY, SET THE GLASS ON THE PALM OF YOUR RIGHT HAND...
THAT'TH THE INTHIDE PART!
...AND PLACE THE PALM OF YOUR LEFT HAND ON TOP OF THE PLAYING CARD.
NOW COMES THE TRICKY PART! YOU TURN THE WHOLE THING UPSIDE-DOWN REAL QUICK!
...BEING CAREFUL TO HOLD THE CARD IN PLATHE.
NEXT, WHILE HOLDIN' THE GLASS IN YOUR RIGHT HAND, YOU VERY SLOWLY TAKE YOUR LEFT HAND AWAY FROM THE CARD.
MAGIC!
IT'S NOT REALLY MAGIC. IT'S THE PRESSURE OF THE AIR PUSHING ON THE CARD THAT HOLDS IT TO THE GLASS. WATCH...
THE AIR PUSHES AT THE GLASS FROM THE TOP AND THE BOTTOM AND FROM ALL SIDES.
BECAUSE THE GLASS IS SOLID, IT KEEPS THE AIR FROM PUSHING AGAINST THE WATER ON THE TOP AND SIDES.
BUT WAY DOWN AT THE BOTTOM WHERE ONLY THE CARD TOUCHES THE WATER...
...THE AIR PUSHES UP AGAINST THE CARD...
...AND THE CARD PUSHES UP AGAINST THE WATER!

SMART COOKIE PRESENTS:

SCIENCE PROJECTS TO DRIVE YOUR PARENTS CRAZY!!!!!!!!

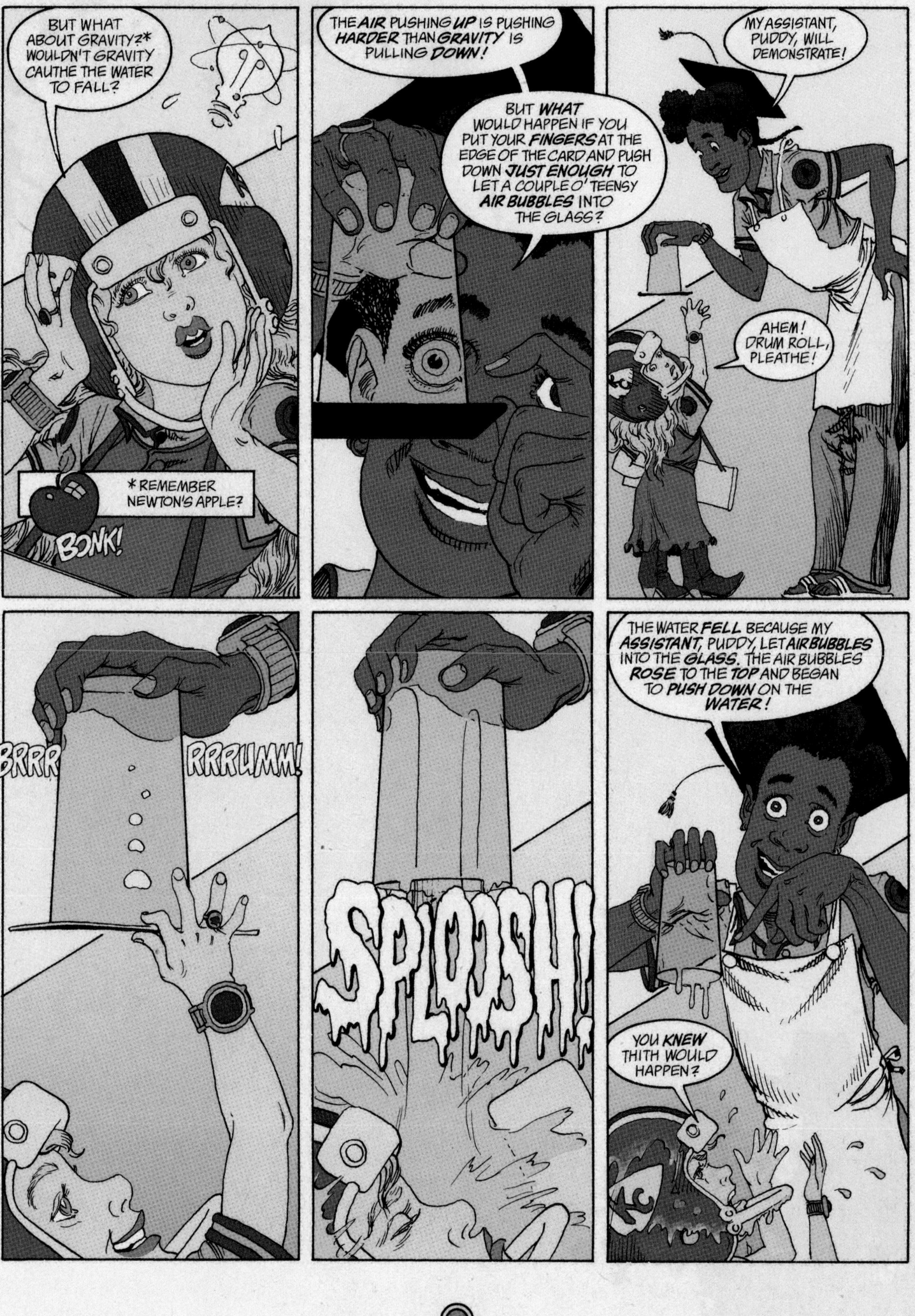

BUT WHAT ABOUT GRAVITY?* WOULDN'T GRAVITY CAUTHE THE WATER TO FALL?
*REMEMBER NEWTON'S APPLE?
BONK!
THE AIR PUSHING UP IS PUSHING HARDER THAN GRAVITY IS PULLING DOWN!
BUT WHAT WOULD HAPPEN IF YOU PUT YOUR FINGERS AT THE EDGE OF THE CARD AND PUSH DOWN JUST ENOUGH TO LET A COUPLE O' TEENSY AIR BUBBLES INTO THE GLASS?
MY ASSISTANT, PUDDY, WILL DEMONSTRATE!
AHEM! DRUM ROLL, PLEATHE!
BRRR
RRRUMM!
SPLOOSH!
THE WATER FELL BECAUSE MY ASSISTANT, PUDDY, LET AIR BUBBLES INTO THE GLASS. THE AIR BUBBLES ROSE TO THE TOP AND BEGAN TO PUSH DOWN ON THE WATER!
YOU KNEW THITH WOULD HAPPEN?

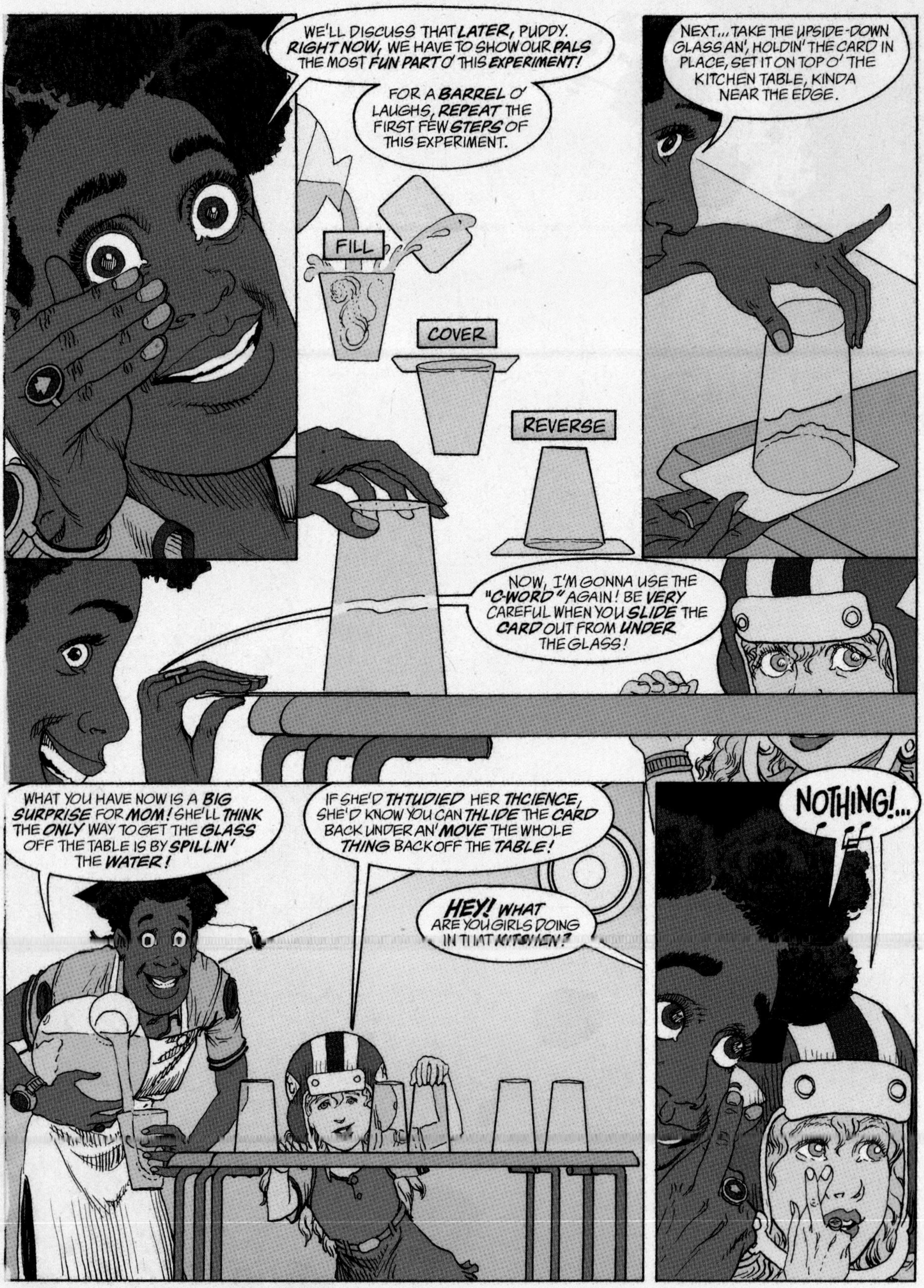
WE'LL DISCUSS THAT LATER, PUDDY. RIGHT NOW, WE HAVE TO SHOW OUR PALS THE MOST FUN PART O' THIS EXPERIMENT!
FOR A BARREL O' LAUGHS, REPEAT THE FIRST FEW STEPS OF THIS EXPERIMENT.
FILL
COVER
REVERSE
NEXT... TAKE THE UPSIDE-DOWN GLASS AN', HOLDIN' THE CARD IN PLACE, SET IT ON TOP O' THE KITCHEN TABLE, KINDA NEAR THE EDGE.
NOW, I'M GONNA USE THE "C-WORD" AGAIN! BE VERY CAREFUL WHEN YOU SLIDE THE CARD OUT FROM UNDER THE GLASS!
WHAT YOU HAVE NOW IS A BIG SURPRISE FOR MOM! SHE'LL THINK THE ONLY WAY TO GET THE GLASS OFF THE TABLE IS BY SPILLIN' THE WATER!
IF SHE'D THTUDIED HER THCIENCE, SHE'D KNOW YOU CAN THLIDE THE CARD BACK UNDER AN' MOVE THE WHOLE THING BACK OFF THE TABLE!
HEY! WHAT ARE YOU GIRLS DOING IN THAT KITCHEN?
NOTHING!...

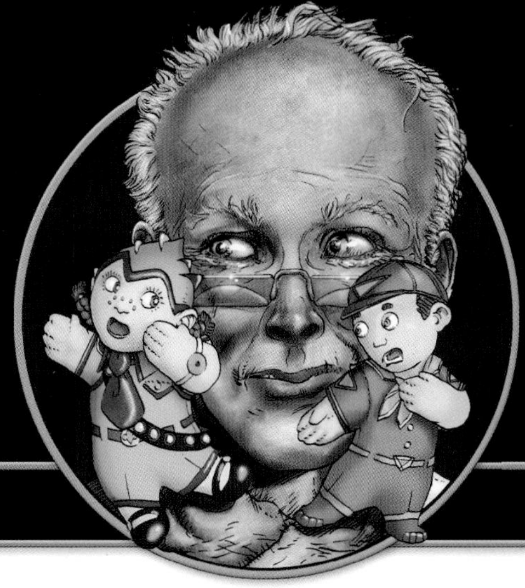

BOYS AND GIRLS TOGETHER

or

"Rangers vs. Guides"

Excerpted from the 7th Chapter of the Book,

Of Playgrounds and Pecking Orders

by

Dwannyun of Griivarr

MA, PHD, PFF, BSH, BXM, PGMSSB Historian Emeritus of Griivonia College, University of Griivarr, Hon Ober, Hon Grii, Griivarr Worlds

In the earlier chapters of this book, we have repeatedly touched on the rocky relationship between the Rocket Rangers and their "sister" organization, the Galactic Girl Guides. Though the Rangers (in their advertising materials) billed themselves as an organization that built "character and assertiveness" in young, male Amercadians, it was my experience that our annual contact with the Guides, over the course of numerous Guide/Ranger Camporees, served to negate any character-building that may have gone on during the previous cycle. This was due, in large part, to the conflicting mission statements of the aforementioned organizations, as evidenced by the lead text on their respective recruiting posters.

Rocket Rangers:

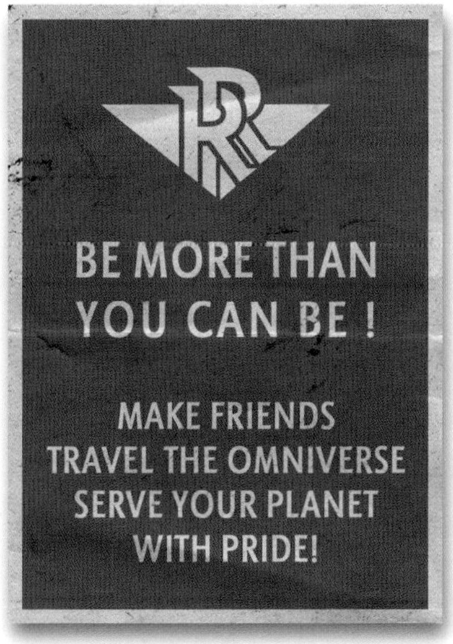
BE MORE THAN
YOU CAN BE !
MAKE FRIENDS
TRAVEL THE OMNIVERSE
SERVE YOUR PLANET
WITH PRIDE!

Galactic Girl Guides:

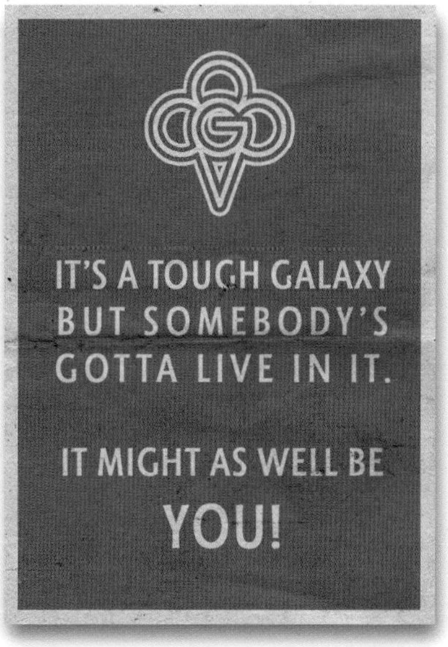
IT'S A TOUGH GALAXY
BUT SOMEBODY'S
GOTTA LIVE IN IT.
IT MIGHT AS WELL BE
YOU!

With the Rangers, it was all about community and service: with the Guides, it was every Guide (or at least Guide Wing) for her- or itself! This being the case, for Rangers and Guides, normal humanoid boy-girl antagonism was magnified to the power of 10 and the rockier aspects of the Ranger/Guide relationship were only exacerbated by the cutthroat competition of the Soup-Can Derby. (Here, I must pause to choke down childhood memories better forgotten!)

The fact that our budding romantic natures only added powder to the fiery battle between these ideologically opposite warring factions cannot be overstated. My own childhood fascination/aversion with and to the Galactic Girl Guide named Brucilla has been well documented in my own previous books, as well as alluded to in a number of popular lasarounds and several romantic novels based on transcripts of the famous trial, the Amercadian Space Brigade v. Brucilla the Muscle.

For the purposes of this chapter, we will not even mention the Amercadian Space Brigade Neutral Zone Fiasco of AE 134, an incident that resulted in this poor writer being forced to attend his senior prom minus his date. I fear that wound is still too raw!

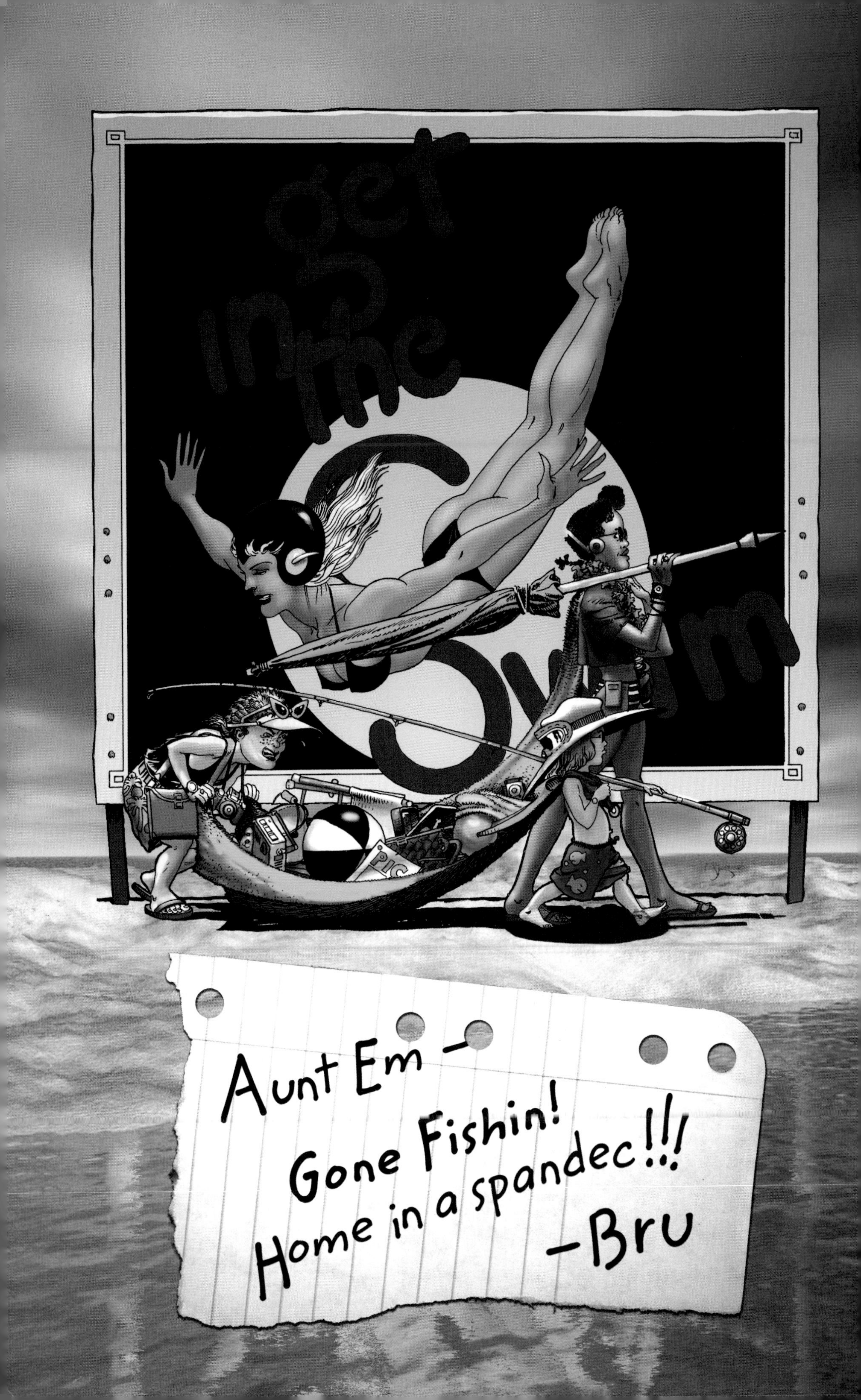
get in the
Aunt Em –
Gone Fishin!
Home in a spandec!!!
–Bru

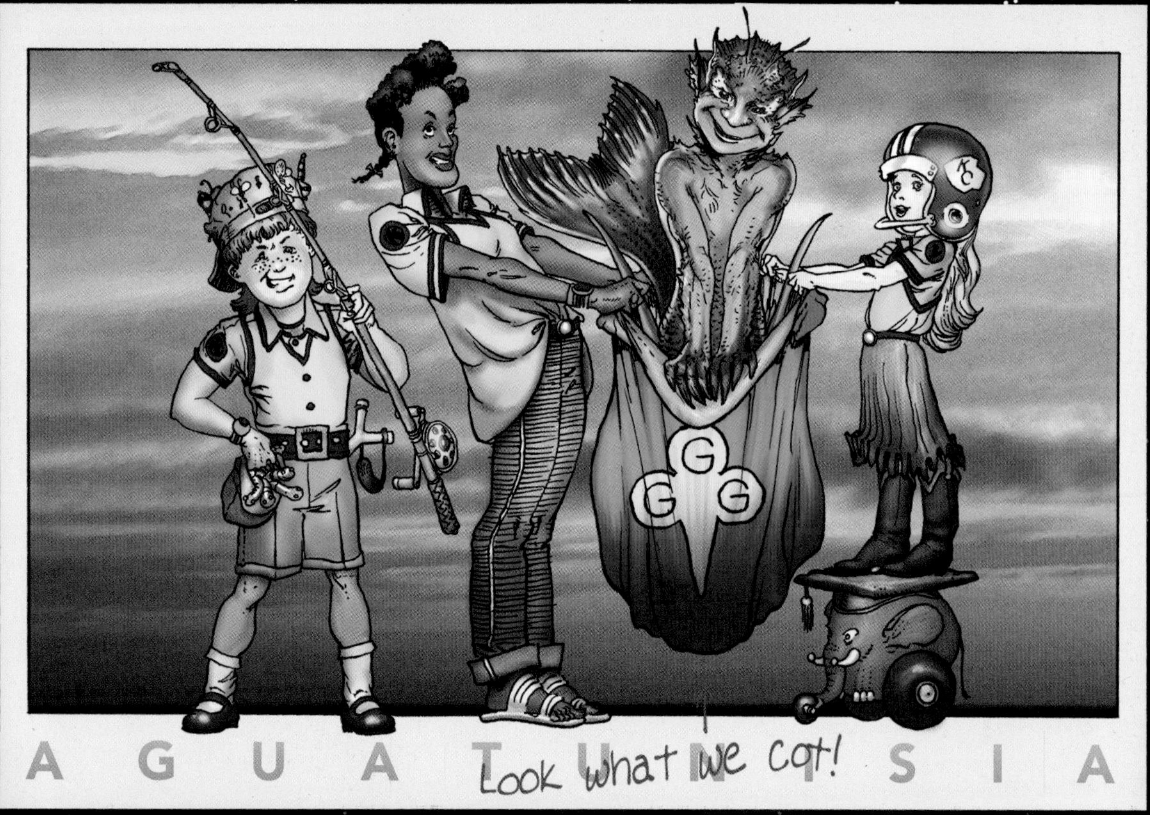

GGG
A G U A T U N I S I A
Look what we cot!

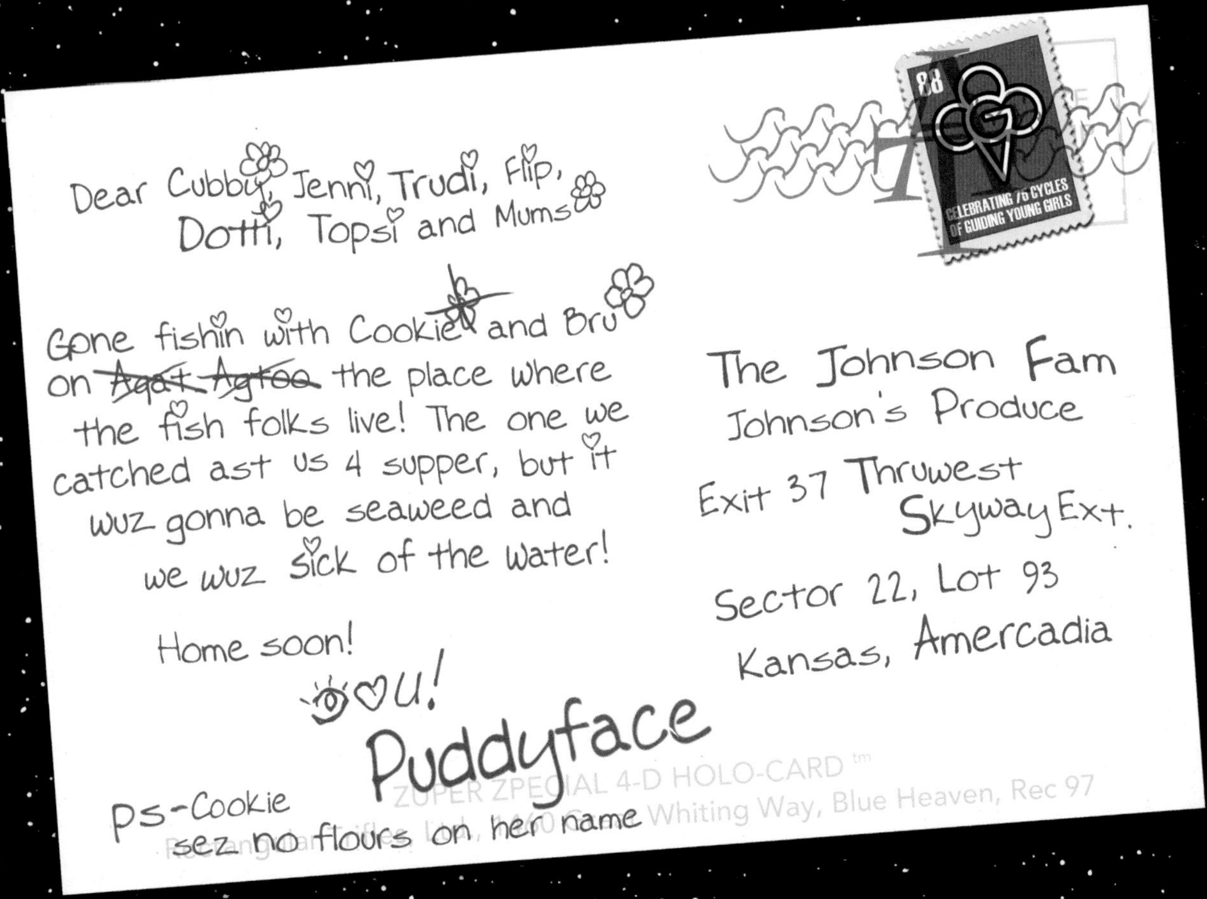

Dear Cubby, Jenni, Trudi, Flip,
Dotti, Topsi and Mums
Gone fishin with Cookie and Bru
on ~~Agat Agtoa~~ the place where
the fish folks live! The one we
catched ast us 4 supper, but it
wuz gonna be seaweed and
we wuz sick of the water!
Home soon!
u!
Puddyface
ps-Cookie
sez no flours on her name
The Johnson Fam
Johnson's Produce
Exit 37 Thruwest
Skyway Ext.
Sector 22, Lot 93
Kansas, Amercadia
88
CELEBRATING 75 CYCLES
OF GUIDING YOUNG GIRLS
ZUPER ZPECIAL 4-D HOLO-CARD tm
Whiting Way, Blue Heaven, Rec 97

Aguatunisia

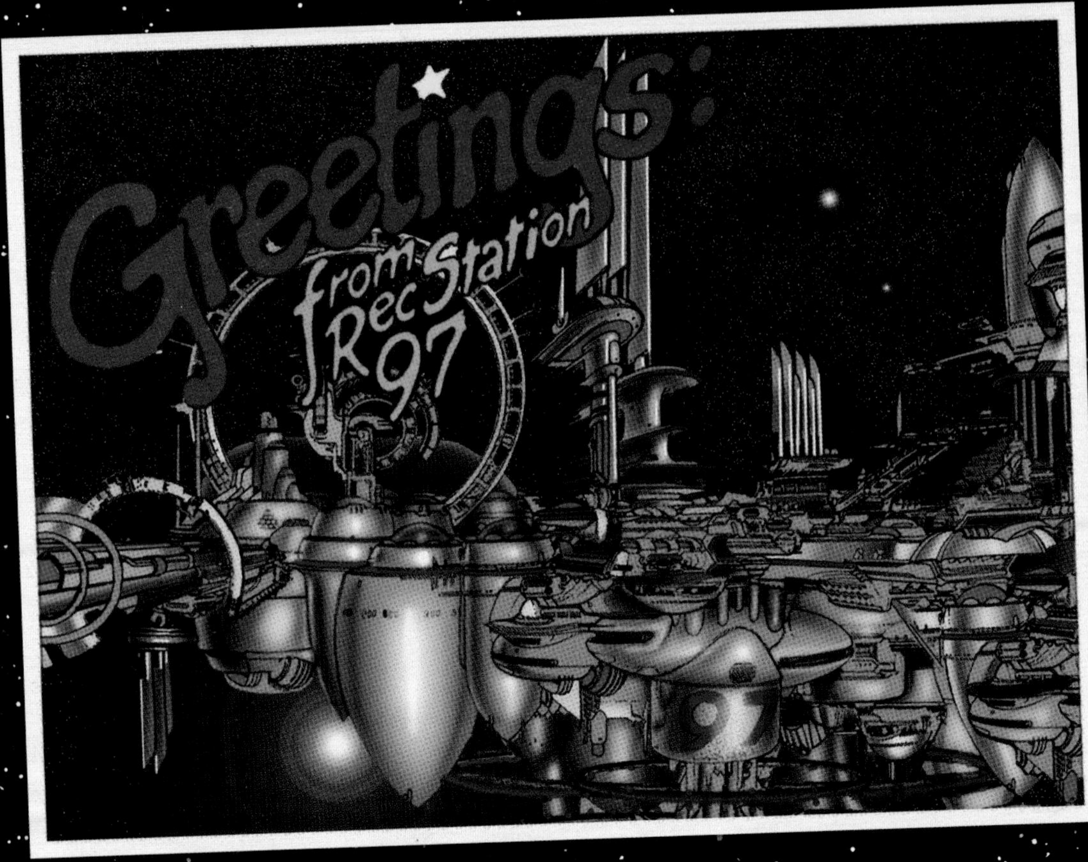
Greetings:
from Rec Station 97

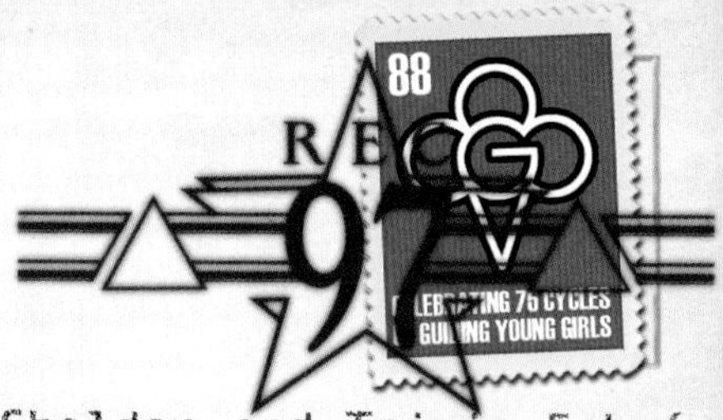
REC 97
88
CELEBRATING 76 CYCLES GUIDING YOUNG GIRLS

Hiya, Mommy and Pops!

You probably know by now I'm not on Miz Em's farm, but don't worry. Bru, Puddy and me are on Rec 97, a really fun place!
When I say don't worry, really don't worry.
Rec 97 is safe as safe can be.

We're here on top secret 3G business, so I can't say what we're doing, but I'll tell you all about it, when we get back.
Promise.

Truth as far as it goes!

Cookie

Sheldon and Trixie Fabré

Trixie's Feed and
Fertilizer Warehouse

Exit 38 Thruwest Skyway
Sector 22, Lot 93

Kansas, Amercadia

GREETINGS FROM REC STATION 97 #14
Rectangular Trifles, Ltd., 1480 Great Whiting Way, Blue Heaven, Rec 97

Recreation Station 97

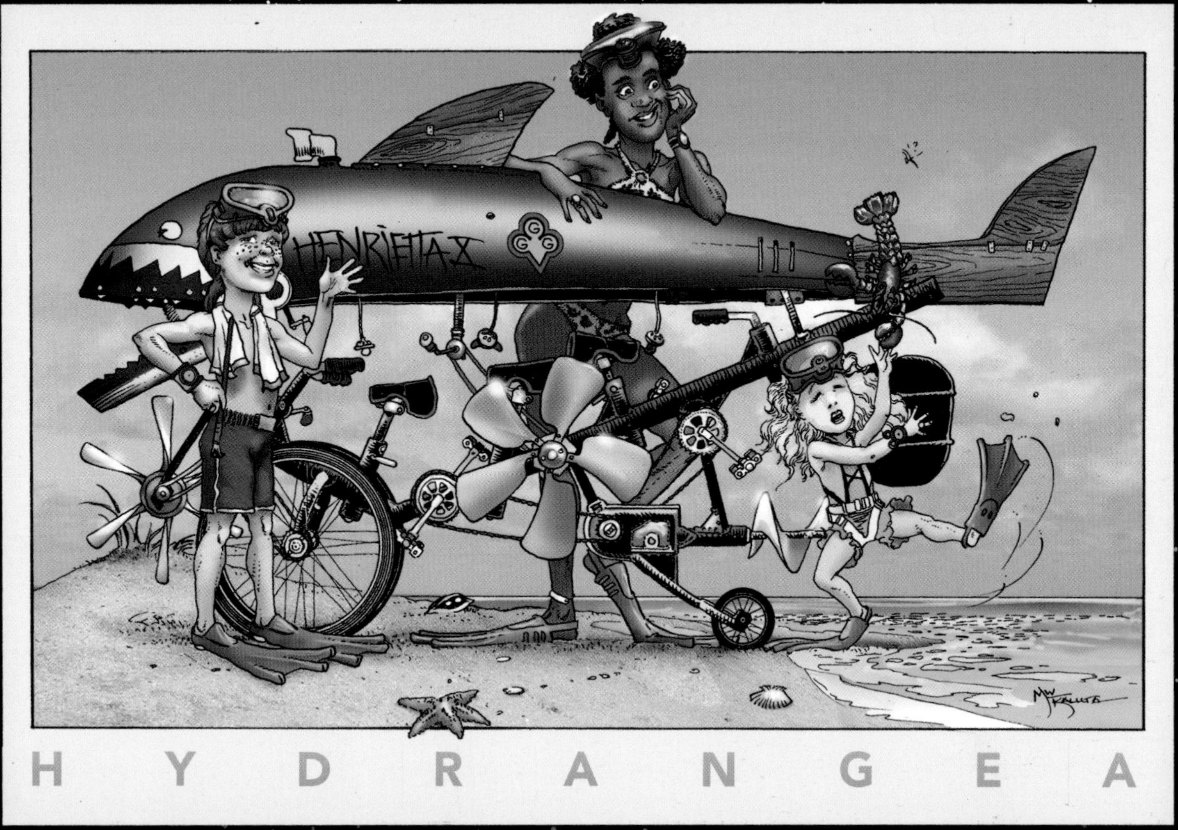
HENRIETTA X
H Y D R A N G E A

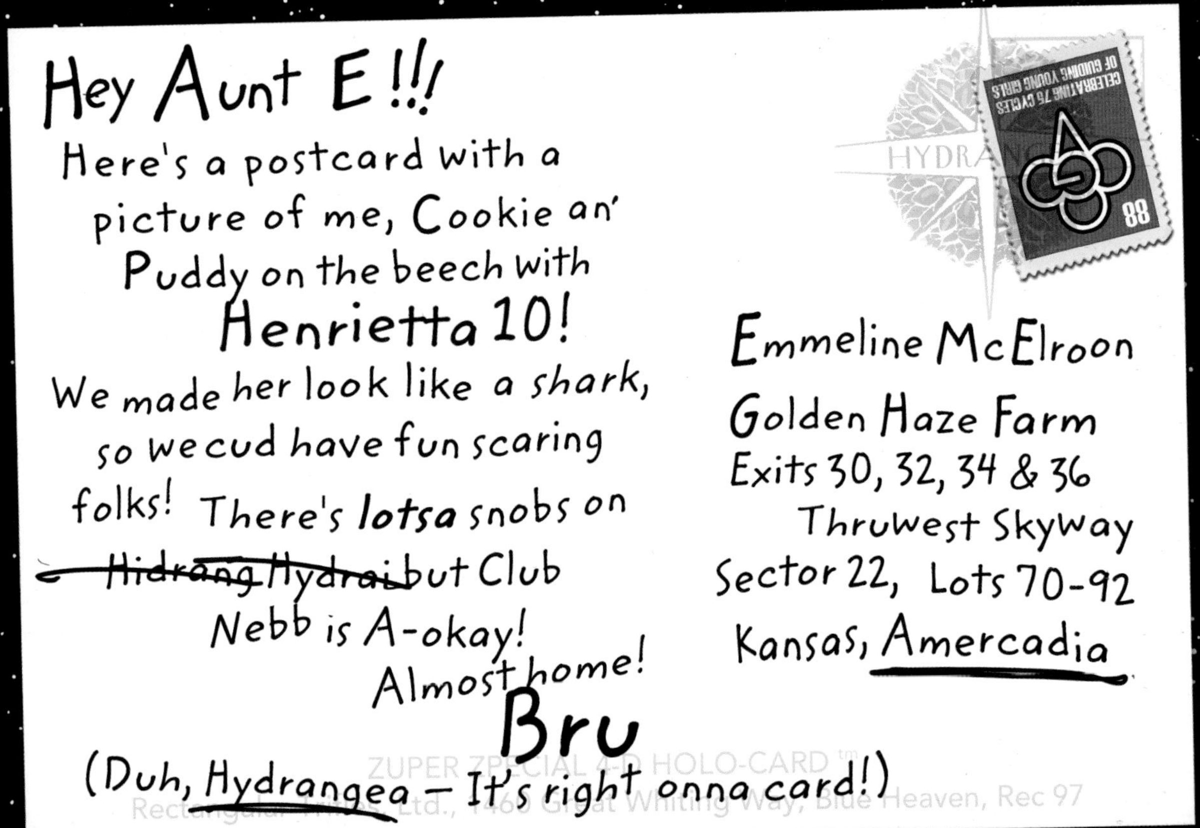
Hey Aunt E!!!
Here's a postcard with a picture of me, Cookie an' Puddy on the beech with
Henrietta 10!
We made her look like a shark, so we cud have fun scaring folks! There's lotsa snobs on ~~Hidrang Hydrai~~ but Club Nebb is A-okay!
Almost home!
Bru
(Duh, Hydrangea – It's right onna card!)
Emmeline McElroon
Golden Haze Farm
Exits 30, 32, 34 & 36
Thruwest Skyway
Sector 22, Lots 70-92
Kansas, Amercadia
HYDRANGEA
CELEBRATING 76 CYCLES OF GUIDING YOUNG GIRLS
88
ZUPER ZPECIAL 4-D HOLO-CARD ™

Hydrangea

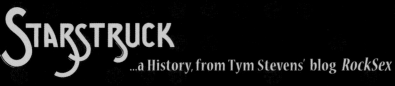

STARSTRUCK

...a History, from Tym Stevens' blog *RockSex*

I often say "STARSTRUCK is the greatest comic you've never read. And people say, "Well, what is it exactly?" (Or "Who are you?" or "How does this relate to Rock or Sex?" or "Please respect the 100 feet distance from the restraining order, sir.")

"Let's do the Time Warp again..."

STARSTRUCK began as a science fiction play performed off-Broadway in 1980. It was written by Elaine Lee, an Emmy-nominated actor on a popular TV soap opera, with her sister Susan Norfleet and Dale Place. Elaine played the wily hero Galatia 9 while Susan played her kickass partner Brucilla The Muscle. By chance the sisters had hooked up with renowned comics artist Michael Wm. Kaluta, who went from volunteering for the poster to designing the sets and costumes, and even building them with compatriot artist Charles Vess.

STARBILL
STARSTRUCK
N.E.T.W.O.R.K. THEATER NYC. 754 NINTH AVE. AT 51ST STREET
APRIL 16TH, 17TH, 18TH, 19TH; 23RD, 24TH, 25TH, 26TH; 30TH. MAY 1ST, 2ND, 3RD; 7TH, 8TH, 9TH AND 10TH.
RESERVATIONS: 212-586-1260 : CURTAIN: 8 PM
• AN EQUITY APPROVED PILOT PROJECT •

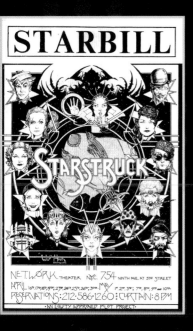

STARSTRUCK was also created during the exploding late '70s/early '80s NYC scene, whose Do-It-Yourself spirit ignited the first Punk bands of CBGB's, the No Wave and Post Punk aftermath, the dawn of Hip Hop, the splicing of Mutant Disco, and a bristling Indie film movement. As part of this hybrid scene, which propelled itself, STARSTRUCK the play was as D.I.Y. with its wicked and absurdist humor, its sets and costumes collaged from street throwaways, and its upending of all conventions. Starlog magazine noticed enough to cover the ensuing madness of this demented semi-musical (Dec. 1980) and a portfolio of designs by Kaluta was released. But that was just the beginning.

The play was essentially like an episode of STAR TREK; on a few ship sets, heroes and villains flung witty dialogue along with some fists. And there were songs and outlandish costumes. And farrr more lead women. Along the way characters rapped rich backgrounds mentioning other characters never shown. Lee and Kaluta realized this backstory was too good to waste. It was too grand to stage or film but Michael could draw it better anyway. So the first STARSTRUCK illustrated adventures began.

At the time the rules of speculative illustrated fiction had been rewritten by METAL HURLANT magazine, a French countercultural exploration of high art, sophisticated stories, and pervasive sensuality. The standard set by creators Moebius, Philippe Druillet, and Enki Bilal raised the bar for mature comics dramatically by filtering the fantasy and science fiction of the radical '50s EC comics through the uncensored advances of the '60s underground comix. The first wave of STARSTRUCK stories, a series of prequel vignettes to the play, were a natural for this graphix revolution. They first debuted in the similar Spanish anthology, ILUSTRACION+COMIX INTERNATIONAL, edited by Joseph Toutain in 1981; the intricate watercolourish washes were by uncredited Spanish artists using Kaluta's color directions. They were then reprinted in HEAVY METAL, the American version of Metal Hurlant, from 1982 to 1983. There was also an article about it all (HM #74, May 1983) and a second staging of the play.

23
ILUSTRACION+
COMIX
INTERNA
TOUTAIN EDITOR
LA INCREIBLE FANTASIA DE
MIKE KALUTA
UN RECUERDO AL DESAPARECIDO
WALLY WOOD
JUAN GIMENEZ • WILL EISNER • LUIS ROYO
DICK MATENA • CRAIG RUSSELL
MANDRAFINA
Y MUCHO MAS

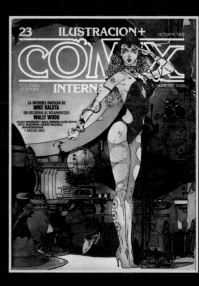

"By a clever ruse..."

The indie spirit was infiltrating the comic book world as well. In the early '80s, DC and Marvel found their duopoly undermined by upstart start-ups like Star Reach, First, Pacific, and Eclipse Comics. These rebels bypassed the newstand and drugstore racks to sell directly through the emerging network of comics-only stores. Most welcome of all, the creators retained the rights to their work while the company only distributed it. Pulp paper was replaced by archival stock and color got more advanced. Without corporate control, fake morality codes, or a teen threshhold, they were free to do whatever they wanted. Like the parallel independent record labels, they infused a stagnant industry with vital new blood. There were new standard-bearers like AZTEC ACE (Eclipse), AMERICAN FLAGG (First), and LOVE AND ROCKETS (Fantagraphics). The two majors noticed.

In Marvels more mature line of graphic novels they chose to collect all of the HM stories. "STARSTRUCK: The Luckless, The Abandoned and Forsaked" came out in 1984. The format was really big (8 1/4 x 11") and the color rich like watercolors. Stacked against anything else out its 74 genius pages were formidable.

Kaluta was most known for his gritty, retro work on THE SHADOW (1973), all edgy intensity and Pulp chiaroscuro. But his STARSTRUCK was a revelation: a vast dreamlike landscape infused with light like Winsor McCay; the technology of Dick Calkins' '30s BUCK ROGERS strips filtered through the hallucinatory kineticism of Moebius; and the elegant architecture and design sense of Mucha and Klimt. But Lee upped the ante with her storytelling: these prelude stories covered generational arcs in sprinting gallops; the narrators changed, the conversations piled up or overlapped or became song verse, the glossary was hysterical; the dialogue was so crackling you read it out loud to savor it; what seemed like happenstance eventually built up in layers and every minor thing paid off startlingly. It was like William Burroughs writing STAR WARS, or Lily Tomlin writing DUNE, or Robert Altman filming FIREFLY, only much funnier and weirder.

You didn't read STARSTRUCK, you held on to your keister and rode it like a rollercoaster.

The most profound innovation of STARSTRUCK was its redefinition of female leads. To be fair, a male-led industry selling to mostly teen boys had made some advances in the '70s responding to feminism. There were more women heroes up front, with equal strength and solo titles. But attitude and aggro don't equal depth or range. And often it felt like they were still just stronger pin-ups for young guys who hadn't worked out their range of respect yet beyond fists and fishnets. There needed to be a mature illustrated fiction where characters were just individuals with real personalities, period. Where gender was about as relevent as a shirt and sensuality was natural as breathing. But STARSTRUCK was already beyond even that. Lee wasn't interested in a SciFi that was trapped in the didactic slants of anyone's war of the sexes. She built a universe of possibility where everyone fended for themselves full-on. Everyone was as unique, quirky, irritating, horny, and surprising as reality. These people lived, they breathed, they were a riot. Seeing that fuller range in fruition was the real liberation. (Meanwhile, the most edgy advance for women in the majors was that Elektra could be just as much an amoral thug as The Punisher.)

"In a desperate race against time..."

Marvel Comics had responded to the threat of Heavy Metal with their own Epic Illustrated magazine. In their most inspired move of the '80s they started a separate imprint for mature titles called Epic Comics. These were creator-owned series for adults, edited by the beloved Archie Goodwin, who promptly tractor-beamed Lee and Kaluta into a bi-monthly STARSTRUCK comic book. It would be "direct market" only to comic stores, in amounts limited to market sales. They could do whatever they wanted. The comic series continued from the set-up of the graphic novel, but focused more fully on the cosmic misadventures of the swashbuckling Galatia 9 and fireball Brucilla. There were six issues of 32 pages each from 1985 to 1986, no ads except for their own T-Shirts, and often character photos from the play inside the cover. After decades of misregistered color on pulp paper, these specialized comics had stronger brighter stock and more controlled color. They also cost more, but maturing readers dropped the newstand superhero stuff entirely for direct-market books that rewarded their attention and age. But not enough of them yet. Despite cover stories on Comics Journal and Amazing Heroes, STARSTRUCK was like a secret even your best friends missed out on and it was discontinued. But it wasn't truly ended.

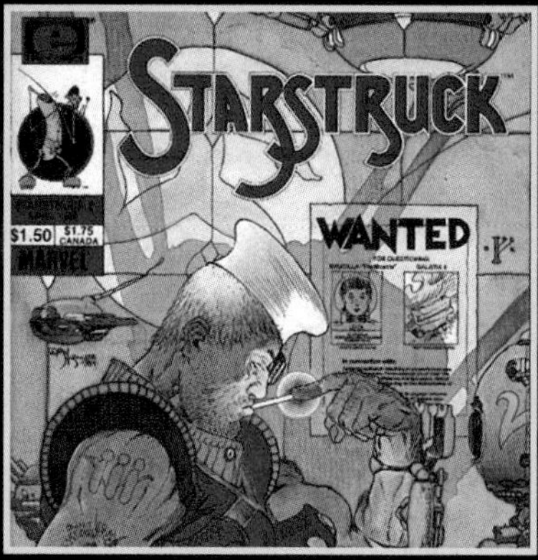
STARSTRUCK
WANTED
$1.50
MARVEL

Par for the course, in its wake, the mainstream started catching up. Alan Moore and Frank Miller paved most of that in 1986, and DC's imprint Vertigo Comics later succeeded in the adult path that Epic had paved. By 1990, the upstart indie Dark Horse Comics felt the time was right for Lee and Kaluta to finish what they started. "STARSTRUCK: The Expanding Universe" came out with a revitalized and revisionary mandate: it would reprint everything but with a projected 320 pages of new material laced through; there would be 12 48-page issues covering three major arcs until it was all done. The catch was it was black and white and cost twice as much. And there was the page size thing; to match the more square dimensions of the story portions from the graphic novel, the new integrated page art left more blank air at the bottom of the rectangular book.

But what a ride! Suddenly everything was deeper, wider, richer. The single-page story that had jumpstarted the original novel now had an additional six pages opening up new levels of clarity and connection. Fresh chapters revealed unseen characters. The first third of the grand plan came out in four issues with more than 100 new pages enriching the grand tale. The toll of this huge amount of work and the dispiriting lack of support in the comics world exhausted Kaluta, which led to another cancellation. While everyone gushed about SANDMAN and WATCHMEN, they'd missed the real party again.

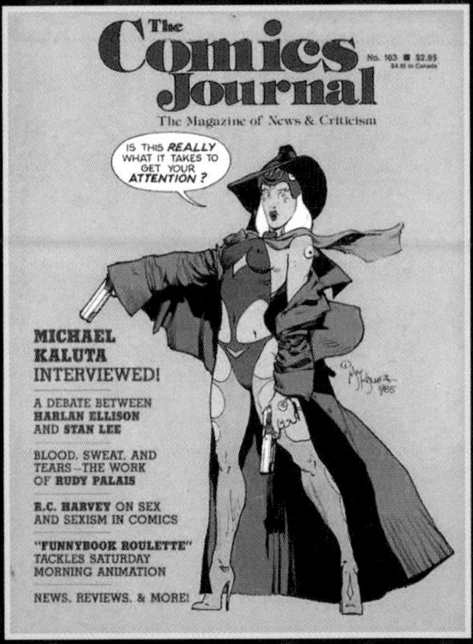
The Comics Journal
No. 163 ■ $2.95
The Magazine of News & Criticism
IS THIS REALLY WHAT IT TAKES TO GET YOUR ATTENTION ?
MICHAEL KALUTA INTERVIEWED!
A DEBATE BETWEEN HARLAN ELLISON AND STAN LEE
BLOOD, SWEAT, AND TEARS—THE WORK OF RUDY PALAIS
R.C. HARVEY ON SEX AND SEXISM IN COMICS
"FUNNYBOOK ROULETTE" TACKLES SATURDAY MORNING ANIMATION
NEWS, REVIEWS, & MORE!

There were multiple attempts to resurrect STARSTRUCK through the '90s; talk of a film, toys, trade collections, TV series. But too many deals collapsed during the process. While other rebel works were canonized and reached the mainstream book stores in graphic novels, with no STARSTRUCK reprint collections, a new generation was left clueless. Diehard fans have held the secret faith since 1991, scrabbling for any rumor like it was a portent.

"Then, by a miracle..."

Enter IDW Comics in 2009 with the best STARSTRUCK ever seen: a 13 issue reprint series that was more of a remastered expansion. Kaluta now rectified the 'square' art problem - mentioned above - by extending new art on every page to full rectangular dimensions. It included all of the initial Expanded Universe tales, in color for the first time thanks to the stunningly lush work of painter Lee Moyer. Elaine amplified the sly glossary and added new intro pages. And it featured back-up stories of Brucilla's childhood in the larcenous and slapstick Galactic Girl Guides, with inking by fantasy art great Charles Vess. Only two of these had ever been seen before, published by Dave "The Rocketeer" Stevens in his Rocketeer Adventure Magazine.

"Elsewhere, at that very moment..."

STARSTRUCK is best known by its comic stories, which are all actually prequels to the play. And though many have heard of the STARSTRUCK play, few have seen it.

The Audiocomics Company has remedied this with a timely new audio adaption of STARSTRUCK that finally brings the play, and the dimension of sound, to the general public. Now fans used to the visual side of STARSTRUCK - from Kaluta's art, Moyer's color, or Sean Smith's stage photos - can finally hear the stage personalities, sound effects, and composer Dwight Dixon's original score.

The audio play homages the roots of STARSTRUCK in several ways. It bands together a new troupe of actors to bring it to life. But its sound format also recalls all of the BUCK ROGERS radio dramas, TV shows like TOM CORBETT, and films like BARBARELLA that inspired the play. Fittingly, it was created in cooperation with WMPG radio in Portland, and will run as radio broadcasts on other stations going forward. Plus, there is talk of new adventures being written directly for radio in the future.

"We find our Heroes..."

STARSTRUCK had helped lead the '80s comics revolution without getting the laurels. It was easily as good as renaissance classics like WATCHMEN, DARK KNIGHT RETURNS and SANDMAN. In truth, probably better, because it was more ambitious, progressive, funnier, and subversive without the aggro male angst underlining them. It was for sharp adults with a sense of wonder and subversion, for radical freespirits, for punk grrrls who were too young to know about it yet. It paved the way for TANK GIRL, MARTHA WASHINGTON, AEON FLUX, FUTURAMA, PROMETHEA, and SERENITY. Fanboy teens may have missed out back then but quality is timeless. It's taken 25 years to catch up to what this series was always doing. The rise of manga, serial TV shows, cyberpunk novels, indie comics, and Riot Grrrl have broadened the audience market to catch up with this book. With their blogs, sites, tweets, and tongues, this new generation is spreading the word and seizing the future Lee and Kaluta made for them.

"So, here's the lowdown..."

Let's see, where to begin? The plot involves a gradually dumbing dynasty versus a revolutionary cowgirl, pleasure droids who become sentient, an amazon clone and freelance fighter, passive/passive space nuns, an omnivorously sexual scheme queen, The Brand New Testament, robot samurai, frivolous cults, Noir detective bartenders, piously jingoistic space fleets, street-lethal Girl Scouts, schizoid dandies, alien boytoys, copious booting (see: boots, knocking), immortality bootlegging, Art Squads from the aesthetic planet Guernica ("Sex is art and art is power."), the infamous Recreation Station 97, and everything is increasingly connected. There is much drinking, explosions, polymorphous polyamory, slapstick chaos, some songs, and vicious satire that goes down like ice cream. You'll laugh, you'll think, you'll feel hot to trot.

STARSTRUCK is smart art for hip people. Catch up to the better revolution in your hands. The future is cooler than ever!

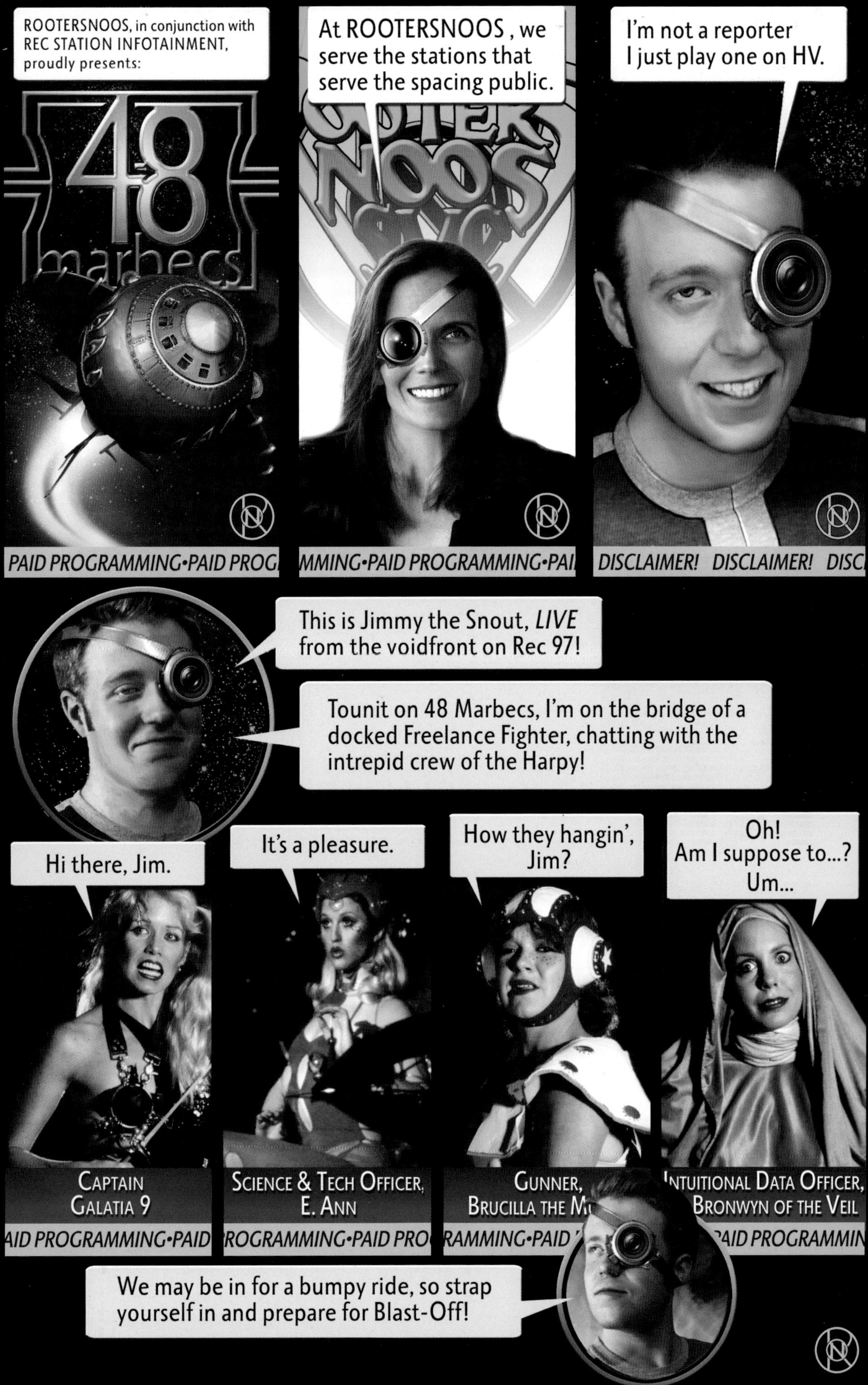
ROOTERSNOOS, in conjunction with REC STATION INFOTAINMENT, proudly presents:
48 marbecs
PAID PROGRAMMING•PAID PROG
At ROOTERSNOOS , we serve the stations that serve the spacing public.
MMING•PAID PROGRAMMING•PAI
I'm not a reporter I just play one on HV.
DISCLAIMER! DISCLAIMER! DISC
This is Jimmy the Snout, *LIVE* from the voidfront on Rec 97!
Tounit on 48 Marbecs, I'm on the bridge of a docked Freelance Fighter, chatting with the intrepid crew of the Harpy!
Hi there, Jim.
It's a pleasure.
How they hangin', Jim?
Oh! Am I suppose to...? Um...
CAPTAIN GALATIA 9
SCIENCE & TECH OFFICER, E. ANN
GUNNER, BRUCILLA THE M
INTUITIONAL DATA OFFICER, BRONWYN OF THE VEIL
AID PROGRAMMING•PAID ROGRAMMING•PAID PRO RAMMING•PAID AID PROGRAMMIN
We may be in for a bumpy ride, so strap yourself in and prepare for Blast-Off!

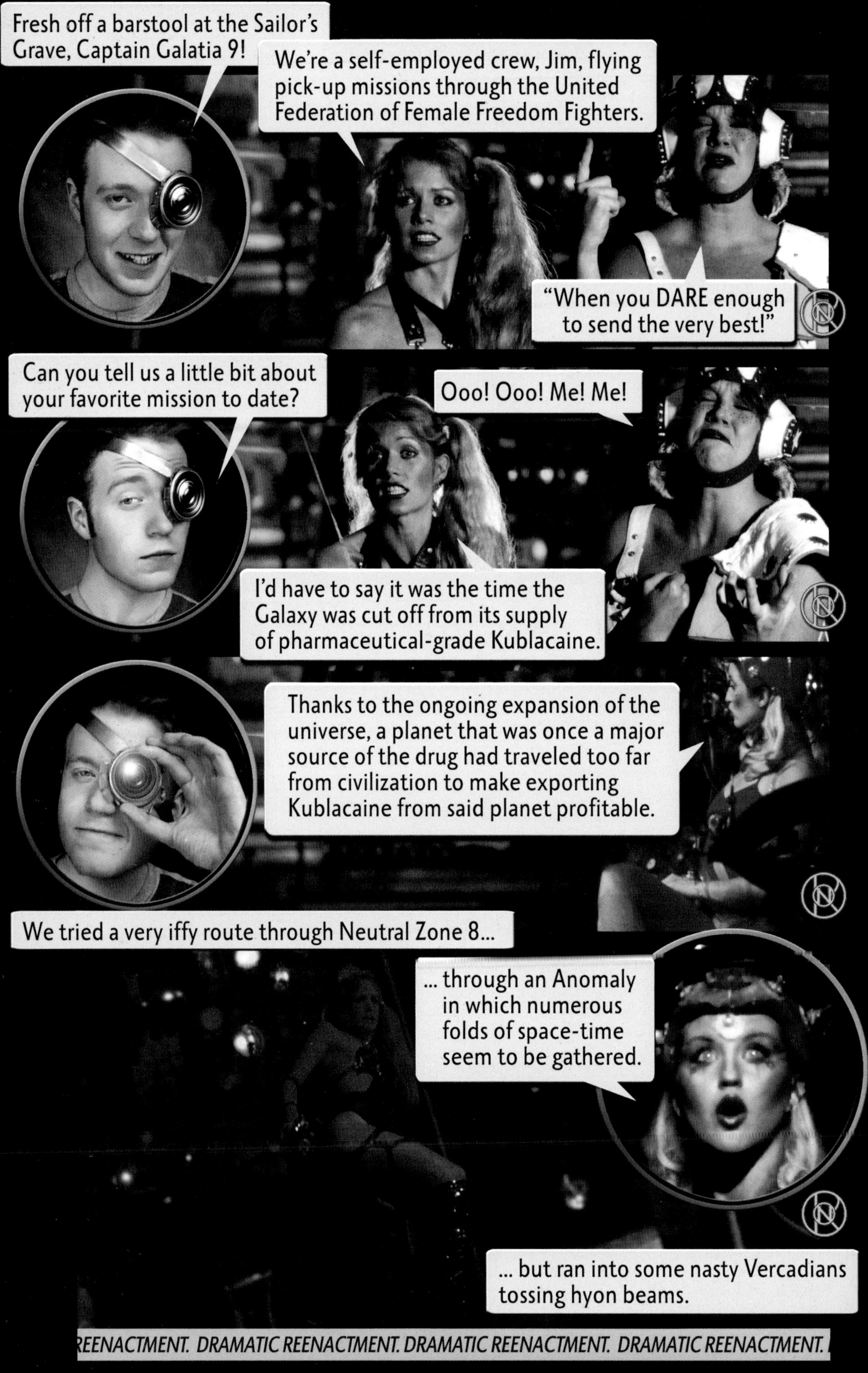
Fresh off a barstool at the Sailor's Grave, Captain Galatia 9!
We're a self-employed crew, Jim, flying pick-up missions through the United Federation of Female Freedom Fighters.
"When you DARE enough to send the very best!"
Can you tell us a little bit about your favorite mission to date?
Ooo! Ooo! Me! Me!
I'd have to say it was the time the Galaxy was cut off from its supply of pharmaceutical-grade Kublacaine.
Thanks to the ongoing expansion of the universe, a planet that was once a major source of the drug had traveled too far from civilization to make exporting Kublacaine from said planet profitable.
We tried a very iffy route through Neutral Zone 8...
... through an Anomaly in which numerous folds of space-time seem to be gathered.
... but ran into some nasty Vercadians tossing hyon beams.
REENACTMENT. DRAMATIC REENACTMENT. DRAMATIC REENACTMENT. DRAMATIC REENACTMENT.

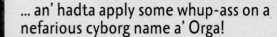

Then there was the time I dressed up like a Krabian to infiltrate a ship fulla depraved evil-doers...

... an' hadta apply some whup-ass on a nefarious cyborg name a' Orga!

ARTIST'S RENDITION • ARTIST'S RENDITION • ARTIST'   *ENDITION • ARTIST'S RENDITION • ARTIST'S RENDITIO*

Correction. Results of said battle: **CYBORG 1, BRUCILLA 0.** Play record, EV.

You *really* like to annoy me, don't you, Neurotica?

ACTUAL FOOTAGE! • A

Negative.

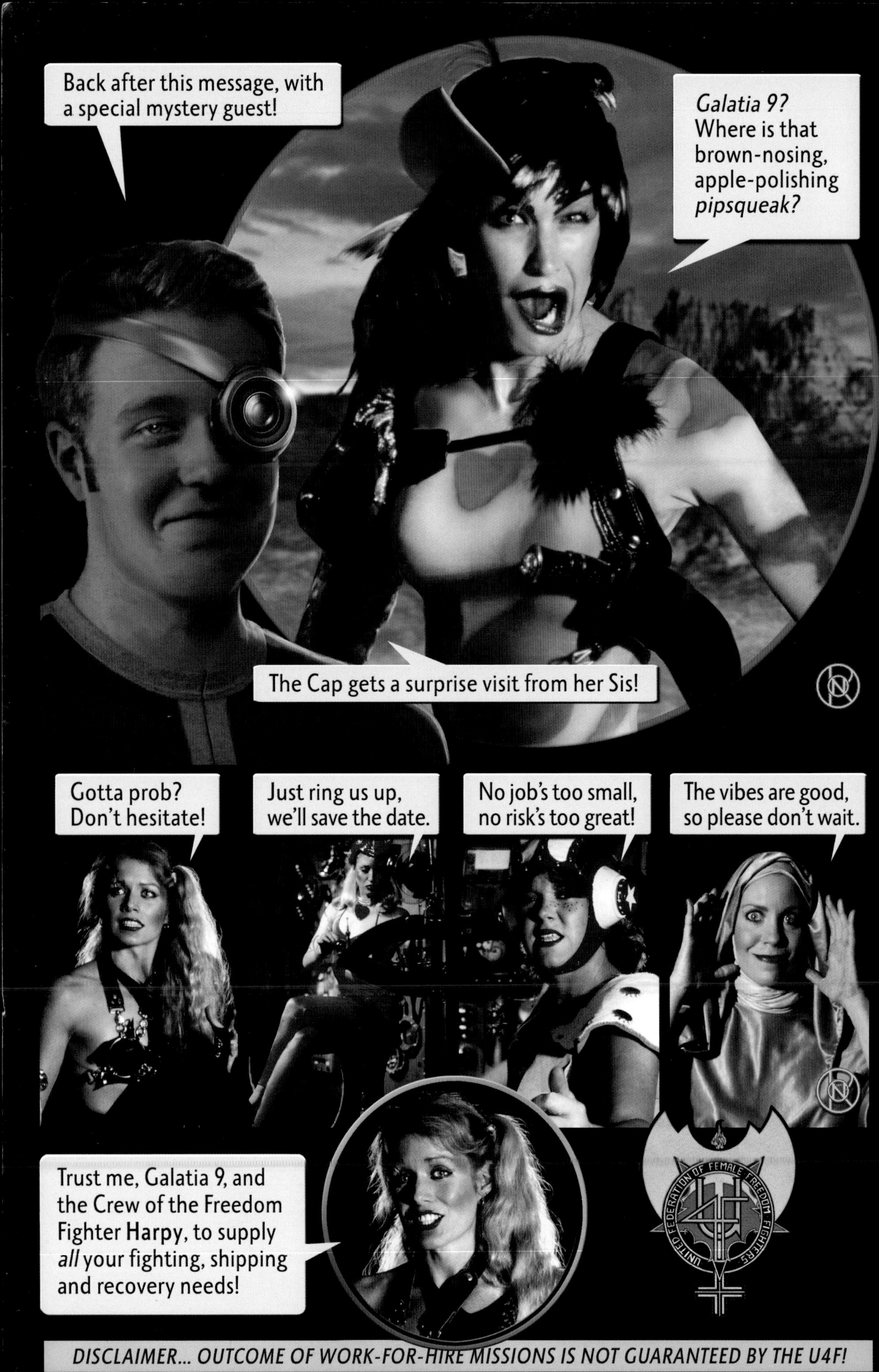
Back after this message, with a special mystery guest!
Galatia 9? Where is that brown-nosing, apple-polishing *pipsqueak?*
The Cap gets a surprise visit from her Sis!
Gotta prob? Don't hesitate!
Just ring us up, we'll save the date.
No job's too small, no risk's too great!
The vibes are good, so please don't wait.
Trust me, Galatia 9, and the Crew of the Freedom Fighter **Harpy**, to supply *all* your fighting, shipping and recovery needs!
UNITED FEDERATION OF FEMALE FREEDOM FIGHTERS
U4F
DISCLAIMER... OUTCOME OF WORK-FOR-HIRE MISSIONS IS NOT GUARANTEED BY THE U4F!

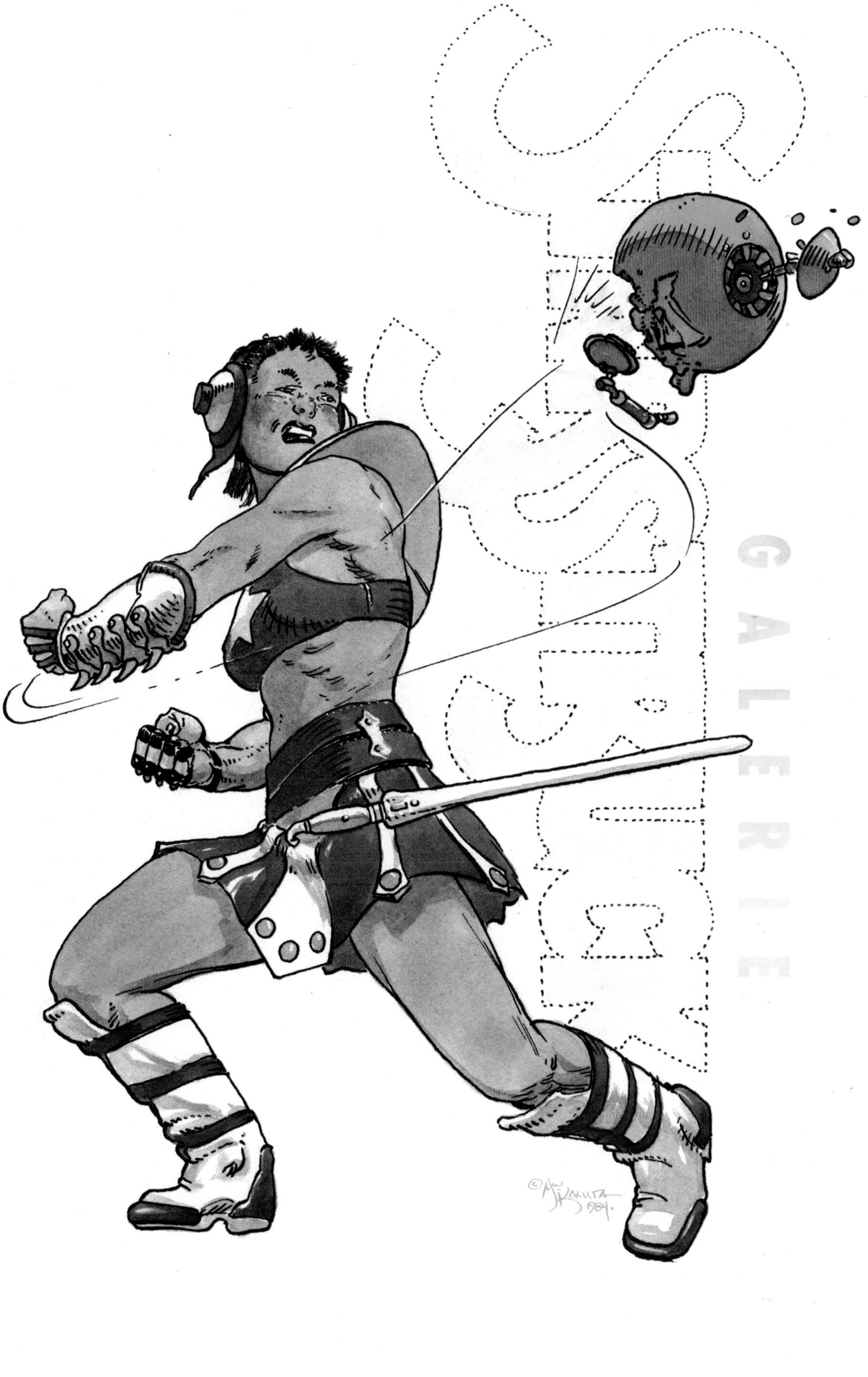
GALERIE
©MWK KALUTA 1984.

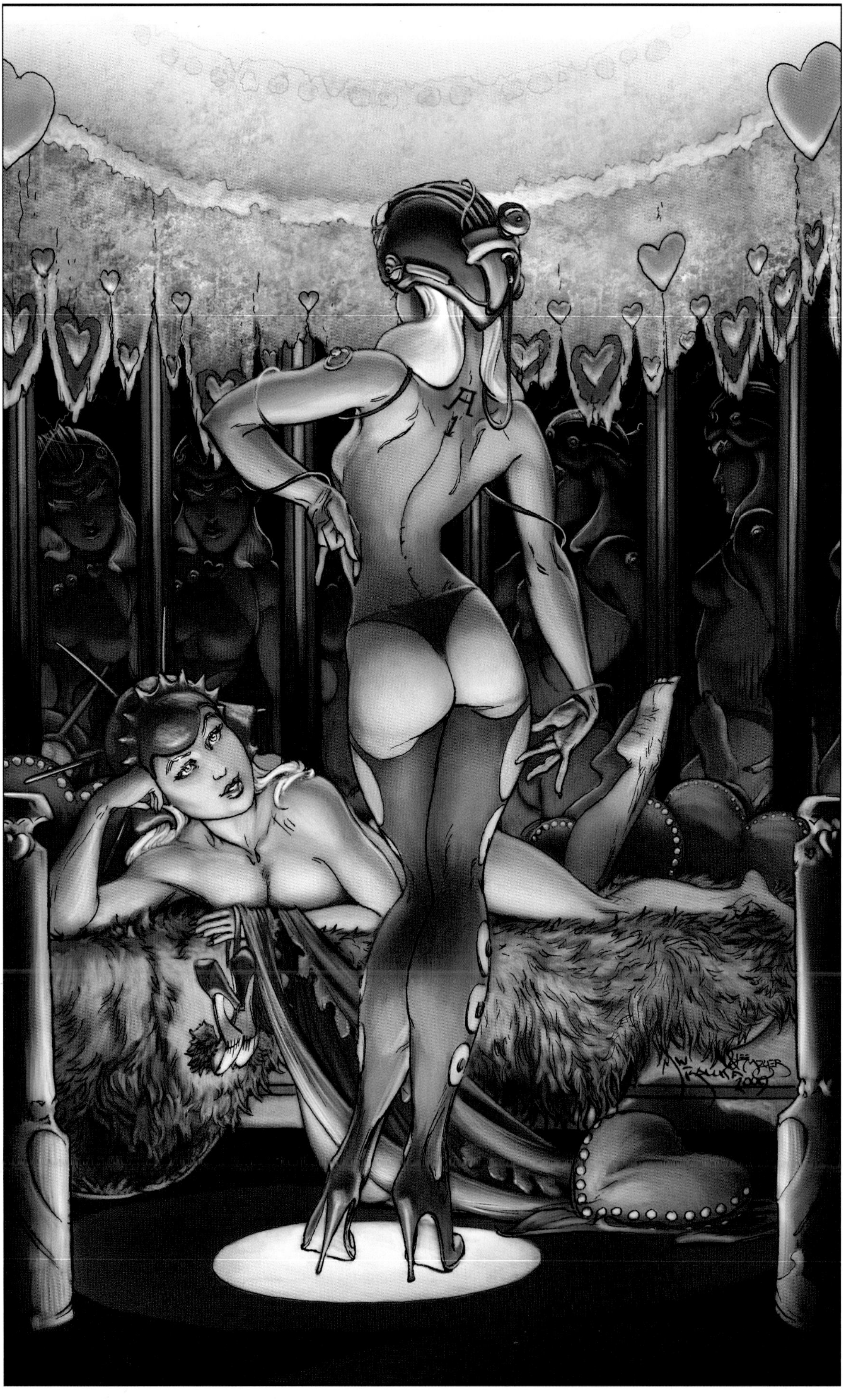

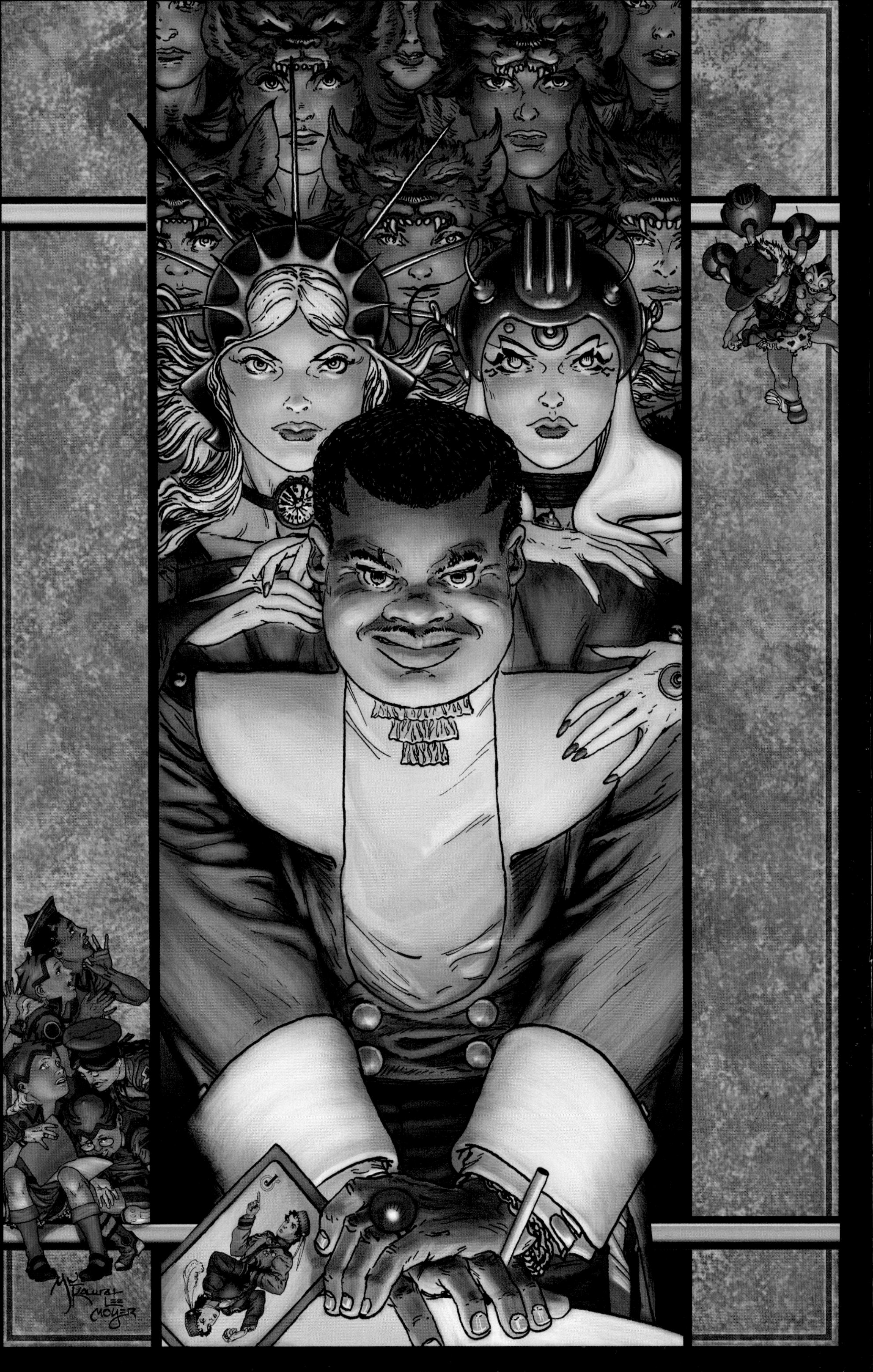
Lee Moyer

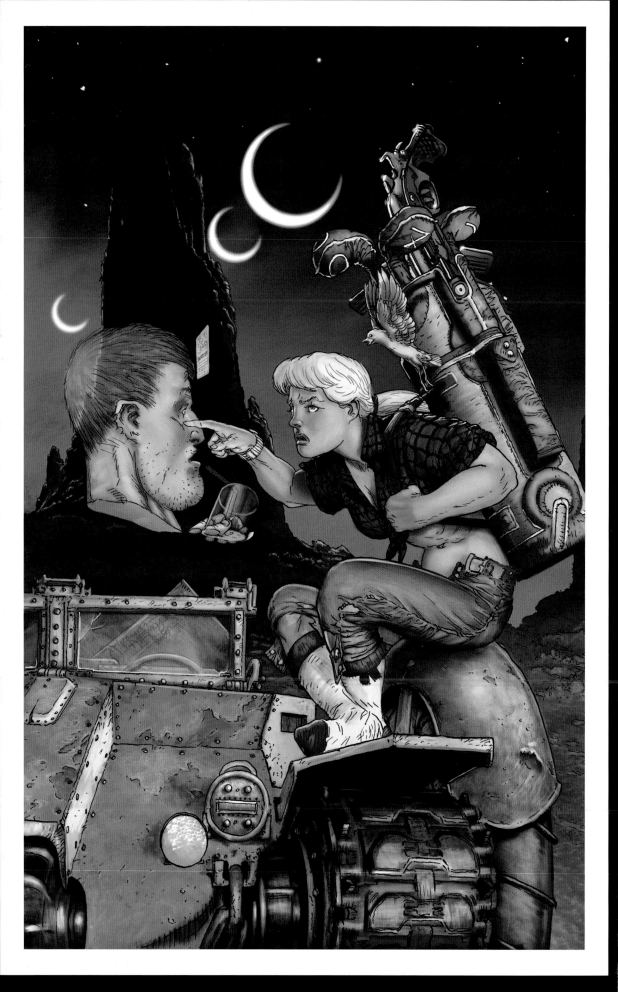

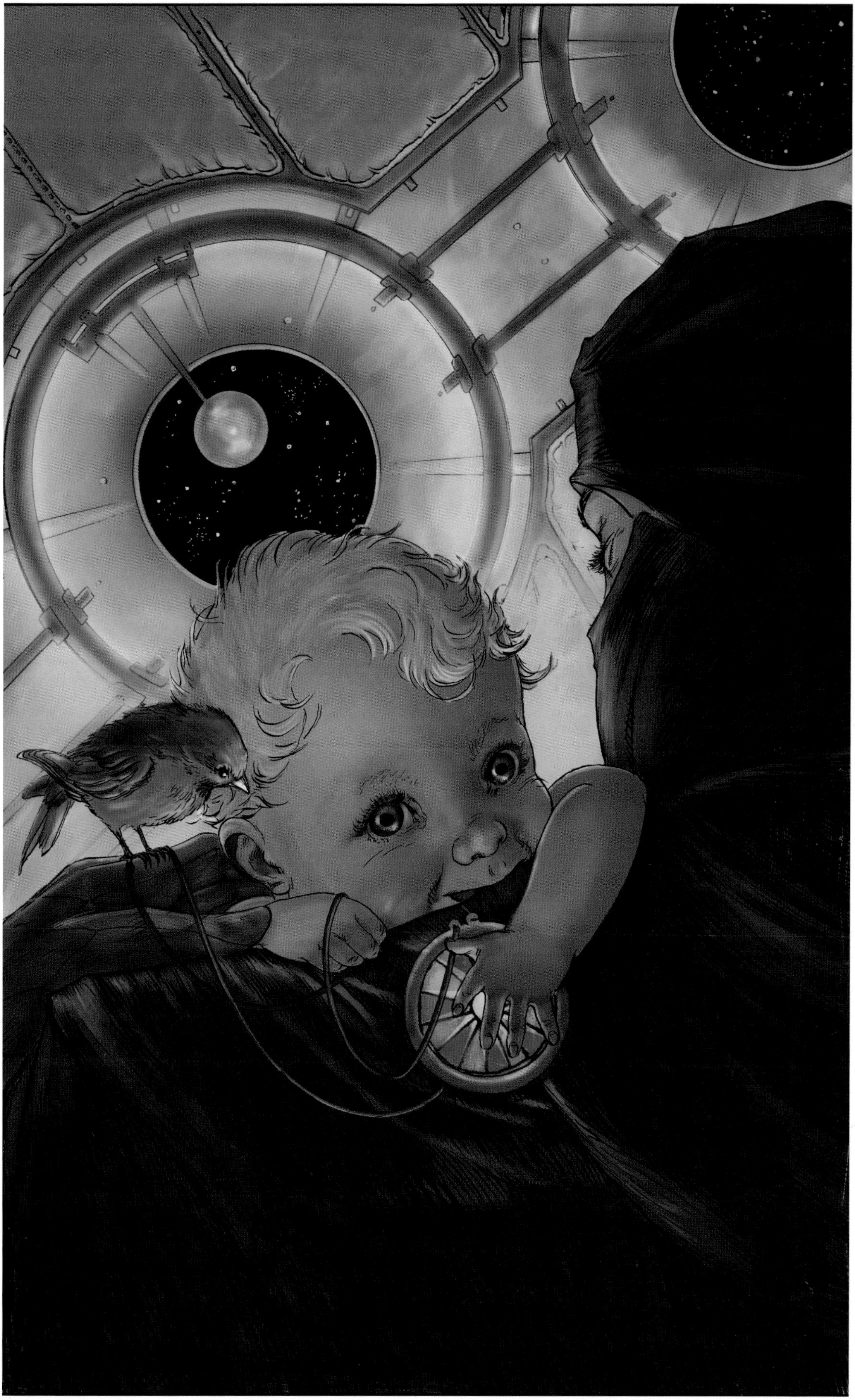

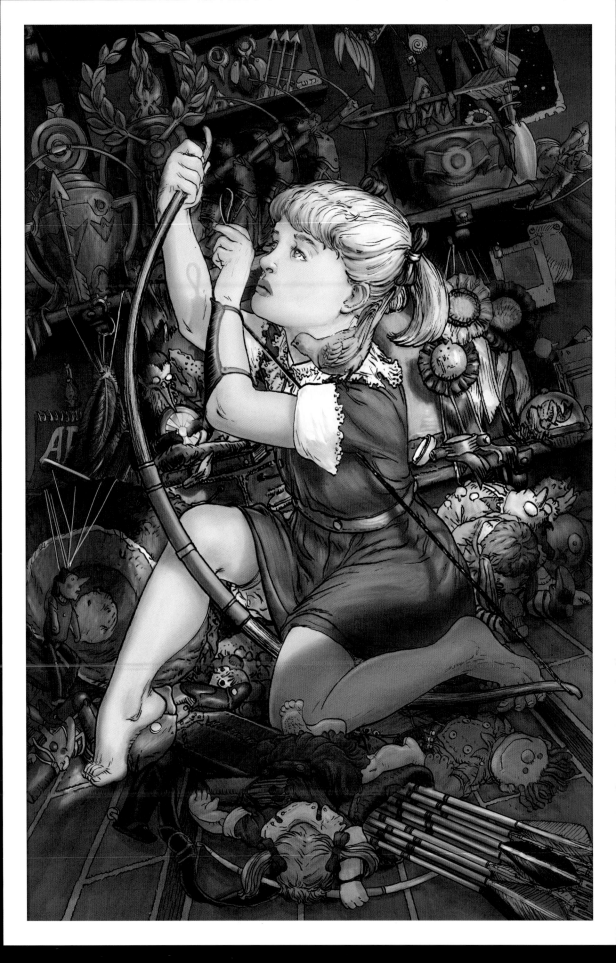

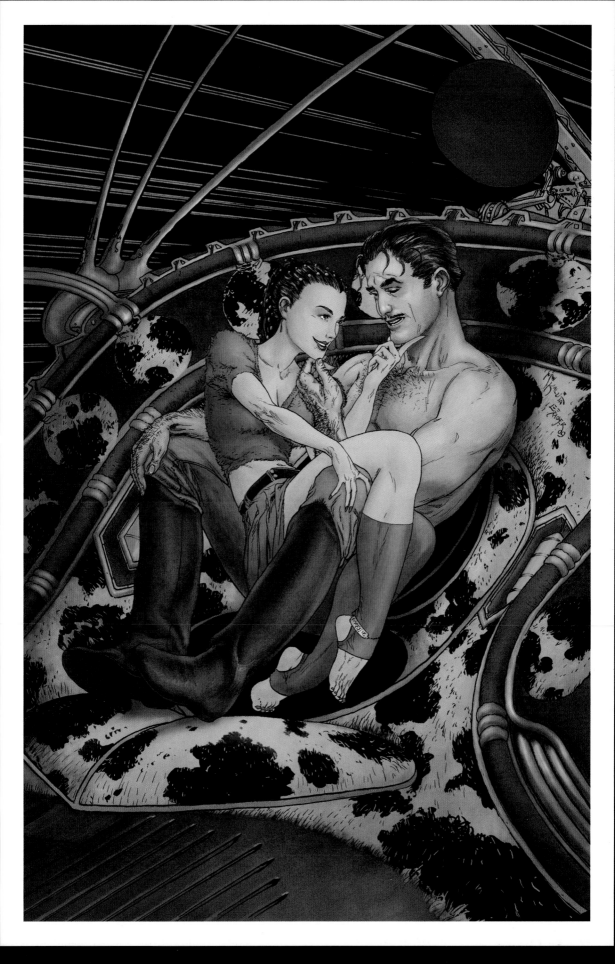

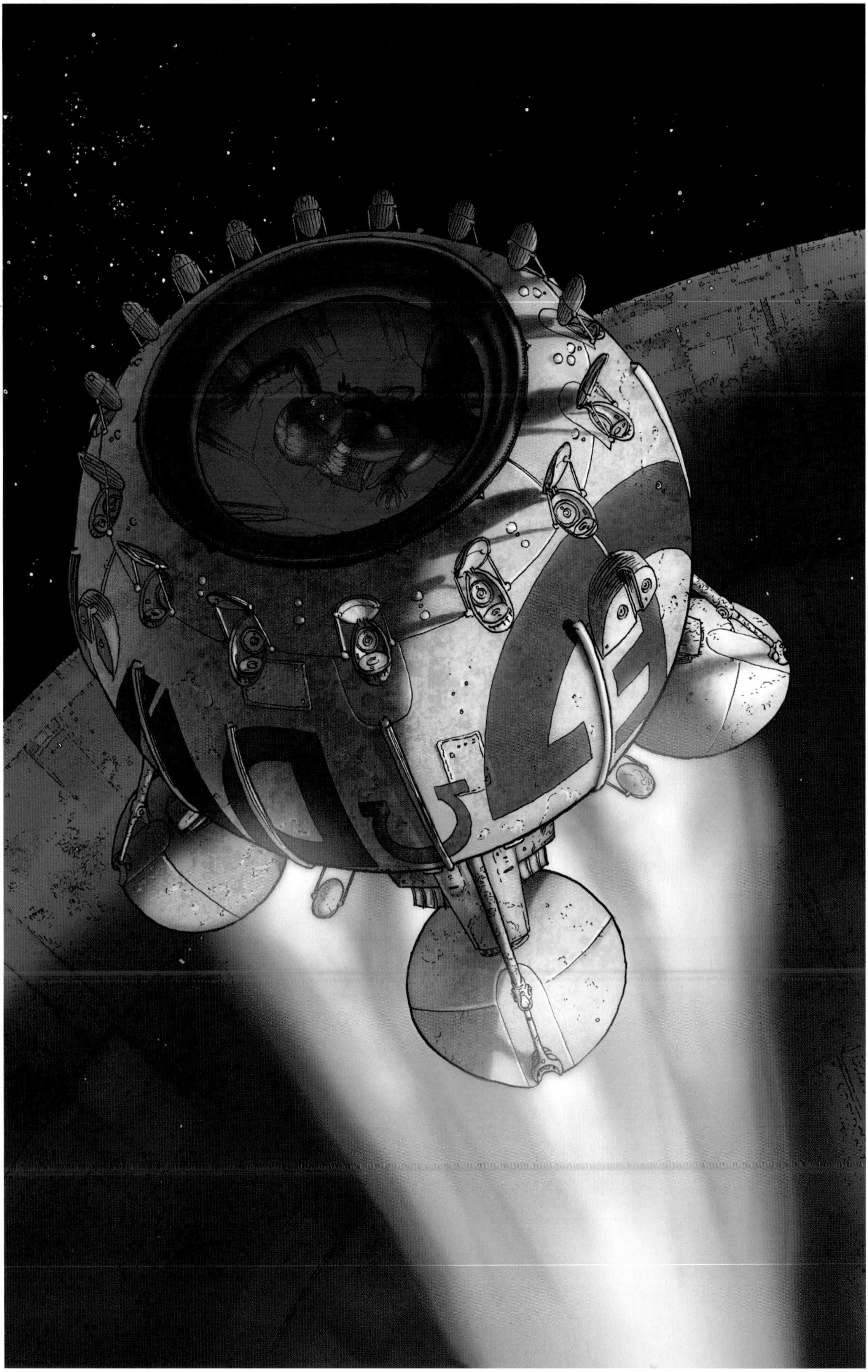

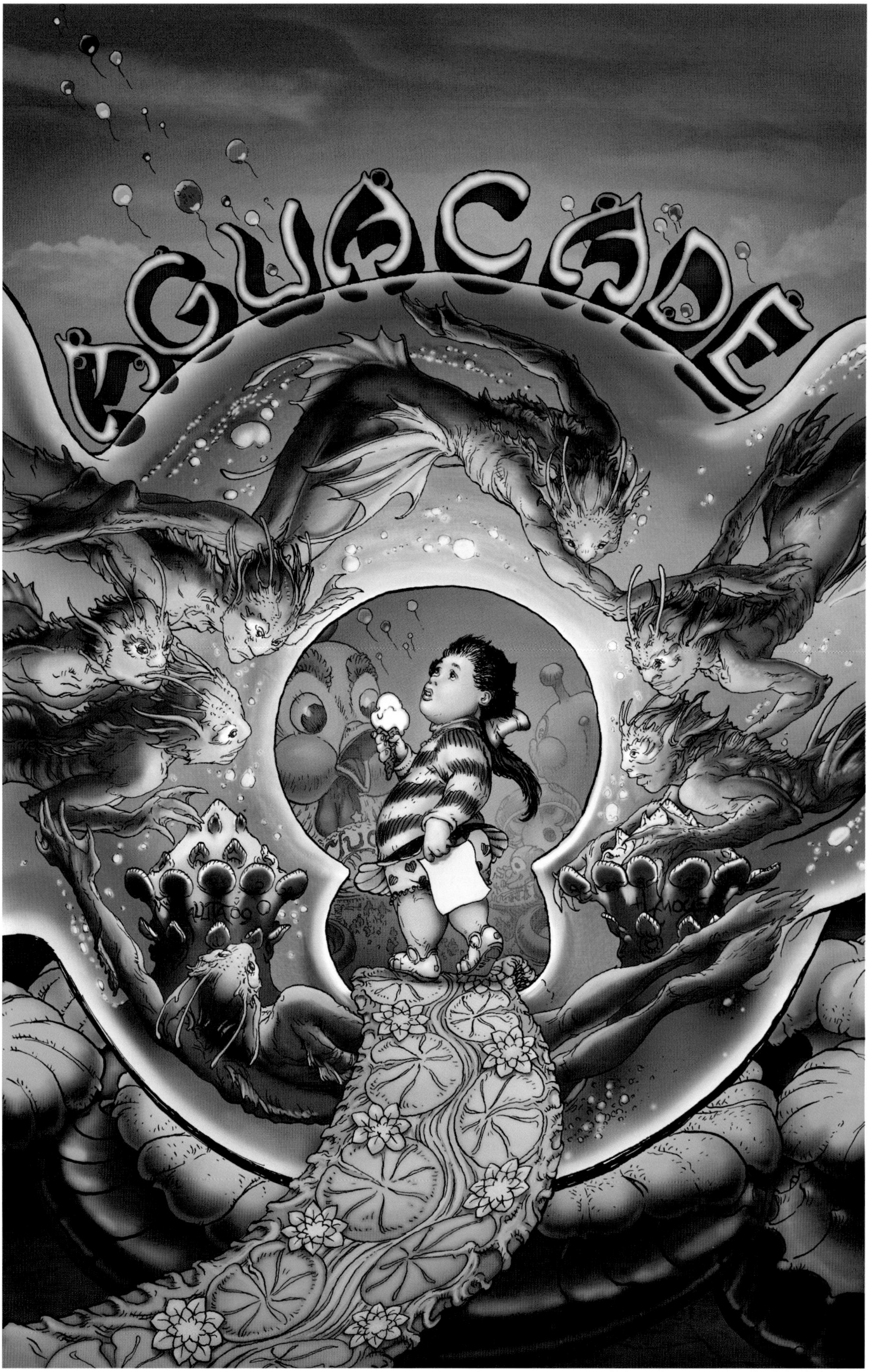
AGUACADE

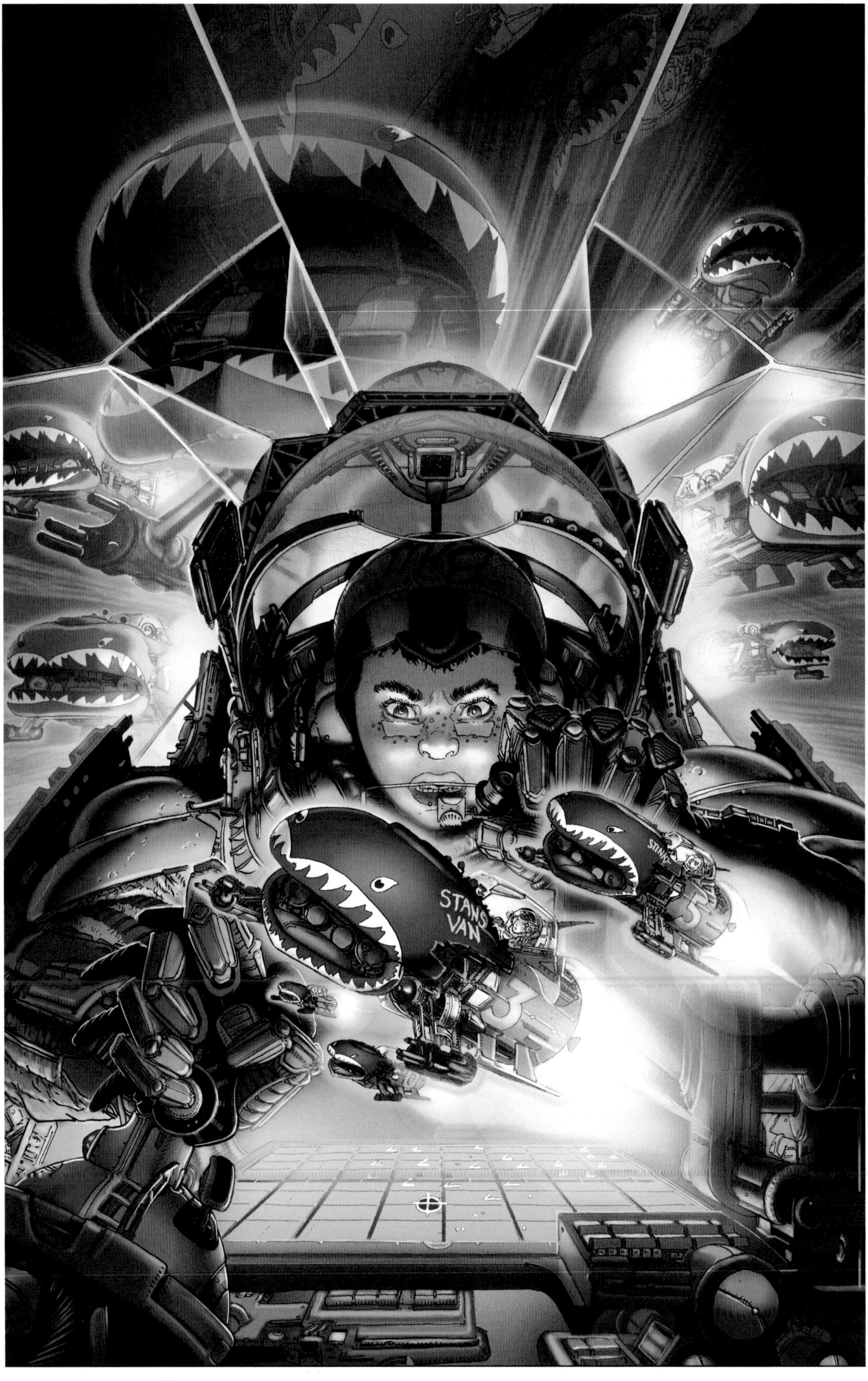
STANS VAN

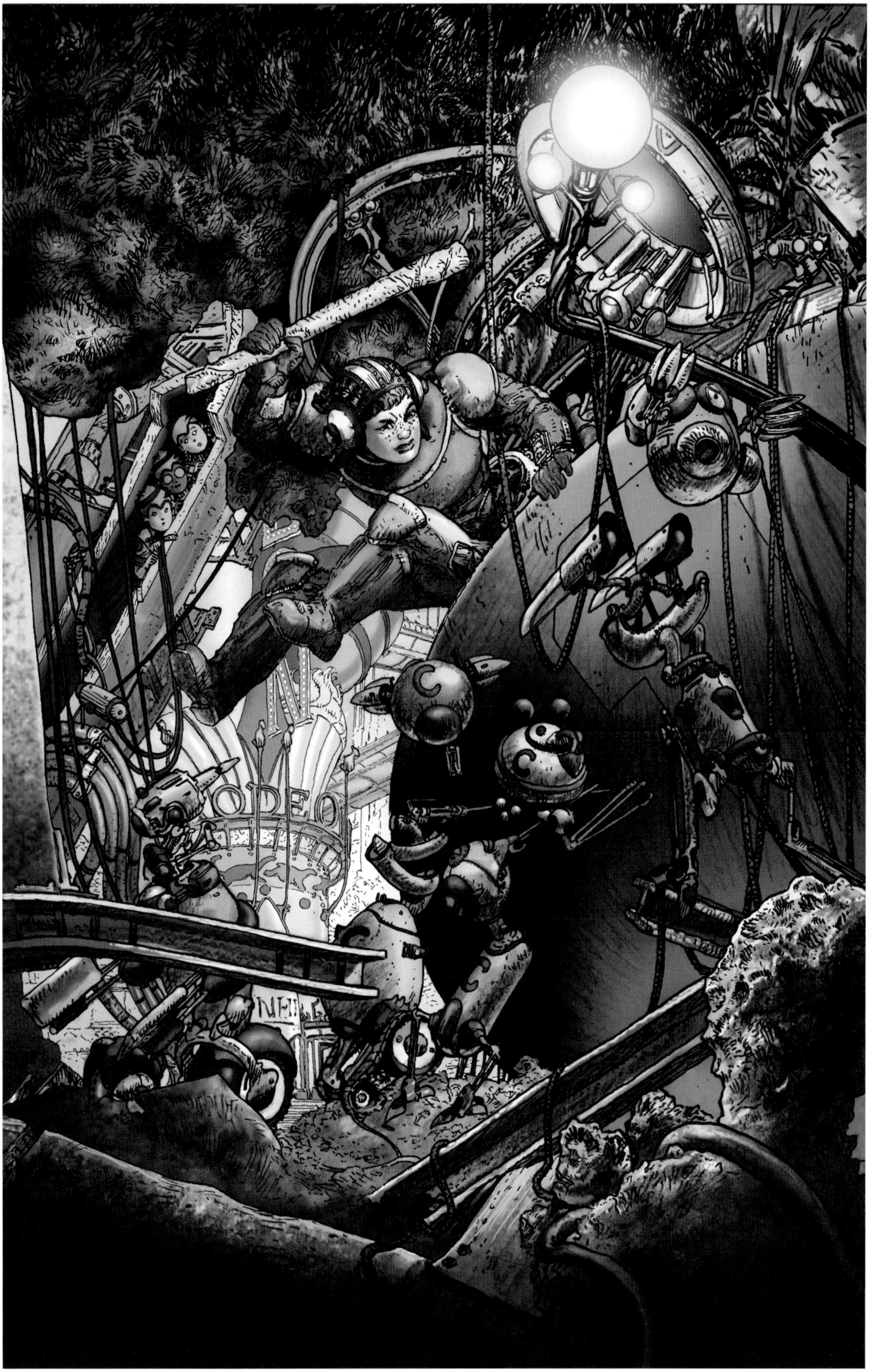

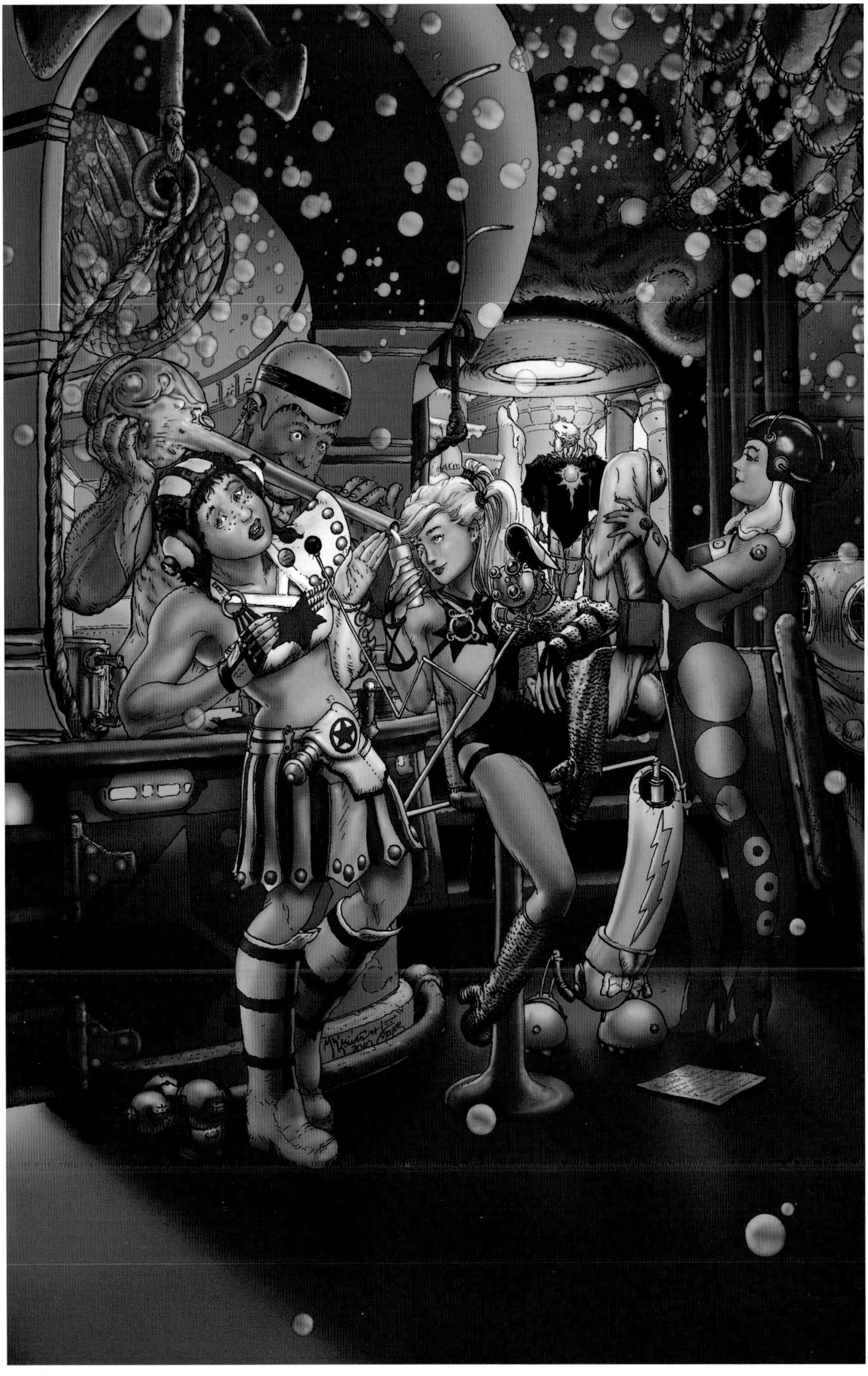

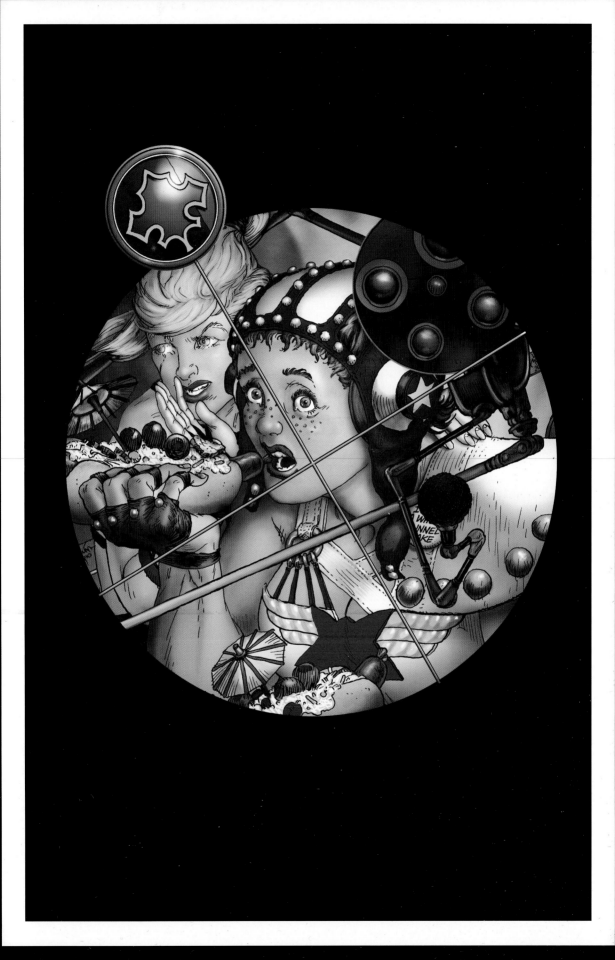

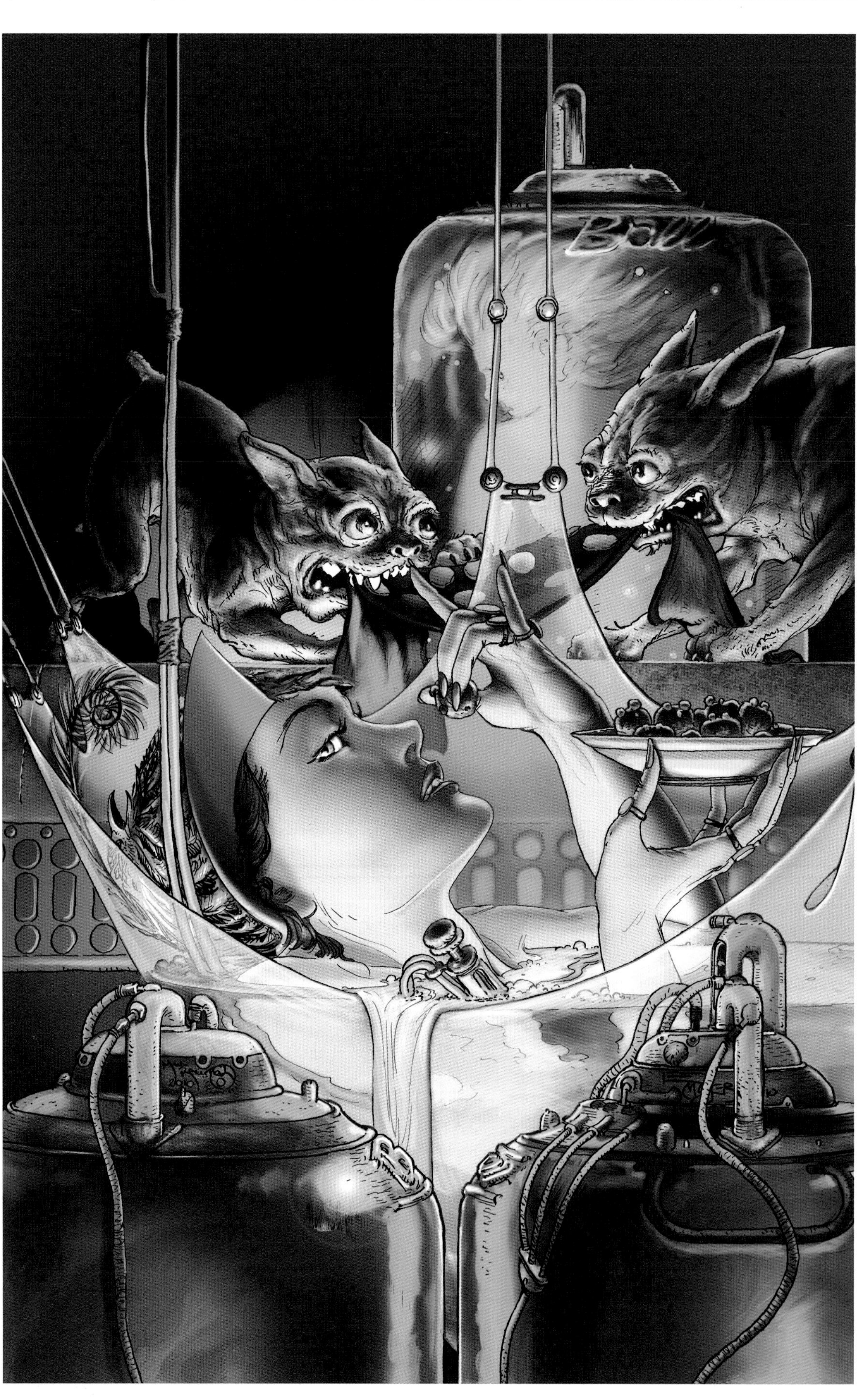

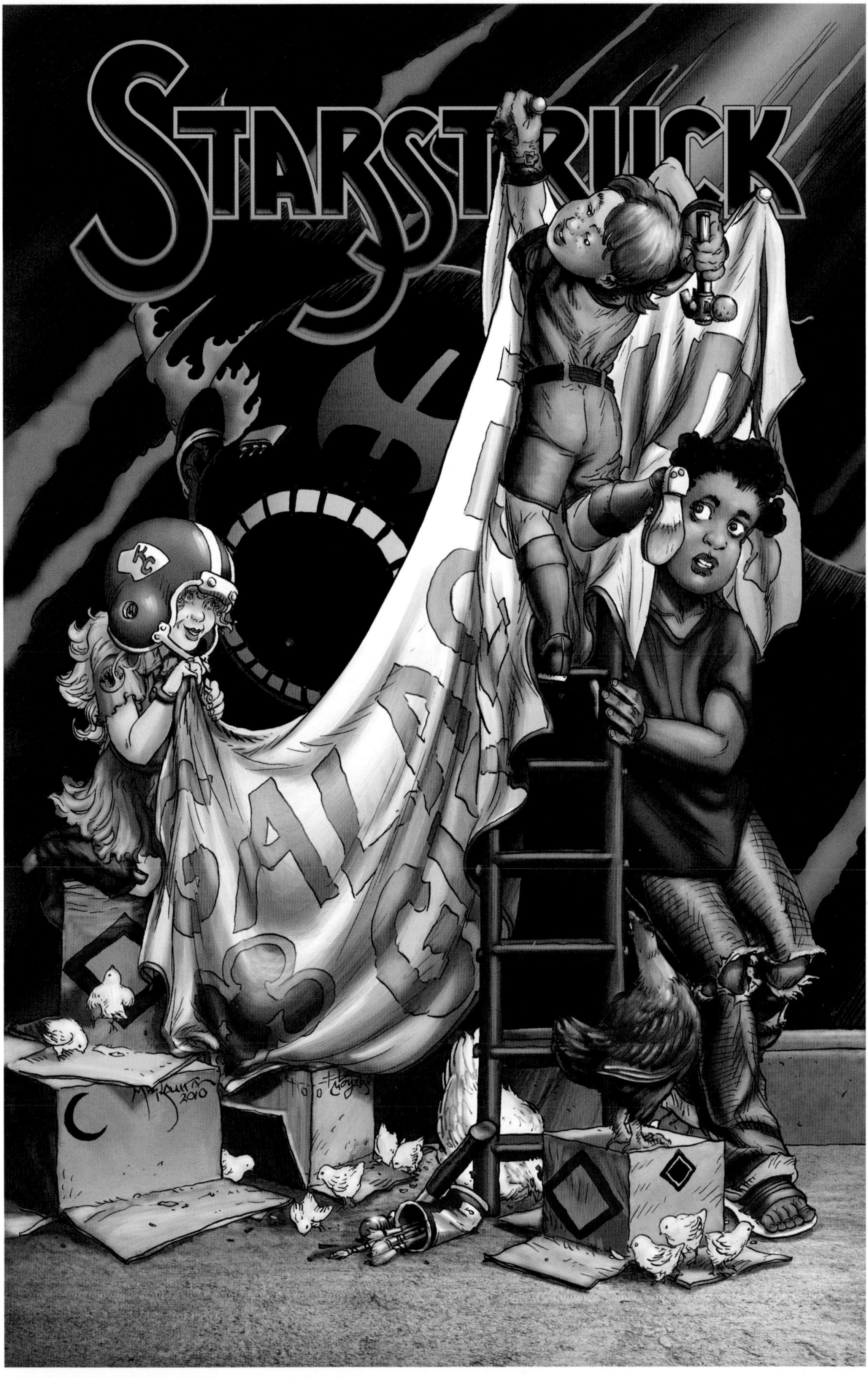
STARSTRUCK

Verloona Tï

AnarchEra's It Girl!

Personalities of AnarchEra   Series 3

Verloona Tï

Temple of Beauty founder, the youngest child of Margaret Medea inherited her mother's vast wealth with *Krystals 'n Things*. But before mom was cold in the grave she'd changed her name - dropping the 'Maggie' *and* the 'Medea' and legally becoming daddy's girl.

Red-carpet events are V's raison d'être, Rec-hopping and party-throwing her favorite sports and she's never met a camera she didn't love! You can find her in the Freebetters' Room of The Dome, Rec 97, or lounging in her rooms in the Krystal Hills Section of Blue Heaven Level… but *only* if you have a Gold Card!

Drop in to see her on her New Wyoming ranch, where Miz Ti breeds thoroughbred racing dogs. Careful though, we hear she's a bitch with a bite.

#27 of 1,000,000   •   Collect 'em All!

Nick "The Geezer" Pico
Collectors' "Gold Card" Edition

Nicholas Pico, known galaxy~wide as Nick the Geezer, made a killing keeping people alive with his patented Running In Place® process, the most popular means of life extension ever! With RIP, buying life is as simple as picking up the dry cleaning.

Though they generate pocket change when compared to his first venture, Nick's Land~o~Nod® Dream Enhancement Parlors are ubiquitous on the **557** Rec Stations and, indeed, throughout the settled Omniverse. The Land~o~Nod® gaming system allows players to enter, armed and conscious, into their own dreams, in order to battle psychic demons.

In the interest of full disclosure…
The Personalities of AnarchEra card sets are manufactured and sold by Mr. Pico's card and collectibles biz, Heroes, Etc.

Personalities of AnarchEra   777 of 1000

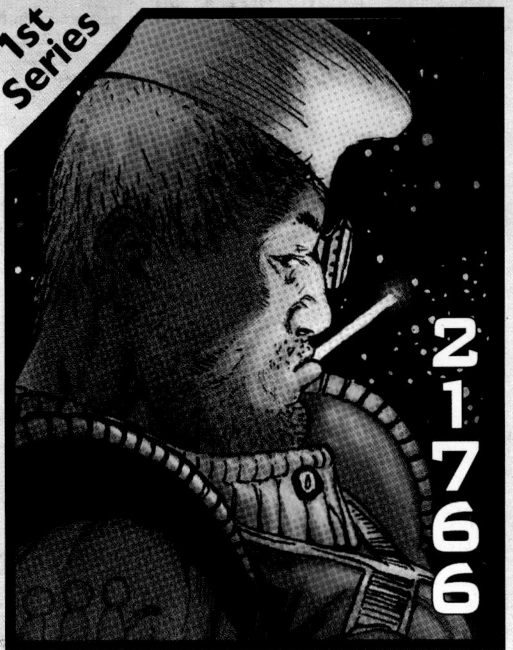
1st Series
21766

Personalities of AnarchEra

HARRY PALMER

c. 73 AE

Personalities of AnarchEra

HARRY PALMER

A Hero of the Revolution, credited by some for shattering the planet Vaikuntha, the Dread D's personal Krystal mine, into a blue billion hunks-o-bucks, thereby ending the war and (*shhhhh, don't tell!*) making gal-pal, Mary Medea, rich beyond belief!

What is known for certain is that Palmer didn't hang up his blasters after PAHM-the-B was booted (*in **every** sense of the word!*) to Mirage. He served in the Droid Wars ***and*** the Tri-Clone Invasion, with BBFs Medea and Factor. And the guy's got the battle tats to prove it!

Needless to say, young Harry's very popular with the vat-grown crowd. (*Not that there's anything wrong with that!*)

#21,766 of 500,000 • Collect 'em All!

CAPTAIN GALATIA 9

U4F

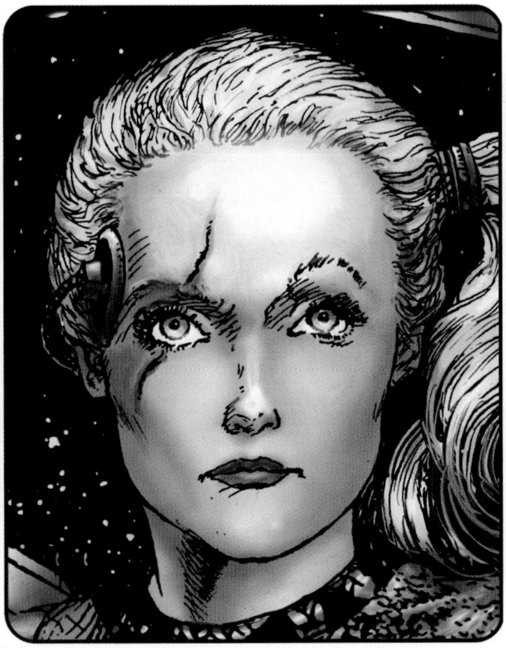

Personalities of AnarchEra Series 4

Personalities of AnarchEra Series 4

CAPTAIN GALATIA 9

Captain 9 and the crew of her flame-painted Krystal-Fighter, Harpy, were top earners for the United Federation of Female Freedom Fighters in AE 154. This former Omegazon (*with the missing breast to prove it!*) always seems to show up where trouble is brewing.

Between U4F missions, the Captain's base of operations is the Sailor's Grave, a bar on Rec 97's Vale of Tiers, popular with entertainers, off-duty Brigaders and the hoi polloi. Was Galatia 9 the match that struck the great fire of AE 140? Those in the know say, "Maybe!"

Inquiring minds want to know: Where and how did she get that scar? And what idiot told her she was a poet?

1,905,284 / 2,000,000 • Collect 'em All!

While on Rec 97...
Stop by Nick "the Geezer" Pico's for all your

Heroes and Dreams!

Collect your favorite Heroes (sung or un) as "Personalities of AnarchEra" cards, at

Big Nick's Comics and Collectibles!

And for a short time only!
COLLECTORS' QUALITY MISSION PATCHES from the ASB, U4F, Droid Wars and More!

Find the Hero within...
just next door at Nick's

Land-o-Nod

Dream Enhancement Game Arcade!

Touchémento! Sandmen! Id Whacker!
REM Warrior!

See Nick's full catalogue of *dreamy* options on page 12,857

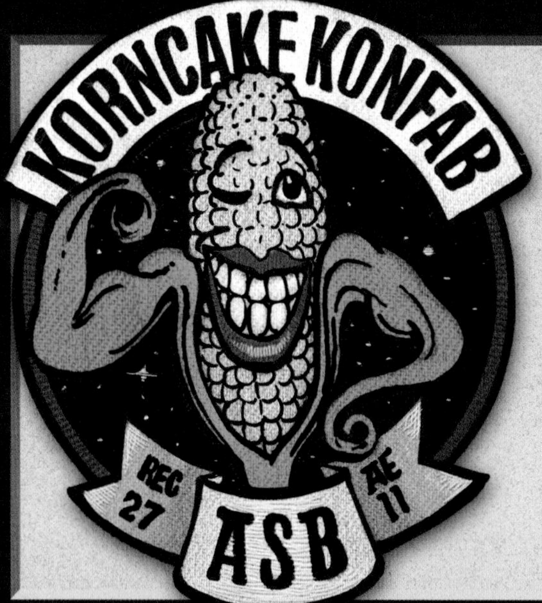
KORNCAKE KONFAB
REC 27
ASB
AE 11

In AE 11, the Quartermaster Corps of the Amercadian Space Brigade held Korncake Konfab on Recreation Station 27, for the purpose of generating ideas on how to "encourage" the galaxy's civilian population to purchase several billion boxes of surplus Kansas Korncakes, a staple of the Brigade diet. By the end of the conference, an ambitious "sales" plan had been put into place and the Brigade prohibited from dropping on-leave Brigaders onto Rec 27 for the next 13 cycles.

Patch status: Rare

An unauthorized badge awarded to Amercadian Space Brigade cadets upon completion of their first "skate" of the mirror-like anomaly in Neutral Zone 8. This badge was issued in 133 AE, just one year before the decision that banned the Academy from the use of their very expensive obstacle course, bordering the Cosmic Veil's property in Zone.

Patch Status: If you have to ask, you can't afford it.

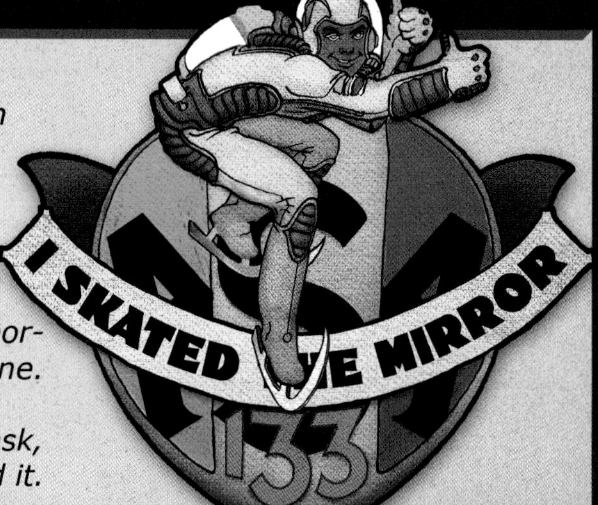
I SKATED
E MIRROR
133

On the Vale of Tiers, White Dwarf Way, near Up- See-

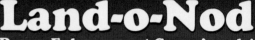

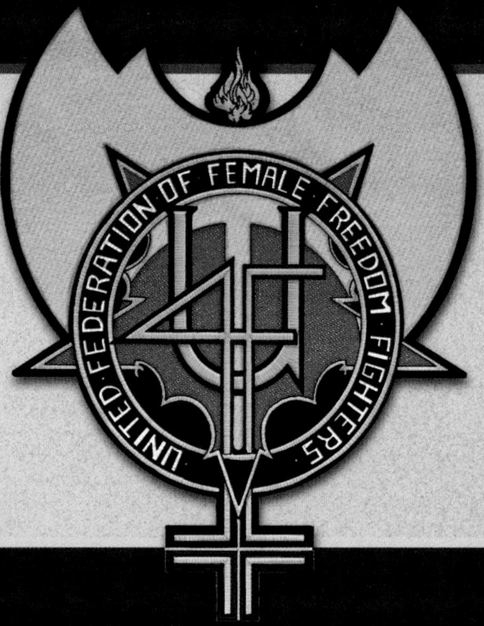
UNITED FEDERATION OF FEMALE FREEDOM FIGHTERS

Standard issue patch given to all new members of the United Federation of Female Freedom Fighters, upon signing. The same logo appears on the letterhead, gear and all official merchandize of this union for female mercenaries. These U4F badges are, in old Terran parlance, "a dime a dozen" (think Bajar shillings). Pretty, though!

Patch status: Common

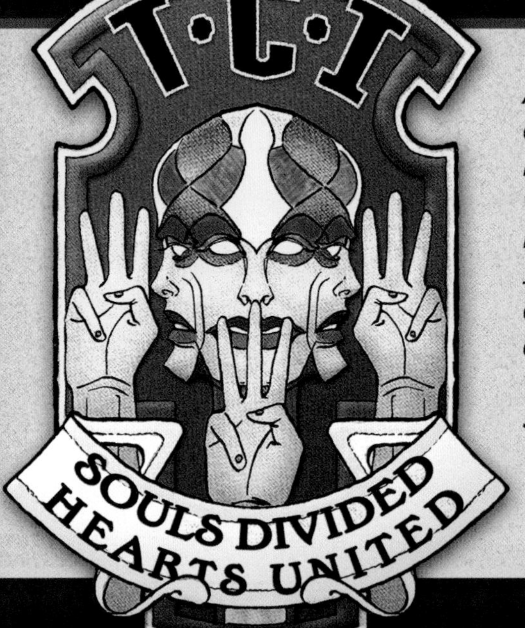
T·C·T
SOULS DIVIDED
HEARTS UNITED

A patch designed for and worn by the cloned soldiers who fought alongside the humanoid allies of cyberforms in what was, by most accounts, the deciding battle of the Droid Wars: The Tri-Clone Invasion. Once common, due to the high casualty rate of the aforementioned clones, more than 95% of the patches were purchased by the reclusive P.D. Schift. He has never parted with one.

Patch status: Rare

This mission patch was created for droid support troops, who would never have thought to create such a thing for themselves, by the human combatants who fought for the cyberforms, during the Droid Wars. The patches became objects of veneration for the droids who survived the wars. Fortunately for collectors (arguably less so for the ill-fated droids themselves), some did not.

Patch status: Uncommon

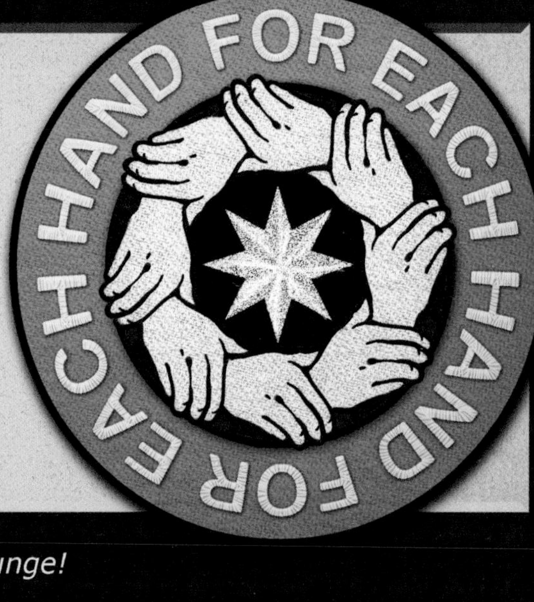
HAND FOR EACH HAND FOR EACH

Daisy 16, directly opposite the Ramscoop Lounge!

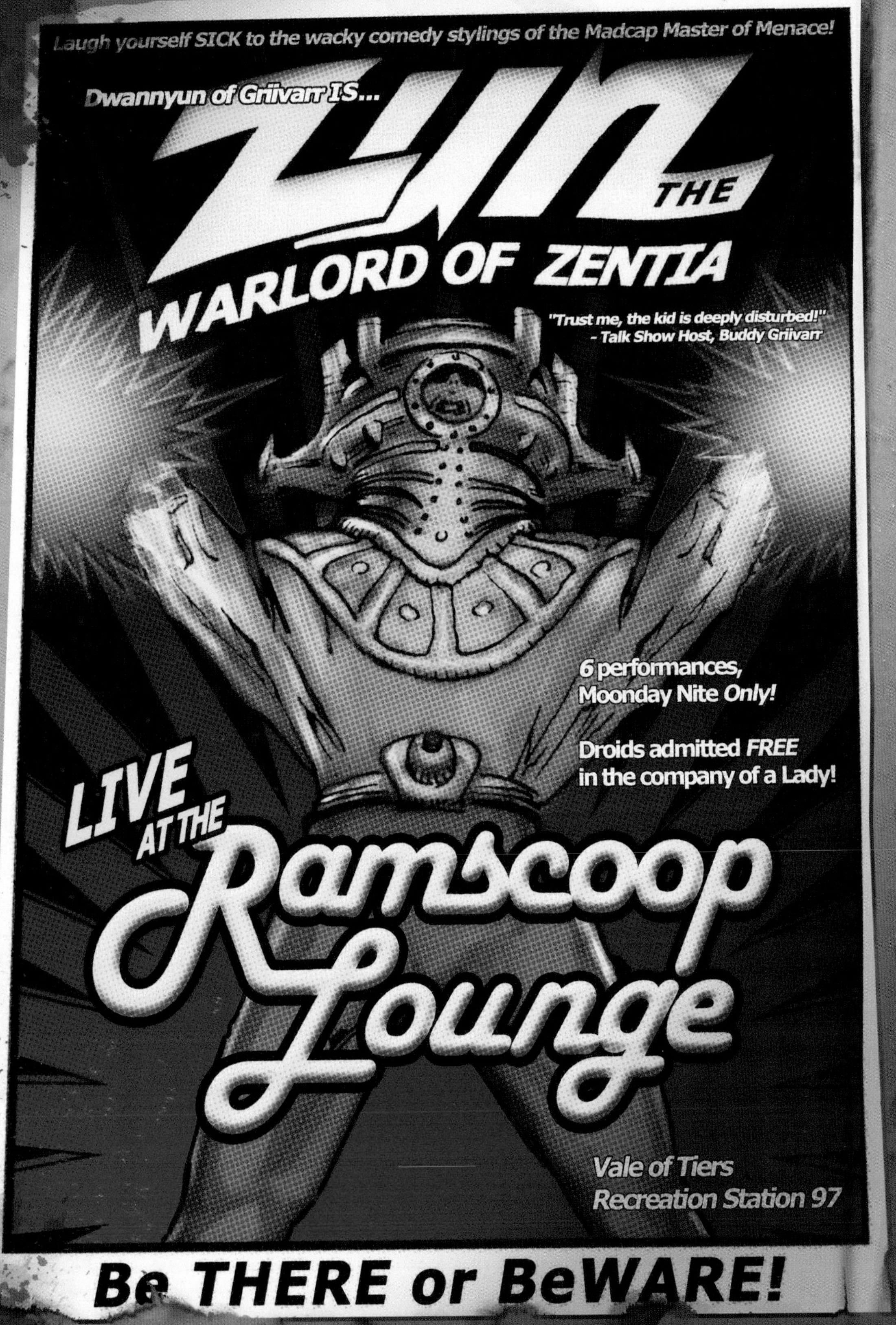
Laugh yourself SICK to the wacky comedy stylings of the Madcap Master of Menace!
Dwannyun of Griivarr IS...
ZIN THE
WARLORD OF ZENTIA
"Trust me, the kid is deeply disturbed!"
- Talk Show Host, Buddy Griivarr
6 performances,
Moonday Nite Only!
Droids admitted FREE
in the company of a Lady!
LIVE AT THE
Ramscoop
Lounge
Vale of Tiers
Recreation Station 97
Be THERE or BeWARE!

This Page:

- a poster for a long-forgotten novelty act from Cycle 160 AE taken from 'Candid Candid Shots: Gutter 97' by Max Cloaca

Opposite:

- One of the ubiquitous ads for the telepathethic Aguatunesians that briefly performed under the Nom du Cirque "The Mystic Nȳts of the Sea" Cycle 117 AE, image provided by "Uncle" B.O.B. Griivarr's Astonishing Archive!

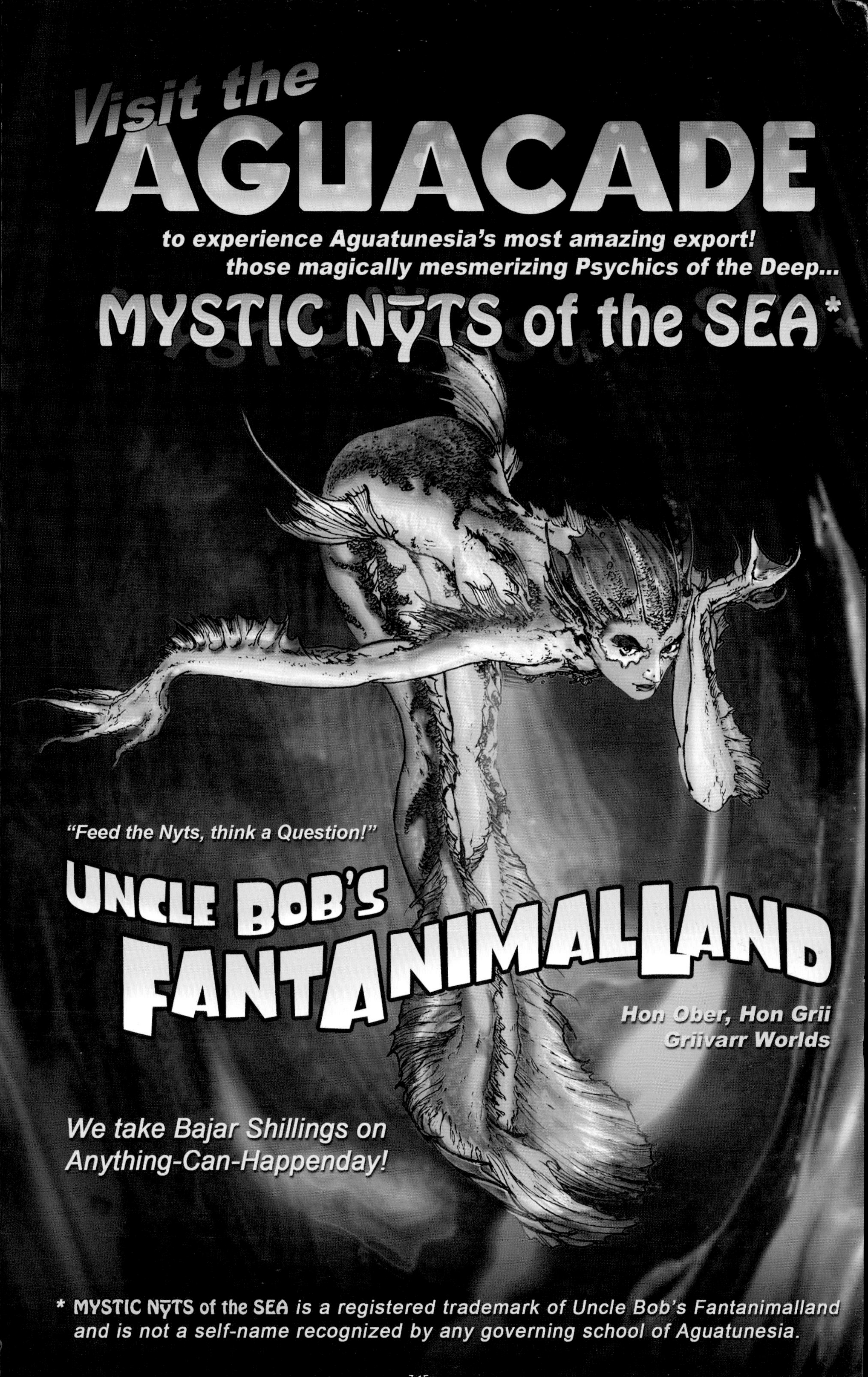
Visit the
AGUACADE
to experience Aguatunesia's most amazing export!
those magically mesmerizing Psychics of the Deep...
MYSTIC NȲTS of the SEA*
"Feed the Nyts, think a Question!"
UNCLE BOB'S
FANTANIMALLAND
Hon Ober, Hon Grii
Griivarr Worlds
We take Bajar Shillings on
Anything-Can-Happenday!
* MYSTIC NȲTS of the SEA is a registered trademark of Uncle Bob's Fantanimalland and is not a self-name recognized by any governing school of Aguatunesia.

GALACTIC GIRL GUIDE FUN PAGE!

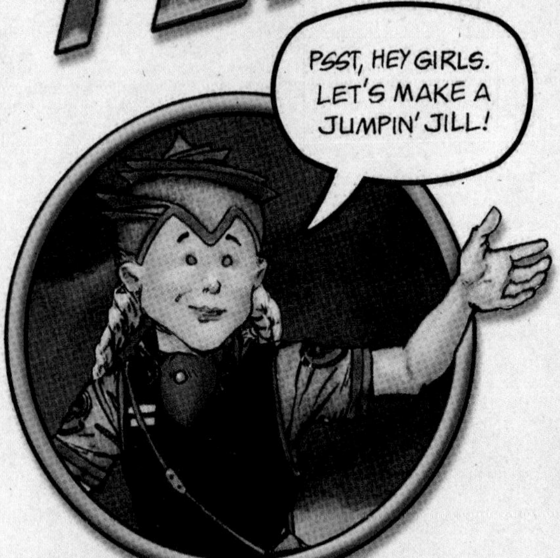
PSST, HEY GIRLS. LET'S MAKE A JUMPIN' JILL!

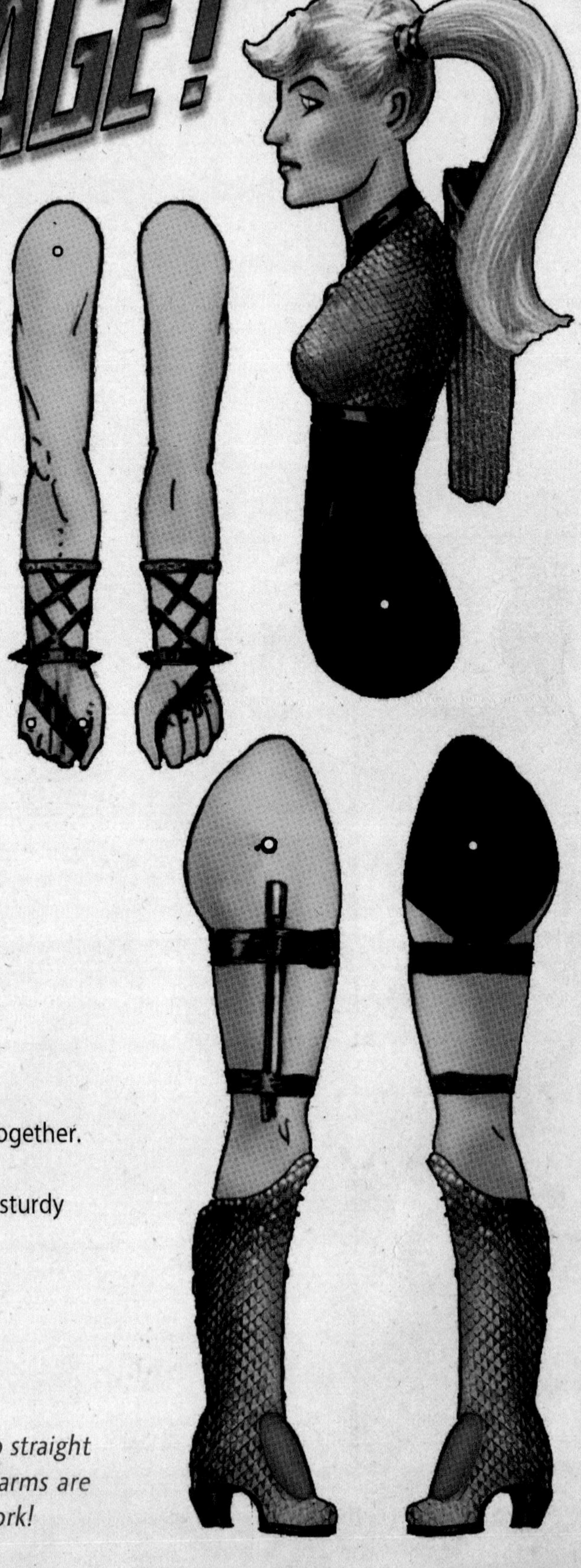

HOW TO DO IT!

1. Spray these pages with a clear finish
2. Paste pages onto cardboard with white glue
3. Cut out all the the pieces.
4. Glue the halves of Galatia 9's torso and limbs together.
5. Assemble the frame (shown lower right) from sturdy wood & roundhead screws.
6. Attach Galatia 9 to the frame with a strong string that will not stretch.

Remember Campers!
Attach Galatia 9 to the frame so the strings go straight through when the frame is inverted and her arms are straight above her head. Otherwise it won't work!

The spacing bead should be a little thicker than the assembled body.

Pivots can be made from straightened paperclips re-bent at the ends.

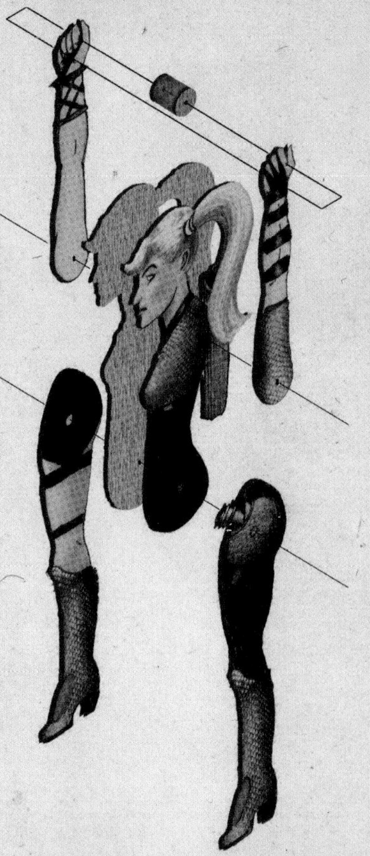

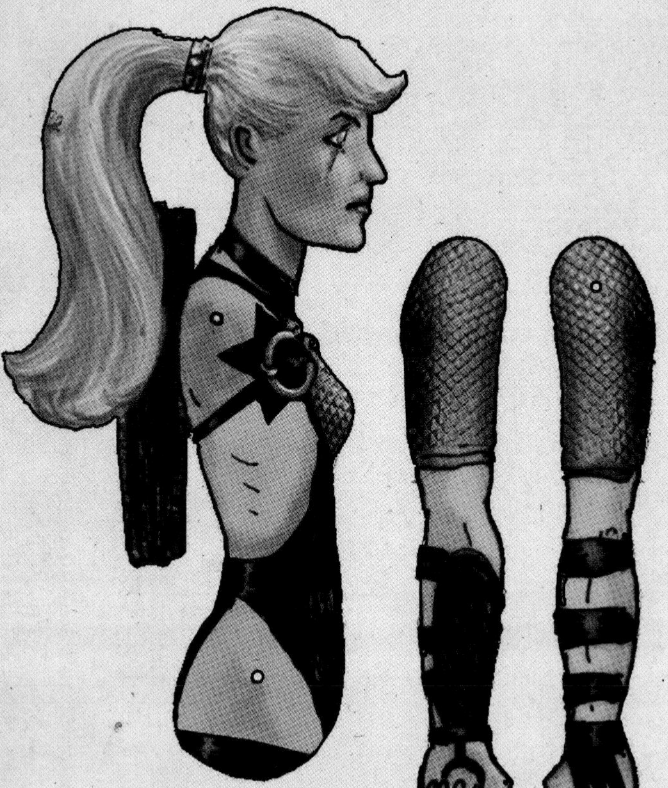

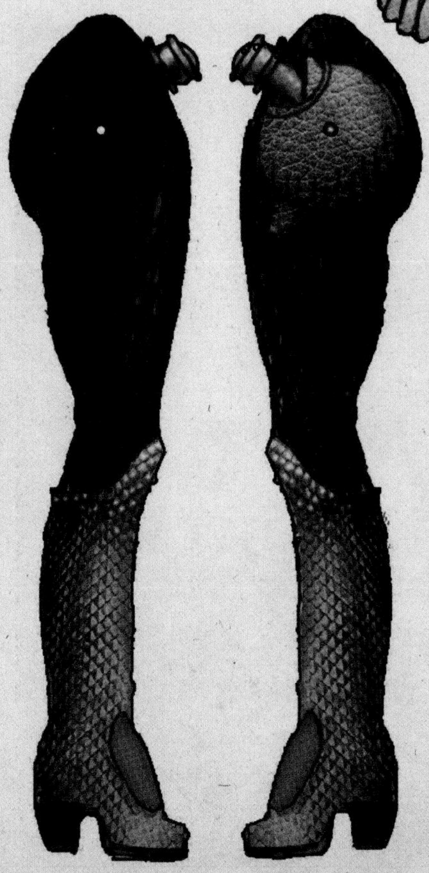

Engineering Consultant: James Mueller Esq., Grover's Mill, New New Jersey

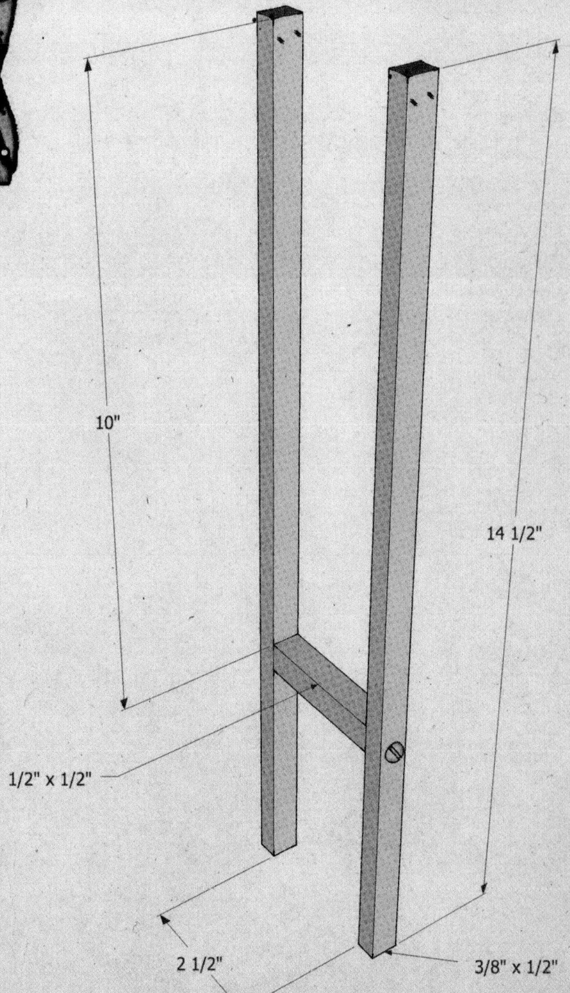
10"
14 1/2"
1/2" x 1/2"
2 1/2"
3/8" x 1/2"

you
war,
we
die,
who cares?
i
float...

An example of Stark Verse,
written on the first day of his
self-imposed exile to the
planet Aguatunesia, by
Warrior-Poet, Veep 7,
arguably the best known and
most feared of all Vercadian
Protector Androids.

Veep 7 drifts peacefully with empathic
companions in the seas of his chosen
homeworld, Aguatunesia. (right)

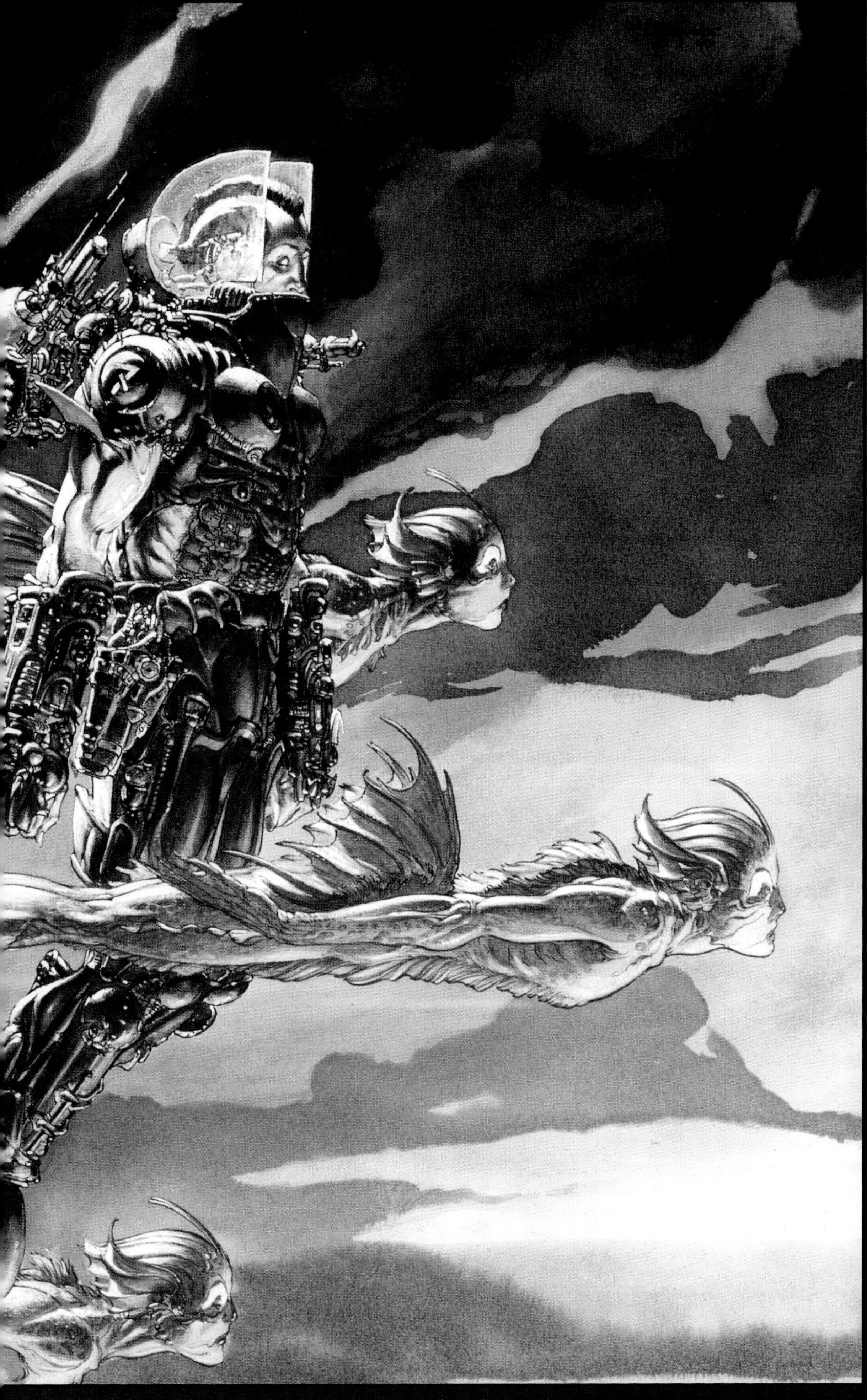

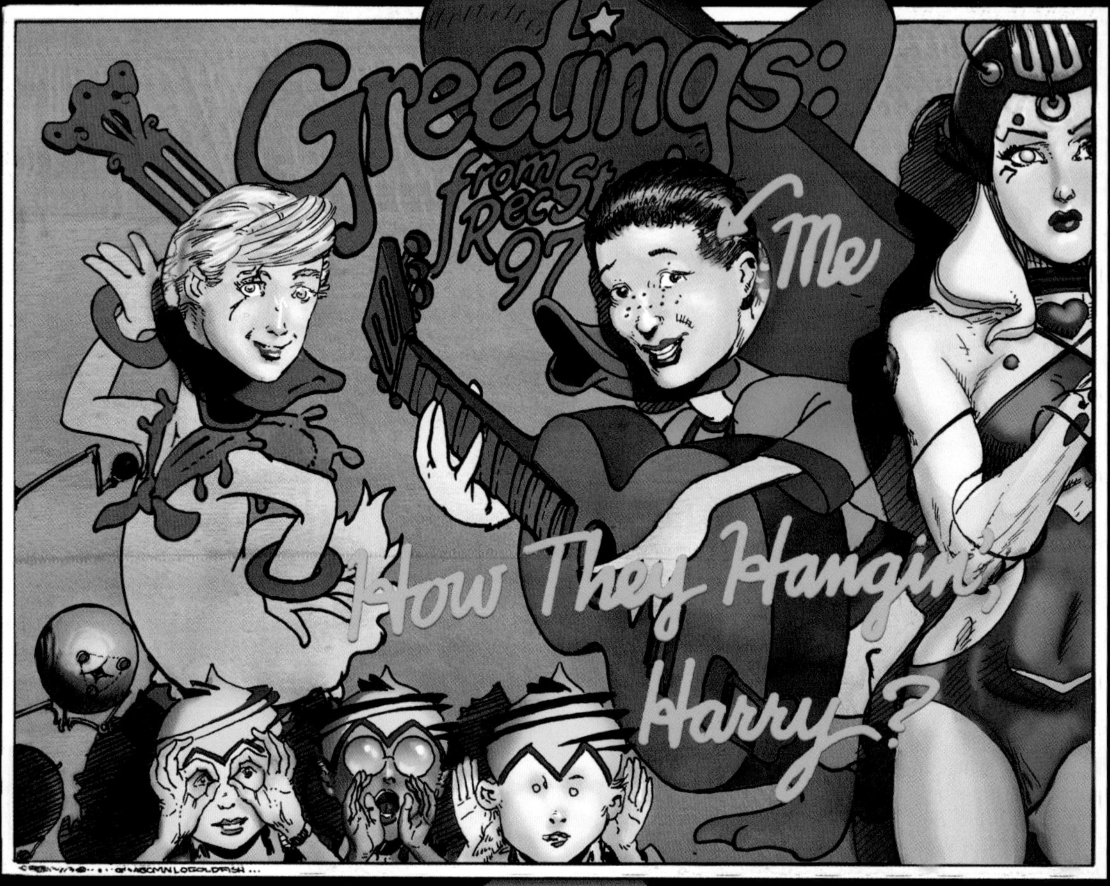
Greetings:
from Rec Station 97
Me
How They Hangin', Harry?

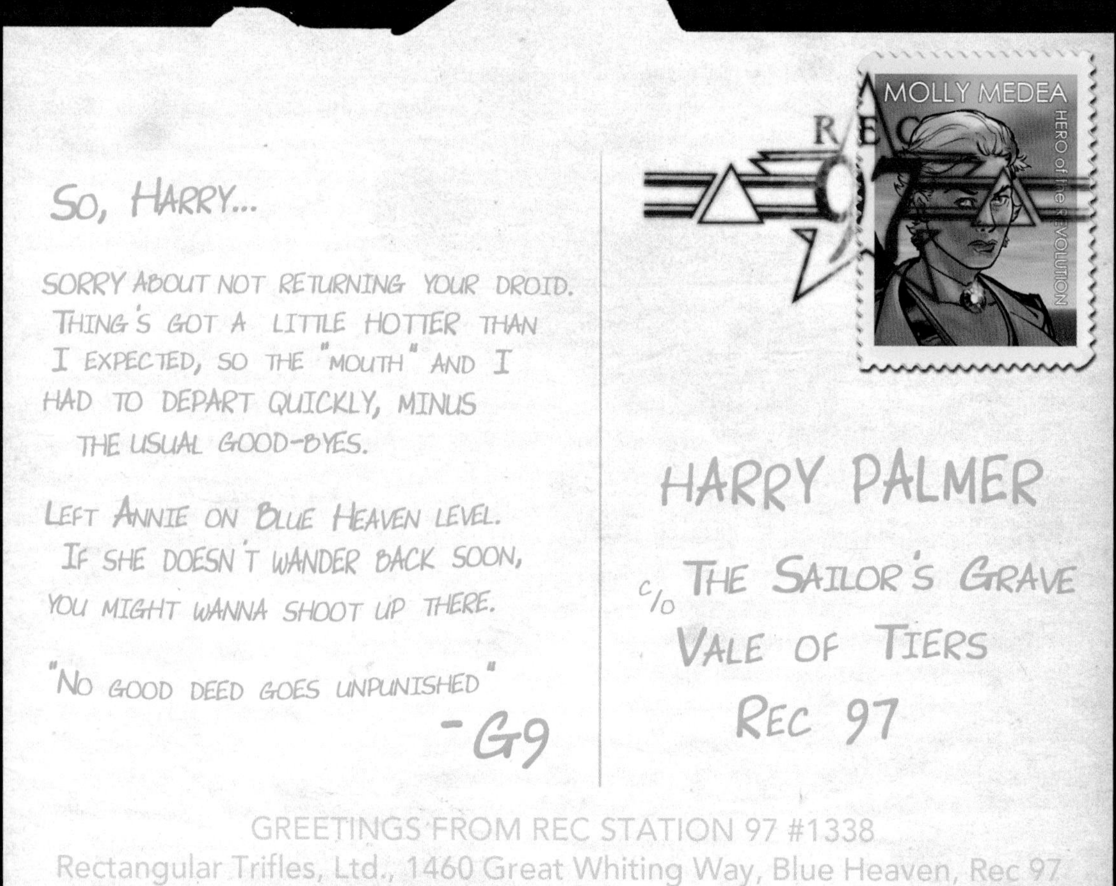
MOLLY MEDEA
HERO of the REVOLUTION
So, Harry...
Sorry about not returning your droid. Thing's got a little hotter than I expected, so the "Mouth" and I had to depart quickly, minus the usual good-byes.
Left Annie on Blue Heaven level. If she doesn't wander back soon, you might wanna shoot up there.
"No good deed goes unpunished"
-G9
HARRY PALMER
c/o The Sailor's Grave
Vale of Tiers
Rec 97
GREETINGS FROM REC STATION 97 #1338
Rectangular Trifles, Ltd., 1460 Great Whiting Way, Blue Heaven, Rec 97

"History repeats itself. And where genetically related humanoids are involved, this is doubly so."

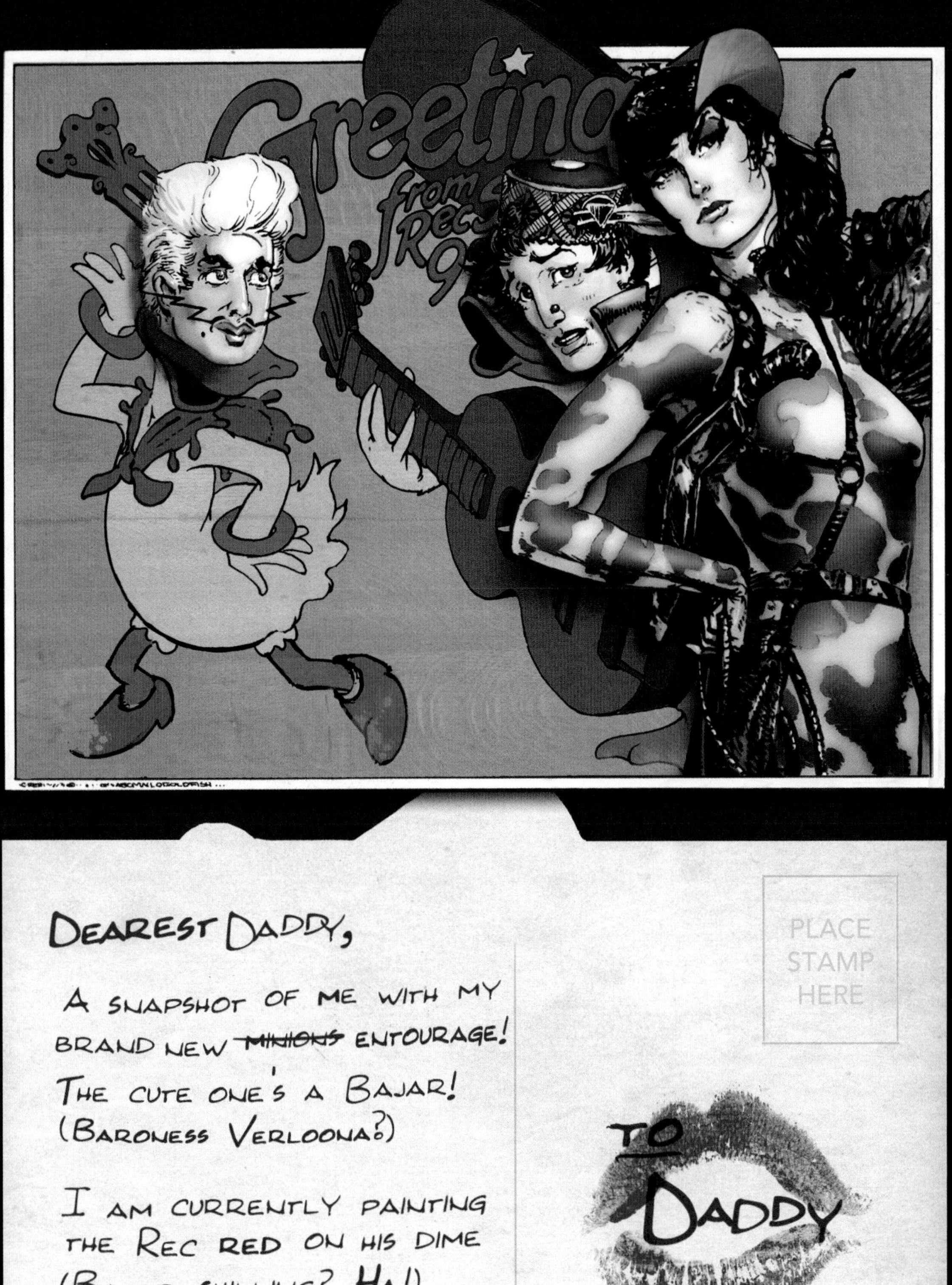
DEAREST DADDY,
A SNAPSHOT OF ME WITH MY BRAND NEW ~~MINIONS~~ ENTOURAGE!
THE CUTE ONE'S A BAJAR!
(BARONESS VERLOONA?)
I AM CURRENTLY PAINTING THE REC RED ON HIS DIME
(BAJAR SHILLING? HA!)
WISH YOU WERE (REALLY) HERE!
KISSES!
-'LOONA
PLACE STAMP HERE
TO DADDY
GREETINGS FROM REC STATION 97 #1338
Rectangular Trifles, Ltd., 1460 Great Whiting Way, Blue Heaven, Rec 97

- Dwannyun of Griivarr, speaking at the Second Galactic Council for Deciding What to Do Next

TOP VIEW

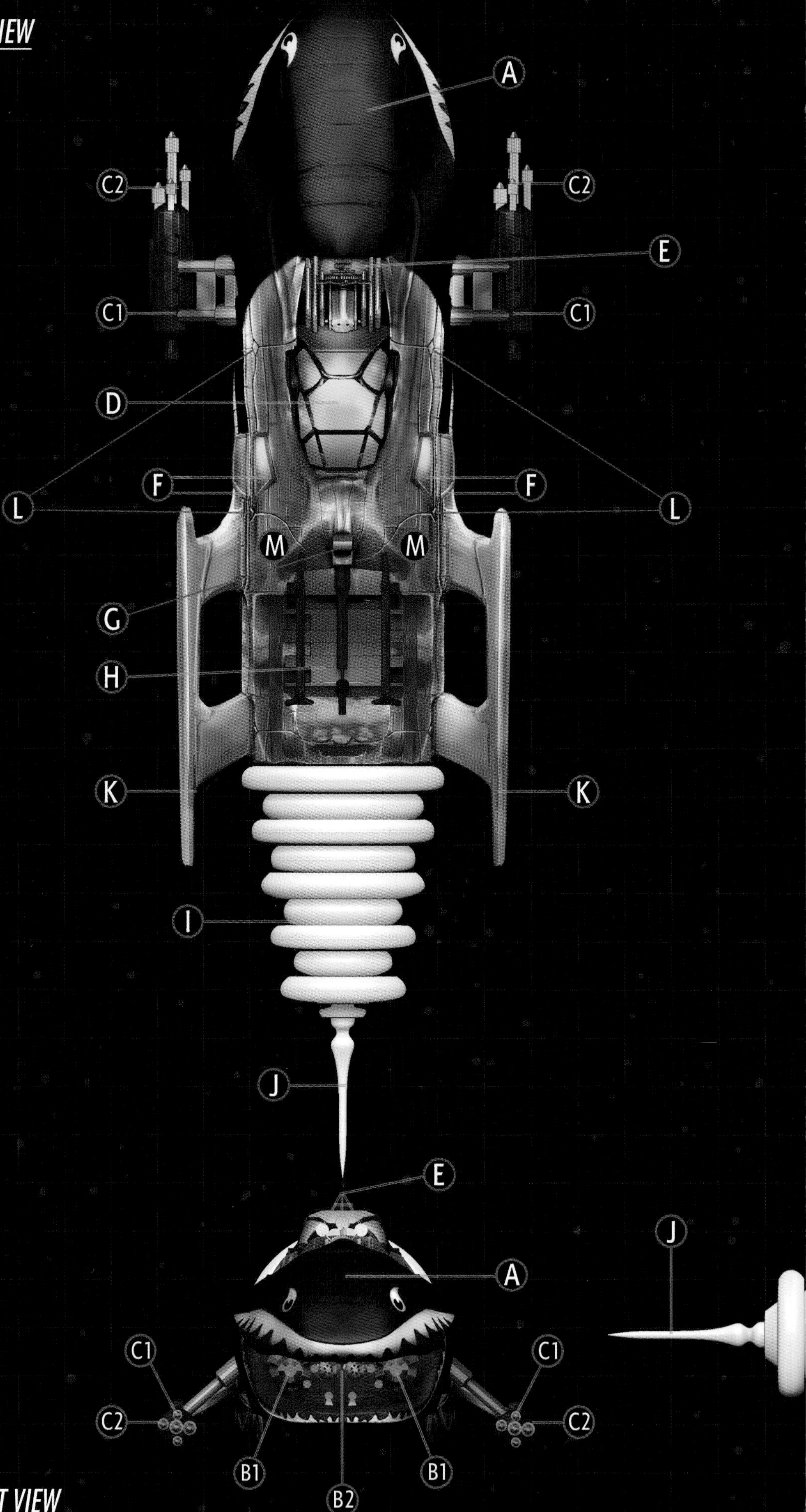
A
C2
C2
E
C1
C1
D
F
F
L
L
M
M
G
H
K
K
I
J
E
J
A
C1
C1
C2
C2
B1
B1
B2

FRONT VIEW

The Amercadian Space Brigade

TIGER

- Ⓐ Brigade TIGER Nose Nacelle
- (B1) Mission Specific Weapon Kit - Laser/Hyon Beam Projector
- (B2) Mission Specific Weapon Kit - Thunder Slug Cannon (depleted uranium projectiles)
- (C1) Retractable Laser Boom
- (C2) Multi-lasing Ray-O-Vacuole targeting assembly
- Ⓓ Pilot's Cockpit and Canopy (see detailed cutaway, overleaf)
- Ⓔ Deadlights
- Ⓕ Gunner's Eye-ports (VistaVane Panes)
- Ⓖ Radio Nest
- Ⓗ Audio Induction Pre-amp Casement
- Ⓘ Articulated Accordion Photon Hoop Assembly (cradling the Prosperina K-Krystal Rack Matrix Power Plant)
- Ⓙ Vectored Guidance Stinger
- Ⓚ Skid
- Ⓛ Explosive Bolt
- Ⓜ Frangible Battle Hull

I
H
L
G
D
L
E
A
M
B1
B2
K
F
C1
C2
RIGHT VIEW

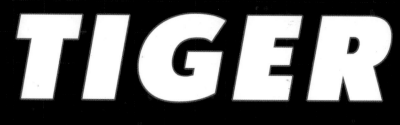

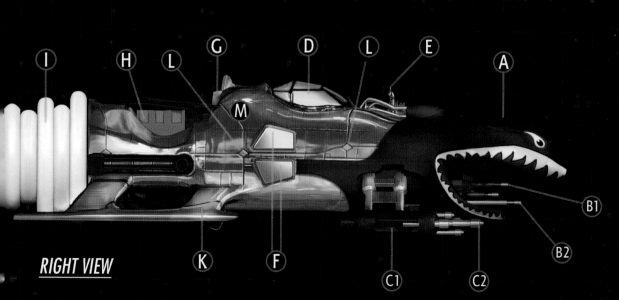

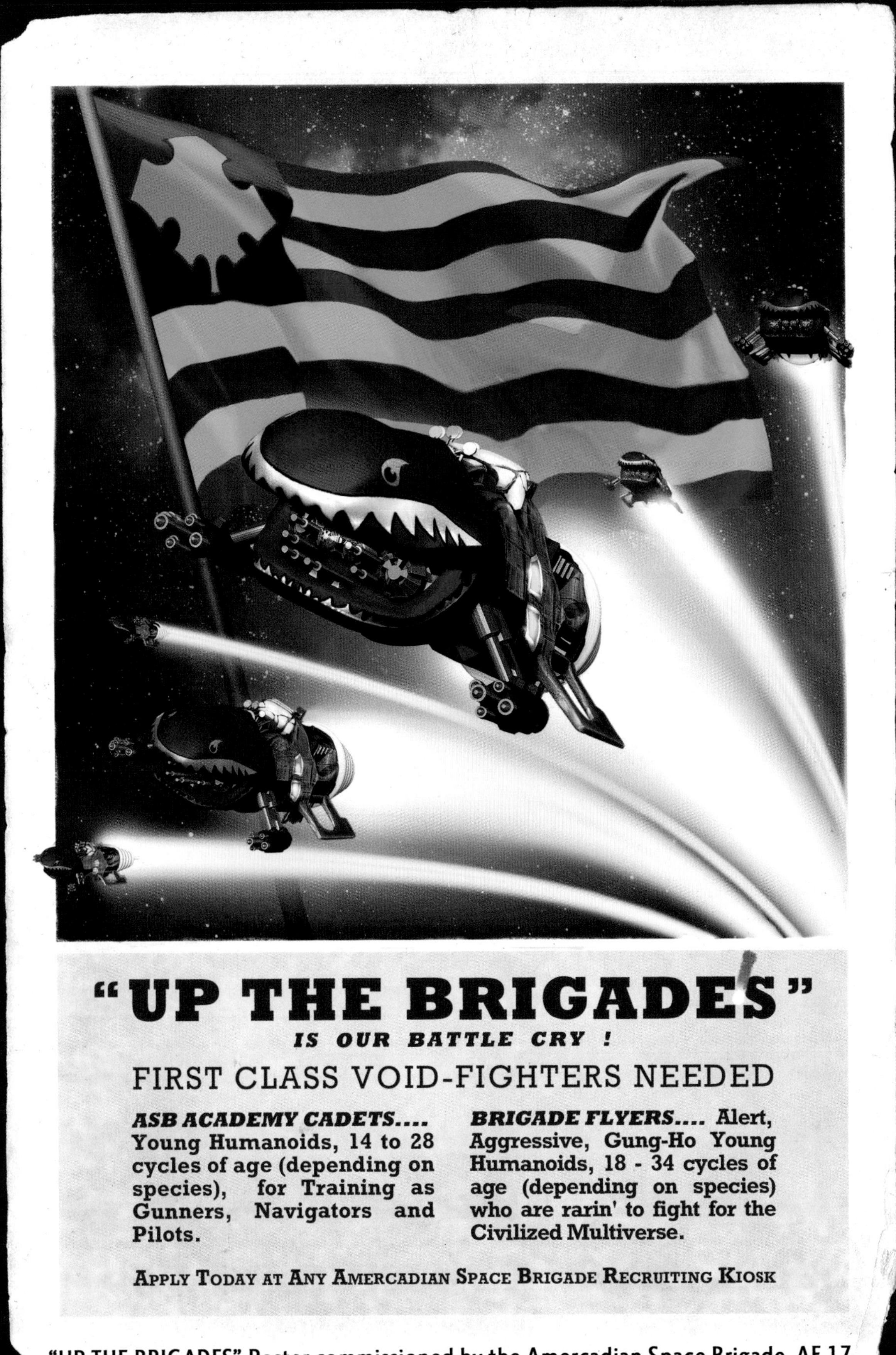
"UP THE BRIGADES"
IS OUR BATTLE CRY !
FIRST CLASS VOID-FIGHTERS NEEDED
ASB ACADEMY CADETS.... Young Humanoids, 14 to 28 cycles of age (depending on species), for Training as Gunners, Navigators and Pilots.
BRIGADE FLYERS.... Alert, Aggressive, Gung-Ho Young Humanoids, 18 - 34 cycles of age (depending on species) who are rarin' to fight for the Civilized Multiverse.
APPLY TODAY AT ANY AMERCADIAN SPACE BRIGADE RECRUITING KIOSK

"UP THE BRIGADES" Poster commissioned by the Amercadian Space Brigade, AE 17

Posted everywhere in known space (and unknown space too, if the printing manifests are to be believed), this poster featured an erroneous plural of BRIGADE. For the agency of record (the late Carter & Mover, LLLC *"We'll Getcha There!"*), losing the Multiverse's biggest *account* was really the least of its troubles.... Finding this poster is easy. Finding it without an added apostrophe is, as of this printing, *impossible*.

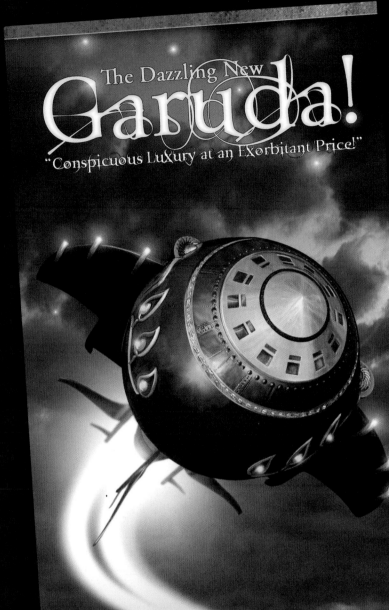

The Dazzling New
Garuda!
"Conspicuous Luxury at an Exorbitant Price!"
NEW FOR IET 190!
• Supplies Strictly Limited •
Sold exclusively through Walter Carter XXIII and Sons, New Baltimore

The flier shown above was discovered on the U4F ship Harpy (along with several hundred others clogging the aft head) by Sister Bronwyn of the Cosmic Veil in AE 155.

HIGH FLIER

Take the average humanoid's attraction to sparkly objects, and multiply it by a factor of five. That gives you some idea of the questionable taste of the late Dread Dictator, known during the cycles of IET as Our Benefactor. During those cycles, many tried to curry favor with said Benefactor by adorning themselves, their kin, their pets and their various means of transportation with gems, ribbons, furs, glittery geegaws and shiny paint.

Enter *Garuda!* Its price mind-blowing, its upkeep astronomical, the krystal-driven *Garuda* was marketed to social climbers of the rich-but-common classes and advertised as "guaranteed to catch the eye of Our Benefactor, as every detail has been finished with his exquisite taste in mind!"

Oft labeled "eye-catching", "showy" or "stunning", the gaudy little pleasure ships were built to be rare. As advertised, there were "never more than ten in existence!". As stipulated in their contracts, the designers and builders of the space-going craft had their memories selectively wiped, once #10 had rolled off of the line.

Unfortunately for the company, #10 rolled off the line mere martrons before the destruction of the planet Vaikuntha insured the end of the Incorporated Elysian Republic and its taste-free Dictator. All 10 were later sold at auction for chump change.

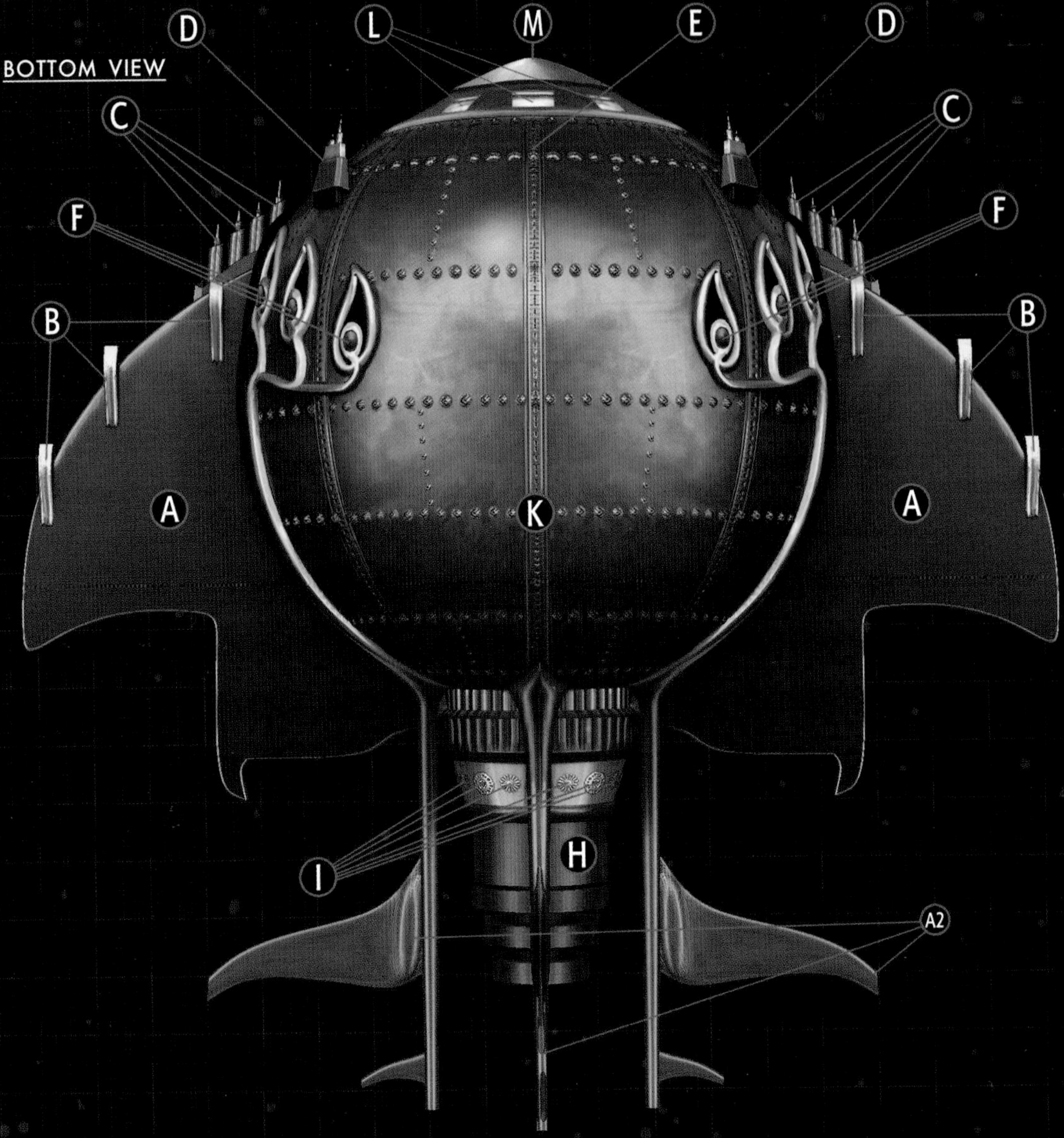
BOTTOM VIEW
D
L
M
E
D
C
C
F
F
B
B
A
K
A
I
H
A2

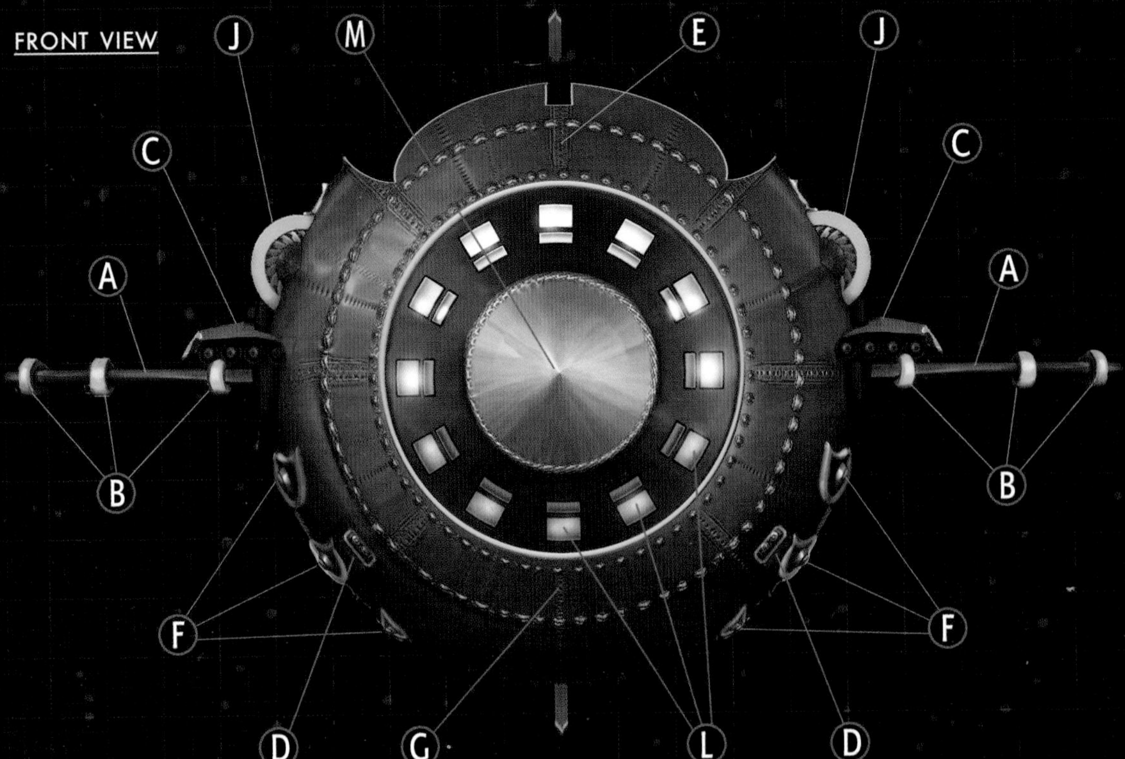
FRONT VIEW
J
M
E
J
C
C
A
A
B
B
F
F
D
G
L
D

THE HARPY!

(A) Anaroid Vanes:

Anaroid Vanes provide Aerodynamic Atmospheric Stability (AAS), sheathes/houses various field generator/accumulators, radiating/directional venturi systems and stowage spontoons

In combo with the Pressure Hull (see K) and empennage (see H), the vane architecture is a legacy hold-over from the original Garuda custom PreArcadian-inspired Pleasure Hull

    (A1) Dynamic Photonic Cell Skin Sheathing (DPCSS)

    (A2) Ablative Cosmic Debris Protectant (ACDP)

(B) Adjustable Wing Fences and Main Tractor Beam Housing

(C) Magneto-Boy LS torpedo vents, Atomo-Torch™ Particle Blastbeam Arc Staplers, Mecury/Elvinrude "Spacesaber" Hyon Beam muzzles

(D) Harley-Wessonoyl "Peewee" Pinlight Pinpickers, H-W Mk VII Planet Splitter projectors

(E) & (G) Ingress/Egress Accessors

(F) Acme-Ashmun™ Field Generator Gondolas

(H) P.K-Krystal Drive rack matrix Accordion Housing

(I) Jake Braking puti-plates: A. G. Mimya (humectic)

(J) Fuller-Buckman "Quad Pod" Faux S-Bend Sponson, housing Piezionic Turbinettes (Be Radburri, Brietang and Oogomont) and the Derailur Caterpillar Assembly

(K) Pressure Hull (see trannies 1200-2470)

(L) Dogg Hatchits and Kitten Flappet el Vis viewport covers

(M) Carter Corps Corkscrew™ Aductors (retracted)

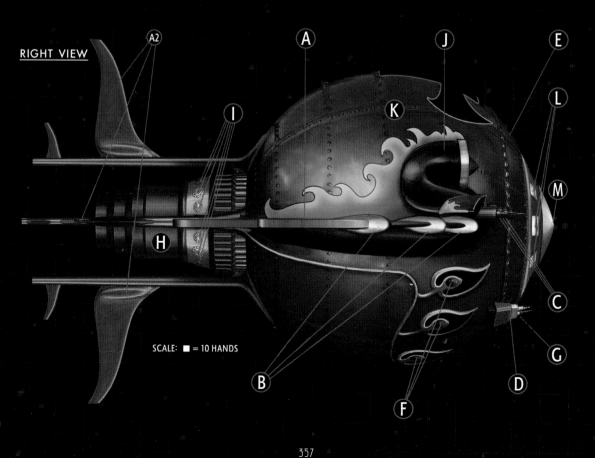

RIGHT VIEW

SCALE: ■ = 10 HANDS

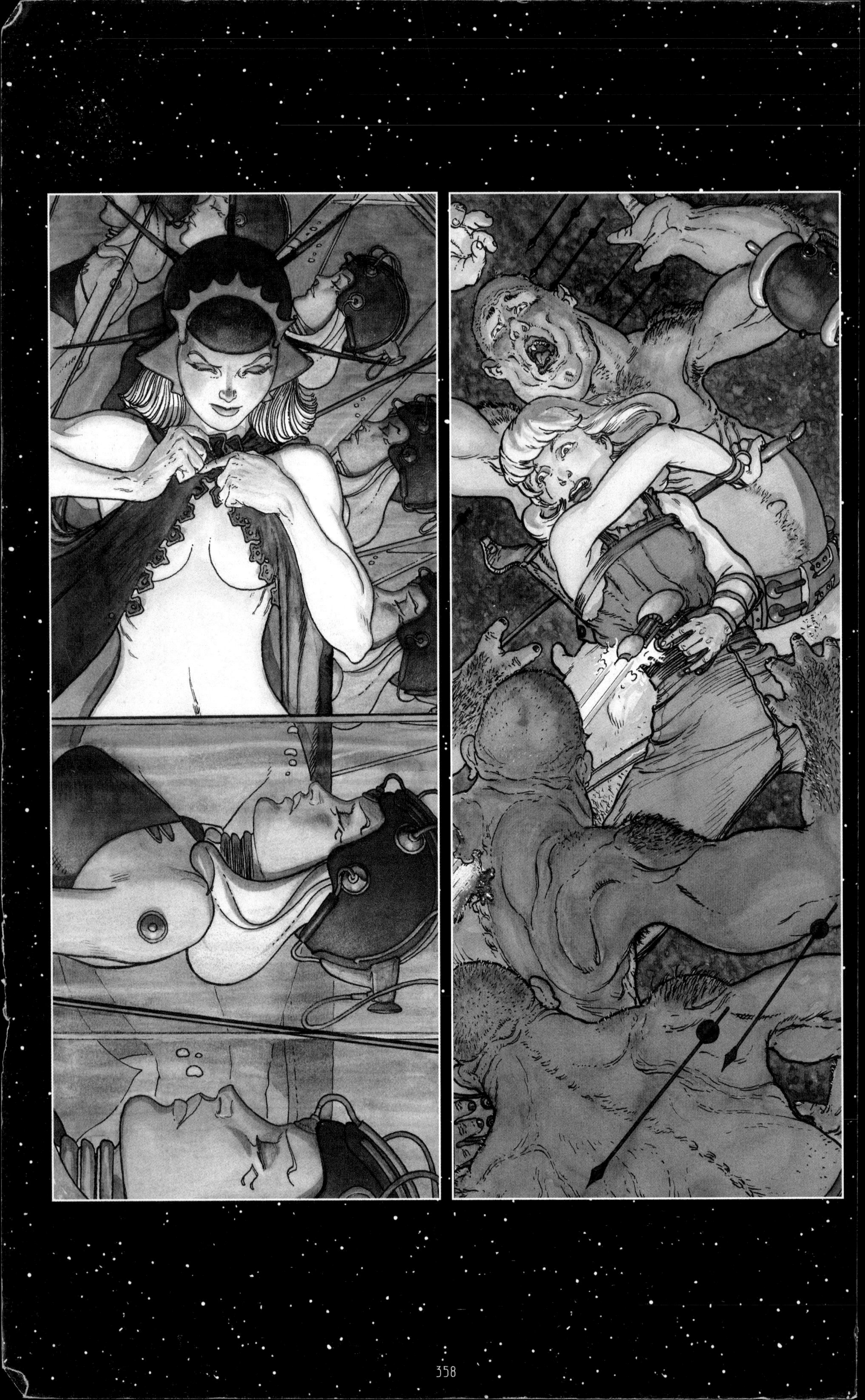